THE FINAL STORM

THE FINAL STORM

A NOVEL OF
THE WAR
IN THE PACIFIC

JEFF SHAARA

BALLANTINE BOOKS

New York

The Final Storm is a work of historical fiction. Apart from the well-known actual people, events, and locales that figure in the narrative, all names, characters, places, and incidents are the products of the author's imagination or are used fictitiously. Any resemblance to current events or locales, or to living persons, is entirely coincidental.

Copyright © 2011 by Jeffrey M. Shaara
Maps copyright © 2011 by Mapping Specialists

Published in the United States by Ballantine Books,
an imprint of The Random House Publishing Group,
a division of Random House, Inc., New York.

BALLANTINE and colophon are registered trademarks of Random House, Inc.

LIBRARY OF CONGRESS CATALOGING-IN-PUBLICATION DATA
Shaara, Jeff.
The final storm: a novel of the war in the Pacific / Jeff Shaara.
p. cm.
ISBN 978-0-345-49794-9
eISBN 978-0-345-52643-4
1. World War, 1939–1945—Pacific Area—Fiction.   2. World War, 1939–1945—
Naval operations, American—Fiction.   3. Pacific Area—Fiction.   I. Title.
PS3569.H18F56 2011   813'.54—dc22   2011003096

Printed in the United States of America on acid-free paper

www.ballantinebooks.com

2 4 6 8 9 7 5 3 1

FIRST EDITION

Book design by Mary A. Wirth

For Brenda
At Last

The story of the end of the war in the Pacific pushes us toward a delicate line between what we know to be simple history (the facts) and what many of us prefer to think *should* have happened. Sixty-five years after the event, many of us sit in judgment on the way the Second World War was brought to a close, some of us wondering if there could have been a better way, or perhaps a more *moral* way to end the war. In the American psyche, those debates are likely to continue for a very long time. But those debates will not be found here.

This story attempts to complete what I began in a trilogy that dealt with the war in Europe. Those stories involved America's first involvement in the fight against the Germans and concluded with the fall of Hitler. Half a world away, there had been another, far more brutal war, against an enemy who was even more successful than Hitler in conquering a vast swath of territory and threatening to slice off an enormous part of the world from our definition of civilization. Had the Japanese been allowed to maintain the empire they sought (and nearly won), all of Asia, including China, Korea, and Indochina, Thailand, Burma, and Malaya, would have become part of an empire that would also have included Australia, New Guinea, the Philippines, Indonesia, and the thousands of islands that spread from those lands all the way east to Hawaii, and north to the Aleutians. What might have followed is speculation, of course. Would the Japanese have invaded the United States (which was one purpose of the conquest of the islands in the Aleutian chain, to serve as a base for such an operation)? Or, strengthened by the raw materials drawn from the riches of the lands under their control, would the Japanese have been strong enough to shove their armies across India, or drive southward to Central and South America?

The urgency of meeting the challenge in the Pacific seemed to many Americans to be secondary to the threat posed to our allies by Hitler. Despite the grotesque insult inflicted upon the United States by the Japanese attack at Pearl Harbor, the government, particularly President Roosevelt, understood that Germany's conquest of Europe, including England, was a more immediate threat. And so greater resources were poured out of American factories toward that part of the world. But the Pacific was hardly ignored. After Pearl Harbor, the United States struck back at the Japanese, and in what now seems an amazing feat, fought both wars simultaneously, against two very different enemies, in two very different ways.

Though my plan had been to complete this story with Europe, I could not just walk away without touching upon the Pacific. (I was also inspired by letters received from a number of Marines, who were quite vocal that "ignoring" *their* story was altogether inappropriate. It's hard to disagree.) Some have written to me, expressing frustration that I am not attempting to tell the entire story of the Pacific campaigns through another complete trilogy. There are reasons for that, which include the requirements of my publisher. My choice was to follow *No Less Than Victory* in rough chronological order, and move through the spring and summer of 1945, to the final collapse of Japan. Thus this story deals with the extraordinary fight on Okinawa, and then, an event unique in world history, the dropping of the atomic bomb on Hiroshima. The points of view vary considerably. Some are familiar: Admiral Chester Nimitz, President Harry Truman. Others are perhaps less well known: Colonel Paul Tibbets, General Mitsuru Ushijima, General Curtis LeMay. And then there are the unknown: Marine Private Clay Adams, Dr. Okiro Hamishita, whose voices have carried me far deeper into this story than I expected to go.

If you are looking for either a strident argument in favor of the atomic bomb, or an apology for American immorality, you will find neither here. This story is told through the eyes of the participants, whose perspectives and decisions and experiences reflected what was happening around them. There is no judgment in hindsight, no moral verdict on my part. That just isn't my job (and never will be). Libraries are filled with volumes that pursue an agenda, political or otherwise, about our role in ending the war. I am merely a storyteller, and this story is as accurate historically as I could make it, told by the voices of the men who made the decisions, who gave the orders, and who took their fight to the enemy. There was only one world for them, a world in which the enemy had to be defeated at all costs. That's why I wanted to tell this story.

Every day, we lose countless numbers of those who participated in this fight. In every case, when I have spoken with veterans, they remind me that once they are gone, their memories will go with them. Unless, as one GI said, *someone tells the damn tale*. Fair enough. This is my attempt.

JEFF SHAARA
April 2011

CONTENTS

LIST OF MAPS

SOURCES AND ACKNOWLEDGMENTS

The following is a partial list of those original sources who provided voices for this story:

THE JAPANESE

Dr. Michihiko Hachiya
Saburo Ienaga
Prime Minister Hideki Tojo
Colonel Hiromichi Yahara

THE AMERICANS

Private First Class George J. Baird, USMC
Jim Boan, Sixth Division, USMC
General Simon Bolivar Buckner, Jr., USA
Sergeant George R. Caron, 509th Composite Group, USAAF
Lieutenant General James V. Edmundson, USAAF
David E. Frederick, USN
Dr. Jack Gennaria, USN
Captain Hank Harmeling, 106th Infantry Division
Sergeant Andrew Hettinga, 164th Regimental Combat Team
Private First Class Irvine Johnson, Second Infantry Division, USA
Sergeant Mack Johnson, 501st Anti-Aircraft Battalion, USA
General Curtis LeMay, USAAF
Sergeant Bill Lorton, Eleventh Field Artillery, USA
General Douglas MacArthur, USA

William Manchester, Sixth Division, USMC
Private First Class Dick Mitchell, USMC
Admiral Chester Nimitz, USN
Journalist Ernie Pyle
Captain Lawrence Renfroe, USN
Lieutenant Louis Claude Roark, USAAC
General Holland M. Smith, USMC
Major Rick Spooner, USMC
Sergeant Robert Stanfill, USMC
General Joseph Stilwell, USA
Seaman Richard Thelen, USN (USS *Indianapolis*)
Colonel Paul Tibbets, 509th Composite Group, USAAF
President Harry S. Truman
Ken Vander Molen, 182nd Infantry Regiment, USA

The following have graciously and generously provided me with research material. Thank you to all.

Bill Baird, St. Petersburg, Florida
Bruce Breeding, Lexington, Kentucky
Dr. Celia Edmundson, Sarasota, Florida
Charles Fannin, San Jose, California
Edward Figlewicz, Jr., Skokie, Illinois
Jared Frederick, Blacksburg, Virginia
Major Richard Gartrell, USMC
Dr. C. R. Gennaria, Winchester, Virginia
Colonel Keith Gibson, Virginia Military Institute, Lexington, Virginia
Hill Goodspeed, National Museum of Naval Aviation, Pensacola, Florida
Scott Hardy
Pete Harmeling, Danvers, Massachusetts
Rick Henderson, National Cryptologic Museum, Fort George Meade, Maryland
Vern Hettinga
Vice Admiral Gerald L. Hoewing, USN (Ret.), Pensacola, Florida
David Hoffert, Wabash, Indiana
Captain William P. Hogan, USN (Ret.), Bellevue, Washington
Phoebe Hunter, Missoula, Montana
Victoria Hurd, Sarasota, Florida
Helen Hutchison, Tallahassee, Florida
Jack Ingram, Columbia, Maryland

Dennis Lorton, Winter Haven, Florida
Ken Lummus, Indio, California
Cole McCulloch, Martinsburg, Virginia
Cope Mitchell, Colorado Springs, Colorado
Joe Moser, Long Beach, California
Bruce and Linda Novak, Needham, Massachusetts
James Ormsby, Leesburg, Georgia
Bruce Poole, Hagerstown, Maryland
Jim Reeb, USS *Torsk* Maritime Museum, Baltimore, Maryland
Liz Renfroe, Tallahassee, Florida
Stephen Roark, Denver, Colorado
Bob Roffler, North Yarmouth, Maine
Mort Rubin, USN
Margaret C. Smith, Merritt Island, Florida
Jim Tollerton, Sarasota, Florida
Ken Urbach, Lake Mary, Florida
Ray Voet, Ionia, Michigan
Kay Whitlock, Missoula, Montana
Mike Wicklein, Baltimore, Maryland
Bill Zeilstra, Grand Rapids, Michigan

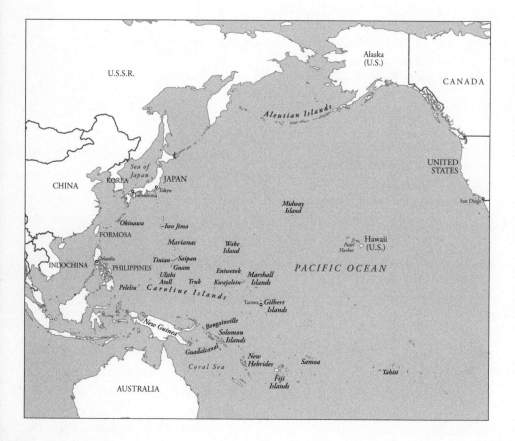

INTRODUCTION

Contrary to what many of us are taught, the Second World War does not begin on September 1, 1939, with Hitler's army invading Poland. In fact, by that time, a war has already been fought on Asian soil for eight years.

In the summer of 1931, the most militant among the Japanese Imperial High Command fabricate an incident that, to them, justifies an all-out invasion of Manchuria, China's northernmost province. More "incidents" are revealed, which lead to attacks against the major Chinese cities of Shanghai and Nanking. The primitive Chinese army is no match for the well-trained and well-equipped Japanese, and in mere months, vast swaths of Chinese territory fall into Japanese hands. By the mid-1930s, Japanese aggression has inspired the League of Nations to offer what amounts to a slap on Japanese wrists. But the Chinese begin to counter, and under the command of Chiang Kai-shek, the Chinese army begins at least to slow the Japanese down. Though the political ramifications of a war between such distant (and foreign) cultures produce few concerns in the West, it is the massacres of Chinese civilians that begin to draw Western attention. The numbers of dead and the ferocity of the Japanese soldiers are staggering, reports causing President Roosevelt to issue a partial embargo on raw materials allowed to enter Japan. As the brutalities against Chinese, Korean, and Southeast Asian peoples escalate, Roosevelt ups the ante by freezing Japanese assets held in the United States. The Japanese respond with loud indignation and claim the need for self-protection from such aggression. They sign the Tripartite Pact, aligning themselves with Germany and Italy, each nation pledging to come to the aid of the others in the event of further hostility from their new enemies.

In 1940, with war now spreading across Europe, a new power emerges in the Japanese government, whose civilian voices have grown increasingly weak. The army assumes increasing authority, and from that army comes General Hideki Tojo. Tojo is vehemently anti-American, a philosophy he imposes on Japanese culture whenever possible. Tojo also commands the Japanese secret police, a force that stifles dissent among the moderates, whose voices are all but snuffed out. In September 1940, building upon a reputation for ruthlessness in Manchuria, Tojo becomes war minister. Immediately he puts his harsh feelings for the United States into strategic planning. Tojo believes that both America and Britain have been weakened considerably by the war in Europe, and all signs point to Germany's eventual victory. Thus a confident Tojo begins to plan for the ultimate achievement, a war to conquer the vast resources of the United States. It is not a view shared by the Japanese navy. Admiral Isoroku Yamamoto delivers a scathing report that calls any engagement with the Americans utter foolishness, and he is supported by many of the admirals who know they will be on the front lines of a fight that must inevitably span the entire Pacific. Despite Yamamoto's reluctance, Tojo orders him to create a plan that will ensure a swift and decisive victory. Yamamoto knows that boldness and surprise are the twin ingredients of success against a formidable foe. He plans to make exceptional use of both. Despite discussions between Japanese and American diplomats in Washington, Tojo has no intention of reaching any peaceful solution. Aware that Yamamoto's plans call for a sneak attack at the very moment their diplomats are talking peace, Tojo remarks, "Our diplomats will have to be sacrificed."

What the Japanese do not know is that the Americans have broken their communications code and are fully aware that soothing words in Washington belie what is taking place in the Pacific. American intelligence knows that Japanese warships have put to sea, but there is no specific word of their mission. Regardless, on Hawaii, the two Americans in command, Admiral Husband Kimmel and General Walter Short, are informed that hostilities with Japan could begin at any time. Though he is warned that the Japanese seem poised to attack the Philippines or Borneo, Admiral

Kimmel never receives word that Washington believes Hawaii to be a target as well. Thus his preparations are minimal, ordering two attack aircraft carriers away from Hawaii to ferry aircraft to Midway and Wake islands. It is the only stroke of luck the Americans will experience. With no reconnaissance planes searching for trouble anywhere close to Hawaii, the American commanders are blissfully unaware that nine major Japanese warships, along with six aircraft carriers and a scattering of smaller escort ships, are steaming toward the U.S. fleet from the northwest. At 6 A.M. on December 7, 1941, the first of two waves of Japanese dive bombers, fighters, and torpedo planes begins an attack at Pearl Harbor that will cost the United States twenty-one ships, more than three hundred aircraft, 2,400 dead, and 1,100 wounded. Despite the isolationist sentiment that still pervades the mind-set of a vast number of Americans, the Japanese attack on Pearl Harbor shatters American complacency. America is in the war.

Even while the smoke rises from Pearl Harbor, Japanese invasion forces surge into the Philippines, virtually obliterating a powerful force of American heavy bombers and fighter planes commanded by General Douglas MacArthur. MacArthur's ground troops, totaling 100,000 Filipinos and 25,000 Americans, are routed completely, and despite a valiant American defense on the Bataan Peninsula and the island fortress of Corregidor, the Japanese prevail. Though MacArthur escapes, the combined forces, under American general Jonathan Wainwright, are forced to surrender, and thus begins the transfer of the prisoners to Japanese prison camps in what will become known as the Bataan Death March. Sixty thousand Filipinos and fifteen thousand Americans endure unmasked brutality and torture along a sixty-mile course that transforms how most Americans view their new enemy. Where barbarism and massacres in China had seemed a distant problem, now the realities of Japanese atrocities come home to the United States.

Throughout late 1941, the Japanese surge engulfs Thailand, Korea, Hong Kong, and Indochina. In the Pacific, the American island of Guam falls, as well as the great chains of islands spreading all across the south and central Pacific, which now become Japanese strongholds. To the south, the Japanese conquer the British fortress at Singapore and sink two British battleships, *Prince of Wales* and *Repulse,* which were thought invincible. The combined blows are a knife in the morale of the British, who had believed their power in that part of the world was unassailable. But the Japanese continue to press forward, and by early 1942 they occupy and fortify the

Dutch East Indies, the Solomon Islands, and New Guinea. Though Wake Island also falls, some five hundred Marines on the island make a valiant though hopeless effort to hold the Japanese away. What is only a minor thorn in the Japanese side becomes a significantly heroic symbol that gives hope to the Americans that the Japanese might not be unstoppable after all. That optimism is further fueled by two enormous engagements, one at sea, the other in the air. In May 1942, the two opposing navies engage in a slugfest in the Coral Sea, northeast of Australia. Though the American and Australian navies suffer the greater loss in warships, the fight ultimately prevents the Japanese from carrying out their planned invasion of Australia. Farther north, in June 1942, the Americans confront a massive Japanese fleet attempting to complete the work begun at Pearl Harbor. The Japanese attempt to lure the American carrier fleet into a trap near Midway Island, northwest of Hawaii. But planes from those carriers instead devastate the Japanese fleet. The loss of their largest and most modern warships, including most of their aircraft carriers, is a blow from which the Japanese will never recover.

At home, the Japanese people and much of their military are being told that the engagements against the enemy are one-sided victories, that the Japanese effort is meeting only with success. With senior commanders believing the tale, the Japanese military loses the sense of urgency that their situation ought to demand, and little effort is made to shore up the devastated fleets. The same is true for Japanese airpower, which has been badly shaken by the increasing skills of American pilots and the improving technology of American aircraft.

On April 18, 1942, the Japanese people receive their first taste that what their government is feeding them might not be the complete truth. Sixteen American B-25 medium bombers are launched from the carrier USS *Hornet,* and make a one-way bombing run over Tokyo. The raid, led by Lieutenant Colonel Jimmy Doolittle, is both success and tragedy. All but one of Doolittle's planes are lost, though many of the crews survive. The raid has no real tactical effect, but to the Japanese people, the sight of American bombs falling on the Japanese capital is eye-opening in the extreme.

In Washington, the American strategy begins to gel. If there is a push to be made against the vast territories now in Japanese hands, it will come from two spheres of control. The more southerly sphere, based in Australia, is commanded by General Douglas MacArthur. The more northerly, because of the vast amount of ocean involved, will be commanded by Admiral Chester Nimitz. Thus begins a two-prong campaign aimed at driving hard into the Japanese bases, which both men believe are overextended. In August 1942, the American First Marine Division, led by General Alexander Vandegrift and supported by troops from Britain, Australia, and New Zealand, launches an invasion of a part of the Solomon Islands anchored by the island of Guadalcanal. The goal is to drive a wedge into the Japanese supply lanes that threaten Australia, and isolate Japanese troops based on New Guinea and surrounding islands. Moreover, the Japanese are rapidly constructing a major airfield there, which will only enhance their presence through that entire part of the Pacific. What begins as an invasion of a single island eventually grows to a fight that involves the ground, air, and sea arms of both sides, and becomes the first extended combat action of the Pacific war. The losses to the Japanese are horrific, and when the fighting ends, the Japanese must face the reality that the tide has turned against them. Both Nimitz and MacArthur realize this as well.

On the mainland of Asia, a different war is being waged. Beleaguered Chinese forces under Chiang Kai-shek are surviving only with the assistance of the British and Americans, who have created two supply routes for sustaining Chiang's army. One, through Burma, is too vulnerable to Japanese attack and so can barely be sustained. The other, far more dangerous, is "the hump," an air route from India across the Himalayan Mountains to China, where fleets of planes and some of the most illustrious pilots in American aviation history haul much needed supplies for the Chinese. But Chiang's army is receiving help from ground and air forces as well, led from India by American general Joseph Stilwell, and inside of China by the Flying Tigers, an American fighter plane wing led by General Claire Chennault. But the two Americans never work effectively together, and Stilwell in particular alienates the British, whose assistance he needs to continue the flow of supplies out of India. Seeds of dissension are sown as well by Chiang, whose corrupt officers and brutal training methods cannot ever put a fighting force into the field to match the Japanese. Worse for Chiang, in China's north there is a new rival leader emerging, whose own army is doing what it can to combat the Japanese. His name is Mao Tse-tung.

In the Pacific, the Americans seem to be falling into the exact kind of strategy the Japanese are now hoping for: a piecemeal, grinding assault against a vast scattering of Japanese island outposts. With sea and air power decidedly in their favor, the Americans believe that overwhelming bombardment of Japanese positions will allow the Marines and army ground troops an advantage in sweeping ashore in so many of these crucial outposts, where airfields and deepwater anchorages await.

The Japanese have purposely expanded their empire into lands where precious war materials, especially oil, rubber, and metal ores, can be ferried to factories in Japan. Cutting those supply lines becomes a priority, mostly for MacArthur, who knows that the Japanese have established large and powerful bases all around resource-rich New Guinea. MacArthur continues his drive up toward the Japanese forces, which results in several sharp engagements, including the Battle of Bougainville, costly for both American and Australian troops.

By this time, it is apparent that a competition has developed between MacArthur and Nimitz, most of that energy coming from MacArthur, who has as his primary goal the liberation of the Philippines. Despite strategic considerations that seem to point more to mainland Japan as the most desired goal, MacArthur insists that his efforts be directed at recapturing the nation to whom he has pledged his *return*. MacArthur has significant popular appeal, especially with the troops in his command, and in Washington not even the chiefs of staff are willing to back him down. Thus the two-prong strategy of the Americans begins to resemble something more like a race.

While the complex strategies and vicious campaigns continue, one particular disaster befalls the Japanese. Code intercepts reveal to American intelligence that Admiral Yamamoto will be traveling a certain route at a certain time through the area approaching Bougainville. In response, American fighters rise to intercept the Japanese admiral and his escorts. They are successful. On April 18, 1943, Yamamoto's plane is shot down, and Japan loses arguably its greatest military planner of the war.

While MacArthur's forces press the fight through the Solomons, still close to New Guinea, Admiral Nimitz aims his spear on a more direct trajectory toward Japan. In November 1943, the next major assault in the chain occurs at an island atoll called Tarawa. Led by General Holland "Howlin' Mad" Smith, two Marine divisions struggle mightily to erase the Japanese positions, which are assumed to have been badly chewed up by heavy naval gunfire. Instead the Marines wade ashore only to find themselves in one of the most costly fights of the Pacific campaign. One more experience awaits them as well. Facing certain defeat, enormous numbers of Japanese soldiers engage in banzai attacks, hordes of men throwing themselves en masse into the Marine positions. The cost in human life is staggering, and the Americans begin to realize that the Japanese are very different indeed. Young Marines embroiled in pitched battles suddenly confront the bizarre, screaming waves of enemy troops pouring into Marine positions with murderous intent yet also an astonishing eagerness to die. When faced with utter defeat, the Japanese choose suicide over surrender, seeking a kind of honor that few Americans can understand.

In the United States, the casualties absorbed on Tarawa are made public: more than a thousand Marines dead, with twice that many wounded. Whether or not the American public fully appreciates the kind of enemy they are fighting, they are rudely awakened to the kind of sacrifice the Marines are being asked to make.

In early 1944, the fights continue, with MacArthur jamming his troops through the Admiralty Islands close to New Guinea, while Nimitz's carriers and warships support the Marines in the Marshall Islands, primarily on the atoll of Kwajalein. By February 1944, Nimitz pushes farther toward the next great chain of islands, the Carolines. There the Japanese maintain one of the most fortified bases in the entire Pacific, the island of Truk. Over time, superior American air and sea power obliterates the Japanese fleet in Truk Lagoon and destroys more than three hundred Japanese aircraft.

In June 1944, the greatest amphibious invasion of all time is coming to fruition a world away, on the beaches at Normandy. Though the American newspapers focus almost exclusively on what General Dwight Eisenhower's forces must accomplish, Admiral Nimitz is engaging in a Pacific campaign that will rival Normandy in its significance. The last great chain of islands that secure the waters far from Japan are the Marianas, and while Eisenhower's army and airborne troops slug their way through the French countryside, Nimitz launches assaults on the island of Saipan, a two-week campaign that claims 14,000 American casualties, two-thirds of them Marines. Less than two weeks after Saipan is secured, Nimitz orders the start of an assault on Guam, to recapture the American island lost so early in the war. At nearly the same time, the Marines and soldiers on Saipan press onward, a short few miles to the island of Tinian. While the fight for Tinian proves not nearly as costly as Saipan, Guam is another matter altogether, with a loss of 8,000 American casualties.

By September 1944, the Normandy campaign draws to a close, and Allied commanders are well aware that Germany's defeat is only a matter

of time. In the Pacific, both MacArthur and Nimitz are accomplishing victories as well, but for MacArthur the big plum still awaits: the Philippines.
For Nimitz, the island hopping continues, the next target a fortified Japanese outpost in the Palau Islands, called Peleliu. Protected by underground
fortifications, the Japanese have strengthened their position on Peleliu to
one of invincibility. But the Americans proceed as they always have and
bombard the island with enormous firepower. On September 15, expecting a stroll on the beach, Marines advance onto Peleliu only to learn that
the Japanese are still waiting for them, protected from the navy's shelling
by a network of underground hiding places. The fight that follows lasts
more than two months and becomes one of the most vicious of the entire
war. The First Marine Division alone suffers more than 6,000 casualties.

Despite the extraordinary cost to the Americans who continue their
drive toward the enemy's homeland, that drive produces results, including
the resignation of the humiliated Hideki Tojo.

With the Mariana Islands now in American hands, long-range B-29
bombers can make strikes directly onto mainland Japan, and begin to do
so with perfect regularity. It is a symbol that few Japanese can misinterpret.
But the airfields are not adequate for the sheer volume of planes the American forces know they must use to bring Japan down. Closer to Japan lies
another atoll, Iwo Jima, where the Japanese have already constructed an
airfield the Americans know they must have. The value of Iwo Jima lies in
its closer proximity to Japan and the fact that American bombers have
demonstrated a woeful record of mechanical failures, which have sent hundreds of crewmen into the sea. What the Americans do not know is that
the 20,000 Japanese troops burrowed into the small chunk of volcanic
rock have learned the lessons from Peleliu and Saipan. Dug into a thousand or more caves and supported by an enormous battery of heavy artillery, the Japanese await the inevitable invasion with perfect calm. The
island is small enough, barely four miles long, that Japanese defenses
spread like a fine spiderweb through the entire island.

On February 19, 1945, more than 60,000 Marines and soldiers make
their landing, only to confront a firestorm that pins them to their beaches.
The ensuing fight lasts six weeks, ending on March 26. The losses to both
sides are staggering. On Iwo Jima the Japanese once again demonstrate
that few will readily accept surrender. Of the 20,000 troops who defend
the island, fewer than three hundred are taken prisoner. But the fight to
the death has accomplished what the Japanese now seem to prefer. The

Americans suffer 26,000 casualties, more than a third of their force. The numbers are so appalling that American newsmen are not given the figures, so that the American people will not learn of the astounding cost of the fight for several months.

With the losses so astoundingly high, the Americans know they cannot sustain many more fights like Peleliu and Iwo Jima. Though MacArthur sticks to his guns and drives into the Philippines, Admiral Nimitz and the strategists in Washington understand what the generals in Europe have learned as well. Waging a *safer* fight from the air will not be enough to win the war. But the airfields close to Japan are crucial, and the islands are essential for basing troops for the eventual invasion of Japan. The maps show plainly that one more island lies in their way. Far larger than Iwo Jima, with deepwater shipping and a dozen airfields, the island is in fact a country, occupied by some quarter million natives, along with their Japanese overseers, estimated to number close to 150,000. This fight will be the first where American troops will strike at a place many Japanese consider their own soil. It is called Okinawa.

PART ONE

1. THE SUBMARINER

The boredom was overwhelming. Even in the darkness, with a low warm breeze, he felt the restlessness, held the sharp stare at what should be the horizon. It was hidden, of course, black water meeting black sky, no hint of the dawn still several hours away. They had patrolled these waters for more than two weeks, some calling it an adventure, the eagerness the crew felt to be back on the search for the scattered Japanese supply ships. Two months before, they had been assigned to *rescue patrol,* close to mainland Japan, a vigilant search for downed American pilots, or even the Japanese. But enemy pilots were very few now, the Japanese air force so depleted, or more likely, so wary of the superiority of their enemy that they seemed to avoid dogfights with the American fighters completely. He hadn't paid much attention to that kind of talk, the newsy communications that filtered down through the chain of command. He was much happier thinking about the American pilots they had rescued, his crew cheerfully hauling aboard coughing breathless men, soaked and shivering, desperately happy to be alive. It was a genuine thrill to rescue a pilot, every sailor feeling that special pride, more so if the man happened to be from a carrier, a naval pilot, and so, one of their own. The pilots were more than just grateful, and in their momentary euphoria they made loud promises of lavish gifts, nights on the town for everyone aboard the sub. The promises usually included a rendezvous in Honolulu or even San Francisco, talk that every crewman enjoyed. The job had been made worthwhile by the beaming gratitude of the men they had saved. It didn't hurt either that as the rescued pilots were returned to their aircraft carriers, they were often *exchanged* for tubs of ice cream, a luxury few submarines carried on their own.

The pilots of the newer American fighters had found that their planes were considerably more agile, and significantly more armored than the legendary Zero, and so the fights grew increasingly one-sided. After long months of terrific casualties among its pilots, Japan seemed to pull the Zeroes out of the sky, holding them back for some purpose no one thought much about. Now the rescues were usually B-29 crews, more likely the result of some mechanical failure in the air than the direct result of combat. Though the B-29 was the largest and most modern bomber of the war, the plane could be a curse to fly. The B-29 had chronic problems with the engines: overheating, flameouts, which might be just as deadly as an accurate strike of an enemy anti-aircraft gun.

The sub rolled slightly to the side, riding a crossing swell, the captain caught off guard, a slight stumble against the steel of the bulkhead. All right, stay awake. But the empty seas were intoxicating, dreamlike, and he thought of the hard bunk down below. Not yet. After dawn you can catch a few winks, but right now your job is up here.

He never fully trusted the instincts of his younger officers, though he knew that his exec, Fred Gordon, was a good man, would likely have his own boat one day, and maybe sooner than the captain preferred. Combat losses to the submarine crews weren't catastrophic, not compared to many of the aircrews above them. Many of the men simply rotated out after several months at sea, fatigue playing a huge part in their decreasing efficiency. But there were combat losses, and the officers who came from Annapolis seemed to feel that far more deeply than their crews. He thought of the *Tang*, sunk a few months before, could see the face of Ed Beaumont. Never thought you'd be the one, Eddie. Lucky in love, lucky in poker, and your fish gets sunk by your own damn torpedo. Happens I guess, and by God you took a few Jap bastards with you. Something to be said for that, I suppose.

The *Tang* had gone down in the midst of a chaotic fight in October the year before, after plowing straight through a Japanese convoy. Her skipper, Dick O'Kane, had already gained a reputation for pure audacity and brilliant success, having sunk nearly two dozen Japanese ships. But on that one night, after causing havoc among a Japanese merchant fleet, the *Tang* had been struck by one of her own torpedoes, some kind of malfunction that sent the torpedo on a circular course. It was a horrific dose of irony to a crew that had poured so much devastation into their enemy.

They say the skipper survived, he thought. Didn't know O'Kane too well, but Eddie loved him. Scuttlebutt says O'Kane will probably get a Medal of Honor, but I doubt it matters much now. Sure as hell doesn't matter to the men who went down with the damn ship.

The communications intercepts indicated that at least a dozen of the *Tang's* crewmen had survived and were being held in Japan. From all he had heard, his friend Beaumont was not among them. So what's worse, he thought. If it's up to me, I'd rather have a lung full of water than some Jap bastard beating the crap out of me every five minutes. That's gonna be the best day of this damn war, the day we can spring our boys from the Jap POW camps. It'll happen, sooner or later. He slapped the steel beside him. How much more can those bastards throw at us? No ships out here, no convoys anymore. The Japs have gotta feed their people, and every piece of their army needs gasoline and oil, and whatever else it takes to keep going. That's my job, isn't it? Send that stuff to the bottom. Hell, here I am, a boatload of torpedoes, and a crew full of piss and vinegar. He stared hard into the darkness. So where the hell are *you*?

The navy had ordered many of the submarines to keep close to the Japanese mainland, still on rescue patrol, the overwhelming number of bombing missions still a priority, and those subs would continue to pluck unfortunate aircrews out of the water. Some performed the task within clear sight of the Japanese coastline, a risky maneuver, made more so by the vigilance of Japanese patrol boats, who sought the same prize. The game was a vicious one, some of the subs engaging the Japanese in firefights on the surface, in water too shallow for diving. Whether rumors and reports of outrageous atrocities were true—all that talk of torture and beheadings by their Japanese captors—the determination to save the downed fliers increased with every bombing mission.

As Japanese convoys seemed to scatter into oblivion, speculation increased through the American command that the Japanese were in desperate straits, food and fuel being parceled out to the military in a trickle, and even less to the civilians. The Americans began to understand how seriously they were strangling the Japanese homeland. The search for seagoing targets became even more intense. Despite the ongoing need for air rescue patrols, many of the subs were ordered away from Japan, back toward the shipping lanes around Formosa and the Philippines, where the Japanese freighters had once traveled unmolested. The greatest challenge now was for the sub commanders to find a target.

The submarines had played a far greater role than most back home would ever know, very few glowing reports in the newspapers, no flow of interviews reaching the home front in glamorous dispatches from men like correspondent Ernie Pyle. As the navy began to be more successful in reaching and breaking the flow of Japanese supplies, the subs borrowed a tactic from the Germans, wolf packs, prowling the seas along the Chinese coast, out through the islands to the east, and then around mainland Japan itself. The Japanese had no effective counter, and the losses to their merchant shipping had been devastating. Their convoys had mostly stopped, and the Allies knew from secret code intercepts and the firsthand accounts of the submarine patrols that the Japanese were quite simply running out of ships. Even the Japanese warships had ceased to be a major threat. Nearly all the great naval battles in the central Pacific had been decidedly one-sided affairs. From Midway to Leyte Gulf, Truk Lagoon and the Coral Sea, the superiority of American carrier-based planes and the warships they supported had crushed the Japanese naval forces, forces that now mostly remained within the safety of their own ports. But Japanese submarines still patrolled the sea lanes, searching for targets that were far too numerous for the Americans to completely shield. The Americans knew that the Japanese technology in radar did not measure up, but their torpedoes were superior, a game of catch-up the Americans were just now realizing. Japanese submarine crews were well trained, considered elite units. The American sub commanders knew that it was their counterparts who had the tools and the skills to strike back, their stealth making them the most formidable foe the Japanese could still bring to the fight.

The sleepiness had gone, a second wind the captain usually felt after midnight. He had gone below for only a brief respite, a quick trip to the head and a handful of chocolate bars. The crew was as alert as he was, the late-night shift the best men he had.

He pulled the wrapping from a piece of chocolate, tossed it down the hatch. No trash overboard, his own rule. They would never leave anything behind, no clue that the Americans had ever been here. A candy carton or a piece of paper floating on the waves might be the best stroke of luck a Japanese lookout could have.

The air was still warm and thick, the light breeze barely any relief. He stood upright in the conning tower, stretching his back, the warm chocolate leaving a sweet film in his mouth. There was sweat inside his shirt, and he thought, after daylight, I'll get a shower. He laughed at the thought, his admonition to the rest of the crew. No one showers before the cook. I'm not going to smell anyone's BO in my damn pancakes.

A sudden swirl of wind engulfed him in the stink of diesel exhaust and he fought the cough, the breeze returning, carrying the exhaust away. The salt spray came now, another shift of the wind, catching the white trail of wake. Dammit, he thought, make up your mind. These are supposed to be trade winds, blowing in one damn direction. So they tell me. Idiot weathermen. Come out of your comfortable office at Pearl and see this for yourself. This damn ocean makes up its own mind, and takes the wind with it. The sub rolled again in a slow, steady rhythm, riding the soft swells, the seas still mostly calm. He glanced to one side, the shimmer of reflected moonlight, a thin sliver coming up low to the east. He judged the size of the wake, thought, twelve knots. We'll keep that up for a while. No reason to worry about getting anywhere fast. No place to go. He thought of the binoculars around his neck, useless. For now the best eyes the sub had were down below, the careful watch of the radar man, Hockley, a boy who seemed to be good at only one thing. Fortunately for the crew, that single talent was spotting the enemy on the radar screen, separating out the noise and blips of whatever might interfere with those blips that actually mattered. He glanced at the microphone to one side. No, if there's something to say, they'll let me know. As he kept his stare on the invisible horizon, there was a familiar twist growing inside of him, anxiousness, the silence unnerving. How in hell can we be the only people out here? There's not even an American fish anywhere close by, not that anyone told me about. The *Queenfish* is well south of us, pretty sure about that. The *Grouper* and the *Pompon* are closer, but not that close. They're doing the same thing I'm doing, wondering where the hell the Japs have gone. Any one of our boys gets near us, I know damn well that we'll pick him up first. They know it too. He laughed quietly, thought of the ongoing bet he had with several of the sub captains. We'll spot you before you spot us. One more thing that kid down there is good at. The sub's name lingered, *Pompon.* That damn Bogley already owes me fifty bucks. I'll meet you at Guam, Captain, and you better fork it over. You don't want me broadcasting all over hell and gone how I snuck up on you from astern within five hundred yards and scared hell out of your sonar guy.

He turned, scanned the ocean in all directions. This is one big damn bunch of water, and somebody else *has* to think this is a good place to be. I'd be a lot happier if I had somebody to chase. Beats hell out of wandering around in the dark. He usually took to the open air of the bridge when the night came, and the other officers knew to leave him alone, unless he asked someone to stand with him. They'll think I'm a real jerk if I bitch about my quarters, he thought. I've got the luxury suite on this bucket, and those boys have to sleep a dozen to a berth, and share each other's farts and BO in the process. He glanced below, faint red light glowing up through a haze of cigarette smoke. No one bitches, at least not so I can hear 'em. And my exec hasn't said anything. I guess we're a happy lot. Yo ho ho. That's it. We ought to put up a Jolly Roger. Nah, I bet the Japs wouldn't have the first idea what the hell that was. I'm guessing they don't watch Errol Flynn movies in Nipland. The playfulness was forced, and he knew that, was still feeling the uneasiness, the itchy tension. Dammit, something just isn't . . . right. Too much ocean and too much of nothing. Down below, the lower level of the open-air bridge, the anti-aircraft guns were unmanned. No Jap planes on patrol out here, he thought, not at night. That's for sure. He focused, blew away the thoughts from his brain, stared hard at the black silence. Okay, Captain, you better let them keep all that cockiness in those offices at Pearl. All it takes is one lucky Jap bastard to drop his eggs too close to us, or spot us underwater. What idiot thought that painting our subs black would make them invisible? This damn water is so clear, a black sub looks like some big damn sea monster. Might as well have been sending up flares, to make it easier for them to spot us. *Black.* How many shouting matches did Admiral Lockwood have to have with those War Department morons before someone figured out to paint these things to match the damn water? Gray's not perfect, but sure as hell beats black. He glanced up, the tip of the two periscopes above him. And then someone decides we should paint the subs pink. *Pink* for God's sake. Supposed to blend in with the ocean. I haven't sailed this tub through one patch of pink water. But what the hell do I know? I'm just out here fighting the enemy. Those engineers and design folks have the tough job, figuring out how much cream to put in their coffee. Now they say we sank every damn ship the Japs have. I'm not believing any of that, not for one second. Somebody's gotta know we're out here, and maybe they're watching us, some smart damn destroyer captain shadowing us. He scanned the blackness, thought, okay, stop that. Hockley would have raised hell down there if anything was around us. And you don't need to show anybody on this crew a case of the jitters. Most of them are too young, too green to know just how human I am. A sub captain's got ice in his blood, yeah. That's it. Ice. Nerves like steel wire. That's what they're told anyway. That's how they think I got this job.

He thought about that, wasn't really sure how he got the job. Yep, I wanted it. It was a plum job, of course, a sub commander ranking among the navy's most elite. Nearly all of us are Annapolis grads, the *elite,* by damned. Yeah, that was tough, worth it for sure. My parents were all gooey about it, my old man bragging to his neighbors. Hell, why not? His boy did good, not like some of those clowns I grew up with. He recalled the graduation with a smile, hats thrown in the air, all the slaps on the back, loud, boisterous calls for what was next, all that *glory.* But that was nearly a decade before Pearl Harbor, and nobody knew anything about what was *next.* Ask my buddy on the *Tang.* Or those poor bastards on the *Growler,* or the *Swordfish.* Glory, my ass.

"Captain. Radar reports a sighting, sir."

The noise jolted him, the voice of Gordon, his exec. He grabbed the microphone, held it to his mouth, pressed the button.

"What is it, Gordy?"

"Sighting at two four zero, moving . . . um . . . zero four zero . . . looks like ten knots."

It was a bad habit Gordon had, that first burst of excitement, tossing out estimates before he had the precise numbers.

"Slow down, Lieutenant. What's their range?"

"Sorry, sir. Seventeen thousand yards." He paused. "Ten knots confirmed."

"Stand by, Gordy. Send Fallon up here."

"Aye, sir."

He glanced toward the compass, his sub moving almost due north, and he stared out toward the direction of the sighting, behind him to the left. Ten miles. Nothing to look at yet. But he's heading roughly toward us, might cross behind us. Ten knots is pretty damn slow. Must be a real piece of junk. He had a sudden flash, his mind fixing on a new thought. Or he's on the *prowl*, looking for something. Yep, that's a whole lot better. If we can get the jump on a Jap warship, that's a whole lot bigger prize than sinking some tub full of rice.

The young seaman, Fallon, rose up through the hatch, a nineteen-year-old who had a knack for precision, and the sharp eyes to match. Fallon stood stiffly, said in a low whisper, "Sir?"

"Richie, man the TBT. We're too far away to see anything, but that's about to change."

"Aye, sir."

Fallon turned close to the high-power binoculars, affixed to the railing of the conning tower, what the navy called the Target Bearing Transmitter. The binoculars were connected electronically to the instruments below, part of the system that impressed every officer in the fleet. It was called the TDC, for Torpedo Data Computer, a bulky piece of equipment near the radar station that, in combination with the radar system, could compute a target's speed and heading, which would translate that information for the precise heading and speed the sub should maintain when firing torpedoes. The captain never pretended to know how it worked, and as long as he had crewmen who knew how to operate the thing, that was fine with him. They had already been credited with sinking seven Japanese merchant ships, and if the man who invented the TDC wanted a pat on the back for that, the captain was ready to offer it.

He looked at the glow on the hands of his watch.

"Three-thirty, Richie. We've got maybe two hours before visual. I'm not waiting."

He reached for the microphone, pressed the key.

"Helm. Left full rudder, go to heading two seven zero, maintain fifteen knots."

"Aye, sir. Left full rudder, two seven zero, at one five knots."

"Lieutenant Gordon, secure the radar."

The exec's voice came back immediately, Gordon expecting the order.

"Done, sir."

No need for anyone to pick up our signal, he thought. Jap equipment isn't too hot, but they can sure as hell pick up a radar beam. He settled back against the steel of the bridge's railing. Now, we wait. As long as they don't change course, we'll run right into them.

The sub was in full turn now, and he braced himself against the steel, the young seaman doing the same. He ignored the compass, knew that the helm would get it right. Done this too many times. So, who the hell's out there? Is he alone? Too far away now, but we'll know pretty soon. We'll keep the radar off for twenty minutes, then give another quick look. Hockley's got a good eye, can pick out whatever the hell it is in a flash. Japs can't home in on us if we're quick. I like good surprises, not bad ones. He stared out toward the unseen vessel, his thoughts beginning to race. What the hell are you, and where the hell do you think you're going? This is *my* damn ocean, pal.

He had dropped down into the cramped conning tower, leaned close to the radar station, had to see it for himself. Above, his executive officer had replaced him in the open air of the bridge, alongside the young seaman, Fallon. There was a high tension throughout the tight space, the hard familiar odor of grease and bodies, young hands on the switches and controls, every man doing his job in perfect silence. Below his feet, in the ship's control room, he knew it was exactly the same, a little more room, but men elbow to elbow, perched at their various stations, waiting for any order that would put them into action. The captain bent low, stared at the dark screen, said, "All right, Hockley, activate radar. Five seconds only."

Hockley flipped the switch, the round green screen flashing brightly, both men staring intently, the blip prominent.

"It's moving closer, sir. Eight thousand yards, ten knots. She'll pass in front of us . . ."

"Secure radar. I know where she's heading, son. We'll get a real good look in about fifteen minutes." He turned toward the sonar station, saw another young man, Gifford, earphones clamped to his head. Gifford had his eyes closed, intense concentration, and the captain knew what was coming, waited for it. Gifford's eyes popped open and he looked toward the captain, nodded, a low voice.

"It's a freighter, sir. Pitch too low for a destroyer. The screws are too heavy." He seemed to catch himself, puzzled, and the captain waited for more.

"It sounds like . . . two ships, sir. Two different rhythms."

The captain looked back to the radar, said, "Activate radar. Five seconds only."

The green light reflected through the small space, and he saw clearly a single blip.

"Dammit. Secure radar. What the hell, son, there's one blip. They riding piggyback?"

"Sorry, sir. But it sounded pretty distinct . . ."

"You sure it's not wax in your ears, Gifford? Radar shows one ship."

Gifford was sweating in the musty heat, and the captain could see the frustration, uncertainty. The Japanese ships had a variety of rhythms and varying pitches depending on their speed and the size of their engines, but the captain knew that his instruments weren't perfect, that often the best instrument they had was the sharp ear of the sonar man. It wasn't something you could train, not completely anyway. There was a peculiar talent that every sub captain valued, the keen ear that could separate the blend of sounds, especially when there were several approaching ships. But Gifford was only nineteen, had come aboard the sub on this most recent patrol, replacing a man the captain was sorry to lose. Gifford might have the skills, but the captain knew he had not yet been under fire. He felt growing frustration, glanced up toward the hatch. They'll be able to see something pretty soon. And we'll get spotted ourselves if someone's paying attention out there. Gifford had his hands clamped on the earphones, eyes closed again, shook his head. The captain watched him, thought, be certain, son. It matters. Gifford looked up at him again, a hint of fear, the telltale lack of confidence.

"I swear . . . there are two ships, sir."

The captain slapped him on the shoulder, said, "All right, we'll look for two ships. We'll figure this out pretty quick."

He climbed the ladder to the open bridge, emerged out of the smoky heat into the soft warmth of the breeze, the exec, Gordon, making space for him.

"Nothing to see yet, Skipper."

"Patience, Lieutenant."

To one side, Fallon had his hands clamped on the TBT binoculars, anxious, frozen in place, knowing his part in this elaborate operation. He was, after all, the eyes, would be the first man to actually see whatever it was that would soon come into visual range.

The captain turned east, a hint of gray on the horizon, thought, all right. Time for some light on this show. He said to Gordon, "Go below, Lieutenant. Prepare to dive on my order. Sonar could be wrong about that thing being a freighter, and I sure as hell don't want a surface fight with a destroyer. Maintain this course until we get a good look at whatever's coming. We should intersect at about two thousand yards, but we'll see him way before then. And sure as hell, they'll see us."

Gordon moved to the hatch, descended, a clipped response.

"Aye, sir. Preparing to dive."

Beside him, the young seaman seemed to jump, leaning into the mounted binoculars.

"Got her, sir!"

The young man knew the drill, immediately stepped aside. The captain leaned close, stared into the TBT binoculars, saw it for himself now, the low gray silhouette. He felt his heart beginning to thump, sharing the young seaman's excitement. There was never a thrill quite like that first glimpse, when a target first appeared. The fox and the hound, he thought. Or better, the mountain lion and the deer. Yep, like that one better. Going for the throat. He kept his eye on the distant ship, reached for the microphone, said in a low voice, "Activate radar, but just for range. Make it quick."

He waited, then heard the words.

"Four thousand, sir. Closing at ten knots."

There was a small tug in his brain, a hint of warning. Why so damn slow? A Jap merchant can make eighteen to twenty, most of 'em anyway. He could see the silhouette more clearly now, definitely a merchant ship. This is too easy. Okay, fine. Give us a gift. I'll take it.

He knew the calculations in his head, had been through this too many times before. The sub had approached east of the merchant ship, the light of the dawn at his back, the breaking sunlight acting as camouflage. Even on the surface, with the sub positioned straight at the merchant, it made almost no silhouette at all, and if a sharp-eyed Jap lookout saw her, it would be too late to do anything about it.

He leaned away from the TBT, the young seaman taking over. He stepped back, stared at the horizon, the lightening sky betraying the Japanese ship to the naked eye. Now the instruments took over, the odd mechanics that had already plotted the target's trajectory, range, and speed, and the ideal moment when he would give the order to fire the first spread of torpedoes. He knew that in the bow, the men had already received the order to load the six torpedo tubes, the training and the experience coming into play. He gripped the steel beside him with one hand, took the microphone in the other, waited, could see a hint of diesel smoke rising from the distant ship, her course taking her directly perpendicular to the sub's bow, a perfect broadside. Yep, he thought. The deer, unaware, helpless, perfect.

The voice came now, from below, Gordon, too loud, nervous.

"Prepared to fire, sir. Optimum range in ten seconds."

He didn't respond, thought, easy, Gordy. He ticked the seconds off in his mind, then said, "Fire one."

"One away, sir."

There was a slight lurch beneath his feet, and he stared past the bow, a hint of a wake, but little else.

"Fire two."

"Two away, sir."

He felt the chill, the sweat in his shirt, the pure thrill. Come on, dammit. He had a stopwatch in his pocket, but his exec did as well, and he knew that Gordon was staring at it now, measuring, counting down, sweating, as he was. No radar needed now, no earphones on the sonar man, everyone on the sub doing exactly what their captain was doing, waiting, pulsing tension, feeling the seconds tick away. He kept his stare at the distant ship, thought of firing a third, no, not yet. Unless something screwy happens, this should be . . .

The flash of light burst high, striking amidship, engulfing the ship quickly, and then another, close to the bow. He clenched one fist, punched the air, pure joy, heard a cheer break out below. Beside him, the boy kept his stare into the TBT, held his composure, still did his job. The freighter was hidden completely now by a fiery cloud of black smoke, and he slapped the young seaman on the back, said, "Good work, son." He keyed the microphone, his words louder than usual, the momentary lapse in his composure.

"Good shooting, boys! Cigars for breakfast." He watched the fire, could see the bow of the ship rising, telltale signs that the ship was in pieces.

"Let's get over there, see if anybody's floating around."

Below he heard the voice of the exec, still the loud excitement.

"Ahead one-third, keep your eye on the prize."

Suddenly the speaker beside him erupted, the voice of Gifford.

"Sir! Sonar contact! A second ship!"

"Radar! Hockley, you got anything?"

"No, sir! No contact!"

He understood now, felt supremely stupid. The second ship, detected only by sound. Because she's *submerged.*

"Prepare to dive!"

He yanked at Fallon's shirt, pushed him toward the hatch, the young man obeying, dropping down quickly. The captain gave a last glance toward the burning merchant ship, thought, ten knots. Perfect target. Bait. It worked, and I'm a dumb son of a bitch.

He dropped down through the hatch, his feet scrambling for the steps of the ladder, and with one motion he pulled the hatch closed above him.

"Dive!"

The order was repeated, the telltale *whoosh* of the ballast tanks, the ship immediately dropping her bow. He saw the faces turned toward him, Gifford and his earphones. The captain said nothing, thought, he was right. And I should have figured it out. Damn fool. All right, do your job. Let's get our asses out of this mess.

"We level out at periscope depth, go to silent running! Nobody sneezes, nobody farts! We've got a Jap sub on our ass!"

The voice of Gordon came in a hard whisper, the exec speaking into a phone receiver, the word passing throughout the ship.

"All hands. Silent running."

Gordon was still on the intercom, listening, a faint voice on the other end of the line, and the captain knew it was the helm officer down below, in the control room. His exec looked at him now, gave a quick thumbs-up. The captain nodded, thought, all right, periscope depth. Now we sit and see what this bastard is going to do. He moved to the main periscope, one hand resting on warm brass. The heat around him seemed magnified by the silence, and he felt the sub tilt slightly, rocking gently in the slow-moving current. He wiped the sweat from his face, looked at the others, some staring at Gifford, others at the instruments close in front of them. No sound, he thought. Nothing. Don't let that bastard have any more advantage than I already gave him. He scanned the crew, looked down toward the hatchway to the control room, thought of the galley. That's where it happens, he thought. Too much tin in too small a space, and the cook was probably getting breakfast together. He couldn't avoid the slight cringe, expecting the sound of something banging the deck, a pot, any piece of silverware carelessly unsecured. But there was only silence, and he let out a breath, thought, all right, maybe an extra cigar for the cook.

His shirt was soaking wet, and he fought the furious helplessness, looked again at Gifford. The sonar man was unmoving, his hands clamped against the earphones. After a long, deathly pause, Gifford looked up at him, wide eyes, a slow nod, and said in a whisper, "Five hundred yards to port, bearing across our stern, sir. No change in course or speed."

The captain nodded, no orders, not yet. Gifford seemed to stare past him, his head turning instinctively, toward the port side of the sub. The captain waited, still angry at himself, thought, point-blank range. Dammit! But if he hasn't fired at us, he may not know where we are. Nothing to do but . . . sit here. The sub was deathly silent around him, no other sound in the conning tower but the hard breathing of the men around him. He knew that conditions would get worse quickly in the tight space, no ventilation, the air growing more foul by the minute. The captain felt the dripping wetness in his shirt, stinging in his eyes. He cursed silently, kept his stare on Gifford. After a long moment, Gifford pointed out, forward to port, said in a whisper, "He's . . . Jesus . . . he's right there, moving past. Two hundred yards!"

He felt Gifford's excitement, acknowledged with a short nod, felt a burst of giddiness. Captain Nip has no idea where we are. None. He tried to imagine the conning tower of the enemy sub, their captain sweating in the stifling, smoky heat, giving his own orders, discipline and precision that came from the best training the Japanese could give their naval officers. But he doesn't have our sonar, not even close. He's pissed off, baffled, wondering where the hell we went. I'll tell you where, you Jap son of a bitch. We just switched roles. Now I'm hunting *you.*

He felt his breathing, hard and heavy, fought to silence it, but it didn't matter now, the others in the conning tower watching him. He kept his eye on Gifford, who looked up at him from the small seat, one hand rising, pointing out to stern, mouthing the words, "Should cross our stern in about three minutes . . . no change, sir. Distance increasing."

The captain nodded, pointed to the young man's earphones, the silent, unnecessary order: stay focused, son. He looked at Gordon, pointed to the intercom.

"Load aft torpedo tubes. Quickly! Quietly!"

The emphasis was unnecessary, his fingers curled into fists, impatience while the lieutenant gave the order. He felt the periscope against his back, had a burst of an idea, a short debate in his brain. It's a risk, dammit, but I've got to see you, make sure you're still moving off. I want to see it for myself. This is a shot of a lifetime, but if you're too close, this could blow us both to hell. He looked toward a seaman, the young man's eyes on him, his hand on an instrument panel, seeming to anticipate the order.

"Up main periscope!"

"Aye, sir, main periscope."

The switch was thrown, the hydraulics silently sliding the fat tube upward. The captain knelt slightly, wrapped his hands around the grips on either side, rose up with it, spun it around quickly to stern, stared, focused, felt a burst of cold, delicious surprise. He wanted to laugh, could see with perfect clarity a single spear pointing upward, moving slowly away from him. Well, hello, Captain. You seem to be looking the wrong damn way. Another whisper, a quick motion with his hand.

"Down periscope."

He stepped closer to the sonar station, Gifford still wide-eyed, his ears full of the whining rotation of the Japanese engines. He looked up at the captain now, nodded furiously, and the captain touched the earphones, Gifford removing them. The captain leaned low, said, "Give me a thumbs-up when he's thirty seconds from dead astern. Tell me if he changes course one degree!"

Gifford nodded, his eyes staring again into the distance, his ears doing the work.

He tried to imagine the scene on the Japanese sub, frantic orders, their perfect trap maybe not so perfect now. But you ought to be circling, you stupid ass. Unless you're putting too much faith in your instruments. You have to think we hauled it out of here, that we ran like hell when we heard you coming. Why the hell else would you be moving off in a straight damn line? Especially after what you just pulled off. It was a hell of a good plan, Captain, I'll give you that. Shadow your own merchant ship, trying to see if your enemy might come along and blow her to hell. Wonder what your merchant captain thought of that idea? Or did he even know you were there? Okay, so I obliged you. But you haven't won anything yet. Right now, I'm the cat.

He fought to breathe through the thick hot air, felt the pounding in his chest, that perfect moment coming very soon, the *opportunity.* He looked toward Gordon, who moved close.

"Aft torpedo tubes loaded and ready, awaiting your order."

"Wait for it, Gordy."

"Sir."

He thought of the aft torpedo room, knew there was silent chaos there, some of the men sleeping in the bunks, packed in around the torpedoes. They're awake now, that's for certain. With the order for silent running, he knew the officers would have spread all through the ship, that even the sleeping day shift would be aroused with urgency, no chance of a loud cough, no chance a man would drop something from his bedding.

The heat was increasing, driving the captain's temper, and he stared hard at Gifford, no change, his breathing in hard, short punches. The captain did the same, thought, please don't be too damn clever, you Jap bastard. Gifford caught his eye, gave him an exaggerated thumbs-up.

Good, very damn good, he thought. He leaned close to the TDC operator, the man staring hard at the gauges.

"Got him?"

"Got him, sir. If he maintains course, he'll be dead astern in no more than thirty seconds."

If he maintains course.

The cold chill ran through him, a stab in his stomach. He made one more glance toward Gifford, who stared back at him, sweat on the man's face. Steak dinner for you, kid. He turned to Gordon, who held the intercom phone in his hand, no need for quiet now.

"Fire one."

He heard the telltale swish from the tube in the stern.

"Fire two."

He caught motion from Gifford, the sonar man hearing their own torpedoes, tearing the earphones from his head, and the captain nodded, thought, smart. We're awfully damn close. He thought of the stopwatch in his pocket, no, we'll know pretty quick . . . the sub suddenly rocked hard, a shock wave that seemed to roll her over to one side. He fell against the pipe railing of the periscope station, saw others staggering, some tumbling from their seats, reaching for pipes and bulkheads, scrambling back to their positions. He felt a sharp pain in his ribs, ignored it, the sub still rolling like a slow-motion bucking horse, gradually righting itself. Gordon pulled himself upright, had blood on his face, and the captain ignored him, moved close beside Gifford, shouted, "Earphones! Anything moving?"

The young man obeyed, the captain watching him, aching with the tick of long seconds. Then Gifford removed the earphones, said, "Nothing, sir. He's gone." Gifford seemed to grasp the meaning of his own words, the others as well, fists pumping, backslaps, and the captain said, "Stand down from silent running."

He looked toward Gordon, who wiped blood from a wound to his scalp, said, "You okay, Gordy?"

The exec nodded, no explanation necessary. Every crewman knew the sub was one dangerous obstacle course, especially if you lost your footing.

He reached for the intercom.

"Dive control. Take her up. I wanna see some oil."

The order was given, and beneath his feet in the control room, the helmsman responded, the crew going through the routine again, the sub's bow tilting upward. After a full minute the signal came from the dive officer, and he climbed up, spun the wheel on the hatch, pushed it open through a light shower of salt water. He shielded his eyes from the burst of new sunlight, climbed up quickly. Behind him there was a clattering of activity, gunner's mates coming up right behind him, more of the routine, the men who would man the smaller deck guns and the anti-aircraft guns close to the conning tower. He stood upright on the bridge, sucked in a lungful of cool fresh air, the wetness in his shirt cool and sticky. He peered out to stern, nothing but dark blue ocean, wide soft swells, the sun just above the horizon to the east. He grabbed the microphone.

"Right full rudder. Reverse course. Ahead slow."

"Aye, sir. Right full rudder, reversing course, ahead slow."

The sub began to turn, and he saw it now, a spreading stain, the glistening sheen of oil on the surface, streams of bubbles. He raised his own binoculars, scanned the water's surface, saw pieces of debris. Direct hit, he thought. Busted her all to hell. He glanced at the compass, thought of the merchant ship, gone as well, a debris field a mile out beyond the oil. We should check that out too, see what we can find. Could be survivors.

"Exec to the bridge."

He knew Gordon was anxious for the order to come topside, to see it for himself. In seconds the executive officer was up beside him, scanning out with his own binoculars.

"Not a thing, Captain. Just junk. Holy mackerel. He never knew what hit him."

The captain leaned both hands on the steel rail of the bridge.

"Wrong, Gordy. He knew exactly what hit him."

Gordon looked at him, and the captain saw the bloody handkerchief held against the wound, the smiling face. Gordon said, "Pretty good day, eh, Skipper? Two for the price of one."

The captain said nothing, could see the second debris field more clearly now. Other men were coming up into the morning coolness, the rescue teams, led by another of the lieutenants. It was routine after a sinking, men spreading along the sub's deck fore and aft, searching for life rafts or someone in the water. Beside him, Gordon said, "This calls for a hell of a party, Skipper. A merchant *and* a warship. Can't get much better than that."

Gordon's words sank into him, and he tried to find the thrill, to share the lieutenant's enthusiasm. But there was a strange emptiness, unexpected, overpowering the man's excitement.

"Yeah, I guess. Give the crew some extra dessert tonight. Whatever."

"You okay, Skipper?"

"Yeah, sure. Two quail in one bag. Gotta love that."

"You don't sound like you love it."

He kept his stare on the oil slick.

"Haven't sunk a sub before." He kept the rest to himself, the odd change in his mood. Merchant ships never gave me a minute's thought. Sinking *steel,* that's all. Tonnage, equipment, supplies, *numbers.* Never gave much of a crap about the crews.

"Oh, hell, Skipper, you got a warship! We'll be bragging about this one!"

"Maybe. Yeah, fine."

"You thinking about . . . the crew, Skipper? Hell, they're just Japs. Just 'cause they were on a submarine . . ."

"That's why they matter, Gordy. This one wasn't about steel and the junk it takes to fight a war. That could have been us. Nothing but an oil slick."

Below him, on the deck, a voice called up.

"Nothing to report, Captain. Just bits of cargo and timbers. Looks like she went down with all hands." The captain nodded, said, "Bring your boys back up. Let's get under way."

"Aye, sir."

Gordon said, "With your permission, sir, I'll go below. Cook should have some breakfast ready about now. The crew deserves a toast, even if it's just bad coffee." The captain stood aside as the rescue teams came up onto the bridge, the men filing down through the hatch. Gordon began to follow, said, "Lieutenant Green is on first watch. I'll send him up. Breakfast, Skipper?"

"In a minute. Go on below. Tell helm, resume course zero three zero, maintain twelve knots. Double-check the torpedo count, fore and aft. We need to keep hunting."

"Aye, sir."

Gordon disappeared, and the captain was alone now. The morning was cool, the breeze light, the sub rocking gently through the long, deep swells. He kept his eye on the oil slick, thought, nice try, Captain. You almost pulled it off. I was careless, cocky, all ready to gloat about one more great victory, sending some piece of junk merchant ship to the bottom. You were counting on that, weren't you? Smart enough to know I might be careless. I should have listened to sonar. Gifford knew you were there, knew there were two ships. I won't make that mistake again.

He couldn't shake the thoughts of his friend Beaumont, the *Tang*. Maybe he never knew what hit him either. Best way to go. Best way for any of us. He saw a man coming up through the hatch, another of his officers, Green, followed by a crewman.

"I have the watch, sir. Lieutenant Gordon said to tell you that breakfast is in your mess."

"Thank you, Steve."

"Good shooting this morning, sir. We nailed those bastards but good."

"Yep. Good shooting."

He made one more glance toward the oil slick, knew that he would not forget this. The curses were always there, the insults, *Nip bastards, Jap sons of bitches*. Yeah, maybe, he thought. They're the enemy and we hate their guts. *No good Jap but a dead Jap*. But that one was a sub captain, and he was sharp, and if he'd had better equipment . . .

He turned away, moved toward the hatch, thought, lucky for all of us, he won't be around to try that again.

2. NIMITZ

He took careful aim, squeezed off a round, the .45 jumping in his hand. He squinted, could see the impact on the target, a small hole just right of center. He aimed again, fired one more round, the small hole punched square on the paper target's crosshairs. He turned, glanced toward his Marine guard with a self-satisfied smile.

"Sixty years old, dammit. Eyes like a hawk. Anybody feel like taking the old man on?"

The Marines knew the routine, their sergeant offering a polite smile.

"Thank you, sir, but my men don't get their pay for another three days. I can't have any of them coming to me for a loan because the admiral's cleaned their pockets."

Nimitz turned again to the target, smiled, had heard that answer before. He thought of refilling the pistol's clip, but the heat was stifling, even the late afternoon cloud cover not enough to hold back another day of sweating misery. He glanced up, saw no sign of rain, shook his head, said aloud, "Another scorcher. And this is supposed to be spring. I really don't want to suffer through this place in July."

There was no response from the Marines, the eight men who followed him everywhere he went. It was the standard procedure, handpicked body-guards, the best security force Nimitz could imagine. On Hawaii there hadn't really been much of a need for this kind of security, other than pro-tection from the most pesky of newspapermen, or the occasional GI, fu-eled by a little too much liquor, who had decided that airing his grievances straight into the face of the highest-ranking officer available might be a good idea. Even at Pearl Harbor, Nimitz hadn't seen much of that, the Ma-rine guards more brutally effective at their job than they would want him to witness.

He holstered the pistol, wiped a handkerchief across his brow, turned again to the Marines. He had tried to memorize their names, knew the sergeant was O'Neal, a huge plug of a man from Chicago, who might be just as happy in a police uniform, bashing in the skulls of pickpockets. The others weren't much different, thick, dangerous-looking men, chosen for both their appearance and their marksmanship. He knew that an eight-man guard might have been overkill on Hawaii, but on Guam it was en-tirely necessary. Guam had been declared *secure* the preceding August, but almost daily the American patrols that pushed cautiously through the hills and thickets of jungle found themselves confronted by pockets of stubborn Japanese troops who refused to end their fight. To the hazard and the ex-treme annoyance of the Americans who sought them out, the Japanese who took the deadly risk of confronting the Americans didn't stick around long enough for the Marines to do much about it. They seemed to vanish straight into the earth, into a labyrinth of caves and tunnels the Marines had found on nearly every island where the two sides had met. To the Americans, it was a curious mix of frustration and bewilderment, as it had been after every American victory. No matter how brutal the slaughter, no matter the horrifying casualties, the Japanese seemed oblivious to the utter defeat their army had suffered. It had been the same way on Guadalcanal, on Peleliu, Saipan, and Tinian. Guam was no different. As dangerous as the stragglers and holdouts continued to be, Nimitz had a grudging respect for their tenacity, and their cunning. He knew they had to be desperately hungry, short of ammunition and anything else a man needed to survive in these inhospitable places. And yet survive they had, holding out in make-shift sanctuaries, able to evade the constant American patrols. For months now, enraged Marine commanders had used a variety of tactics, some in-sisting on the brute force of tanks and flamethrowers. Others chose a more subtle approach, employing snipers who worked alone, perched in treetops and carefully disguised thickets, hoping that the last hint of daylight would encourage an impatient Japanese soldier to betray his hiding place. But more often the Japanese came out after dark, scavenging silently through supply dumps and garbage pits, melting away at first light, only to emerge again the following night. Some were no more dangerous than the rats and other vermin that plagued the mess halls and kitchens, just hungry men who slit tent walls to grab the occasional loaf of bread. Others had shown a brazen curiosity, one report coming to Nimitz's office that during the showing of a much-sought-after Dorothy Lamour film, the Seabees in attendance were suddenly aware that along the back of the open-air tent, a handful of Japanese soldiers had gathered in rapt attention, sharing the Seabees' admiration for the pronounced curves of the actress. The Seabees had made a chaotic effort to capture the trespassers, mostly to no avail. The reaction from Nimitz's staff had been a mix of outrage and laughter, but Nimitz knew that there was nothing funny about any of this. Japanese soldiers meant Japanese weapons, and there would be no humor at all if the commander in chief of operations in the central Pacific was suddenly gunned down by a sniper, or confronted by a bayonet-wielding enemy during the admiral's morning jog.

Nimitz had loved Hawaii, certainly, and though he appreciated the enormous responsibility he carried for the staff work and warehouses of paper that engulfed his command, he had quickly grown weary of the vast sea of minutiae that accompanied every move his forces had made. His excuse, one that not even Admiral King in Washington could argue with, was that, with the upcoming campaigns pushing closer to Japan itself, Nimitz needed to be *out there.* The move to Guam had come in January, after a not so discreet shove to the Seabees who had begun building his headquarters on a site he had chosen months before. With most of the vast ocean now between the admiral and the suffering officers who dealt with so much of his paperwork, Nimitz had brought a relaxed atmosphere to his new headquarters. To the surprise of every senior officer who happened to visit, Nimitz had allowed his men to adapt to the hard tropical heat by wearing shorts. Neckties were almost nonexistent. Even the admiral himself could be spotted during his morning routine, keeping trim by a long, vigorous run on the beachside road, bare legs and bare-chested, the Marine guards who ran with him wisely keeping any commentary to themselves.

One member of his staff had been indispensable and so had made the trip to the new headquarters. Nimitz heard him now, the manic fierceness of his schnauzer, a fairly vicious dog who seemed to dislike everyone but his master. Even the Marines respected the schnauzer's temper, each man freezing in place as the schnauzer galloped past. Nimitz turned, watched with a smile as the dog bounced up to him, stopping abruptly, spinning in the sand, rolling over in a desperate request for a belly rub. Nimitz could never resist the dog's show of soft affection, something few of his officers had ever witnessed. He leaned low, stroked the dog's exposed stomach, the schnauzer's tongue hanging loosely out of its mouth.

"Damn you, Mak, you're too spoiled. Just once I'd like to try this little maneuver of yours with my own staff. They think you're some kind of damn werewolf. Hell, I can't even get my wife to do this to *me* . . ." He stopped, thought of the Marine sergeant, kept the indiscreet thought to himself. He stood straight again, the schnauzer bounding away once more, and Nimitz looked to the west, the sun melting into the far horizon like a fat blob of orange ice cream. The Marines kept to their usual boxlike formation, most of them keeping their gaze on the distant trees. He enjoyed talking to the men, but there was little opportunity for that beyond the walls of his compound, and there the guards understood that their job didn't include socializing with the brass they were supposed to protect. He enjoyed their generals far less, the men like Holland Smith, known by all as Howlin' Mad Smith, the Marine commander who had headed up the slugfests that tore Guam, Tinian, and Saipan from Japanese control. Smith's command now included the forces that were completing operations on a dismal slab of lava rock called Iwo Jima, and Nimitz knew that the horrendous Marine casualty counts would throw Smith into a hot temper directed toward anyone in his command who had failed to live up to Smith's own standards. It wasn't a bad trait for a commander to have, but Smith had made few friends among the brass from the army and navy he was supposed to be working beside. Nimitz knew that Howlin' Mad's days were numbered in this part of the war. Even out here, a good general could create problems for himself if he didn't respect politics. Smith would have no role at all in the upcoming invasion of Okinawa, that job placed into the hands of army general Simon Bolivar Buckner, Jr. Buckner had been a surprise choice to some, and Nimitz knew he was despised by Douglas MacArthur, who had made it clear that he wanted Buckner far removed from MacArthur's own command to the south. But Buckner seemed to be a man who understood that it was possible, even necessary, to combine army and Marine forces into one cohesive unit, without making enemies

in the process. And, as Nimitz had been quick to observe, Buckner was a
man who understood that his superiors, namely Nimitz himself, had the
last word.

He turned back toward the headquarters buildings, saw the usual
rumblings of activity, jeeps coming and going, men on foot, some of them
MPs. But it was the heavy equipment that caught his attention, men up on
bulldozers and excavators. The Seabees were continuing to improve the
Guam command post, adding buildings and storage areas as the need
arose. Nimitz enjoyed watching the massive machines, green steel and
black smoke. He knew the Seabees carried a chip on their shoulder for the
lack of attention the newspapermen gave them. Just because a man rides a
bulldozer doesn't mean he can't get shot to hell, he thought. They've sure
as hell taken their share of casualties too. But if I need an airstrip or a harbor cleared, there's no one as good at it as those boys. They're probably
pretty sick of getting razzed by the Marines, but any Marine worth a crap
who's watched these boys turn a swamp into a mess hall learns to keep his
mouth shut. And if one of those bulldozer jockeys busts a rifleman in the
mouth for smarting off about driving a tractor . . . well, I haven't put one
in the stockade yet.

He glanced again at the setting sun, heard a storm of barking from the
schnauzer, looked that way. He had expected to see Buckner, the army general often timing his frequent meetings to coincide with Nimitz's afternoon cocktail hour. But the man he saw now was shorter, moving toward
him with a hurried determination. Nimitz knew the uniform of the air
corps, watched as the man pretended to ignore the dog, who now circled
him in a show of temper, neither the man nor the beast allowing the other
to intimidate him. Nimitz knew that might be the smartest move his dog
could make. The man was Curtis LeMay.

LeMay walked more toward the pistol target than Nimitz himself,
said, "Not bad, Admiral. I hear MacArthur can't hit the side of a barn."

"Good afternoon, General. Care for a little target shooting?"

"No chance. You'd embarrass me. Won't stand for that."

Nimitz smiled, thought, no, you wouldn't stand for that at all.

LeMay was a gruff bulldog of a man, hated anyone's inefficiency, and
had no hesitation spouting off about it. He had spent most of his career spouting off about nearly everything, and if you didn't agree with

LeMay's manic dedication to the army air force, you were most likely to be disrespected in a way that most senior commanders wouldn't tolerate. Nimitz knew that LeMay didn't much care for him at all, probably disliked anyone who had *webbed feet,* the man's casual insult to anyone in a naval uniform. But Nimitz knew that despite his irritable disregard for anyone else's authority, LeMay carried a frightening dedication to destroying the enemy. As long as LeMay brought results, Nimitz could care less what the man thought of him, and would ignore LeMay's utter lack of social graciousness.

LeMay commanded the Twenty-first Bomber Command, and in the often strange configuration of the American military's chain of organization, he was the only general officer serving in the central Pacific who was not technically under Nimitz's authority. It was the ongoing mystery of just how the War Department handled their air force; no one was really sure just who should be running that show, other than the airmen themselves. But the targets for the air force were spread out over the entire theater of the war, from Joe Stilwell's command in the China/Burma campaigns, over MacArthur's area throughout New Guinea and the Philippines. It wasn't a practical solution to have the air force fall under the single authority of anyone on the ground. Nimitz had come to accept LeMay's independence, knew better than to concern himself with the views of either Stilwell or MacArthur. He had a large enough sphere of authority without worrying about nagging controversies in Washington that never seemed to fade away. From the air force's first days, there had been outright hostility between those who saw enormous value in airpower and those who considered airplanes a waste of resources. Though the air force was technically under the umbrella of the army, the senior air force commander, Hap Arnold, had rarely accepted anyone's authority other than the president. In Washington, Arnold had shown sufficient stubbornness and had earned enough clout with members of Congress that most in the War Department conceded to him his place in the military's hierarchy, virtually equal to that of George Marshall and Admiral Ernest King. That arrangement had worked well enough in Europe, where the value of airpower had long proven itself. There General Eisenhower had avoided any controversy over the independence of Jimmy Doolittle and Tooey Spaatz. But those men had made it a point to work in full cooperation with the Allies' European commander. As far as Nimitz could see, Curtis LeMay had little interest in cooperating with anyone. Like many in the air commands, LeMay seemed to believe that the war could be won by dropping as many bombs as possible on the enemy. With his extraordinary success in obliterating so much of the Japanese capital, LeMay would only grow more vocal about fighting the war precisely as he pleased. The soldiers and Marines who slogged ashore into vicious fighting on so many of these disease-infested islands were just a time-consuming sideshow.

L eMay leaned close to the paper target, said, "Work on the grip. Hold it a little looser. You're tugging it to the right."

Nimitz already knew how his marksmanship compared to the other ranking officers on Guam, or anywhere else, and didn't really need any coaching from an air force man.

"I'll keep that in mind."

"Nah, you won't. Nobody listens to much of anything I have to say, so I try to keep my mouth shut, usually."

But not today, Nimitz thought.

"You come by for a shot of bourbon, General? Or maybe some dinner?"

LeMay didn't smile, nodded.

"Dinner. That's good. I thought you might like to see the reports from Tokyo. Recon flights confirm what I predicted. I turned that place into one big damn cow pasture."

Nimitz glanced at the Marine sergeant, who seemed to perk up at the words.

"Let's take this inside, General. I'm getting too old for the heat. My cook's supposed to be throwing together some fish recipe he picked up from the natives. Top-notch, if you don't mind some spice."

"That'll do. Lead the way. Anything you got here has to beat the slop your supply boys throw my way. Not as bad as MacArthur though, I'll give you that. His people spend more time trying to poison us than feed us."

Nimitz knew better than to open that door, thought, let it go. He has a permanent bone up his ass for MacArthur, and I don't really want to hear about it. I hear enough of that as it is.

"Y ou could have sent the reports over here, you know. No need to deliver them yourself."

LeMay sipped from the glass, seemed to appraise Nimitz's liquid offering.

"No chance. I wanted you to hear it from me, not some ass-kissing toad who thinks being a messenger will get him a medal." LeMay paused. "Word is, your boys are rationed a bottle of booze a week and a case of beer to boot. We don't get a damn drop. No alcohol ration at all. Not your doing, I guess. Someone back in Washington thinks air boys don't need any favors." LeMay tipped up the glass, emptied it, appraised again, nodded slowly. "Good stuff. Hate to see somebody in my command do a commando raid on your supply depot, liberate a few hundred cases of this stuff." He stared at Nimitz, still no smile. "Just kidding."

"So. Reports? Photos?"

"Right here." LeMay held the folder in his hand, hesitated, looked at Nimitz again. "Bomb 'em and burn 'em until they quit. That's been my motto and my strategy since I earned this command. So, here, Admiral. Take a look at this." LeMay took a long, self-satisfied breath, and Nimitz knew the presentation had been well rehearsed.

"On nine March we threw two hundred seventy-nine Superforts right into Tokyo. I took a new approach, ordered them in at night, flying low, under ten thousand feet. My boys weren't too happy about that, thought the Jap anti-aircraft fire would chew them to bits. But I knew better. Coming in that low, a few planes at a time, would catch the yellow bastards with their pants down. They wouldn't know what the hell to do. For whatever reason, they don't seem to have the kind of ack-ack the Germans threw at us, don't seem able to adapt to different attack altitudes. I had to convince my boys that the advantages outweighed the risk. Even persuaded them to make room for more payload by reducing weight. Thought it would be a good idea to remove most of the machine guns, and the gunners too. Jap fighters haven't done much damage to us in night raids, so what the hell do we need all that extra weight for? The boys weren't too keen on that, but I convinced them."

Nimitz thought, you didn't convince anybody of anything. You just ordered them to do whatever the hell you wanted.

LeMay continued.

"The low altitude gave the B-29s a greater bomb capacity, and I loaded up those sons of bitches with incendiaries. No more of this high-altitude tiddlywinks, playing hit-and-miss with targets that are too far below us to pinpoint. This time we didn't need to pinpoint anything. The target was the whole damn city. Hard to miss that one." He slapped a folder of papers against his leg. "It worked too. We should have been doing this to those Nip bastards from the beginning. We've gutted Germany's war machine, and now we're doing it to the Japs. But this is even better. You know what their damn cities are made out of? Paper and wood. I wish I'd have seen it myself, especially at night. Had to settle for the recon reports, but I've got 'em right here. In the last ten days, we've incinerated what looks to be fifteen or sixteen square miles of the Japanese capital. *Incinerated. Gone.* Flat damn ground. We have to assume that the number of enemy casualties is in the high tens of thousands, maybe double that. They're not likely to give us that information on their own. But dammit, Admiral, this is how the war ought to be fought. It worked in Germany and it's working here. Problem is, I'm having trouble getting an adequate supply of incendiaries from the mainland. Damn pestiferous supply bastards keep telling me that the factories can't produce them as quick as I'm dropping them. What a load of crap. Some asses back home need to be kicked."

LeMay tossed the file on the table, reached for his cigar, resting on the nearby ashtray. He jabbed the cigar in his mouth, sat back with a self-satisfied grin, a rarity.

"Learning to smoke these things. Not bad. Prefer a pipe, but can't keep the mold off 'em out here in this tropical hellhole."

Nimitz ignored the cigar smoke, pulled the folder close, opened, saw the reports, the number of sorties each night, the bomb loads, and then high-altitude recon photos of the aftermath, the enormous city showing a great gray stain, as though one large hand had simply wiped it away. My God, he thought. How many civilians? He knew LeMay wouldn't listen to any lecture about casualties, and Nimitz had already heard intelligence reports about Japanese factories spread all through civilian neighborhoods. LeMay knows that too, he thought. So, who do we blame? He's right on that count. They are *all* the enemy.

LeMay seemed to wait for the pat on the back, and Nimitz sat back in the chair, sipped the bourbon.

"Amazing. Impressive."

"You bet your ass it's impressive. I don't know what the hell's going on in Washington, rather not know. But Hap Arnold needs to shove this report and these photos under every face in the War Department, maybe give FDR a good look too. I'm so damn sick of . . ." He paused, seemed to catch himself.

"Sick of what, General?"

LeMay's face curled into a hard, silent growl.

"You know as well as I do that we should have passed by the damn Philippines and put all our energy right into Japan. You *know* that, don't you? MacArthur is wasting time and men and supplies to liberate his private little kingdom. He's taken months away from our timetables, when you know damn well that if he had given you his people, his ships, his planes, you'd be kicking down Hirohito's palace door by now."

Nimitz knew that if LeMay was smoking that same cigar in front of MacArthur, it would be Nimitz who was being blasted for whatever incompetence LeMay felt like blasting. Nimitz said slowly, "Whether I agreed with the War Department's decision to go along with Doug's invasion of the Philippines isn't as important now as what he's accomplished there. I've gotten word that Manila is in his hands, that the Japs are routed pretty badly. The harbor is usable, and we're moving supplies in there as quick as we can. I'm used to him getting the headlines. All the headlines. He needs it. Fortunately for me, strutting across a stage on Broadway has never been my ambition."

"Oh, there's only one stage, Admiral. Doug won't allow anyone else up there, you can be sure of that. But this war would be over . . ."

"You don't know that. Hell, the war's not even over on *Guam.* Right up in those hills, there are Japs who still haven't given up, who are dedicated to fight and die for their emperor. I sure as hell don't understand that, but then, it doesn't matter whether I understand the Jap brain at all. My job, and yours, is to kill as many of them as we can, and by doing so, end this war." He raised the file of papers. "I give you credit, General, this is impressive as hell. But even this isn't going to make those bastards surrender. Every transmission, everything we intercept says they're going to go down swinging. We know damn well they're running out of gasoline and rubber and steel, but try telling that to those poor sons of bitches on Iwo Jima, or Peleliu. Or right here. We had a squad ambushed a mile up in those hills two nights ago. Four men didn't make it. Try telling their families, oh, well, hell, the Jap is beat. Any day now he's gonna throw up the white flag."

LeMay shook his head.

"I don't disagree with you, Admiral. The Japanese is a different breed, nothing like the German, nothing we've ever fought before. MacArthur thinks he can *intimidate* the Japs into ending this war. Never happen. You can't intimidate a fanatic into doing a damn thing. That's why I keep telling Arnold and anyone else who'll listen that the only way to end this war is to wipe those bastards off this earth. I appreciate what your web-foots . . . what your boys have done by blowing hell out of their merchant ships. Fine, you starve 'em, all you can. That's your job, isn't it? You're, what? Ten days away from hitting Okinawa? I've been ordered to give you all the help you need, whether I think there's a better way or not. I do need those airstrips, for two reasons. We're still losing too many B-29s who have to ditch on the trip back home. Okinawa is that much closer, helps us a hell of a lot if my boys need to put down in a hurry. And once you give me those strips, we can put a thousand more fighters close enough to make strafing runs on those Jap bastards in their own beds. By adding fighter escorts around the B-29s, there's not a Zero that'll get anywhere close, and we'll have full dominance over every square inch of Japan. But . . ." His voice was rising, the usual show Nimitz was accustomed to. LeMay paused, the hard scowl unchanging, his anger adding fuel to the hiss in his words.

"I need supplies. Incendiaries. For now, all I've got is steel, and we've already figured out that TNT doesn't do crap to Jap positions. I'll bomb anyplace you want me to with steel, but once I get those incendiaries, I'm going back to work on those Jap cities. If MacArthur wasn't out there fighting his own damn war . . . if he'd have pushed toward Okinawa instead of Manila, linked up with you, made a combined effort . . ."

Nimitz knew it was time to throw the leash.

"Let it go, General. The plans were put in the books months ago. I've had too many arguments with Washington about strategy, and when it comes to Okinawa, I've got the backing to do the job I want to do. Five days ago, Iwo Jima fell into our pocket, and it won't take long before you'll have your airstrips there in top shape. I'm heading out there in a couple days, see it for myself. We took some hellacious casualties there, and I need to pat some people on the back. With all due respect, General, right now my attention is on the men who have to cross those beaches. And the next beaches we're hitting are on Okinawa."

"I told them we should have used gas. Still can."

Nimitz knew this conversation too well. It had begun with a loud call coming from newspapers in the States that poison gas would quite simply save American lives.

"Not on my watch, General. Until the president tells me he's tossed the Geneva Convention in the crapper, gas is not an option. You already know that."

LeMay nodded.

"It would work. Pretty sure of that. But, fine. Just . . . if there's anybody you can talk to . . . Admiral King, Forrestal, hell, William Randolph Hearst, I don't care. Find a way to get me some more incendiaries."

Nimitz was growing weary of LeMay's surly energy.

"How about I find a way to get you those airbases closer to Japan? Right now there are several thousand Jap planes anchored on Formosa and Kyushu, and God knows where else, and every damn one of them is fired up to go out in some asinine blaze of glory. I'm scared as hell of those kamikaze strikes. You hear what they did to the *Franklin*?"

LeMay shook his head, still scowling, and Nimitz said, "I just received the report this morning, General. The Japs took a hell of a swipe at us, after you bombed those airfields on Kyushu." Nimitz felt his own heat rising. "Five carriers took direct hits from those sons of bitches. But the *Franklin* got it the worst. More than seven hundred sailors were lost, blown to bits, burned to hell. So, if you're having trouble getting incendiaries, then use high explosives and give me a hand somewhere besides Tokyo. Just because you can beat the hell out of somebody doesn't mean you should. The Jap civilians aren't our priority right now. The Jap troops waiting for us on Okinawa are. I don't want my boys going across those beaches worried about what's about to drop on them from the air. You want air superiority? So do I. So let's start by giving it to those boys who have to worry more about Jap bayonets than Jap fighter planes. I'm authorized to call upon you for B-29 support, and I'm doing just that. Put your people over those Jap airbases, drop a thousand mines in the Jap harbors, keep their warships the hell out of our way."

LeMay seemed to sulk.

"No B-29 is going to stop any damn kamikaze. We blow hell out of their airfields, and they take their Zeroes or their crop dusters or whatever the hell else they're using back into the brush, hide 'em until we're done. I've seen those reports too. We bust up an airfield, and slave labor fills in the holes the next day."

"No arguments about this, General. I know your orders. Until the Okinawa landings are completed, and that island is secure, your bombers will do everything I need them to do. Supply will catch up, and I'm certain that you'll get your incendiaries. But right now . . ."

"Fine. Put your staff in touch with my logistics officers. For now, there's not much else I can do."

"Plenty you can do. Just do it for me, instead of Hap Arnold. I promise you, he won't mind. He doesn't want Admiral King beating down his office door, bitching about your lack of support." Nimitz paused, thought he saw a hint of a smile from the man who almost never smiled. Nimitz had calmed, took a sip of the bourbon, savored the sweet burn. "General, how about we put every ounce of energy into capturing Okinawa? You'll have your emergency airstrips, and you'll have your staging area for your fighters. In no time we'll have that place fixed up so your boys can get back to work on those Jap cities. I know damn well you'll pin a medal on the first fighter pilot who machine-guns the emperor's front door."

LeMay seemed to ponder the image, nodded slowly.

"Yep. Suppose I will. Look, Admiral, I'm not oblivious. I know what it's going to cost to rout a hundred thousand enemy soldiers off Okinawa. I know what it cost to take Tarawa and Peleliu and all the rest. All I want is for you to give me the airbases, get me close enough to do my job like it needs to be done. Hell, I'll bomb MacArthur's headquarters if it'll end the war any sooner." Nimitz flinched, and LeMay seemed to know he had crossed the line. LeMay lowered his voice, one fist slowly pounding the table in front of him, his words following the steady rhythm.

"You send that damn Buckner out there to get me those airstrips. That's what *I* want." He stood, clamped his hat hard under his arm. "One more thing. When you go out to Iwo Jima, pat a couple of those Marines on the back for me. We've got a hell of a flock of Superforts who need those landing strips, and I know your boys got beat to hell grabbing them. Hope it's not as bad on Okinawa."

3. ADAMS

"Bust him up!"

"Left hook! Come on! One more!"

Adams heard the roar of voices, ignored them, his brain focused only on the man in front of him, a flicker of motion from the curled brown glove, a lightning jab that whistled past his ear. He ducked, too late, another jab thumping hard straight into his face, square on his nose, watering his eyes. He backed up a step, the man coming forward, closing the gap, sensing some vulnerability, but Adams was angry far more than he was hurt. The jabs had been a nuisance, nothing more, but had kept him off balance just enough to keep him from setting his feet, getting in the good shot of his own. He ducked again, moved to one side, frustrated, but kept his focus, an unshakable stare on the man's chest, the one place the fighter couldn't feint. Adams tried not to look at the man's gloves, knew to ignore the flickers of movement, the quick shift of the man's head, all the fakes designed to mislead. Adams held his own gloves up tight to his chin, his elbows in against his ribs, protection from a man who was becoming less and less of a threat. There had been a few hard punches, one catching Adams flush on the side of the head, but there had been no thunder behind it, no effect at all, and from those first few moments, Adams knew it was only a matter of time. Adams continued to back away, watched as the man pursued him with a clumsy bobbing of his head. His opponent was tall, lean, spiderlike arms, his best asset, used them perfectly, keeping Adams away with the jabs to his face. But there was no damage from that, just the massive annoyance, infuriating frustration from the man's pecks and probes, the occasional attempt at a heavier shot into Adams's face. But the man's lack of power had seemed to discourage him, and as the fight moved into the third round, the gangly man worked harder to keep Adams away. Adams had seen this before, a man no longer fighting to win, but just to survive. The jabs continued to come, flickers that mostly slipped past Adams's ears, bouncing off his gloves, anything to keep Adams out of close range, keep him off balance. In his corner the sergeant was spewing out words, instructions, advice, words that melted away with the shouts and cheers of the Marines on the open deck around them. Adams had forgotten about the *plan,* the careful strategy, the sergeant's instructions meaningless now, the only thought in his brain the search for the opening, seeking the gap, the space, the target. He saw the man glance away, toward his own corner, and Adams jumped, no time for thought. He sent the left out in a sharp curl into the man's ribs, heard the grunt, the man's gloves coming down slightly, helpless reaction. Adams saw the opening, moved with perfect instinct, rammed a short hard right hand to the man's chin, opening his mouth, twisting his jaw, a spray of blood coming off the man's wounded lips. The man bent low at the waist, staggered back into the ropes, another glance toward his corner, seeking . . . *help.* Adams dropped his arms for a quick second, flexed slightly, fighting the stiff pain, the exhaustion in his muscles. The man was shaking his head, blinking hard, scrambled eyes, trying to focus, and Adams saw the flash of fear. The man pulled his gloves up to his face, feeble protection, and Adams was there, ignored the one weak jab, the man's last desperate punch. There were no more feints, no dancing, the man still against the ropes, and Adams moved closer still, his eyes on the man's chin now, made a quick short step to the right, and in one motion turned into the man, driving his right hand past the man's left, a compact bolt of lightning against the man's exposed jaw. The left followed, a tight upward swing, but there was no target, only air. The tall man had gone down, crumpling into the ropes, rolling over onto his back. Adams leaned low, ready, his arms cocked again, the anger spilling onto the fallen man, words in his brain, get up! I'm not done! The man still held his hands up in front of his face, pawing the air, but there was nothing else, blank eyes, his brain off in some other place. Adams was breathing heavily, felt a hard arm across his chest, pulling him away. He turned, furious, cocked his right again, *I'll kill you, you bastard* . . . but the distractions came, his brain letting go, a green shirt, the referee, holding a steel grip on his shoulder, the referee's other arm waving, shouting the words, "Seven . . . eight . . . nine . . ."

The hand released him, and the sergeant was there, hands on his shoulders, a happy grin, a flood of words through stinking breath. The sounds engulfed him, and Adams glanced around, beyond the small roped-off square, saw hands in the air. A hundred Marines were standing, wild eyes and wide smiles, cheers and shouts, all directed at him. He began to feel his fists relaxing, the agony of desperately tired arms, sniffed through blood in his nose. He tried to escape the sergeant's breath, looked for his victim, saw him sitting slumped on a short-legged stool, tended to by a corpsman. Adams pushed that way, through the arms of the sergeant, saw the beaten man staring down, still unseeing. Adams stopped, nothing to say, saw blood on a towel, another corpsman coming through the ropes, words . . . *broken jaw*.

He felt a hard slap on his back, the sergeant pulling him toward the ropes. Adams stopped, resisted the man's grip, looked out at the Marines, not as much cheering, their attention drawn away to the next pair of fighters. He saw them coming up close to the ring, towels on their heads, the boxing gloves laced up, ready, the next act in the show. Adams tried to feel the joy, victory, but the dull soreness in his arms was taking over, the blood clogging his nose. He bent low, the sergeant helping him through the ropes, stepped down off the plywood, the single step to the steel of the deck, a towel now wrapping his shoulders.

"Nice job, kid. Like to see you take on Halligan next. Thinks he's a tough guy. You can loosen a few teeth in that big damn mouth."

Adams looked toward the sergeant, saw confidence, businesslike, and then a corpsman was there, cotton in the man's hand.

"Hold still, Private. Let me get you cleaned up."

Adams didn't protest, felt the sergeant working on his hands, removing the boxing gloves, while the corpsman stuck something into Adams's nose, cleaning out the blood.

"There. You breathe okay?"

Adams pulled air through his nose, nodded, and the corpsman was gone as quickly as he had come. Behind Adams, a voice came from the ring, the lieutenant, the names of the next pair of fighters.

"All right ladies, simmer down. Next bout. From Greenville, South Carolina . . ."

Adams stared out across the deck, the open sea, the sun low on the horizon, salt spray in the air. Above him sailors lined the railings, more of the audience, men staying close to their anti-aircraft guns. Higher up he saw faces on the bridge, but only a few. The men running this ship had better things to do than watch Marines on the deck below beating the hell out of each other.

To one side, Adams saw another ship, like this one, moving on a parallel course, more ships beyond. He wanted to stay on the deck, loved the open air, the ships, but the wet towel around his shoulders was growing heavy, cold, and a chill ran through him. He moved through a hatchway into a short corridor, saw a single sailor coming toward him, passing by, a quick glance.

"You win?"

"Yeah. KO."

"Figures. Marines."

The man moved away, and Adams flexed his tired arms, took a long deep breath. He could hear the cheers behind him, the new fight beginning, and one part of his brain wanted to watch, but his legs wouldn't move any other way but down, the exhaustion complete. As he moved farther into the ship, the smells returned, grease and paint and the stink of diesel fumes. He thought now of the shower, one minute of blessed hot water, and then his bunk, his quarters, the tight squeeze with forty other men. But there would be space for him, someone making way, a show of respect coming even from the men who had stayed below, who cared nothing for boxing. They knew his name now, knew he had proven something they all wanted to prove, that he was *a tough son of a bitch*. He passed another sailor, the man ignoring him, and Adams saw the ladder, leading below, felt for the railing with a stiff hand. He started down, gingerly, tired legs, thought, yep. KO. Another one. I'll be damned.

The boxing was a ritual, something Adams had needed. He felt it the moment he arrived at the Marine base at Guadalcanal, after he endured the automatic look of disgust on the faces of the men who had never left the islands, who had weathered all those bloody storms against the Japanese. He had wanted to tell them, all of them, that he was not new, not a green idiot, that if it hadn't been for some ridiculous disease, he never would have left them, would never have been shipped home. Adams was desperate for a way back in, a way to prove that to the men who barely remembered him. It was the sergeant, Ferucci, who had opened the door. Ferucci was a tough goon of a man, who came from the hard streets of Jersey City. He knew something of boxing, what he called the *sweet science,* had talked long and often of Joe Louis and Max Schmeling and Jack Dempsey and Jack Johnson, and the message to Adams was clear. He had missed out on so many of the Marines' great fights, and so he would make fights of his own. He would put on the gloves, stand in front of whatever fool felt the same need, and the better fighter would bloody the other into submission. In eight bouts, Clay Adams had been the better fighter. He had been afraid at first, but his desire was too great, erasing that part of his brain that spewed out all that annoying *common sense.* He refused to understand what a man's fist might actually do to your face, that some of these Marines might actually enjoy hurting him, and worse, they might be damn good at it. As the sergeant trained him, Adams had asked all those questions, what it *felt* like, but Ferucci was wise enough not to answer them. So Adams stepped through the ropes with no idea how much it could hurt to be knocked out, if it hurt at all. And until he saw it for himself, he had no idea that another man's teeth could end up around his own feet. But Adams's teeth were still intact. He had surprised the sergeant, and himself, by his smooth talent for slipping away from the fists. And, to both men's surprise, Adams had another talent as well, the coordination you can't teach, the instinct for dropping a thunderous shot into a man's jaw with a perfect right hand. He had knocked out every man he had faced, but unlike the animal cheering that came from the Marines in his audience, Adams felt no special joy in drawing another man's blood, or watching the man's eyes roll up into a frightening oblivion. It was never about victory, as much as it was about being one of them, being accepted back into the Twenty-second Regiment. Whatever he had to prove when he had returned from San Diego, he had done a pretty good job of it. In a few short weeks back on Guadalcanal, no one in the unit confused him with one of those replacements.

He had spent too many months stateside, and when Ferucci and the others accepted that he was in fact one of their own, he could finally join in the general displays of disgust for the replacements that had come with him. They sailed to the islands full of that mindless spirit that had been driven into them at the Marine training centers, and once he joined them on the transport ship, Adams quickly learned to avoid them. He could identify them as soon as they spoke, all the talk of adventure and conquest, how they were oh so eager to face the Japs, so much asinine talk from men who had no idea what kind of *adventure* they were headed for. But the transport carried veterans as well, and Adams felt the same guilt that infected so many of those men, mostly the wounded who had been shipped stateside for recovery and recuperation. Not all of the men from the hospitals would return, of course, many of them too damaged, Purple Hearts and a train ticket home. And not all the veterans who were shipped back out on the transports were as eager to rejoin their units as Adams was. Some had seen too much already, had recovered from what they had hoped were *million-dollar wounds* that would get them out of the fight. But the Marine Corps's nasty secret was that they were losing men at such an alarming rate that the training camps could not keep up with the gaps in the line. If a wounded man had healed well enough to fight again, he would. There was griping about that at first, men who dared to show the fear, who had no desire to go back *out there,* who believed they had already done their share. No one had patience for that kind of talk, and certainly none of the officers. Most of the veterans passed their time in silence, or occupied their thoughts with poker and dice and letter writing, anything that would keep their thoughts away from what they had seen and done, and what they might be asked to do again. They tended to keep separate from the replacements, and Adams had done the same, trying to avoid the idiotic talk. But there was one hitch to the camaraderie he shared with the veterans, a fear he carried every day. He wondered if they knew, if anyone could see through the hard glare he tried to show them, that it all might be counterfeit. Adams had not actually been in a fight, had never fired his rifle, never even seen a Japanese soldier. In early 1944, when the Twenty-second moved ashore through the ring of islands called Eniwetok, Adams had already been chewed up and spit back to San Diego by a disease he had never heard of.

I t was called *filariasis,* and an enormous number of Marines had been afflicted with the parasite from their first days on whatever tropical waste-

land they had been ordered to land. Adams had been one of the first in his
unit to suffer the awful misery of what some had begun to call *elephant disease.* More properly, the doctors knew that filariasis could cause elephantiasis, and might not be curable at all if it stayed in a man's body for any
length of time. As a result, the medical staffs took the disease seriously.
Adams had been pulled off the line in Samoa, hauled by transport ship
back to San Diego, and to his groaning dismay, he had been confined to
the naval hospital there for nearly four months. When the disease was explained to him in detail, his griping about abandoning his buddies was replaced by something else: abject terror. The risk that the disease would
bring on elephantiasis might have inspired jokes among those who had
never suffered from it, since the most grotesque symptoms included
greatly enlarged body parts, most notably a man's genitals. The jokes had
been obvious and crude, but Adams had seen the photographs, offered in-
discreetly by a drunk corpsman, who thought it might be funny to shock
the afflicted Marines with the potential horror of what they had con-
tracted.

But the doctors in San Diego had done their work well, and after suffering through an extended recuperation period, he had been assigned to
an office, faced with the horror that all his Marine training had gone to
one good use: He would excel as a file clerk.

The men who shared his purgatory knew very well what was happening to the Marines in their own units far out in the Pacific. No one could
keep hidden the carnage that had spread across so many islands, names
now familiar to every Marine. To the wounded, those names had come
back to them in nightmares they could not escape, jungle and swamp and
jagged coral reefs, shrapnel and machine guns, places where a friend had
gone down, or where the captain or the sergeant had led their platoon into
annihilation. Adams had escaped it all, but the guilt of not being there
caused nightmares as well. The letters had come, one in particular, from
his captain, that Adams's close friend, a tall mosquito of a man everyone
called Bug-eye, had been killed on the rocky coral reefs at Eniwetok. Word
of the man's death had been unreal, a strange joke, but the joke was never
funny, and as he shuffled the papers in the nameless office within sight of
the vast ocean, Adams had grown more angry and more guilty by the day.

By now every one of the Marines who had been held back on the
mainland knew that even in victory, the Marines had been gutted in battle
after battle. Most of the assaults had been amphibious landings, the news-

reels in American theaters displaying with patriotic pride the grand show of landing craft swarming ashore in so many obscure places, places where the Japanese waited, places that someone at the top had labeled *important.* Adams heard the talk from the hospital beds, some of it loud and stupid, the men who begged to go back out there, to join the party, killing Japs as though it were a bird shoot. There had always been that kind of talk, through boot camp, through training in San Diego, more training on Guadalcanal. There, in September 1944, the Twenty-second Regiment had been assigned as part of a brand-new Marine division, the Sixth, created from what some in the other divisions thought to be dregs, leftovers, the crippled and shot-up remains of other units. But the brass knew differently and made sure the men who formed this new combat unit knew it as well. The Sixth was commanded by a fire-breathing dragon, General Lemuel Shepherd, who had organized the various ground troops and engineers, the corpsmen and tankers, into a solid fighting force, and had done it on Guadalcanal by re-creating what could only be called another boot camp. The training had been fierce and brutal, especially for veterans of the combat regiments who thought they had already faced their worst challenge from the enemy. Shepherd had been a hero at Belleau Wood in the First World War, earning medals before most of his command had been born, but having a hero at the top didn't stop their griping. Even the officers who carried out Shepherd's orders had begun to wonder if the general's pride was going to brutalize these men far beyond what they could expect from the Japanese.

By the time the rigorous retraining had concluded, the officers knew what Shepherd had already known, that this new division would put up the best fight the Marines could offer. There were rivalries, of course, the other Marine divisions always certain that *they* were the best, the toughest, the most feared by the Japanese. The brass ignored most of that, focused instead on where all of this angry spirit could best be used. By late 1944 the planning had been complete, the bases established primarily on Guadalcanal and Guam. As the War Department's two-prong strategy ripped away the island bases from the grip of the enemy, what men in Washington knew only as pins on a map, the Marine and army divisions had suffered in horrific and costly battles. Every month brought some new plan, another invasion, another beach, another jungle. Individually, the regiments that now formed the Sixth had been engaged in fights that began with the disastrous defeat at Corregidor in 1942, right up through

the conquest of Guam two years later. But since the summer of 1944, the
Sixth had been the focus of General Shepherd's intense training, all units
brought up to full fighting strength, rested and refitted for yet another
campaign. While they did their work at the base on Guadalcanal, other
Marine divisions had continued the fight across the islands, the most recent the bloodletting on Iwo Jima, the fight that the newsreels were already
trumpeting as America's most heroic success. But the Sixth was continuing
to strengthen and prepare, receiving an influx of veterans from some of the
earlier campaigns, men who had crossed the beaches at Peleliu and Saipan.
Throughout the entire Corps, new recruits were being sprinkled into the
veteran regiments so that no commander would have to lead completely
green troops into battle. On paper the Sixth might be a brand-new division, but they carried too many veterans to ever be labeled untested. Only
the commanders knew what that test would be.

Adams had joined the Corps shortly after Pearl Harbor, had spent
what seemed to him to be an eternity in the training bases stateside
before his opportunity had come to sail westward. The indignity of the filariasis had been more than a health scare. Adams carried a kind of pride
that only a few of the men around him would understand. He was the
youngest of two, his brother serving in the army as a paratroop sergeant.
Jesse was older, and in Clay's mind, tougher. When Clay announced to his
brother that he had joined the Marines, Jesse seemed to understand even
then that the younger brother had something to prove, to make up for all
the fistfights, all the youthful bullying that Jesse had been called upon to
prevent. In the mining town of Silver City, New Mexico, a man was defined by his toughness, and Clay had not been the biggest or the strongest,
not in school, and not in his own home. Their father was a vicious brute
of a man, who hated life and struck back at his own misery by striking first
at his sons. When Clay enlisted and announced to his parents that he
wanted to go to war, his father's response had been an uncaring shrug, no
ceremony, no pride. Neither Clay nor his brother had been surprised. Far
more difficult for both boys had been the tearful wrath of a terrified
mother, the woman who had stood as much ground as her frail spirit
would allow, absorbing the endless abuse from the man she had married.
Clay had never shaken that from his mind: one awful night after dinner,
his proud announcement that he had enlisted to be a Marine, and his

mother's response, a shocking surprise, this quiet-suffering, soulful woman exploding with angry tears. Clay still didn't understand that, the furious attack aimed at her youngest son. To the eighteen-year-old, it had seemed grotesquely unfair that his mother would expect her precious boys to stay close at hand, and that just by leaving, he was abandoning her to a life she could not escape alone. Jesse had been as supportive of Clay as any older brother could be, had stood between Clay and his mother with calm assurances that everything would be fine, that the Marines would do Clay some good, teach him to be a man, teach him to be a better man than her own husband. And so Clay had had no second thoughts, had made his escape, had taken the train westward to San Diego. He could not know that within months, Jesse would fight that same battle again, this time for himself. Clay had wondered if it had been worse for his older brother, if Jesse had been infected even more strongly by the guilt of abandoning the family. It was a horrifying dream to realize that his mother expected either of her boys to stay in that horrific place, to *be* her family, sacrificing any boyhood dreams only to work in the copper mine, destined to mimic the suffering and the decay of their father.

But his mother had finally softened, and within weeks of his enlistment, her letters began to reach him. The first piece of news was that Jesse would go to Europe, would jump out of airplanes, and later, Clay learned only that his older brother had quickly risen to sergeant in the new Eighty-second Airborne Division. Clay had been amazed by that, but then, he knew his brother would have something to prove as well, would have to accomplish anything that would prevent him from sinking back into their father's life in the copper mines. Clay had wanted to hear all about that, the whole idea of jumping out of airplanes not only wondrous but utterly insane. But there could be no letters directly between them from a world apart, just the tidbits of news his mother would pass along. It came mostly in a trickle of sadness, but Jesse was at least alive, had fought through the campaigns in Sicily and then Normandy. As Clay labored in the clean white offices of San Diego, there had been a glint of sunlight in one of her letters, a cheerful announcement that Jesse was coming home, the paratrooper's war over. But Clay did not want to write to his brother, not yet, not while he endured the embarrassment of sleeping on white sheets in soft beds. Once free of the hospital, the office work had drained him of his dignity. The daily routine had seemed to be designed to inflict a more agonizing death on an eager Marine than any enemy weapon could. Clay could never admit to his brother what his duty had become, and so he lied about it by not writing at all. He had the perfect excuse of every Marine who toiled in some godforsaken jungle, or on some atoll that no one could find on a map. Mail was chancy at best, letters requiring long weeks to reach their destination, if they arrived at all. For months Clay kept silent from his own family, ashamed that he had failed to do what his brother had done, to fight the good fight, to earn his stripes. Certainly there would be the secrets the paratrooper would never share with his mother, the stark horror of all that he had seen, how many of the enemy he had killed, how many friends were lost. If there was a hot spear in Clay's back, driving him out beyond his recuperation and his soft bed, it was that. He wanted to be that kind of warrior, sharing those stories with his brother, comparing the different enemies, the fears and miseries and triumphs, a link the two of them could have for the rest of their lives. He knew that their shared respect would be a perfect shield against the fury of their father, and give solace to the woman who only wanted her sons to survive, to return, to be her pride in a home where pride had long disappeared.

When word came of the formation of the Sixth Division, Clay had pulled every string a private can pull, had begged and cajoled, made ridiculous speeches to indifferent officers. The process took agonizing months, and then word had come of something new and strange and wonderful. Somewhere in some white office in Washington, the decision had been made to allow women into the Marine Corps. Soon they had begun to arrive in San Diego, their duty freeing those men who agonized to join or rejoin combat units. When the first women arrived at his own post, Adams felt the giddy excitement that finally, he would go back *out there*. Once he had his orders in hand, all those newsreels and casualty counts were forgotten, all the sights and sounds and smells from the hospital put aside. Finally Clay Adams would hold the steel in his hands, and this time he would face the enemy.

OFFSHORE, ULITHI ATOLL, CAROLINE ISLANDS
MARCH 27, 1945

"Anybody know where the hell we're going?"

"Shut up. The captain's on his way."

The talk continued, different fragments of scuttlebutt from the men blending together into utter confusion. Sergeant Ferucci lay in his own bunk, said nothing, doing what the other sergeants were doing, letting the

men blow off steam, the crowded compartment thick with the stink of cig-
arettes and socks. Adams had been shooting craps in one corner of the
cramped space behind one of the hammocklike bunks, but the dice had
not been friendly, and he moved away, left three other men to their game.
Above him a cloud of cigarette smoke hovered over the bunk of Jack Welty,
another of the newly arrived veterans.

"They strip you clean, Clay?"

"A couple bucks. Not really in the mood. You got anything to read?"

"Nothing I wanna share with you."

Adams enjoyed Welty's Virginia drawl, the young man barely nineteen. He knew that Welty's family had money, but Welty seemed embarrassed by that, seemed to resent the lavish care packages of odd food and
clothing, most of it completely inappropriate for a Marine. The greatest
laugh had come at Welty's expense only a month before, a large box addressed to Welty that had been his family's obvious attempt to help him *fit
in* with his *comrades*. It had been a case of beef stew, small cans not much
different from the prime ingredient in their K rations. After the humiliat-
ing howls from the others had subsided, the stew disappeared. Adams had
a strong suspicion that Welty had tossed it overboard.

Welty sat up, let his feet dangle just above Adams's head. All around
them men were sitting with their backs against the steel bulkheads, or
sleeping fitfully in tiny bunks, trying to ignore the chorus of conversation,
most of it wild speculation of their next port of call. Across from Adams,
another man lay against a gap between the bunks, his helmet liner low over
his eyes, and said in another soft drawl, "Tokyo Bay. Heard a sailor saying
something about minefields there."

The responses came from around the cramped space, the usual skepti-
cism, opinions from men who knew that they had no idea what they were
talking about.

"You know how far it is to Tokyo Bay? We'd get bombed to hell before
we got halfway there."

"Formosa. I heard Formosa. Found it on a map."

"Hell no. We're going to China. Japs have been kicking ass, and they
need us to take the ports back. Gotta be better than getting blown to hell
trying to take Tokyo Bay."

"I been bombed plenty of times, shelled and machine-gunned. All I
know is that Tokyo Bay is in Japan, right? That's close enough for me."

"He's right. Let's hit 'em where it hurts. Get this thing over with."

"I wrote my sis I was in Ulithi, and the censors sent it back to me. Top secret. How can a place nobody ever heard of be top secret?"

Adams let the talk flow past, adjusted himself to the hard surface under his rear end, tried to find a comfortable way to sit. He looked up at Welty, saw freckles and red hair, the white smile that never seemed to go away. Adams said, "Hey, Jack, where you think we're heading?"

Welty shrugged.

"Someplace else. Can't say I'll miss our glorious week on Ulithi. A sand bar with palm trees. Not much to get excited about there. Rather go back to Guadalcanal."

The attention turned from the argument over geography, one man catching Welty's words.

"Hey, Red. I bet you loved all those island girls? They ain't never seen anything like you. They thought your head was on fire."

Welty shook his head, ignored the man, who returned to the manic discussion of their next mission. Adams still looked up at the red hair, said, "I don't remember seeing too many girls on Ulithi. Guadalcanal, different story."

"You can have 'em, Clay." Welty tapped his shirt pocket. "Got all the gal I need right here. She's back in Richmond writing me right now. Gotta write her again too, before we get all wrapped up in whatever we're doing next. My parents aren't too happy about it, but not much they can do about it now."

Adams left that alone, knew Welty wouldn't go into details about his parents at all. And he had seen the photo Welty kept in his pocket, a bright smile on a pretty blonde, every letter coming with that soft scent of some kind of perfume.

"Yeah, well, can't argue that one. Agree with you though. These island dames don't do a thing for me. Most of 'em got no teeth, or too much of everything else."

Welty lay back in the bunk, his feet still dangling, and Adams closed his eyes, tried to avoid the arguments around him, thought, I've seen a few of these island girls that weren't too damn ugly. A few. Not sure what I'd do if one of 'em pounced on me.

He had heard plenty from the combat veterans, warnings that the natives on any of these islands could be as dangerous as the enemy soldiers they helped to hide. The words had been drilled into them all, first by the company commander, Captain Bennett, then Sergeant Ferucci. Stay the hell away from the indigenous people. He still didn't know exactly what *indigenous* meant, but the meaning was clear enough. Out here, anyone not a Marine could be looking to kill a Marine. Simple enough.

"Listen up!"

The voice came from the hatchway, and Adams saw Captain Bennett lean in through the oval opening, followed by the platoon commander, Lieutenant Porter. The men shifted across the tight space, gave the officers room to stand, and Bennett said, "All right, it's time to let you in on the big secret. Though why anything needs to be so damn secret out here is a mystery to me. Any of you know where Okinawa is?"

There was a hum, some men suddenly aware that the secret wasn't secret anymore.

"Didn't think so. If you've heard jack about what the First went through on Iwo Jima, you know that place was nothing but a hole in the ocean, one tiny hot rock. Some of you found the same thing on Peleliu. Not much to look at, not much to fight over. But we fought over it anyway, because it was our job. This one's different. A hell of a lot different. Okinawa isn't some four-mile lava pile. It's a damn country. Sixty miles from top to bottom, maybe a dozen miles across. There are several major airfields there that the top brass wants, and a load of Japs defending them. As bad as that ought to be, there are a hell of a lot of civilians there who have been under the Jap boot heels for years. One of our jobs will be to fix that, liberate those people. I've heard about how many of you have been shooting your mouths off how anxious you are to get started on our next mission. Well, good. I want to see you *enthusiastic* about your jobs. Whether you got your training at Parris Island or San Diego, or whether you had to eat sand for General Shepherd on Guadalcanal, everything you were taught about fighting the Japs is about to be tested." The captain paused, gave a sharp nod to Lieutenant Porter, who stepped forward, shouted, "Which way do you run your K-bar knife into a Jap's gut?"

The response was immediate, a chorus.

"Up, sir!"

"What do you do when you pass an officer on the line?"

There was a slight hesitation, then a smattering of responses, all the same.

"Nothing, sir!"

Porter seemed satisfied but Bennett said, "That's right. Nothing. No salutes, no *yes sir, no sir*. No *sir* at all. I'm not going home in a box because you ladies suddenly decide to show me some respect within earshot of a Jap sniper. No officer is to use binoculars. That shows authority, and Japs will target anyone they think is in charge. No radio operator is to let his antenna show, no walkie-talkie operator is to stand in the wide damn open. The Japs have shown us what kinds of targets they prefer, and this company isn't going to offer them up on a platter." He paused. "Lieutenant, finish the briefing. I've got four more platoons on this boat, and every one of them is uglier than the last one. That makes you special, ladies. You were first."

The captain turned, slipped out through the hatchway. Porter stood with his hands on his hips, eyed the men slowly.

"Right now, we're headed for Okinawa. We cross the beach on one April. We'll go in alongside the First Marines, and south of us, two army divisions are going in with us. Two more will be in support, and one more Marine division will be in reserve. You don't need to know any more details than that."

The inevitable laughter came, one man raising his hand.

"Sir, has the army finally learned that it takes a whole lot more of them *ground pounders* to do the job . . ."

"Can that, Marine! This is no damn beach drill. There could be a hundred thousand Japs on that island, and we don't know exactly where they are. For the past few days, the navy's been shelling hell out of every inch of that place, and the air boys are dropping every bomb they can haul there. The word that's come down to us is that you might wade ashore into one big damn mess of Jap bodies. Don't count on that. I'm betting it'll be hot as hell. Japs have already shown us they can dig holes, and recon tells us that there are holes all over that place. Lots of concrete too. The captain mentioned the Okinawan civilians. There's hundreds of thousands of them, innocents, likely to be caught in the crossfire, or, if they're stupid, helping the Japs fight us off. They're not savages. A lot of farmers, and there are regular cities too. Nobody in this platoon has ever fought an enemy door to door. The navy says they'll level every building for us, but I've heard that before. You don't need to know this, but I'll tell you anyway. We're hitting Okinawa for one very good reason that the captain didn't mention. That damn island is three hundred fifty miles from the Jap mainland. We secure that place, and we've got us one hell of a good staging area for an invasion of Japan. But that comes later, and you're not supposed to think about that. Me either. Our primary mission is to get across the damn beach as quick as possible, establish a hard perimeter, and hold off any Jap counterattacks. By the second day, we'll make a hard push inland, extend the beachhead into the farm country. By the third day, we are expected to occupy and secure the Yontan Airfield. You won't need any maps. It'll be right in front of us."

He stopped, seemed to wait for the mission to sink in. No one spoke for a long moment, and then Ferucci said, "Sir. What's the army doing there? They backing us up?"

There were low comments, and Porter did not smile.

"Quiet. Once we establish control of the airfield, we will drive north, securing the northern half of the island. The army divisions will come across the beaches to our south, and once they establish their own beachheads, they will drive south and do the same thing. The objective is to divide Okinawa into two theaters of action, driving the enemy in both directions until their backs are to the wall, so to speak. We do not expect the enemy to surrender. So far, he never has. Command anticipates a great deal of banzai attacks, and a whole hell of a lot of hari-kari when we pen those bastards up in a tight space. You want points with me, you bring me back a hari-kari knife. I want a whole damn collection of those things." He paused, now a smile. "I got a bet going with an army lieutenant. Old pal of mine from Baltimore. I told him my boys would scoop up a whole pile of those fancy-assed knives, and he's told his boys to do the same. Whoever gets the most gets a night on the town when we get back home. I might just bring some of you along with me. Don't let me down, boys. Can't let any damn *ground pounders* show us up!"

The response was loud, raucous, Adams joining in, punching a fist in the air. Porter had his hands on his hips again, nodded in approval, then silenced them with a wave of one hand.

"One April. Four days from now. You get a chance to go topside, do it. Take a good look at what's around us. We'll be part of the biggest damn fleet ever put together. Bigger than what they did at Normandy. One April is 'L-Day.' In case you're wondering, *L* stands for *love*. Somebody back at Guam came up with that, thinking it would confuse the Japs." He paused. "None of those admirals asked *me* what I thought of that idea."

The noisy cheers came again, and Porter held up his hand.

"One April, well before dawn, we'll board landing crafts and head straight into the beach. The coral reefs are not nearly as big a pain in the ass as we've had to cross before. It'll be a sight. If any Japs survive what the navy's doing to 'em right now, there'll be so many of you ugly bastards hitting that beach, you just might scare 'em away." He paused again, seemed to realize the stupidity of his comment. "But I doubt it. Use your rifles, use your K-bar, use your damn fists if you have to. Those of you . . . well, some of you know what the Jap is all about. Kill those bastards, every damn one of them. 'Cause they sure as hell will be trying to kill you. All right, I'm done. Go back to whatever the hell you were doing. You sergeants . . . keep these boys under control. No fights, and keep the damn gambling under wraps. Anybody in this platoon ends up in the brig . . . well, I'll make sure *you're* the first ones across the beach. You got that?"

Porter didn't wait for a response, turned, leaned low through the hatchway, and was gone. Adams felt the thick silence, the fog of clarity that spread through them all, the men absorbing the briefing. One man said in a low voice, "Four days."

Ferucci responded, "April Fool's Day. The joke'll be on those Japs. If there's any left. Leave it to the navy to blow hell out of those bastards and spoil all our fun."

The talk began again, nervous chatter, the voices louder, an urgency no one could avoid. Adams thought back to San Diego, studying the maps that hung on the office walls, killing time by searching for the islands whose names had become so well known. He had seen Okinawa, wished now he had studied the place in more detail. He couldn't avoid a strange excitement, knots in his gut. That's close to Japan, he thought, closer than anyplace we've been yet. I guess that's good. He felt a shiver, but it was not the sweat in his shirt. Beaches, he thought. Finally. Killing those Jap sons of bitches. The words rolled through him, pushed by the energy of the others. Through the hum of anticipation, there was something else, unspoken, no one offering those mindless cheers. Too many of these men were veterans, and those men knew that every assault brought casualties. There were glances, the curious, the angry, morbid examination of the men around them. Who would not come back? Who would do the job . . . who would fail? Adams saw men looking at him, brief, cold stares. He knew the meaning, looked down, his hands pulled tight, arms crossed, holding down the thunder in his own heart. They're wondering about me, he thought. Just like the damn replacements. When we get out there . . . cross that beach . . . what'll I do? He could not answer his own question, felt the shiver again. He glanced toward Ferucci, the sergeant leaning back in his bunk, staring away into some other place. Follow him. He knows . . . he's done it before. Just kill the damn Japs. That's all you have to think about. Adams avoided the others, the low talk, the probing eyes. Men close to him were looking down; he knew that some of them had done this before. They're as scared as I am, he thought. Scared of what? Being a Marine? He chased that away from his mind. Dammit, Marines aren't scared. We're the toughest bastards in the world. He shivered again, his arms tightening into a harder grip across his chest. He looked at his boots, his boondockers, clean, the soles barely worn. *New.* Not for long. He took a breath, loosened the grip against his chest, looked up toward Welty's bunk. The redhead had put on his wire-rimmed eyeglasses, was sitting upright, staring silently at a photo in his hand.

4. USHIJIMA

The barrage from the warships had slowed, then finally stopped completely, thick clouds of smoke drifting up from the coastline, all through the hills. The artillery fire had lasted for more than an hour, and he knew it would come again, like the perfect chime of a precise clock. There would only be a short time for his men to emerge from the cover of the caves. His officers knew it as well, and the orders had been given, the soldiers scrambling out over the hillside, some retrieving wounded, others doing what they could to secure and strengthen the camouflage that blanketed most of the troop positions closest to him. For more than a week now the barrages of fire from the great warships had been a magnificent spectacle, aimed at every part of the island, streaks of red and white light, bursts of fire, thunderous shaking that sent dust even through the deepest caves. But the caves were secure, no cracks in the concrete, no sign of weakness in the rocks that surrounded him. He knew that several times the Americans had been lucky, direct hits, a single shell coming down straight into a cave. The results were catastrophic for the men inside, entire squads blasted to bloody shreds, sometimes nothing left at all. But those were rare, and all over the island his men kept their positions, low in the earth, far back in the natural and man-made caverns that ran beneath so much of the island like some great honeycomb.

He had no fear for himself, knew that no matter how much artillery came down around him, or burst into the enormous walls of the castle above him, there was almost no danger. The cave behind him wound deeply into the hillside, a labyrinth of offices and living space for hundreds of his troops. No one had yet seen a bomb or a shell from the great warships that could penetrate a mountain. And yet, he thought, they continue to try. Can they truly believe that we would spread ourselves out on open ground, that I would position my army in shallow trenches, perfect targets for their fire? They must believe it, or they would not continue this . . . absurdity. Day after day the fire begins precisely on schedule, as though we will have forgotten the shelling that came the day before. The Americans are an amazing people, possessed of wealth and resources and utterly without wisdom. He stepped forward to the very edge of the cave's opening, watched the quick work of the men down below, most of them already scampering back into hiding, the hillside growing quiet again, no movement but the drifting smoke. He raised his eyes to the sea again, still marveled at the amazing variety of ships, and their number. No country on this earth has a navy this large, he thought. The British perhaps. But the Americans have outshone even them, and now they send those ships to me, anchor them around my island as though I should cower in fear, as though I should be intimidated by how superior they are, and how hopeless our fight will be. No, I will never be intimidated. Arrogance does not defeat an enemy, and certainly, by this grand show, they display their arrogance. He scanned the ships, spread out far to the horizon, the smaller patrol boats, torpedo launchers, supply and troop carriers, and farther away, the warships, destroyers and cruisers and the enormous battleships. It was those that intrigued him most of all, hulking giants whose fire engulfed each ship in enormous clouds of smoke, their heaviest guns launching artillery shells that rolled through the air like railroad cars. The impact of those shells had thundered beneath his feet, as though the whole island quivered from the mighty blasts. Many of those heavier shells came closest, and he knew why, thought, they are trying to find me, my staff, my headquarters. They know we are up away from the beaches, and they must believe that this great castle above me is a symbol that we will grasp in our hands until they force us to let it go. Perhaps we will. But they can fire every shell in their arsenal and they will not harm us, no matter what they do to our symbols.

He focused on the smaller ships, closer to shore, could see motion, newly arrived transports, moving in behind and beside the destroyers that would protect them. He had asked the question already. How many are there, how many ships can they bring to this one place? He had tried to count them himself, but his field of vision was limited to the southern coasts. Someone on my staff will have done that by now, and I will see the number on paper, but then, tomorrow there will be more, as there have been every day for a week. He shook his head, a wave of despair. There are some in Tokyo who still believe the Americans will strike us at Formosa, that all of *this* is merely a feint. Those people hold so tightly to their own arrogance, and perhaps they have more arrogance than our enemies. They read my reports and dismiss my staff for exaggerating, insist that we are in a panic because of a *few ships*. Who among them will come here and see this? Who will stand on this ledge and watch what I have watched? How many of them still believe that all we must do is stand up and wave our swords and cry out the name of our ancestors and the Americans will melt away into the sea?

They were foolish questions, answered months before, when he had been assigned to command the enormous garrison on Okinawa. In the beginning he had more than a hundred thousand troops on the island, good troops, veterans, skilled commanders. But the Imperial High Command was not confident that the enemy would come to Okinawa, Japanese intelligence reporting often that there was debate in the American headquarters, that Formosa could be the target instead. And so the order came, the order he fought bitterly against, to remove the Ninth Division, twenty-five thousand of his finest soldiers, and transfer them to Formosa. And now, he thought, when it is so clear what the Americans have planned, will I receive those good men back here? Of course not. It is too late. It would be suicide to send those transports through the American fleet. He rolled those words over in his mind. Yes, that is after all what I am being asked to do, what every soldier in my command is being asked to do. We will be sacrificed in the desperate hope that we will draw the Americans down with us, that by giving up our lives for our emperor, we might also kill so many Americans that they will give up this war.

That . . . is arrogance.

The first puff of smoke came again, a small gunship close to the beach to the north, and he knew it was a signal, that in seconds the entire fleet would begin their shelling again. He knew the staff would be concerned, the secretaries fearful, knew that his aides were lurking anxiously in the earthen corridor behind him. But the larger ships were not yet firing, and he had learned the routine. The smaller ships would pepper the beaches first, intense clouds of smoke rising up far below. Yes, he thought, they are certain we are there. It is an assumption I would make, in their place. Strike hard at the first line of defense, obliterate any troops along the water, those men I *should* have put close to the landing places, where their troops are the most vulnerable. He made a weak smile, allowed himself one small piece of satisfaction. There is no one there, you foolish people. All your admirals and generals and the brilliant minds that design your assaults . . . you think you know the Japanese ways. You think we are predictable. But I will surprise you, as you have been surprised so often before. You do not learn. You have been bloodied on so many islands where you thought you would waltz ashore to festivals of half-naked native girls. So, now you will correct that mistake by erasing us with your artillery, as though we would sit in our holes along the beach and wait to be destroyed. Good. Waste your ammunition. Convince yourselves that we have been annihilated. And then, when you do not find our bodies among the sand and rocks, you can wonder if we have run away. Perhaps we have been so frightened by you that every night, thousands of us have slipped off this island and fled back to Japan.

He knew his tactic was controversial, that his instructions from the Imperial Command in Tokyo had forbidden any unopposed landing by the enemy. He had been furious with the inflexibility in Tokyo, was furious about that now. You tell me how to fight this enemy and then you cut off my hand, strip me of a quarter of my strength. You tell me that this island must not fall and then you offer me no way to prevent that, no way at all. So I will fight the Americans with the weapons I have, not the weapons that you dream of. Every man in my command will give up his life by taking ten of theirs. That is the fantasy I must believe. That is the fantasy my army already believes. And the decision makers in Tokyo will never dirty their minds with the truth. They will continue to play with maps and pretend that we are invincible.

"Forgive my intrusion, sir!" The voice was loud, as it was always loud, the fat-faced man pretending to grovel toward Ushijima's authority. "I see the enemy still chooses to spend his wealth by killing snakes and snails! Your plan is brilliant in its execution, sir. It will ensure total victory!"

Ushijima said nothing, respected the honesty of his subordinates. But he understood quite well that General Cho's words held no honesty at all.

I samu Cho held the same rank of lieutenant general, but the command on Okinawa belonged solely to Ushijima. Cho had accepted the position of chief of staff, had served Ushijima with perfectly annoying deference. Ushijima knew more about Cho than he would ever discuss with the man, that Cho had been a fiery militant whose activities throughout the 1930s had nearly branded him a traitor. He was a rabble-rouser from the army's most disgruntled ranks, the men who thought the emperor too passive, renegade officers who insisted that the Japanese army should destroy every enemy with a swift and bloody hand, whether or not that strategy had any basis in reality. Implicated in various plots to overthrow the army's more moderate command, Cho had survived politically only by accepting a post in China during the earliest days of the brutal invasion of Manchuria. Later Cho had been a primary force behind the destruction of the Chinese city of Nanking, which included the slaughter of its citizens, an act of barbarism that had shocked even the most aggressive militants in Tokyo. But there was little soul-searching in the Japanese army, their mission accepted by the careful and utterly efficient indoctrination that spread to the entire Japanese people. Every schoolchild had been taught of the *shido minzoku,* the outright cultural and genetic superiority of the Japanese race. That the Japanese should claim territories far beyond their island borders was accepted as perfect justice. The civilians had been educated to believe that it was only by a cruel trick of fate that the Japanese islands had been denied the wealth of natural resources, and so oil and rubber and iron would be taken from those inferior lands who had been so unjustly blessed. If the people of those far-distant lands were not grateful to assist in strengthening the Japanese culture, then the Japanese army would subjugate them and use them for labor. Already armies of slave labor had been used to build the bridges and roadways and airfields necessary for Japanese transportation. It mattered little to the Imperial Command if some of those laborers were in fact enemy prisoners of war. The Geneva Convention was an inconvenient irritant when the priority was to put food into Japanese mouths and fuel into their homes. What the civilians had not been told was that if any of those hordes of slave laborers became unfit, by disease or the abuse of their captors, few of the Japanese commanders in the field had any qualms about eliminating them altogether. The viciousness among the Japanese soldiers who dealt with the captives had concerned some in the Imperial Command, but no one there had issued any kind of order that it be stopped. The army's militants were far too powerful and far too dangerous to the moderates in Tokyo. And many of those who fought a private war of conscience had come to accept that Japan's desperate need for raw materials meant that sacrifices had to be made, and that no one outside Japan was qualified to judge Japanese morality.

As Japanese forces extended their empire to the limits of what their military could support, there had been the rare circumstances where Emperor Hirohito had blunted the behavior of his armies, holding back the sword, which the army saw as an annoying compromise. When the eyes of Tokyo looked elsewhere, those officers would often continue with the same viciousness against their conquered peoples that the more moderate officials in Tokyo found appalling.

The navy was entirely different, but in the Japanese hierarchy that mattered little to the army commanders. The two branches of the Japanese military were completely separate, no overlap of authority. And so there was very little cooperation in the various campaigns that had spread Japanese troops, ships, and planes across such a wide swath of the hemisphere. As difficult as it was logistically to maintain Japanese successes across Burma and Indochina, New Guinea and the Philippines, as well as China and the ocean of islands to the east, the lack of cooperation between the two services also produced a crippling handicap for their overall strategy. The army and navy commanders spent too much of their time and energy competing for the resources each needed to make war. To the disgust of the senior admirals, the army more often prevailed, and everyone close to the emperor understood why. Emperor Hirohito had a much greater grasp of ground tactics than anything that happened at sea. If the army had needs, they would be met.

Cho stood to one side, allowed him to pass, Ushijima adjusting his eyes to the lower light from the bulbs along the walls of the corridor. Behind him the larger guns from the battleships had begun their shelling again, the rumble coming up through the floor as the shells impacted.

"The Americans will run out of powder before this is over, don't you think?"

Ushijima did not look back, let Cho's idiotic glee drift past him. He saw the light of an office ahead, turned through the doorway, saw four women, neatly dressed, perched behind a row of desks, working in unison at typewriters. Standing behind them, like a mindful schoolmaster, was Colonel Yahara, who, after General Cho, was Ushijima's most senior staff officer. Yahara seemed to avoid looking at Cho, made a short bow toward Ushijima, said, "Sir! We have nearly completed the reports of enemy activity from last evening. I have alerted the radio room to be prepared to transmit. Is there anything you wish to add?"

Ushijima had enormous affection for Yahara, the man totally opposite in personality from the abrasive and conniving Cho.

"Nothing to add. The Americans will certainly continue their shelling until it is too dark to see. They take pride in their work, and certainly their admirals wish to see the damage they are inflicting on us. Today should be no different than yesterday."

"We shall drive their pride into their bellies at the point of the bayonet!"

Ushijima avoided the bombast coming from Cho, but the man did not wait for a reply, was quickly gone. Yahara seemed not to notice, moved close to the back of a chair, leaned over the shoulder of one of the secretaries, a pretty woman who did not acknowledge him.

"Yes, you may complete that for my signature."

"As you wish, sir."

Ushijima studied the woman's face, saw no fear, thought, good. She is not one of the *playthings*. And Yahara is not so crude. We will all leave that to General Cho.

"When you have completed this task, Colonel, come to my room. I should like you to give me your latest reports on the progress of the construction of the caves."

"I shall be there in two minutes, General, if that is acceptable."

Ushijima tried to maintain the formality, but Yahara was far too likable, a cheerfulness in the man that showed clearly how much he loved his work.

"You may have three. I do not wish you to break an ankle running through these dark hallways."

"Do you miss your days in the classroom, Colonel?"

Yahara was still standing in the doorway, seemed surprised by the question.

"I am pleased to be here, General."

"Sit down, Colonel. This is not an inquiry. You may relax. If General Cho insists on joining us, then we will button our coats and stand at attention. Please. Sit down."

Ushijima was seated on a small rug, his legs bent inward, a small cup of tea beside him. Yahara made a short bow, sat across from him, and Ushijima pointed to the teapot, said, "Pour yourself a cup. I'm not in the mood for alcohol just now. Is that acceptable?"

"Of course, General. Thank you. Tea is always acceptable."

"Relax, please. Perhaps I should have brought you some sake. It is not necessary that you be so nervous around me. General Cho has secured a case of rather outstanding Scotch. I can summon him, if that would be more to your liking."

Yahara seemed to know that Ushijima was toying with him, shook his head.

"I would not ever consider depriving General Cho of his fine whiskey. I have learned that when he is in a festive mood, it is best to stay in my quarters."

"I would never admit this to anyone else, Colonel, but Cho makes me somewhat uncomfortable as well. I suppose he does that to everyone. I think he rather enjoys that. I would suppose that when he was a boy, he was the schoolyard bully."

"I would agree with you, General. But, no, I have come to respect General Cho, and to obey him when it is appropriate."

Ushijima laughed.

"When is it not appropriate?" He saw hesitation, laughed again. "Yes, I understand. If I tell you one thing and he tells you another, you know very well whom to obey. I cannot fault General Cho for his enthusiasm. He is the picture of the samurai, is he not? He will attack anyone at any time with complete disregard for himself. Is that not what we are all supposed to do?"

Yahara seemed puzzled.

"Yes, certainly, sir."

"So, what's wrong? Is the progress on the caves in the south going well?"

"Oh . . . yes, quite well, sir. I have tried to employ the Koreans and the

Okinawans whenever possible, rather than overwork our own troops. But our people are much better at the labor. I am sorry to say that within the last few days, our schedule has been altered by the arrival of the Americans. I do not believe we will have time to complete my design before their ground assault begins."

"No, we will not. They will come any day now. But not today. As long as their cannons fire, their troops shall stay put. Perhaps tomorrow. They do prefer dawn."

Yahara looked down, ignored the teacup.

"I must admit, sir, that I do not believe we can defeat them."

It was a rare show of honesty, but Ushijima knew that he had Yahara's trust, and had tried to use the man as a confidant as much as any commanding officer could.

"Why? General Cho believes we will drown them in their own blood. General Cho is very good at quoting history. The Japanese people have not suffered a military defeat in twenty-three hundred years. Did you know that? Well, certainly you do. You had to teach that to your own students at the military academy. I certainly did. They wrote down every word I said with delightful enthusiasm. Some of those boys are right out here, in this mountain. I have no doubt that every man in this army has faith in our future, in our inevitable victory. Isn't that how General Cho puts it?"

"I am sorry I spoke, sir."

"Never mind. I am not mocking you, Colonel. I speak only what we are to believe. Tokyo has never accepted that we can be defeated, and General Cho supports that philosophy. He certainly believes that the louder he shouts about it, the more genuine it becomes. Perhaps if we scream out our dreams, they become real." He paused, sipped the tea. "You don't agree."

"Sir, the reports from Tokyo continue to insist that the Imperial Navy is on its way here, to relieve us, to destroy the American fleet. If *shouting* that will make it true, then I will shout it until my voice is gone. I have seen nothing of our fleet, or of the great flights of bombers that were promised us. Every morning I go to the mouths of the caves and I wait for the enemy to begin his assault. The enemy has their own plan, and once they begin their landings it will be too late."

"Not according to Tokyo. It matters little what the Americans are doing on our soil. Once their fleet has been blasted to smoking wreckage, the Americans will have to admit defeat. Yes, I've heard everything you've heard. I recall hearing much the same after our attack on Pearl Harbor.

Didn't you? I recall hearing the reports of our great victories in the skies over Midway, our navy's great triumph at Leyte Gulf, and only last week I received word that General MacArthur has had his army butchered in the streets of Manila. I have asked myself the question: How is it that we have struck such triumphant blows at the Americans and yet they manage to anchor a thousand warships off my beaches?"

Yahara blinked at him, and Ushijima knew the man would not say the words.

"Is it possible, Colonel, that we are not being told that this war has been lost?"

Yahara lowered his head, said in a low voice, "I have refused to believe that, sir. I . . . cannot believe it. But I felt a great despair when we had to abandon the islands, when the Americans took our bases in the Marianas. I have thought that once they broke through our inner ring, we could not drive them away. Is that what you believe as well?"

"No. We lost this war when we attacked Pearl Harbor. If we had kept our focus on Southeast Asia, if we had invaded Australia, if we had penned the English up in India, this war would be over. Nothing could have prevented us from establishing our new boundaries over lands that would become our new empire. But it was decided by those far more *wise* than I am, that instead of consolidating our strength in those places we could control, we should creep up upon the world's greatest monster, and chop off his tail. And now, right out there, we are facing the monster's wrath. Were you not told that the attack at Pearl Harbor destroyed America's ability to fight at sea?"

"Yes, sir."

"Then who might those ships belong to out there? Did the great monster cower away, only to produce a twin whose *tail* is quite intact?"

Yahara continued to look down, and Ushijima knew what the man was feeling.

"Colonel, you took the same path in your younger years that I did. You chose to teach young soldiers the art of war. Teaching is a noble profession. Educated soldiers make for educated officers, and educated officers make for a superior army. We have that army. You should be proud."

"I am, sir. I did enjoy teaching."

"Ah, but look at all the time you wasted. Men like Cho, they spent their time serving themselves. They chose to advance their careers instead of shaping the careers of others. There is no blame for that. Cho is ambitious, and an excellent commander. He believes we will win this war and he will do everything he can to make it so. Of course, we do not agree on how that should be accomplished. Your plan for the defense of this island is our best chance to delay the enemy's invasion of Japan. That is their goal, of course. Everything they have done shows us that they will not stop until American troops stand on Japanese soil. I know very well that General Cho considers your strategy here to be . . . unacceptable."

"He is far more vigorous in his criticism, sir. He believes that my plans here are traitorous. He believes that we should meet the enemy at the water's edge and prevent them from landing a single soldier on these beaches."

"Yes, yes, I know all that. I have heard his arguments. He would sacrifice our good men in the sand. He is not skilled in mathematics, is he? You know as well as I do how many Marines the enemy is capable of sending to our beaches. You have seen their warships. Your strategy is our only chance to prolong this fight so that some good may come of it. But that good will be of little consequence. Now, of course, General Cho insults me with his deference to my decisions, because unless he chooses to assassinate me, he has no choice but to obey."

"Sir . . . do you believe . . ."

"No. General Cho has chosen to fight the best fight he can, and he has inspired this army to do the same. He will die in his efforts." He paused, saw a slow nod from Yahara. "So, you are prepared as well?"

Yahara looked at him, a sadness in the man's eyes.

"Certainly, sir. I know my duty."

"Ah, yes. The words of the samurai. We do not ask about the wisdom of our mission. We seek only the opportunity to die with glory."

"Of course, sir."

There was no enthusiasm in Yahara's words. Ushijima emptied the teacup, reached for the pot, poured again, said, "General Cho believes that there is shame in putting up an effective defense. He would have us charge to our deaths in one great blaze of fire. I will no longer entertain his musings on that subject. Your men have positioned themselves as I have instructed, and we shall do what we can to make this a good fight. I do not concern myself with what will follow. The end is inevitable, and the only variable is time. I no longer concern myself with anything Tokyo will say, and I do not care how history will judge what we do here. There is no confusion or doubt what all those American ships mean to us. They have come here to kill us. In that, Colonel, the Americans will do us a favor."

5. NIMITZ

H e tried to lose himself in the music, closed his eyes, conducting the orchestra with his fork, but the distraction didn't help. The specter of what he had seen on Iwo Jima had stayed with him, no escaping that what the Marines had done there had come at a dreadful cost. It had become a recurring theme in nearly every battle for the islands. The enemy fought as though they had no other alternative, and the Marines had come to understand that when the enemy had no intention of surrendering, you had to kill every man you saw.

Nimitz had very little appetite, forced himself to finish the meal. The orderly waited to one side, prepared to take away his plate, and Nimitz sat back, waved his hand, spoke over the music.

"Go ahead, son. I've had enough. Tell the cook he did another fine job. It's just my gut. And send Lieutenant Lamar in here."

The man moved quickly, the table cleared.

"Right away, sir."

Lamar came in now, seemed to hold his position right outside Nimitz's dining room. There was no surprise in that. Arthur Lamar had been the admiral's flag secretary since early in the war, and Nimitz knew there was no one on his staff more dependable.

"Sir. Was the meal acceptable?"

"You know it was. Sit down. Bourbon?"

"Perhaps later, sir. We're monitoring communications from Okinawa, and I've been told to expect a report from Admiral King's office."

Nimitz kept the frown to himself, thought, King is the crankiest son of a bitch I've ever met. Thank God he's eight thousand miles away. If he decided to leave Washington and put his office out here, I'd probably end up saying something really stupid, cost me my career. How can one man make so many people so damn miserable? At least he didn't feel obliged to join me on Iwo Jima. That was rough enough.

He poured a shallow pool of bourbon into his glass, moved one hand in time to the music, a reflex he didn't notice. He saw a slight wince on Lamar's face, knew the music was loud, louder to the young man with the sharper hearing.

"All right, turn it down. Just a little. Don't screw around with Mozart."

Lamar complied with a grateful nod, leaned over toward the record player, adjusted the volume. Nimitz held the glass in his hand, said, "Iwo Jima surprised us all, Arthur. But we'll save some lives now. LeMay's already putting some of his B-29s down there. I saw one busted to hell, tail nearly shot off. Amazing the thing could still fly. Oh hell, you were there. You saw the thing."

"Aye, sir. Terrible sight. Very happy the crew survived that one."

Nimitz sipped at the bourbon.

"Hell of a place though. Not a tree standing, nothing but rocks and smoke. Not sure when the casualty counts will be complete, not for the public anyway. Hard to convince some mother in Iowa that having her son blown to hell will save lives. Doubt it matters much." He looked to one side, the letter still on the table. He stared at it, the words dug into his mind.

You killed my son . . . and every year on this day . . . I will write you to remind you what you did . . .

"Very sorry, sir. I'll remove that."

"Leave it be, Arthur. I'll never fault a mother for blaming me, or anyone else in this place for what we're doing. You can't expect a civilian . . . a *mother* for God's sake, you can't expect them to understand that death can be positive. Don't ever say that to a newspaperman. He'll twist it around, make it sound like I'm the grim reaper, that I love killing people. Nobody loves killing, Arthur, nobody. Not LeMay, not MacArthur, not Howlin' Mad Smith. It's the job. And in case anyone forgets, we didn't start this thing."

"Aye, sir. I know, sir."

Nimitz downed the rest of the bourbon, looked at the young man, saw calm and confidence, something he rarely saw from his most senior commanders. Comes with the territory, he thought. Whoever said that thing about the squeaky wheel never met these characters I have to handle out here. There's not enough *grease* in the world to keep these people from shooting off their mouths. Or starting feuds with one another. Good thing Halsey and LeMay are in two different branches of the service. They'd probably end up fighting a duel. Nimitz glanced around behind his chair, said, "Where's Mak?"

"Must be in the mess, sir. The staff keeps feeding him table scraps."

Nimitz laughed.

"Trying to fatten him up so they can outrun him. Won't work. If he can't chase you down, he'll ambush you. Never saw a dog who so enjoyed biting people in the ass. Reminds me of Halsey."

Lamar stifled a smile, said nothing.

"Sorry, Arthur. I'm just jabbering. That trip to Iwo Jima set me off a little. I knew it was bad, but I wasn't sure it would be . . . well, what it was. We won the damn place, gave LeMay his airstrip. But I sure as hell wouldn't want to spend any time there."

"Did you see the sulfur springs, sir?"

"The what?"

"On Iwo, sir. The place is still pretty active as a volcanic island. There are hot springs scattered about in the old lava beds. Some of the Marines were taking advantage. I saw lines of men waiting at one of those places, a steaming pool. Seemed to be a pleasant surprise . . . after what they went through."

"Sulfur hot springs? Like some damn health spa? Well, I guess that's good. Any man who can find some way to have liberty on that rock deserves it."

Lamar nodded in agreement, leaned over to the record player, adjusted the volume again, lowering the music another notch.

"What you do that for?"

Lamar straightened, said, "I thought . . . you were talking and . . . my apologies, sir."

"You know damn well I'm a little deaf. You and no one else, right?"

"Aye, sir."

A man appeared at the door across the room, one of the aides.

He glanced at the record player, stiffened, said, "Excuse me, sir. We have received Admiral King's communication. He has forwarded a copy of General MacArthur's report from Manila."

Nimitz let out a breath, looked at the empty glass, only a film of the dark liquid in the bottom. No, let it go. It shouldn't take a bottle of bourbon just to read something from MacArthur. He saw the paper in the man's hand, pointed to the dining room table.

"Drop it here, son."

The man placed the stack of papers carefully, and Nimitz nodded toward him, the silent dismissal. He glanced at Lamar, saw no emotion, said, "Sometimes, Lieutenant, I feel like I've got dogs chewing on both my ankles." He paused. "Don't repeat that."

"Never heard it, sir."

The reports coming from Manila were far more gruesome than Nimitz had ever expected. MacArthur had succeeded in securing the primary airfields and most of the once-grand city, but the casualty counts had surpassed even the most pessimistic estimates. The worst catastrophe came from the body counts of the Filipino civilians, tens of thousands massacred by the Japanese, and nearly that many more falling victim to the heavy shelling MacArthur had thrown into the city itself, the city he claimed to love.

Nimitz turned the pages, shook his head. That had to hurt like hell. Doug's a lot of things, but he does love those people and he does have his sentimental streak. He'd rather be in the Philippines than anyplace else on earth, and he had to blow hell out of most of the place to chase the Japs away. Not sure what he expected to find there. Can't imagine that he thought all he had to do was show up and the Japs would hand him the place. But I know damn well he's overdoing it, trying to scrape every Jap out of every cave. It's costing us casualties we shouldn't be losing. He has to know that. And he has to care about it. But he just can't help . . . being Doug.

He put the papers down, looked toward the suddenly silent record player, the Mozart complete.

"Look through that stack of records, Arthur. I need some Tchaikovsky."

The young lieutenant obeyed, and Nimitz waited for it, a soaring burst of brass and strings. He looked again at MacArthur's report, thought, I'll probably have to go there. Sure as hell he'll set up some formal reception, where all the brass can offer him their congratulations. Not looking forward to that. He'll put on a whale of a show, try to put a smiling face on what was nothing more than a disaster that should never have happened. But . . . he's that much closer to Japan, and somewhere in Tokyo, somebody's gotta be scared as hell of that. I imagine it's just like Patton, big mouth and big guns ripping hell out of everything in the way. As long as you win, that kind of noise works, and no matter what Jap general is over the next hill, they'll be paying attention. I don't care how much propaganda they throw out to their people, every Jap general has to dread any thought of mixing it up with Doug.

He leaned back in the soft chair, the music rolling over him, a passage that always made him stop his work. He set the papers aside, closed his eyes for a brief moment, pushed MacArthur away. I've got bigger things to think about, he thought. Much bigger things. I should be out there, watching it, making sure. He glanced at Lamar, still sitting across the room, jotting notes on a pad of paper. He sat up, thought, no, Okinawa is *not* where you need to be at all. Let them handle it. Some of the best officers I've got. But, by God . . . it's *tomorrow.* And it's out of my hands.

He had wanted to be there, to see the bombardment, the largest armada ever assembled, *his* armada. The reports had come to him regularly from Admiral Turner, from the USS *Eldorado,* and even the admiral's flagship had contributed to the astonishing volume of destruction the navy had inflicted on Okinawa. Turner would command the invasion and support forces, while General Buckner, also on board the *Eldorado,* would command the Tenth Army, the combined army and Marine divisions that would drive ashore.

Nimitz pictured Buckner in his mind, tall, gray hair, the picture of what a general should look like. Not sure how the Japs feel about him, he thought. For all I know they never heard of him. No, the best thing we have going for us on Okinawa is the Marines. I'll bet it doesn't make a bit of difference to the Japs that two-thirds of our people there will be army. By now they have to think that anybody coming across a beach is a Marine. That can't hurt. He knew that the offices in Washington had as much anxiety about the invasion as he did, thought, King's pissed as hell that MacArthur gets the headlines. Not much I can do about that, except my job. King's gotta be busting at the seams for us to get our people on Okinawa, grab some attention for ourselves. Hell, Iwo Jima wasn't enough?

He knew it wasn't. Despite any glorious photographs that reached stateside, the newspapers would not be told the casualty figures from Iwo Jima, at least for a while. The same would happen in the fight to come. That's not the kind of press we want, he thought. MacArthur can disguise that kind of news by being . . . well, MacArthur. Out here, there's not much else we can tell anyone. We fight like hell to take an island, and get chewed up doing it, and that's pretty much the whole story. Hard for any newspaper to crow about our wonderful conquest of someplace they can't even spell.

There was a sharp rap on the door, and he looked up, saw another of his aides, a red-haired ensign.

"Sir, sorry to interrupt you . . ."

"I'm done here. What is it, Greg?"

"Report just received from General Buckner, sir."

Nimitz glanced at the empty glass of bourbon, his second, thought about filling it again.

"Yeah, I'll bet he's jumping around like he stepped on a beehive." He passed on the bourbon with a hint of reluctance, pulled himself from the chair.

"I'm coming, Greg."

The man stood aside, and Nimitz led Lamar out into the warm hallway, both men turning quickly into the radio room.

"Well, Arthur, what do you think? Is Buckner annoying the hell out of Admiral Turner? Bad idea to put two senior commanders on the same ship." He saw a slight frown on Lamar's face. "Yeah, I know, Lieutenant. It was my idea. All right, Ensign, what's Buckner saying?"

"Just a general update on their preparedness, sir. The boys will be loaded onto the landing craft very soon. The offshore islands are secure, and we've captured a whole fleet of suicide boats."

"Good. He'll crow about that for a while. I promise you, later on, his after-action report will point out how the army saved the navy from certain destruction. He's big on *those* kinds of details. That's a West Pointer for you. Anything else I need to read?"

Lamar held the report in his hand, seemed to hesitate, and Nimitz knew the signal.

"Give me the damn paper."

Lamar handed him the dispatch and Nimitz read, his eye catching the word.

"Civilians? Again?"

Lamar was looking down, did not respond, the others at the radio desk looking away. Nimitz read more of Buckner's words, his anger growing.

"What the hell's the matter with those people? This is Saipan all over again! Where did this happen . . . okay, yeah, Kerama Retto. They blew themselves up? We didn't do a damn thing to them, and they just . . . blew themselves up?"

It was a memory he had tried to forget, visiting Saipan the summer before. Admiral King had been there as well, the usual high-ranking inspection of a successful campaign. What Nimitz did not expect to see was the place called Marpi Point, where hundreds of terrified civilians had fled the advance of the American Marines by hurling themselves off the cliffs onto the rocky coastline below. The Marines who had tried to communicate their friendliness to the civilians had been stunned by the horror, and Nimitz had seen firsthand how effective Japanese propaganda could be. Those few civilians whom the Marines had prevented from leaping to their deaths spoke of the cannibalism of the Americans, how every child was certain to be raped and killed. Their terror had made it clear that the Japanese would spread the same propaganda to the occupants of every island. And now Nimitz saw the same kind of report. As Buckner's troops from the Seventy-seventh Infantry Division swept over the small islands off Okinawa's southwestern shore, the civilians there had reacted with the same blind fear. Unlike Saipan, on the small cluster of islands, the Japanese had supplied the people with weapons, mostly grenades. The troops who had witnessed the suicides had thought they were being fired on, but it was quickly apparent the civilians were using the grenades on themselves. Once again, Japanese propaganda had been amazingly effective.

"Damn. It could be this way all over Okinawa. How in hell do we stop this?"

It was a question no one around him could answer.

Nimitz continued to read, more of the same efficiency from Buckner, troop counts and landing craft specifics that Nimitz already knew. There were details of the shelling of the island as well, Buckner's gleeful expectation that the Japanese defenses had been completely destroyed. Nimitz took no joy from the general's optimism, had heard too much of that before. Dammit, if bombs and artillery are all we need, why in hell are you out there in the first place?

Nimitz was growing weary, the end of a long day, knew that tomorrow would be longer still. He couldn't help the tension, felt it from his entire staff, the same tightness they all felt the night before every major operation. He scanned the rest of Buckner's report, and his eye stopped at the end of the last page, a single line of type. Nimitz felt a cold stab in his stomach. No, not this crap again.

"Tomorrow we start on a great adventure."

6. ADAMS

"Eat up! All you want. Grab it and growl!"

The line snaked back along the corridor, the men inching their way past the amazing bins of hot food. Adams could smell the meat, saw men coming back past him with trays of steak and scrambled eggs, bowls of ice cream, steaming coffee. The smells were wonderful, hunger overcoming his bleary-eyed lack of sleep. He glanced behind him, saw Sergeant Ferucci, said, "What time is it, Sarge?"

"Just past three. You better eat up. Might not get anything for a while."

In front of him one man stepped out of line, moved the other way, down a stairway, stumbled, held himself against the railing, was suddenly sick. Around Adams there was a chorus of groans, low curses, the scene too common on the transport ships. Ferucci prodded him gently, said, "Ignore that. Eat what you can. Some of these boys are too smart for their own good. They ain't eating 'cause they know what's coming. More'n' likely, you'll just be borrowing those steaks. Seen too many boys give it all back before we hit the beach. Not me. I see this much grub, I grab all I can. You

oughta do the same. If it stays down, you'll be better off. If it doesn't . . .
well, won't matter much."

Behind the sergeant, another man said, "Funny as hell, Sarge. How
the hell can you eat anything at three in the morning? I'm done. You can
have my share."

Adams turned, saw Gorman, one of the veterans, a sickly look on the
man's face. They called Gorman "Pops," though Adams knew he couldn't
have been much older than the rest, maybe twenty-five. Gorman had been
in four major engagements, and Adams had envied that, knew that Gorman should be someone to watch, would know what to do in a tight spot.
But Gorman was getting sicker by the second, and Adams watched as he
stepped out of line, made his way to the same stairway, dropped out of
sight. Ferucci said, "He shoulda gone up, gotten some air. He'll be okay.
Just means more steak for the rest of us."

Ferucci moved up to the long table, his plate filled quickly. At the far
end of the table, Lieutenant Porter waited, watching, and Adams saw a
silent nod toward Ferucci. The lieutenant held a grim stare, a glance
toward Adams, then the others as they came up behind. Adams liked
Porter, kept that to himself, knew the men didn't talk kindly about officers
very often. But there was something solid about the man, the kind of energy that Adams hoped was contagious, the look in the man's eye that
Adams interpreted as concern for his men, and more, an officer who could
lead. He didn't know what kind of action Porter had seen, how many men
he had led into horrible places, how many of those had gone down. The
man kept just enough steel in his stare to keep the questions away, and
Adams felt the same confidence that the rest of the platoon seemed to expect. They might still make jokes about officers, but in this platoon, Porter
was in charge.

Behind the table, a row of sailors were dishing out the food. Behind
them stood an officer, the source of the ongoing pep talk.

"Eat up! Put a steak in your pocket if you want to! When was the last
time you had ice cream? There's plenty."

More of the men were filling their plates, and Adams smelled the coffee now, caught the officer's eye.

"Belly up to the table, Private! Take plenty!"

Adams was close to the massive pile of steaks now, the sailor across
from him holding a long, thin fork.

"How many?"

"Just one, I guess."

Behind Adams, another man fell out, soft words, "Can't do it."

Adams tried to ignore him, knew it was another of the veterans. The sailor smiled at him now.

"One more for you, Marine. Here, take two."

Adams felt the weight dropping on his tray, moved farther along the table, saw the eggs, piled high, another sailor holding a large spoon.

"Here you go. Fresh from the navy's own chickens. Bet you didn't know we had a henhouse. The captain gets his over easy, every morning."

The other sailors laughed at their own joke, the food passing from spoon and fork to the tin plates on the trays, the line continuing, coffee poured into tin cups. Adams saw the heavy tubs of ice cream, stared at the mountain of food on his tray, saw a wave from the lieutenant.

"This way, Private. Through the hatch. Find a place to sit."

The words were automatic, Porter's face still grim, tight, and Adams followed the instructions, moved through a hatchway into a cramped mess hall, benches and narrow tables. Men were sitting tightly against one another on the benches, some on the floor, and Adams searched for a spot, saw no space, leaned toward a bulkhead beside him, put his back against the steel. He picked up his fork, probed the eggs, the steak beneath the yellow heap, hesitated, looked out across the mess hall, saw men staring down at their plates, almost no one eating. One man stood, left his tray on the table, hurried out quickly, past him. No one reacted, and Adams realized the room was silent, no sound of tin plates, no one talking at all. He wanted to say something, to ask, but something in his brain told him to keep quiet. Three A.M., he thought. Guess it's kinda tough to eat much. I'd rather be sleeping.

He had felt the tension all night, few men talking at all. But when the mess call came, everyone had reacted as they always reacted, orderly, automatic, following the lieutenant to their designated mess. The food had been an amazing surprise, but many of the veterans were angry at that, a strange reaction. He saw the same anger now, the faces staring downward, one man suddenly throwing his fork against a bulkhead, a sharp clatter, no one responding. The man still sat with fists curled on either side of his tray, said, "Another *last meal.* How many more times we gotta do this?"

Adams saw movement beside him, the lieutenant coming in through the hatchway.

"Knock it off, Yablonski. You don't want to eat, don't eat. You got a bitch, you air it to me. Let these men eat."

Adams had never liked Yablonski, the man always angry, always trying to pick a fight. Adams had obliged him, faced the man in a boxing match that Adams had won easily, a thunderous right hand into Yablonski's temple that had knocked him cold. Yablonski hadn't spoken to him since, seemed to pretend Adams didn't exist, that the fight had never happened. Adams had heard from the others that Yablonski had been in more fights than anyone in the platoon, mostly outside of a boxing ring. Nearly everyone seemed to be afraid of him, and Adams heard talk that he was flat-out dangerous, with a manic need to kill someone, hopefully the enemy. Adams had seen that look in Yablonski's eye, and the knockout hadn't done anything to change it.

Porter waited silently for a response, kept his eye on Yablonski's back. Yablonski seemed to ignore the lieutenant, said, "I'm sick of this! How many times they expect us to do this?" He turned, faced the lieutenant now. "I made it this far . . . how many lives you think I have left? Any of us? We've lived through fight after fight, and the ones who made it this far are just plain lucky. So, they're gonna keep sending us in until we get it? Is that the way this goes?"

"Outside, Private. Now."

The lieutenant stayed calm, the order coming without anger. Adams felt a cold chill in Yablonski's stare, the man rising slowly. Yablonski stepped back away from the bench, moved away from the lieutenant, toward the far hatchway. Adams waited for the order bringing Yablonski back, sending him below, but the lieutenant said, "That's right. Go topside. Get some air. All hell's about to break loose, and you might wanna watch that. See what we're doing to those yellow bastards."

Yablonski didn't respond, disappeared through the hatchway, and Adams felt the cold still, the man's anger hanging in the room. Most of the men kept their stare on their untouched food, no one looking at the lieutenant. Adams couldn't look at the tray, his appetite gone, could feel it now, more than ever before. Men were shivering, hands shaking, one fork rattling in a manic chatter against a tin plate.

"Easy, boys. We'll be on that beach soon enough. You start shooting Japs, you'll feel a hell of a lot better." Porter paused. "Look at me! All of you!"

Heads turned slowly, and Adams saw the eyes, some with tears. The lieutenant stepped close to one table, reached over a man's shoulder, picked up a steak from the man's plate, held it in the air, grease dripping from his fingers. Porter seemed to wait, had their full attention, then made a quick shout, pulled at the steak with both hands, ripping it in half. He stuffed one piece in his mouth, ripped away the excess, threw it hard over their heads, a wet slap against the bulkhead. Adams stared at the lieutenant with wide eyes, saw a glimmer of madness, and now Porter finished chewing the meat in his mouth, then began to laugh, a low chuckle. He held his hands out, the juice still dripping, "That's what I'm going to do to the first Jap bastard I see! How about you!"

He pointed at one man closest to him and the man responded, "I'll rip those sons of bitches in half!"

The mess seemed to explode with voices, the others responding. The lieutenant kept up the calls, one fist pounding the table, and Adams knew it was calculated, but he couldn't help himself, was caught up in the flow of emotion, the curses and shouts, the anger and fear turning outward. Men were ripping meat from their teeth, more steaks thrown against the bulkheads. Adams grabbed a blob of melting ice cream, held it out toward the lieutenant, then threw it hard to the deck, straight down, a splash of white on his boondockers. Porter watched him, the same steel in the man's eyes, the lieutenant poking his finger close to Adams's face, the words in a low, hard hiss.

"What are you going to do on that beach, Private?"

"Kill Japs, sir!"

"How many Japs, Private?"

"All of them, sir!"

Porter looked back across the mess, the faces changed, the tears gone, men standing, no time for food now. Porter gave them direction, harnessing the outburst, pointed toward the hatchway, the only order they needed. Plates clattered, food falling to the floor, men stepping up and over the tables. Adams saw Ferucci now, the sergeant pushing a man in front of him, out through the hatchway, the sergeant turning back with a quick glance at the lieutenant, a silent signal, yes, good. Adams was caught up in the flow of men, but he understood now, felt his heart racing, his hands shaking. The fear was in all of them, paralyzing, but the lieutenant had pulled it out of them, putting it to use, directing it where it needed to go. Porter still pointed the way, the men filing quickly out through the hatchway that would take them topside. Adams followed, was suddenly stabbed by a hard jolt of thunder, the echoes of artillery fire. It rolled down around them all, thumps and thuds, echoing through the steel corridor. The Marines rushed to the ladders, pushing toward another hatchway that took them out into the cool night air. They poured out onto the deck of the transport ship, and it was Adams's turn now. He ducked low through the oval hatchway, smelled the stink of smoke, saw flashes of light. The guns were firing on all sides of them, blinding light, the mass of faces reflecting the glow. Each thump punched him, the deck beneath his feet vibrating, the entire ship engulfed by the violence of the enormous fleet around them. Adams moved with the men around him, toward the railings, the men packing in tightly, their eyes adjusting, seeing the streaks of fire cutting through the last shadows of the night. The firing all went in one direction, and Adams fought to see above the heads in front of him, to see the target, the place that now had a name. The darkness had begun to lift, a hint of gray. The horizon was uneven, low hills, peppered with splashes of fire. The smoke was swirling over the deck, and Adams felt his eyes watering, wiped furiously, tried to breathe, covering his mouth. But the smoke couldn't hide the massed fire from a thousand guns, ships far out on both sides pouring fire toward a narrow span of beach, and the hills beyond.

Whether the navy had done this every day for a week made no difference to the men who watched this now. With the first hint of dawn, the men could finally see Okinawa, the landing zones blasted, erupting into flashes of fire and rock and mud. Adams stood with the men of his platoon, his company, his regiment, some of them seeing this before, who knew what this meant, and others who had no idea what would happen next. Through the vast crowd on the deck there was still fear, but it was held away by the spectacle. They watched with anxious excitement, tight stomachs, and for some, still the sickness, the tears. But for many the fear was gone, at least for those who were not yet ready for what daylight would bring. As the warships threw their vicious fire onto the beaches, Adams shared the same exhilaration of many of the men around him. They were captivated by a magnificent show.

7. ADAMS

No one spoke, the rumble of the landing craft pushing them through the water's surface in a slow, sickening roll. Adams did as the men around him, kept his stare on the back of the man closest to him, trying to ignore the stink of vomit, the helmet that would suddenly drop low, the sickness pulling a man to his knees. He felt the pressure from men behind him, pushed up tight against Adams's backpack, as tight as Adams was pressed into the man to his front.

All around them the shellfire continued, but much lighter now, the bombardment from the navy's smaller patrol boats that rolled forward alongside the landing craft. The smoke was there again, washing over them, mixing with the exhaust from the churning engine of the landing craft. Above, Adams heard a new sound, planes close overhead, some of the men looking up with him, a glimpse of the blue Corsairs, the navy's best aerial weapon. One man let out a cheer, but no one joined him. The gunboats close by continued to fire, sharp thumps, but then, nothing, the guns silent. Adams peered up, saw the closest boat veering away, as though its job was done. The landing craft rocked to one side, then rolled the other way, the men trying to stay upright, wedged together, a shout behind them, and suddenly the landing craft jerked to a stop. Adams fell forward, driven by the man behind him, curses, the stink from the sickness around their feet rising up through the sharp, salty breeze. In a sudden rush of motion, the bow of the craft fell away, a hard slap into shallow water, the beach and the hills now visible, close, less than a hundred yards. One voice rose above the noise, the lieutenant, standing at the opening, a hand in the air.

"Let's go! Follow me!"

The lieutenant was out and down into the water, still waving, and behind him the men surged out of the craft in one mass, a cluster of helmets and rifle barrels and overstuffed backpacks. The open bow of the craft sloped downward, bouncing against black coral, and Adams stared at the beach, saw a mass of men in the water, far out in both directions. The water was mostly shallow, knee-deep, the men pushing forward to a narrow stretch of dull gray sand. He saw the hand in the air again, Porter calling them forward, and Adams splashed down into the warm water, his boots hitting the uneven rocks, stumbling, fighting for balance against the weight of the ammo, the weight of the backpack. He kept his stare toward the beach, straining to see the flashes of fire, to hear the sounds he had been told about, the hiss of machine gun fire into the water around him. But there was no firing at all, the men around him splashing forward, no one aiming, no targets anyone could see, and better, no one seeming to target *them*. The tension turned his stomach over, and he wanted to be sick, fought it, focused on each step, angry at himself, the warm water not easing the cold inside him. He pulled his arms in tight, gripping his rifle, his mind racing, thoughts of everything, nothing, ignored the men around him, stepping forward, as he was. They pushed closer to the beach in manic splashes, and he felt salt water on his face, stinging his eyes. Beneath him the rough coral had given way to hard sand, easier footing, and he kept his stare toward the beach, saw men up on the sand, more hands in the air, waving them on. As far out as he could see, Marines were flowing up out of the surf, swarming across the narrow stretch of open ground, an enormous green wave moving forward toward the low hills. Adams slogged through the water with heavy automatic steps, but the water and the fear had drained him. He struggled to breathe, his chest heaving, and still he stared up into the thin brush, past the men who were on the beach. Most of them kept running, disappearing; others dropped down onto dry sand, fighting with themselves, finding their wind. They were back up now, prodded by screaming sergeants, shoved forward into the brush. Adams blinked through the salt and sweat in his eyes, was clear of the surf now, tried to push his legs harder, to run, hard wet sand, turning softer, dragging at his boots. The pain in his legs was paralyzing, but he would not stop, passed by one man who had collapsed, the man struggling to rise, another man pulling him up. He kept his eyes forward, toward the low hills, the men staggering ahead of him under the weight of their packs, more of them falling, seeking cover in the low rocks, pockets of coral, fresh craters from the shelling. He moved past them, saw the lieutenant, Porter, still pulling them forward, and Adams forced himself to keep running, the terror in his mind giving way to a strange exhilaration, the excitement ripping through the fear, inspired by the lieutenant, no hesitation, the man doing his job, *leading* them. He followed Porter up onto a low rocky hill, the men around him still running, Adams keeping the pace, the energy coming back. They reached a row of bushes, a field of waist-high brush, and Porter waved them down, the signal every man knew. *Take cover.*

Adams tumbled down, the weight on his back rolling him over, men coming down close to him, rifles jabbed forward, expectant, the only sound the scuffling of men on rock, grunts and hard breathing. Adams crawled forward, close to a fat ragged boulder, brush on one side, good cover, and he rolled onto his back, sat, tried to catch his breath. The faces were there now, wide-eyed terror and exhaustion, most from his own platoon, the names rolling into his brain. Ferucci was on his knees, peering up, then dropping down, the man who had done this before, who knew what to expect. Adams saw Welty lying on his side, wiping the water off his glasses. Close beside Adams was Yablonski, wide-eyed fury, aiming his rifle, but not firing. No one spoke, all of them doing what Adams was doing, gathering themselves, finding their wind, checking their rifles, some seeking targets. Ferucci crawled forward, probing the brush, and Adams felt a stab of fear, no, stay back . . . and now Ferucci shouted, "Here! Jap trenches! Good cover!"

Adams saw Porter responding, holding up his hands, low words, "Wait here!"

The lieutenant disappeared into the brush, and quickly there was a shout, passed on by the sergeants, more calls out in both directions.

"Move forward! Into the trenches!"

Adams rolled to his knees, followed the others through the thorny thickets, the ground suddenly opening up in front of him, a narrow ditch of sand and rock. Men were sliding down, rifles ready, good cover from the depth of the trench and the rocks and patches of brush beyond. Adams looked for Ferucci, saw the sergeant aiming his carbine, the others mimicking him with their own weapons, the longer M-1s laid up on flat ground, men seeking targets. For a long moment no one spoke, and Adams felt himself flinching, expecting . . . something. Now Porter was there, slipping along the wide, winding trench.

"Stay low! Keep to this cover! I'll find Captain Bennett! He should be to our right!"

Adams watched Porter scramble away, was suddenly scared for the man, stay down, dammit. The fear built up in a thick wave, the calm and the silence around him unnerving, unexpected. Adams pulled the M-1 close to his chest again, laid back against the side of the trench, saw out to one side, a wide dugout, a slab of concrete. Words filled his brain, the logic, an artillery emplacement, but there was no sign of the artillery piece at all, no blasted parts, no twisted steel. His mind focused on the flow of men still coming up behind him, the trench filling rapidly, men now calling out, sergeants, pulling their men through the narrow brush, dropping down, lining the trench, the gun pit. Close to him, Ferucci said, "The damn Japs gave us a gift! I'll be damned!"

Another man, a sergeant Adams didn't know, said, "You sure about that? They could have mined this thing, booby-trapped it. They start tossing grenades on us, we're dead."

"If that was true, we'd already be blown to hell, wouldn't we? And there's not a Jap in sight. I think we wiped these bastards out, or scared them off this beach. The damn swab jockeys did their job."

Beside Adams, Yablonski said, "I don't see any guts. No bones. Nobody got wiped out here, Sarge. They ran."

Ferucci peered out again, shook his head.

"To where? That's what we gotta worry about."

Adams saw movement, men pulling in their legs, making way for the lieutenant. Porter crawled low, a quick scramble down the trench, red-faced, breathing heavily.

"Sergeants, gather up!"

The men came close, Ferucci, the others, and Porter waited for them, then said in a hard whisper, "Listen up! Captain says there's been no resistance so far. Radio reports from down the beach all say the same thing. The Japs left these works empty. Gun emplacements all down the beach, but nobody's home! So, they gotta be laying low. But nobody gets careless, you got that? We're to push up through that brush field out ahead. There's some rocks up beyond that, more good cover. The Japs might be waiting for us there, so keep low! Space your men . . . five yards between 'em. Our mortar crews are already setting up in those low rocks to the left. If all hell breaks loose, they're watching us, and they'll give us support. Take five minutes to catch your breaths, then wait for my command! That's it!"

The sergeants spread out, moving back to their squads. Adams could see both ways, thick clusters of green, no one talking, a light breeze whispering through the brush behind them. Men still aimed their rifles, but others did as Adams was doing, sat with their backs against the hard, rocky sand. He felt something pressing painfully against his hip, rolled slightly, his hand finding his gas mask.

"Get rid of that stupid thing." He saw Ferucci holding up his own gas mask, and the sergeant continued, "Ditch those gas masks. You're carrying too much crap. Before this is over, you'll wish you hadn't grabbed all that ammo. Every damn one of you is carrying enough junk for a Boy Scout campout." He glanced up, the sun well above the horizon. "Wait till that sun starts to bake your asses. Every bit of that junk will be left behind. Seen it every damn time."

Adams looked at the gas mask, wasn't completely convinced, but beside him Yablonski tossed his mask back into the brush, other men doing the same. Adams felt the belt of clips across his chest, thought, no, I'll keep these. Yablonski seemed to read his mind, said, "They said take all the clips you can carry, and that's what I'm doing. You wanna get caught out there with an empty weapon, you go right ahead. Every clip means eight dead Japs. All it costs me is sweat."

Ferucci said nothing, tossed his own gas mask out in front of the depression. Adams lay back against the softness of his pack, glanced at the M-1 again, water beading on the oiled steel. Beside him Yablonski was moving the brush aside with the barrel of his rifle, still seeking a target, a low voice, more angry words.

"Where the hell are you, you yellow bastards. Stick your head up, just one time. Give me one clean shot, you sons of bitches . . ."

Adams said nothing, knew better than to interfere in the man's angry monologue. He saw Ferucci watching Yablonski, a cold, uncertain stare, the sergeant not doing anything to break the man's frightening concentration. Adams lay back again, Yablonski's words fading, silent, and Adams took a long breath, tested himself, the fear not as bad as he expected. Welty was on his other side, and Adams turned, saw the glasses, Welty slowly peering up above the lip of the trench. Welty was the only man in the squad that Adams felt was his friend, and he was curious, had never seen Welty in any kind of dangerous situation. He wondered if Welty was as scared as he was, wanted to say something, reassuring them both, put a hand on Welty's shoulder.

"We made it, Jack. On the beach. We got our beachhead."

Welty didn't respond, was in some other place, held his rifle up at his chest, staring away, his face sweating. Ferucci said, "Leave him be. He knows what's about to happen. Never seen a man more in charge of himself, once the fighting starts. We'll all be okay. So far, this is just . . . strange."

Behind Ferucci, Gorman popped his head up, the older man calm as well, appraising the land around them.

"Hey Sarge, the tanks oughta hit the beaches right behind us. That's usually the drill. That'll make our job a whole hell of a lot easier."

Ferucci pointed a thumb back over his shoulder toward Gorman, said to Adams, "Pops has done this more times than anybody. Listen to him, Private." He turned. "Hey, Pops. You got Gridley's stuff?"

Gorman didn't smile.

"You have to ask? He can't fire that damn Browning without me. I wouldn't let him down."

Gridley was farther down the line, the heavy BAR standing upright against the sandy embankment beside him. Gorman was Gridley's ammo carrier, the older man somehow earning the right to go into combat with a carbine and heavy boxes of cartridges. Adams had yet to understand why any of that was a privilege.

The sergeant began to move, pulled himself up to his knees, anticipating the lieutenant's order. After a long pause, it came, a sharp wave, the crisp shout, "Let's go! Move! Spread out!"

The men surged forward out of the trench, following Porter in a crouching run across the uneven ground. Adams pushed through a thicket of brush, stiff and thorny, scraping his legs. To both sides the men ran with him, Gorman moving close to Gridley, Yablonski beside them, Ferucci's squad mostly together. There was sweat on every face, grim purpose, some ignoring the order to keep their distance. All around him the wave of green pressed forward, the only sound the boots on rock, hard breathing, and the crunch of the brush. The dirt was reeking of the stink of explosives, craters and blasted rock, smoke from small fires, shattered trees still smoldering, wisps of smoke coming from low places. He tried to keep his eye on Porter, was uncertain where he was, no insignia on the man's green jacket, all the men anonymous, running as one, scrambling, stumbling through the rocky field. Then a hand went up, familiar. The men responded, settled low, Adams down to his knees, jagged rocks, dirt and brush, more good cover. He rolled to one side, the weight from the ammo belts pulling him down, and he put his rifle at his shoulder, glanced across the rocks, saw men dropping low all around him, rifles ready, no one talking. Porter watched them come, still motioning to the slower men: *Down.*

Adams's mind searched for sounds, the fear sharpening his senses. What the hell is happening? Where the hell are the Japs? His heartbeat was heavy in his ears, his breaths coming in short, hard gasps. He heard a whisper of breeze, smoke drifting past, and now a new sound, low at first, then coming fast, louder, a high-pitched screaming roar. The terrifying sounds became engines, and he saw the blue Corsair, then another, the planes racing low over the beach. Just as quickly they were gone, up and over the hills. From the rocks around him, men called out, cheers, but Porter shouted them down.

"Shut up! Do your job!"

Adams stared up at the puffs of white clouds, felt lost, confused, grateful for Porter, for anyone who knew what was going on. He had heard too many horror stories, men crossing beaches, ripped to bits before they reached any cover at all. What he hadn't heard from the veterans he had imagined, and none of the fantasies was pleasant. No matter how he tried to fight that, the images were there, driven into him by the bloody bandages and missing limbs of the men he had seen in the hospital. Some never made it out of the water, some had been wounded while still in their landing craft. But we didn't get it at all, he thought. They let us alone, gave us the beach. Did the officers expect that? The navy guns . . . all that bombing. It worked? So what do we do now?

The whining roar of the engines came again, three more Corsairs, the blue gull-winged planes flying along the beach, higher, wings dipping, the planes turning, going inland, like the others. He could see the bombs beneath their wings, felt a jab of excitement, yes! That's why there are no Japs. What the navy's guns didn't get, the carrier planes have blasted all to hell! Only thing that makes sense.

The quiet returned, low talk from some of the men around him huddled in their rugged cover. For now there were only the soft sounds of the beach, a distant calling of birds, and beyond that, silence.

Silence.

HANZA VILLAGE, OKINAWA
APRIL 1, 1945, 11 A.M.

They were walking, two rows of men in the shallow ditches that lined a narrow gravelly road. Adams kept his eyes on the low patches of brush speckled across wide rocky fields, taller hills beyond, rocks and trees. There were more roads that led away, intersections that led into a row of stone huts, straw roofs, some with sheets of tin. Marines were everywhere, more of the landing force moving inland along other roads, into the small villages near the beach. Porter's men moved in silence, each man holding tight to his weapon, waiting for . . . something. Behind them Adams could hear the sounds of engines on the beach, the great invasion continuing, amphtracs and floating tanks driving up onto the narrow shoreline, the larger LSTs unloading their men and machinery all along the landing zone. The tanks were already there, and he knew from the briefings that the engineers and Seabees would come close behind them, more equipment, bulldozers, and tractors. Ultimately they would deal with the airfields, smoothing over the damage caused by the shelling and bombing from the American bombardments, or whatever destruction the Japanese still had in mind.

Adams couldn't keep his heart from pounding, sweat thick in his shirt and short jacket, his backpack growing heavier with each step. The belts of clips for the M-1 draped heavily across his chest, thumping him as he walked, pressing into the grenades that hung from his shirt. Far up in front of him, Porter led the way, another squad behind him, Ferucci's squad bringing up the rear. Every few minutes there were hard whispers from the sergeant.

"Five yards! Dammit, keep your distance!"

Adams focused on the backpack that bobbed along in front of him, Yablonski, the man holding his rifle up, keyed, alert, still a desperate search for a target. Adams could see across the road, an open field cut by a narrow road that led to a small village. Marines were there as well, slipping cautiously into the small buildings, pushing through, shouts of *all clear.*

The sweat stung his eyes, and he wiped them with his sleeve, saw a hand signal, then a low voice passed the word back from Porter.

"Take ten. Stay down in the ditch. No huddling up. Keep your distance."

The men dropped like sacks of flour, and Adams did the same, his knees gratefully giving way, the pack breaking his fall. Welty was closest behind him, the march not seeming to affect the man at all. Welty removed the glasses, wiped them with a sleeve. Adams wanted to talk to him, but there was nothing to say, no answers to the questions. The mystery was complete, no sign of the great Japanese horde that was supposed to meet them, nothing to stop the Marines from moving inland. They had already passed their first day's objective, spreading far beyond the beachhead. There had been *nothing* to slow them down.

As they had moved up the low hills, there had been a burst of fire, off to the south, and Adams had heard the different sound of the Japanese Nambu machine gun, the first clue that there might be anyone else here at all. But the firefight had been brief, a peppering of shots from a few M-1s, and then, nothing. Farther to the south had come a hard rumble, thumps from what sounded like mortars, but if there had been a fight at all, it had been over quickly. The farther they moved inland, the more frequent the exchanges had been. But all of that had been far away, no one firing at *them*.

"Drink some water." Adams turned toward the voice, saw the sergeant holding up his canteen, pointing. "Do it. I'm not dragging your asses up this road because you fall out all dried up. You're sweating like pigs, and I can smell every one of you back here. A barnyard would be a relief."

Adams obeyed, the water in his canteen warm, and he washed away the crust and salt on his lips. He had another canteen, empty now, most of the men carrying two, another of those luxuries offered on board the transport ship. He slipped the tin back into its canvas holster, his mind drifting, the heat working on his brain. He looked skyward, thought of home, *a bluebird day.* Well, not quite like that here. There's clouds. And I haven't seen a bluebird either. Seagulls, and some other brown thing. He wiped sweat out of his eyes, looked toward the front of the column, saw Porter close to the walkie-talkie man, the antenna wobbling out to one side. Porter was talking in a low voice, raised his head, stared out down the road. Adams focused, watched, waited for Porter to tell them . . . something. The conference was quick, Porter now rising.

"Saddle up, ladies."

They rose, some struggling under the weight of the cargo they carried, and Adams was surprised to see ammo belts coming off, tossed into the ditch. He put a hand against his chest, thought, no, not me. In front of him, Yablonski bent low, retrieved one belt, slung it over his shoulder, said, "Thank you, boys. Keep 'em coming. You weak assholes can't hack this, you shoulda stayed home. There's Japs in these hills, I can smell 'em. Don't come running to me when you run outta clips."

Ferucci responded from behind Adams.

"Shut up. You want to haul those belts, fine. The rest of you . . . well, I told you to drop that crap back at the beach."

Porter was already moving ahead, watched the scene with weary annoyance, and another of the sergeants passed the order back to the last squad.

"Move it. Five-yard intervals. The looey says we got someplace to be."

The march continued, the wetness in Adams's boots less noticeable, his legs aching, moving in a slow, plodding rhythm, keeping the five-yard gap from Yablonski. They crested a low hill, Porter slowing them, cautious, but the far side of the hill was different, a cultivated field, waist high and green, and Yablonski said, "Sugarcane. The bastards could be hiding in here."

Adams had never seen sugarcane before, took Yablonski's word for it, followed as Porter waved them up out of the ditch. They moved out in a wide formation, stepping through the soft green stalks, the men separated by at least three neatly planted rows. Adams was focused on the sea of leafy green spreading out for a hundred yards, up and over a rise. The ground beneath his feet was clear, the half-grown stalks a foot apart. To his right, Welty made a sound, a high short whine, and Adams flinched, but Welty was walking slowly, deliberately, staring straight down, his rifle prodding the greenery as he moved. Beyond him, Ferucci said, "Eyes front, Private. Good hiding place for the Japs. Keep sharp. The shooting starts, hit the deck."

Welty seemed lost in his own fear, and Adams remembered now, the briefing, the captain telling the entire company about the snakes on Okinawa, the place famous for the most poisonous snakes on earth. Welty had been one of those who seemed sickened by the fear of that, and Adams had laughed at them, thought, city boys. In New Mexico there were rattlesnakes as big as a man's leg, and even as a boy he had learned to step through rocks and brush with one eye glancing down at each footstep. The thorny brush on Okinawa had brought that back to him, not that different from the hostility of the land near his home. The snakes were different, he thought, but a snake's a snake. As long as you don't step on them, they leave you alone. The others hadn't been nearly as calm about that, some of the men more anxious about snakes than they were about the Japanese. Now, in the sugarcane, the fear had magnified, the progress slow as the men kept their gaze downward, M-1s pointing low. Even on the road, as several of the men had dropped out of line for an urgent call of nature, every one of them had stayed in the wide-open spaces, any embarrassment erased by the fear of what might be waiting in the clusters of brush. Adams was more curious about what the snakes looked like, had yet to see one, a mild disappointment. On board the ship, the captain had spoken of vast numbers of them, as though Okinawa was one great snake pit, no place safe enough to step. That was just bull, Adams thought. They're just keeping us on our toes, keeping these city boys from wandering off into God knows where. I don't want to be lost out in this stuff, for sure. He thought of Yablonski, the man's grim certainty. Yep, he's probably right. There's gotta be Japs out here someplace. I don't want to be the guy who finds them.

They crested the hill, and the lieutenant signaled them to slow down, crouched low himself. They did the same, fifty men in a wide row. Adams glanced back and saw fifty more, the next platoon coming up behind, could see the road they had left, more men there, waiting to join them. Up ahead the sugarcane abruptly ended, giving way to a wide, flat field. The lieutenant glanced back to the second platoon, held up his hand, *careful,* now waved to his own men. *Let's go.* Adams moved at the lieutenant's pace, quick glances down between the greenery, the edge of the field blessedly close. They stepped clear of the cane and Porter stopped them again, the man seeming uncertain, a look of confusion. The lieutenant dropped low, the cane to his back, the others following his lead. Adams dropped to one knee, questions rolling through his head, a stab of fear. What? All I see is a big damn field. He stared out at the hills beyond, saw clusters of trees. To his right, Ferucci said in a low voice, "There's more of our boys. There's some buildings."

Adams saw Marines emerging from distant brush, and barely visible, a cluster of low white buildings. Porter scanned the open ground, motioned to the walkie-talkie man, another quick conversation. Adams saw a smile, strange, and now the lieutenant waved the men out in both directions. The men responded by moving quickly, short steps across the open ground. Adams could see farther out in front of them, the field pockmarked by shell holes. They moved toward the buildings, the other Marines moving in and out, gathering. Adams could see sheets of camouflage up on poles, flapping in the gentle breeze. What the hell is that? Marines were gathering beneath the camouflage, the only shade in the area, and Adams saw now that the poles were arranged in the shape of airplanes. There were wooden crates beyond the strange shelters, stacked in odd configurations. Men were talking, laughter, one man climbing up on the crates, spreading his arms like wings. Adams understood now, the others as well, Ferucci saying it aloud.

"Fake airplanes. The Japs made fake airplanes. I guess . . . it's all part of the joke."

Adams moved closer to the gathering Marines, said, "What joke?"

Ferucci looked at him, a short laugh.

"One April, Private. Seems the Japs have played the world's greatest April Fool's joke on us. A pretend air force. Maybe this whole thing is pretend."

As he moved closer to the camouflage, Adams saw a pile of black wreckage, what used to be a truck. Beyond was more of the same, another truck down in a crater, pieces scattered. Porter moved out past them, a quick order.

"Easy. Stay here, stay alert. We're in the wide-assed open here. Be ready for incoming fire. I need to find the captain."

Porter moved away, and Adams saw one of the Marines moving out toward him, the unmistakable stride of an officer. The two men spoke for a long minute, pointing, and now a radioman appeared. There was more talk, another officer joining the conversation. The curiosity was digging hard at Adams, but he thought of Porter's words, *wide-assed open.* He looked out toward far hills, thought, anyone up there can see us clear as hell. Suddenly, from the officers and the men close to them came a new sound: celebration. Around him the platoon inched forward, the others as curious as he was. Adams still watched the higher ground, nervous, said to Ferucci, "Sarge, what the hell is this place?"

"I guess the looey's gonna tell us."

Porter was walking toward them, shouldered his carbine, beamed a broad smile.

"Congratulations, gentlemen." He glanced at his wristwatch. "Not even noon. Well, it seems that halfway through our first day on this slice of paradise, we've captured our third day's objective. Welcome to Yontan Airfield."

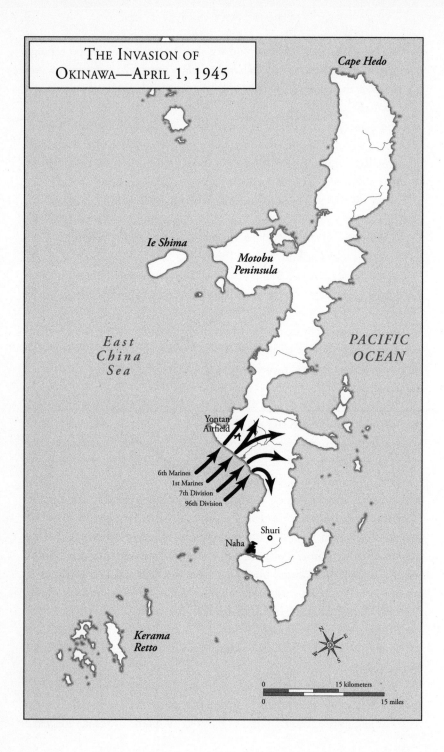

THE INVASION OF
OKINAWA—APRIL 1, 1945

Cape Hedo

Ie Shima

Motobu
Peninsula

East
China
Sea

PACIFIC
OCEAN

Yontan
Airfield

6th Marines
1st Marines
7th Division
96th Division

Shuri

Naha

Kerama
Retto

0   15 kilometers
0   15 miles

8. ADAMS

"Don't stop digging until the two of you can sit with your helmets be-lowground. Snipers are good at picking off helmets, and once it's dark, the Japs will probably move in to take a better look at us. I hear any more bitching about rocks, you can toss me your shovels and dig with your damn hands!"

Porter prowled through his platoon like an angry cat, the smartest men keeping their comments to themselves. Adams worked as they all worked, chopping, digging, cutting down through the tough mix of dense sand and coral rock, hacking and probing with the small shovel. Close be-side him, Welty worked as well, but Adams knew Welty didn't have the strong back, not for the ridiculous effort it took to make a hole in this kind of ground.

To one side, a voice, and Adams glanced that way, saw Gridley, shirt-less, wide shoulders, streams of sweat, digging his hole close to Ferucci.

"Hey Sarge. I'm digging, but I gotta wonder why? There ain't been a Jap anywhere around this place all day."

"Shut up, and keep digging. You heard the looey. That's all you need to know. I've gotta dig my own damn hole, and spend the night with that smelly bastard Hunley and his damn walkie-talkie. Don't give me your beefs. Some Jap up in those hills decides to throw some artillery fire at us, where'd you rather be? Up here on the nice flat ground, or in a deep-assed hole? Get to work. No more stupid questions."

The chopping, hacking, and cursing continued, but gradually the fox-holes grew deeper, the men testing them by sitting upright, squeezed to-gether, facing each other with legs side by side. Adams sat down in the bottom of the hole, the shade welcome. He looked up at Welty, who had his small shovel on his shoulder, and Welty had a look of tired satisfaction.

"Looks good, Clay. I think we're safe."

"Safe from what? I'm with Gridley. There isn't a damn Jap anywhere around this place."

"You heard that firing. I can hear it now, down that way. Something's happening. There's gotta be Japs . . ."

"Or our own guys shooting at rabbits."

Welty clearly was not convinced, dropped down into the hole, kept his stare toward the distant rumbling. Adams had tried to avoid the sounds, had convinced himself it was still naval gunfire, distorted over the great distance.

"We're still shelling the island down there in front of those ground pounders. They're probably jumpy as hell. I'll bet most of those army guys have never been through this before."

"Not like you, eh, Hardtack?"

Ferucci was standing above the hole, no smile with his question. Adams felt suddenly very stupid, said, "Uh, no, Sarge."

"Listen, you lamebrain, a bunch of those ground pounders are veter-ans too, fought under MacArthur, some damn place like New Guinea. Cannibals, boys. How'd you like to spend your night in a foxhole wonder-ing if the next bastard you hear might be wanting to eat your ass? The looey says the ground pounders are running into some resistance down south. That's not fireworks, it's artillery, and if you paid attention, you'd know that none of that sounds like our stuff. Seems we had the easy time of it. But down there, the Japs aren't just sitting back. Maybe they figured out who we are, and decided they'd rather stand up to ground pounders. Now settle in and eat something. The brass wants us up and moving north at dawn. The looey says there's supposed to be Jap positions up that way, and recon says they're just waiting for us to wander by. So, you think we're here to shoot rabbits, don't come bitching to me when some Jap sniper takes your head off."

The absurdity of the sergeant's words made Adams drop his head, hiding the smile. He made a slow nod.

"Aye, Sarge."

Ferucci was gone now, curses directed at another of the foxholes. Welty sat across from him, their backpacks wedged close beside them.

"Don't think he likes you too much, Clay."

Adams thought of the boxing matches, Ferucci treating him like a star.

"He's not supposed to like anybody out here. Just like the looey. Hell, *you're* not even supposed to like me. Nobody's supposed to be buddies. Buddies get killed, and it makes you a crappy Marine. That's what I was told, anyway."

Welty seemed to ponder the thought, shrugged.

"I learned a lot of that kind of stuff in training. Don't see how that makes me a better Marine. I know what to do when the enemy attacks. Kill the bastards. That's what we're supposed to do, right?"

There was no fire in Welty's words, Adams unconvinced that Welty could really kill anybody. He would never forget boot camp, thought charging sandbags with bayonets was easy. Hell, he thought, it was fun. Scream your brains out, curse the sandbag's momma, all so the sergeants would think you were getting tougher. Now we're tougher. Okay, what now?

There was a shout and Adams grabbed the M-1, popped his head up above the rim of the foxhole, heard the sound of an engine, searched the fading daylight. Men were pointing, Welty's words loud in his ear.

"It's a plane! He's coming in!"

Adams stared, mystified, said, "He'll have a hell of a time finding a place to land that ain't busted all to hell."

Nearby, Ferucci shouted, "Lieutenant! We got company!"

The plane rolled its wings slightly, the pilot maneuvering, seeking a clear strip of undamaged runway, the plane dropping quickly. Adams watched with raw amazement, thought, hell of a good pilot. Something's gotta be wrong with him.

The plane made a last bank, a steep turn, putting down onto a narrow strip that led close to the Marines, and they all saw it, the last bit of sunlight reflecting off the plane's wings, and now the fuselage, the bright red circle. Welty shouted into Adams's ear.

"Holy Jesus! That's a Jap!"

Across the field other men had identified the plane already, a swarm of Marines crouched low in a line of fire. The plane slipped its way past the shell holes, moved closer to the buildings at the end of the field, the engine shut off, the prop jerking to a stop. All across the field the rifles and machine guns were aimed, a curtain of silence over the bizarre scene. In short seconds the cockpit slid open, a single man emerging, adjusting his cloth helmet, slipping a parachute off his arms, swinging his legs out onto the wings, dropping down to the ground with a soft thump. He looked around, began to walk toward the first building, then suddenly stopped, turned with a jerk of his head, scanning the field. He seemed to understand now, crouched low, reached for a pistol at his belt. The shots came from close in front of him, and farther across the field, a chattering of fire that crumpled the man where he stood. Close to Adams, one man had fired an entire clip, shouted now, was up and out of his foxhole, running toward the silent plane. It was Yablonski.

"Got him! By God, I got him!"

Ferucci pursued him, others as well, a mass of men moving out from their positions. Adams was drawn with them, Welty following, a quick dash across to the plane. Officers were there now, calling the men back, one older man stepping forward, kneeling at the body.

"I'll be a son of a bitch."

The officer stood, moved to the plane, said aloud, "Well, we didn't shoot it down, but I'd say you boys nailed your first Jap Zero."

Lieutenant Porter moved out close to the older man, said, "Sir, what the hell was he doing?"

The older officer glanced at Porter, and he shrugged, laughed, looked out to the sea of faces who gathered in a tight circle around the plane and its desperately unfortunate pilot.

"Lieutenant, it's happened in every army that's ever fought. There's always some poor bastard who doesn't get the word."

They had tried to sleep, Adams unnerved by the intermittent rattling from distant machine gun fire, the occasional thump of artillery. But sleep did come, both men in their foxhole finally unwinding from the amphibious landing. Welty had been fidgety, and just before dawn, when the low growling call came from Ferucci, Adams was jolted awake to see Welty digging through his own backpack, as though he had not slept at all.

Their breakfasts had been quick and awful, the K rations a poor substitute for the relative luxury of the chow on board the transport ship. As Adams checked his M-1, the routine from the training, Welty had gone out to fill the canteens. Ferucci had called them up out of the foxholes with a sharp curse, and there had been no time for anything but a brief latrine call, men lining up impatiently at a shallow slit trench. The slower men had to handle nature's call out on the march.

They moved out at the first hint of daylight, the various companies flowing northward on the network of roads that led through the smaller villages and farmlands, every piece of ground offering some kind of cover that could disguise a Japanese machine gun nest. The navy recon planes had provided information on a scattering of Japanese positions, the carrier pilots spotting gun emplacements in the hills, most of them tucked into hiding places that no one might find until the guns had done their job. The experienced pilots had come to expect what they saw now, that the Japanese had positioned the larger artillery pieces on railway tracks, or flattened roadbeds, which allowed the guns to fire, then be withdrawn back into caves. The spotters might note the position, but before a Corsair or a naval gunner could zero in, the gun would disappear straight back into the mountain.

It was the same with the Japanese troop positions. All along the low mountain ridges that ran to the northern tip of the island, recon showed troops in motion, but only glimpses. There were no large-scale troop movements, no great masses of trenches where the Japanese seemed prepared to make a stand. The senior commanders could only vent their frustration at the intelligence officers, since no one could accurately count just how many enemy troops were on the northern half of the island. And even when people were located, there was never complete certainty that they weren't just Okinawan civilians, working their fields, tending to what remained of the normalcy of their everyday lives. As had happened around the airbases inland from the landing beaches, it appeared that most of the carefully constructed defensive works had been blasted to rubble and splinters by naval and air force bombardment. Driving northward, some of the Marines stumbled into pockets of resistance, a carefully hidden enemy who could emerge from uncountable holes in the brush and rocky hillsides. The fights were often brief, but the Japanese had every advantage. All the Marines could do was what their commanders insisted: keep going, shoving the Japanese back until the enemy had no choice but to give up that part of the island.

They spent their second day expanding their beachhead, and then expanding it again. Every road became a line of march, the Marines making dusty treks through scrub brush and rocky fields. The fears had begun to subside, the attacks from Japanese snipers or the occasional machine gun nest surprisingly rare. There had been casualties, of course, Adams hearing the manic call for a corpsman from up in front of them, two men wounded as they slipped through a gap in the cover. Others had found enemy soldiers in the small villages, the Japanese troops scampering away at the approach of the men in the green uniforms. Shots were exchanged, outbursts of fire that accomplished little for either side. As the second day drew to a close, Adams began to wonder if the Japanese were looking for a fight at all. The fatigue of the daylong march brought weary, dreamlike exhaustion, Adams fighting the sweat in his eyes, the canteens emptying more quickly than anyone wanted. They stayed mostly on the roads, keeping to the ditches, hundreds of men who followed the lines on a map that someone else had drawn. They were far ahead of the schedule for the assault, and if the Marines didn't know much about that, the men back on the ships did. On the beaches where the men had come ashore, the heavy equipment had followed, continued to follow. The tanks and artillery pieces were already lining the roadways away from the beaches, jeeps and amphtracs ferrying officers inland to their newly established field headquarters. Radio tents had gone up, kitchens and mess stations created, while the heavy equipment of the Seabees was already at work repairing and lengthening the runways on the abandoned airfields that would soon serve the fleets of B-29s and their fighter escorts.

With the second night approaching, the Marines knew the routine, and the shovels had come out once more, the holes dug in the brutal rockiness. While the Japanese had not shown their intentions, the officers who led the Marines had grown more itchy by the hour. There had been too much intel, too much recon, and too many reports of just how valuable this island was to the Japanese and their military. As Adams worked his shovel into the cracking coral, he had questions of his own. It had come to him on the march, aching legs supporting tired bodies, dreamy gazes where the hillsides opened up toward the strands of beaches to the west, soft surf, dotted only by the vast armada of American ships that lay off-shore. The hills had been mostly quiet, as though the occasional Japanese soldier was just an angry tourist, annoyed that these Marines had tres-passed into his private piece of solitude. The weariness in Adams's steps had gone from painful drudgery to annoyance. As the shovel bounced painfully against the coral, the foxhole inching deeper far too slowly, his curiosity had become anger. He thought of the maps he had studied in San Diego, the enormity of the Pacific, so many islands, some of them so terri-bly vital, some of them completely ignored. Who figures that out, he thought. Which Jap general decided which ones he needed, and which ones he didn't? And back in Guam and Hawaii . . . all of those men in their offices, with their plans and committees and secretaries, the men who never dirtied their hands. What if this is one of those incredibly stupid mistakes, another one of those screw-ups that made me a clerk? He wanted to ask Ferucci, but he knew the sergeant wouldn't know any more than the rest of them. But still the question burned, the same question he had asked on the roadway. So damn much ocean . . . so damn many islands. Is any-body sure if this is really Okinawa?

By the third day, American Marines and infantry had divided Okinawa in half and had easily captured the two primary airfields in the island's center. The invasion continued ahead of schedule, the First and Sixth Ma-rine divisions moving northward, the army's Seventh and Ninety-sixth di-visions moving south. On Kerama Retto, the cluster of islands off Okinawa's southwestern shore, the Seventy-seventh Division held its posi-tion securely while the airfield there was made usable for American air-craft. As the invasion had begun, the Second Marine Division had made a feint on the island's east side, an attempt to draw Japanese attention away from the primary assault. Now the Second was back on the transport ships, a floating reserve. The army had its own reserve, the Twenty-seventh In-fantry Division, waiting as well. No one in the American command had any precise idea when or if those reserves would be sent ashore. None of the intel reports had given General Buckner any specific idea how many Japanese troops were still dug into the caves and man-made tunnels be-neath Okinawa's hills.

The Marines began to focus on Japanese positions on the Motobu Peninsula, which jutted seaward to the west, reports coming in from the recon patrols that the Japanese had dug in a considerable garrison there. While some of the Marines would attack the peninsula, others would continue to press northward, driving whatever resistance they found straight up toward the island's northern edge. In the south the army would press against resistance there, with a goal of capturing the island's capital city, Naha, as well as what General Buckner's intelligence officers assumed to be a strong defensive line that ran from the capital across the island to the historic Shuri Castle. The castle sat on a prominent knoll, geographically perfect for a stout Japanese defense. Despite the ease of landing sixty thousand troops on the first day of the invasion, and tens of thousands in the days that followed, not even the most confident American commander believed the Japanese would simply hand the island to the Americans with a courteous bow.

9. ADAMS

"We're missing all the damn fun, you know. I didn't sign up to be a house inspector. This is just another damn ghost town."

"Shut up! Go around to the side. There's a window."

Yablonski obeyed, and Ferucci looked back at Adams, said with a hard whisper, "Get ready!"

Adams had done this too many times to be nervous, hoisted his rifle up to his waist, pointed at the rough wooden door. The others scattered out to one side, Gridley dropping to his knees, Gorman beside him, the BAR aimed at the door. Ferucci raised one foot, pushed slightly against the door, testing, then glanced back again, nodded, and shoved hard. The door opened, Ferucci shouldering his rifle, a quick scan inside, then he backed away, said, "Go!"

Adams moved past him, Welty close behind. They saw Yablonski at the window, a smirk on the man's face, no whisper now.

"Well? You see any treasure? A Jap division maybe hiding under that bamboo thing?"

Adams ignored him, knew the routine, poked his rifle into a pile of some kind of clothing, saw a small cloth sack in one corner of what seemed to be a primitive kitchen. He opened the sack with the muzzle of the M-1, saw sweet potatoes, scanned the kitchen for anything of interest, nothing but crude utensils, one copper pot.

"Nothing here."

Welty moved quickly into the other room of the two-room house, a quick shout, "Ah! Hey! Stop! Don't move! Sarge!"

Adams jumped toward the doorway, saw Welty pointing his M-1 downward, aimed at two old women, seated together in a corner, wedged against the crude wall by the side of a straw-covered cot. The sergeant was there quickly, pushed Adams aside.

"Well, somebody lives here. Howdy do, ladies. Sorry to bother you, but we're supposed to be looking for Jap bastards. You got any around here?"

Adams could see stark terror on the women's faces, one holding feeble hands up over her head, a pathetic show of self-protection, both women shaking, a mumble of words Adams thought to be a prayer. But there was more, the smell rising over him, thick and sour, and he backed away, said, "Come on, Sarge. Just old ladies."

Ferucci shook his head.

"Phew-ee. Ain't had a bath in a while, that's for sure. Well, hey there, ladies, we'll be going now. You see any Jap bastards, you be sure to let us know." He came back past Adams, said, "Let's go. Welty, you go tell the looey we found some Okies. Didn't look like much of a threat to me. The aid boys will wanna check 'em out though. I'm not touching them. God knows what kind of damn tropical crud they're carrying."

They moved back outside, and Adams glanced skyward, the clouds low and black, the wind picking up, raising the dust from the sandy ground. Welty moved away, a short walk through the cluster of houses, to where the lieutenant waited, sitting on an arch-shaped wall of concrete. The other squads were moving among the houses, rifles aimed into windows, more doors kicked in, no one calling out, no hint of alarm. They had been doing this for two days now, each of the small villages perched near cultivated fields, the farmers only occasionally appearing, old men mostly, primitive plows, tending to rows of short green plants.

Adams could hear the sharp rumbles to the south, the first sounds of fighting on the peninsula. The sounds had been inconsistent, nothing like anyone's idea of a pitched battle. There was mostly artillery, any rifle fire hidden by the lay of the hilly land, and now the rising winds. Adams had watched a swarm of fighter planes, twisting, banking, seeking targets along the higher hills, but even those were gone now, chased back to their ships by the change in the weather. Ferucci was beside him now, said, "Yablonski may be right. All the action's down that way. I like the looey, but this job is stupid as hell. We ain't gonna find any Japs hiding out in these places. They see us coming, they're long gone."

Adams thought of the sack of sweet potatoes, could see out past the small houses, a patch of open ground, rows of thick green plants.

"Hey, Sarge, you sure we can't eat the crops? We could cook up some of those sweet potatoes, and I saw a bean field back a ways. If we boiled hell out of the stuff, dumped in a handful of halazone tablets, might make a good soup."

He knew what the order had been, the captain passing word through the company that the vegetables were off-limits. But Adams had suspected it was just some protocol for being nice to the farmers. Ferucci was watching the others, turned to Adams, said, "You know what *night fertilizer* is?"

"Well, I hadn't heard that before the captain said it."

"*People shit.* That make it any clearer? That's what the Okies use to fertilize these fields. You still interested?"

Adams thought a moment, had seen Indians do the same thing near his home.

"Well, if we boil the vegetables . . ."

"I'll boil you, you stupid son of a bitch. Captain says there's all kinds of diseases we can catch, typhoid, or the plague or something. I'm not being your damn nursemaid if you start crying about your guts coming out. We got our own rations, and that's what we're gonna eat. You got that?"

Adams saw others watching him, heard the laughter.

"Got it, Sarge."

He started to move out toward the road, heard Yablonski call out, "Hey, Sarge! I'm grabbing these straw things. Make a good bed in my foxhole. You want one?"

It was Yablonski's usual game, offering to share anything resembling loot with the one man who would otherwise object to him taking it. Adams had heard the lectures about that, the captain preaching about leaving the civilians alone, making friends, so the Okinawans would be more helpful. But Lieutenant Porter hadn't said anything about the minor treasures Yablonski had found, trinkets mostly, stuffed into his backpack. It bothered Adams at first, but he was growing numb to that now, the people mostly filthy and frightened, no one offering any information where the Japanese might be.

Ferucci looked at the thin mat, woven bamboo, said, "Yeah, fine. I'm sick of sleeping on dirt. I bet there's more of them things." He called out now, "Hey! You guys see these mat things, grab 'em. We could use a little luxury."

Beside the road, the lieutenant watched the scene play out, no objection, seemed as impatient as his men, ready to move on to the next village. Adams felt an itch on his leg, reached down, scratched, saw Welty coming back toward him, the other men gathering, their job complete. Adams looked again at the approaching storm, glanced at his wristwatch. It's after five. Time to start digging again. Welty moved toward him, and Adams said, "Another day of fun. Maybe we oughta grab some of those mats too. I still got dirt in my ass from this morning."

Welty shrugged, leaned low, scratched his own leg, said, "There was some cloth back there, maybe sheets or something. I'll grab 'em."

Adams felt a hint of guilt, thought, these damn people don't have a pot to piss in . . . but the itching came again, and he tugged at his dungarees, tried to relieve the discomfort. Yeah, enough of this. They got beds, we got dirt.

The holes had been dug, Adams shifting the dirty white cloth beneath him, not nearly as much padding as he had hoped. He began poking through the backpack for his rations, and across from him Welty did the same. The daylight was almost completely gone, and Ferucci appeared above them, said, "Starting to rain. Grab your ponchos. One man two on, then two off."

He was gone quickly, repeating the words a few yards away. Welty pulled his poncho from the backpack, said, "I hate the rain. You're lucky, New Mexico and all. I'd trade Virginia for the desert any day."

"It's not all desert. We get rain. Monsoon season, comes up from Mexico. It's a bitch. Can't do anything outside but slide in the mud."

The conversation faded away, Adams fumbling with his own poncho, sliding it over his head, replacing his helmet. He put his hands on the cardboard of a K ration box, felt a rumble in his stomach. He hadn't eaten since morning, but had no appetite for the small can of stew, or whatever else the supply people had thought was an amusing addition to their meals. There was a stinging itch on his backside, and he shifted his bottom against the ground, but the itching wouldn't stop. Now there were more, along his belt, and he shoved his hands down his pants, said, "What the hell?"

Welty was scratching at his stomach, suddenly jumped up, said, "Ah! There's bugs! Damn!"

Adams stood as well, looked down at the white cloth, bent low, grabbed it, tugged, said, "Get off this thing. It's infested with something."

Welty was scratching furiously at his legs, and Adams yanked the cloth up, tossed it out of the foxhole. He heard laughter, but now there was cursing, close by, Yablonski, "There's damn critters all over me! Itches like hell! Hey Sarge!"

"Shut up! I got 'em too. It's this bamboo stuff, these mats."

Adams crawled up out of the foxhole, fumbled through the laces on his boots, yanked them off, ripped at his socks, scratching furiously at his legs. More men were coming up from the holes, and now the lieutenant was there, kneeling low, an angry shout.

"Get your asses back in your holes! What the hell's the matter with you?"

Adams dropped down, Welty beside him, still scratching, and Ferucci said, "I don't know! I got bugs on me!"

From the other foxholes, the chorus was the same, and Welty shouted out, "It's fleas! Sir, it's fleas! I know it."

Adams froze for a silent moment, heard more cursing, the mystery of their ailment suddenly explained. But Adams ignored that, stared at Welty, felt a hot burst of fear, the word punching him. *Sir.*

"Damn, Jack. Don't . . . do that."

Welty seemed oblivious, was rubbing furiously at his legs, and Adams eased his head up, looked for the lieutenant, wanted to do something to correct the mistake. It was full dark now, the curses still coming, and he heard rustling, the sounds of the mats tossed up onto the ground, everyone's mistake.

"Don't do what?"

Adams lowered his voice to a whisper.

"You called him . . . sir."

Welty stopped moving, but only for a brief second. But he lowered his voice as well.

"Sorry. No harm done. No Japs around here, least not any we've seen today."

"Yeah, well, you know the order."

Welty said nothing, rubbed his legs again, and Adams said, "I'll take the first two, okay? I'm not gonna eat. My gut's kinda messed up."

"Sure."

Adams stood slowly, knew that all across the rocky ground, the others were doing the same, the two men in each foxhole dividing the watch duty between them. If there was sleep at all, a man could get close to two hours while his buddy kept his eyes out for any Japanese infiltrators. The orders had been specific, the lieutenant passing on what came from above, that the Japanese had already been tormenting some of the army and Marine units by slipping into their positions at night. Makes sense, he thought. If they're that damn good at hiding in this stuff, they could be anywhere. He thought of Welty's error. That could be real bad. If something happens to the lieutenant because one of us singled him out . . .

His knees were bent under him, raising his head up to just above the level of the foxhole. He felt the rain now, the ground around him splattering with hard, fat drops. Damn, this is gonna be one crappy night. He knew the orders, had no choice but to watch the darkness, knew that all out across the stretch of low hills, the other platoons were doing the same, an entire company holding positions alongside the fields beside this one road. The rain was growing more intense, muddy drops splashing into his face. He pulled at the hood of the poncho, the plastic sheeting noisy, made noisier by the rain, small rivers of water finding their way in, slipping down his shirt. Some army guy had to invent these things, he thought. And the ones that didn't work, they gave to us. The itching was still there, and he fought it, thought, maybe the rain will drown those little sons of bitches. Fleas. Who in hell would think the Okies carried fleas? I haven't seen a single dog yet.

His knees were soaked, the water pooling in the bottom of the foxhole, and he tried to lean back, felt soft mud everywhere he touched. He glanced toward Welty, knew better than to say anything, thought, you'll be asleep in minutes. Never saw anything like it. I could be beating hell out of you with a baseball bat and you'd sleep right through it. How'd you even eat in this stuff? The damn stew is bad enough without Okie rainwater . . .

The short quick steps moved right past him, sharp splashes in the mud, and now another, one behind the other. He felt a stab of panic, started to call out, the sounds choked away by the shock. More steps came, quick, running, and he reached for his rifle, tried to bring it up, his hands wet, clumsy, the barrel jabbed into the side of the foxhole. He kicked Welty, but the man had already heard, was up as well, his M-1 pointed back to where the sounds had gone. Out to one side, the shots came, blinding flashes, a spray of fire from a foxhole close by. Adams hesitated, thought of the mud in his barrel, dangerous, but the fear was overwhelming, men shouting, more shots coming farther down. He strained to see anything in the dark, steady rain, and he held his breath, turned his head away from the rifle, fired. There was no clog in the barrel, and he aimed now, fired again, kept his aim low along the ground, kept firing, blinded by the muzzle blast, by the flashes of fire around him. The shooting spread, contagious, the fear in every man pouring out through the weapons, two dozen rifles firing all across the rolling ground. As the magazines emptied, the shots began to slow, and he heard one voice, loud, the lieutenant.

"Cease fire! What are you shooting at?"

The silence came now, no one responding, and Adams heard a hard whisper, a question from Welty.

"Japs?"

Adams wanted to respond, but he didn't have an answer. He stared into the rain, no sounds at all but the gentle splashes around him, the swirling wind, the men all watching, as he was, blind and desperate fear that the enemy had finally come close.

The rain had stopped, but the misery of the foxhole had only grown worse. Adams felt the stiff aching in his knees, his back, his skin raw from scratching at the plague of fleas. The endless night had finally given way, a hint of detail, small bumps appearing in the ground around him, the helmets of the others, men starting to move in the dim light. He could feel the water in his boots, the bottom of the foxhole inches deep in soft mud, every part of him wet beneath the poncho. Welty was up now as well, neither man making any effort to sleep. Welty whispered close to him, "No coffee this morning, that's for sure."

The joke wasn't funny. Adams hadn't had coffee since they left the ship.

He saw one man rising up, crawling toward them, knew by now it would be Ferucci, the sergeant pulling them awake, as though anyone had been able to sleep after the small-scale war they had waged. There had been other shots, scattered farther along the road, panicked men too eager to see enemies in the rain. Ferucci said in a low voice, "Anybody shoots me, I'll kick your ass. Wake up your buddies."

Men responded, the foxholes close by coming alive, low talk. Ferucci stood now, and Adams watched him with a hint of alarm, thought, easy, Sarge. What the hell are you doing? The sergeant moved toward Adams, didn't look down, stepped past in the slop of deep mud, held his rifle low, pointing it forward, and Adams heard Ferucci laughing. Beyond the brush, others were up, and more laughs came, one man calling out, a mocking sound.

"Baaaaah."

Adams heard the familiar voice of the lieutenant, moving through the foxholes, hard whispers, closer now.

"Pipe down! Get back in cover! This isn't a damn playground!"

Ferucci returned, knelt down close to his squad, said, "Well, boys, you've got fresh meat today. Seems the infiltrators you took out last night had fur. You assholes killed a flock of goats."

10. USHIJIMA

"We should not have allowed them to take those airbases. Not without shedding their blood. I offer this only as a respectful suggestion, sir!"

Ushijima did not look at Cho, let the words slip past. He closed his eyes, the smell of the tea comforting.

"You tell me what I already know, General. But the power of the American fleet gave us no choice."

"What power is that, sir? They only bring numbers, they do not bring the code of the Bushido, they are not warriors!"

Ushijima kept his eyes closed, but Cho's energy was poisoning his calm. He took a long breath, tried to relax, but Cho's presence would never allow that. He could hear the man's agitated breathing, opened his eyes, looked up at him from his cushion on the floor, said, "It will take more than spiritual strength to prevail in this war."

Cho crossed his arms, his usual stubbornness.

"It never has required anything else! Never! Not in all our history! You were in China, you saw for yourself how easily we prevailed. There were those in Tokyo who thought that we should never awaken such a massive dragon. What kind of dragon did we find? One who steps aside and bows to our victories. It will be the same again, right here! Sir!"

The added show of respect punctuated every outburst from Cho, a theatrical afterthought. It is mere performance, Ushijima thought, for some invisible set of eyes that are watching us, judging us, in every gesture we make. He felt drained by Cho's energy, but he would never allow Cho to know that. Cho was, after all, his subordinate. He took the small teacup in his hands, soothed by the warmth, tasted the flowery liquid.

"I was not aware the war in China has concluded. From my experience there, we were victorious over armies of poorly armed peasants. We swept away troops who were more suited to fight Neanderthals. But China has changed. There are greater forces against us there, perhaps too great. China has rallied her friends and those friends have brought better troops and better arms. And the Chinese are fighting on their own soil. Never forget that. No matter how weak an army, they are strengthened when they fight to protect their own homes."

Cho bent low, as though testing Ushijima's vision, a mocking test of whether he was ill, and Ushijima thought, he was never in a classroom, he has never studied the great lessons of history. Why do I waste my words?

Cho's response came in a syrupy, patronizing tone.

"We have won every battle. We occupy an enormous amount of Chinese territory, territory in Burma, Indochina, Korea. Soon the entire Asian continent will lie in peace beneath our emperor's flag. The Chinese do not know of honor, of the code of the Bushido."

"And yet they fight us. No one in Tokyo has indicated to me that there is any end to that campaign, that we are close to conquering China . . . we might as well try to conquer the moon. If our army here was to be increased by a handful of those divisions, those good men who are buried in the mud in Manchuria . . ."

"Manchukuo, sir! *Forgive me* for correcting you."

"Yes, yes, Manchukuo. I will play the game. That is what our children will be taught. I suspect the Chinese maps will still read Manchuria."

He knew he had crossed a dangerous line, that Cho still had influence in Tokyo that would treat this kind of talk as treasonous. But Ushijima clearly understood his place now, his role in the spectacle that was being played out for the emperor's benefit. When Manchuria had been conquered, a government had been put into place there, a Chinese aristocrat who of course answered only to the Japanese army that kept him in power.

Cho stood straight, stared past him, the arrogance unyielding.

"If there are Chinese fools who do not accept their fate, then we shall manage that in the only way possible. They would play with maps? We shall burn every last one of them, until they accept their destiny."

Cho's dreamlike confidence was overpowering, and Ushijima had no patience for it. He had not slept well for days now, not since the Americans had come ashore. The preparations for the Shuri defensive lines had been intense and continuous, and he had marveled how the tireless Colonel Ya-hara seemed to be everywhere at once, every hour of the day and night. Ushijima pulled himself to his feet, the tea forgotten, any pleasantness swept away by Cho's noisy version of patriotism. Cho stood back, hands clasped behind his back, rocked slowly on his heels, a show of impatient obedience, waiting for Ushijima to speak. Ushijima tugged at his jacket, straightened his uniform, stretched his back.

"General, let us pay more attention to those things we can control. I agree with you about the airfields. I very much regret that we could not hold the Americans away. But you are certainly aware that if Tokyo had not thought it so wise to take away the Ninth Division, this army would have had the manpower to put up a far more formidable defense. But I will not make excuses. Had we done as you proposed, and manned those positions near the water's edge, those men would have died uselessly. You saw the American bombardment, you saw how they targeted the coastline. As much as I mourn the loss of so many fine soldiers, sacrificing them would not have prevented the enemy landing. We must fight the war with the tools we have been given."

"We have been given the code of the Bushido. That is the greatest tool of all. Sir!"

Ushijima knew there was nothing to be gained by continuing any argument with Cho, thought, does he truly believe that? We shall win because we are more *spiritual* than the Americans? Ushijima moved out of his room, turned toward the map room, a short walk down the hall. Cho moved with him, stayed a pace behind, appropriate. There, two officers were staring at the enormous map of the island, one man with a thick stub of blue chalk, marking a line across Okinawa's narrow center. They were suddenly aware of the commanders, stood back at stiff attention, and the man with the chalk said, "Forgive me, sir. I was adjusting the enemy's position."

"Yes, I see that. Then it is confirmed? They have reached the eastern coast, severed our connection with the north?"

The man seemed to hesitate, a glance at Cho. Ushijima knew why, said, "You may speak, Major. Give me the report. The accurate report."

The man nodded toward the table close to the large map.

"Just arrived, sir. I was going to bring it to General Cho in one minute. I had been ordered to correct the maps as quickly as possible. My apologies for the delay."

Cho started to speak, and Ushijima interrupted him, knew that the major would get a lashing for no good reason. It was Cho's way, bombast and fear, as though no one would do their jobs without the crack of his whip.

"Thank you, Major. Have all the line commanders communicated with us?"

"Those in the south, yes, sir. We have been unable to reach Colonel Udo."

"No, I suspect not."

Cho stepped forward, pointed at the northern part of the island.

"Udo will do his duty. He will bloody the enemy and drive them into the sea!"

Ushijima did not respond, moved close to the map. He had studied every detail of the geography, stared at the curving lines that represented the hills over the northern half of the island. Udo will fight with what he has, he thought, and we can give him nothing more. He knew Udo well, had studied alongside him at the Imperial Military Academy. But Udo had shown very little of the dignity Ushijima had expected, seemed to spend his energies endearing himself to General Cho. Colonel Udo was said to have brutalized the Okinawan civilians in the north, which kept many of them from willingly serving the army as much-needed laborers. Ushijima had planned that the north be lightly defended, and so Udo was given that command, which kept Udo out of the way from the more critical defenses in the south. Ushijima understood that he did not have the luxury of re-placing Udo with another experienced commander. If Udo's *bad habits* got in the way of his performance against the Americans, Ushijima just didn't want to hear about it. After a long silence, Ushijima said flatly, "Colonel Udo knows his duty. He will do what we have asked him to do." He glanced at the paper, troop movements, brief reports from several of the field commanders, all communicated through the radio room nearby. "The American Marines are driving northward, which will weaken the forces who face us here. That is the best we can do with the resources we have. We shall continue to strengthen our position in the south, using this part of the island to our advantage. I expect Colonel Udo to do what he can against the Marines, engaging them at every suitable opportunity. His greatest duty is to allow the passage of time, to keep the Marines far from our strongest point."

"He shall succeed! And he shall accomplish much more! I am certain of it! Sir!"

Ushijima ignored Cho's bombast once more, studied the southern half of the island.

"I am greatly pleased with the work we have done to strengthen our defensive lines." He turned to Cho. "You are pleased with the strength of our lines, yes?"

Cho seemed not to notice the change of subject.

"I accept the shame we must endure by fighting from the defensive, sir. But I must admit that our men have shown the kind of spirit we must have, even as they bring shame upon their ancestors."

Ushijima felt his patience slipping, but there were too many ears in the offices around him, and he would not reveal any anger to the staff, to the many secretaries who labored close to the map room. He held his breath for a short pause, fought to calm himself.

"There will be no shame for any soldier who kills his enemy. You would agree with that?"

"Oh, most definitely, sir! I should expect my own death to come while taking ten or a hundred of the enemy with me! I can think of no greater gift . . ."

"I would rather not have this army meet their ancestors just yet. Even the most junior private understands that if we are *all* dead, there is not much of a fight we can offer."

Cho seemed unwilling to respond, and Ushijima knew the moment had come.

"You are dismissed, General. Thank you for your counsel. Your spirit is most valuable to this army, and I trust you will continue to inspire our men. Perhaps you should inspect the caves closer to the Naha airfields. That is a key position in our defenses . . . in our quest for *victory.* I will have no weakness there. Do you agree?"

Cho seemed to brighten.

"Sir! I will inspect the Naha caves. There will be no weakness! I will stand that ground myself, if the enemy requires it!"

Cho turned crisply, was gone, and Ushijima felt himself sagging, his usual reaction when Cho left the room. He glanced at the two officers, silent, respectful, and he thought of returning to the tea. He stared at the map once more, the thick chalk line across the island's waist. The ground shook slightly beneath him, and he heard a distant rumble, an echo that drifted through the vast network of caves.

"Those are our guns, yes?"

"Yes, sir!"

"Excellent. I must take time to mention this to Colonel Yahara. He has done a magnificent job in building these positions." He moved out into the corridor, thought, I must also apologize to him for ordering Cho to march out there and stare over his shoulder. But one officer's pleasure often comes at another's grief. Right now I have had enough grief for one day.

He looked into one of the smaller offices, an aide snapping to attention.

"Summon the guards to escort me to the opening of the primary cave."

"Right away, sir!"

The man hurried out of the office, and Ushijima saw the others looking up at him, two women, backed by three other men, all of them sitting at small desks, papers stacked neatly in front of them. He knew they were dealing with the enormity of the supply problems, finding the means to move food, water, and medical assistance where it was most required. He felt a stab of guilt, knew that those in the north could not be reached at all. Two nights earlier they had attempted to launch small boats in the darkness, carrying food and ammunition northward along the east side of the island. But the Americans were vigilant, patrol boats with searchlights scouring every beach, every cove. Ushijima had not heard anything more from the small flotilla, had to assume that the Americans had destroyed them. So, those men in the north will fight with what they have.

The guards were there now, eight men, heavily armed, stiff at attention. He moved past them, knew they would allow him ten meters before they marched behind. It was the usual routine, ordered of course by General Cho. Ushijima accepted the added security grudgingly, thought it ridiculous, had yet to hear any reports of assassins lurking in the cave beneath the castle. But he had learned to save his energy for the battles that mattered.

To save power, the offices were dimly lit, and he moved past the doorways quickly, did not want anyone's show of fealty. The thick mustiness of the deeper caves gave way now to fresher air. He glanced to one side, another, smaller corridor, and he changed course abruptly, knew the guards would adjust. Yes, I will see this for myself. Another sharp thump rolled through the corridor, much louder, and he was carried forward by the power, the energy of that. Talk is tiring, he thought. There is much more value in artillery fire. If these men are firing, it means they have a target. I should like to see it. He laughed silently, hid the smile. Cho will tell them I have visited their battery because I am so brave.

The passageway narrowed, and he saw hazy sunlight, heard voices, a quick shout, men suddenly scrambling into position to one side of their gun. He knew he had surprised them, regretted that, had no interest in a show of obedience to some mindless inspection. He wasn't there to see the men at all. The officer stepped forward, and Ushijima put up his hand, said, "Captain, please relax your men. I am here to examine your field of fire."

The man stood straight, a perfect show of respect.

"As you wish, sir. You honor us with your inspection!"

Ushijima knew the man, one of his former students at the military academy, knew the man's family as well. He stepped past him, glanced at the mound of new ammunition, thought, General Wada has done his job, certainly. He will not leave any one of his batteries unprepared.

The piece was one of the larger cannons in Ushijima's arsenal, a 150. The long, heavy barrel was supported by two spoked wheels, which rested on thick wood planks that led straight to the mouth of the cave. He stepped past the muzzle of the cannon, the smoke thinning, felt the heat from the barrel, moved close to the mouth of the cave, the opening shrouded by camouflage cloth, just a small hole visible.

"What is your target, Captain?"

The man moved up beside him, said, "Sir, we have put several rounds toward that destroyer closest to the shore. They have foolishly moved into range."

"Have you been . . . successful?"

"We . . . uh . . . no, sir. I was attempting to adjust the range when you arrived. But I shall do what I must until the enemy has been destroyed. I am confident in these men, sir. We can destroy every ship in the enemy's fleet."

"Is that so? Then please tell me why you have not already done so?"

The captain seemed surprised at the question, and Ushijima stared out again, did not like embarrassing the man.

"Sir, I apologize. We shall find the proper elevation. My orders are to attack targets as they present themselves. Most of the enemy fleet is well beyond the range of this piece. The destroyer moved within acceptable range . . ."

"Never mind, Captain. You must follow the orders you have been given."

"Sir, permit me to inquire . . ."

"About what?" The captain hesitated, and Ushijima looked at him, knew he had been a good student, had a serious mind for military studies. "I assure you, Captain, General Cho is nowhere close. Ask what you wish."

"Sir, I have heard that the Imperial Air Force will arrive here at any time. The reports say that the enemy fleet will be forced to abandon their ground troops by sailing away, and if they do not, their ships will be destroyed. My men . . . the others in our battery are greatly pleased to hear that. I was wondering if you could reveal when this might happen. I do not wish to expend ammunition if it is not called for. We shall require every shell if the ground troops approach our field of fire."

Ushijima appreciated the man's logic, but the question was infuriating.

"Captain, you have heard no *reports*. What you have heard is *rumors*. The Imperial Air Force, along with the Imperial Navy, has been assuring me for many days now that the enemy fleet is to be utterly destroyed by vast waves of our finest planes and a mighty armada of our finest warships. They have not yet provided me with a timetable for such a wonderful scene of destruction."

The man bowed.

"I understand, sir. It is not my place to know such details. I should not have asked about matters beyond my responsibility. Please forgive my impudence, sir."

Ushijima absorbed the man's words, thought, he believes it still. Perhaps they all believe it. And perhaps that is a good thing, good for morale. I wish I believed it.

Thirty-second Army Headquarters
Beneath Shuri Castle, Okinawa
April 6, 1945

It was his favorite lookout, the wide opening of his primary cave, safe from enemy fire only at night. During the day the opening that dug straight into the mountainside was covered by the thick mat of camouflage, designed to look exactly like the brush that surrounded it. Despite the shattering carpet of explosives the Americans had draped across the area, the opening had seemed to escape detection by the American spotters completely.

The sun was just beginning to set, the western sky a blaze of pink and orange, the reflection on the ocean broken by the shadows of the American ships. He held a teacup, heard nothing from the security guards standing in rows behind him, lining both sides of the corridor.

"When this is over, I should look forward to sharing moments like this with all of you. You have been loyal and efficient. Perhaps if I am allowed to return to teaching, some of you would consider attending the Imperial Military Academy. It would require the recommendation of someone in . . . authority." He turned, saw the surprised faces. "I suppose I qualify."

The lieutenant closest to him bowed deeply, said, "Thank you, sir. From all of us. We shall leave this place with the enemy's blood on our swords. I would be honored to learn the art of war at your hand."

"Your loyalty is appreciated. All of you."

Ushijima said nothing more, knew very well he would never see the academy again.

The day had been rainy, but the storms had cleared now, remnants of clouds to the south. He knew that the poor weather had been to his advantage, the rains deepening the mud that would slow any advance by the Americans. For his own men, the rains provided much-needed fresh water, which was lacking in most of the caves. With the setting sun, his work details waited near the mouths of the many caves, preparing for darkness, when they could retrieve the tubs and empty the cisterns. They had learned long ago that there were few wells anywhere near the mountains, but the army had its needs, and on Okinawa the wells were on flatter ground. Thus, whether the farmers offered up the water on their own, the soldiers knew where the wells were found. But carrying the precious water to the caves was a long and treacherous job by night, and nearly impossi-

ble by day. The American fighters had continued their patrols, and so far
the thunderstorms had been too brief to ground the fighters for long. Each
time the thunderstorms subsided, they had come again, a swarm of blue
bees rising up from the distant aircraft carriers. Once it was dark the soldiers could emerge from underground once more, not to do the actual
work, but to supervise the legions of laborers. They were Okinawans
mostly, along with the Koreans and Chinese that had been brought over to
assist in Colonel Yahara's enormous construction projects. Any hope of
building a pipeline had long been dismissed, Yahara as certain as his commander that the American bombs would destroy it in short order. So the
laborers hauled the water in buckets. Ushijima had warned his officers not
to brutalize the Okinawan farmers, that their work in the fields was essential to providing food for his own troops. He knew the order had been dis-
obeyed, suspected that General Cho had overseen some of the occupation
of the farmhouses for officers who remained out beyond the caves. Reports
were many that Okinawan homes had been established as comfort stations
for the officers, local women and their daughters hidden away with one
purpose, to serve the needs of his men. He had known of such things in
China, and everywhere the army had been, most of the High Command
blithely looking away, as though such activities were completely acceptable, so long as the women were not Japanese. Ushijima had forbidden this
behavior around his own headquarters, knew that the women he saw daily
in his offices were performing valuable work. Others, mostly Okinawan,
were serving the army as nurses, a service that could only grow more crucial as the days passed. I cannot stand guard over everything this army
does, he thought, no matter how stupid. The best officers are those who
are educated, and in this army there are too many who have risen to the
ranks because we have no choice but to put them there. Too many good
men are gone, and the luxury of choosing one's own subordinates has long
passed. The field officers who worship men like Cho have learned only the
ways of the training camps, conscripts taught to be soldiers by sergeants
who exercise the authority of the whip and the fist. The soldiers perform
their duties because they are afraid not to. It has become the way of this
army, and that is stupid as well.

He missed teaching at the military academy, missed the brightest
minds, those so privileged to attend, some of those, like the artillery captain, officers under his command. He had tried to convince himself that he
had made the army much more professional, more efficient, more skilled,

but the illusion had been shattered too many times by what he had seen in China. The brutality and savagery of his own men had been horrific and unstoppable, even the officers participating in the worst acts of inhumanity imaginable. He thought of Cho, all the man's talk about victories. How can you claim to have achieved such honorable victory when you destroy a nation in the process? What have you won? You exterminate an entire race of people, just because you can . . . and so you congratulate yourself on your glorious conquest. None of that was in the lessons I learned, the lessons I taught my cadets. And yet men like Cho don't give it a second thought.

He sipped the tea, the taste suddenly unpleasant. Behind him his servant seemed to read him, was close now, a hand holding a small tray. He set the cup down, never looked at the girl, caught a smell of her, some fragrance. He pushed that from his mind, heard her shuffle away, thought of Cho again. There had been talk all through his headquarters of the parties, that despite Ushijima's orders, Cho had made it a practice to abuse many of the women who worked in the offices. The noise had been kept far away from Ushijima's quarters, and he felt paralyzed to press the matter, would not wander down through the labyrinth of caves seeking out the dirty secrets of his officers. He knew that Cho had a loyal following, and those men would accept Ushijima's authority as long as it did not interfere too much in Cho's own world. A knife in the back, he thought, or a pistol shot to the temple. It would happen in my room, in the still of the night, one of the guards perhaps, tempted by glorious promises, a special place in the Yasukuni Shrine. The killer would most likely take his own life right beside me. He felt disgust, Cho's bleating cheers a sickening reminder of the worst of the army. They sent that jackal here to get him away from . . . someone else, someone with more political influence than I have. It is the system. All that talk of Bushido, all the glorious history of the samurai. What we are is *men,* mortal and flawed, and we serve our emperor because it is what we are taught, and there can be no other way.

The sun was sinking low, the bright colors fading. He stared out toward the city of Naha, could not quite see the airfield there, the primary field on the island not yet captured by the Americans. More stupidity, he thought. It is just like this on every place we have added to the vast reaches of our empire. Let us create airfields, countless airfields. No matter that our air force refuses to use them, or perhaps our strength is so depleted that we have more airfields than usable fighters. Ah, but we must take pride in them. And the enemy admires them as well. So, we shall make the Americans happy by offering them such wonderful temptation, so many fine airfields on every island, every outpost, our smiling invitation for the Americans to come, to see our airfields, and should they wish, to take them for themselves. And we shall be powerless to stop them.

He heard the roar of a plane, high above, out of his view, knew the sound. One of their carrier planes, he thought, with the strange gull-shaped wing. We have nothing to compare; not even the Imperial Air Force can maintain the illusion that our Zero is the finest plane in the world. He stared out at the distant ships, thought, Tokyo promised me you would be blasted to oblivion, that the Imperial Air Force would come here as one mighty unstoppable wave, erasing your planes from the sky, showering your ships with bombs until every one was sent to the bottom of the sea. What a marvelous fantasy. It is what comforts our emperor every night when he goes to sleep, visions of our might, our victories, our endless glory, and the glory of our ancestors. A marvelous fantasy.

He heard another engine, closer, and he stepped back from the opening, instinct, but the sound grew louder, passing close overhead. There were more now, many more, and he caught flickers of movement out to the north, planes dipping and rolling, streaks of machine gun fire, combat in the air. He was curious, moved to the edge of the cave's mouth, sought the best view, thought, what is happening? The Americans do not make raids at night, and it will be dark in minutes. But those . . . those are *our* planes. He saw more of them now, rolling up and over the mountain, a swarm of angry insects. The swarm continued to grow, emerging from behind the mountain, some dipping low, flowing out past the city of Naha, past the distant beaches, spreading out in a chaotic pattern, no formation. He began to feel a sharp stirring in his chest, saw a flash of light, a burst of flames, then another. The ships were responding, streaks of anti-aircraft fire rising up, hundreds of ships answering the swarm with a swarm of their own, the streaks lighting the sky like strands of fiery straw. In the corridor behind him were boot steps, coming quickly, but he kept his stare out to sea, to the battle that was erupting right in front of him. Yes, there could be glory here! They have come at last!

"Sir!"

The voice was Colonel Miyake, another of the staff. The man stood silently for a long moment, absorbing the sight, and Ushijima said nothing, watched the distant bursts of fire, the impacts of so many bombs . . .

and then he began to see, the planes were dropping low, close to the water, and the stirring inside of him turned colder, a sudden clarity, the sickening reality. He had seen this before, but only single planes, began to understand what the battle meant.

"Sir! Forgive me for interrupting . . . but we have received a report. What we have been told has finally happened, sir! Tokyo reports the first wave of Operation Floating Chrysanthemum. They are attacking the enemy fleet! It is as we have heard, sir! The Divine Wind! *Kamikaze!*"

Ushijima had received the coded messages from the Imperial High Command that the air force was mobilizing every available plane, an attack that was as the rumors described, wave upon wave of assaults upon the American fleet. So far the reports had been empty promises, rumors that inspired the men, and frustrated the one man who had the responsibility for defending Okinawa against what he now knew to be the enemy's overwhelming superiority. He had kept the hope inside of him, his own fantasy, that someone in Tokyo would live up to the promise, that the ocean would be cleansed of the massive fleet. But the anti-aircraft fire and the bursts of flame revealed now what Operation Floating Chrysanthemum truly meant. The planes were not dropping bombs. They *were* the bombs.

Though reports had circulated through the American command of scattered suicide attacks by small numbers of Japanese planes, the first organized kamikaze assault against American warships had taken place in October 1944, during the Battle of Leyte Gulf. The apparent willingness of the Japanese pilots to crash their explosive-laden planes deliberately into the American ships had shocked the American commanders and inflicted considerable casualties, sending five ships to the bottom and damaging thirty-five others. As horrified as the Americans were, those attacks had been carried out by no more than a few dozen specially chosen pilots. At Okinawa the Japanese sent more than three hundred fifty planes against the American fleet and produced devastating damage to several small vessels. Despite the enormity of the attack, the results were not nearly the crushing blow that the Imperial Air Force had promised. The Americans had long ago broken the Japanese intelligence codes, and when the first wave of Operation Floating Chrysanthemum left their airfields, American fighter planes were waiting for them. Half of the Japanese planes were shot down far out at sea, and many of those who survived the gauntlet were shot out of the sky by a storm of anti-aircraft fire. With so much firepower aimed their way, the Japanese pilots mostly ignored their orders to target the largest ships, the carriers and battleships, and instead launched themselves at the first ship they saw. Because of the configuration of the American fleet, those ships were most often the outer ring, the picket line, including smaller gunboats, patrol boats, transports, and supply ships, and the occasional destroyer or light cruiser. Though the most valuable prizes were largely missed, the destruction on the smaller American craft was horrific. Hundreds of sailors were killed, and several ships were sunk.

As the carnage played out in front of him, Ushijima received word that he had long discounted, a communication from Tokyo that the Imperial Navy was finally fulfilling its own promises. They were coming to Okinawa as well. Most of the Japanese army commanders still believed that the navy far outclassed and outnumbered their enemies, but the admirals understood that the greatest naval battles they had fought were mostly one-sided affairs, and the Japanese fleets had suffered severely. What most Japanese never could be told was that the power of the Japanese fleet, the battleships and carriers, was simply gone. But there was one exception, one survivor, a ship that by its very size and strength inspired the Japanese people, their military, and their emperor. On April 6, that ship sailed out of the protection of her port and, accompanied by a fleet of support ships, made her way directly for the American anchorage at Okinawa. The Americans knew her to be the fiercest weapon the Japanese had in their arsenal, the largest and most heavily armed battleship ever built. It was called the *Yamato*.

The first American ship to spot the *Yamato* was the submarine USS *Threadfin*, who radioed that the mammoth warship had emerged from her home port of Kure, on Japan's inland sea. She was accompanied by nine smaller ships: eight destroyers and one cruiser. It required very little imagination for the American command to predict the *Yamato*'s destination. The *Threadfin* could not keep up with the faster-moving warships, and so the Americans responded by launching spotter planes to keep discreet track of the Japanese vessels. As the *Yamato* drew within two hundred fifty miles of Okinawa, the Americans were astonished to discover that the small fleet was steaming straight toward the island completely naked of air support. The response was ordered by Admiral Raymond Spruance, in overall command of the task force that included the fleet around Okinawa. The Americans launched an attack force of nearly three hundred planes, from eight different aircraft carriers.

The worst challenge for the American pilots was weather, a dense rain and cloud layer that kept their targets mostly hidden, but openings in the overcast were found. Midday on April 7, low-flying Helldiver bombers struck the first blows, followed by Avengers, who launched torpedoes as they skimmed toward their target barely above the water's surface. The results were immediate and devastating. In a battle that lasted barely five hours, the Japanese cruiser and four of the accompanying destroyers were sunk, with the loss of more than a thousand crewmen. But the Japanese sailors who survived the carnage were witness to their final catastrophe. Stung by torpedoes and a continuing rain of bombs, the *Yamato* began to list severely, and in one great gasp, she rolled over and sank. As she disappeared beneath the sea, her magazine ignited in a mammoth blast that sent a fiery plume a mile high, a blast that ensured the end for more than three thousand of her crewmen. Those few Japanese sailors who survived the lopsided battle were rescued by their own ships after the American planes had gone home. Whether those rescued sailors regretted the complete absence of lifeboats, no one would dare complain. It was tradition on board Japanese naval vessels that lifeboats were a symbol of defeat, that sailors who did not die with their ship would suffer a shameful indignity if they survived.

On Okinawa, word quickly reached Ushijima of the catastrophic naval battle. The particulars told him what he had suspected all along, that the navy had used the *Yamato* as a grand sacrifice, another show of glory for Japan's legacy. It was a poorly guarded secret that the *Yamato* had not been given enough precious fuel for the round trip that would return her to her home port. Ushijima already understood what the others in Tokyo had to accept. The great attack against the American fleet was planned as a one-way trip.

What the Japanese commanders could not know was that this most crushing of defeats had come at a cost to the Americans of only twelve pilots.

11. ADAMS

On April 1, the initial landings for the Sixth Marine Division had been staged by the Fourth and Twenty-second regiments, while the Twenty-ninth Regiment had been held back, to jump into the fray should major problems arise. With the invasion so strangely uncontested, the Twenty-ninth had come ashore ahead of schedule, and now, alongside the Fourth, they had been given the task of sweeping enemy resistance off the Motobu Peninsula. Some units of the Twenty-second were sent in as a backup, mainly to perform mop-up operations, tackling those stubborn pockets of Japanese resistance that always seemed to escape detection. Other companies of the Twenty-second were sent farther north, their original mission to confront and then clear out any Japanese resistance, all the way to Okinawa's northern tip.

They marched as before, the beaches below them to the left, gentle hillsides of low, fat palm trees, the road undulating with the curves of the rolling countryside. The farms were still there, but not as many, and as they moved farther north the villages grew smaller. But they were no longer ghost towns. With the fighting so sporadic, civilians had begun to emerge, many of them old, some younger mothers with small children. Though the Marines obeyed the order to be as unthreatening as they

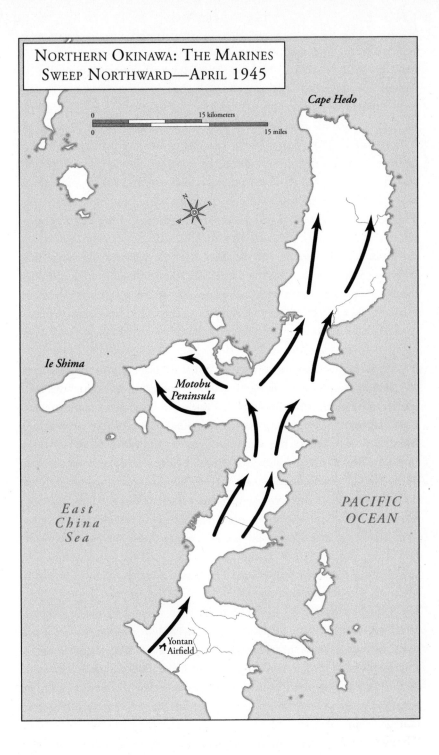

NORTHERN OKINAWA: THE MARINES
SWEEP NORTHWARD—APRIL 1945

Cape Hedo

0   15 kilometers
0   15 miles

Ie Shima

Motobu
Peninsula

East
China
Sea

PACIFIC
OCEAN

Yontan
Airfield

could, offering food and an open hand, the Okinawans were mostly terrified. But hungry civilians had gradually accepted the handouts from the
Americans, mainly the packages of food sent forward by the supply teams
on the ships that had prepared for exactly this kind of operation. With the
food came medical care, teams of corpsmen and doctors establishing aid
stations, offering safe haven for the sick and injured far behind the lines of
combat. To those Okinawans willing to accept American hospitality, special Marine and naval units trained in civilian relations sought to communicate that the Americans were in fact liberators, and not the enemy.
Though some Okinawans still reacted to the advance of the Marines by retreating in a mad scamper back into the hills, many more were too hungry,
too injured, or too fed up with the abuse from the Japanese. As more of the
civilians found shelter with the Americans, the smiles appeared, and even
though they were held in wire enclosures close to the airfields and beaches,
many of the Okinawans seemed happy to accept the Americans as liberators. At the very least, they were much more content to be fed and cared
for than ordered about.

With the doctors and corpsmen came interpreters, and to make matters easier, many of the Okinawans spoke English. The debriefings were
useful, some of the Okinawans explaining where their rabid fear had come
from. Japanese officers had taken great pains to portray the approaching
Americans as savages of the worst kind, rapists and cannibals. The American cause had not been helped, of course, by the weeklong bombardment
of the island, which caused significant numbers of civilian casualties. It was
then that terrified Okinawan civilians had learned that the Japanese caves
were mainly for use by the Japanese. Many of the Okinawans had to endure incoming shellfire by taking cover where there was no cover at all,
hunkering down in their homes, or in the concrete burial tombs that
spread around nearly every village. The tombs were a uniquely Okinawan
tradition, crescent-shaped mausoleums where the remains of their ancestors would remain close to the families who revered them. During the
bombardment, the concrete had become revered for another reason. It had
been the best available protection for thousands of Okinawan civilians. It
was not difficult for the American chaplains to understand that what some
had expected to be the primitive heathenism of the Okinawan faith had
actually proven powerfully accurate. Their ancestors had indeed protected
them.

The conversations with the Okinawans also revealed how the Japanese treated these people, long regarded as second-class Japanese citizens. The intelligence officers learned of the brutality, so many of the villagers made to dig in the hillsides, hauling dirt and rock for the Japanese tunnel system. The Americans had heard these kinds of stories before. The lack of young women among the refugees was testament to the particular usefulness that kept them hidden away alongside the Japanese troops. The young men were mostly gone as well, and the Americans were told that although the Okinawans might not want to take up arms against the Americans, with Japanese officers leading the way, and Japanese bayonets at their backs, they might have no choice.

NORTHERN OKINAWA
APRIL 12, 1945

"Hit the deck!"

Adams didn't need the instructions, dropped down hard. He held his breath, dirt in his face, the rocky ground beside him cracking into splinters. He started to move, to scramble back, a desperate slithering crawl, his heart racing, looked for any kind of cover, but the firing came again, a hard *ping* off the rock beside him. He lay flat again, paralyzed by the terror, felt like screaming, the spray of lead now slapping the rocks just behind him. He spit out the dirt in his mouth, gasped for air, a loud shout down the hill behind him, Ferucci.

"Get back here! Run!"

Adams started to rise up, heard the crack of the bullet past his ear, lay flat again. The burst from the Japanese machine gun came again, tapping high on the hill like a woodpecker. Ferucci continued to shout, a manic tirade.

"Where is that son of a bitch? Anybody see him?"

No one responded, the spray of lead splitting the air overhead, still pinning Adams tight to the ground. He was breathing dust, choking, the terror freezing him, Ferucci again, "Find that bastard! Where's the BAR? Give him hell!"

The rock beside Adams's head cracked again, a shower of lead ripping past just above his back. Behind him rifle fire began, men taking aim at nothing, peppering the hillside, desperate, useless. The machine gun continued, seeking new targets, and Adams's brain screamed at him to move, to run. But there were other voices too, Ferucci again, "He's gotta be hit! Lay down fire! I'll get him!"

Adams tried to think, his body still frozen, his arms pulled in tight, and he shouted through the dust in his throat, "No! Stay back!"

The men behind him kept up their fire, and Adams closed his eyes, utterly helpless, his face jarred by the thumps and pops in the rocks. The machine gun kept firing, shattering the ground just past his feet, seeking targets farther down, the men along the road behind him. His brain tried to work, fighting through, shouting orders . . . *maybe the Jap thinks I'm dead.* Don't move, don't do anything. He's shooting at *them.* Just . . . wait.

And then, the machine gun stopped.

"Run! Now! Get down here!"

Adams waited for a long second, stayed perfectly still, his brain focused on the silence from above. The springs uncoiled now, and he pushed himself up with his arms. One hand still gripped the rifle, and he crawled backward, slid down the slope on his stomach, his dungarees ripped by the rocks, scrapes against his knees. But he was down now, tall grass, larger rocks, saw the faces of the others, the entire squad staring at him, more men out beyond the road, still searching for a target, aiming up at the unseen gunner. He tried to breathe, still spitting dirt, coughed again, Ferucci's voice, close to him, "You hit? You got blood on your face."

He realized Ferucci was talking to him, but he couldn't speak, coughed violently, put a shaking hand on his nose. He looked at the blood on his dirty fingers, saw the torn pant legs, more blood at his knees, took a breath, no pain, no other blood on his clothes.

"I'm okay, I think. Bloody nose. I think that's it."

"Get a corpsman up here! I'm not losing anybody today! Why the hell didn't you run? I told you to get your ass back down here!"

Adams felt helpless, like a small child, still shaking, said in a stammer, "I don't know. I couldn't . . ."

He saw the lieutenant crawling toward them, the officer making a sharp glance toward Ferucci, who said, "He's okay. Not hit. We couldn't spot that bastard. He's up in that brush somewhere."

"Sergeant, next time you want to designate somebody for recon, use your damn brains! You sent him up there in the wide damn open!"

"Aye, sir. But we hadn't seen any Japs . . . I thought . . ." Ferucci stopped, frozen by the lieutenant's stare. "Aye, sir."

Porter looked at Adams, seemed to scan him.

"All right. Maybe that son of a bitch is gone, crawled back into his hole. Unless we give him another target. Let's stay in cover, keep close to the ditch, get past this guy. He can't be the only damn Nambu gun in these hills, so stay low, use whatever cover you can. And keep your distance. Five yards apart! Move out on my signal. Walkie-talkie!"

"Sir!"

The man crawled along the rocky depression, pulled the equipment from his back, handed it to Porter.

"Charlie six, this is Charlie two. We're taking Nambu fire. You hear it?"

The response was a crackling garble, the words just audible.

"Roger, Charlie six . . . a clump of trees . . . two hundred yards above . . ."

Porter spoke again, "Charlie two, we're moving out. Watch your flank. The enemy is still up there, but looks like a lone duck. Pretty sure we missed him."

A new voice came now, and Porter's reaction was different, his authority fading. It was Captain Bennett.

"Charlie six, negative that. We can't leave him in our rear. Charlie two, move up the hill. Charlie six, do the same. Find him!"

Porter lowered the walkie-talkie, seemed to pause, stared down, thoughts Adams couldn't read. Then Porter said, "Aye, sir. Charlie six . . . out." The lieutenant handed the walkie-talkie to Hunley, the carrier, said in a low voice, "Guess we've got a job to do." He peered up briefly over a low flat rock, no fire coming down. In the ditch across the road, Yablonski called out, "If that bastard is still up there, I'll draw his fire. I poured two clips into those trees. I saw something move, but that's it. I mighta hit him."

Porter pointed a finger toward Yablonski, toward the others on that side of the road.

"Whether you hit him or not . . . you're our cover! We're going up, and if that bastard opens fire again, lay down as much return fire as you can! Where's the BAR?"

Gridley was across the road as well, responded, "Here!"

"Good! Use it, son. Anything moves up there, blow hell out of it! Watch out for Charlie two. They'll be moving up on our right, beyond that rise."

The lieutenant took a long breath, glanced both ways, the others on the near side of the road watching him. Adams saw something new in the lieutenant's eyes, a hard glaze, staring right through the men closest to him.

The words came out slowly, precise, a slight wavering, and Adams realized now, the man was afraid.

"Keep low. Use the cover. That bastard fires, hit the deck, let these boys nail him from back here. They might see him before we do." He paused, looked to the right, where the road curved away, the direction they had just come. "Maybe Charlie two will get him first, save us the trouble." He looked both ways, pulled his carbine close to his chest, a long second, said, "Let's go!"

Porter moved first, crawled up over the flat rock, dove into brush, and now Ferucci followed, a hard shout to the others.

"Move your ass!"

Adams was still spitting dirt and blood, coughed again, made a quick glance at the M-1, felt a quiver in his knees, the paralyzing fear again. But the others on both sides of him leapt up, crawling uphill, slipping into the thin patches of brush. He watched boots working frantically, one man driving up on his belly, moving away. Adams gripped the M-1, tried to stop the shaking in his chest. He heard another one of the sergeants farther along the road, pulling his men up onto the hillside, and behind him the muzzles of the rifles in the ditch were up, silent and still, ready for a target. His heart was pounding wildly, and he hesitated, but the others were moving on up the hill, and he shouted to himself, his own order, get moving! The springs uncoiled again, and he launched himself up and over the rock, stayed on his feet, running uphill, bent low, pushed past the brush, stepped over someone, saw a larger rock, no one there, dove headlong, hit the ground with a gut-busting grunt.

Up the hill there was no response, and Porter was close to Adams, hidden by a bush to one side, said in a low growl, "Where the hell is that bastard?"

The others responded, short calls.

"Nothing!"

"No sign of him!"

Adams felt pain in his chest, the impact against the ground, the hard breathing, saw the others spread out across the hillside, some in good cover, some protected by a wisp of brush. Porter was up suddenly, running farther up, boots kicking up dirt, and he went down again, more cover, looked back at his men, scanned the hillside with a manic jerk of his head. Adams saw the man's eyes, furious, terror, and Porter shouted, "Dammit! Find the bastard!"

Adams pushed up with one arm, ran after the lieutenant, and from the trees above them came the sound again, the *tap tap tap* of the woodpecker, closer now. There was no cover in front of him, but he flattened out again, and now the response, down the hill, the heavy thumping of the BAR. The Nambu was silent again, and Adams saw the lieutenant rise, firing the carbine, then moving up again, another low rock, falling in a heap of dust. Adams's legs reacted, following, and on both sides others were moving as well, short bursts of motion, then down. But there was little cover, the rocks small, the brush too scattered. They were close to the clump of trees, thin pines along the hilltop, and Adams hugged the ground, jerked his head to one side, looking for Porter, waiting, his chest heaving against the hard ground. There was a new burst of fire, from the right, pops from an M-1, then more, and now came shouts.

"Got him! Got him!"

Adams breathed the dirt, choked again, rose with Porter, who stayed down on one knee, still aiming the carbine. Adams mimicked him, pulled the M-1 up to his shoulder, scanned the trees, small spaces, and Adams saw movement, men in the trees, saw . . . green. Marines. Porter yelled out, "Hold your fire!"

The men in the trees were waving, but others had come up from the right, were swarming past them, cautious, taking position along the ridgeline, searching for more targets in the pine thickets. The lieutenant looked out to both sides, his own men spread out on the hill, said, "Easy! Keep low! Eyes on anything that moves!"

He rose up, stepping quickly, and Adams followed him to the trees, some of the others coming as well. The men from the other platoon were in position, and Porter moved close to one man, both of them on their knees. Adams knew the man, Sergeant Long, and Adams kept his distance, stayed down in line behind Porter, scanning the hillside. He looked back toward the road, saw the men there in good cover, dark spots of rifle barrels, the men there still aiming up the hill. Up beside Porter, the sergeant said, "Right here! Saw him poke his Nambu up out of this hole."

Porter said only, "Stay down. Could be more. I see the bastard."

The two men crawled up past some low pines, and Adams felt a burning curiosity, followed, tried to ignore the pain in his scraped knees. The sergeant sat, facing Porter, raised a machine gun up from the brushy thicket, stood it upright on its butt, a look of pure joy on his face.

"Look at this piece of crap. That the best they got?"

Adams moved closer, staring at the machine gun, could see the enemy soldier now, the dull brown uniform, coated in blood, the man lying face-down beside what looked like a small round foxhole. The lieutenant eased over close to the hole, stared down, said, "Spider hole. Not big enough for a rabbit. These sons of bitches could be all over the place. I bet we've been walking right past them."

"Not this one. I'll take credit for him, but I know your BAR ripped hell out of the trees, could have nailed him too."

The sergeant was beaming, the star of his own show, his squad gathering up through the trees. He stood now, still held the Nambu, aimed it upward, his words directed toward his men.

"Pretty light weight. If this is the best they can do, it's gonna be a short fight."

Adams saw Porter looking away, toward his own men, ignoring the sergeant's bluster. Porter seemed to freeze now, pointed past Adams, said in a low voice, "There!"

Adams followed the man's eyes, saw a fat tuft of grass, a patch of raw earth a few yards away. He felt a jolt, a nervous stab in his stomach, pointed the M-1 at the odd clump. He stepped slowly, aiming, saw it was another hole, round and deep, like a home for some giant worm. Porter moved out to the side, covering him, and Adams said, "It's another one!"

Behind them, the sergeant was dismissive, said, "Passed a few more on the way up here. Looks like they skedaddled, left this one stupid asshole behind to keep us honest. Guess it didn't work."

Porter moved up close to Adams, examined the hole, ignored the sergeant's arrogance.

"Let's get moving."

Long pointed back into the trees.

"My looey sent his walkie-talkie guy with us. He's right back there. You wanna use it?"

"Use your head. We're on a damn ridgeline. Anybody holding a walkie-talkie is a target for every Jap around here! We're not sightseeing. Get your asses back down to the road. Your looey and I need to fill in the captain. But not from up here."

Long was still holding the Nambu, admiring his trophy, but it was too large, too clumsy for a souvenir. He tossed it aside, and Adams was drawn back toward the Japanese soldier, could smell a sweet stink, blood and filth, felt a turn in his stomach. Long was watching him, still with the smile, suddenly launched a hard kick into the body, a sickening crunch against the dead man's side.

"You ain't seen too many of these, have you kid?"

"No."

"Well, I seen a bunch. Before this is over, there'll be so damn many, you can make a necklace out of their teeth. Nice gift for your girl, huh?"

Adams wasn't sure if Long was kidding or not, said only, "Sure."

Adams tried to avoid the wide smile on the sergeant's face, didn't know what else to say. Long leaned out closer to him, put one foot on the Japanese corpse, said in a whisper, "Give your looey credit. He led you guys up here. Mine stayed down on the road. Mine might be smarter, but yours has bigger balls!"

Adams nodded, and Long laughed now, waved one arm toward his men.

"Let's go!"

On the hillside behind him, Porter had waved the men back down the hill. Adams began the descent, blew more dust through the crust of blood in his nose. He tried to spot Porter, but there was just the green, no faces, every man moving quickly through the stubble of brush. They settled back down on the roadbed, no one standing, all of them returning to their cover. He eased himself off the large flat rock, dropped down, grunted from the pain in his leg, saw he was next to Porter again, the lieutenant looking both ways, a silent head count. Adams wiped a rough hand on the crust of blood on his face, saw Porter look back up the hill, then he looked at Adams, said, "No casualties, thank God. But you . . . you're one lucky son of a bitch. That sergeant is full of it. Jap weapons might not measure up, but don't let anybody tell you they can't shoot. Only reason that bastard didn't rip you to pieces was because he thought he'd gotten you. Yep, you've got luck on your side. I'm betting a twenty on your next fight."

Adams nodded toward the lieutenant, wasn't sure how to respond.

"Uh . . . thank you."

Porter moved away, past the others, to the head of the platoon, toward the walkie-talkie. But there were sounds on the road behind them and Adams saw Captain Bennett walking a short distance behind the other lieutenant, Berkeley. Berkeley's platoon spread out in the ditches, most down on one knee, some with canteens, faint clouds of cigarette smoke. Porter came back, and Adams heard him take a deep breath, moving close to the captain, and Porter said, "Problem solved. Charlie two got him."

"Yeah, I saw. Good job, all of you. I want us out of this hilly stuff, where we can dig in tonight and watch our flanks. Maps show a road that goes down the hill, flatter ground closer to the beach. We've got two more companies joining us along the way and the colonel is making sure we get some heavy support pretty quick. Recon reports that the enemy was seen in force all over the next hill, just beyond the intersection. They seem to be pulling away from us every step of the way, but in case they decide to stick around, there are some 75s coming up on the road behind us. The artillery boys will raise hell all over that place, bust up whatever might be there."

Porter nodded, and Adams looked at the other lieutenant, who kept his distance. Adams thought of the sergeant on the hilltop. Yep, I guess your looey's smart. One mortar shell comes down right here, and we'd be in a fix.

Bennett turned, scanned the road in both directions.

"We get to the intersection, the whole company will go to the left. Once we're on flatter ground, I'll set up a CP on the beach side. The colonel will give us orders, probably in the morning. Let's not lose anybody tonight. Eyes sharp!"

Bennett moved away, and Porter said, "Saddle up! Let's go! Keep your gap!"

Adams saw Ferucci, realized he hadn't seen him on the hillside. The sergeant was pulling thorns out of his pant leg, said, "Well, we got the bastard. The looey's right though. You're one lucky son of a bitch. But for chrissakes, wipe that crud off your face. You look like hell."

Adams obeyed, a rough sleeve scraping the crust around his nose. Ferucci moved away and Adams waited for the prescribed five yards, and then began to move as well. The road made a wide sweeping curve to the right, dropping down into a narrow gully, out of the line of sight of whoever might have been in the trees above. He moved down the hill, kept a close watch on the brush and rocks above him, could see the beach far below. He felt the cold wetness in his shirt, soaked with his own sweat, realized now, his pants were wet. He had tried to ignore that, knew it had come when he had been pinned down by the Nambu gun, so close to being hit. He cursed to himself, carried the rifle low across his front, glanced across the road, saw Yablonski, the others, no one staring at him, no humiliation, at least not yet. He thought of Ferucci's words. Lucky? Maybe so. Maybe stupid. You wanted someone to climb up on that rock and see what was beyond those flat rocks. And so I shot my mouth off. Private Adams, *volunteer.*

Next time, don't be Mr. Stupid Ass Rock Climber. If the sarge wants to see over the next hill, let him climb his own damn rocks.

Welty came up close, violated the gap between them, hard breathing, a hand on Adams's arm.

"Damn, that was something. Surprised hell out of me, that's for sure. You did good."

Adams looked back at him, was beginning to wonder if the whole world had gone stupid.

"*Good?* That Jap nearly blew my head off. I stood up there like a damn lighthouse, for all the world to see. And then I froze, didn't know enough to get my ass in gear. If the other platoon hadn't found that damn Jap, he might have shot hell out of all of us. You see those holes up there? Could have been dozens of them, just waiting for us to walk past them. We're stupid as hell!"

He realized he was nearly shouting, Welty backing away, his response coming in a low voice.

"Well, yeah. He coulda killed a bunch of us, but he didn't. Seen a lot of that happen before. Saipan."

Adams was surprised, had never heard Welty mention anything about Saipan. He waited for more, the redhead silent now, dropping back, had said all he wanted to say.

They reached the intersection, and Porter held them up, a low rise in front of them, one fork of the road dipping away to the left. Adams still felt the wetness in his pants. Damn you, anyway. You a coward? You gonna piss on yourself every time you see the enemy? He thought of the sergeant, Long, casual hatred, the man utterly immune to the death of the Japanese soldier. He *wanted* to be the one who killed him. He was *proud*. God, I need to be like that. I need to be the tough son of a bitch. He glanced at his right hand, made a fist. Yeah, they think you already are. Hey, put boxing gloves on him and he beats the crap out of everybody. Must be a really *tough guy.*

Up ahead the men were following Porter to the left. Adams looked down, the stain on his pants. Yeah, you asshole, there's a good story to tell your brother. Hey, Jesse, a Jap shot at me and I pissed my pants. Pretty impressive, huh? He stared ahead, focused on the distance between him and Ferucci. It happens to everybody, right? Everybody's scared. You saw it in the looey's eyes. Maybe that sergeant, before that Jap was killed, maybe he pissed his pants too. Adams looked across the road again, the others spread out in line, no one looking his way. Damn you, he thought, you better not be a coward, not out here, not when everyone will know. You better find a Jap and blow him to hell, and maybe make one of those necklaces that sergeant bragged about. He thought of the Japanese soldier, the blood and the stink, could not hide from that. That sergeant was proud, he thought. He *liked* it. That's what I need to do. That's what a Marine's supposed to be. Dammit, you better get good at this.

12. ADAMS

The darkness was already oppressive, more of the same routine, one man in each foxhole standing watch while the other tried to sleep. Adams stared out, the ground more flat than the rocky hills, but far out to the east he could see the taller ridgeline, thickets of pine trees. He held the M-1 close, ready, obeying the harsh instructions from the lieutenant, as though no one had done this before. Porter had seemed rattled after the experience with the Japanese machine gunner, and whether anyone else paid attention or not, Adams had seen something he didn't want to see. Porter was a veteran, like so many of the others, had done all of this before, Saipan mostly, or Guam. Like Welty, the lieutenant didn't seem interested in telling his stories, that loudmouth baloney Adams had heard from that other sergeant, Long. Adams had paid much more attention to the *eyes,* both Welty and the lieutenant showing hints of that odd stare that the men in the hospital had talked about. Not sure what that's about, he thought. I know a little about Saipan, I guess, stuff I heard in the hospital. He stared into darkness, thinking about Welty, yeah, he'd know how much of the newsreel stuff was crap, and how much wasn't. But I can't ask him about it. I just can't. That's what the new recruits do, happy stupidity, gee, Buddy,

what's it like? How many Japs did you kill? Well, we killed one today.
Doesn't seem like something to tell the grandkids about. I know damn well
Sergeant Long will tell somebody about that, part of his *big adventure*.
Some of these guys . . . that's just how they are, and that's what the recruits
want to hear. But if the lead starts flying, I'd rather be close to the lieutenant, or even Welty. If one of them grabs his ass and hauls it the other
way, pay attention to that.

He had finally been able to eat, but the K rations were just as awful as
ever. Welty had given him a chocolate bar, but that didn't sit any better in
his gut. Before dark the lieutenant had gone through the platoon telling
them all not to forget their Atabrine tablets, what was supposed to protect
them from malaria. Maybe that's what I got, he thought. Not sure what's
boiled up in my gut, and I don't know what the hell malaria's supposed to
do to you. I've seen a few of the others taking a haul-ass squat in the brush,
and nobody's said anything about some tropical disease. Funny how nobody's scared of snakes anymore. Haven't seen a single damn one, and that
Nambu gun changed a lot of these idiots. Yeah, there's worse things to
worry about. He poked his stomach, felt the painful response, thought,
no, you're not sick. Just tied up in knots. Some of these green beans they
got in those fields would help, for sure. Hell, I don't see why that fertilizer
should change anything. The damn Okies seem fine, and they eat this stuff
all the time. Their own crap. He pondered that for a long moment. Well,
maybe I'll skip the beans. He thought of the unfortunate goat herd, all that
fresh meat we blew to pieces. Nobody ate any of that, but hell, if the Okies
raise them for food, they can't be all bad. It's just meat. Real meat, not this
stuff in the K rations. Hell, maybe we been eating goat all along. They're
not gonna tell us one way or the other. He felt his stomach rolling over, a
hard knot down low, whispered, "Oh hell."

He probed Welty with his foot, heard a low grunt, Welty awake, alert,
sitting upright.

"What is it?"

"Sorry. I gotta hit the head. Bad."

Welty was up on his knees quickly, the M-1 coming up. He leaned
close to Adams, the whispers staying low.

"The password . . . you remember the password?"

"Lollygag."

"Say it out loud."

Adams knew the routine, that if any man left his foxhole in the dark, he had better make sure his buddies knew who he was. The password was one of those delicious pieces of lore that inspired someone's clever inventiveness. The intel officers had spread the word that the Japanese couldn't properly say the letter *l*, and so every password contained a mouthful of *l*'s. Yeah, he thought, I guess if some Jap overheard our password, and hollered out *rorrygag*, it wouldn't be too good for him. Adams felt the turmoil increasing in his gut, tried to see the small pile of dirt that marked the hole they had dug, just beyond arm's reach of the foxhole. The luxury of a slit trench for the whole platoon was a thing of the past now, each duo digging their own small latrine close by. It wouldn't do for anyone to get lost in the dark, password or not. He stayed still for a brief moment, then forced the word out loud.

"*Lollygag.*"

The sound burst through the silence, another voice responding, Ferucci.

"Why?"

"Head."

"Make it quick."

Adams pulled himself up out of the foxhole, one hand already on the buckle of his belt. He waited for the silence to return, knew there were eyes in the dark, that he was probably a dull shadow to the men close by, every one of them nervous, their weapons ready for any kind of deception.

He crawled to the hole, knew it wasn't deep, but the urgency was getting worse, and he pulled at the belt, was startled by muffled footsteps, saw a shadow in front of him, moving quickly. What the hell? Somebody using this hole? Wait a damn minute! The shadow had moved away from him, but then came the sound of a stumble, a startled cry in one of the foxholes. The shouts were loud, a scream cutting through the darkness. Adams stayed frozen, low on his knees, strained to see, heard a shot, a flash of fire coming from the next foxhole. He was blinded, but he knew that the shot would bring more, a lot more, and made a fast crawl, tumbled down onto Welty, who cried out as well.

"What? What's going on?"

The struggle continued nearby, and now another cry, shouts again, another shot from farther across the field, and then the chaos began, flashes of fire from every direction. Adams pulled hard on Welty's shirt, tried to right himself, Welty fighting him off, and then a hard whisper, "Pull your K-bar!"

The shooting stopped, shouts from the lieutenant, others, and Adams felt for the knife, unsheathed it, his heart exploding, held the knife close to his chest, stared up into the darkness, waiting for whatever was coming. Welty was crouched low, motionless, and Adams wanted to get to his own knees, but there was no room, and there could be no sound. After a long moment, a voice broke the silence, Porter.

"Whose foxhole?"

"Yablonski here! Son of a bitch fell in on us! We got him! Gridley's hurt!"

Adams heard a low curse from Porter, and the lieutenant said, "Bad?"

"No! Stuck me. I stuck him back!"

Adams knew Gridley's voice, deep, thunderous. Yablonski said, "Got a cloth on it. Shoulder! Can't see!"

"No lights. I'm coming up! Corpsman!"

"Here! Lollygag!"

Adams eased his head up, heard the scamper of boots, a shadow rushing toward Yablonski's foxhole. There were low voices now, another shadow from behind them, and Adams thought, the corpsman. Around Gridley's foxhole the men lay flat, no profile. Adams heard a hard groan from the big man, the talk around them low, intense. There were whispers in every direction, every man up, focused, searching the dark. One man crawled away from Yablonski's hole, disappeared into the dark, and now the other man, a low slither to the front, and Adams knew it had to be Porter. The passwords came now, each man making his way back to his own place, no other sounds. Ferucci called out, several yards to Adams's right.

"How bad?"

The voice that responded was deep and furious, Gridley.

"Bayonet in my shoulder! Son of a bitch just dropped on us. He's lying out here, next to the hole! We stuck him good, both of us. Got his stinking blood all over me."

"Shut up! If there's one, there's more!"

"Quiet! Stay sharp!"

The streaks of fire came now, white tracers, scattered, a flurry high above, some lower, ripping into the ground. Adams had rolled to his knees, kept his head below ground level, saw a line of blue-white light directly overhead, fading quickly, and Welty said, "Jap tracers!"

No one spoke, the machine gun fire coming from far away, different from the woodpecker tapping. Adams knew from the briefings it had to be the heavier pieces, something close to the fifty caliber. Welty whispered, "This is good! No infiltrators now. They wouldn't fire if they had a squad of guys out here crawling around. As long as they keep this up, we can get some sleep."

Adams stared at him in the dark, saw faint reflections from the tracers, Welty pulling himself down into the corner of the foxhole. And then the firing stopped. There was no sound at all for a long minute, every man waiting for what might happen next. Adams had forgotten the problems in his gut, the cramped misery replaced by the sudden reality. That Jap was . . . right here. He could have come into our hole . . . probably would have. Stay alert, dammit! Welty was sitting again, a low whisper.

"Damn them anyway. I need some sleep."

Adams eased his head up, trained his eyes on the terrain, tried to recall the familiar lumps and bulges of the low brush. Out in front of the foxhole, something seemed to move, a larger bulge, something new, and he reached for Welty's arm, missed, and out front came a sharp *thump*. He brought the rifle up, and now the darkness was blasted by a flash of fire, a thunderous explosion. All around them M-1s responded, and Adams closed his eyes, blinded, fired once, Welty doing the same, then Welty's hand on his arm, pulling him down again.

"Jap grenade! Stay down."

The streaks of fire came all across the field, more shouts, farther away.

"Got him! Got him!"

"Shut up! Cease fire!"

Again the firing died down, the panic passing. Ferucci shouted, "Grenade! Anybody hit?"

"Just missed us here!"

Adams knew now what the thump had been, the one part of the briefings that the veterans had repeated often. Japanese grenades were primed by a hard knock straight against the fuse, Japanese soldiers usually knocking them against a rock, or their own helmets. He leaned close to Welty, said, "I heard it!"

Welty said nothing, and Adams felt the familiar shivering, spreading out from inside his gut, his hands gripping the M-1. He rose up again with Welty, stared hard into the darkness, his night vision coming back, could smell the explosives, the dust. Welty tugged on his arm again, startling him.

"I can hear your teeth chattering. Sit. Keep the K-bar out. There could be more of them. They jump in here, cut 'em hard and fast!"

Adams obeyed, felt a strange calm from Welty, the mild-mannered man now taking charge. He shifted himself against the bottom of the fox-hole, heard voices, the sergeant, the lieutenant, communicating in single words.

"Hurt?"

"None."

"Morning."

Adams translated, thought, we'll see what the hell happened in the morning. God, Gridley's hurt. We need his BAR. Somebody else will have to carry it. Maybe he's not too bad.

He gripped the K-bar knife hard in his left hand, kept it pointing up-ward, his right hand resting on the trigger guard of the M-1. The questions rolled through his brain. How many more? They gonna do this all night? Maybe we should shoot every now and then. What happens if they get the lieutenant? He stared ahead into black dark, glanced down toward Welty, could barely make out the shape of the man curled up beside him. He stared out again into the darkness, his brain working, feverish, every man in the platoon asking the same questions.

APRIL 13, 1945
DAWN

There had been no sleep for Adams, the night creeping past in an agoniz-ing torrent of images, waking nightmares that skipped through his mind, scenes of blood and death, questions of what they would see in the light. The darkness had been alive with motion, his imagination playing terrify-ing games, dancing figures in the dark, small brush suddenly running away, then there again, unmoving. With the first hint of gray, he had cursed anxiously at the darkness to go away, felt desperate relief as the ground revealed itself. His vision increased by the minute and by the foot, finally to where Yablonski and Gridley lay, then farther, a dull shadow tak-ing shape, more, until the images were no longer just in his mind. Beside Yablonski's foxhole lay the dead soldier, blood all through his uniform, Yablonski's manic work with the knife more efficient than it needed to be. In front of Adams lay another Japanese body, no more than twenty yards away. With more daylight the man's dark form took shape, and Adams could see that the man had no head, everything above his shoulders a bloody mass of shredded cloth and skin. On both sides helmets were rising up, the rest of the platoon taking it in, the daylight erasing the nightmares. To the left, out in front of the next squad, he saw a third body, bareheaded, lying faceup, his arms twisted in some bizarre contortion, as though the man had tried to tie himself in a knot.

"Nobody move. Stay down in your damn holes! Remember those machine guns!"

The men to that side obeyed their sergeant's command, even the most curious settling back into the ground. The talk began now.

"We got 'em!"

"Hell, I got him! He was right in front of me!"

"One got himself!"

Adams settled back into the hole, sat, saw Welty doing the same, the redhead now digging into his backpack.

"Chocolate bar? I got plenty."

"No thanks. God, did you see the one right out front? What do you think happened?"

Welty looked at him, and Adams could see the man's face, just enough light to show the reflection of his glasses. Welty said, "Seen it before. Jap goes to throw his grenade and the fuse goes off too soon. Blew his damn head off. Their grenades must be crap."

"Wonder where he was throwing it?"

"Don't. Doesn't matter."

"I saw three dead ones. Think there were more?"

"Yep."

Welty ripped open the cardboard of the K ration box, scattered the contents beside him. He poked, appraising, said, "God, I could use some coffee."

Adams felt grit in his mouth, his tongue like cotton.

"I need water. My canteens are empty."

Welty said nothing, and Adams thought, if he could spare some, he would say so. There's gotta be a water truck or some barrels around here somewhere close.

Welty put a thick cracker in his mouth, said, "The CP's not too far behind us. Captain will make sure we get some water."

To one side, a voice called out.

"Holy God! Would you look at that!"

Adams heard a hoot, another man, "I'll be! Take a look at that! She come for breakfast?"

Adams peeked up, saw the woman now, walking across the open ground, a slow march closer to the foxholes. He could see her short black hair, could tell she was young, small and thin. But he could see clearly that she was not a child. She was naked.

Other hoots came now, her audience appreciative, curious, some of the comments vulgar, and now, one man was up, moving toward her, took off his helmet, made a mock bow. The girl kept walking, closer, and Adams could see more details, her face showing nothing, staring straight ahead, doing her best to ignore the calls of the stunned men around her. Another man rose, then his buddy, crawling up from their hole, and the man waved the others back, said with authority, "Back off. We'll wrap her up in something."

And now one more voice above the clamor, the lieutenant.

"Get the hell away from her! Get back in your—"

The shots came now, slow and precise, single pops in the distance, the dull crack of lead as the carefully aimed shots impacted each of the men. They dropped in perfect rhythm, one by one, tumbling clumsily, helmets rolling away, motionless, the voices gone, the vulgar hoots replaced by the sounds of horror in the men who watched, surprise and fury. The girl was still there, paralyzed, standing with her eyes closed, and then there was one more shot, and Adams saw the girl collapse. He felt a hand on his arm, a hard tug, Welty yanking him into the hole.

"Get down!"

He felt queasy shock, wanted to see, and Welty rose up, kept his hand on Adams's shoulder, holding him down.

"Snipers! Nobody's moving."

The order came in a manic high pitch, the voice of the lieutenant.

"Goddammit, stay put! It came from those far trees!"

Adams heard Porter's voice again, this time low in his foxhole, and Welty said, "He's on the walkie-talkie. We need some help. Maybe some 75s, or some tin cans. Somebody needs to blow hell out of that tree line." Welty paused. "God bless those damn fools."

The tanks rolled close, a half-dozen machines, rising up off the road, spreading into formation. Adams could smell the exhaust fumes, smoke trailing each of the Shermans, and around him the men responded, the lieutenant pulling them up from their cover, advancing them toward the distant tree lines. The men were pulled into packs close behind the tanks, natural instinct, no one objecting. Behind them the officers had gathered briefly in a shallow gully, kneeling low. Adams was close to Welty, Ferucci guiding them into line, the sergeant staring back where the officers spoke, and Adams ignored that, looked across the open ground to the cluster of bodies, the four Marines now wrapped in ponchos, only their boots protruding. The girl was there too, a piece of cloth tossed across her, someone's gesture of decency that seemed to contradict the obscenity of what she had been made to do. Adams had stepped past her, had seen the thin legs, the prettiness of her face only partly covered. He had focused more on the stain of blood on the cloth, thought, no one volunteers for that. She's got to be an Okie. Behind him a man moved up to the bodies, stopped, and Adams hesitated, saw his face, older, sad eyes, the man making a brief sign of the cross. Adams knew him, the chaplain, nodded toward the man, got no response, the chaplain's attention on the bodies.

"Get moving!"

Adams turned, saw Ferucci waving at him, moved away, thought, nothing I can say . . . the chappy knows his job. Didn't even know he was out here.

The services had been conducted somewhere every Sunday, even on the Sunday two weeks before when they began the invasion. Then, the chaplain had been on the ship, administering a ritual to anyone who cared for it. There had been many that day, many more than usual, and Adams had assumed that a chaplain shouldn't cross the beach until it was secure. But the man was there now, doing his job. Adams had a curiosity about the girl, wondered if the chaplain would say something for her. Well, yeah, we're all God's children, all of that. She ended up as bait. Wonder what God thinks of that?

Adams saw Welty waiting for him, the tanks slowly moving away, and Adams pushed himself forward, realized the lieutenant was up beside him, moving fast, taking himself to the front of his platoon. Adams was swallowed by the exhaust, the agony in his stomach only worse, worse still by what had happened to the four Marines. He fought through the sights and sounds, the girl, the utter shock of that, felt more angry at the men who died than the enemy. We did just what the Japs thought we'd do. We'd either ogle her and be jackasses, or we'd try to help her. Either way, we'd let down, for just a second. Who can just pretend there's not a naked girl walking by? Smart sons of bitches. And then they were done with her. She was just . . . another weapon.

There had been no more from the Japanese since the Marines were killed, since the sun had risen completely. The Marines had poured out their own anger in a storm of fire from the M-1s and BARs, a machine gun battery moving up as well, a half-dozen thirty calibers peppering anyplace where the Japanese might be. No one knew if there had been any effect from that, but the firing had released the anger, and when word came quickly that the Shermans were coming, the men had responded with cheers.

A gust of wind took the exhaust smoke away, and Adams could see the ground in front of them clearly now, the pine trees and low squat palms. One of the Shermans erupted in machine gun fire, blasting a cluster of palms. The men on foot gathered closer, no one sure what to do, no targets. The Sherman closest to Adams suddenly accelerated, the turret shifting to one side, its cannon cutting loose. The explosion burst into a clump of short trees, fire, smoke, and then three more tanks began to fire, ripping away at the strand of woods. The Marines were being left back, and no one ran to keep up, the tanks suddenly taking full command, turning, maneuvering, one crushing right through the palms, more machine gun fire, all of it from the Shermans.

Adams felt a hand on his shoulder, startled, turned, saw Ferucci, pointing back. He saw now, behind them, a row of amphtracs moving up, the vehicles that had carried some of them in from the ships. Now they were rolling on land, each one equipped with a heavy machine gun, a fifty caliber, the crews inside protected by the steel bulkheads. The first amphtrac rolled by, men looking out at the Marines, fists pumping the air, any cheers silenced by the belching roars of the engines. The amphibious machines moved up closer to the tanks, and around him the Marines were called forward as well, the lieutenants continuing the advance. But the M-1s were silent. The larger machines were doing the work. The battle seemed to spread out farther, the tanks fanning outward. Around him the Marines continued their advance through the trees, wood and grass fires boiling up around them, the stink of explosives, and beyond, the tree lines gave way to upsloping ground, the larger hills. But the tree line had been cleared and the tanks stopped their advance, curled around, came together in a formation, keeping a safe distance between them, poised in a soft chugging of their engines, the amphtracs doing the same. Adams saw Porter waving him forward, heard pops of rifle fire, men shooting straight down into holes in the ground. He searched frantically, the words etched into his brain, the lieutenant's description, spider holes. Close to one side an amphtrac had halted, lowered the wide steel door, six men pouring out, keeping together in pairs. Adams saw the fat tanks on the men's backs, the strange weapon they carried, like a thin rifle, but it was no rifle at all. It was a flamethrower.

The battle had been brief and mostly one-sided. The Marines had found targets, but not many, and the work had been done mostly by the tankers and the flamethrowers, few Japanese soldiers willing to come up to the surface to fight on terms the fresher recruits had expected. For many there was little to do but wait and pick out targets as they emerged from the caves. Some came out as prisoners, but not many. The Japanese who emerged with their weapons did not live long enough to aim them, some holding grenades they never had a chance to throw. But those had been few as well. There was no way to know how many of the enemy were in the ground around them, and how many might still be alive. But Adams had watched with horrified fascination as the liquid flames shot deep into the small cavelike tunnels, and the one-man spider holes were either empty or held the body of a Japanese soldier too stubborn to run away.

With the fight drawing to a close, the artillery batteries had been brought closer, the distant hills now splattered in a cascade of fire, aided by the good work of the dive-bombers from the carriers offshore. The Marines were pulled back, Captain Bennett's company regrouping on the flat ground above the beach, ground that was too familiar. To everyone's relief, the bodies of the four Marines had been removed, and one of the foxholes had been filled in, marked by a trail of stained brown dirt that Adams had to guess was all that remained of the girl. Before the darkness came again, there were more officers, jeeps and amphtracs, command posts set up, aid stations for those few who had been wounded in the attack on the Japanese positions. As the men settled back into their makeshift encampment, there had been a shocking surprise, which not even the officers expected. Along the beaches, small patrol boats moved in close, some of the Marines not even noticing them until the voices came, broadcast on loudspeakers. The men who worked at their foxholes were brought to a halt, no sergeants griping, no orders from the lieutenants. The loudspeakers carried a message, a solemn announcement that no one could ignore. Franklin Delano Roosevelt had died.

Like most of those around him, Adams knew little of the man beyond what he had heard on the radio, or what the newsreels showed, a president who was more like a kindly grandfather than their commander in chief. After Pearl Harbor, it had been Roosevelt's words that inspired Adams to join the Marines, inspiration shared by hundreds of thousands of young men across the country, including many of those who shared the foxholes above the beach. The announcement threw a strange cloud over the men, some of them reacting by not reacting at all, others invigorated to work harder, to dig the foxhole deeper, better. Some just sat and cried, as though they had truly lost a member of their family. No one interrupted that, there was no teasing, no embarrassment to anyone who had grown up knowing no other name who meant so much to the nation. After a time the emotions passed, replaced by a silent gloom, and there were few conversations, almost no one thinking about the new man in charge, most not even knowing that his name was *Truman*. With the fading daylight the Marines climbed down into their holes, awaiting the darkness again, staring at shadows, keeping watch against the infiltrators, fighting the panic and the nightmares that rolled through them all night long.

And the next night, they would do it all again.

13. NIMITZ

For the next several days, the fights rolled northward, the Japanese making their stands in a way that only invited defeat. Rather than attack the Americans with guile and sound tactics, the Japanese mostly held their ground, and were overwhelmed by the crushing superiority of the Marine tanks, artillery, and naval aircraft. Each night the infiltrators would come, small-scale strikes against the dug-in Marines, rattling the nerves and trigger fingers of the men who were suffering mostly from heat and the lack of sleep. But the Japanese seemed content to wage a piecemeal war, rather than the massed horror of the banzai assaults, the chaotic slaughter that so many of the veterans had seen before.

As the Japanese withdrew or were crushed by sheer strength of arms, the Marines continued to exceed their own timetables, pushing toward the northern tip of Okinawa far ahead of schedule. To the Marine commanders, who had feared the kind of casualty counts that had come on Iwo Jima, the lack of a stout Japanese effort was welcome.

On the Motobu Peninsula the job for the Fourth and Twenty-ninth Marine regiments had been costly. The enemy had seemed far more willing to offer a sharp struggle on a piece of land that was subject to ongoing bombardments from air and sea, as well as the relentless push by the Marines. The casualty counts had been somewhat severe, but by April 20 the peninsula was declared secure. The combat units who had taken punishment were allowed some rest and refitting, while the remainder of the Sixth Division and the bulk of the First continued driving north. Up the spine of the island, the Marines did their job, made a relentless push into whatever enemy they could find, or whatever resistance was thrown up in their paths.

Despite ongoing mop-up operations, the success in securing the Motobu Peninsula allowed General Buckner an opportunity to crow about a victory, and so crow he did. But the news that reached Nimitz was not all good. To the south the first two army divisions had been bolstered by their reserves, but all three were becoming bogged down against a far stronger Japanese effort. Though no one in the American command had been able to predict exactly what the Japanese strategy would be, it was increasingly apparent that General Ushijima had positioned his greatest defensive strength in the south, along the line that ran from Shuri Castle westward to the Okinawan coast. General Buckner painted an optimistic portrait, but Nimitz was hearing something very different from the naval commanders, particularly Admiral Turner, whose ships were bearing the brunt of the increasingly destructive kamikaze attacks. With the army's casualties mounting on land, and Turner's sailors beginning to absorb a horrifying pounding offshore, Nimitz could no longer accept Buckner's assurances that everything was going according to Buckner's planning. With obvious friction growing between army and navy commanders, Nimitz knew the time had come to see the situation for himself. He would go to Okinawa.

The kamikaze attacks had come continuously, though some were small in scale, sometimes a single aircraft. But it had become clear that there was a method to the Japanese tactics. Every seven to eight days now the attacks were launched toward the American fleet in a massive wave, hundreds of aircraft of every imaginable type ramming their way through the American defenses. The destruction was becoming astonishing, both on board the ships and to the Japanese pilots, almost none of whom survived. Throughout the war, naval casualties had been comparably light, even during the most brutal battles in the Coral Sea and at Leyte Gulf. But now the navy was absorbing losses they had never experienced, and though the most prized targets, the battleships and carriers, had taken some hits, it was the smaller escort and supply ships that were receiving the worst punishment. Dozens of American ships were being sent to the bottom, along with far too many crewmen. The losses were doubly horrifying because they had been so unexpected, and yet the Americans continued to be baffled by Japanese logic. If Tokyo had any expectation that their planes would either destroy the American fleet or drive them away from Okinawa, the tactics being used seemed gruesomely absurd. Radar and lookout stations monitored the incoming waves of Japanese planes, allowing gunners on board the American ships to prepare for the onslaught. The carrier aircraft could combat the incoming Japanese waves before the kamikaze pilots could even see their targets. With Japanese losses in aircraft numbering in the hundreds, the Americans had to wonder just how much more of this kind of attack the Japanese could mount. The loss in pilots alone had to mean that the planes were being flown by men with minimal training, whose sole mission was to end their lives by a desperate gamble that Americans would die in the process. The number of aircraft the Japanese were losing added to the mystery. How many more planes could the Japanese air force sacrifice before they simply ran out?

COMMAND POST, TENTH ARMY, OKINAWA
APRIL 23, 1945

He climbed from the jeep, returned the salutes, waited as Vandegrift slid out the other side. The Marines who stood guard seemed to recognize their highest-ranking commander, most of them showing a little more starch in their salutes toward Vandegrift, a little more enthusiasm than they had for Nimitz. Nimitz smiled to himself, had no objections to that at all. Vandegrift had just received his fourth star, the first Marine general to ever reach that rank.

In an active war zone, a gathering of high-ranking commanders usually did little more than annoy the men on the ground who were trying to do their jobs. Nimitz had suggested to Vandegrift that the Marine Corps commander spend more of his time visiting his battle-weary divisions, the Fourth in particular, who had been badly mauled at Iwo Jima. Vandegrift had obliged him with a barely disguised anger, the general expecting to be allowed free rein over his units no matter where they might be stationed. After several days with the Fourth in Hawaii, Vandegrift had visited the exhausted Third Division, which held station on the newly secured Iwo Jima. By the time the Marine commander returned to Nimitz's headquarters on Guam, Nimitz could see that the exposure to the tattered remains of two of his best divisions had worn a hole in Vandegrift's patience.

Nimitz realized that, annoyance or not, if Nimitz was going to Okinawa, he had no right to prevent Vandegrift from accompanying him. To Vandegrift's obvious delight, Nimitz had conceded that there was probably no one in the entire Pacific theater who had earned a greater right to visit his troops, no matter where they might be.

Alexander Vandegrift was two years Nimitz's junior, bore himself with that distinctive straight-backed demeanor that Nimitz always respected. He was a Virginian, the descendant of a survivor of Pickett's Charge, and surprised no one by his desire to pursue a military career. But the number of influential Virginians who pushed for appointments to the military academies had left Vandegrift behind, and instead he began his own path by attending the Virginia Military Institute. Rather than the army, Vandegrift chose the Marine Corps, serving in the First Division. At Guadalcanal in 1942, Vandegrift commanded that division, and his heroics there caught the attention of Admiral King in Washington. In a short time, Vandegrift's star rose considerably, and by early 1945 he had become commandant of the Marine Corps. But office politics and a fat desk had not tamed the man known by his officers as "Sunny Jim." On the long flight to Okinawa, Nimitz had already chastised himself repeatedly for ever assuming Vandegrift would be a pain to anybody.

Across the open ground, Nimitz could see tents and hastily built metal and wood huts, scattered through a smattering of low-slung palm trees. Anti-aircraft guns ringed the entire compound, the gunners closest to him curious, mostly with their eyes on Vandegrift.

Nimitz had seen the same kinds of faces on board the USS *New Mexico* the night before, where he had dined with Fleet Admiral Spruance. The gunners on board the great battleship were nervous, angry men, who focused much more of their attention on the skies than on a parade of brass who strode along their decks. It had surprised Nimitz that little effort had been made on the battleship to hide the stacks of cots, other than to shove them into any nook where they wouldn't be in the way. It was a clear sign that most of the sailors were using the open deck for sleeping. Even on those days when the rains came, the extraordinary heat prevented anyone from sleeping in the stifling misery of their quarters belowdecks. Nimitz focused now on the faces closest to him, as he had on the ship. He saw the same faces he had seen at sea, fatigued, sad eyes, men going about their jobs with automatic movements, no joking, no laughter. Low morale was as obvious here on the island as it had been on the ship. It was not a surprise. Nimitz knew that the loss of President Roosevelt had certainly cast a heavy dose of gloom among the troops everywhere, but then, there had been one more dreadful surprise, news of a completely unexpected tragedy. Nimitz received the word, as had every commander in the theater, that on April 18 newspaper columnist Ernie Pyle had been killed while accompanying a patrol of the Seventy-seventh Infantry Division on one of the smaller islands offshore. Nimitz knew that the president's death would have a far more profound effect on the conduct of the war. But the loss of Ernie Pyle would have a devastating effect on the men in the ranks. Of all the reporters who had accompanied the troops in all theaters of the war, Pyle was by far the most beloved. From North Africa to Europe and now to the Pacific, the columns Pyle sent back home had humanized the troops by telling their stories directly, experiences comical, absurd, and tragic. He gave the troops their own voice, when most other reporters were far more interested in snuggling up to the brass. By naming them and offering a nod to their hometowns, Pyle had sent a reassuring hand back to relatives who might otherwise never know of the fate of their own, since mail service took far longer than Pyle's own dispatches. Everywhere he went, Pyle obliged as many of the troops as he could, moving among the men with his trademark typewriter slung over his shoulder, offering good cheer and an eagerness to listen that the average GI had found nowhere else.

Nimitz still returned the stares, hard, cold eyes, thought, that's what this is. So many of these men are veterans, have seen these islands come and go, have faced a viciousness in the Japanese that none of us expected. They're losing friends in every fight, and Ernie Pyle made himself a friend to every one of these men. Damn it all, I want this fight to end.

"Ah, Admiral, welcome! Sorry, I was just dealing with a . . . radio matter. Messages coming in from offshore. Admiral Turner is checking on you, making sure your party arrived safely. I don't hear much from him, you know. Prefer it that way. Not that he's a pest or anything. It's just that . . . well, his communications can be . . . well . . ."

Buckner was digging himself into a hole, and Nimitz held up both hands, said, "I understand, General. No need for explanations."

"Ah, General Vandegrift, welcome! Congratulations are in order. Welcome to the thin air at the top, if I do say. Please, I may not be the first, but I'll shake your hand, if you'll allow it."

"Thank you, General. I'm at your service."

The pleasantries were already strained, Nimitz wanting to move into whatever passed for Buckner's headquarters, Buckner's obvious cheerful-ness a poor mask for his anxiety that Nimitz had come to Okinawa in the first place. Buckner was a huge bear of a man, roughly Nimitz's age, a shock of white hair over deep blue eyes. Buckner was more fanatical about physical fitness than Nimitz was, something Nimitz admired. But there were extremes to Buckner's devotion to the conditioning of his men. It was one of the major gripes that came from the men who served him, that the general had put even the older officers through so much rigorous exercise that throughout the Tenth Army the senior command suffered from con-stant physical injuries. Nimitz had heard that some of the meetings resem-bled hospital wards, generals with various joints wrapped in gauze or hard casts.

He followed Buckner, glanced at the stiff-backed MPs who stood guard, grim-faced men who reminded Nimitz of his own Marine guard on Guam. He turned over the name in his head, Turner, the admiral who now held overall command around the Okinawan operation. Turner had re-mained on board his own command ship, the USS *Eldorado,* and had seemed relieved that Nimitz had not asked him to come along. There were other reasons why Nimitz was growing increasingly uncomfortable with the man he had chosen to oversee Buckner's Tenth Army and the fleet an-chored offshore.

It had been a particular thorn in Nimitz's side, the scuttlebutt that Ad-miral Turner couldn't stay away from the bottle. But his performance in the fights for Saipan and Guam had been outstanding, and Nimitz knew that performance mattered more than a man's personal habits. But worse for Nimitz, Turner was physically opposite from the lean, hard comman-ders that Nimitz tried to keep in his command. Turner had a soft paunch, a belly that spread out well over his belt line. It made Nimitz wince to think about that, a violation of Nimitz's philosophy that officers should be as lean as their men. That's worse than the booze, he thought, and he should know that. I can't dictate orders about being a slob, when a man comes by it naturally. The drinking . . . well, if I see it's really affecting his performance out here, I'll have to do something. No doubt about it.

Richmond Kelly Turner had been chosen by Nimitz himself to com-mand the overall assault on Okinawa, a decision that even now Nimitz be-lieved had been a good one. There had been failures though, hard grumbling from the Marines that Turner had refused to shell the landing zones at Iwo Jima, causing casualties to the Marines that could have been avoided. That kind of accusation was speculative at best, no one really knowing how much of the Japanese resistance would have been obliterated by naval fire. And Nimitz knew that the others who could have been chosen for the job, men like Bull Halsey, who gathered more headlines than Turner, had their failures as well. No matter whom he had picked for the job, there would be bellyaching. The only problem for Turner would be if Nimitz developed a bellyache of his own.

Nimitz had already briefed the few members of his staff who had come along, some of those remaining on board the *Eldorado* with Turner. Nimitz had confidence that each of those men understood his role, would purposely engage in casual chitchat with the *Eldorado*'s junior officers that might reveal more to Nimitz than what was said in the official meetings.

"Sir, if you please . . ."

Nimitz obliged Buckner, stepped through the doorway of a low concrete block building. Buckner led the way again, past a makeshift office, an aide rising to quick attention, two more standing at their desks, typewriters stuffed with paper. To one side he heard the commotion of a radio room, and Nimitz glanced that way, saw a row of men with earphones, could hear the clatter of a teletype machine. This has got to be for show, he thought. He sure as hell doesn't keep his quarters here, and I bet there are more comfortable places for us to meet. But I'll give him slack. Pretty damn sure he just wants us the hell out of the way.

He followed Buckner into a white-walled room, saw a narrow rectangular table, a half-dozen chairs, one large map on the wall. Buckner gave way and Nimitz sat at the head of the table, Vandegrift on the far end, Buckner now between them. Nimitz caught the unmistakable odor of hot food, and Buckner seemed to wait for that, said, "Once again my cook has outdone himself! We found a few locals who were kind enough to offer us baskets of fresh vegetables, sweet potatoes, and a rather nice string bean. My cook has a way with the vegetables that you should find appealing. The fresh fish is a wonder. The Okinawans certainly don't want for good food. I can have them serve lunch in here, or we can adjourn outside and enjoy the air."

The cheer in Buckner's voice was offset by the counterfeit smile of a man who knew his superior wasn't there for anything *appealing*. Nimitz stared at the map, thought, adjourn? Why don't we *begin* first.

"Is this map up-to-date?"

"Absolutely, sir."

His eyes stayed on the southern half of the island, pins marking the army units that Nimitz knew were bogged down against the Japanese defenses. He avoided looking at Buckner, said, "Tough nut. We knew it could be this way. All that damn optimism after the landing, like we'd beaten the bastards without a fight."

"Yes, sir. We were rather surprised by that. So, how soon would you like lunch?"

"It can wait."

Vandegrift stayed silent, conceding the floor to Nimitz, but Buckner seemed to concede nothing, shook his head, an indiscreet show of disappointment.

"Well, then, perhaps later. Oh, I wanted to say . . . awful shame about Ernie Pyle. Some damn fool colonel, out joyriding, and I suppose Pyle went along to see the sights. Ran slam into a Jap machine gun nest, or sniper. Something. Well, I assume you got the report."

Nimitz turned back toward Buckner, nodded.

"Saw it. I met him a few times. Decent man, I think. The boys will miss hell out of him."

"His death will give 'em a spark, that's what I say. Fire 'em up, kill hell out of the Japs."

Nimitz tried to avoid looking at Buckner's beaming smile.

"We shouldn't need that kind of *spark*. Civilians shouldn't be out here at all. Everybody cut Pyle more slack than usual because he was so popular with the men, and Pyle did his part. But I don't need to hear details about some line officer hauling Pyle's ass into a hot spot. Pyle knew he was taking risks, and he paid the price. Could happen to any of us. It's the risk we all take. If you don't mind, General, can we get this briefing under way?"

Buckner seemed to flinch and Nimitz thought, dammit, no reason to ream him out. Not yet anyway. You're just pissed at everybody. Long trip, and it's been a crappy couple of weeks all around. After a short pause, Nimitz said, "We may have more problems back home than you'll hear about out here, at least for a while." He paused. "I was in Washington, you know, early last month. My daughter got married. Saw the president while I was there. He didn't look good, not at all. But I'd been hearing for more than a year that he was in rough shape. Didn't give it much thought. Now . . . he's gone. Just like that. Hard to swallow. Damn hard. There have been enough pissing matches in Washington between the War Department and . . . well, everybody. This won't help. Forrestal will probably go. I imagine the *new* president will want his own navy secretary. He won't touch King, pretty sure of that. King's got too much dirt on everybody else, and he'll kick down doors before he lets some wet-behind-the-ears president tell him anything. Marshall is bound to stay as well, Hap Arnold too. Truman can't possibly be stupid enough to clean house of the experienced chiefs of staff." He paused. "Truman."

He rolled the name around in his brain. God help us. Buckner seemed desperate to respond, held his hand poised in the air, one forefinger extended, then said, "He fought in the first war, you know. I heard that about him."

"Who? Truman?"

"Yep. Infantry, maybe. Or artillery. At least he knows about fighting."

Nimitz kept his response to himself, thought, you've said enough already. But that's just perfect. A damn infantryman in the White House. Hut two three. Maybe he can come out here and tell Buckner how to kick his people in the ass. Nimitz was out of patience, the windowless room already stifling, sweat soaking his shirt. Buckner seemed not to be sweating at all.

"Well, gentlemen, shall we get down to it? If we're lucky, the cook will still have us some hot chow."

Nimitz glanced at Vandegrift, saw rigid impatience. Buckner suddenly rose, a quick shout to the outer office.

"I need Colonel Harper and his secretary, and I want MPs inside and out! What the hell's going on around here? Lunch can wait! We've got guests. Let's show these men how the army throws out a welcome mat!"

Nimitz let out a breath, thought, we're not guests. I run this damn show. Maybe the *army* has forgotten that.

It was the challenge for every operation like this, trying to blend the different branches in the service into a smooth command. He glanced at Vandegrift, who seemed content for things to run on Buckner's timetable. The two men sat in sweltering silence, Vandegrift focusing more on the map to one side. Buckner was outside now, gone altogether, and Nimitz suddenly realized, he's stirring this pot for my benefit, showing me how hands-on he is. Dammit, I don't need a show. I need to know he's got what we need to handle this operation.

An aide suddenly appeared, two glasses of what seemed to be tea, each with a rapidly disappearing ice cube. The man hustled away without a word, and Vandegrift took a short drink, set the glass down.

"I'm not much for fruit juice. You bring any bourbon?"

"You waited until *now* to remind me?"

There was no humor in the words, Nimitz growing more annoyed, the sweat stinging his eyes. He pulled out a handkerchief, wiped his face, said, "I suppose it's painfully apparent that a visiting blue jacket here is more trouble than he's worth. Not sure I've had anyone under my command communicate that to me before."

"If I may say, Admiral, that's probably the biggest difference between you and MacArthur. You expect all of us to work together, and you assume it will happen because it's the right thing for us to do. Mac would just order everyone to like each other, and he'll expect it to happen. If you don't go along, or perform to his expectations, he gets rid of you. It may be that, with all due respect, the navy has no business telling an army commander how to put troops on the ground. This shouldn't surprise you, sir, but I've been hearing too much scuttlebutt. Bitching has a way of crossing a lot of distance. Something smells here, and I for one want to know what it is."

Nimitz nodded, forced himself to drink the tea.

"I had assumed Admiral Turner to be the man who could keep that from happening. I still believe he's fit to handle this combined operation, but if I'm wrong, I need to hear that from Buckner. And if Buckner's not the man for this job, I'll hear it from everyone below him with enough backbone to speak up. I'm pretty sure that includes your General Geiger. That tough old bird has more medals than anyone in this theater, and if he wants to bitch, feel free to encourage him."

Vandegrift laughed.

"I already know what he wants. He thinks he should be in charge out here, and the army should be tending the goat herds. It's not quite appropriate for me to suggest I agree with him. But there's nobody else I'd rather see handling my Marines than Roy." He motioned to the map. "He'll have plenty to say about what his boys have done, and what the army boys are supposed to be doing."

Roy Geiger was another of the old bulldogs who was nearly Nimitz's age. Like Vandegrift, Geiger had established an outstanding reputation early in the war. Geiger had been an accomplished aviator, but the powers above him knew he could inspire his men no matter where he served. Now he was in overall command of the three Marine divisions assigned to the Okinawan campaign, and Nimitz knew that in the three weeks since the landing, Geiger had done as well on Okinawa as he had anyplace before.

Geiger had already led Marines into action on Guadalcanal and Bougainville, the Palau Islands and Guam, and in the process had been awarded the Navy Cross and the Distinguished Service Medal. He had also been awarded three gold stars, which Nimitz knew had been embarrassing substitutes for the two higher honors, that Geiger should be wearing at least two Navy Crosses, just for starters. But it was the politics of war, few in Washington, including Vandegrift, wanting to bear the brunt of anyone's jealousy over this rough-hewn Marine getting his name in the paper too often. Nimitz liked Geiger, despite the rough edges, thought, it has to kick him in the ass to be taking orders from an army man. Yep, if there's a problem, he'll tell me about it.

"Sir!"

Nimitz turned, saw one of Buckner's aides in the doorway, making way for an MP. The MP was stern-faced, wore a pair of forty-fives, stared at Nimitz, then Vandegrift, as though appraising whether the two men were a threat. The MP stepped into the room, stood to one side, his back pressed firmly against the wall. Nimitz saw a second MP, another rapid entrance, the two men acknowledging the *all clear* with a brief nod to each other, as though any danger had been neutralized. It was a ridiculous show, the kind of theatrics he knew had been absorbed by anyone who had ever served MacArthur. Buckner returned now, marching in, seemed satisfied that something vital had been accomplished in his absence. He stared down at Nimitz with the hard blue eyes, a show of fierceness that Nimitz had seen before, sat down heavily, his hands folded, a man waiting for some unpleasant task.

Nimitz eyed the MPs, thought, oh, for crying out loud. This is ridiculous.

"General Buckner, will you please ask your men to remain outside. We will summon them if needed."

Buckner seemed suddenly uneasy, as though his bluff had been called.

"Um . . . of course, Admiral."

He turned, the men absorbing a look from Buckner that Nimitz couldn't see. He wants witnesses, Nimitz thought. Maybe he thinks I'm here to relieve him. So, he knows there's a problem. That's a start. The aide was out, then the MPs, one of them pulling the door closed behind him. Nimitz felt the air heating up even more, said, "For chrissakes, General, let some air in here. Unless you believe you've got a security problem in your own headquarters, we don't need to seal this place up like a fuel drum. I assume your MPs won't be lurking outside the door like private eyes, for God's sake."

Buckner turned again, self-conscious, seemed to check out beyond the door.

"No, sir. Certainly not. If we need a staff briefing, I'll summon them."

Nimitz didn't wait, motioned toward the map.

"What's going on in the south, General? Seems to be a lack of progress."

Buckner seemed surprised that Nimitz had avoided small talk. Buckner was immediately defensive, something Nimitz expected.

"Sir, we are facing a dedicated, fanatical enemy, who has all the good ground. The Japanese have created a massed defensive position that takes full advantage of the assets of the island. Naval intelligence . . . our intelligence was unable to tell us exactly where they'd be, but we know their positions for certain now. Their plan was most certainly to distract us in the north while they put up a major front across the southern half of the island that would be difficult, no matter which forces attacked them. It's pretty admirable, actually. I'll give Ushijima credit for a good plan."

Nimitz saw a scowl from Vandegrift, said to Buckner, "What about *your* plan, General?"

Buckner crossed his arms, tilted his head to one side.

"Everything is under control here, sir. Before this is over with, we'll have destroyed every enemy installation, every hiding place, every defensive position. The Japs have nowhere to run. Your navy boys are doing a fine job with their artillery, and I expect that will continue. There won't be a building standing in any town on this whole place. We'll level this place just like Mac did Manila. The enemy will understand that we're not playing around."

Nimitz looked down at the table, thought, Manila? MacArthur devastated a glorious, historic city for no good reason, except that he could. And the civilian casualties . . .

"What of the Okinawan people, General? Our mission here is to capture these islands and eliminate the Japanese. I don't recall anyone in Washington telling us to eliminate the people who live here."

Buckner nodded, seemed to concede the point.

"Damn shame. But they chose their lot, sided with the Japanese. Can't be helped if they're in the way now. I have given this a great deal of thought, I must admit. I firmly believe that once we have secured this place, we embrace the Okinawan people into some sort of protectorate, making them a part of, well . . . us. Though of course they would not be granted citizenship, anything like that. The engineers have assured me that this island can support two dozen or more airfields, and we will certainly benefit from the cooperation of the citizens here, labor and whatnot. We must also look to the future, our operations against the Japanese mainland, and even afterward. We must maintain control here, well after this war ends. This place guards our flanks, so to speak, against any aggressive acts we might encounter in the future, Russia, China, what have you."

Buckner seemed energized by his demonstration of political savvy, and Nimitz was stunned. He had no time to give Buckner a history lesson, knew that the Japanese had occupied Okinawa at their own convenience, without any friendly invitation from the Okinawan people or their civil government. But Buckner's concerns for the future of any political arrangements anywhere in the Pacific were far beyond any planning that should be going on in his own headquarters.

"General, I appreciate the gravity of thought you have given this matter, but your priorities seem to be a little out of sequence. Okinawans are dying in large numbers, many of them by the hands of the Japanese, and many from the impact of our own weaponry. Before we start inviting them to dinner, or welcoming them to the family, perhaps we should liberate them from the enemy." He saw Buckner absorbing his words as though it were an entirely new concept. "The point, General, is that before any other grand global strategies can be put into place, we must do what we can to secure this island, and hopefully, do so without *extinguishing* these people in the process. The longer we take, the more they will suffer, plain and simple. And for that matter, I'd rather not absorb any more of our own casualties than we have to."

Buckner didn't respond, and Nimitz knew this conversation needed to return to the point.

"It's good that you've found the enemy's primary position, and apparently we now understand his strategy. So, how do you plan to drive through his defenses? It seems that frontal assaults against a well-fortified enemy are . . . costly."

Vandegrift shook his head, said, "End run. Amphibious assault. The Second Marine Division is waiting on Saipan and can be mobilized within a couple of days. That's a strong, well-rested force that can come ashore in the south and set up behind the Jap positions you're facing now. Even without any element of surprise, our aircraft and naval guns will keep them in their holes. Once we're ashore on two sides of them, the enemy will be in an untenable situation. They'll have to surrender, or do one of those *blaze of glory* things. Either way, our casualty counts will be minimized."

Buckner sniffed.

"As I said, sir, we have things under control. I would prefer that the Second Marines be kept in readiness for another amphibious operation closer to mainland Japan. Admiral, you are familiar with the long-range planning. Does it not make sense to have a well-rested unit prepared to drive even closer to the enemy's homeland?" He didn't wait for a response. "With the artillery and armor we have on the ground, it is only a matter of time before we blow through the Japanese defenses. With all due respect, General, we long ago reconnoitered those landing zones, and Admiral Nimitz is very aware that it was our conclusion that those beaches are not defensible. The cost in lives could be catastrophic, and I will not participate in another fiasco like Anzio! You must certainly agree that we don't want to see the Marines taking any more casualties than necessary. General, you should be pleased that Geiger's success in the north came so easily."

Nimitz saw Vandegrift straighten in the chair, as though inflating, the blast inevitable. Nimitz waited for it, saw Vandegrift red-faced, forcing himself into composure.

"I have been in communication with General Geiger, and I know personally that the general will happily escort you through the battlegrounds on the Motobu Peninsula. I am confident that you will see that efforts made by my people were made against a scattered, well-armed enemy, who took what we gave them exactly as *they* had planned."

Buckner seemed not to care how hot Vandegrift might be.

"Yes, yes, General, with all due respect, I am well aware of the enemy's actions on Motobu. I admit that at first, we did not understand what the enemy was doing, why they were offering your Marines such a soft defense. General Geiger has reported to me that their plan was designed to draw us into some awful ground, where their small numbers were enhanced by every other advantage. It was their intention to chew us up piecemeal. Well, I'm sure we can agree that their plans didn't succeed. And our casualties there were insignificant."

Vandegrift looked at Nimitz, no softening of his anger.

"There is no such thing, General, even for a Marine. I fail to see why you object to an amphibious assault."

Buckner closed his eyes.

"I must ask you, please do not drag out this debate. It serves no purpose. It would take far too long to mobilize the Second Marines for such an attack."

Vandegrift raised his voice a notch.

"Fine. Use your own people. Unless my intelligence reports are inaccurate, much of your Seventy-seventh Infantry Division is sitting out there holding fort on those dinky little islands playing with sand castles. I heard they're a good outfit. Prove it by sending them into the south. You'll have an enormous amount of air and naval fire in support. To assume disaster is unwarranted. And, frankly, General, it is inappropriate."

Buckner rose slightly in his chair, and Nimitz knew this had to play out before he could interfere. Vandegrift was being energized by the information he was receiving from Geiger, and Nimitz knew that Geiger's Marines in the north of the island would expect to be used where the toughest fight would be. So far, that had not been the case. Vandegrift was doing exactly what his subordinate would hope, and Nimitz felt as though he was refereeing a wrestling match.

"General Vandegrift, the Seventy-seventh Division is where I need them to be, for now. Look, I understand the pride of the Marines. You have earned it, no doubt. But you must admit that the enemy forces Geiger's men faced northward were nothing like what the army divisions are facing now. At worst, your men are suffering every night through *jitter parties,* dealing with infiltrators and snipers. The heat is on down south, and the infantry has the support they need to get the job done."

Vandegrift was still red-faced.

"Your troops have been drawn into the same kind of soft defense my boys were, only you're facing the bulk of the damn Jap army! Fine, forget the Second Division. Geiger is prepared right now to shift as many units as are needed from the north as quickly as you give the order! If those men were down there, they'd be finding a way to cut past those dug-in bastards in their deep-ass caves. We've been in too many costly engagements on these islands, General, and we learned a long time ago that relying on artillery and dive-bombers to pour high explosives all over hell and gone, trying to rearrange the landscape . . . just doesn't do the job! The Japs are like moles, and they've adapted to all that steel we drop on them by lying low. When the blasting stops, they come out again. Your people should be learning that right now!"

Buckner shrugged.

"My people are learning exactly what they should be learning. We are rapidly moving the artillery into proximity to the enemy's strongest positions. Armored units are rolling into place even as we speak. But if it satisfies you, General, please know that I have already considered my options. If I feel it is necessary, I will order General Geiger to move his Marines southward, to lend a hand."

Nimitz didn't wait for the response from Vandegrift, held up a hand, said, "Enough. General Buckner, I would suggest . . ."

"Sir, forgive me, but I am not in favor of navy commanders issuing instructions as to how the army should go about its business. I deeply regret the cost the navy is suffering from the Japanese suicide assaults. Those strikes have caused us to lose two supply ships, which have contributed to our difficulties. But in time, those difficulties will be solved. The army knows its business, Admiral. Please allow me to do my job. If you order me to change my strategies, then of course, I will follow those orders. But I will vigorously protest that kind of interference." He looked hard at Nimitz, a cold blue glare. "Sir, we have the firepower in place to carry out this operation just as planned. Every day we make forward progress."

Vandegrift interrupted.

"A foot at a time."

Nimitz knew the Marine had a point. But he understood Buckner's strategy and his stubborn adherence to every piece of training he had received. It was simply the army way, move steadily forward by overwhelming the enemy with firepower. The Marines had maintained a completely opposite philosophy, that movement should be lightning quick by men on foot, and the artillery and tanks could come in afterward to clean up. Nimitz understood more clearly than ever why MacArthur mostly left the Marines out of his own picture. It was far easier doing things his own way, without having to hear dissension from his subordinates. They're both right, he thought. And, probably, both wrong. No wonder Turner hides in a bottle. He's staying the hell out of the way.

"General Vandegrift, I appreciate your frustration, but General Buckner is in command here. Your men have performed extremely well, as I expected. But the Marines cannot be the point of every sword. I know the numbers, know how much devastation we can bring to any enemy position. General Buckner, your forces are engaged with an enemy you are expected to defeat, without any more delay than necessary. Delay means casualties, as we all know. It was anticipated that Okinawa would be secured in a month. You have one week left in that timetable, and from the looks of things, you're not even close to making it." He glanced at Vandegrift, who seemed to recognize Nimitz heating up. The Marine leaned forward, clearly hanging on Nimitz's anger. "We're losing a ship or more every day to the damn kamikazes. Men are dying at sea, and men are dying on these hills. Too many men. You've got a week, General. If you can't make a significant breakthrough, I need to find someone who will."

Buckner started to protest, and Nimitz knew he had trespassed into Buckner's authority more than any army man would normally tolerate. But Nimitz could read the energy of both men, and there was just enough muggy heat in the room to light his own fuse. Even Buckner seemed to understand that there was little he could say. Nimitz tried to calm down, fought the unpleasant wetness in his clothes.

"Simply put, gentlemen, the army's difficulties in the south must be solved. I do agree with you, that our success here is only a matter of time. The problem of course . . ." He paused, studied the table in front of him, chose his words. "The problem, General Buckner, is that *time* is not measured *out here.* It is measured in Washington. And Washington is tapping its foot."

14. ADAMS

NEAR CAPE HEDO, NORTHERN OKINAWA
APRIL 28, 1945

The rain finally stopped, but the mud around him continued to ooze downward into the base of the foxhole, deepening the pool of goo beneath him. He stared at Welty, saw the same misery, but more, Welty scratching at his pant leg, futility against the constant assault from the fleas. The roads had been nearly impassable, and so today there had been no kitchen trucks. Their only alternative was K rations, and even the lieutenant had grumbled at that. It was a mystery to Adams that Welty never seemed to mind the K rations, and he watched his friend digging merrily through the boxes, picking out whatever seemed to suit his tastes at the moment. But the fleas were relentless, not even Welty's quiet cheerfulness protecting him. Adams rubbed his own legs in reflex, said, "The oil works. I'm telling you. The sarge was right."

Welty shook his head.

"I'm not wasting my gun oil. My piece is more important than any damn bugs. If this weapon doesn't fire when I need it to, it ain't gonna make much difference how many fleas are on me."

"Fine. I haven't fired at a damn thing in a week, and right now, I'd rather keep from being eaten by bugs. It'll be dark in an hour, and then the mosquitoes'll be here. I might try the oil on my face. This is about the worst damn place I've ever been."

Welty looked at him without comment, but the message in Welty's expression was familiar. *You haven't seen a damn thing yet.*

When it wasn't raining the heat returned, and when the heat gave way to sunset it was the insects. Several of the men had come down with dysentery, and the lieutenant had relayed word from above that malaria was showing itself as well. The Atabrine tablets were plentiful, along with salt tablets, sucrose tablets, and a variety of medical stations where the men could have every ailment treated. The pills were an easy remedy, and Adams was as curious as Porter had been why so many of the men bolted at the thought of swallowing a tiny pill that could prevent a miserable sickness, especially since doing so was an order. Welty devoured something from the cardboard box, crumbs on his face, looked again at Adams, a slight smile, and Adams said, "You're right, dammit. I got no reason to bitch. This hasn't been too tough, no matter what some of the others say."

Welty began scratching again, said, "I'm sick of hearing Yablonski and those other guys bellyache about how the Fourth and the Twenty-ninth got all the fun while all we did was walk. I heard Yablonski say the looey musta been a chicken since he didn't volunteer us to join those boys on that peninsula fight. Who the hell thinks like that? Stupid as hell. I don't care how much they hate the Japs, taking casualties ain't ever fun."

Welty stopped himself, seemed to withdraw, and Adams let it go, knew that Welty wouldn't talk about anything he had seen on those other places, the other fights. He seemed to focus more on the fleas, pulled up his shirt, deep red streaks on his belly.

"I'm telling you, Jack. Gun oil. Try it."

"I got a better idea. We get much more rain in this foxhole, we'll be up to our necks. That'll drown 'em. Nothing's been biting my ass since we've been sitting in this slop."

Adams shifted himself, knew he had to rise up from the mud, that his clothes were already too wet, and with the night would come the biting chill. Shivering in the darkness was bad enough as it was, the unending fear that an infiltrator would sneak up, drop a grenade in the hole.

The veterans were still speaking in low voices about the ease of the operation so far, how most of the Japanese had been wiped out without making much of a fight. The Marines were taking casualties, of course, but nothing like the commanders had expected. That message had been clear, driven home by the number of medical crews they had seen around every command post, every makeshift field hospital. Navy corpsmen were plentiful, and when there were wounded, the corpsmen had always responded with what seemed to Adams to be a complete ignorance of the danger around them. Adams had no idea how many of the medical men were supposed to be assigned to each company or battalion, but the others talked about it with surprise, that there were far more of them now than some of the men could ever recall. As the Twenty-second pressed northward, anchoring control of the northern tip of the island, Adams had marched past a number of command posts, had seen the men with the red crosses on their helmets in clusters, playing cards or, on those rare sunny days, catching naps in the sunshine. It hadn't taken any officer to explain what the men could see for themselves. The brass had expected those corpsmen and the medical staffs to be in action, far more action than they had seen. It was a strange and uneasy blessing, so many medical staffs with so little to do. Some of the newer men began to talk, all of that loud cheerleading about the Marines and their reputations, as though the Japanese had been so afraid they had scampered underground, to await their deaths in peaceful submission to the flamethrowers. Adams paid more attention to the veterans like Welty and the sergeant, others who had gathered on the northern tip of the island, happy to accept the victory that had been handed them. If the Japanese had decided not to defend Okinawa by rushing headlong into the Marine positions, no one was objecting.

Along the heights that led them northward, the land had been stunning in its beauty, a lush tropical paradise. But the beauty was erased too often by the soaking rains. With the fighting in their area almost nonexistent, Captain Bennett's company had been ordered to dig into the flat fields that overlooked a cliff, a sheer drop to the ocean below. Adams had slung the small shovel into the soft ground, staring out toward waves rolling up on soft beaches, breakers lapping across lines of coral offshore. Beyond, the ships stood guard, as they had all throughout the campaign, smaller gunboats up close, supply and mostly empty troop ships in the distance, and beyond that, the mammoth warships. In the rain the ships were hidden, but when the sun came out, as it was coming out now, the ships speckled the broad blue sea like a painting, some artist's glorious impression of war that didn't seem real. Every night there had been incidents, infiltrators sweeping through their positions. Some sought out the careless glow of a cigarette, zeroing in on chatter from the men who thought themselves safe. The infiltrators were as stealthy and as determined as they had always been, intent on killing anyone they could find, dropping a grenade or themselves into a foxhole. Others were raiding the supply and ammunition depots, some of those shot down as they sought out food or a weapon. When the Marines got lucky, when an infiltrator was taken down, the morning would bring the examination, and nothing had changed. The Japanese were ragged, unkempt men, showing signs of malnutrition or the effects of days in the wet, muddy caves. But the Marines knew that whether they came for blood or bread, the enemy's dedication to the job was absolute. Even with the northern half of the island declared secure, the Marines spent their nights in their foxholes, wary of the sounds, the shadows, cursing the vermin that swarmed out of the ground around them, or the rain that seemed to wait for those times when the men had barely found sleep. The rain seemed to pass right through the shelter halves and ponchos, and no matter how much care the men used to ward off the water, it found them anyway, every man engulfed in mud and misery.

And then it would stop, as it had stopped now. The winds had picked up, and Adams could see patches of blue sky, the clouds above him drifting away, as though shoved aside by the sun. Welty was eating something from a can, ravenous enjoyment, and Adams couldn't watch him, said, "I'm peeking out. Sun's coming out, and dammit, I'm too wet and too cold to just sit here. Maybe I can change into some new underwear before the sun goes down."

Welty shrugged, spoke through a mouthful of something brown, "Ain't been any snipers all day. Up to you."

Adams put his hand down into several inches of soft mud, pulled his soaking boots under him, stood slowly. He was surprised to see men moving around, some not in their foxholes at all. Some were gathering close to the edge of a cliff, wringing out shirts, shaking mud from ponchos, every man seeking some comfort from the sudden gift of a setting sun. He saw Porter now, the lieutenant walking quickly past, eyes focused downward. He's in a hurry to go somewhere, Adams thought. Glad I'm not an officer. Too much work.

He stood straight, stretched his back, stood waist high in the muddy hole, slung mud from his fingers, wiped them on a shirt that was muddier than his hands. To the west the sun was an enormous orange ball, the reflection spread out on the water in a great sheet of silent fire, broken only by the ships. Adams pulled himself up, sat on the edge of the foxhole, reached down for his M-1, slung it over his shoulder. He stood up, felt water running down his legs, thought, yep, clean underwear. They sure as hell better send us a supply truck up here soon. Ran out of socks this morning. He stepped toward the others, stared out past them to the sun, and Ferucci was beside him now, said, "Pretty damn impressive, ain't it? This would be a hell of a place to bring a gal. Sit up here and drink a little beer, put your arm around her waist, tell her all kinds of poetic crap. She'd melt right on the spot, give it to you without a second thought. Course, then it would rain like hell, and a flea would bite her on the ass, and you'd have hell to pay."

The sergeant laughed at his own joke, moved closer to the cliff, said something to the row of men seated there. Adams heard the sound of a jeep, looked toward the road that wound southward down the hill. All across the green hillsides, steam was rising from the great thickets of dense trees, and now he saw a fire, high above, black smoke in a heavy column, knew it had to be from one of the patrols. He thought of the flamethrower, thought, hell of a thing. Damn glad I don't have to haul that around. Gotta make you a target for sure, if the Japs see you coming. The Japs gotta know what's about to happen to 'em, and seems like most of the time they just sit tight till we burn 'em to death. I don't care how much you wanna die, that ain't the way to go.

His eyes turned back to the sea, the sun just now touching the horizon, seeming to melt like some fat wad of orange butter. He squinted, thought of Ferucci and his gal. He's probably right. But damn if I'm coming anywhere out here for a vacation. I'll settle for Albuquerque. Maybe that cute blonde, Loraine Lancaster. God, I've loved her since I was a kid. But now I've got this here uniform. "Hey, baby, how 'bout you and this big-time Marine hit the big city?" Oh yeah, you jackass, and she'll look at you like she always did, like you ain't even there. I always figured she had the hots for Jesse or some of his buddies. Any gal that special could get anybody she wanted, even the older guys. Now Jesse's home, big war hero, tough-guy paratrooper. He's probably already had her up on Lover's Hill, in one of those little caves. Damn it to hell. She won't even remember my name. That's what I get for being the little brother. He'll get the good-looking ones, and I'll have to settle for some fat waitress who spits tobacco.

He heard a hum now, far behind the hill, the noise growing into a sharp roar. Men were turning to look, and the chatter came now, unmistakable, machine gun fire. They burst into view just above the hilltop, two planes locked in a twisting duel, one tight behind the other, and he could see the markings of the lead plane, the distinct red meatball on its wings.

Men were calling out now, "A Zero! And that's a Hellcat! Get him!" "Knock the bastard down!"

Adams saw a burst of fire, the Japanese plane nosing down, straight into the water. It impacted with a fiery splash, the men responding with raised fists, salutes for the Hellcat's pilot. But now there were more planes, some much farther away. They seemed to drop down like a swarm of flies, dipping, turning, more flickers of fire as the American fighters moved among them. Adams watched in amazement, an enormous battle in the skies spreading out toward the north, past the cape. More planes came over the treetops on the hill, a new swarm, dozens, some pursued by the Americans. But many more were not, and they came down low, following the contour of the island, racing down toward the water's surface, some of them dipping in a sharp roar right past the cliff. Some of the men scrambled to their foxholes, but there were no bombs, no strafing runs. The planes ignored them, moved out to sea, some of them dropping close to the water, like schools of airborne fish. Others were much higher, barely in view, but then they began to dive, some in great sweeping arcs. As the planes moved out past the island, the American fighters did not follow. They seemed to disappear, pulling away, leaving the Japanese pilots to a new fate. He saw it now, streaks and specks of fire rising from every ship, close and far away. The men around him were returning to the cliff, no danger on the ground, the great battle now unfolding between plane and ship. The sun was nearly gone, but the fading glow still reflected off the planes, a chaotic shower of specks, dancing, swirling, all moving toward the ships. Close offshore, a smaller frigate was firing every anti-aircraft gun, the streaks erupting off the ship like some sickening fireworks display, and he saw their target now, coming down in a tight corkscrew, impacting the water closer to shore. Now another, the plane low to the water, dipping downward, coming apart, tumbling into pieces on the water's surface. They continued to come, and Adams felt a strange panic, helplessness, silence from the men around him, the awful show continuing to unfold, the Marines useless bystanders. The noise flowed past them, the thump and chatter of anti-aircraft fire, another wave of Japanese planes swarming across the sky, spreading out, seeking targets. The roar came close overhead, and he saw the plane, a steep dive, pulling up just off the beach, driving straight for the frigate. The guns on the ship poured out low, and he saw one wing suddenly breaking off, the plane rolling over, but the plane was too close to its target, and it plowed low against the waterline, a sharp blast square in the middle of the ship itself. Beside him he heard soft words, Welty, couldn't look at him, couldn't turn away from the fireball. Now the sound reached them, a hard rumble, and Adams flinched, felt the sickening knot inside his gut. There was another blast, a surprise from a plane he hadn't seen, striking the ship close to the bow. The frigate was swallowed by fire, black smoke hiding the gruesome horror. But the anti-aircraft fire from the more distant ships continued, the skies darkening with the sunset and the vast plumes of smoke. He understood now, the insane simplicity of it. The officers had talked of it, how the Americans would meet the incoming waves of planes with as many of the carrier fighters as could be launched. But the Hellcats and Wildcats and Corsairs could only do so much, and those Japanese pilots who survived the gauntlet in the air could not be pursued into the storm of anti-aircraft fire from panicky naval gunners. Many of the Japanese planes would plunge harmlessly into the water, most with pilots already dead, but even in death, some of the pilots had put their planes into a fall that would reach a target. Not even the largest and most heavily armored ships were completely immune to the shock of the explosives that had been stuffed into the Japanese planes, and so any ship that was struck suffered damage that could be fatal, if not to the ship itself, then to many of her crew. Adams stared at the burning frigate, and he felt the thickening silence, the darkness putting an end to the fight, the battle over, the waves of aircraft either fulfilling their mission or dropped into the sea. Beside him, Welty, "My God. Those sons of bitches."

Adams kept his stare on the flames, the skies now dark, the sun only a faint glow of light, the sea lit by the fires from a dozen ships.

NEAR CAPE HEDO, NORTHERN OKINAWA
MAY 2, 1945

The rains had stopped, the ground drying, the mud now turning to a fine red dust. Adams cursed, rubbed the small oily cloth over the barrel of his M-1, turned sheepishly to Welty, who said, "Yeah, fine. Here. I told you. Use only a little. The looey says we'll be getting more, but who'the hell knows when."

Adams took the small vial of gun oil, squeezed a single drop into the open breech of the rifle, rubbed the cloth in the tight circle against the steel.

"I never saw this kind of stuff before. It gets into everything."

Welty blew hard into the breech of his own M-1, said, "Coral. Like the grit on sandpaper. Plays hell with the truck engines too, the airplane engines, anything like that. The mechanics go nuts with this stuff. Don't think I'd wanna be a pilot chasing some Jap Zero while this crap is grinding my engine down to nothing."

"Jesus! Bitch bitch bitch! You ladies need a backrub, make all your little pains go away? I'll find one of the Okie gals for each of you."

Ferucci was standing over them, and Adams focused more on the rifle, pretended not to hear him. The sergeant bent low, stared at the breech of the M-1, said, "Clean it again. You must be out of practice. This damn vacation we've been on's made you careless. Then get ready to saddle up. The looey says regimental is sending us a potload of trucks. We're going for a ride."

Adams looked up, the sergeant's face framed by the piercing glare from the sun.

"We going south?"

Ferucci straightened, hands on his hips.

"We're not going *north,* you moron. Unless you wanna drive a truck off that cliff."

Welty worked the action of his rifle, said, "Guam, I bet. They're sending us back to the beach we came in on."

Others were nearby, the word *Guam* attracting attention. Yablonski came closer, the big man, Gridley behind him. Both were shirtless, and Gridley carried the BAR across his shoulder, wore the bandoliers across his bare chest, the wound from the Japanese infiltrator hidden beneath a small white bandage on his shoulder. Yablonski said, "Guam. That's what I heard too. We done the job. So they're sending us back to do some more training. Pain in the ass. Hardly saw an anthill of Japs up here, and they think we oughta rest up."

Ferucci said, "So complain to your damn congressman. Next time we'll stick you in the hottest place we can find. That make you feel better?"

"Yeah, it does. I didn't sign up to go on a Boy Scout camping trip. I still got clips they gave me on the damn transport ship. My damn piece ain't even been warmed up yet. If I don't heave a grenade at some Jap's belly, I may heave one at these two idiots. You clean that damn piece good enough, redhead?"

Welty replaced the butt of his rifle, the cleaning kit put away, looked up at Yablonski.

"You better aim that grenade where it'll do some good. Before it goes off, I'll sling this bayonet right into your damn big mouth."

"Shut the hell up, both of you!" Ferucci turned away, suddenly distracted. "What the hell? Now what?"

Adams heard the sound of a jeep, peered up over the edge of the foxhole, and Ferucci said, "That's the colonel. And Bennett."

Adams kept his eye more on Yablonski, had developed a healthy fear of the man. Yablonski moved off, back toward his foxhole, Gridley following like some oversized pet. Welty stood, watched the officers gathering, and Adams looked that way, saw three of the lieutenants joining them, Porter among them. Ferucci said, "I knew it. We're not going to Guam. They're talking about our next mission, and it ain't a camping trip. Nobody's smiling. Look, the colonel's flunky's got a map. I been thinking about this. I bet they're laying out the next assault, another island. Maybe Japan itself. We cleaned out the Japs pretty good here, and the high brass knows we didn't get chewed up too bad. They're gonna send us to Japan. I knew it!"

Welty was up now, curious, stood close beside Adams as they watched the officers, the map unrolling onto the hood of the colonel's jeep. Adams said, "Japan? You think so?"

Ferucci seemed completely sure of himself, arms folded across his chest.

"Damn right. Time to take this fight right into the Jap living room. I been waiting for this, hoped like hell I'd be a part of it. All that bitching about how we missed out, well, we're not gonna miss out now. You just wait."

Adams heard the rumble, far down the road, a cloud of red dust rising up. The trucks came into view now, a long line of deuce-and-a-halfs. The meeting of officers broke up, the colonel climbing into his jeep, moving away into the dust cloud, and the others fanned out quickly, Porter coming up the hill toward his own platoon. Adams felt a strange dread, examined the rifle with a quick glance, saw more of the fine red film on the barrel, a new layer of coral dust already sticking to the oily sheen. Dammit! Porter stopped, scanned the foxholes, said aloud, "Gather up! Keep to those rocks, but get where you can hear me! Don't bunch up. There's still some Japs in these hills, and this is no time for stupid casualties."

Adams obeyed, the others as well, some of them emerging from foxholes, some already holding backpacks, prepared for the move. Porter dropped to one knee, waited for them to gather, some squatting, sitting, finding low places that might serve as cover, cover none of them thought they'd need. Adams moved toward a fat sago palm, saw Yablonski slip into the shade before him, knew better than to object. Welty was close to the lieutenant, squatting between two low rocks, and Adams moved that way, sat, one hand on the ground, coated now with a fine grit of red.

"All right, listen up! Those trucks are taking us out of here. The whole damn division's mounting up."

"Ha! I knew it!"

The voice came from the palm tree, and Porter looked that way, annoyed.

"Shut up! You don't know jack. I've heard all the crap you idiots have been tossing around. You're expecting hula girls and cold beer. Forget it. The army's been getting their teeth kicked in down south, and the generals have decided they need us to move down there and replace them. That shouldn't surprise any of you. We knew that we'd end up with the heavy lifting, and my guess is some dumbass on some ship out there had his map upside down and sent us the wrong way. The real heat's down south, has been from the beginning. The army boys can't handle it, so you know what's gotta happen next. The First Division is already on the move, and we're going in behind them. I haven't been told exactly what they're gonna do with us, but you know damn well it's not gonna be pretty."

The trucks were pulling into a wide field, the engines shutting down, the clouds of dust pouring up the hill toward the platoon. Across the field, other platoons were getting the same briefing, loosely spaced clusters of men listening to their officers. Porter glanced toward the trucks, said, "Grab your gear and mount up. Fifteen to a truck, so we'll fill three of 'em. I'll be up front with the radio. If you need water, there's a truck coming up with some barrels. Fill 'em up. It's a long drive."

The trucks had no canopies, the dust swirling around them in suffocating clouds of heat and blinding grit. Adams had his head down, eyes closed, his helmet the only shade. Close beside him Welty did the same, and even the most vocal knew better than to open their mouths. Even if their complaints could be heard at all, the dust would find any opening, a mouthful of the crushed coral adding more misery to what was already a rumbling bouncing hell.

Adams had no idea how long they had been in the trucks, had bounced and rocked in rhythm with those around him, swaying with the turns, cursing silently when the truck hit a sharp hole. He tried to open his eyes more than once, tried again now, was surprised that the air seemed to be clearing, the dust not as bad. He felt a sharp breeze in his face, looked across to the man opposite, Gridley, the big man staring past him, his eyes ringed with white circles. More of the men raised their heads, the air clearing, and Adams saw flat fields, sugarcane, the small farms they had marched past many days ago. Beside him Welty spat a hard wad of something thick into the air, past Adams's head, stared up and over, trying to see more of where they were, the others doing the same. Adams heard a croaking voice at the back of the truck, the last man on the bench, Ferucci.

"Airfield. Maybe Yontan. We're stopping."

Adams felt the truck slow, a hard squeal of brakes, could see a sea of trucks already in place, parked in neat rows. Just as quickly the trucks at the far end of the field began to move, one after the other, the caravan resuming. The truck beneath him rumbled to life, curses rolling through the men, the usual voices, Yablonski, "What the hell? Somebody can't make up his mind?"

Adams ignored him, was more curious than angry, the truck lurching forward, following the next one in the long, snaking line. The road away from the airfield was wider, smoother than the coral trail they had endured, and he kept his gaze outward, saw another row of trucks, some with canopies, coming the other way, toward them. Beside him Welty said, "Hey, where the hell are they going?"

The truck slowed, dipped to one side, easing off the road, the entire caravan shifting over, allowing the northbound trucks to pass. Some of those trucks were covered, but others were open, and Adams could see the men now, faces peering out, as curious as he was. But there was a difference, something in the faces that seemed gloomy, lifeless. Some of the Marines began to call out, waving, simple greetings, but the greetings weren't returned, and now Ferucci said, "Army! Sure as hell! Those are ground pounders!"

The men on both benches rose up, and Adams heard the calls coming from the trucks in front, the usual hoots, insults and joking, and now the men around him began the same routine.

"Hey, doggie, doggie! Woof!"

"Too tough for you boys down here? You doggies need some *men* to take over for you?"

"Hey! You scared of those little Japs?"

The calls continued, and now the convoy moving past slowed even more, then stopped, engines still running, a jam in the traffic somewhere up ahead. Adams tried to think of his own insult, something appropriate, unique, knew that every army man everywhere was thought of as a *doggie*. The barking took over now, a chorus of insults, and through it all, he heard a voice, Ferucci.

"The Twenty-seventh! Those guys are the Twenty-seventh! You bastards!"

There was hesitation in the catcalls, some of the Marines hearing the words, comprehending. The shouting erupted again, different, far more hostile, even Welty, standing now, surprising Adams.

"You yellow sons of bitches! You no-good yellow bastards!" Welty continued, the volume of his fury growing, and after a long minute he dropped down, seemed exhausted by his own anger, repeated the words quietly. "Worthless no-good bastards. Worthless. We oughta shoot every one of them."

Adams looked at the redhead with driving curiosity, wanted to ask the question, but the shouts of the Marines stifled him. All along the caravan the wave of menace seemed to grow, furious cursing, insults and jeers. The trucks were no more than a few feet apart, and when the words were not enough, the Marines began to throw things, cartridges, pieces of scrap from the floor of the truck, anything they could find. There was nothing playful, the objects hurled with baseball precision, a rain of debris into the army trucks in a one-sided assault. Adams stared in horror, saw one face from the other truck, a quick glance outward, fear in the man's eyes. The face disappeared now, ducking low, and now the trucks began to move. Another truck crept past, canvas hiding the men, no one looking out, the shouting from the Marines still relentless. Adams felt a strange fear, thought, this is stupid. Somebody's gonna start shooting. What the hell's going on? The trucks kept moving, picking up speed, belching smoke, kicking up clouds of dust and gradually the noisy display from the Marines began to quiet. Welty seemed much more subdued than the men around him, and Adams leaned close to his ear.

"What the hell?"

"Yellow bastards. The Twenty-seventh was on Saipan. They just fell apart. Ran like hell."

Adams heard the words drift away, knew the sign, that Welty wouldn't say anything else, and Adams knew not to ask. But he was deathly curious, had heard only bits and pieces of the scuttlebutt about Saipan. He had heard the insulting descriptions for the army divisions, the Twenty-seventh in particular, had assumed the insults had been just another one of those rivalry things, all Marines giving grief to all GIs, sailors giving grief to them both. But this was different, far more intense than any rivalry. On the other side of Welty, a face leaned out, looked at Adams, the older man, Gorman.

"They're no good, pal. Worst division in the army. A lot of Marines died because of those sons of bitches. I heard Howlin' Mad had their general fired. I don't know what the hell they're doing here. They shoulda been sent to MacArthur, where they belong. If they're moving north, it's cause they screwed up again. We sure as hell don't need 'em here."

Ferucci joined in.

"Pop's right. That's gotta be why we're going south. Replacing those bastards. I bet they're either going up north or they're getting hauled out of here altogether. They do a little dirty work and some general gives them a vacation. I bet they'll sit up north and use our foxholes and slit trenches. Too lazy to dig their own."

Adams saw Porter now, the lieutenant climbing up on the back of the truck.

"You boys through acting like assholes? Listen up. Captain says we're heading down a little farther. Once these doggies get out of our way, we'll be rolling again."

Porter dropped down, was gone, hustling back to the next truck in line. The last truck in the army caravan passed by now, a swirl of dust engulfing it, the canvas pulled tightly closed. Ferucci said, "Those bastards know to keep their asses hidden. I'd like to have a little chat with General Buckner, or whoever else thought any army dogs could do this job. They probably took one mortar shell and the whole line collapsed."

The trucks rolled to life again, the road in front clear. The men rocked against one another, the bumping rhythm returning, more dust, the sun straight overhead now. They rumbled for another half hour, and then, just as before, they slowed, moving into line alongside dozens more. But this time the engines did not shut down. Adams blew the dust out of his nose, coughed it out of his throat, wiped at the grime in his eyes, saw Ferucci up, jumping down, out the rear of the truck. The others followed, filing out through the stink of exhaust, men slapping at the red dust in their clothes, and Porter was there, pulling them off the road.

"Get out this way! The company's in this field. Space out, dig in, and wait for orders!"

The lieutenant moved away to the next truck, the same instructions, and Adams dropped down off the truck, held his backpack in his hands, his rifle slung on his shoulder. He saw Ferucci eyeing him, then looking toward the others in the squad.

"All right, you heard him. Let's go."

As the trucks emptied, they moved away in a roar, the empty caravan rolling back northward. The Marines had been unloaded on a broad hill and to one side were the unmistakable signs of a distant airfield, low buildings and rows of tents, scattered patches of camouflaged netting. Around him the men moved past, most of them with heads down, still spitting out the dust of the miserable ride. Adams began to move, the hillside drawing his eye, and now he stopped, along with a half-dozen men from the truck. On the far side of the hill, away from the airfield, the hill fell away in a gentle slope a mile long, maybe more, and just as wide. To the right he could see the ocean, and southward, in the far distance, he could see a wide swath of smoke settled along another ridge. There was smoke in the deepest part of the valley as well, thin and drifting, and beneath it, the snaking line of a river.

"Move it! Dig in!"

He followed Ferucci, kept his eyes out to the long hillside, caught a smell now, carried on the soft breeze. Around him some of the men were reacting to it, a stink like nothing he had ever experienced. As they moved out into the field, the smell grew worse, the wind driving toward them from the south. The lieutenant had spread them in one section of the wide hilltop, men already digging in on the slope of the hill that faced the airfield. He moved that way, then closer to the ridgeline, the smell curling his face, sweet and bitter and sickening. He stepped up onto the highest point, could see all across the wide sloping ground, saw that the ground was churned and blasted, trees ripped to splinters, shell craters small and large.

"Let's go! Get off that ridgeline! The enemy can see these heights!"

Adams turned, saw Porter moving along the high ground, waving at him, at the others who had been as curious what lay in front of their new position. Porter moved up past him, slowed, said, "There's gonna be hell to pay, kid. Right out there . . . that's Jap-land. The party's over."

PART TWO

15. USHIJIMA

He had allowed a rancorous debate between his staff officers, unusual for someone in his position. But in the end, no matter how passionately Colonel Yahara had argued against it, Ushijima knew that, finally, he would go along with General Cho's fiery insistence on launching a significant offensive counterstrike at the Americans.

The banquet had begun late, nearly midnight, a feast to celebrate the commencement of the great battle. The display of luxury had been rare and wonderful, platters of fish and meats prepared by the Okinawan servants, supervised of course by Ushijima's own chef. Throughout the late evening, the spirits had flowed, sake and the homegrown Okinawan wines, dulling the talk, so that in the early morning the conversation among some of the staff officers had become jovial, almost giddy. The energy for that had come not only from Cho's boisterous mood but from the girls who served them, who brought the food and drink, who lingered even now, cooing with birdlike compliments for the bravery and the manliness of their Japanese masters. Most of that had been directed at General Cho, who would appreciate it more than anyone on Ushijima's staff. He had long accepted Cho's *bad habits,* mainly because he had little choice.

Ushijima had drunk far too much sake himself, but that had stopped two hours ago, when he had withdrawn from the greater festivities, returning to his private room. He sat now, his usual pose, knees bent, his feet pulled in tightly, fighting off the effects of the sake. With the attack not more than a couple of hours away, he needed clarity, a sharp mind. He pulled out his pocket watch, nearly four. His energy was returning, the effects of the partying wearing off, and he focused on the planning, on what was to come. Less than two hours, he thought. And then we shall have our say, we shall find out what kind of enemy faces us.

For several days the spies and observers had brought in word of a major shift in the American deployment. Across the southern front, many of the American infantry units had absorbed a terrific pounding from his well-fortified and perfectly camouflaged artillery. The Japanese machine gun placements, engineered by Colonel Yahara, had been brutally effective, and for the most part the American army units had made impressive assaults into positions that almost guaranteed failure. But still they had come, and slowly Ushijima had consolidated his defenses, driven back meter by meter by the infantry units he had come to respect. Cho did not share his feeling of admiration for the American tenacity, and Ushijima understood that the ploddingly slow progress of the Americans was costing their infantry enormous casualties. They do not respect death, he thought. They find no glory in sacrifice, and so they will find another way. With their resources, they will merely pull the depleted units away and replace them with fresh men who have not yet run from our guns. And that is why we must strike now. For once, General Cho is correct.

Ushijima knew that the American commanders would be agonizing over their lack of progress, that surely no American general had the stomach for such a high casualty rate. Unlike the Japanese, who fed their people only what the Imperial High Command chose to reveal, he knew that the American newspapers were sure to announce openly the kinds of losses their soldiers were suffering. It is astounding, he thought, that they believe such openness is a positive thing. War is not about truth. It is about morale and spirit and what officers can drive their men to do. The civilians have no place in such things, and the Americans can never understand that the cost of waging war is honorable death. None of their generals can withstand the pressure that will come from that. Japanese mothers are inspired by the emperor to sacrifice their sons, knowing that every death brings glory and honor. The Americans fight for . . . what? Because they hate us?

Because we humiliated them at Pearl Harbor? That kind of inspiration has no solid foundation, and so, if we kill enough of them, *their* mothers will not be so accepting. Washington does not have the power of our emperor, or our high command. They will listen to the mothers. And that is perhaps our only advantage.

Cho had insisted that the Americans were losing two thousand men every day, a number that Ushijima knew was ridiculously high, but he did nothing to correct his chief of staff, even if the bluster of that made Colonel Yahara cringe. The Americans might know how high their losses are, but surely they are listening to our communications. Someone out there might believe Cho's figures, or at least might believe it is possible. If their soldiers who kneel in mud and filth stop believing what their generals tell them, we will have won another kind of victory. We may defeat their morale. Cho's boasting is certainly improving our own. If we receive no more support from Tokyo, morale might be the only thing my army will have left.

The shift in the American position had been carefully documented, reports confirming that the battered infantry was being pulled back, especially along the western flanks. Ushijima knew that those lines were now filling with Marines who were being trucked down from the north. The first to arrive had been the Marine First Division, filling the positions vacated by the badly mauled Twenty-seventh Infantry. Directly behind the First, he knew that the Sixth Marine Division was moving into place, and it was inevitable that once those forces were in position to attack, they would. He shared the grudging respect many of his commanders felt for the Marines, knew that all throughout the Pacific island campaigns, it had mostly been Marines who had come across the beaches and crushed the Japanese defenses. Whether Tokyo acknowledged that or not didn't matter. On Okinawa his own defenses had held up well, despite being vastly outmanned by American infantry, and the toll suffered by the Americans had been deeply satisfying. It was after all his primary mission, that if his precious Thirty-second Army was to be sacrificed, they would take as many Americans with them as they could. But the butchery inflicted on the American infantry had not sent them scampering back to their ships as Cho had long predicted. With fresh troops moving in to face him, Ushijima had finally consented to Cho's wishes that the Americans be attacked in a massive show of Japanese force. Despite Colonel Yahara's passionate opposition, Ushijima had to accept Cho's logic, that with so much shifting of troops, there could be confusion and uncertainty in the American lines. There might be no better time.

A young girl appeared in his doorway, holding a tray, made a short, respectful bow. He waved her in, and she moved close, bent low, offering him a single glass of sake. He shook his head and the girl backed away, a silent exchange that had been repeated for the past couple of hours. She shuffled slowly away and he watched her, focused on her colorful floor-length dress, the slight shift of her hips, hidden by the soft silk. She has no place here, he thought. None of them. Even the nurses. If Cho's plan is a failure, this army can prepare itself for what we must do. If we fail, it will mean an inevitable withdrawal southward.

He tried to drive those thoughts from his mind, punched the side of a fist into his leg. You owe your army more confidence than this, more faith in what they can do. What is wrong with you? Is it the sake? He had tried to convince himself that Cho's counterattack would accomplish all that Cho insisted it would. But I am not a dreamer, I do not embrace fantasy. There is a simple truth to this plan. I sanctioned this attack because it will be our best opportunity, perhaps our only opportunity to extend this campaign. He saw the girl at the doorway again, holding another tray, some kind of food. He shook his head, tried not to notice how pretty she was, a small flower who was there only for him.

"You may retire. I have need of nothing further."

She bowed again, a flicker of disappointment in her eyes, disappeared into the corridor.

He felt a strange sense of pity, thought, I am not her master, I am not her sanctuary. I cannot be anything to her, to any of them, except . . . protector. Of everything that surrounds me here, the girls are most vulnerable. If our army does not succeed in driving the enemy back, this place will become far more dangerous than it is now. Whether or not these girls are innocent, whether or not they are here by choice, I will not allow them to be slaughtered alongside our soldiers.

T he ongoing disagreements among his staff had come to a noisy head on April 29, the occasion of Emperor Hirohito's birthday. The insistence on a change of strategy had been bolstered by Cho's emotional appeal that a sharp counterstrike at the enemy could be offered as a gift to the emperor that would demonstrate Ushijima's unwavering dedication. Colonel Yahara had been outraged that Cho would tie the two together, as though by waging the most logical and intelligent kind of defense against an overwhelming enemy, they were somehow insulting Japanese pride, violating sacred traditions. The arguments had risen to hot-tempered confrontations between Cho and Yahara, and it was not the first time Cho had belittled Yahara for his emphasis on defense. This time Cho expanded his arguments, even going so far as to badger Ushijima with the uselessness of Yahara's war of attrition. It had been indiscreet and insubordinate, but to Yahara's disgust, Ushijima had allowed the display, had encouraged a surprised Cho to present his plan in detail. Throughout the campaign thus far, Yahara had been the primary engineer, the colonel operating with Ushijima's blessing, both men understanding that the power the Americans brought to Okinawa could not be defeated by old ways, by what had worked in China. But Ushijima was now taking Cho's arguments to heart, not because of the absurd patriotism Cho was ramming down their throats, but because Ushijima knew that with the infusion of fresh power on the American side, the inevitability of total defeat for Ushijima's army had just been amplified. Despite Yahara's intensely effective defenses, the Americans had shown far more tenacity than Ushijima had expected, and with the sinking of the *Yamato,* Cho's arguments took on new significance. The sacrificial loss of Japan's greatest warship had been a clear sign that the Imperial Navy had made its last best effort, and in the end, that effort had been a terribly useless waste. Now, with no great battle fleets to protect the supply ships, those ships would not come at all. Despite the cheery radio messages from the Japanese mainland, Ushijima also understood that the only air support his men would receive would come from the *Divine Wind* flights. Operation Floating Chrysanthemum had certainly wounded a number of American ships, but thus far, despite all the mindless optimism from the mainland, the suicide planes had done nothing to drive away the enormous American fleet.

Ushijima had finally silenced Yahara's protests by pointing out that Cho's arguments carried an unusual amount of military logic. A sudden counterattack would certainly catch the Americans completely by surprise. The results could be spectacular, an all-out strike that might so shred the American positions that they would have no choice but to retreat. Cho's song had not changed, the man still believing that kind of retreat would take the Americans all the way back to their ships. But Ushijima had finally allowed himself to be convinced that if this fight had an inevitable outcome, his duty lay in the most effective way he could damage the enemy. If the Americans could be thrown into chaos by a sudden counterattack, it would buy precious time. The longer the campaign, the greater the number of American casualties. Ushijima knew that, ultimately, those casualties were the only gift he could hope to offer the emperor.

It would not be a mindless banzai attack. There was a plan, carefully structured, and despite Yahara's grumblings, Ushijima had demanded his participation. Yahara was the best strategist in his army, and if the colonel did not believe in the plan, he was still obligated by duty and Ushijima's order to help carry it out. For four days the troops had been prepared, the artillery furnished with as much ammunition as could be gathered, Japanese tanks put into position for the most effective strike they could launch. As the time drew closer, Ushijima had allowed himself some optimism, had accepted Cho's suggestion for the banquet celebration as a tribute to the men who would put this plan into motion. For once Cho's fire had warmed Ushijima to the possibility of success.

He glanced again at his watch. It could work, he thought. It is all we can do, and so it must work. Even Yahara will celebrate our success, will understand that sometimes we must do the outrageous, throw our sound, sensible strategies to the winds and do the unpredictable, the reckless. If it does not work . . . we are no worse off.

"Ah, General, here you are! You should come out and see these girls do their dance. I offer credit to the Okinawans. They show remarkable . . . um . . . flexibility."

Cho's shirt was partially open, his uniform a sloppy mess. He staggered slightly, steadied himself against the wooden beams that framed Ushijima's doorway.

"I am quite satisfied to remain here. Thank you."

"Oh, come, come, General! A little revelry is a wonderful tonic! And tomorrow there will be celebration like we have not yet seen! Victory is in the wind, I feel it! I smell it." He hesitated, laughed, his knees giving way for a brief second. He tossed a wink toward Ushijima. "I have *tasted* it!" His laughter continued, and Ushijima smelled the party in the man's clothes, perfume and alcohol, had all he could take.

"Please return to your revelries. I am fine here. I would rather sit alone, for now."

Cho shrugged, sagged against the timbers.

"If you insist, sir. But we shall soon toast the emperor in his palace! There will be medals and gifts for us all. You will see! Ask your Colonel Ya-hara, the soft little man with all those papers. He will tell you, he will go behind my back as he always has, and he will tell you that I stood tall in front of my men and told them that I have wagered my life on their suc-cess! Victory is assured!"

Cho half fell back out of the doorway, disappeared into a chorus of happy calls. Ushijima closed his eyes, blew out a breath, tried to cleanse himself of Cho's odor. A girl staggered past the doorway, stopped, seemed as inebriated as Cho, said something he couldn't understand, a slur of words, then staggered away. I should not have allowed this, he thought. This is not a celebration, it is debauchery, and no matter what Cho says, the emperor would not find this appealing at all. He had nearly recovered from the effects of the sake, felt a wave of sadness. What we have done tonight is celebrate a *plan*. And if it is a good plan, then we shall die a lit-tle later. If it is a bad plan . . . then it will not matter. It is all we can do.

The artillery barrage began at four-fifty in the morning, a cascade of shells into the American position that was met at first by return fire from the American ships. But the Japanese guns did not do as they had done every day before. They did not fire a quick burst and then slide back into their holes. The guns stayed put, kept up their fire in a torrent of steel that caught the Americans by complete surprise. After more than an hour, the fire subsided, many of the guns exhausting their ammunition. But many more were silenced by the very act of keeping up their assaults. With the big guns staying outside the protection of their hiding places, their muzzle blasts offered the naval ships clear targets, and so frustrated Amer-ican gunners suddenly had an opportunity they had never expected. For Ushijima's artillery, the results were a disaster. Guided first by the flashes of fire, and then by the awakening daylight, the Americans pinpointed their targets so effectively that a majority of the largest artillery pieces were com-pletely destroyed. All across the rugged hillsides, so much of the Japanese firepower that had devastated the American ground forces was now oblit-erated.

The same was true for the Japanese armor. The Japanese tanks were primitive compared to the Shermans, but any tank can be a deadly threat

to ground troops. As the Americans hunkered low in their foxholes, enduring the shelling from Japanese artillery, the Japanese tanks rolled forward
to do their damage as well. But outside their cleverly designed cover, crossing open ground, they were no match for American anti-tank weapons,
aided by more of the navy's accurate fire. In a matter of hours, the bulk of
Japanese armor charged with leading the counterattack had been destroyed.

As the Americans scrambled to react to the surprising change in Japanese tactics, the Japanese ground troops began their assault. At first daylight waves of men emerged from their perfect camouflage and swarmed
headlong into the American positions. A few of the advances by individual
regiments were effective, punching holes in the American lines, driving past
stunned and panicked troops, pushing into supply depots and rear echelon
positions. But those successes were few. As the Japanese troops rushed
headlong into the guns of the Americans, most of them met the same fate
as their armor. Entire units were virtually wiped out. Despite the enormous losses, the Japanese pushed forward for a full day and into the night.
The next morning what was left of the Japanese offensive forces obeyed
their officers, who obeyed the plan given them by General Cho. They attacked again. Though the tenacity of the Japanese impressed the Americans who faced them, the outcome was never in doubt.

BENEATH SHURI CASTLE,
THIRTY-SECOND ARMY HEADQUARTERS, OKINAWA
MAY 5, 1945

He read the latest report, Yahara standing close, impatient.

"It is a disaster, sir! Here, look! Captain Oka reports his troops are
completely surrounded. He does not expect to survive. It is the same in
every part of the field. You must stop this!"

Ushijima looked at Yahara, a stern glare.

"You do not tell me what I must do."

Yahara lowered his head.

"No, certainly not, General. Please forgive me."

Ushijima looked at the others, the men standing alongside the map,
no one speaking. The gloom was in all of them, the men who knew the reports, whose job it was to record the progress of the attack on the great
map. But the men had been silent for some time now, nothing on the maps
for them to change.

"Where is Cho?"

One of the aides close to the doorway said, "I will summon him, sir."

"Yes, summon him." He did not look at Yahara, said, "Return to your office. I will call for you shortly."

Yahara made a quick short bow, was gone without a word. Ushijima saw the expectant looks on the faces of the aides, said, "I shall be in my room. When General Cho arrives, send him to me."

"Yes, sir."

He moved out into the corridor, slipped quickly into his room, hesitated, leaned his back against the wood that lined his earthen walls. A hard knot rose in his throat, choking away the air, and he fought it, straightened, stretched, forced air into his lungs. He felt dizziness, pulled himself away from the wall, reached down, settled on the mat on the floor, his usual place. I need water, he thought. He knew the servants would hear him, but the words did not come, and he scolded himself, no, do not bother them. You should be made to suffer for this. Do not bother anyone. They all know what this day means.

"Sir! You sent for me?"

Cho stood stiffly in the doorway, and Ushijima said, "You were not in your office."

"No. I was at the mouth of the great cave. The radio there continues to send in reports, though most of the reporting stations have been lost. So, General, is it time for us all to die?"

There was a strange levity in Cho's voice, and Ushijima looked at him, saw the hint of a smile, said, "You are aware that we have not been successful?"

"I know our situation, General. If this is to be the end, then it is ordained for us to die together. I welcome my place at the great shrine. I have done my best for the emperor."

Ushijima understood now, thought, so, he is abdicating any responsibility for our failures. This was all part of his glorious plan.

"General Cho, despite your eagerness to join your ancestors, I am not yet ready to die. There is still a fight to be had here, a duty to perform."

"If you insist, sir."

"I do insist. Return to your office. Remain there until I summon you again. I want you close, in the event our situation requires some immediate action."

"Of course, sir."

Ushijima heard the sarcasm in Cho's show of obedience. He was gone now, and Ushijima felt the anger, Cho's smugness digging into him. He tried to relax, stared at the bare floor, took several long breaths. The lump in his throat was growing, a pain in his chest, and he clenched his fists, no! I will not be a *victim* of this disaster! He continued to breathe heavily, the pain subsiding. Outside there were voices, and he waited, knew someone would appear. It was Yahara.

"Sir, we have received a report from Colonel Kujima. He has been forced to withdraw from his forward position. He claims he has no choice but to return to his original position."

Ushijima thought of Kujima, another of the academy graduates.

"He is a good man. If he has withdrawn it is because it was the right thing to do. I will find no fault with him. With any of them. But this must end." He paused, thought of Cho, the man's eagerness to throw himself into the glorious abyss. No, I will not make it so easy for him. His plan did not work, but, still, he cannot be embarrassed. He would lose his effectiveness as a commander.

"Colonel Yahara, as you predicted, this offensive has been a total failure. Your judgment was correct. I am determined to stop this. You will see that my order to every field commander is communicated in the most effective way possible. I am ordering a . . . temporary halt to the offensive." He paused, saw the undisguised anger on Yahara's face. "You have been frustrated because you believe I have not used your talents wisely. In that you are correct. Sometimes a man in my position must do the unwise, in the hopes of a positive outcome. But I do not wish this army to commit meaningless suicide."

Nothing in his words calmed the anger in Yahara's eyes. He knew how valuable Yahara was, felt suddenly like the father who has disappointed the son. He avoided Yahara's stare, said in a low voice, "What else would you have me do?"

Yahara did not respond, and Ushijima felt a sudden wave of emotion, tears in his eyes, the hard shell cracking for just a brief moment. He lowered his head, tried to hide it, said nothing for a long minute. Yahara waited patiently, and Ushijima felt the control returning.

"Our main force is largely spent. But our fighting strength remains. This army is loyal and dedicated to our cause. If we must, we will withdraw to the southernmost hills and make our final stand there. I will require your assistance, Colonel. Your logistical skills will be crucial. Do you understand?"

"I do, sir."

There was cold in Yahara's words, and Ushijima still avoided his stare.

"I want you to see to our position as it stands now, and draw in our lines to the best possible defense. The Americans will come again, and this time they know we are wounded. Make the best use of those assets we have, most especially this ground."

"I understand, sir."

"Is General Cho in his office?"

"I just saw him, yes, sir."

Ushijima nodded, knew that Cho's proximity meant that he had heard everything Ushijima had just said. He glanced that way, toward the wall, thought, he is standing close, making sure he misses nothing. Good.

"I am not ready to end this fight, Colonel. I was sent here with specific orders that we not destroy this army by engaging in one massive suicidal charge. Those kinds of attacks are no longer appropriate, and as you know, they do nothing at all to bring victory." He raised his voice, aimed the words at the ears of Cho. "A *military* victory." He paused. "We have one duty now, to kill as many of the enemy as it is possible to kill. I am count-ing on you to see that we accomplish that."

"I understand, sir."

There was a commotion behind Yahara, an aide, holding a piece of paper. The man seemed agitated, excited, and Ushijima said, "What is it?"

The man stepped into the room, tried to hold himself at attention, his energy making that impossible.

"Here, sir! A message has just come through from the Imperial High Command."

"What is it, Lieutenant?"

The man held out the folded paper, and Yahara took it, passed it on to Ushijima without looking at it. Ushijima opened the paper, read.

The Imperial Command informs General Ushijima that the Imperial Air Force is prepared to launch a glorious assault against the Americans who now threaten your position. Our glorious emperor has been advised of this plan and has expressed his complete confidence to General Ushijima that this attack will utterly destroy the American fleet. General Ushijima

is ordered to hold fast to his position of strength on Okinawa and continue to inflict devastating losses to our enemies. Success is assured.

He stared at the message, the characters blurring, felt the tears returning, a mix of sadness and overwhelming anger. He crumpled the paper in
his hands, threw it hard against the wall.

16. ADAMS

The rains had come again the day before, and with so much of the vegetation and clusters of trees already destroyed, the ground and the roads that cut through the countryside were becoming a sea of deepening mud. The Sixth had advanced southward into an area vacated by the First Division, those Marines moving more to the east. Beyond the east flank of the First, two of the American army divisions, the Seventy-seventh and Ninety-sixth, held the ground all the way to the far coast. There had been more griping about that, so many of the Marines insultingly dismissive of the army's work, but the infantry who stood beside them had nothing to be embarrassed about. Throughout May 4 and 5, the unexpected Japanese counterattack had been directed mostly into army positions, and despite low expectations from the Marines, the army had held their ground with as much ruthlessness as the Marines themselves. No one in the front lines knew how badly the Japanese had spent themselves, and how many more of the enemy still waited in their hiding places among the low hills. But the army units were just as prepared to resume their forward advance as the fresher Marines who had moved in alongside them.

The truck was sliding, tilting to the right, then farther still, the men on the high side tumbling over, falling into the men whose backs were now to the ground.

"Get out! Move it!"

He saw Porter yelling the order from outside, the lieutenant standing in knee-deep mud. No one had to be told twice, the truck balanced precariously with two wheels completely buried. They bailed out as quickly as each man could move, some stumbling, backpacks and weapons hitting the mushy ground. Immediately they were engulfed by another horror, the rain and mud blanketed by a pungent stink, the smell of the earth revealing some hint of what lay hidden beneath it. Adams felt his face curling up, fighting the smell, far worse than before, others reacting as well. But he saw the lieutenant high-stepping through the mud as quickly as he could, waving his arms.

"There! That shallow dip. Get there! Now!"

The men flowed clumsily away from the trucks, Adams aware of the urgency in Porter's order, and he saw the lieutenant staring away, down another long hillside. Even in the driving rain, Adams could see men dug in everywhere, the soft ground pockmarked by foxholes and narrow trenches. In the shallow bowl where Porter had sent them, other men were waving them on, officers certainly, anonymous in their ponchos. But the authority was there, the men who *knew something,* who were assigning Porter's platoon and the rest of Bennett's company to a place where they could dig their own holes. Adams felt the mud pulling at his boots, tried to keep his balance, stepped as quickly as he could. He heard a new sound now, a sharp rip in the air above him, the shell impacting off to the left, near some of the men on the far flank. The shell didn't explode with much vigor, the blast throwing up more mud than fire, but the men close to the blast reacted as any man would, diving headlong into the miserable slop. The rumble from the artillery reached them, their pace picking up, the boots trudging as quickly as they could through the vast sea of oozing ground they had been assigned to.

"Dig in!"

Porter dropped down, obeying his own order, his walkie-talkie man cutting into the mud with the small shovel. Adams saw Welty, already working at the soft goo at their feet, and Welty said, "Here! Come on! Dig!"

Another crack split the air, two more to one side, shells striking the hillside behind them, near the trucks. Adams ducked, useless instinct, and Ferucci was there, moving past, his own shovel in his hand.

"Dig! No cover up here! They're looking at us, you jackass!"

Adams swung his shovel down like a pickax, but the angled blade just sank into the mud, nothing like the rugged coral they had chopped through before.

"Straighten it out! Dig!"

Welty seemed furious, and Adams felt immensely stupid, fumbled with the shovel's head, loosening the clamp, straightening the blade, the shovel now . . . a shovel. He began to scoop the mud, tossing it to one side, another scoop, the slop filling the hole as quickly as he could clear it away. Welty was doing the same, manic motion, another shell coming down fifty yards in front of them, the hillside erupting into a bright flash, a wall of brown goo coming down around them. Adams felt his heart screaming in his chest, worked the shovel, gradually the hole deepening, the softer ground hardening the deeper they went. The hole began to take shape, deepening further, Welty now down inside, punching the ground with the small blade, Adams kneeling on one knee, the poncho billowing out in a gust of wind, no protection at all, the rain blowing hard into his face. There were more shells coming in, some bursting high above, flashes of fire in the dark rain. Others came down straight into the mire, throwing up more curtains of mud. Welty yelled at him, "Get down here! Help me!"

Adams dropped down, the bottom of the foxhole already filling with water, softening, easier to dig. Adams tried to find room for his own shovel, worked in rhythm with Welty, digging while Welty tossed away the dirt. The hole was almost waist deep, both men struggling, the mud seeping in, but not as quickly as they tossed it out. Adams worked as rapidly as Welty's movements allowed, let himself be guided by the redhead's speed, and soon the hole was more than belly deep. Deep enough.

Welty jerked at his backpack, shouted at him, "Shelter half! Try to spread it out over the hole! Come on, you know how to do this!"

Adams pulled his slab of canvas from his pack, unrolled it, felt water running down his neck and back. He did as Welty did, anchored the corners of the shelter half on either side of the hole, saw a rock lodged in the

mud, reached out, pulled it onto one corner of the canvas, searched frantically for another. But the ground had hidden anything on the surface, and
he mimicked Welty, the man scooping a mound of mud onto the other
corner of the shelter, the best they could do. The canvas was across the hole
now, overlapping in the center, and Adams knew it wouldn't hold, that the
rain would simply flow right into the sagging center.

"We need a tent pole, anything."

"You see any damn tent poles?"

Adams felt stupid again, glanced at his rifle, useless, too short, and he
didn't want the barrel in the mud, or filling up with water. Welty sat at one
end of the rectangular hole and Adams dropped down, facing him, both
men exhausted. Adams fought for his breath, tried to slide the poncho beneath him, some protection from the muddy bottom, but he was already
soaked, his dungarees thick with the filthy water. Above them the shelter
halves were sagging low, water pouring through in steady streams. Adams
shifted his position, tried to avoid a rivulet that came down on his legs,
splattering against his boots. He looked at Welty, hoped to see a smile, the
man's calm humor reassuring. But Welty had his head down, his eyes hidden by his helmet, water dripping off the brim. Adams felt a thump in the
ground, knew it had to be an artillery shell. More came in now, the soft
sides of the foxhole shaking, mud tumbling in around their legs. He heard
voices, distant, urgent, tried to hear . . . who? But the words were swept
away by the wind and rain, and Welty did not move.

"Did you hear that? Somebody might be hit."

Welty raised his head, his eyes peering out toward him from beneath
the helmet.

"Yep. Artillery attack. That's what happens. We're safer right here than
anyplace out there. You crawl out there and you'll catch hell from the
looey, I promise you. Just pray for luck. We'll be okay unless a Jap shell
comes down right on top of us. If that happens . . . well, it won't matter
much."

Welty seemed resigned, his strange calm returning, and Adams said,
"What do we do now? I'm cold. Damn! You smell that? What stinks so
bad?"

Welty looked at him with a tilt of his head.

"Don't think about that. No telling what's in this mud. The cold'll get
worse. What we do now is . . . wait. They need us to move, they'll let us
know. That's what officers are for. The looey's as miserable as we are."

Adams looked at the side of the foxhole, close to his face, the mud oozing downward, the smells engulfing him. The question rolled through his
brain. What's in the mud? Oh God. Dead Japs. He wanted to ask, felt stupid again, no, keep your mouth shut. If it's dead Japs . . . maybe the rain
will help. God, maybe it won't.

He shivered again, felt the water deepening beneath him. He kept his
stare on the mud close to his face, thought, blood? That stink . . . gotta be
something dead. How long we gotta sit here and just do nothing? I'd rather
be up there marching, maybe shooting at somebody than just sitting here.
He clamped his arms in tight, trying to push heat through them, useless,
the shivering growing worse, the smells sickening, images of dead bodies.
He closed his eyes, tried to think of anything else, any distraction, but the
first image he couldn't erase was the dead sniper, and then the men with
the flamethrowers, roasting the enemy in their caves. God, how much
worse can this get, anyway? This place . . . who the hell picked this place
to fight over? He opened his eyes, saw mud flowing onto his legs, slowly
burying him. He jerked his knees toward him, wiped at the mud with his
hands, looked at it, the shivering coming from fear, a stab of nausea. Across
from him, Welty pulled at his backpack, said, "How 'bout some stew?"

They were on the move again, this time on foot, no truck able to nav-
igate the deep mud of the trails, none daring to move across the
open ground. Some had tried to use the primary roads, and Adams had
passed by them, watching the engineers at work, bulldozers extricating
mired vehicles from mud that seemed hip deep. In front of them the Japanese artillery was peppering another open hilltop, but the near side of the
ridge was cut with limestone gullies, large rocks scattered about, thickets of
brush. It was excellent cover, and Adams could see clearly that the river of
mud led them straight toward that hillside.

There had been no briefing, no senior officer telling them where they
were going, what the plan might be. The lieutenant knew more than they
did, of course, whether through the walkie-talkie or word from a runner,
one of the amazingly unfortunate men who had to move quickly across all
kinds of open ground just to pass some command to the frontline officers.
Runners were labeled the *suicide squad,* their life expectancy in battle as
bad as the lieutenants who were supposed to lead their men into every assault. If the runners had one advantage, it came from a lack of a shovel.

They rarely stayed in one place long enough to worry about digging a fox-hole.

The march had begun with a hard shout from Porter to move up out of the soggy protection of their foxholes. Once the men had emerged, a sea of dull green shapes, Adams had seen the lieutenant hurry away toward a huddle of other men who were sheltered by the shadow of a tank. The tank had seemed unoccupied, quiet and still, its treads half buried, but when the brief meeting had ended, two of the anonymous poncho-covered men had crawled up on the turret, and with a smoky belch the tank had come to life, churning frantically, its riders barely able to hang on. But that tank was long gone, and to Adams's dismay, it had gone in the opposite direc-tion from where they slogged their way now.

The flashes of artillery fire still came toward them, but there was no precision, the patterns brief, scattered. It was like before, and Adams had heard enough to know that the bigger guns were probably firing in single shots, then disappearing back into their hiding places. The shells that came down within sight were mostly ineffective, the mud and driving rain keep-ing the artillery from igniting any fires, the thunder from the impacts mostly muffled. But no one slowed to watch, the entire company moving up as quickly as they could into this new cover, the ravines and rocks, men spreading out, guided by more men in ponchos, no one showing a face. Adams began to climb, put one hand on a fat wet rock, pushed himself up a steep slick path. Men were closing in behind him, no one paying atten-tion to the order to keep their distance, the five-yard rule forgotten, at least for now. The rocks were the first real cover they had seen since the trucks had pulled away, every man searching for his own bit of safety.

He glanced upward toward the crest of the hill, a mistake, rain and sweat in his eyes, a small flood washing down his neck. But he had seen men up there, faceless helmets staring down at them, dug into the rocks and thickets of brush. Close in front he saw one man pointing out to the side, a glimpse of the man's face. Porter.

"Move out that way! Find some cover. Use your shelter halves, or dig in if you can!"

Adams slipped up close to an embankment, the ledge above jutting out over his head, sat, cradling his rifle across his knees. Others were mov-ing close against the same rock face, sitting, some moving farther on, dragged by someone else's order. He saw Welty moving down into a low place in the rocks, heard a shout coming up from the crevice.

"Find your own damn hole!"

Adams knew the voice, Yablonski, and Adams watched as Welty backed away, stared into the low place with a look that spoke of pure exhaustion, and no patience at all. Adams called out, "Over here! Good spot!"

Welty seemed to hesitate, and Adams started to call again, but a shock jolted him, rocks showering down, a deafening blast that raised him off the ground. He stared toward Welty with wide-eyed horror, crawled out toward him, the smoke clearing quickly, driven away by the rain. He saw Welty still standing, staring back at him. Others were calling out now, Ferucci, "Get your ass down!"

Welty staggered forward, seemed to see Adams for the first time, scampered quickly now, dropped down hard against the rock face. Adams grabbed him, said, "You okay? God, I thought you were blown to hell!"

Welty nodded furiously.

"Me too." He held up both his arms, seemed to do an examination, flexed his fingers, slapped both his legs, put one hand on his crotch. "Son of a bitch. They missed me."

"Not by much! Good God, that shell hit right above you!"

"Yeah. I heard it. Guess this was my lucky day."

Porter was there now, wet and furious.

"Shut up! I need ten men! Where's Ferucci?"

"Here!"

"Gather up your squad. Bennett's up above us, needs a little firepower to go along. Where's a BAR?"

"Here!"

Gridley rose up from Yablonski's hole, Gorman beside him, and Adams could see the tension in Porter's face, a manic flow of words.

"Good. Ferucci, get your men together, and follow me up that path to the right. Bennett's up there. No talking, keep your damn heads down. The Japs know we're here. The First has had boys up here for two days, and they're pulling out, leaving this hill to us. But the Japs only know that we've got people all over this place, and they're not happy about it. We're watching them just like they're watching us. First man in this platoon gets his brains blown out gets a kick in the ass."

Adams saw no hint of a smile from Porter, the odd joke nonsensical, spoken by a man who was anxious, as nervous as Adams had ever seen him. *Afraid.* Porter watched as the men moved closer, said, "Ballard! Your squad hold back, give us fifty yards, then follow. Mortensen! Follow Ballard. Fifty yards. Got it?"

Adams didn't know where the other sergeants were, knew only that close to him the ragged hillside was alive with men, every rock, every nook now in motion. Farther back, out in the muddy flat ground, he could see more men, some digging in, a squad of tanks plowing through the deep mud. Trucks were there as well, some struggling to move on what was left of the road, others buried up beyond their axles.

"We're way the hell up."

His words came out unexpectedly, and beside him, Welty said, "Yeah. Great view of hell. You bring a picnic? Good vacation spot."

"Shut up, you morons! Let's go!"

Adams followed the sergeant, saw Porter already moving up ahead through the rocks. The trail was no trail at all, just a slick wet gap that wound in a snaking path toward the top of the ridge. Adams did as the others in front of him, stayed low, tried to keep his head below the tops of the rocks. There were open gaps along the way, and he caught the stink of explosives, saw patches of gray and black, rocks splintered into small shards. He climbed up past another black smear in the rock, a flat dishlike depression, his eyes caught by something new, something that didn't belong. It was a helmet, one side smashed, a hole ripped through the top. He forced himself not to stare at it, knew it was American, put a hand on his own helmet, pressing it down, foolish instinct. Some of the men had thrown their helmets away, ridding themselves of one more encumbrance, along with the gas masks and snake leggings. Stupid, he thought. Stupid as hell. But . . . well, that one didn't work too well. Not getting rid of mine though. Never.

The path began to spread out, the larger rocks behind him, the hill cresting into a narrow plain, thick grass, deep cuts, bare ground washed white by the rain. Porter was squatting, moving them out to one side with a wave, motioning them to lie flat. Another man moved past, ignored the lieutenant's signal, and Adams saw the poncho, glistening wet, no smears of mud, no dirt at all. He moved right past the lieutenant, seemed to ignore him completely. New man, Adams thought. Or an officer. *Brass.* Adams found a small depression in the thick grass, hard rocky ground, no puddle, lay down. But he kept his head where he could see the officer, saw more men gathering, a low table-like rock. He could see the faces now, Captain Bennett, the new man, older, another coming up quickly, another clean poncho. Porter and the other lieutenants seemed to hold back, keeping their distance, but Bennett spoke to them all, his voice audible in the hiss of the rain.

"There it is, boys. Right below us. What do you think, sir?"

Adams cringed at the word, *sir,* but the men were on top of an enormous flat-topped hill, and he glanced around, thought, unlikely as hell any Japs can hear him. I guess the orders don't apply to captains. The older officer pulled a pair of binoculars from his jacket, moved forward on his stomach, shoved his way through thick grass, glasses downward. He turned back toward the others, slid closer through the grass, said, "We sent foot patrols out last night. They found what I expected, that the bridge is mostly blown to hell, and the river along that span is about four or five feet deep, soft silt, but fordable. The span will never support a tank, and likely not even a supply truck. They're hoping we'll try to use it, and you can bet every gun on that far hill is trained on it. So we'll build another one, just downstream. We won't need more than a footbridge for now, to get some of your men across, and they can wade if the Japs make it hot. After dark my men will slip down there and do our part of the job. I'll call for a covering force to keep an eye on us, in case the Japs decide to go night hunting. By early tomorrow morning you should be able to cross over. But there's almost no cover anywhere close to the river, so don't delay. Get your men out there well before daylight. My engineers will keep recon officers on this side and give you as much help as we can. We'll build more bridges for the armor as quickly as we can, but your objective is to get the hell over to the other side, and establish a bridgehead. I'll radio back to Colonel Schneider. He's given me the authority to put my people in the water, and once we're done I'll pass the word to him. You should get his order to cross as soon as my people are back onshore. Can't waste time. Even if the Japs don't know we're coming across, by dawn they'll see that footbridge and try to blow hell out of it. You'll have to get over pretty quick."

Adams saw Bennett nodding, "I've been told that, yes, sir."

The engineer turned again toward the river, the binoculars coming up once more. Bennett said, "Sir, I wouldn't do that too often. Binoculars draw fire. Even in this mess, the enemy snipers can catch a reflection. Any glimpse of something like that on this ridgeline could . . . um . . ."

The binoculars dropped, and Adams saw the older man's face, a hard frown.

"I know my job, Captain. Your concern is noted, but I've been staring at Jap positions for a month now. I'll do my job, you do yours."

"Of course, sir."

The engineer didn't linger, no more conversation. He slid past Adams on his backside, then stood in the rocks below, disappeared quickly down the hill, another man following close behind him. Adams felt impressed, thought, yep, engineer. Gotta know his stuff, for sure. He felt movement at his feet, saw Welty slipping up beside him.

"That's Colonel Wakeman, I think. Saw his men do some pretty keen work on Saipan. I couldn't hear them. What's the hot dope?"

"They're gonna build a bridge. I guess the river is pretty close to us."

Welty seemed to chew on the words, put his face down, said nothing.

Porter slid down near them now, scanned the men closest to him, pointed toward a man to one side, Ferucci.

"Let's move back down, Sergeant. Engineers have some work to do, and we need to be ready to move out in short order. Find good cover in those rocks and gullies in case the Japs open up on us again. Make sure your men get some rest, eat something. It'll be a short night."

Porter moved off in a low crouch, and Adams felt the lieutenant's excitement, felt it himself. One word rolled through his brain, a *mission*. Finally! Something to do, something more useful than sitting in a mud hole. He knew what was coming next, Ferucci's barking command, and he started to move back along the pathway. But Welty didn't follow, and Adams stopped, tapped Welty's leg.

"Let's go. Gotta find a good spot to spend the night."

Welty looked at him, and Adams saw a gray mask of dread, anger on Welty's wet face.

"What's wrong?"

"Are you stupid or something?" Adams was mystified, didn't know what to say. "That engineer colonel . . . his men are gonna build a bridge? That means we're up here for one reason. We're gonna cross the river."

Ferucci moved up close, slapped Adams on the back.

"Right. That's why we're here. Japs ain't on this side, they're over there. It's our job to go get 'em."

Adams felt a rush of exhilaration, said, "Yeah! Right! About damn time we can bust up some Japs instead of everybody else getting all the fun!"

Ferucci stared at him, unsmiling, then looked at Welty.

"I keep forgetting, he hasn't done much of this before. Tell you what, Adams. When it comes time to hit that water, you can be the first one in."

17. ADAMS

He had seen the engineers and their work crews moving out, disguised by the wet darkness. The rains had still not subsided, but there was no time now for sitting in muddy foxholes. Despite the dense mire of the flooded roads, fresh supplies had reached the hill. But the trucks stayed far back, would not risk either the mud or Japanese artillery. Instead the supplies were carried forward on foot, men hauling crates of grenades, rations, and fresh ammunition on their backs. Every man in the company was encouraged to grab as many grenades as he could carry, the word passing throughout the Twenty-second Regiment that the soldiers and Marines who had first confronted the enemy in these hills had spent more time lobbing grenades than firing their rifles.

Even with supplies coming to them, the officers sent their own men back along the same muddy trails, concerned that a few boxes of K rations wouldn't support men who were about to cross a river that would in effect cut off their lifeline. Adams had gone back, along with several of the others, on orders from Captain Bennett that the company load up on anything the trucks had brought close, including the desperately needed drinking water. Adams had hauled a cluster of canteens, had made his way along a faintly marked trail, guided by hidden voices, whispers, the supply officers seemingly more frightened of Japanese snipers than were the Marines who actually faced the snipers on the front lines. The canteens had been filled beneath a camouflaged tent, which shielded a half-dozen drums of fresh water, steel barrels that had been rolled into the mud off the back of a truck that was still there, hopelessly bogged down, the driver cursing every drop of rain that kept him away from the dry tents of his supply depot. Adams had done his job, filling the canteens to the top, had tried his best to ignore the bitching of the supply troops who had sacrificed little more than a pair of dry socks. But there were more rants to come. Finding his way once more through the absurd rivers of mud, he had reached his own platoon. Almost immediately, as the canteens were passed out to anxious, thirsty men, there came a new round of curses, directed at Adams himself. As soon as the canteens were raised, the water was spat out, some of it directly on Adams. He had been baffled, stunned at the response, but then, even in the rain, the smell of the water on his uniform had given him a clue. With furious amazement he had tasted the water himself, his full canteen giving off the same odor. Like the others, he couldn't swallow, the pungent taste revealing what the others had quickly learned. Speculation ran wild, that there had been sabotage, that the Japanese had succeeded somehow in poisoning the water supply. It took the experience of the men like Porter, who realized with perfect dread that what the men were drinking had come from drums that had once held oil, drums that, for reasons no one could fathom, were not cleaned before they were filled with water. Porter reassured his men, as did the other officers across the dismal muddy hills, hundreds of men who now had to rely on their canteens regardless of how awful the water could be. It wasn't completely poisonous after all, just disgusting. But it was all they would have until new drums could be brought forward, until new supply trucks could slog their way through the mud that was deepening every hour. Word was passed back by the runners, radioed by furious line officers, and somewhere a supply officer finally got the word. But for the men who waited in the rain, who sat in the mud and stinking filth of a churned-up battlefield, the fury was complete. If there had been any way for the men to find that supply officer, oil would have been the least of his worries.

NORTH OF THE ASA KAWA RIVER, OKINAWA
MAY 10, 1945, PREDAWN

Porter had waited for orders, the low crackle of a radio, and after midnight had led his men back up to the ridgeline. The narrow pathways had been no less muddy, no less slick, and the tall grass along the ridge bathed each man in a shower of water that soaked their already wet clothes. On the ridge itself they could only wait, Porter and the other officers close to their walkie-talkies, alert for any emergency that might suddenly erupt below them. The hill fell away to flat ground, an open plain that they would have to cross to reach the river itself. With the first sign of darkness the engineers had moved out, and no one had seen any sign of the kind of work they were trying to do, the darkness and the driving rain disguising their labor. As the men around him waited in soaking-wet darkness, Adams focused his gaze down toward the hidden river, thought about those men, building some kind of bridge. Footbridge, he thought. What the hell is that? Pieces of something laid end to end, I guess. More questions rolled through him, but he would not ask, knew that close by, Ferucci sat, waiting, the others, Welty right behind him. They think I'm an idiot, he thought. Bad enough I brought them undrinkable water. Now we're about to do . . . what? They probably think I'm a screw-up no matter what happens next, the new guy who's not new. I shoulda been there with them all along, shoulda been with Welty on Saipan. Some stupid-assed disease, and now I'm no better than those slick-faced replacements they sent out here with me. Welty's gotta be scared, the sarge too, all of them. It can't just be *me.* He glanced down at his chest, hidden by the poncho, thought of the lumbering weight hanging from his shirt, the extra grenades. Hell, we never trained in anything like this. It never rained like this in San Diego, days at a time. The deepest mud was over my ankles. This stuff . . . you could drown in it, and they'd never find you. Sure as hell, no one ever told us we'd need a dozen damn grenades. All that bayonet practice, all us tough guys, cutting up a cloth dummy. No one's shown me a single reason why these Japs are *dummies* at all. Most of these guys have done all this before, and I bet they're watching me, keep an eye on the idiot, the *new guy.* The guy who peed his own damn pants. Well, maybe so. But I bet every one of these guys up here is as scared as I am. I sure as hell hope so.

The words rolled through his brain in a quivering wave, silent chatter, more questions. If we can wade, why do we need a bridge? Who decides who uses the bridge? Is that for officers? Five feet deep, that's up to my neck. Welty's shorter than me. Damn, I better keep an eye on him. The Japs know we're coming? Well, maybe not. He stared into the rain, the steady hiss, and suddenly there were streaks of fire, red lines, then blue, the odd color of the Japanese tracers, pouring out in clusters from the far side of the river. The men flattened out, but the fire was aimed low, toward the water none of them could see. There were short calls, the officers keeping their men in silence, orders not to fire, not to respond. Adams pushed himself flat against the soggy grass, but the only sound came from the rain, none of the pops and cracks from the distant machine guns, no other sound at all. He took a breath, peered up, saw the tracers aimed far below them, only a few machine guns, the rain deadening their chatter. The engineers, he thought. The Japs must have had lookouts or something, must have heard something. Oh God, get those guys out of there. All this for a stupid damn footbridge?

And then the streaks stopped, the Japanese holding their fire. Adams was breathing heavily, heard low talk, close beside him, behind, men in nervous stammers, speculating what had happened. He wanted to tell them, shut up! The Japs heard those guys! They might hear us too. But there was nothing else now, just the rain, and Adams felt his stomach turning over, flexed his fingers, realized he was shaking, the cold and the fear eating at him again.

He heard a rustle in the grass, a man moving up from out in front, a low voice.

"Saddle up. Follow me. Nobody fires on this side of the river. There's nobody here but us, nobody shoots, you hear me? Keep track of your buddy, whoever's beside you. Nobody lags behind."

Porter was already moving away, down into the thick grass. Adams waited for a shadow to move past him, fell into line behind the man. The grass gave way to more rocks, slices in the hillside, narrow gorges of coral and limestone, uneven footing. He felt a high wall on one side of him, tripped on something, stumbled to one side, rammed his ribs into a jutting rock, made a hard grunt, the man behind him doing the same, more grunts. He heard a hard whisper from the lieutenant.

"Quiet, dammit!"

There were no replies, Porter again pushing out in front of them. Adams felt the ground flattening, easier stepping, and now the mud was there, his feet slurping their way with the others. The mud grew deeper, the going slow. He stared at the back of the man in front of him, a shadow struggling forward, kept his distance, winced from the hard slurps of their steps. His legs began to burn, sweat blending with the rain in his eyes. He wanted to look around, to see if someone was behind him, his own footsteps now drowning out the sounds of anyone else. But even a glance to the side could cost him his balance, and he kept his head down, stared blindly at the knee-deep goo.

The mud began to harden, and he felt himself climbing, a low rise, gravel now beneath his feet. The noise echoed all along the line, and he glanced to the side, caught a glimpse of men, many men, columns spread out in formation, heard the soft crunch of the gravel. He tried to soften his steps, but it was useless, the boots of dozens of men around him stirring up the wide field, the strange image in his shivering mind of walking in a vast field of corn flakes. He stared ahead, thought of the engineers, the tracers, Japanese lookouts, and now, in front of him, the closest man had stopped. Adams halted just before running into the man; behind him others were coming up close. Men were kneeling, and he dropped down with them, saw one man still up, standing, silent, seeming to wait. No one was speaking at all, the only sound the rain on helmets and ponchos. He blinked water out of his eyes, but there was no rest, the men responding to a quiet order he didn't hear. The crunching began again, and he could see wide-open ground all around, no sign of cover, felt a hand on his arm, a brief tug, and now he saw the river, a wide black stain, peppered by the rain. The bank was thick with men, and he watched as one man moved out into the water, others following in line, one man behind the other. Then, to the left, another line, another leader. He thought of the footbridge. Where is that? Did they build it? Why are we . . . a hand grabbed his shoulder, pushed him up close to another man, a low grunt he had heard before . . . Ferucci. There were no words, the message clear. *Get moving.*

The streaks of red and blue came again, the far side of the river, higher up, reflecting on the water, the sounds reaching him, too close to be disguised by the rain. Adams followed the others out into the river, his knees bent, loud splashes all around him, quick steps into deepening water, the chopping of the machine guns rolling toward them from places he couldn't see. The streaks were closer now, the aim improving, a ripping slice in the water to one side. He pushed quickly forward, as quickly as the man in front would allow, the water up to his knees, then deeper, to his groin. The machine guns kept up their fire and he pressed forward, as much of a run as the water would allow. He realized now, the water was warm, surprising, soothing the chill in his legs, and he felt the soft mud of the bottom, the current not strong, easy to keep his balance. He stayed close to the men in front, the fire now mostly above them. Men settled low in the water, the best cover they had, a sea of helmets moving together, hands holding rifles high above. His knees kept driving him forward, men pushing up close to him from behind, driven by the same fear that tried to paralyze him now. The tracers lit the water from above, and he could see the lines of men on both sides, waves on the surface increasing from their movement, the water deepening, over his stomach. He held the rifle just over his head, shuffled his feet, working to keep his balance. How much deeper, he thought? Why in hell aren't we on that bridge? Forget that. We're all down in this stuff. He wanted to turn, to find Welty, but the men were moving in slow motion, driven by the machine gun fire, everyone keeping the rhythm, the lines pressing forward. To one side came an enormous splash, a plume of spray that blinded him, another now out to the front. The sounds followed, distant thumps, the rain deadening the rips and screams. More shells impacted far to the right, others whistled close overhead, striking the gravel and dirt behind them. The water was below his waist now, then his knees, and in front of him men began to run. He was on gravel again, his own legs kicking into motion, a blind scamper, pulled by the men scrambling forward, the ground visible only from the sprays of tracer fire. The mud came again, his feet slowing, bogging down, fire in his legs. He stumbled, the ground dipping low, fell to one hand, fingers in mud, pushed himself up, men moving past, calls, voices, urging the men forward. The machine gun fire began to slow, the tracers only to the right now, one Nambu gun still sending out a steady stream of fire. In front the guns were suddenly quiet, and he kept moving, screaming pain in his legs, his chest, hard breaths. He tried to see anything at all, rocks, hills, but the rain still blinded him, stinging his eyes. There were only shadows, some men stumbling, falling, grunts and low words. He felt the ground rising again, a hill, hard, ragged coral, heard men moving up in front, some calling out to the others. Cover! He pushed into any opening he could find, climbing with every step, saw some men falling into holes, cuts, the hillside gashed with the deep crevices, just as before, men filling the gaps, some stepping on each other as they fought for cover. He slipped in behind a rock, brush around it, heard a voice, felt a man push up against him, but there was no anger, no curses, both men doing the same thing. He sat still now, strained to hear, the man beside him silent, breathing heavily. We made it, he thought. We crossed the damn river! Downstream the single machine gun stopped its fire, and now the only sound came from the rain, and the pounding in his ears from his own heart, his breaths. He was shivering again, the warmth of the river turning cold, flexed his arms, held the rifle out, then pulled it close, anything to keep moving. He thought of the lieutenant, the others, the men who led the way, who took them across. Where are they? They know what we're supposed to do. What happens now? We wait for daylight? Maybe the Japs will come after us, make a charge. He felt the rock with his back, tall, above his head. Good cover. Good cover. Okay, I'm ready. For what?

Beside him the man shifted position, rolled over away from him, peered up over the rock. Adams leaned that way, said in a low whisper, "Get down! You nuts?"

The man settled back down, sat heavily, said, "Maybe. You an officer?"

"No. Private Adams."

"Adams. Yeah, the boxer. Won ten bucks on you last month. I'm Captain Bennett."

SOUTH OF THE ASA KAWA RIVER, OKINAWA
MAY 10, 1945, DAWN

The mortar fire began at first light, incoming rounds that shattered into the coral, blowing rocky shrapnel through the men who tried desperately to hold on to their advance position. Near the mouth of the river, where it spread wide into the ocean, the obliterated road bridge stood as a shattered monument to the effectiveness of what still remained of Japanese artillery. On the north side of the river, frustrated tank commanders brought their vehicles close to the water, hoping to support the Marines who had made the crossing, but without the bridge, the tanks could do nothing more. The river itself would swamp any machines that tried to drive across. As the tank crews waited impatiently, the engineers attempted to build a bridge strong enough to support the weight of the armor. But the Japanese had a perfect field of fire, and immediately the engineers were targeted, soaring plumes of water taking a horrific toll on the men who did their best to build yet another bridge. Even the footbridge was targeted, not by artillery but by bands of Japanese soldiers who rushed the bridge wearing satchel charges, suicide squads whose work was stunningly effective. As the engineers tried to respond with hastily fired carbines, they could not prevent the Japanese from accomplishing their goal. The footbridge was blasted to rubble by men who gave their lives for that one simple task.

As the hours passed, the determination of the engineers prevailed. Despite ongoing artillery fire from the hidden Japanese positions, the heavier bridges took shape, and the tanks began to roll. Offshore, in perfect testament to the effectiveness of the navy's firepower, the cruiser USS *Indianapolis* provided supporting fire against the Japanese guns that dared to show their position for more than a few seconds. With the tanks finally able to lend support, the Marines on the south side of the river received the orders the officers had expected all along. Crossing the river wasn't enough. Now it was time to continue the drive. To the east, the army divisions and the Marine First Division were facing Japanese defenses anchored by the Shuri Castle, and other strong positions dug deep into networks of low hills. To the west, closer to the coast, the Sixth Marines were facing one of the primary goals of the entire campaign: Okinawa's capital city of Naha, and just beyond, the city's major airfield.

Before first light on May 10, the Marines who hugged to whatever cover they could find began to suffer from incoming mortar fire, their positions revealed by the light of green flares, which burst over them, effective even in the driving rain. There was a new weapon as well, already familiar to the soldiers who had spent so many days close to Japanese positions. Enormous numbers of Japanese soldiers were equipped with a *knee mortar*, so called because its lightweight portability meant that it could be fired from nearly anywhere, anchored against the ground by a man's knee. But the small size did not diminish its brutal effectiveness against troops within close range. Hidden by ridgelines and any obstacle they could find, the Japanese troops began to pour fire into anyplace the Marines were trying desperately to seek cover. The low hills outside the city of Naha were now crawling with Marines, but very soon they learned that close in front of them, behind them and beneath them, the hill was crawling with Japanese troops as well.

They slid forward through the shallow mud, thick pools of stench that had flowed into low places in the coral. Adams stayed close to the soles of Ferucci's boots, knew that Welty or someone else was close behind him. Together they snaked their way through a deep draw, cut into the face of a hill that was no more than forty feet high. Around them the more open ground was a sea of uneven wreckage, earthen hills plowed up by artillery shells, any vegetation long since obliterated, the rough ground offering shallow sanctuary for the Marines. Their goal had been a hill, what Bennett's map had shown to be Charlie Hill, but naming the mound of rocky coral did not mean it was that much more prominent than most of the undulating wasteland around it. As they reached the base of the hill, Adams had glimpsed a single landmark, one lone pine tree, rising above the ragged ridgeline, knew that somewhere an artilleryman was sighting on it as well. The shellfire had come all morning, some from the American 150s back near the river, or from the *Indianapolis*. The tanks were assisting as well, rolling up in support of the men who crawled their way through the cut coral. But as the Marines slipped and squirmed their way onto Charlie Hill, the big guns had to stop. Whatever targets there might have been were mostly underground, and the only thing the gunners and their observers could spot now were the specks of dirty green.

The rifle fire was relentless, most of it coming from rocks and crevices above them, keeping the Marines low in their cover. In front of him Ferucci had stopped, no progress now, nothing to do but wait for an opportunity. The shelling had seemed to come in bursts, Adams wondering if the Japanese inside the caves and holes knew the timing and so kept low while their gunners did the job. But no one had answers, and there was no time for *conversation* about anything. He thought of the lieutenant above them, just beyond a hump in the rocks. He'll know more than I do. He'll tell me to shut up and keep my head down. Getting good at that. The rocks close to his left hand shattered, and he hunched his shoulders in, thought, God, they see me! He wanted to move, anywhere, any direction, but the men around him were in no better position, no better cover than he had now. We can't just sit here! Dammit! He realized now that a roar was coming from below. The sound was familiar, clanking steel, a belching rumble. He eased his head around, saw down the hill, far out in the open, the black smoke, the machine rolling up and over the uneven ground.

"Sarge! A tank!"

"Shut up. I hear it. There's a crack in that rock above us. Jap rifles there. If the tank can send one shot in there, we can rush it!"

Adams gripped the M-1, held it close to his chest, saw the men down the hill behind him, some curled into muddy depressions, shell holes, no one seeming to want to *rush* anything. He watched the tank coming closer, felt a surge of thankfulness, the Sherman keeping back from the base of the hill. Now another appeared, its turret rotating, seeking targets, both machines drawing closer, stopping, and above him, Adams heard the voice, Porter, "Come on, damn you! Put one up on this ridge! Son of a bitch, where's the walkie-talkie?"

No one responded, the rifle fire from the Japanese above them continuing, the sudden chatter from a Nambu gun, somewhere close. Adams lay as flat as he could, heard the whining crack, a dull *whump* from a Japanese rifle, so many odd sounds, different kinds of weapons. He had no choice but to keep flat, sharp coral beneath him, his face turned to the side, dirt in his ear. The rifle fire seemed to increase, more Japanese joining the fight, some response from below, the rattle of a BAR, pops from the Marines who crouched along the base of the hill, waiting for their own lieutenant to order the advance. The Nambu gun kept up its fire, a spray that ricocheted across the coral just behind Adams, and he heard shouts, a short scream, "I'm hit! Doc!"

Ferucci did not move, shouted, "We've got wounded up here! Corpsman!"

Others took up the call, voices from behind, "Corpsman!"

"Get a doc up here!"

"Got him!"

Adams let out a breath, the rifle fire close again, a splatter on a rock beside him, and he pushed against Ferucci's boot heel.

"We gotta move. They see us!"

Ferucci didn't speak, crawled away up the trail, a short scramble, and Adams stayed close to him, the smell of powder rolling over them. From below a tank fired, the shell passing overhead with a sharp whistle, impacting against the hilltop. Adams felt the ground shake beneath him, turned toward the tank, could see smoke from the barrel of the tank's 75. Yes! Again! Blow them to hell! He saw movement now, close to the tank, a man, another, emerging from some hidden place. They moved with quick steps, scurrying toward the tank. The uniforms were light, tan, and his heart leapt in his throat.

"Sarge!"

But there was no time, and two more Japanese soldiers appeared, the men running low toward both tanks, a mad crawl right under the belly, and now the blasts came, one quickly after the other, bursts of fire and black smoke. Adams stared in horror, swung around with his rifle, but there were no targets, the tanks engulfed in fire. He saw one hatch open, a man scrambling out, billowing smoke from inside the tank, but the Nambu guns were taking aim, the man falling, cut down by the Japanese fire. Another tanker emerged, bloody, bareheaded, staggering up out of the machine, was punched backward by the machine gun fire, fell in a heap to the muddy ground. Adams stared, sick, expected more men to emerge, the smoke coming out of both hatches in a thick plume. But there was only silence now, the fire curling up around each tank, a thump of a blast as a gas tank ignited, fire now spewing straight up through the open hatches.

"Sons of bitches! Satchel charges!" Adams looked at the voice, Welty, below him.

Adams said, "They just blew themselves up!"

Welty said nothing more, turned toward him, black calm on the man's face, and above him, Ferucci said, "Stay down!"

Porter shouted now, from his hidden perch.

"Give me covering fire! I'm going up!"

Adams wanted to shout out, no! Going up . . . where? He looked past Ferucci, saw the lieutenant emerge from a shallow hole, a grenade in his hand. The men responded with fire of their own, Adams raising his rifle to his shoulder, aiming up toward the ridge, nothing to see, no targets at all, just cuts in the rock. Porter seemed to pause, and Adams saw his face, red, bathed in sweat. He leapt out now, ran up over the rocky hillside, fell flat again, and now Adams saw the rifle barrel just above him, the Japanese soldier showing himself. Porter tossed the grenade up, into the opening, then rolled away. The blast came, a thumping billow of smoke and rock, and Porter was up again, threw another into the same hole, then stood, fired his carbine into the narrow gap. Ferucci yelled, "Let's go! Move!"

The sergeant rose, moved away quickly, darting into the shallow cover, closer to Porter. Adams followed, automatic, no thought, his eyes on the black ground, rocks and mud and smoke.

The rifle fire came from the left now, a burst from another machine gun, the rocks around him erupting in small splatters. Adams fell flat, no cover, men stumbling beside him, one man crying out. The Marines answered, M-1s from below, firing into the new target, no target at all. There was no other sound, just the steady firing from both sides, and Adams felt the paralysis, immobile against the rocks, staring sideways, a man's body close beside him. Run, you stupid . . .

He leapt up, climbed frantically, searching wildly for anyplace to come down. There were small rocks in a heap, and he moved that way, dove, landing hard, rolled over them, saw a crack in the hard rock, slid that way, more fire, close by. He hugged the rifle close to his chest, terror holding him hard against the rocks, the crack inviting, a small cave. And now he saw the helmet, eyes staring back at him from inside the rock. He yelled, animal sounds, jammed the rifle forward, fired, fired again, kept firing until the clip clinked out of the M-1. Smoke filled the narrow gap, blinding, and he heard noises, voices, more men farther back in the rock. His legs tried to pull him away, to run, but there was no other place to be, and he dropped the M-1, no time, grabbed a grenade, jerked it from his shirt, blind instinct, pulled the pin, threw the grenade into the hole. He ducked now, just below the opening, the voices louder, a hard shout, but the blast came, knocking him backward, rolling him away from the rocky face. His ears were ringing and he tried to stand, saw splinters of rock around him, the Japanese machine guns still seeking him, punching the ground close to him. He scrambled back up into the cloud of dust and smoke, hugged the rock, saw the M-1, grabbed a clip from the cartridge belt, jammed it home.

"Pull back!"

"No! Japs! Right here!"

"Pull back!"

He knew Porter's voice, but the words seemed to echo from very far away. The smoke cleared around him, and he saw movement down below, the men moving back down the hill, some in a run, some dropping, rolling, some not moving at all. He coughed from the smoke, wanted to see inside the rocky opening, to see the Japanese soldiers, the dead, *his* dead.

"Pull back! Get back! Move it!"

The hillside was alive with movement, men crawling down, some firing up toward the crevices, the enemy answering, flashes from the hidden places, smoke drifting past him in thin, stinking clouds. He kept his back to the rocks, heard more voices now from behind him, more men inside the rock hole, the voices urgent, silly, meaningless words. He grabbed another grenade, jerked the pin, held the grenade for a long second, his hand shaking, then with one motion stood back from the rock and threw the grenade hard inside. He ducked again, braced for the blast, one hand on his ear, the rocks jumping under him, a fresh cloud of blinding smoke.

"Pull back! Now!"

The smoke was all around him, a cloud of camouflage, and he dove down through it, struggling to keep his feet, jumped down to the crevice, past the rocks, more muddy holes. There were bodies, Marines, and he hesitated, reached down, grabbed a man's hand, *no one left behind* . . .

"Get down! Pull back!"

The hand did not move, and his own momentum pulled him away, the Nambu gun chipping the rocks, whistles and cracks around his head. He released the hand, no choice, saw a low place in the rocks, jumped down, the hillside flattening, deeper mud, shell holes and torn ground. There were others moving around him, pulling back, no one stopping, and he kept running, tripping, stumbling, a desperate scamper, saw more of the others, men all across the muddy uneven ground, settling into cover. Faces watched him, terrified, some with dead eyes, and he saw Ferucci, on his knees, the sergeant cursing him, waving at him.

"Here! Take cover!"

Adams slid to a stop, felt mud inside his shirt, the sergeant grabbing him hard, pulling him flat to the ground.

"You stupid bastard! You hear the order to withdraw, you withdraw!"

Adams didn't know how to respond, wanted to say something about the Japanese in the rocks, but there was no voice, his breathing in furious gasps, the smoke still in his lungs. There was a calm moment, strange, no firing, a wafting black cloud rolling past, the stink of the smoke that poured toward them from the tanks. Adams tried to sit, roll over, see up the hill, but the order came from far down the line.

"Tanks are coming up! Withdraw!"

The words seemed nonsensical, foolish, someone's stupid mistake. Tanks get blown to hell! He searched the faces, saw some with helmets low, staring into the mud, some looking back up the hill, some with rifles aimed. The tanks came with hard rumbles, the squeaking of steel, and the big guns fired, a steady thumping rhythm into the hill. He thought of the bodies, could see them, splayed out, filthy green heaps, but the tankers aimed high, were blasting the crest, and now a hand jerked his shoulder, sharp words.

"Let's go!"

He rose up with the others, the Japanese opening up again from hidden machine guns, the firing from the tanks continuing, their own machine guns answering. The Marines flowed back away from the hill, into the undulating ground, thick deep mud, some men seeking cover around the tanks, but the tanks did not stay, were already in motion, pulling away, their machine guns continuing to fire, offering cover to the retreating Marines. Adams scrambled to keep up, searing pain in his chest, legs bogging down in the mud, saw some men jumping up on the tanks, grabbing on, some sliding back off, the bouncing motion of the tanks too unsteady. He followed the men on foot, no faces now, just backs, helmets, rifles and carbines and BARs, a mad scramble away from the hill, the hill they couldn't take.

18. ADAMS

The brief respite from the rains had ended, a new storm washing over them with a fury that felt like the clouds were making up for lost time. The winds were blustery, sweeping away the shelter halves, no kind of cover for the muddy holes strong enough to keep the storm off the men who kept low in their foxholes. From hills and hidden places in what seemed every direction, the Japanese continued to choose their targets, anyone leaving his hole likely to draw attention from a dozen machine guns, a hail of rifle fire. And so the men stayed put. They were getting used to the oily water, but only because they had no choice.

In the foxholes themselves, the misery of the mud was made worse for another more personal reason. Those, like Adams, whose guts were twisted into sickening turmoil, had no place to go to relieve themselves, no latrine, no slit trench. But their pants came down, brief seconds of embarrassing hell, the new stink adding to the mud and water in the only place they could stay, the only place there was cover from the Japanese guns, the only kind of *comfort* there could be.

The stink had come from other sources as well, and no one had to ask why. The answers lay all around them, shreds of clothing, uniforms of the soldiers from both sides who had fought over this same ground for weeks now. Worse were the bones, and what was still hanging from them, some identifiable, an arm, hand, leg, some just blobs of black filth. The shovels had done quick work, the foxholes easier to dig in the mud, gaps in the coral. But the shovels continued to chop through the remains of the men who had died there. The sickening crunch of bone was never ignored, even by the men who had done this before, who seemed immune to almost any other horror. With every hour the smells had grown worse, had become a part of them, their soggy uniforms, their food, infesting every brain, driving some of the men into nightmares of what . . . and who . . . they sat in. The nightmares were brief, most of the men not able to sleep at all, and if they found themselves nodding off for blessed moments in the foot-deep water, the Japanese flares would come, shattering the darkness with harsh green light. The flares usually meant a mortar barrage, the blasts sudden and unpredictable, since the telltale sounds of the knee mortars were disguised by the storm. The Marines had withdrawn as far as the brass considered necessary, but no matter their distance from Naha, or the hills they still had to assault, the Japanese were there. In the dark they came as they had before, but in far greater numbers. The rain disguised any sound, no shadows caught by starlight. The grenades and satchel charges were their weapons of choice, stunning blasts of blinding light, enough to terrorize the men in their foxholes, but enough as well to silhouette the enemy who was often so close, some of the Marines claimed they could smell them. When the individual attacks came, it was rare that the Japanese soldier did any more than sacrifice himself, falling straight into a foxhole with an armed grenade, taking away his enemy and himself, fulfilling his glorious mission. With the American tanks moving up in a vain effort to support the Marines, the infiltrators would go after those much more valuable targets, the men on the ground ordered to keep watch for any hint of Japanese soldiers whose sole mission was to throw themselves and their satchel charges beneath the belly of the tank. Already the armor officers had pulled many of the Shermans farther back, conceding that the Japanese suicide assaults were infuriatingly effective. In the rainy darkness it didn't matter how many Marines kept watch, some sheltered by the tank itself. When the Japanese came, those men were just as likely to become casualties themselves.

Along the muddy front, the orders from the lieutenants were direct and harsh. At least two men per hole, and as before one had to remain alert, keeping watch, whether there was anything to be seen or not. The ponchos that still held together were all they had for protection, and with no way to dry out clothes or skin, sickness had begun to spread through the men, made far worse by the filth they could not escape. The enemy was suffering as well, but no Marine gave that much thought, knew only that any attempt to leave the foxhole would likely draw fire. The Japanese seemed to wait in every low place, rising up from some invisible nook, seeking out the vulnerable, the careless, the unwary, and if any of the sickest men had the desperate need to find a corpsman, or make it to an aid station, it was just as likely he would run headlong into a band of infiltrators. And with the driving rain muffling the passwords, the danger was more intense than ever that he might be shot down by a jittery hand from his own unit.

NORTH OF NAHA, OKINAWA
MAY 11, 1945, MIDNIGHT

Adams knew the rot had crept down from his groin, a stinging agony, sore and raw, all the way into his boots. He had tried to ignore it, as much as he could ignore anything around him. But he could not ignore Welty. The redhead sat down slowly, settled into the wetness, his two-hour watch complete. Adams began to pull himself upright, the M-1 a crutch, and he saw the shadows of Welty with his backpack, heard the muffled sound of the man rifling through, searching. Adams straightened his legs, the sharp pain in his groin grabbing him, and he made himself stand straight, ignored the M-1 he couldn't see, had given up on whether it was clean or not. But it was his turn to take the watch, two hours of rain flowing down his neck, splattering his helmet, blowing into his eyes. Welty pulled something from the pack, and Adams heard the rip of soggy cardboard.

"Oh God, are you kidding?"

Welty completed the task, the sound of the tin can opening, replied in a whisper.

"Gotta eat."

"No, you don't. I don't. Can't even think about it. What the hell is that?"

"Stew I think. Don't much matter. The rain fills up the can fast as I can eat it. It's like . . . seconds."

Adams had grown used to Welty's amazing ability to ignore his surroundings, but this was pushing him too far. He felt the twist in his stomach, bent low, a convulsive surge driving hard up through his throat, the sharp groan. But there was nothing inside of him, just the painful grip of his stomach muscles.

"Hey, you got the dry heaves again? Oh crap. You want me to take your watch? Sit back down."

Adams tried to relax his insides, stood slowly, knew he was exposed from the chest up, ignored that, nothing at all to be seen in the thick wet darkness. He tried to take a deep breath, find some way to cleanse the air in his lungs. The smells were a part of him, had filled his brain and his insides to capacity, but the thought of Welty's stew and rainwater had been the last dismal straw.

"I'm okay. You enjoy your dinner. You twisted bastard."

Welty ignored the insults, had heard them before.

"You'll get used to it. You're not a newbie anymore. And no matter what you feel like now . . . you gotta eat. At least drink some water. Got a full canteen here. What you don't drink, you can lube your piece. Or hell, rub it all over your skin. You're the one who thought gun oil would keep the damn fleas off you. The stuff in this damn canteen's gotta be pretty close."

Adams stared into the rain, water dripping from the brim of his helmet. He had done all he could to ignore Welty's strange behavior, had kept the thoughts away that Welty seemed to like this, or that maybe he was just going nuts. It had happened to others, men suddenly crawling up out of their holes, calling out to someone, a girl, their mothers, the brutal conditions so complete that their brains had just abandoned them, gone off somewhere else. Most of those men did not survive long, and the ones who had were back in some place Adams didn't want to think of. He had known a few of those in the hospital in San Diego, the ones who had gone *Asian,* who simply fell apart. It was a fear he still held on to, that it might be him, that the paralyzing panic would eat away at what sense he had left. But now, in the driving rain, with his buddy chomping down rain-filled stew, Adams could not escape the fear that he might be the only sane man left in the platoon.

With the gray light came the same amazing scene, rolling muddy hills, blasted clean of brush, the rain revealing even more bones, scraps of cloth, pieces of bodies. Adams kept his helmet low, peered up every minute or so, nothing changing but the slow drift of dense fog. Close to either side of him, the tops of helmets were just visible, some men moving inside the sanctuary of their foxholes. He examined the M-1, dripping water, mud on the stock, on the barrel, thought of the drill sergeant, nameless now, some huge monster of a man who tormented the recruits in San Diego, who would find the slightest smudge on a rifle barrel and punish you by making a man lick a dirty rifle clean. But saliva wasn't clean, of course, so the recruit would then use his own toothbrush, soaked in gun oil, then, when the rifle was thoroughly brushed, the DI would make the man brush his teeth. It was obscenely idiotic, and Adams remembered every detail now, stared at the mud and rain on his rifle, wanted to laugh. Hey, asshole, what about this? You want me to lick this son of a bitch clean? Fine, but you gotta come out here and show me how. Where the hell are you, anyway? Warm bed, or sitting on the beach, watching the girls? Toughest bastard in the Corps, that's what you wanted us to believe. If I ever find you, I'll ram this piece right up your cocoa hole. He focused, the daydream shattered by a flash of light, far to the front. More came now, a splattering of blasts in the mud that seemed to come in a line, straight toward him.

"Mortar!"

He splashed into the bottom of the hole, Welty shrinking himself against the far end, shoulders hunched, nothing else to do. The ground shuddered with each blast, mud tossed in on them, a half-dozen thumps coming in close to the network of foxholes. And then, silence. Adams rose up from the thick goo, Welty beside him, listened for the inevitable, and now it came.

"Corpsman! Doc! Doc!"

One man was screaming, a high thick whine, another voice, trying to calm him. But the scream continued, and Adams searched through the mist, saw a fresh heap of smoking mud, dug up by the mortar shell. From behind a man moved up, crawling quickly, closer to the churned earth.

"Coming!"

"Doc! Oh hell!"

The corpsman reached the smoking hole, lay flat, peered down, seemed suddenly headless, an unnerving sight, Adams blinking it away. The screaming came again, the corpsman working furiously, still lying flat outside the blasted hole, and within a minute the screaming seemed to drift away, then stopped. The corpsman rose up, rolled over to one side, motionless for a long second, black mud on his arms, his face. Adams saw a glimpse of the man's eyes, empty, staring at nothing, then a slow shake of his head. He began to crawl away, back to his own safe place, and in a thick low voice, Welty said, "Nothing he could do. I bet."

"How do you know? Maybe he gave him some morphine, shut him up."

"Yeah. Maybe."

"Doc! Doc!"

The voice came from the distance, somewhere in the fog, beyond a short rise. Adams saw the corpsman stop, turn, still on his knees, the man's head hanging low, resignation to the awful task. He moved that way, and now another man crawled out of a hole, moving with him, keeping his distance a few paces behind.

"Doc!"

The corpsman didn't speak, just crawled toward the voice, climbed slowly up the incline, the second man moving up faster, sliding in beside him, a carbine in the man's hand. The corpsman peered over, trying to see, to find the foxhole of the wounded man, and now the shot punched the air, the corpsman collapsing in a heap, flat, motionless. The second man ducked low in the mud, then fired the carbine, emptied the magazine, stayed low, reloaded, fired again. Adams watched in horror, saw no movement from the corpsman, the other man still reloading, spraying fire from the carbine out beyond the muddy rise. The man slid back, reached out for the boot of the corpsman, dragging him, and now another man rose up, scampering close, another hand on the corpsman's boots. They slid him through the mud, plowing a shallow furrow back through the foxholes. More men climbed up, but there was a harsh voice from the man with the carbine, sending the men back into their holes. Adams could see now. It was Porter.

The two men pulled the corpsman back past Adams, who stared, frozen, a new sickness, felt a hand on his shoulder, Welty, pulling him down.

"They're right out there, sport. Keep your damn head down."

"They shot the doc!"

"Japs know some English, Clay. *Doc's* an easy one. Don't ever call out a name, the Japs will call 'em right back to you." Adams looked at him, Welty's eyes cold, the same grim stare. "The doc shoulda known better."

Adams looked back, the men already gone behind another low rise, the corpsman's body hauled somewhere off the line.

"Known better? How?"

Throughout the day the positions were shifted, units sliding to one side or another, pulled into position for new attacks on the hills the Japanese still controlled. The fire from the Japanese positions had come in waves and spurts, whenever targets had appeared. Their aim had been mostly ineffective, but not always, and all through the muddy fields, the men who dared to show themselves for more than a second or two were sprayed with a barrage from machine guns that no one could see. The mortars would come next, no aim at all, their destructiveness by pure chance. If a shell came down directly into a foxhole, even the corpsmen knew not to take chances examining the victims.

By midday the fog had mostly cleared, but the rains still came, and with no hope of moving supply trucks forward, the men had to make do with the food and ammunition they carried. No runner could hope to survive by hauling anything across the open ground in daylight, and when the order came for a new attack, each platoon had been sorted out by their lieutenants, who made sure each man had grenades, and enough clips for his rifle to be effective. Then more orders came, and Adams had seen Porter sitting upright on the edge of his foxhole, wiping down his carbine, as though the danger had passed, that anything they had gone through so far was only a taste. The Marines all along the lines were pulled up into position for the assault again and again, striking at the low rocky hills that served as the strong points along the main Japanese defensive line. Porter had told his own men only what had come across his radio, that the brass was growing more impatient watching casualties hauled back to the command posts, that dead men wrapped in ponchos meant that something more had to be done. It was an easy conclusion to draw by men who stayed dry under their camouflaged tents. But Porter spread the word to his men, who, for once, agreed with their commanders. There was no victory to be had as long as the Marines were sitting still. For two long days they had absorbed a horrific toll trying to take hills that the Japanese seemed expert at protecting. Adams had seen the corpsman die because the man was doing his job. Others had watched friends close by ripped apart by shrapnel, cut down by the fire of the Nambu guns, helmets cracked by the deadly fire of a sniper. They knew with perfect certainty that they were facing a very capable enemy who had only one goal: to die by killing as many Americans as he could. The Marines understood what had to happen well before their officers made it official. No matter that they had been driven off the hills, they had no choice but to try again.

NORTHWEST OF "HILL TWO"
MAY 12, 1945

Around them the entire battalion had gathered, brought closer together for an assault someone far behind them seemed to think would end their problems. Charlie Hill now lay to their east, the place assaulted repeatedly, but this time, when the men of Bennett's company had been marched through the muddy fields, it was more to the west, away from the familiar ground they had expected to climb. In the darkness there were no features to the ground at all, beyond the dips in the terrain, and the familiar mud. The only light came from the strange storm of flares, mostly in the distance, silhouetting the distant hills, or star shells, American, sent aloft to aid the artillery and tank fire. The rumble from the big guns had been almost continuous, and as Adams plodded along, keeping his boots in the sloppy tracks of the men before him, he had stopped hearing the peculiar differences between all the varieties of shells. He had still not been able to eat much of anything, had munched down a brick-hard cracker from a K ration box. The oily water had become a part of the routine, the nauseating taste just another piece of the torturous test of endurance that to most of the Marines had become normal. But the crack-up cases were increasing, Adams watching as one man from Porter's platoon suddenly leapt out into the rain, running in wide circles, shouting at the nonexistent sun, outraged that there hadn't been any sign of a sunset. It was a ridiculous show of utter insanity, the man attracting a storm of machine gun fire, standing perfectly upright in the wide open, arms raised, fists shaking, curses directed at no one else but the man's own decaying version of God. He had been tackled finally, completely unharmed, but the corpsmen had sedated the man, and in minutes the strange rant was now just one more nightmarish memory to the men who still had their job to do.

The column in front of Adams slowed, halted, the men dropping down, no instructions necessary. Adams did as the others did, knees in the mud, the poncho serving as a small makeshift tent. He tried to see anything at all, caught only shadows in the rain, realized that a man was moving up close to him, hard whispers.

"Check your weapons. Grab every grenade you can carry. Moving out in five minutes."

Adams saw more figures, heard the splashing thud of a heavy crate. He caught a new, oily smell, suddenly realized there was a tank a few yards in front of them, a silent, hulking mass, men climbing up, boxes unloaded. The men around him began to move, and he followed, mindless, his legs stiff, cold, achingly sore. The grenades were uncrated, the men dipping down, filling their hands, pockets, shirts, anyplace they could be stashed. Adams did the same, gave it no other thought, the order logical, the obedience automatic. The voices around him were low, serious, none of the cursing banter of the men. Near the tank he caught a low conversation, stepped that way, knew the sound of officers, perked up, curious, heard Porter, others, and now, Captain Bennett.

"No more than a third of them are left up there. The Twenty-ninth is shot for now, and we've got to move in to replace them. The colonel says to get to the top, hold on for everything we can. At dawn the navy will help, unless we can make it all the way up there first."

"How the hell is the navy supposed to know that? You want me to stand up and wave?"

The question rolled through Adams's brain in sleepy logic. He stepped closer, had to hear the response, expected some kind of punch line, like a bad Bob Hope joke, nonsensical lunacy. *Wavy at the navy.*

"Just get your people up that hill as quick as you can. The colonel is watching from his CP, and I'll have a radio. There's probably a bunch of wounded up there. Nobody really knows. That's why you have to get there quick. Do whatever you can to scrub those Jap bastards off that hill. Dawn should come in a half hour. Now, move out."

The men began to separate and Adams felt a strange disappointment, nothing funny at all in the officer's instructions. But the nonsense of it all still rolled through him, and he tried to form a picture, his brain dancing strangely. Scrub a hill? This whole damn place needs scrubbing. This rain keeps up, the whole place might wash into the sea. The new image flickered through his brain, soldiers suddenly caught in some giant whirlpool, a flow through the great drain of a sewer, sliding down a long chute of mud, the entire island, airfields, straw huts, rats, snakes, and people, all washed out to sea. *Wavy at the navy.*

"Now!"

The word punched him, close to his ear, and he seemed to wake, blinked through rain in his eyes.

"What?"

"Move out, Private. You waiting for a taxi?"

It was Ferucci, and Adams realized others were close beside him, the familiar smell of Welty, distinct now, a low voice, "Got him, Sarge. Let's move out."

Adams felt his feet in motion, tried to blink through the fog in his brain, heard Welty beside him.

"You going crackers, sport? What's so funny?"

Adams tried to sort out his friend's words, said, "What? Nothing."

"You were laughing like hell, couldn't get you to stop. The looey was about to call for the doc to check you out."

Adams felt his head clearing, the march awakening him, the thumping weight of the grenades throbbing against him with each step. He had a surge of panic, thought of the crack-ups. No, God no. Not now. Can't leave these guys. He sorted through the officer's words, a hill to take, our guys up there. Wounded. That's bad. Gotta help 'em out.

"I'm okay. Just fell asleep I guess."

"Here. Eat this."

Adams took the cracker, softened by the rain, felt a different rumbling in his gut, healthier. It was actual hunger. He wolfed down the cracker, said, "Damn. Pretty good. You got more?"

"You've got plenty, you idiot. Your backpack's full of K rations. I saw 'em. No time to eat now. We've gotta move. Somewhere, another hill. Light's coming soon."

The clarity seemed to flow through him, and he put a hand on a pocket of his jacket, felt a heavy wad of grenades. Good.

"You got a D ration?"

"Jesus, Clay. Been trying to feed you for days. Now you're hungry? Hang on, I'll grab one out of your pack. I know damn well you've got those too."

Welty reached under the poncho, pulled something from Adams's backpack, stuffed it in his hand. Adams ripped off the thin cardboard, stuffed it in his mouth. The chocolate bar was syrupy and delicious, and Adams felt an urgent need to eat a dozen more.

"Shut up! Space out!"

Adams knew Ferucci's growl, savored the last thick taste of the choco-late, felt energized now, clamped his arm against the M-1 that hung from his shoulder. He raised his head, peered out past the hood of his poncho, saw the green glow of a distant flare, a clear image of the hill. But the sky was lightening, the first hint of sunrise, and he realized the rain had stopped. The men in front of him were visible now, shapes more clear, hel-mets and ponchos, rifle barrels, one man with a BAR slung up on his shoulder. More columns marched out beside them, a few yards away, and he saw a machine gun crew, three men, hauling the weapon, with the tri-pod and ammunition boxes. He looked out the other way, saw faces mostly looking down, the men spaced apart, more columns, all moving together, realized they were in the hundreds. The officer's words came back to him, *battalion.* That's us. Several companies. All going . . . where? A hill. He looked forward again, fog and mist, but the sounds were increasing, louder, the steady chatter of machine guns. He felt his heart beginning to race with a new energy, something he hadn't felt before. He could see only glimpses of the hill, the fog thick, drifting. The machine gun fire opened up suddenly to the right, from some hidden place, some of it American, hard shocks from artillery shells coming down far into the fog. More of us, he thought. He shivered, the wetness still chilling him, but the excitement was growing as well. Across the rolling fields, in every direction, Marines were moving as he was, toward the same place, the fight that continued to spread out all across the ground he couldn't see. He wanted to run, to jog, the aching stiffness in his legs gone, the energy building. It's time, Clay. Look at these guys. And the Japs. They gotta know we're coming. The fear was still there, the officer's words coming back. So, this is very bad. We're chewed up. They're killing corpsmen, for God's sake. *Scrub the hill.* He thought of a prayer, something he rarely did, but he couldn't form the words, nothing meaningful. God doesn't care, he thought. This is about men. Kill the bastards. We'll tell God about it later.

The scream of an artillery shell came straight past him, coming down close behind. More came now, hints of red streaks in the dull light, com-ing toward them from far to the left. The calls went out, the men hurrying their pace, the impacts coming in closer, enemy gunners in far places find-ing the range. But there was no cover, no stopping, no orders to dig in. He saw Porter doing as others did, waving his men forward. Adams crossed a two-rut trail, a road thick with mud, the wreckage of a jeep, something else, black metal, destroyed, swallowed by the mud. Beyond the narrow road was open ground, and through black smoke he could see a round pit, nothing like a shell hole. It was wide and clear, and men were moving down into the natural cover. The edges were neatly formed, concrete in a circular arc. He had seen this before, in the north, one of the many tombs the Okinawan people had constructed for the interment of their ancestors. The C-shaped depressions were a natural defense for avoiding shrapnel, but as every lieutenant had pointed out, a direct hit would likely shred every man in the depressed hole. The sergeants were moving quickly now, cursing shouts at the men to get up out of the concrete cover, to keep up the advance. Some obeyed, but Adams saw others, lumps of green, helmets and ponchos, sitting motionless against the low solid walls, too terrified to move. He ignored them, could not be angry at them, knew the fear, the terror, tried not to think of that. The tombs were everywhere, like some oversized cemetery, spread out across the open ground. Each one held men now, the shellfire driving them into cover. Adams wanted to follow, pure instinct, the luscious allure of a concrete wall, saw Porter yelling something, waving still, pulling his men past one of the round gaping maws. Above all the sounds, one rose, louder, the freight-train roar coming closer. Adams didn't hesitate, dropped flat, the shell passing close to one side, erupting with a deafening concussion of fire and smoke directly in the arc of the closest tomb. He hugged the muddy ground for a long second, the ringing in his ears sharp, painful, but he saw men rising up, Porter again. The lieutenant was moving back through his men, grabbing them, pushing them forward, and Adams saw his face, furious eyes, a glimpse back at Adams, a sharp nod, words, and Adams was up again, blew mud from his mouth, breathed in a lungful of smoke, fought it with a violent cough. He looked toward the tomb, concrete in huge pieces, scattered around a smear of black in the circular arc, pieces of . . . men.

"Move!"

"No stopping! Keep moving!"

He kept his eyes on the bloody awful scene, boots and a gathering pool of black . . . something. He turned away, tried to find the energy, saw Porter again. Adams saw him look into what remained of the tomb, of the men who had sought safety there. Adams felt a punch of fear. Who? Does he know? But there was no time for that, the lieutenant waving again, pushing his men past the awful scene. The shellfire came down in a new pattern now, to one side, splattering rhythmically into the muddy ground, bursts of water and dirt tossed skyward. One shell struck a piece of steel

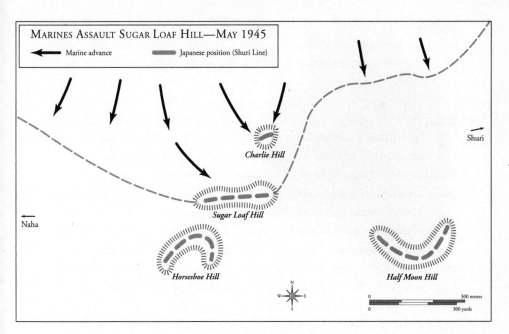

MARINES ASSAULT SUGAR LOAF HILL—MAY 1945

Marine advance   Japanese position (Shuri Line)

Charlie Hill

Shuri

Sugar Loaf Hill

Naha

Horseshoe Hill

Half Moon Hill

N
W · E
S

0   300 meters
0   300 yards

wreckage, and he saw men going down around it, like petals of a flower, blown out by the burst of shrapnel. Adams tried to ignore that, pushed his legs forward, searched for Porter, anyone familiar, but there were no faces, just smoke and mud and fire. The hill was close, squatting in the rolling plain like a fat loaf of bread, no more than forty yards high. Out in front of the hill there was no cover at all, just a gently sloping plain, streaks of tracer fire ripping across from several directions. On the hill itself came flashes from the muzzles of a hundred rifles, more, every rocky hole alive with men and guns. He hunched his shoulders, as though fighting off the rain, ran forward, following another man, rapid steps, muddy splashes, saw a fat rock at the base of the hill, men huddled low. Behind it one man was lying flat, blood on his head, the uniform ripped away, the man's arm . . . gone. Machine guns ripped the air all around him, pinging on the rocks, the smell of burnt coral, the pop and whine of rifle fire, mortar shells coming down all out across the open ground behind them. Adams glanced around, panicked, didn't know what to do, saw men falling around him, some diving for bits of shelter, some just collapsing. He leapt past the rock, saw men climbing, this hill so much like the one before, deep crevices and shallow cracks, overhanging rocks and jagged edges of coral. The smoke was thick, blinding, suffocating, every kind of projectile flying past, steel and rock. The blasts were growing in number, fiery eruptions small and large, the thumps and thuds and cracks blending together into one great deafening roar, punctuated by screams, shouts, the broad hillside its own perfect hell.

The bombing and shelling of the hill from American air strikes and naval guns had gone on for several days, long before the Marines had actually reached the hill itself. American artillerymen and tankers had naturally assumed they had so badly damaged the Japanese position that few of the enemy would be left to offer any kind of heavy resistance. That foolishness had been erased days before as the Sixth Division's Twenty-ninth Regiment and one battalion of the Twenty-second had attempted to capture the position, only to be ripped apart by the mostly unseen enemy. With those Marines so badly mauled, another battalion of the Twenty-second had been ordered in to make another attempt, continuing what had become a massive slow-footed assault against the entire Japanese defenses, what the maps now labeled the *Shuri Line.*

But Hill Two was becoming more than just a number on a map. The network of hills that lay behind it was part of the interconnecting defenses that ran in an undulating line through the Japanese strongholds that belted the entire southern half of the island, the extraordinary defensive wall created by General Ushijima, crafted by the perfect efficiency of Colonel Yahara. Since the American command had dismissed the notion of bypassing the line with amphibious assaults, General Buckner's troops were under orders that made it clear that if the Japanese defenses were to be broken, it would be up to the two army divisions now to the east, the Seventh and the Ninety-sixth, and the two Marine divisions, the First and the Sixth, to ram headlong into whatever the Japanese had prepared for them. Against Ushijima's eastern defenses, the army divisions faced the same kinds of bloody challenges, while in the center, the First Marines pushed toward the enormous stronghold anchored by Shuri Castle. But none of the Americans were finding easy success. In the west, what was now the right flank of the American drive, the Sixth Marine Division was charged still with securing the low hills that offered artillery protection for the city of Naha, and then capturing Naha itself. But the rugged rocky formations held far more power than the Marines had expected. Once they finally rolled over Charlie Hill, they encountered a larger, more elaborate section of the Japanese defenses, the maps showing only a series of low hills that seemed to resemble an arrowhead, aimed directly at their advance. With perfectly interconnecting fields of fire from the three hills, the Japanese had anticipated that any American assault would be decimated before any of the hills could be taken at all. Thus far, they had been right.

With orders to continue, the American field officers directed the attacks from command posts where the smoke ran thick. Those men did more of their work with binoculars than maps, and so the numbers and grid lines were not as important as what they could see for themselves. Quickly, labels on maps were replaced by names that more perfectly described the shapes of the obstacles the officers and their men could actually see. The names were mostly innocuous, but they gave memory to the struggles, would resonate with the fighting men far more than any simple number. Across the rear of the arrowhead, the larger, more spread-out promontories were now referred to as the Half Moon and the Horseshoe, each one labeled with perfect obviousness. But at the point, Hill Two was very different. Some described it as a half watermelon, a red-rock dome that rose little more than fifty feet high and three hundred yards long. But the name that stuck, the name the Marines would remember, was Sugar Loaf Hill.

SUGAR LOAF HILL, EAST OF NAHA, OKINAWA
MAY 14, 1945

They made progress in inches, feeling their way up into any kind of low cover, but no hole was safe, no rock or slash in the coral secure. The hill was draped and shattered with shellfire, small arms close by, artillery shells coming down on the Marines from distant caves, mortar shells impacting from knee mortars that could be anywhere at all. The low hilly formations beyond Sugar Loaf might have seemed to be an arrowhead, but to the Japanese artillery officers they created the other two points of a triangle, each one offering hidden gunners easy range toward the entire position, protecting the Japanese soldiers who the Marines now realized were right beneath them. Sugar Loaf Hill was hardly a solid chunk of rock. The Marines were assaulted from a network of caves and tunnels that made the hill more like a great fat honeycomb, hollow in ways the Marines were just figuring out. For most of the day they had no choice but to lie flat, seeking cover while trying to fight an enemy who might be anywhere at all. Some who had managed to reach the ragged rocks higher up the slope soon found rifle fire coming at them from behind, Japanese troops firing through narrow slits and spider holes that a man could step right over. Out in the open fields, American tanks attempted to drive close, but other than scattered shots at fleeting glimpses of targets, the gunners had little to do. The Marines were spreading out right in the midst of their enemy, and any shellfire would just as likely kill friend as foe. Worse for the tanks, the Marine riflemen who had been ordered to stay close, protecting the armor from suicidal Japanese soldiers, found that the tanks offered no protection at all from the impact of mortar shells. The tanks themselves were immediately vulnerable to a new threat, expertly aimed anti-tank weapons, fired, like everything else, from carefully disguised positions. Realizing their chaotic predicament, the tanks that were not quickly destroyed were forced to withdraw, seeking shelter far back from the network of hills. Most of the Marines were too occupied with survival and raw combat to notice that the tanks had left them to fight on alone. But any Marines who remained out on the open ground, or who attempted to reach the base of the hill, suffered the worst. With nowhere to hide, many of them were simply swept away in a storm of fire.

The rain came again, but only a brief shower, muddying the already wet soil beneath him. Adams had squeezed himself between two sharp rocks, filling a gap no more than the width of his chest, the ledge beneath his feet less than a yard wide. Around him men were firing in every direction, some lying flat in shallow remnants of burned brush, others rolling over in the mud, then rolling again, trying desperately to avoid the enemy fire as they fought in the wide open. Adams had reached the narrow ledge by climbing up past several of the other men, no one paying any attention, each man fighting his own war. He had given himself a single minute of rest, trying to catch his breath, to gather his senses, the roar of shellfire and weapons around him relentless. After a painful moment he loosened himself from the tight squeeze, struggled to pull a clip from the belt across his chest, rammed it into the M-1, stared straight up, a craggy rock jutting out a few feet over his head. There had been a stream of fire coming from above the rock, and he was close enough to hear hints of shouting in Japanese. Already Adams had tried to warn anyone who drew close, but his own shouts were useless, drowned out by the noise, the men below him mostly beyond his sight, focused solely on avoiding the steady storms of machine gun fire. A fresh cloud of smoke flowed along the face of the hill, settling into low pockets in the rough rock, and he struggled to breathe, the smoke offering momentary cover to the men most vulnerable. He saw flickers of motion, some of the Marines below him trying to move up, to advance away from the flatter depressions, several climbing up where he could see them. There were familiar faces, all of them plastered with dirt and sweat, staring up and out with wide-eyed terror. To one side, beyond the rock that jammed against him, he knew Yablonski was there, and close below him, Gridley had the BAR. Adams caught a glimpse of the big man's helmet, had seen Pop Gorman's face, a brief glimpse of the man who fed the BAR, more fear than Adams wanted to see. Within his limited field of vision, Adams caught sight of rifle barrels, heard the close rattle of a thirty-caliber machine gun, a crew somehow hauling their weapon up through the rocks. In the moments of calm, brief seconds of silence, Yablonski's curses came from the left side of him, a chorus of furious yelling, more frustration than anger. Adams couldn't see where he had gone, what kind of cover he had found, but Yablonski was firing his M-1 in a manic attack all his own. Whether Yablonski had any actual targets, Adams had no idea.

He leaned slightly away from the rocks, the rifle ready, no one in sight but glimpses of Marines. He realized he hadn't seen Ferucci since the climb had started, or Welty, had no time to pay attention to faces and names as he scrambled up into cover. Above him there had been a steady mix of Nambu fire and the distinct pop of a carbine, plus scattered rounds coming from M-1s in places Adams had not yet seen. He thought of Porter, hadn't seen him either, felt the usual stab of panic, thought, if he's dead . . . what do we do? How in hell does anybody give orders up here? His brain fought with itself, forcing his panic away. Just do what he said. Climb. Get to the top. Kill Japs. He repeated that to himself. *Kill Japs.* But you're safe here. Right here. Maybe. The bastards are everywhere. But so are we. This is stupid as hell! Is this what we're supposed to do? Porter would know. Welty knows. He's done this before. Where the hell is he? He can't be dead. Can't be. Dammit, I can't just stay here.

From his wedged-in position, Adams could see nothing but smoke, movement out to one side, in one low depression, the thirty-caliber, the men changing position, one man holding two ammo boxes. Good. Ammo.

Use it! The man suddenly crumpled, as though the boxes were too heavy, dragging him down at the knees, but Adams shook his head, one word, "No!"

The others in the crew pulled the man into someplace Adams couldn't see, and he pressed himself back into the craggy gap, closed his eyes. I can't just watch this. That man was shot. Dead maybe. What the hell do I do? He felt like crying, the fear draining everything away, and he tried to keep the shivering away, furious at himself. Coward! Do something! His best view was straight up, the rock, the Japanese voices, and the Nambu gun began to fire again, the woodpecker chatter close above him. He stared at the rock, black, thick, ugly, caught movement at his feet just below the ledge, and he jerked the M-1 that way, terrified surprise. He saw the helmet, the poncho, a hand on the ledge, gripping rocks, one leg swinging up on the ledge, the man rolling close to Adams's wedge in the rocks. The man was on his knees, low on the narrow strip of flat rock, and the face turned up toward Adams, a shock for both of them. He saw white circles around the man's eyes, his face blackened with mud and ash and a smear of blood. It was Ferucci.

"Sarge!"

Ferucci stared at him with pure frozen hate, said nothing at all, seemed confused, but then came clarity, recognition, and the sergeant nodded toward him, still silent. Behind him, below the ledge, a mortar shell suddenly erupted, showering both men with muddy ash, Ferucci down flat on the narrow slab of rock. Adams blew the dust away, blinked through the smoke.

"Sarge!"

Ferucci rose to his knees again, didn't seem to be hit, and Adams was crying now, didn't know what else to do. Ferucci stood suddenly, fell hard against Adams, pushing himself into the narrow crack, jamming Adams back even harder in the rock, hissed sharply into Adams's ear.

"Shut up! Japs everywhere! Everybody's scared! Get over it, you piece of shit!"

Adams said nothing, fought for control, the wind crushed out of him from Ferucci's pressure. The sergeant was breathing heavily, a low growl, "Sons of bitches. They're everywhere! Nobody's getting off this hill until nightfall. Anybody moves out into the open, they're chopped into meat! I'm not ready to be wrapped in this damn poncho!"

"Sarge, where's the looey?"

"Why? You think he knows what the hell we're supposed to do?"

"I just thought . . ."

"Shut up. Your job is to kill Japs, not think."

The words made an odd kind of sense, and Adams cleared his brain, focused on the sergeant's rifle, the grenades Adams could feel pressing against him. He whispered close to Ferucci's ear, "Right above us. That rock ledge. There's Japs right there. Nambu."

Ferucci turned his face, inches from Adams's.

"I know that, you idiot. What the hell are you doing about it? You got grenades?"

The question required no answer, and Ferucci pushed himself off Adams, backed away, into the open, the ledge, crouched low, looked up at the rocky spit above them. He yanked a grenade from his shirt, pulled the pin, backed up another step, Adams wanting to pull him back, new cracks of fire striking the rocks beside his feet. But Ferucci held his ground, reached one arm out, tossed the grenade up high, then collapsed back into Adams. The blast was muffled by so many others, but the burst of smoke came now, blowing out above them.

"That's how it's done, you jackass! Now let's get up this damn hill!"

Ferucci backed off him again, stared up, frantic eyes searching for a way to reach the larger rocks above. He crouched low, moved to one side, looked up again, and Adams saw the ball of steel, the grenade coming down, bouncing once, rolling right between Ferucci's feet. The sergeant saw it as well, reached down low, but the grenade exploded, blew against Adams as a punch of mud and splinters of rock. He cried out, animal sound, pain and terror, waited for the smoke to clear, felt nothing, no wounds, no pain. He pried himself out of the rocks, saw what remained of Ferucci, the man's legs gone completely, his crotch split open, a river of blood flowing down the rocks below. The man's face showed shock, his mouth open, and slowly the sergeant's torso rolled over, tumbled down the hill, disappeared, hidden suddenly by another blast, a mortar shell, that drove Adams back against the rocks. He covered his eyes, wiped at the dust, felt sick, tears, deafened, blinded by more smoke, shoved himself harder into the tight crack in the rocks. Another grenade suddenly appeared, dropping off the rock ledge, bouncing down, but away, below, into the burnt brush, and he lowered his head, the explosion adding to the dust and smoke. His chest was heaving, pain in his throat, a desperate need to cry out, the horror searing through him, changing now to anger. They

killed the sarge! They killed him! The fury grew, exploding in his chest, raw
red hatred, and he felt a sudden desperate need, an urgency to kill them, to
kill anyone, to grab the enemy and tear the man in half. His brain froze for
a brief second, a strange image in his mind, the ship, the lieutenant, ripping the steak into pieces, throwing it hard against the bulkhead. Adams
stared into the smoke, new blasts around him, and he sobbed for a long
minute, helpless again, yelled out, "Porter!"

It was stupid, and he knew it, no way the lieutenant should respond,
if he was there at all. Adams fought to control the panic, the fury, heard a
sound, right above him, like some twisted echo.

"Porter! Porter . . . come out!"

He wasn't fooled, knew it was the Japanese. The voice made him focus,
the enemy suddenly real, close, a target. The horror had turned into a sick
game now, and he called back.

"You first!"

From below the BAR suddenly erupted, splattering the rock he lay
against, the far side, and he was frozen, paralyzed, wanted to scream out,
it's me, you damn idiot . . . but then the body fell, straight across in front
of him, rolled down, through the pool of slop that was Ferucci's legs. The
man was Japanese.

"Got him!"

The voice belonged to Gridley, and now a new voice came, from
somewhere below.

"Let's go! We don't move up, they're coming down!"

It was Welty.

The Marines below Adams responded, a surge of motion, another
burst of fire from the BAR, a Japanese soldier tumbling down out of the
rocks just above him. The M-1s began to fire, upward, far above him, and
he saw the men emerging from their cover. The rifle fire continued, answered by the Nambu gun, others, farther along the hill, and Adams pulled
himself free from the tight squeeze, frustrated and furious, knelt low, some
of the fire from the others striking the rocks dangerously close to him. He
crawled forward, to the edge of the drop-off, saw the Japanese body, the
smoke blending with a sour, rotten smell, the sergeant's blood on Adams's
boot. He spun around, aiming his rifle at the craggy rock. But he was still
too close, underneath it, remembered Ferucci's toss of the grenade, tried to
reach a clumsy hand into his baggy pocket. But there was movement close
beside him, from beyond his hiding place, and he jumped, surprised, saw

a Japanese soldier, wide eyes staring into his. The man seemed not to know what to do, too close for his own weapon, too close for the M-1. A shot burst out from below Adams's feet, a crack against the rock close to the man's head. The man seemed confused, a brief second, the fatal pause Adams had seen before. He did as he had always done, the right hand coming hard in a flash of lightning against the man's jaw. The man fell backward, his helmet knocked away, tumbled upright into the crack where Adams had hidden. Adams's fists were still clenched, and he stepped toward the Japanese soldier, saw nothing in the man's eyes, *out cold.* Adams relaxed the fist, reached low, pulled out the K-bar knife from its sheath, waited. He wanted the man awake, wanted him to see, to feel it, but there was no time, the rifle fire growing, coming closer, the Marines below him rising up to the narrow ledge and beyond, voices. Adams ignored them, put the knife point against the man's throat, shoved it in hard, then made a twist, a slice, now jammed the knife harder, severing the man's spine, his head flopping forward, down, across Adams's chest, blood flowing out on Adams's hand.

19. PORTER

The Japanese grenades rolled past him, most of them tossed from high above, beyond the crest of the hill. His own perch was a dangerous basket for any kind of projectile, a muddy bowl set back close to the rocks, hemmed in by burnt brush. He gasped for air, had reached the spot pursued by the cracking fire of a Nambu gun, somehow found the energy to climb what seemed to be a sheer cliff. His legs ached, a rip in one side of his boots, but there were no wounds, nothing to stop him from continuing the climb. But that thought had been erased quickly, the ground out to both sides wide open, flat rock, and just above him the Japanese seemed to target every open space with perfect precision. You're not fighting a one-man war, he thought. You've got to get the rest of those boys up here, find a way to move higher still, silence as many of the enemy up there as we can. His breath was calming, and he glanced out, saw just below him, to one side, a crew working a thirty-caliber machine gun, firing almost straight up, the men straining to hold the gun in an awkward position so the gunner could draw some kind of bead on the enemy caves, which dotted the hillside close above. He watched them with pure admiration, knew that no one had been trained to fire a tripod-mounted piece anywhere but forward, but his admiration had been tempered by fear, the men and the precious gun constantly targeted by Japanese mortars. The blasts shook the rocks around him, the machine gunners still trying to make their weapon work, the same kind of desperation he could see from the others, some of the men in his own command, scampering from shallow cover across exposed rock where there was no cover at all. The Japanese grenades had come from no more than a few feet above him, men who probably had no idea exactly where he was. For now he had kept silent, no orders called out, no voice of authority, knew that if any Japanese soldier suspected he was an officer, someone would find a way to drop one right in his lap. He had used the carbine instead, the shots blending easily with the torrents of fire rolling up across the hill. An entire magazine had been emptied at the opening of the cave, far more from his own frustration than marksmanship. There had been hints of movement there, a brief glimpse of the barrel of the Nambu gun, but the angle was too severe, the cave facing out away from him. Even if his fire struck the rocks around the mouth of the cave, it did little to keep the Japanese from doing their job, taking aim at the men, *his men,* as they tried desperately to push up the hill. Not even the thirty caliber was effective from their position farther down, no one able to shove the Japanese back into their holes for more than seconds at a time. All along the hillside Japanese troops fired from what seemed to be every angle, heads popping up from narrow holes, rifle barrels appearing in shrubs. He had watched for that, frustrated and furious, as though playing a deadly carnival game, trying to aim his carbine with a quick jerk, seeking a single shot at a head, an arm, motion in the brush where the Nambu guns fired. But the longer he remained in his hiding place, the less fire he could offer. The belt around his chest held only three magazines, and he knew that with at least two more hours of daylight, there could be no more ammo, no supplies at all sent anywhere close to where he huddled with his men. He had a clear view of the beleaguered tanks out in the flat plain, watched as they withdrew, no choice but to abandon the Marines they had tried to support. Streaks of fire had poured out of the hill from a dozen Nambu guns, some of that coming out of rock faces and brush piles a few yards above him. He knew that there were others like him, higher up, scattered among the Japanese, had picked up the telltale pop of their M-1s or the distinct fire of a Thompson. There was another thirty caliber off to the left, and like him the Marines who had reached more than halfway up the hill were spread out in shallow cover, pressed into small gorges, all along the face of the hill. But there was one great difference between most of those men and him. The men closest below him were *his* to command, to gather and organize and complete the mission. He was supposed to *lead.* There were other officers across the hill, of course, most of them frontline lieutenants. But he knew that some of those men had gone down, had seen one in particular, Dawes, ripped apart by heavy fire from a machine gun as he led his platoon into a thicket just above the base of the hill. Porter had been stunned by the sight of that, had known Dawes since officer training, but there could be no stopping, no help, Dawes's own men continuing to scramble up, braving the Japanese guns to retrieve their commander. As Porter reached higher ground, he had been amazed that runners had found him, desperately scared men who had been sent from below, whose single mission was to find any officer. They brought urgent word that command was desperately needed in other places, to expand their commands to include men who had become leaderless. Word came that at least two captains were dead, and Porter thought of Bennett, had last seen him down close to the base of the hill, directing fire with a radio, calling back to gunners and observers for the larger guns that were supposed to be helping them out. So far those guns had been no help at all, no artillery officer wanting to risk killing Marines who struggled too close to the Japanese targets.

The Nambu guns closest to him were aimed in a downward slant, ripping through the pockets of brush that still remained on the hill, or chipping away at the rocky crags that hid the Marines still trying to find their way to the top. He had tried to move out next to one of the hidden craggy spaces, the mouth of what seemed to be a cave, had seen too much firing there for a single gun crew. The men close below him had taken a full hour of fire from that one opening in the rocks, and he knew what that meant, that the cave had to be part of a larger network, where carriers could move unimpeded, Japanese troops back in the hill supplying all the guns with ammo and replacement barrels, or maybe switching out the guns with fresh ones. Down below, some of his men had fired back, but those men who dared to reveal their position, to fire even a single round had been struck down in a shower of lead. He had watched with sickening helplessness as the wounded Marines were retrieved by men who seemed to ignore the danger. He knew that some of those were corpsmen, but others were simply doing the job, obeying their own conscience. But those men were not always lucky, and they had gone down as well. Some of the dead had been pulled back into cover, others still laid out on open rock, bloody wounds from mortar shells and the Nambu guns that ripped open bodies, took away limbs. After dark, he thought. We'll get those men back down when it's safe. Somebody will. Somebody has to.

The training had been driven hard into all of them, no man left behind, *no man,* and he had seen the extraordinary effort even his own men had made to pull the casualties back down the hill. To the officers, the emotional lesson had come from a textbook, that the officers would inspire their men on their own if necessary, retrieving any man who went down. But there was nothing inspirational in watching his own men get shot to pieces. He had felt useless, angry, building a hate for the Japanese and for himself, the lieutenant who was supposed to take care of his boys. From his perch, he could *monitor their progress,* one of those duties spelled out in another textbook, but the Nambu gun in the cave was too close to him, too utterly infuriating, too dangerous and deadly, and was killing his men with casual ease.

The perch also gave him a perfect view of the fighting out to the side, someone else's men, more of the bare rocky places peppered with the bodies of Marines, mixed alongside dead Japanese, black bloated corpses that might have been there for days. The Marines would certainly retrieve their own, but he could see clearly now that the Japanese had no such priority. All up through the ragged hillside, bodies were laid out in grotesque shapes, some disguised by the mud so that a man wouldn't know what was there until he crawled across it. The rain had washed some of that away, but not in the low pits, the shell holes and flat places like the one that held him now. Beneath him the mud seemed to be more like stinking black oil, what was left of three Japanese machine gunners, the rags of their uniforms holding shattered bones close by in a cluster of burnt brushy stubble. He had tried to ignore them, knew that whatever artillery shell made the hole that gave him protection had probably been the same shell that killed the three men, and so they might have been there for a week or more. He pulled himself to the farthest corner of the muddy pool, but beyond was flat open rock. He had tried moving that way already, to escape the small piece of hell, only to draw fire from another Nambu gun that seemed suspended in the rocks no more than twenty feet above him. From the mud hole he was just back at an angle the gun couldn't reach, and the enemy seemed to know that, and so, for now anyway, ignored him.

The Nambu in the cave sprayed out fire again, and he thought of the nickname someone had come up with to describe the sound, the chatter of a woodpecker. Doesn't sound anything like that from here, he thought. Sounds like something I need to blow to hell. He had kept his attention mostly on that one place, expected that the Japanese who occupied the cave might still try to erase him with a grenade. Until more of his men could make their way closer, there was nothing else he could do but wait, and so, with his ammo running low, he had made that one Nambu his single purpose. The carbine rested on one knee, its muzzle barely above the stubble, waiting for anyone at the cave mouth to show himself. Instead they kept their fire on the men down the hill, who still struggled to push upward inches at a time.

He rose up slightly, looked below, Marines in every corner of every gap, some firing upward, some just hunkered down. Dammit, he thought, sure as hell some of 'em are waiting for *me*. They need something, someone to get them moving. The longer they sit, the worse it's going to get. The mortars will find them, even after dark. He raised his head a few inches higher, saw farther below, more men along the base of the hill. They were just reaching the incline, the Japanese greeting them with waves of fire, the first scattering of rocks seeming to burst into pieces around them, mortar blasts dropping down in random patterns, men going down, some just . . . gone, obliterated by Japanese artillery fire that rolled across from distant positions. Farther out, on the wide-open ground, more men were moving up toward the hill, the scampering march into what had become, pure and simple, a meat grinder. He clenched his jaw, watched them falling, no cover at all. More dead lieutenants, he thought. The Japs know that, and those poor bastards are the first target. He had seen too much of that in every fight. So often, in the wide-open spaces, the Japanese had an uncanny knack for dropping the officers first.

For a long minute he kept his stare out to the open ground, watched those men slogging forward, pushing past plumes of mud and fire, the impact of mortar and artillery fire. He had no idea who they were, who their officers might be, Bennett not telling him any more than he needed to know. They continued to come, emerging out of each blast of smoke, but some were chopped down in the mud, the wounded still moving, some crawling, the sound of their agony erased by the steady roar of the shelling. He couldn't look away, the surge of men pushing to the edge of the hill, another part of the battalion moving up into the ragged crags. As they climbed, many were hidden by the same gaps and slices in the coral that had protected him, and he knew they were filling every space, slipping into holes and muddy hollows, sliding in behind rocks. Some men were better at hiding than others, and he was helpless to change that, saw boots dangling out from rocky perches, drawing the fire of the sharpshooters and Nambu guns. A mortar shell came down close now, just below him, jarring impact into a thick brushy hole. He was knocked back, hit the rock behind him hard, knocking his breath away, gasped for air, curled up tightly, angry at himself. No time for sightseeing. From the brush below there were screams, then another blast, straight into the same hole, the screams gone. His breath came back, and he struggled to lean forward, nothing to see, the hole just a rolling cloud of dust and smoke. Too many of his men had already tumbled off the hill, victims of the grenades, the mortar fire, some picked off by Japanese sharpshooters, a weapon that seemed to him more dangerous than any other. The single crack and ping had come past him several times, aimed somewhere below, and once he had reached the muddy bowl, so close to the tall rocks, he felt safe from that. But the men hidden down below were completely vulnerable, and the careless man who peered up would probably never hear the well-aimed round that struck the helmet, the helmet that was supposed to protect them. The snipers scared him more than the mortar rounds, something he had learned from the fights he had gone through before. The training had drilled that into him, of course, that any officer who revealed his identity by the careless slip of a show of authority could be the first man to die. They died on Guam, he thought. They're dying here. The stupid go first. Maybe that's how it's supposed to be.

He sat back against the rock, no way to keep his legs out of the stinking black mire, pulled the carbine to his chest, thoughts racing through his brain, what he should do, what orders to give. He had felt this kind of fear before, knew it was never acceptable, that he had to find the iron inside of him, make the move, put himself out *there,* do whatever it took to draw the rest of the men farther up the hill. Dammit, it's time to be . . . what? In charge? Those boys are waiting for me, and no matter how many of them are left, they can't do this on their own. Some will try, some have already tried, the brave and the stupid, no idea how deadly the Jap fire can be. Some of those are the replacements, believing the ridiculous propaganda that the Japs are half blind and subhuman, that all we have to do is shoot at them and the battle is won. No, they need someone to show them just what the hell we're doing up here. And that's *you.* He still held the carbine tight against him, stared again at the opening of the cave a few yards away, his useless vigil. Figure this out, Lieutenant. Figure it out right now.

I t seemed odd at first, that no matter how *normal* it was supposed to be, he had never become quite used to every enlisted man saluting him, calling him *sir*. But not out here, not in the battle zones, that order given to the men before any other. On Guam he had seen the mistakes, a careless reflex, a salute followed almost immediately by the snapping crack of a man's head. The Japanese snipers had been amazingly accurate on both Guam and Saipan, and no matter the constant patrolling by the Marines, they seemed to be everywhere, doing their damage and then vanishing into thin air. The binoculars could be deadly as well, another agonizing lesson. The new lieutenants were the worst, straight-backed men right out of training, who thought leadership meant that in every confrontation with the enemy they should stand out like some statue on a battlefield, glassing the countryside. The image stayed with him even now, one statue in particular, blackened bronze, so distinctive at Gettysburg. The officer candidates had been hauled there on a field trip, training on the ground of the country's bloodiest battle, lectured about the bad tactics of the Confederates. He had noticed what most hadn't, what even the instructors ignored, that out there on Little Round Top, General Gouverneur K. Warren stood in perfect repose, out in the wide open, holding his binoculars, gazing out with what Porter had felt was stuffed-shirted pomposity, as though daring the Confederates to come up on his hill. Even then Porter knew the obvious, that if he became an officer, and joined the fighting, the tactics at Gettysburg involved muskets, not the weapons they would likely face from the Japanese. And yet in every battle, every island, he had seen the same pose, fresh-faced officers leading men for the first time, one distinct memory from Saipan, a green lieutenant rushing ashore, eager to find that good vantage point, scampering up that first piece of high ground to strike that pose. If those men were unlucky enough to be anywhere close to a Japanese sniper, they went down so quickly, their own platoon never even learned their name.

He knew those men had long gone, that any officers on this hill now were veterans. But we're being chewed to pieces, he thought. They'll be sending us help, damn sure of that. Replacements coming in all the time. But if they keep trying to climb this thing in broad daylight, none of those boys will survive long enough to find out what it's like to do this . . . to watch your own men die while you sit in a pool of someone's guts.

He thought of calling out, giving the loud order they would hear. But there was a shout below him, someone else giving an order of his own, and he saw a burst of activity, a flurry of M-1 fire aimed toward the cave, splats on the rocks above him. Men were in motion, a quick run across the open patch of rocky ground. They jumped down, tumbling into brush, and the Nambu gun responded, but too late, and now the M-1 fire slackened, the mission accomplished. But the Nambu kept up its fire, ripping across the rock, then into the brush, and he pictured what was happening in the cave, the Japanese gun crew, one more belt of ammo consumed. The cries came, the only words he had heard for some minutes, the cry he had heard before, in every place he had pushed through, all the way up the hill.

"Corpsman!"

"Corpsman!"

He pounded one fist against his leg, furious, aimed the carbine, fired one round across the opening of the cave, useless. His anger was aimed as much at himself as the enemy in their hole. Damn it all, do something! At least let the boys know you're here, that you know what's going on! Oh, yeah, then what? You gonna holler at them to keep their heads down? Yeah, a real leader. *Be careful boys, you might get hurt.* They're your responsibility for God's sake. He glanced back at what remained of the Japanese corpses, felt overwhelmed by the stinking ooze that coated his legs, his boots. Enough of this.

The thirty caliber opened fire again, below him and to the left, and Porter eased his head forward, saw a frustrated glimpse in his direction from one of the men. It answered a mystery. Okay, yeah, they know I'm here. But they're in no place to do any good. None of us are. To his right the Nambu gun opened again, and Porter slid that way, to the edge of his cover. The rock just above him splintered, a hard *crack,* and he dropped low, his face in the mud, his helmet jarred to the side. He cursed himself, thought, somebody else knows I'm here too. But that sounded like M-1 fire. If I get killed by one of my own boys . . . Okay, then don't. He pulled his helmet straight, spit the filthy mud from his mouth, clamped down on the gag rising in his throat. He punched his arm in the air, a quick short wave with the carbine. See? It's one of *us,* you idiot. In front of him the Nambu fired again, the wisps of smoke drifting out of the cave's opening, and he stared that way, thought, that son of a bitch is right there, perched for all the world on his rocky little hole, thinking no one can get to him. He scanned the hill above the gun, no place to go, no footholds but open rock, putting him in the wide open, knew the Japanese up higher would see anything he tried to do. Dammit! The grenades in his pocket jabbed against his leg, and he felt a sudden spark, a burst of an idea. The grenade was in his hand now, and he gripped it hard, the idea growing, leaping through his brain. He laughed, manic tension, thought, well, how about a little slow-pitch softball? He glanced back at the narrow pool of black water, his shallow pit of cover, thought, this might work. It might kill you in the process, but if you're any good at this, it could take that bastard out. He held tight to the grenade, pulled the pin, took a breath, counted in his head, practiced the rhythm of seconds, one . . . two . . . three . . . okay, that's about right. Play ball.

He eased up to his knees, the grenade handle still gripped tightly, then he opened his fingers, the handle popping out, igniting the fuse, and he counted out loud, "One . . . two . . ."

He lobbed the grenade in a high arc, underhanded, like a softball, the slow pitch, then rolled back into the mud, pulled himself as low as he could. The blast came in midair, out in front of the rocks, and he raised his head, stared through the smoke, grabbed another grenade, ready for the same trick. But there was a new sound, a grunting cry, and suddenly a man rolled forward, straight out of the rocky face of the hill. The man tumbled down, gathering rocks as he went, slid to a stop in a patch of thorny stubble. A cheer came from below, but Porter kept his head down, heard cheers close by as well, the crew of the thirty. I'll be damned, he thought. It worked. Slow-pitch softball. They don't call it that in training, of course. Proximity blast. That's how it's done. He knew that the one silenced gun wouldn't give them relief for long, stood now, letting the men below see him clearly. The men responded, no sounds, just movement, some of them climbing up from hidden holes and cracks, scampering upward, toward him. Immediately the blast of a mortar erupted down to one side, then another, another Nambu gun, farther along the slope, another grenade tumbling down from above him. The Marines responded with fire of their own, another thirty, farther down, M-1 fire, and he waited for the smoke to thin out, thought, at least it's something. They found new targets. Just keep those bastards above me in their holes, just for a few seconds . . . let me get to that cave. Sure as hell, there are more Japs in that cave moving up to take that gun crew's place. He kept a low crouch, saw men still in motion, using the smoke for cover, moving past fresh bodies, wounded men, rifle fire coming down from above. The M-1s answered, and now another thirty caliber, farther away, the rocks overhead pinging, shattering, a body suddenly rolling down right in front of him, past his perch, crashing on hard rocks below. He raised his fist, a salute, stupid gesture, but the good shooting of the machine gunner was energizing, would inspire his men as well. The thirty kept up its fire, the cover they needed, and he shouted, "Move up! Go!"

They came out of their cover and he waited, watched them, saw that most of the ponchos were gone, some of the men shirtless, their skin shining like white torches in the black rock. But there was no time to chew anyone out, the thought flashing through his brain: It's going to rain again, you idiots. Then what? We'll stop the war so you can get a raincoat? Morons. You can't all be *my* boys. But, right now . . . get your asses up this hill.

He watched them through the smoke, saw faces, eyes peering under helmets, staring up, the men moving closer. More men were coming from farther down, across the open rocks, and he wanted to halt that, stop them, but there was no time, the men following each other automatically. The distant Nambu gun found them now, shots in quick succession, more rifle fire from above. Some of the Marines reached the brushy holes, but others simply fell, some rolling away, two men lying where they dropped. He closed his eyes, cursed loudly, glanced toward the cave, no sign of anyone new, shouted out, "Up here! Brush along the rock to the right! Climb like hell!"

He had sent them in the direction of the thirty's crew, knew only that the cluster of cover there seemed to hide those men for a longer time than he had been in his own perch. Whether they heard his order or not, men were moving up that way, and he saw a handful of men reaching the brush, sliding forward, some right into the machine gunners' laps. The mortar shells came again, the Japanese far above reacting to the new surge of movement, and the blasts ripped all across the hillside, but mostly farther down, into the fresher men who had just begun their climb. He watched the men closer to him coming up, the distant Nambu gun ripping into them, more men collapsing, some just hitting the deck, taking cover where there was no cover, no other place to hide. Another mortar shell impacted, closer up the hill, blowing dust and rock skyward, and he dropped down again, splashing the watery filth. The cries came again, wounded men, hopeless requests for a corpsman. The shock of the blast drifted away, and the fury returned, different now, thoughts of generals and their *plans*. This is bullshit! This isn't a plan, it's raw perfect stupidity. He recalled Bennett's words, passed along from the colonel. *Get to the top.* Straight up. Sure, any other time this hill is a hefty jog, a good training run. Did somebody back in those tents forget there's a million damn Japs up here? He had long understood why enlisted men seemed to hate officers, some hiding it better than others. Well, right now, I'm with *you* boys.

He heard a scrape on the rocks, was surprised to see faces appear, three men, filthy, wide-eyed, clambering up the rocks toward his watery crater. They saw him now, gasping relief, tumbled forward, splashing close to him. They seemed oblivious to the stench, low breathless voices, one man familiar, and Porter knew it was the loudmouthed jerk, Yablonski.

"There's Japs right above us! Saw 'em. They just sat up there and watched us come." Yablonski seemed to realize who Porter was now, but his expression didn't change. The man had carried an angry stare with him for the eighteen months Porter had him in his platoon. "So, looey, what you want us to do now?"

Porter looked at the others, one man unfamiliar, the other, the redhead, smudged glasses, the name coming to him. Private Welty.

"Well, we can't stay here, that's for sure. They probably watched you so they know where you were gonna end up. Grenades will be next." Porter paused, stared up, thought of leaving the precious nest, gave out a long breath. "The cave, over there. We make a dash for that. Each of you, pull a grenade, have it ready. Hell, pull the pin in case we come face-to-face with those bastards. One thing, they'll be surprised. Might be the only advantage we have."

"Pull the pin?"

The third man stared at him as though the lieutenant were completely insane.

"Yes! Pull the pin. Hold tight to the damn thing. It won't hurt you, son, until you release the handle. You did this in training a thousand times."

"No, sir, I didn't. I'm a cook."

The others looked at him, and Porter said in a hard whisper, "Don't ever call me *sir*! What the hell are you doing up here?"

The cook glanced at the other two, who seemed as baffled as Porter.

"We couldn't get the kitchen truck up close enough last night, the mud and all. Captain Lomaz told us to grab a rifle and come up here, try to help you out."

Porter realized the man had no weapon at all.

"What rifle?"

He saw tears now, running down the man's filthy face, could tell he was very young and very scared.

"Dropped it. Stepped on somebody . . . dead. Couldn't see . . ."

"How the hell did you get up this far? Yeah, okay, shut up. War is hell. You got a forty-five?"

"You mean a pistol?"

Yablonski had said nothing, but rose up now in front of the man, knelt facing him, and Porter saw the fist go out, a hard punch across the younger man's jaw. The cook fell to the side, his face splashing into the mud, an audible cry. Porter grabbed Yablonski by the shoulder, didn't know what to say, and Yablonski turned to him.

"He'll get us killed. Best we leave him here. He's . . . injured."

Yablonski didn't wait for any more instructions, moved out past the lieutenant to the edge of the brushy perch, and Porter knew there was nothing he could do about any of this, not here. But, he thought, I'm still in charge of this lunatic. Porter moved up close beside him, said, "Wait for me to get out on the rocks. I'll rush the cave opening. You come in right behind me. Use the grenades, toss 'em hard, back into the cave. If they haven't killed us by then, we should wipe out anybody who's still there."

Yablonski looked at him, still no change in the furious glare.

"If you say so."

"Right. One day *you* can play general, but not today."

He glanced at Welty, who said, "I'm ready."

Porter saw the calm on the redhead's face, the opposite of Yablonski. Another day at the office. Strange little bastard.

Porter focused on the chorus of firing across the hill, unceasing, the M-1s and the thirty still peppering the Jap position above. Down below the thumping rhythm came from a half-dozen Japanese mortars, blasting the rocks and the men who sought cover there. The smoke was rising again, and Porter thought, good time to move. He took a long breath, let it out, leapt out of the cover, muddy boots slipping on the rock, the slope flattening out, a narrow ledge. He ran hard that way and above him, the hill came alive with fire, another Nambu gun, answered by fire from below, M-1s, the thirty, Marines in position to see the three-man attack. Smoke still seeped from the cave mouth, and he hesitated, a brief second, then heaved the grenade around the edge. The seconds passed, eternity, and the cave erupted in a billowing fountain of smoke and debris. He didn't wait, rolled into the narrow opening, tried to hold his breath, impossible, the fumes choking him. There were loud voices farther back in the cave, and he clawed his way past the shattered remnants of the Nambu. The cave was no more than four feet across, and not much taller, but the smoke hid the depth. Yablonski was there now, pushed past him, the cave still a fog of dust, and Yablonski threw the grenade, then fired his M-1 in a quick burst, emptying the clip. All three men dropped flat, the blast much farther back, more dust flowing past them. Porter raised his head, stared at the smoke, saw now, the cave fell downward, a steep slope, said, "Grenade! Throw it hard!"

Welty obeyed, the grenade flying past Yablonski, bouncing, tumbling away, all three men collapsing again against the rocks. The blast came, much farther back, and now Yablonski threw another one, slow seconds, one more blast. Porter grabbed his leg, "Enough!"

Yablonski didn't turn, kept his stare into the billowing smoke, slapped a clip into his M-1.

"Let's go!"

The command came from Yablonski, and Porter blew through the stink of the explosives, the smell of something horribly rotten, said, "No! Stay here!"

Yablonski turned now, animal fury, said, "This cave might go right into the center of this hill. We can take out the whole damn thing, wipe out a flock of these bastards!"

Yablonski turned away, seemed ready to carry out his own idea, and Porter kept his grip on the man's leg.

"With what? There's three of us, Private! As narrow as this cave is . . . we're easy pickings for one Jap back there with a pop gun. We're backing out of here! Let's keep moving. The idea is to get to the top, remember? Both of you . . . you get out into the open, start climbing, find cover anywhere you can. The boys down below see us, they'll cover us, and I'll try to signal them to come up too."

Yablonski seemed to calm from Porter's unyielding grip on his leg. He turned again and Porter saw the disgust, knew Yablonski had only one way of thinking, that this cave might go all the way to Tokyo. Behind the lieutenant, Welty said, "We need to get more men up here. Those Japs above us know we're here. Right now we're just stuck in a hole."

Yablonski seemed resigned to his lost opportunity to end the war, slid backward, knelt in the narrow gap.

"Okay, boss, what now?"

Porter moved back close to the mouth of the cave, desperate for fresh air. He waved the carbine outside, hoped it would attract the right kind of attention.

"Saddle up. We're climbing."

He stepped out of the cave, navigated the sharp drop immediately in front of the opening, slipped quickly to one side, making room for the other two. Below, the men were responding as he had hoped, rapidly making their way up through the morass of uneven hillside. Yes, dammit! Let's go! He crouched, spun toward the crest of the hill, scanned quickly, searching for the Japanese, saw nothing but the jagged ridgeline. Where are you, you bastards? He kept the carbine at his shoulder, ready to put out any covering fire his men might need, felt Yablonski beside him, doing the same. Yablonski had the same questions, said, "They're up there! I saw them!"

"Stay on 'em. Anything moves, blow hell out of it."

Welty was there as well, a third muzzle aimed upward, and Porter could hear the sound of the men coming up from behind, said, "Time to climb. Let's get to that ridge."

He rose from his knees, still in a crouch, the carbine pointed forward from his waist. He stepped up past a muddy hole, a lump of rock, the footing slippery, uncertain, kept his eyes sharp on the ridgeline. The sounds of the fight still rolled over the hill, an echo he had grown used to. The roar seemed to grow, closer, machine guns, rifle fire, men screaming, but he tried to ignore that, kept his eyes on one place, where the Japanese had been, where they would certainly be again. Behind him the others were gathering quickly, following him, a surge of two dozen men, led by the man in charge, the man who knew what to do. The ridgeline was less than ten feet above him, the flatter ground now rising in a sharp incline, and he dropped his eyes, searched for a foothold, his boots kicking into soft rock. There was a flicker of movement to one side and he glanced that way, a cut in the rocks, a narrow crevice he hadn't seen before. He started to turn that way, the carbine swinging around, caught the glimpse of a rifle, saw the muzzle, a small black eye pointing toward him. The shot struck him in the chest, tearing through him, a punch knocking him back. He staggered, fell to one knee, and now new sounds came, a sudden burst of rifle fire, close by, the response from the men beside him. His eyes tried to stay on the crack in the rocks, the rifle barrel gone, and he tried to stand, but there was nothing there, no strength, no feeling at all. He took a breath, choked away, reached down with his hands, steadying himself, but his face came down hard on the rocks, no pain, just the hard choking twist in his throat. The shots were growing dull, the roar in his ears fading, a soft silence, and he struggled to breathe, to move, thought of the men, the orders, the crest of the hill. There was no feeling at all now, a glimmer of sight, a last frantic search, a glimpse of blood, flowing away, adding to the pool of black mud.

20. ADAMS

He tried to catch his breath, stared up in perfect horror, saw Welty squatting down, close to the body of the lieutenant. Others had stopped, too many men trying to help, nothing anyone could do. Adams moved closer, up the rocky hill, stared at the lieutenant's face, the eyes still open, empty stare, the skin already a pasty white.

"What happened?"

The question went beyond the idiotic, but no one responded, Welty upright again, a hard shout.

"Up the hill! Move it!"

More men were coming up through the defiles and muddy gaps, few stopping to see the body, who it might be. But Adams stood frozen, a long desperate moment, wanted to pull Porter up to his feet, to help the man, do *something*. The voice came from in front of him, the ugly sneer from Yablonski.

"He's meat. I got the Jap. Let's go."

Welty was close to him now, pulling his sleeve.

"Clay! We gotta go. We're in the open. Let's make the ridgeline. The Japs are in every damn hole! Come on!"

Adams saw the men moving by him, heard the grunts, the scuffing of the boots. He looked at Porter once again, but there was nothing else to see, the oozing blood coming from the man's chest, staining the rocks beneath him. Porter was gone.

"A corpsman. We need to find . . ."

"There ain't any corpsmen, Clay! They're all gone! Get your ass up the hill!"

Welty jerked him hard, and Adams began to move, following, the flow of men rising up and over the jagged coral. He had no strength in his legs, but somehow he kept up, a slow plod. Welty was still in front of him, and Adams forced the words out, "They got the sarge too. Right in front of me. A grenade."

His harsh breathing stopped the words, and he heard a grunting response from Welty.

"Saw it."

They climbed the sharper incline now, a ridge of coral, thick with mud and broken shards of rock that made any climb difficult. He tried to focus, to wipe the image of Porter from his mind, saw that some men were holding grenades, arms cocked, and Adams felt for his, stumbled on the coral, lost his grip on the M-1. The rifle clattered against the rock, and he grabbed it quickly, urgent fear. The ridgeline was close above him, and he realized it was where the Japanese had been, where they had dropped their grenades down on him, the grenade that killed Ferucci. The others were going up and over the sharp ridge, and he followed, pulled himself up with one hand, noticed the thick crust on his skin, his sleeve soaked with the blood of the Japanese soldier. He swung his legs over, saw a narrow ditch, hand-tooled, not just the craters from American shellfire. The trench extended in a snaking curve, following the terrain, dipping lower far to the right, where the hill opened up with shallow ravines, narrow cuts. The trench was a perfectly constructed hiding place for sharpshooters, a perfect place to toss grenades down on men who struggled to reach the position. They pulled back, he thought. Where the hell did they go? He looked up, beyond the trench, saw the rolling crest of the hill, the top, the place they were supposed to go. His mind focused on that, but there was too much activity around him, a dozen more Marines making their way into the narrow slit, as surprised as he was, every man grateful for the halt to their climb. They continued to come, some by themselves, staggering up to the trench, panting, exhausted, the shirtless glistening with sweat, others soaked in their clothes, some still in their ponchos. The faces searched the men already there, seeking a friend, or some authority, someone to tell them what to do. Up past the trench the hill was cut with crevices, shell holes, and blasted rock. But no one was moving up that far, the men close to him dropping to one knee or lying flat, all of them seeming to know that, for the moment, on this one small piece of Sugar Loaf Hill, the Japanese had abandoned the fight.

Adams knelt, tried to catch his breath. The rains had not come all day, and he glanced up, a gray shroud of clouds, thankful. He realized now the fighting all along the higher part of the hill had become more sporadic, brief bursts, single shots and mortar blasts, small firefights. Some of the sounds came far out beyond the hill, the flat muddy ground where the roads led to the city, Naha. But here, on this part of the ridge, the firing had stopped altogether, the thick wet air strangely quiet. Adams heard voices around him, Welty coming up close to him, saying aloud, "We need to spread out, keep tight in this trench, hold our position here until someone tells us what to do."

Several men seemed to hang on Welty's words, one man responding, "Ain't that you?"

Welty shook his head.

"I'm just a private."

"Well, hell, Private, you seem to have more brains than anybody else on this hill. What you think we oughta do?"

Adams saw more faces turning toward Welty, knew the redhead was sensitive about the glasses, all the old insults from training, *hey, Four Eyes*. But Adams knew something about Welty's calm, his experience, thought, that man is probably right. Welty searched the faces, another cluster of men rolling up and over the craggy ridge, grateful for the shallow trench. Welty focused on one man, said, "You! We need you!"

The face was familiar to Adams, the man moving closer, past the others, staring at Welty.

"For what?"

Welty lowered his voice.

"You're a damn sergeant, right?"

"Yeah."

"Well, until somebody says they outrank you, I guess you're in charge."

Adams recognized the man now, another of the platoon's squad leaders, Sergeant Ballard. Ballard glanced around, said, "Where's the looey?"

Welty seemed frustrated, made no effort to hide it.

"He's dead! He's on those rocks down there."

Ballard nodded slowly, said, "Wow. Who's your sergeant? He here?"

"Ferucci. He's dead too. Dammit, this ain't any time to take roll call."

Ballard seemed to gather himself, still scanned the men in the trench. Adams felt a new burst of gloom, thought, he doesn't have the first idea what to do. He moved closer to Welty, perfect earshot of Ballard, said, "Maybe *you* should take charge, Jack."

Ballard looked at Welty, seemed to agree with Adams's suggestion. Welty seemed ready to explode, said to Ballard, "Look, you're in charge. We should spread out, down both flanks of this trench. There's two thirties that have made it up so far, we should put one on each flank." He scanned the others, and Adams saw Gridley, huffing over the rocks, still carrying the BAR. Behind him came Gorman, the older man helmetless, sweating, breathing heavily. Welty pointed, said, "BAR! Right here! Watch that ridgeline! Everybody, pass the word. Stay down along this line. Good cover. Watch for snipers, nobody get careless! They could still be down behind us!"

Gridley seemed puzzled, glanced at the others, said, "If you say so, Redhead. Where's the Japs at?"

Welty looked again at Ballard, who had clearly abdicated any authority. Welty wiped his glasses with a filthy sleeve, hooked them back over his ears, said, "They skedaddled out of here. But it'll be dark soon, and they'll be coming, sure as hell. For now they gave us this cover, so we oughta use it. Keep low, but keep ready. This is a hell of a good place for somebody to toss a grenade. You see one, try to toss it back."

Adams stared at Ballard, who nodded, said, "Yeah. Good idea."

Welty was ignoring the sergeant now, said, "I'm going up there, take a peek at the ridge, maybe get a look at the other side. Somebody come with me." He turned to Adams, then looked past him. "Clay . . . and you two."

Welty climbed up past the trench, stayed on his knees, then slipped to his belly. Adams moved out with him, the other two Welty had chosen, and Adams saw the exhausted fear in both of them, mixed with curiosity. Good question, he thought. What's on the other side? Welty pushed himself farther up what seemed to be the last bit of incline. The mud was deeper, shell holes full of thick brown water, rocks tumbled about, the remnants from a handful of artillery barrages. Welty stopped, motionless, and Adams eased up close, could see far beyond the hill, a vast sea of mud, and in the distance, less than a quarter mile away, the other two hills in the arrowhead. Their shape was far from distinct, and he realized now that the other two were less of a single hill than Sugar Loaf, more spread out, far more uneven, dips and creases and rough remains of timber. But both hills were alive with activity, men in motion, some scampering away from Sugar Loaf, Japanese troops out in the open spaces, some emerging from hidden places Adams couldn't hope to see. Beside him, Welty whispered, "The brass wants us to take those hills too? This is the stupidest attack I've ever seen. Some damn general drew this up without having any idea what this place . . ."

He froze, no words, and Adams probed the silence, heard voices, Japanese, straight down the hill, distant, out of the line of sight. Welty slid backward, the others doing the same, no need for orders. It was only a few yards back to the trench, but Welty stayed on his belly, the others mimicking him. In the trench again, more men gathered, and Adams saw a new wave of men coming up into the trench, saw another of the sergeants, Mortensen, men speaking to him with low urgency, hands pointing toward Welty. Mortensen was a lean, lanky man, older, a touch of gray hair, rough face and sharp blue eyes. He was breathing heavily, carried a Thompson on his shoulder, one of the few men in the company who preferred the weapon that was only practical at close range. Welty moved close to him, seemed dwarfed by the man, said quietly, "Lots of Japs down below. Looks like we drove them back."

"We didn't drive anybody anywhere. They gave us this ridgeline so they can cut us off. Pretty sure of that. There's caves that probably go straight through this damn hill. They can hit us from anyplace they like. The caves we passed coming up here are still full of 'em, and we could be in a pile of shit up here. We found several narrow caves out to the right, and one of my men thought he'd check it out, and got blown to hell. Our grenades just chased the Japs in deeper. Unless somebody sends up some relief, we're probably done for. I plan to go down fighting, if I have to kick hell out of every one of those yellow bastards with my boot heels." He paused, and Adams saw nothing to suggest that Mortensen didn't mean exactly what he said. Mortensen scanned the position, said, "What's on our right flank?"

"Two thirties made it up this far, and I sent one down that way, where that brush begins. Looked like good cover. The other's out to the left, but the rocks are smaller. There's a passel of Japs right down below us on the far side. Lots of activity on the far hills too."

Mortensen nodded toward Welty, said, "Good job."

Welty hesitated, glanced around.

"Uh . . . Sergeant Ballard was here. Not sure where he went."

Mortensen didn't change his expression, said, "Doesn't matter where *he* went. You seen Porter?"

"He's dead."

Mortensen lowered his head.

"Damn. At least four more looeys down to the right got it. Saw the stretcher bearers, and the Japs hammered them too, sons of bitches. The corpsmen ran out of stretchers down that way, and were using ponchos, but then we ran out of corpsmen. One colonel got it too, I heard. You heard from Bennett? You got a radio, anything?"

"Uh, no. Sarge, I'm only a private."

Mortensen absorbed that, shook his head.

"Even the Corps makes mistakes. Unless somebody tells us different, we spend the night right here. You're in charge from this point left. I'll go back to the right. My own squad is mostly gone. Maybe one or two still alive. Never seen anything like this one. No place to hide, nothing to use for cover. The damn mortars . . ." Mortensen seemed to catch himself, raised up, the sea of faces close by watching the conversation. "All of you . . . you listen to this man! Until I say different, do what he says!"

The order was as short as it needed to be, no one objecting, except Welty.

"Sarge . . ."

"You call me that again up here and I'll break your glasses *and* your teeth. Dark in an hour. Nobody sleeps."

The sergeant looked at Adams now, studied his shirt, the blood crusted thick on Adams's sleeve.

"Damn, son, you okay?"

Welty seemed to notice the gory mess all over Adams now, said, "What the hell happened to you? You wounded?"

"Just a knife fight."

"I bet you won. Good for you. You sure you're not wounded?"

Adams shook his head, and Welty said, "A few wounded made it up here, but I haven't seen any medical bags."

Mortensen glanced around, called out a single word as a question.

"Corpsman?"

Faces looked his way, but no one answered. Close by, Gridley was wiping down his BAR, said, "Saw two get hit. Ain't seen no more."

Mortensen shook his head.

"Too damn easy a target for these bastards. Anybody gets hit up here, we'll have to make our own aid station." Mortensen stared beyond the trench, toward the crest of the hill. "The top, huh? Well, that's where they wanted us to be. I guess somebody *back there* will call this a *victory.*"

Welty led Adams along the ridgeline, the crest of the hill not more than a few yards above them. The Japanese works had simply faded away, the hillside now cut up by deeper holes, some of them made by American artillery. The mud was as it had been all across the hill, thick black pools gathered in the low places, most of those places now occupied by Marines. Welty moved quickly, appraising the position, men looking up at him as though appreciating his authority, even though almost none of them had ever seen him before. They moved past a thicket of brush, more burned stubble, a deep pocket, sharp rocks that opened into a miniature valley that was cut several feet deep into the hillside. In the bottom was a cluster of Marines, a thirty caliber, metal ammo boxes scattered around them. The tripod of the machine gun was broken, one leg supported by a well-placed rock. Welty stopped, the men staring up at them with dull, tired eyes. Welty said, "You're not the thirty I sent down here. Where'd you boys come from?"

The men looked up at him with puzzled glances toward each other, and one man said, "We come from down the damn hill. Where you come from? Mars?"

The smell of the men reached Adams now, sour, filthy, the wetness around them thick with the same horror that seemed to fill every low place. Adams nudged Welty, said, "They've been here awhile."

"Yeah, we've been here awhile. You think we can just go marching up and down this damn place like we own it?"

Welty glanced toward the ridge above them, stepped down into the depression, and Adams followed, the smells growing, could see how the hole could hold these men in good protection. The machine gun was tilted to one side, the rock not quite level for the tripod, and Adams could see a carpet of spent shells, spread all past the muddy bog the men seemed anchored to. Close beside him, Adams flinched, saw two corpses, men wrapped in ponchos, boots sticking out toward him. Marines. Welty said, "What's your unit?"

"You got the password, Captain Four-Eyes?"

"Hell no. Ain't had one for a couple days. How about 'Lala palooza'?"

"Close enough. Zeke here's been waiting to stick somebody who can't get the *l*'s right. Ran out of grenades last night. You got some you can spare?"

Welty fumbled through the baggy pockets on his jacket, Adams doing the same, each man pulling out a pair.

"Here. Take these. We got a few more. There's a few dozen of us up to the right, a Jap trench, or something like it."

The closest man took the grenades from Welty's hand, passed them to the others, spoke for the first time, a low, hard whisper.

"These won't last long. Full dark, the rain will come. After that, they'll come for us. Not much we can do."

The man's voice was different, and even through the whisper, Adams could hear his words distinctly, clear, the telltale sound of an education. Welty focused on that man as well, said again, "What unit?"

"Doesn't matter now. We're Marines."

Welty glanced back at Adams, then said, "Twenty-ninth? You been up here for . . ."

"Three days."

Adams stared at the well-spoken man, saw age, a glimmer of serious-ness he had seen before. He moved closer, squatted, said in a whisper, "You're an officer."

The man stared at him, shook his head slowly.

"Nope. Not anymore. Lost my whole damn company. My bars went with 'em. They followed me up here, and I got every man killed. Some of 'em got hauled off somewhere, an aid station maybe, but pretty sure they didn't make it. Mortars caught most of us. Too much blood, too many heads half blown off. I didn't get a scratch. I assumed somebody's trying to tell me something. So, I thought I'd better listen. I lead men, they die. So no more of that. I'm stuck up here with these two boys, and I assume somebody put me here for one reason, to fight. No more fancy uniforms." He looked at Welty, and Adams saw the dead calm in the man's eyes, a deep hint of madness. "So, how about you?"

Welty shook his head, said only, "Private."

"Well, Private, welcome to our corner of the war. I'm guessing some-body sent you down here to check on us. Fine by me. You're in command. We heard your boys coming up on those rocks out there. Can't say it's a very good place to be, once the rain starts. There's a few more of us down farther, deep ground, like this. Caves everywhere, Japs inside, waiting for dark. I hope you've got a hell of a lot more grenades than what you gave us. The rain oughta start any time now."

Adams was baffled, glanced skyward, the darkness sifting over them, but the air was clear, no rain at all. He heard a sound, far up on the crest, a low voice, scuffing on the rocks. He put a hand against Welty's arm, the redhead looking that way as well. The three men didn't look up at all, slid back farther into their muddy grotto, pulling the thirty with them. The man they called Zeke said, "Half a box. All we got left."

The officer shrugged, said to Welty, "We'll hold out here as best we can. We can keep the infiltrators away for a little while. But once the rain starts, we're probably finished. You will be too, unless you get the hell out of here. The entire Japanese army knows we're here."

The sounds above them were increasing, low voices, and Adams heard the dull thump, familiar, a grenade jammed on a helmet. There was an-other, more thumps on the rocks. Welty grabbed his arm, yanked him hard through the stinking mud, pulling him back into the deepest part of the hidden hole. The grenades came down now, tumbling, bouncing, one landing close to the corpses. They ignited in a scattering of blasts, and Adams pulled his knees up tight, the M-1 against his gut, the blasts blow-ing mud and dust into him, the ringing of shrapnel on the rocks around him. Above the position, the Japanese could be heard clearly, shouting out, single taunting words, names.

"John! Joe! Hey Doc!"

Another wave of grenades tumbled down, some farther away, the hill-side erupting in bursts of fire, more mud and shrapnel, one of the gunners close to him grunting, a hard groan. Adams wanted to move, to help the man, but the grenades did not stop, continued to bounce and thump on the rocks out past the entrance to the odd hiding place. Adams held his knees as tightly as he could, his helmet tilted down toward the worst of the blasts, heard the sudden eruption from the thirty, the gunner firing a brief burst into nothing, a streak of red reaching far out into the dim light, the gun silent now.

"Come on down, you yellow bastards!"

"Time for me to go, boys."

The words came from the officer, and in the last glimpse of daylight Adams saw the man crawling forward with his carbine, wanted to shout at the man to keep back. The grenades came down farther away again, a carpet of blasts to the right, one sharp scream, a man crying out. The officer seemed oblivious, moved out beside the mangled corpses, leaned down, pulled the ripped ponchos over one man's body, straightening the legs. He stood now, climbed up from the low hole, stepped out onto the rocks. Adams stared in horror, no one saying anything, the officer a clear shadow, silhouetted by the blasts of fire down below. He aimed the carbine high, fired a burst, made a strange sound, calling out, not words, just a cheer, a mad *hurrah*. The grenades came now, a half dozen, bouncing around the man. Adams watched as he caught one in his hand, threw it hard back up the hill, the sound of a brief laugh, but the grenades were too many, and before the man could fire the carbine again, the ground around him erupted into a burst of fire. Adams ducked low, felt impacts against his legs, his helmet, heavy wet slop. All along the hill the grenades kept falling and the Marines answered by tossing up their own, up and over the hill, the two sides only yards apart, spread along opposite sides of the muddy ridgeline. There was almost no rifle fire, no targets for the M-1s, the enemies too close for mortars, too close for artillery. Some of the fights erupted face-to-face, knives and bayonets, but when the two sides kept their distance, there was no effective weapon except the handheld bombs. Throughout the long night, men on both sides surged up and out of their hiding places, seeking any glimpse of their enemy, but few were adventurous enough to leave the fragile safety of their own side of the hill. While the supply of grenades held out, they flew back and forth over the hilltop, coming down on their unseen targets like rain.

T he trench had been no trench at all, not in the way any Marine had hoped. Welty kept them in place, but less than an hour after full darkness, the mortar shells had come. They were carefully aimed, unusual, but the Japanese clearly had the range on this particular part of the hill. The mortars came down on both sides of the snaking trench, and then, dead center, men shredded and cut apart, Welty immediately pulling the survivors back down the hill. From the right flank Mortensen had sent word that the Japanese had come up from behind, a hidden tunnel the

Marines still couldn't locate. Adams had heard the thirty caliber offer bursts of fire for long seconds at a time, and then silence, only the pops of the rifles, the dull eruptions from grenades from both sides. The thirty caliber machine gun Welty had sent to the left had never been heard from again, and there was no time to investigate that, no hope of finding anyone in the dark. It had to be bad, no one optimistic that any gunner who suddenly stopped firing had done so by his own choice. The chaos was absolute, any Marine who could was waging his own war, seeking targets from bursts of fire, or emptying magazines and tossing grenades in a desperate hope that the enemy was there. The wounded were many and loud, the voices drawing more fire, grenades mostly, from Japanese troops who had slipped in among the American positions. With Welty forced to bring the men down, Mortensen did the same, and in the muddy defiles and ragged rocky heights, men began to slide and tumble and scamper back down through the places they had climbed the day before. Some did not stop until they made the bottom of the hill, and even then, the fire from Japanese guns on the far hills took aim at landmarks already established in daylight. As the Americans pulled down and off Sugar Loaf yet again, the vicious fire from what remained of the enemy's artillery spread flashes of light over the mud and wreckage of the bare landscape, and showed the retreat for what it was, a desperate escape for the Marines.

On the hill, men still hunkered low, lost, digging into softer dirt, wallowing in the filthy mud, the smells of the corpses not nearly as pungent as the smells from the explosives and the smoke that surrounded them. Some of those men tended wounded, would not leave them behind, strangers offering whatever help they could give, help that more often was a ripped shirt or a syrette of morphine. The dead offered one last gift, ammunition, men forced to tear through the horrifying remains, stiff or bloody corpses that might still be holding ammo belts and grenades. Throughout the night the fight continued, the Marines who remained on the hill engulfed in a blind war with an enemy who seemed to lust for death, as long as that death took Americans along for the ride. The Japanese made no secret of their tactics, loud shouts, often in English, taunting the Marines with name-calling and threats, the Japanese seeming to know they had the Marines exactly where they wanted them. As more grenades rolled down into shallow cover, the casualty count continued to grow. From distant officers word filtered up the hill that a general withdrawal had been ordered, but most of the men who sat terrified in their holes had no way of hearing that, and most of those had no will to do anything but sit in one place and wait for the dawn.

Adams had stayed as close to Welty as he could, and the others in their squad, even the ever-hostile Yablonski, had accepted Welty's authority as absolute. Others who had stayed higher on the hill had fought on as best they could manage, an extraordinary game of hot potato as grenades flew across the crest of the hill from men on both sides. But the Japanese had the advantage, greater number, and, apparently, greater supply of grenades, fed to them from the supply caves on the south side of the hill. With the grenade war becoming a lopsided affair, many of those Marines who could still move had done what Welty had done, obeyed the panicky instinct to pull back to some kind of safety, every man hearing the order in his brain, whether passed on to him by an officer or not. *Get off the hill.*

The flash of fire blinded him yet again, a cascade of broken rock and mud burying them, the smoke burning his lungs. Adams waited for it to clear, holding his breath as long as he could, kept his face straight down into the soft, putrid dirt. He raised his head, blinked through the blindness, the flecks in his eyes, knew that with each blast the enemy had come forward, low scampering shadows who waited for their own mortars to clear the way before launching themselves straight into wherever the Marines might be. He pointed the M-1, searched frantically for movement, did not fire. With no targets, a flash from his own rifle would just tell the closest enemy where he was, and it was a certainty that a grenade would follow. Welty was pulled up beside a small rock pile close to him, a makeshift barricade Welty had gathered in the first minute they had stopped. Adams kept himself flat in the muddy depression, desperate optimism that a wad of uprooted brush might protect him, still tried to dig himself in wherever it was soft. Behind them Adams knew there were others spread out in a low gash in the rock, some beyond, up the far side. In the lowest place wounded had been dragged, a gesture of desperation, no corpsmen or medical bags to be found. Those who were conscious had done an admirable job of keeping quiet, muffled cries from men whose limbs were shattered, whose chests had been battered by shrapnel from a grenade or ripped by the shards of steel from a mortar shell. Adams kept his stare on a bare rocky plane, sloping ground that led away into nooks and crevices he could not see. He glanced toward Welty, knew Welty was doing as he did, pointing the M-1 outward, would pour a clip of fire toward anything that could be Japanese. Adams gripped the K-bar knife in his left hand, clamped against the stock of the rifle. It was awkward, a clumsy way to shoot, but marksmanship meant very little now, and having the knife ready for immediate use was more of a priority now than it had ever been in a foxhole.

He let out a breath, good night vision, searched with stinging eyes for any flicker of motion. Without any warning another mortar round came down, a hard blast down behind him, the force jarring him off the ground, something hard striking his feet and legs. He yelped, pulled his feet up close, panic, rubbing one hand on his legs, wiping through mud and filth. But there was no pain, no sign that he had been struck by more than the debris tossed out of the deeper hole by the round. But then a new thought came, no, my God . . . and he jerked his head around, stared into smoky black dark, wiped his face, saw flickers of flame on the already burned brush. The scream came now, too loud, the sound piercing the dark.

"Oh God! Oh God! Doc! I need a doc!"

Welty slid back away from his small rock pile, down into the hole, right into the thickest smoke from the blast. Adams whispered, "You okay?"

"Do your job!"

There was no other response, and Adams was frantic now, turned back, searched the ground in front of him for any sign of movement, still trying to hear through the ringing in his ears, wanted to call out, to ask how bad it was, but there could be no sound. He wasn't sure how many men had been down in the deeper hole, had pulled one of the wounded down there himself, helped by another man, anonymous in the darkness. Adams tried to breathe, to clear the misery of smoke and burning powder from his lungs, heard the man cry again, softer, could hear a flurry of muffled motion, and now, one more word, a faint, gentle sound.

"Mama . . ."

No one spoke, a long second, and then a familiar voice, from beyond the low place, the growl Adams knew well: Yablonski.

"We gotta shut him up!"

Welty responded, an angry whisper.

"Shut you up! He's done!"

Adams looked that way, felt swallowed by the smells from the low ground, the explosives blending with the awful soup of what remained of

the men. He knew the deep place had been crowded, the wounded laid together, thought of the men who had tried to help them, no one he knew.
He heard more scuffling, a low curse from Welty. Out the other way, along
the hillside, Adams heard a soft rustle, and now, a few feet away, a low
voice.

"He want mama? You want mama?"

Adams jerked around, nothing, darkness, but the accent was too clear
and he yanked the M-1 that way, groped for the trigger, felt the grenade
drop onto him, a dull *thunk* that jarred his helmet. Adams made a shout,
desperate fear, felt the grenade with his hand, flung it out toward the voice,
dropped his face to the mud, the blast immediate, close, splinters of steel
ripping the soft ground around him, a punch striking his arm. He yelped
again, pulled the arm in tightly, heard another cry, could see movement in
the darkness, the Japanese soldier stumbling, a noisy stagger, falling away,
groaning. Adams felt his heart exploding in his chest, fired the M-1, the
flashes blinding him. The clip popped out of the rifle, and he rolled, tried
to reach the cartridge belt, realized his arm was burning, sharp pain. His
fear turned again to panic and he heard a sharp whisper, close beside him.

"You hit? Get back here!"

Welty was there now, pulling Adams by the pant leg, lower into the
hole, and Adams hooked the unhurt arm through the strap of the M-1,
grabbed the wound with his free hand, was shaking, the panic unyielding.

"I'm hit! My arm! Jap was right there!"

"Shut up! Get down here."

Adams let Welty pull him down, hit level ground, his feet sliding hard
into another man, no protest.

"Sorry . . ."

"Shut up. Nobody alive here. Just sit tight. Might have to use the bodies for cover. Some of 'em are fresh. It'll be different tomorrow."

The smell of the bodies was overwhelming him, combining with the
fear, the sweet sickly smell of blood and insides, a powerful odor of excre-
ment. Adams held the arm tight against him, tried to ease his feet off the
body, waves of sickness rolling through him. Welty pulled on his arm,
Adams resisting, but relaxing now, Welty wrapping something on the
wound, a soft whisper, "Best we can do for bandages. It's not bad, doesn't
feel like you're bleeding much. You need morphine?"

"No . . . don't think so."

An M-1 popped twice from out beyond the low place, where Yablon-

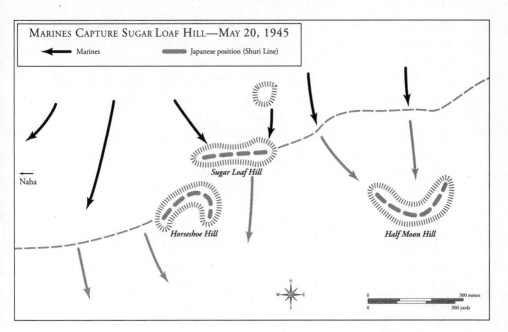

MARINES CAPTURE SUGAR LOAF HILL—MAY 20, 1945

Marines Japanese position (Shuri Line)

Naha

Sugar Loaf Hill

Horseshoe Hill

Half Moon Hill

300 meters

300 yards

ski had been, and now the thunderous clap from the BAR rolled across, streaks cutting across the hillside. The sounds jarred him, some kind of cheer from Yablonski, and Adams tried to grip the rifle, the wound in his arm like a stabbing torch, his feet now pressed hard into the soft pieces of the man just below him. He stared up into the darkness, skyward, nothing at all, hints of shadows from the rocks, the rolling rattle of shellfire from the fight that still spread across the hill, more from down below, on the flat ground. He couldn't keep the shivers away, tried to answer that, you're not dying, it's just a small wound. Get control of yourself. The enemy is right up there! He slid the gun up the slope, realized it was empty, felt a new panic, one hand fumbling against the cartridge belt. But the shaking in his hands was too much, the shaking now in his brain, pulling him to some other place, warm and dry. The ground beneath him was different now, soft, like a bed, holding him, someplace *safe*. He stayed with the feeling for a long moment, but something brought him back, a hard crack, a gunshot, startling, dangerous. He tried to fight the dream, gripped the rifle, stared into the darkness. Stop this! Stay awake! But it wasn't sleep, his eyes wide, alert. His heart began to race, the pain and the wetness returning. He thought of Welty, needed help from his friend. From what? What's happening to me? The dream came again, angry this time, and he wanted to shout, the anger rolling over into horror, pieces of bodies, faces, Ferucci, laughing at him, more laughter, his own, sharing the joke, a deep echo inside his brain. The laughter was louder, unstoppable, and he felt a hard claw wrapped around him, pulling him out of the mud, carrying him away. The darkness gave way to more images, faces, men he didn't know, some just pieces, all of them laughing, his brain erupting with too many images, the claw suddenly letting go, dropping him into a great black hole, a surging river of blood and filth and madness.

The assaults on Sugar Loaf Hill had been many and futile, and after each failure to drive the Japanese away, the number of Marine casualties grew to a staggering percentage of each unit engaged. Using darkness as the only protection they had, the platoons who still had their lieutenants, or squads that could depend on a sergeant, obeyed the orders that trickled up the hill from runners and the occasional walkie-talkie: withdraw. In the daylight, from the distant hills to the north, American observers could see the Japanese swarming back out into their positions, positions the Marines had no choice but to abandon. Offshore, the enormous battleship the USS *Mississippi* used its massive guns to pour a horrific dose of fire onto the Japanese positions, not only on the south slope of Sugar Loaf, but on the other two hills that spread out behind, as much as the navy could do to obliterate all three corners of the triangle. The cost to the Japanese was horrific, but, as always, their greatest number had scrambled back down into the deepest caves, which protected them from even the heaviest artillery.

The Marines who could make the withdrawal did so, but many of the wounded could not yet be evacuated, and so the American artillery unwittingly did what the doctors could not: erased their suffering. On the open ground of the hill itself, the bodies of men from both sides could be seen by the observers, and by the men who gathered out beyond the base of the hill, preparing for yet another frontal assault. Though the Marines did all they could to obey their passionate duty to *leave no man behind,* the bodies of the dead were spread throughout pockets of dead Japanese, a scattered mass of rotting decay, the ongoing fights not allowing either side to offer rescue or assistance to so many of their fallen.

The fight on Sugar Loaf Hill continued for nearly a full week, with much the same result: conquest and withdrawal, all the while increasing the astounding casualty counts on both sides. By May 20, the vicious pounding from American artillery had silenced most of the heavy Japanese guns that had directed fire from Half Moon and Horseshoe, the other two hills. Finally, waves of American tanks swung southward, circling behind the hills themselves, trying to pierce through supply lines to the Japanese on Sugar Loaf and adding their firepower to the struggle that would soon follow on the base of the arrowhead. Pockets of Japanese troops still occupied many of the caves, but the tanks brought a new weapon to the fight. Many had their 75-millimeter cannons replaced by long-range flamethrowers, the tanks accomplishing what many of the men on the ground could not. Entire squads of Japanese troops were obliterated while still holding position deep in the rocky caves.

To the east, the First Marine Division had pressed their attack hard against the heights closer to the Shuri Castle, and the castle itself began taking heavy fire from American artillery, an assault that required several days to complete. To their east, the American infantry divisions accomplished the same goal, surging toward more of the high ground the Japanese generals had assumed would resist any attack. The cost to all the American divisions was extraordinary, entire companies wiped out, officers swept away en masse, yet in every case the Americans continued their push, inflicting casualties on the enemy that equaled or exceeded their own. The difference of course was that the Americans could bring in replacements, fill holes in the line, replace officers with new men coming in from the ships that continued to arrive offshore. The Japanese had no such luxury.

The men of the Sixth Marine Division who survived Sugar Loaf Hill were given little time for recovery. The city of Naha and its valuable airfield still lay in their path, and with furious pressure on General Buckner to complete the conquest of Okinawa, a campaign that had already exceeded its timetable by several weeks, even the squads and companies that had lost so many of their number on that dismal hill were still needed, still pressed into action. This meant that the men with the light wounds would still be called upon to do their part. No matter their number and their enthusiasm, the replacements could not be as dependable as the men who had already faced some of the worst fighting of the war.

In a bizarre postscript to the campaigns that punched hard against the primary Japanese defenses, word had come through the commanders, passed along through the ranks, finally reaching the men who held the rifle. On May 8, the war in Europe had ended. Hitler was said to have died, and the Germans had officially surrendered. In towns across America, streets filled with celebration, a nation grateful that in that one part of the war at least, sons and husbands would finally return home. On Okinawa, the announcement of *VE Day* was virtually ignored.

21. USHIJIMA

He had received word of the German surrender with the same stoic resignation he had felt for weeks now. Though others around him seemed injured by the news, as though a good friend had been lost, Ushijima understood that the alliance with Germany had been only one more enormous miscalculation. It was a familiar song, years of soothing reassurances from Japan's Imperial High Command that all was well, that Japan's destiny was being fulfilled. The decisions to expand Japan's inevitable empire by striking hard into China, by striking hard at the British and the Americans, were made by men in grand offices in Tokyo, who drew lines on maps without ever facing the pure devastating reality of what their decisions had done to their glorious army, their invincible navy. The alliance with Hitler had been one more of those *wise decisions,* aligning Japanese interests with Germany's, both nations seeking to spread their superior races over a vast empire that would eventually divide the world into two mighty spheres of influence. No one in Tokyo had revealed to Ushijima what might occur if those two spheres happened to collide. Now that mattered not at all. Germany's sphere had been smashed to rubble, and Ushijima shared none of Tokyo's illusions that Japan could avoid the same disastrous defeat. Yes, he thought, one more miscalculation.

Ushijima walked slowly, carefully, through a shallow pool of water that spread down through the main headquarters cave, a gently flowing creek that poured into the cave from the earthen walls near the main entrance, thought, how many *miscalculations* does it take to destroy an empire? Was it difficult to convince the emperor that Hitler would be a reliable ally, that Germany's enormous war machine could withstand what the Allies brought to the fight? Is the emperor aware, even now, how many miscalculations have been made by the men he has trusted to expand his glorious empire?

Above him the Shuri Castle had finally been blasted to rubble, the inevitable result of days of constant shelling from the heavy guns of the Americans. The rains had returned the day before, and the shattering devastation to the hills around him had caused ruptures in the carefully constructed supports of the caves. There had been no major failures, not yet anyway, the timbers still preventing any kind of general collapse, but Ushijima could see the result now, the floor coated with a gentle flow of rainwater, a muddy creek that sifted through the dirt above and beside him. He stood silently for a long moment, still thought of the Germans, had never really known any high-ranking German commanders, his counterparts, but there had to be *this,* he thought. After so much destruction, even the earth punishes us. Surely, in Berlin, in Munich or Frankfurt, there were generals who stood in their luxurious headquarters and mourned the great loss, helpless to hold back the tide. Did they cast blame on their subordinates, or did they stand tall and accept that Hitler had simply *miscalculated*? He thought of the book, sitting high even now on a shelf in his room. He had used Sun Tzu's *The Art of War* at the military academy, had kept it with his possessions all throughout his travels. There was annoying irony to Ushijima that Japan would employ so much cultural propaganda about the Chinese, using that as their pretext for the invasion of Manchuria. And yet, he thought, for twenty-five hundred years, there has been no one with a clearer understanding of the art and science of war than a man who was . . . Chinese. Sun Tzu's most poignant lesson was painfully obvious now, even more so than it had been in his classrooms. *Know your enemy.* Whether the enemy fights with sticks and arrows, or whether he brings tanks and vast fleets of warships, the lesson must be obeyed. In that we have failed, and that failure will cost us our army, our emperor, perhaps our nation. Men like Cho do not read the lessons. Cho believed the Americans would be defeated by the sight of their own blood. Perhaps Hitler believed that as well. The Americans must certainly teach the wisdom of Sun Tzu to their generals. Perhaps they are better students than we are.

The return of the rains was a blessing that Ushijima knew he had to take seriously. All along the entire defensive line, the American drives had so weakened what remained of his army that the fighting could be brought to a close within a week. The most significant breakthrough for the Americans had come to the east, the Japanese right flank, a tenacious effort by the American infantry divisions. That was a surprise, no one in the Japanese hierarchy believing that infantry could mount as stubborn an offense as the Marines. Our strongest defensive efforts against the entire front were fruitful, he thought, for a while at least. Their casualty counts have to be astoundingly high, and surely there is hand-wringing, an agony of conscience among the American generals that so many men have died where we invited them to come. I feared the Marines, but I did not expect the American infantry to be as formidable. Sun Tzu speaks again. I did not know them. That is no one's failure but my own.

He moved slowly forward, shuffled his feet through the shallow sheet of water, mud on his boots, the wetness soaking through. He glanced into the map room, men working as they had always worked, doing their duty, no one reflecting his own gloom. But they know, he thought. There can be no cheerfulness now. He realized how bleak the offices seemed to be, thought, of course, it is the *flowers*. They are gone.

The seeping rainwater had quickly brought deterioration to the sanitary facilities in the caves, one more reason why the women who worked there had been sent away. Whether or not General Cho's recreational activities had been interrupted, the shrinking supplies of food and fresh water emphasized to Ushijima that the time had finally come. The order had gone out through Colonel Yahara that the caves be cleared of all females, including nurses, the women sent southward to a much safer part of the island. Many of the women had protested, had displayed an admirable willingness to die alongside the soldiers. But Ushijima had entertained no argument. What the women could not know, of course, was that there was a greater plan already rolling into play, a plan designed yet again by Colonel Yahara. The withdrawal of the women was only the first step.

Ushijima stared down at the thick brown water, his boots, knew that farther down into the vast network of tunnels the water was much worse. He had come out into the corridor to travel once more to the mouth of the

great cave, and Cho had of course notified the guards to accompany him.
But Ushijima had sent them away, a change of plans, had stood in the wetness of the softening earth and scolded himself for the romantic notion
that he should find any enjoyment from a visit to his favorite vantage
point. The lofty perch that gave him a view of Naha, the distant beaches,
the vast American fleet, had become itself a far too dangerous place. American tanks were within range now, and any movement on the rubble of the
hillside, any sign of a break in the carefully designed camouflage could
bring a torrent of shelling. For a brief time he had considered the inevitable
assault on his lookout as somehow appropriate. The plan had formed in
his mind, and he retrieved his best-preserved uniform, his medals, had
thought that finally, the time had come. He would march to the mouth of
the great cave, would pull aside his curtain of protection, and stand there
in full view of the Americans who drove toward him. His death would
come as one glorious show of defiance, something to inspire his troops,
and perhaps they would stand tall and face the enemy with no fear, nothing but a brutal certainty that death was welcome. But that fantasy had
slipped away, replaced by the practical. The teacher found one more reason
to scold himself, knew that ultimately his leadership was still more important than martyrdom. The shrine will still be there, he thought, and my
ancestors can wait a bit longer.

No matter the overwhelming strength of the Americans, his men continued to do what they could to hold their ground, vicious fights from
dwindling forces, the dedicated struggle to offer their lives by taking as
many of the Americans as they could. It was one advantage of the rains,
that the Americans would have to keep their aircraft grounded, could not
advance their machinery with as much force. The soldiers would again be
swamped by oceans of mud, deepening once more, neither side able to maneuver effectively, an advantage to his men, who kept to their wonderfully
designed hiding places. The reports continued to come in from the field
that the Americans were adding new equipment to the fight, equipment he
had seen himself. His own artillery was nearly nonexistent. What had not
been destroyed in the great failure of his counterattack had been virtually
obliterated by the ongoing assaults from the American naval guns, or the
dive-bombing runs of their carrier planes. Now the tanks had come, and
there was little he could do to keep them away. For the first time the deadly
attacks on the American armor had almost ceased, not because his men
were unwilling to die in the process, but because the supply of satchel

charges had been almost completely consumed. The suicide squads no longer had the tools to carry out the job.

He stepped back to his room, could not escape the water, a thin and slippery pool, mud oozing down the walls everywhere he looked. On the desks, the maps, the tables and chairs, a film of dank wetness coated every surface. On a small table to one side, a sheaf of papers rested on a china plate. He stared at them for a long moment, knew that once more, Yahara had done the amazing. The papers were a carefully detailed description of three alternatives that remained for the remnants of his army, each part of each plan detailed step by step. Yahara was as meticulous as always, but Ushijima knew that two of those alternatives had been detailed for one very good reason, to convince General Cho that they were two very bad ideas. One of those alternatives was to hold the Shuri Line, allowing the Americans to envelop what remained of his Thirty-second Army, forcing them into certain destruction, far sooner than Ushijima had hoped. Yahara knew that General Cho would likely favor that strategy over any other, but Ushijima did not want that debate, not while he believed that his army still had a fight to give, could still force the Americans into more costly frontal assaults. To his surprise, Cho's fiery nihilism had seemed to temper, brought down perhaps by the great failure three weeks before of his glorious counterattack. The second *bad choice* involved a general retreat, to the Chinen Peninsula, the southeastern corner of the island. On the maps, Chinen would seem logical, but the landmass there was not large enough to allow Yahara to spread the army into a cohesive defensive position. Yahara already knew that Ushijima had sanctioned the third alternative, and Cho had agreed completely to abide by the plan, adding nothing of his own. Ushijima was more surprised when Cho responded to Yahara's proposed alternatives with a shrug of acceptance, offering the meek explanation that, after all, Yahara was the chief strategist. The colonel's strategy would be put into motion within two days, the length of time it would require for the staffs to organize the paperwork of the headquarters for travel. Everything left behind would, of course, be destroyed. Once the staffs were ready to move, they would withdraw from beneath the remains of the Shuri Castle and relocate in a series of temporary headquarters as they made their way to the Kiyan Peninsula, the southernmost tip of the island. Within a very few days, the senior commanders would follow along with the bulk of the army, withdrawing from the battlegrounds that even now the Americans were pushing through. The Kiyan area would be difficult for the Americans to assault, was protected by high bluffs that rivaled or exceeded the strength of the heights that had already cost the Americans so much blood. Even an assault from the sea could be a serious challenge, much of the southern tip of the island protected by tall cliffs that could easily be defended. Yahara had added one more element to the plan, drawing on tactics he had studied from Napoleon to Rommel. The withdrawal of the army away from the Shuri Line had been carefully designed so that overconfident Americans would assume their enemy had simply scampered away. Instead two powerful forces would remain hidden at each end of the line, and as the Americans advanced, those forces would launch a sudden attack against the Americans on both their flanks. It was a desperate gamble and would most likely sacrifice some of Ushijima's best frontline troops. The *victory* would come if the inevitable American advance was delayed, for days or even weeks, Yahara predicting that the apparent indecisiveness of the American generals would be heightened over the uncertainty of any other surprises the Japanese might have in store. The added time would allow Yahara to position what remained of the army in the most advantageous defensive posture down south, to maximize the last great effort they could make to bring down as many Americans as possible. If the army was to be sacrificed, Ushijima believed that Yahara's new plan would make that sacrifice as effective as possible.

To the west, along the coast, the Oroku Peninsula held the major airfield west of the city of Naha, and Ushijima was well aware that the American Marines on that part of the line had both the city and the airfield as their goals. The city itself was mostly ruins, a victim of constant bombardment by American ships and planes. But west of the city, in carefully designed fortifications, the peninsula held some three thousand Japanese naval troops, troops over which Ushijima had no direct authority. Their commander was Admiral Minoru Ota, who had enthusiastically offered his men for whatever operation Ushijima might appreciate. Despite Ota's willingness to help, Ushijima knew that the naval troops had almost no training in the field and weren't likely to fare well against the Marines. Up until now the sailors had only been used as part of small infiltration squads. But as the fight dragged on, even those efforts had been futile at best. Too often the effectiveness of their raids had been a complete mystery, since once they went into action, no one had ever heard from them again. Even if they weren't effective fighters, Colonel Yahara still believed they could be effective in adding manpower to the defense of the Kiyan

USHIJIMA WITHDRAWS FROM
SHURI LINE—MAY 29, 1945

American   Japanese

Marines

Infantry

Shuri

Sugar
Loaf Hill

Naha

Chinen
Peninsula

Naha
Airfield

East
China
Sea

Mabuni

PACIFIC
OCEAN

New
Ushijima
HQ

Ara Saki

0   5 kilometers

0   5 miles

Peninsula by moving south with the army, hopefully escaping the American drive that was sure to engulf the capital city. Admiral Ota disagreed, feeling that his men would best serve the Japanese cause by keeping to their well-designed fortifications on Oroku. Added to the naval force were five thousand Okinawans who had been pressed into service supporting the navy's defenses across the peninsula. Whether those *troops* would be effective as fighters mattered little now. Ushijima could not order the admiral to comply with any plan, so, for now anyway, the naval troops would make their stand by keeping to their artillery and automatic weapons dug into the rough ground closer to the airfield. The goal on the Oroku Peninsula was much the same as throughout the entire campaign, to delay the Americans, this time the Marines, in their inevitable efforts to capture the airfield. Also, Ushijima knew that any fight that kept a full division of Marines bogged down on Oroku meant fewer Americans joining the ultimate assault against Ushijima's bastion down south. Any delay would prolong the fight.

The plan was as sound as any that Ushijima could have imagined, but there was nothing in Yahara's strategy that predicted a defeat of the Americans, none of Cho's manic boastfulness that this time the Americans would be driven back to their ships. The plan had one inevitable outcome, no matter if it was successful by Yahara's standards or not. Ushijima knew that it was his army's final effort, their last stand.

MAY 29, 1945

They escaped from the Shuri Heights through a thicket of artillery blasts, slipping in the darkness down treacherous pathways that led through hillsides of rubble. For the first few miles, the artillery had continued, terrifying rips through the night sky, the Americans blanketing the entire area with firepower that the Japanese could never equal. But luck followed them, Ushijima and his senior staff making their way mostly on foot until the most immediate danger of the American artillery was past.

He rode now in an old truck, Yahara and Cho piled in like so many farm laborers, their dignity erased by the urgency of the escape. As they moved farther south, the roads became better, less of the paralyzing mud, harder surfaces. But the truck itself was wholly unreliable, one more symptom of the diminishing supplies. As though on schedule, the truck's engine had gasped into silence, the officers disembarking onto the wet roadway once more.

Ushijima moved away from the turmoil of his aides, the men fumbling beneath the truck's open hood, desperate to remedy the problem. Cho was there, would do as he had done before, stand watch behind the men, as though by his threats of punishment the truck itself would be as fearful as the men and respond with proper behavior.

Ushijima wandered farther from the chaotic scene, listened instead to the artillery, a barrage coming down closer to the sea, along the western coast. There was little noise from the south, a good sign, the advance staff reporting that the American fleet had not anchored any of the larger warships off the island's southern tip. So far, he thought, they have ignored those places we have not been. But surely they must know we will occupy the high ground there. Surely they know I will not surrender to them, that the peninsula is the one place I will gather my army, that we shall end this the only way we have ever ended any fight. *Surely* they know that.

He moved out through a thin stand of trees, some kind of orchard, the land around him undisturbed by shelling. The wet smells washed over him, and he glanced back, caught the shadow of a single guard. The man kept his distance, and Ushijima knew that the guard would be Cho's idea, assigned no doubt to make sure Ushijima did not wander off or stumble into some dangerous place. There is no danger here, he thought. No Americans, certainly. The worst we have encountered are the civilians, and they must endure a danger far greater than our own. They are, after all, not Japanese. They do not appreciate the sacrifice we make, that it is the most positive end we can seek.

The civilians had poured out onto the roads from Naha and the smaller villages, a dreadful parade of filthy, frightened people in a mass exodus that led anywhere the shells did not fall. His troops had been unmerciful in moving them aside, the army's retreat far more of a priority. Colonel Yahara had issued instructions that any civilians encountered be ordered to clear the way by moving to the east, to the Chinen Peninsula, the one place on the southern half of Okinawa where there would likely be no fight. Some of them actually listened to the officers, slogging along muddy roads with wagons and carts, or carrying what remained of their possessions on their backs toward a place many of them had never seen. But many others ignored the officers, and so endured brutal punishment by the army who moved past them, all of them heading to the south. Most of the soldiers were as desperately ignorant of their destination as the civilians, the agonizing misery of a march through mud that to some would end along the way. Unseen by Ushijima were the vast fields of civilians, shoved off the roads by the army. Many seemed too bewildered to obey anything the officers told them; they huddled along the muddy ground, enduring sickness and wounds, caring weakly for children or the very old, watching the Japanese retreat with blank hopelessness, or utter disinterest.

As their retreat passed through the smaller villages, Ushijima had seen some of the civilians up close. The sight of young men had grabbed his attention. Those were few, and usually they tried to shirk away, to be unnoticed. Ushijima said nothing, gave no orders to anyone on his staff to gather those men into the army's ranks, ranks they may have deserted. He knew they would serve very little usefulness now. Whether they were laborers or had been issued a Japanese rifle, Ushijima knew that those men would know the truth about what was happening to their island. They would know that the army was retreating, and if they believed the outrageous propaganda fed to them about American brutality, they would be far more desperate to escape, would seek out their families and their homes. Despite what Tokyo had preached, the Okinawan people had no loyalty, no patriotism for Japan's *great cause*. He also knew that General Cho would have had any deserters executed, had Ushijima allowed it.

Ushijima felt a slight breeze drifting through the trees, the rain a heavy mist. In the distance the rumble of artillery continued, muffled by the rustling of the leaves above him. The air was strange, pungent with the soggy earth, and, he realized, it was *clean*. He had not experienced fresh air for many weeks, thought, do not forget this moment. The new headquarters will be . . . less than perfect. Yahara is full of apologies for that, but it cannot be helped. The caves at Shuri were the best we could have provided, and that has passed. While this fight continues we will once again huddle low in the stink of our own making, dug into the earth like rats, awaiting our fate. He glanced toward the truck, thought of Cho. Even he has accepted the obvious. He rides alongside me in a broken-down truck, and instead of his ridiculous speeches and rabid pronouncements, he endures this journey with patience and silence and reflection. Ushijima could not help a small laugh, thought, well, there is a first time for everything.

He focused again on the artillery, a low thunder, a strange kind of silence to it. He looked up, the mist on his face, thought, for one brief moment, this war is very far away. But you are not allowed to think that. This war is inside you, you carry it with you even now. The Americans are still pouring out their vast firepower. But we will surprise them. So many of those shells are falling on empty spaces, caves we have already left behind. This might actually be working, he thought. So far there is no indication that the enemy knows what we are doing. General Buckner must believe that we have been crushed beneath the weight of his steel and that the Shuri Line is just a mopping-up operation. The rain has helped us, has kept his reconnaissance planes on the ground, and so has kept him blind to our plans. Yet he knows he has all the advantage. A good general would have been prepared for a final blow, would have sensed our collapse. He would keep strong reserves in position to push past the worst of the fighting, seeking what lay behind. Buckner relies on his eyes in the sky, and of course, that is his greatest advantage. But the weather is ours. If there is anything about this miserable island that I should be grateful for, it is that the weather has helped equalize the fight, has given us precious days, lengthened our war. Now we will lengthen it again.

The truck erupted in an uneven rumble, coming to life, success for his aides. He stared out through the black mist, took a deep breath of the soggy air. His guard was still there, patient, waiting, and Ushijima moved that way, the guard letting him pass, then following him to the truck. The guard joined the others, climbed up in the rear of the truck. Inside the truck itself, Ushijima pressed in close beside Yahara, Cho just behind them, and Cho said, "It is not wise to drift off in the dark like that. We thought you had gone over to the enemy!"

"That would leave you in command, General Cho. Tell me this. If I was to present myself to General Buckner, what should I tell him? What great secrets could I carry to the Americans that would label me a traitor? Oh yes, I forget. Just by the act of surrender, I am a traitor. That is one of my own lessons, of course. I taught that to many of the officers who still fight in those hills. Do you truly think I would . . . wander off?"

Cho's joke was silenced now, his reply unusually meek.

"I would not suggest that any of us would do such a thing. Forgive me for my poor judgment."

It was the wrong word, and Ushijima knew that beside him, Yahara would chew on that, would know that Cho's *judgment* had been the greatest failure of this entire campaign. Ushijima leaned forward, tried to see the driver's face, knew only his name, Inko. Yahara seemed to read him, said, "We have four kilometers to the next station, sir. There is a radio there, with reports of the flank attacks. I admit, sir, that I am anxious to receive whatever word awaits us."

"You should be."

Ushijima sat back, tried to be as comfortable as possible on a seat that had not offered any kind of comfort for years. The truck rattled along in total darkness, no lights of any kind, the road scattered with the glimpses of moving shadows, no way to see if they were soldiers or civilians. The next station, he thought. Well, we might receive some good news.

Yahara held his ear to the radio receiver, stared down. Cho stood close to him, energized, rocking back and forth on his heels, staring at Yahara with brutal impatience. Yahara spoke into the radio, said, "I have received your report, Colonel. I shall communicate it directly to General Ushijima. You have performed your duty with glory and loyalty. There is no greater gift you can give our emperor."

Yahara set the receiver down slowly, a deliberate pause, and Ushijima could see now that the man had tears in his eyes. Cho was in the colonel's ear now, an impatient shout, "What? Are we successful?"

Yahara seemed to slide away from him, turned to Ushijima, composed himself.

"I regret to inform the commanding general that our retreat-and-attack plan has not been a success. The forces we positioned on the enemy's flanks were not sufficient to accomplish the task we assigned them. The enemy has succeeded in destroying our efforts while preventing us from driving into their positions with much effectiveness. Our losses have been substantial. We just did not have the artillery to support our troops."

Ushijima absorbed the words in stoic silence, had suspected this might be the result of Yahara's grand plan, though, he knew, Yahara had to make the effort. It was, after all, sound strategy.

"No excuses are required, Colonel. It was necessary that we do everything we could to inflict doubt and uncertainty on the enemy. Our troops have surely made a valiant effort. Do we know if the enemy advance has been slowed at all by our efforts?"

Yahara shook his head.

"That is something of a mystery, sir. Colonel Ieko reports that the enemy was not making much effort to advance at all. They seem more engaged in consolidation, and there is little evidence that they know we have abandoned the front. If they are aware, they are not making any significant effort to pursue our retreat."

Cho stepped close again, the old fury showing itself.

"Then your grand flank attack should have caught them by complete surprise! What kind of treachery is this? We fail to inflict losses on an enemy who does not plan a fight? Colonel Ieko shall be pulled by his ears to my headquarters . . ."

Ushijima held up a hand, a clear signal that for once Cho obeyed, the fury silenced.

"I will not condemn the men who made this effort. Colonel Ieko was once a student of mine. He understands tactics, and when he says we could not give him artillery support, that is a sufficient explanation. The Americans have secured every advantage, in men and in machines. In case you have forgotten, General, that is why we are making this retreat."

22. ADAMS

"Good God, what are you two doing here?"

Clay sat up on the bed, stared in amazement, the two Marines in front of him more like filthy scarecrows than men. Welty had not shaved in days, his red beard more like a growth of some odd fungus, and beside him, Sergeant Mortensen looked older and leaner than any time before. Welty smiled, said, "Got leave to come get you. The captain checked with the brass, and they said a lot of the cases . . . the guys who got sent back . . ."

Mortensen shook his head, the older man interrupting.

"Some of the nut jobs aren't in such bad shape after all. Like you. The captain called back here to some chief headshrinker, and the guy said you hadn't gone totally *Asian,* that he thought you were fit. He said you just needed a few days on some white sheets, maybe a nurse or two to rub your feet, trim your toenails, and you're good as new."

Welty seemed embarrassed for Mortensen's lack of delicacy.

"Look, Clay, they said you could come back to the outfit. That okay with you? You doing all right?"

Adams felt a strange rush of glee, smiled broadly.

"No disrespect intended, Sarge, but you two are about as ugly as a mule's asshole. I gotta say . . . damn, it's good to see you. Yeah, the doc here says I'm okay." He was already wearing the uniform, tried as much as possible not to *fit in* with the others, who mostly kept to the rows of beds. Most of them were army, the hospital itself in the army sector, the pair of psychiatrists army doctors. He tugged at the waistband of his new dungarees, showed a wide gap from the thick cloth to his belly. "I musta lost twenty pounds out there. The doc says all I needed was to fatten up a little bit, eat a few squares, and it would help out my head. I guess I shoulda listened to you, Jack, eaten some more of that stew you always carry around."

"I got plenty. You need a can of stew, or anything else, you just ask."

"Thanks, Jack. Damn, I'm glad you're okay."

"You scared hell out of me. We hauled you off in a poncho, and I thought I'd never see you again."

Mortensen spat out a wad of something brown, an amazing shot out through the opening of the tent.

"You two oughta have a real nice honeymoon when this is over with. Hand in hand down some main street in Tokyo. Damn! Now listen up, Nut Case." Mortensen straightened, mock seriousness that inspired Welty to assume the same stance, an attempt at dignity. "Private Adams, as your new squad leader, I have been authorized by Captain Bennett to get you the hell out of this place, and bring you back to the company command post." Mortensen looked around, as though expecting someone to stop him. A much older man came close now, a white coat draped over an army uniform. Mortensen said, "You the damn doctor?"

"Are you the damn loudmouth coming in here and waking up my patients?"

Mortensen's attitude dropped a notch, and he said, "Uh, aye, sir. We have orders to retrieve Private Adams."

"Fine. He's yours. He's not nearly as cracked up as some of these other boys. Get him the hell out of here. Put a rifle in his hands and let him kill Japs. That's all he's been talking about since he's been here. Better yet, give him his own tank, a few mortars, and the biggest damn cannon you can find. Now beat it. You're stinking up the place."

Adams absorbed the scene with a swelling need to laugh out loud.

Welty smiled at him, a discreet wink, and Adams watched as the doctor walked away. He swung his legs out onto the wooden floor, leaned out closer to the two men.

"Did Bennett really send you down here?"

"That's *Captain* Bennett." Mortensen scanned the large tent, seemed to focus on one particular nurse, who was bending over to attend to a nearby patient. He kept his gaze that way, said, "Just grab your gear. Let's go."

Adams picked up his backpack, newly stuffed with fresh everything, grabbed his boots, slipped them on quickly, laced up the straps with automatic precision. Welty said, "New boots? They gave you new boots?"

"Yep. Burned the old ones. Burned everything else too, I guess." Adams stood now, tried to hide the slight waver, but Welty caught it, said, "You sure . . . ?"

"Let's get him out of here. Talk about it later."

Mortensen grabbed him by the arm, for support as much as a strong pull out of the tent. They were outside quickly, away from the awful smell of antiseptics and sickness. Adams felt giddy, the sky a shocking blue, the heat from the sun swarming about him, sweat already in his shirt.

"They even gave me fresh underwear. Socks, the whole works. Real food too. I musta looked even worse than you two." He grimaced, the foul air surrounding him, the smell rolling up around him from the two Marines. "If I smelled like that, it's a wonder they didn't toss me in the latrine. Damn, Sarge, you two ever gonna take a bath?"

He realized it was a stupid question, but Mortensen surprised him, said, "Right over there. I saw some army boys lining up for a shower. What do you say, Private?"

Welty jumped at the question.

"You betcha."

They kept Adams between them, moved out through the sea of larger tents, distant rows of concrete block buildings and tin huts. The activity passed by them, no one seeing them at all, everyone on some kind of mission, carrying the self-importance he had always seen in the rear echelon. Mortensen slowed, held out a hand, pointing to a small open field, and Adams saw the line, a dozen men, stark naked, standing in front of a small tent. Above was perched a huge barrel on a metal stand, and beside the tent, a crude hand-painted sign: THIRTY SECONDS PER MAN—NO EXCEPTIONS.

Welty was already removing his shirt, said, "That's more than it takes me at home. But if they got soap, I might not wanna leave."

Mortensen said, "One more reason the army boys are so damn soft. They're living back here in the lap of luxury. After this, I'm looking for the tent where the doggies get their massages. I got this little crink in my back."

They released Adams, and he stood guard over the pile of stinking clothes, wondered if there was some way to discreetly haul them to a fire barrel. But this was army ground, no Marine uniforms in sight, and likely, no place to find any. He watched them fall into line, their bare skin as dirty as their uniforms, both men with the smiling anticipation, as though they were getting away with something naughty. To one side Adams saw a group of army officers, a casual conversation, mostly ignoring anyone else. Adams felt a pang of nervousness, thought, this might not be a welcome spot for Marines. But the two men were already at the tent, next in line, the gangly Mortensen taking the lead, and Adams laughed, reached down and dragged their clothes and weapons away from the traffic, a shady spot beside a supply tent. Guess no one will know they're Marines, he thought. Hard to tell once they're naked. Unless Marines smell different.

T he men were clean but in their uniforms there was no way to tell. They moved quickly through the bustle of the supply depot, the three men knowing it would be best if they seemed to be on an urgent mission, no time for chitchat. Adams had left the field hospital with no weapon but his K-bar, and Mortensen had reassured him, no problem at all. The sergeant led the three-man parade, seemed to know exactly where he was heading, and Adams brought up the rear, just followed, trying not to catch the eye of anyone who seemed important. Mortensen suddenly turned, like a hound on a scent, stepped up to a concrete building, paused, a quick glance back at the other two, said, "I'll do the talking. Both of you . . . try to look a little nuts. Like you can't wait to cut some doggy's throat."

They moved through the open door, past a sign that was much less crude than the shower: ORDNANCE SUPPLY.

The building was mostly a vast open space, the thick odor of gun oil, men with clipboards, others moving crates in through a gaping doorway in the rear. Mortensen led them to a desk, a lieutenant busy at some papers, his single gold bar polished to a high sheen. Mortensen said softly, "You in charge here?"

The man did not look up, said, "What do you think?" The odor of the two uniforms caught him now, and he backed away from his papers, said, "Good God, you boys fall in a latrine?"

Mortensen kept his voice low, leaned close.

"This is what the front lines smell like, sir. The fellow behind me in the clean shirt brought us off the line in G sector, and the colonel's hopping mad. Says unless we get some shotguns right away, he's coming down here to rip the asshole out of anyone who gets in his way. Sir, I don't have to tell you what the colonel's like when he's that pissed. We got Japs dropping down in every damn foxhole, and the boys are going nuts up there, taking shots at every officer who walks by. This guy's clean uniform and all, he damn near started his own firefight. Those boys up there are so whacked-out, they're shooting anything that don't look like one of them. The colonel got the word that a bunch of our boys are ganging up to come down here to take care of business with more of you army lads in clean uniforms. My crud-covered buddy here keeps wanting to run his bayonet through this guy, and if I wasn't bigger than him, he'd have done it."

As though on cue, Welty reached down, withdrew his K-bar knife, and fingered it with affection, staring at Adams as though ready to carve a roast. Mortensen grabbed Welty by the shoulder, jerked him around.

"Later! This man's an officer!"

Welty slumped, twitched nervously, the K-bar still in his hand, and Welty seemed to notice the lieutenant for the first time, a broad, lustful smile. Mortensen looked at the officer again, said, "Sir, I'm hauling this one down to the hospital right now. He's done for. You ever see hair turn that red? The colonel said I'm the only one who can handle him, so here we are. But there's fifty more headed down here, and the colonel sent me to load up on riot gear. Shotguns are the best we can do, so I need your help, sir. Three shotguns. A few ammo belts of shells. That's all we need."

The lieutenant sat back in his chair, began to laugh.

"Yeah? What the hell you think we got MPs for? You damn leathernecks pull this crap on me all the time. I might look like some shavetail to you, but I've been doing this job for too long. Get lost."

"I can tell you're a veteran, sir. You've been to the front then?"

"Hell no."

Mortensen glanced out in both directions, their conversation still not drawing any unwelcome attention.

"Surely, sir, you must hear the reports of what's going on up there."

"Nobody tells me a thing, and I like it that way. Now, I said, get lost."

Mortensen leaned out over the man's desk, a scattering of dried mud falling on the lieutenant's papers. The officer stared up at him, more angry now, his face curling even more from the sergeant's odor.

"Sir, with all due respect. I've got men dying by the boatloads. Shotguns are the best weapon against what the Japs are doing up there. If you like, I can have the colonel arrange to send a jeep down, give you a tour. No trouble at all, sir. As many holes as we got in the line, a tough-looking hombre like you could help us out. The platoon leaders we've got coming up are, pardon the expression, sir, as worthless as tits on a boar. We could use a veteran like yourself."

Mortensen leaned even closer, as though showering the lieutenant in as much of his essence as he could.

"I know I can smooth it over with the colonel. I bet you're itching like hell to get out from behind this desk and get out to where the action is, right, sir?"

The lieutenant stared up at Mortensen, a long, silent pause.

"Three shotguns?"

"And ammo, sir."

"And ammo. While I'm gone, clean up this crap you dropped all over my desk."

The man was up now, disappeared down a corridor of steel shelves. To one side several GIs stood, watching the entire scene, all in clean uniforms. One man moved closer, older, and Adams knew the stare of an officer.

"The Marines don't have their own supply depots?"

Mortensen straightened, stepped toward the officer, his smell moving with him.

"We don't have shotguns, sir. The army is blessed with the best weapons, and my boys are fighting it out with knives. I'm hoping you'll allow us this one luxury, sir."

The officer appraised Mortensen, seemed to appreciate his age.

"Your company get pretty chewed up, then?"

Mortensen didn't miss a beat.

"Lost most of the company, sir. Trying to do what we can with replacements. You know how that goes. Pretty tough sledding with these new kids they're sending over."

The older man nodded, still appraising.

"All right, Captain. Tell Lieutenant Moseby to give you what you need. Won't be any paperwork problems on this end."

"Thank you, sir."

"You get your new company together, well, give 'em hell up there. Just . . . next time, stick to your own depot. You're drawing flies."

"Absolutely, sir."

The lieutenant returned, a clipboard in his hand, three shotguns slung on his shoulder, several belts of shells. He saw the older officer, said, "Major, I was going to get this requisition signed . . ."

"Sign it yourself, Lieutenant. Just get these stinking bastards out of here."

"That major thought you were a captain? Hell, Sarge, you can go to the stockade for impersonating an officer!"

"I didn't impersonate anybody. He just assumed. Sometimes a little gray hair is an asset."

Adams sat back, shifted on the hard seat, tried to find some angle that didn't hurt. They had hitched a ride with a truck carrying army and civilian aid workers, the kind of people who wouldn't have any idea where three Marines were actually supposed to be. Adams examined the shotgun in between his knees, saw concern on the faces across from him, tried not to appear too menacing. Beside him Mortensen fingered his own shotgun, said to a man straight across, "Blows hell out of anything in close range. Kills Japs by the dozen. Best damn weapon man ever invented. You oughta see the guts."

Adams tried to avoid the horror on those who stared at them, wondered just what *aid workers* were hoping to do, thought, the best aid we can give the Okies is if we kill every damn Jap on this island. Okies oughta appreciate that, for sure. He slid open the breech of the pump shotgun, had watched the sergeant load his, a great show of expertise, obviously impressing the aid workers, if not injecting them with a bit more fear. Adams did the same, sliding the fat shells into the magazine, then one into the chamber, thought, five. That's not too many. I kinda like eight better.

He had no idea why Mortensen had wanted shotguns at all, and even now with the heavy piece in his hand, he wasn't sure why it was any better than the M-1, or Mortensen's Thompson. But the sergeant showed perfect certainty, and Adams had accepted Mortensen's authority, as much as he had respected Ferucci. Just like Welty, Mortensen was a longtime veteran, and from the grim efficiency in the man's authority, Adams assumed the sergeant had seen and done more than anyone in the platoon, maybe the company. He didn't actually know that, of course, but he understood what that supply officer had seen, why the major had assumed Mortensen to be a company commander. Yep, a little gray hair goes a long way. There's a whole hell of a lot of us that ain't making it that far. Mortensen was a graphic contrast to the replacements, the men who came forward with what seemed to be utter brainlessness, an affliction apparent even in the new lieutenants. In the same truck, four of those men sat in the rear, two across, crisp new army uniforms, the faces of panicked children. They wore the insignia of their units, something any veteran sergeant would immediately rip away when they reached their destination. Their boots were even shinier than Adams's, one man a sergeant, his stripes newly sewn onto a jacket that had never seen the outdoors. Beside Adams, Mortensen seemed to share his thoughts, leaned forward, said, "Any of you boys shave yet?"

They tried to respond by haughty silence, as though their training made them seasoned, too grizzled for such abuse. But one of them broke ranks, stared at the filthy uniforms of Mortensen and Welty, said, "Marines, huh? I hear you boys had it kinda rough. How many Japs you kill?"

The voice betrayed the man's age, and Adams guessed, seventeen, if that old. Mortensen sat back, ignored the man, Welty keeping silent as well.

"Maybe you haven't killed any? That it? Might explain why you're riding up to the line. They grab you for running away? Heard Marines don't like it when their own shag ass."

Adams stared at the sneer on the chalky face, the sound of snottiness in his voice. Something cold and nasty suddenly rolled over in Adams's brain, the man not even looking at him, focused more on the men with the dirty uniforms. He thinks I'm just like him, Adams thought. Clean uniform, so I'm *one of them,* another man who thinks he knows everything, who thinks he knows . . . the thoughts were overrun by his anger, and he slammed the shotgun down between his knees, said, "Listen, you little turd. We've all killed Japs. We're not done killing Japs. If I can, I'll kill every damn Jap on this island, and when I'm done, I'll go to Japan and kill every damn one there. Those sons of bitches killed my sergeant, they killed my lieutenant, and they killed half my company. I killed one with my knife. I blew one up with a grenade, and they nearly did the same to me. They dumped mortar shells on me until I couldn't take it anymore, but I'm taking it anyway! I'm going back up there because my buddies need me, they need every damn one of us who knows what it takes to kill Japs! You hear me?"

He was shouting now, ignored the hand pulling on his arm, tried to stand in the rolling truck, fought the grip from Mortensen, the sergeant silent, pulling him back to the seat. But the words wouldn't stop, the four replacements leaning back away from him, obvious fear. Adams pulled free of Mortensen's grip, leaned closer to the man with the attitude, the attitude erased completely.

"I've seen them kill people I've known since training, and I've seen them kill corpsmen and stretcher bearers . . . I've seen them kill an Okie girl . . ."

He began to stammer, and Mortensen grabbed his arm again, yanked him down hard, and Welty was in front of him, kneeling, shouted into his face.

"Shut up! You hear me? Shut up! You wanna go back to that damn white-sheet place? You crack up on me again and I'll take you there myself. You see that shotgun?"

Welty waited for the answer, and Adams tried to hold back the shaking in his chest, his hands, nodded.

"Look at it!"

Adams obeyed, stared at the cold steel, the fat barrel pointing skyward, the belt of ammo across his chest. Welty grabbed the shotgun, shoved it hard into Adams's chest.

"You know why we wanted these things? 'Cause they work! We got a job to do, and you already know that those Jap bastards wanna make it easy for us, they wanna walk right up to us and stick a grenade down our throats. We have to kill every one of these bastards, every one! Right?"

"Yeah."

"I said, *right?*"

Adams felt the hard grip on his arm, Mortensen still holding him, hard fingers digging into the barely healed wound on his arm. Adams felt the pain, wouldn't flinch, saw Welty still staring at him, hard and cold, the same hint of madness he had seen in the others. Adams understood now, they've gotta know. Am I gonna crack up again? *I've gotta know.* His hands gripped hard to the shotgun, and he realized that what Mortensen said was true, that Welty was right. The shotgun had one purpose. At close range it could blow a man to pieces and take out a half-dozen Japs behind him.

Welty's voice rose, closer to Adams's face.

"You talk like a tough guy, but I'm telling you, I want more than talk outta you! We're gonna kill every one of those bastards! *Right?*"

Adams saw the fury in Welty's red eyes, his friend searching him, a frightening urgency. He felt it now, that they needed to hear they could count on him, that Adams was still ready for the fight. He jerked the shotgun from Welty's hands, knew that Welty shared the memories, the death and the stink, but one memory was Adams's alone, and he embraced it now, that one dismal day, vivid and pure, digging his knife into the throat of the Japanese soldier, the head rolling away, the fountain of blood. He could smell the man's blood still, would always smell it, and for the first time he knew he had to have more, that the hate and the pain were part of the men beside him, part of everything he had become. It was why he had to leave the hospital, why the doctors had allowed him back on the line. If he was nuts at all it was because *that* kind of nuts was what they needed from him. He *had* to go back, he *had* to fight. He returned Welty's stare, no emotion, no fear, the words coming out as perfect truth.

"I wanna kill every damn one."

On June 4, the Sixth Division's commanding general, Lemuel Shepherd, was finally allowed to embark on the kind of mission his men were suited for. Coming in from the sea, the Fourth and Twenty-ninth regiments struck the Oroku Peninsula and tore into the defenses that the Japanese naval troops had thought were invincible. Inland, the Twenty-second Regiment served both as reserve and as the cutoff force, moving into what was left of the city of Naha, sealing off the base of the peninsula against any escape for the Japanese forces who now faced seaward. After four days of slogging through intermittent rain and stifling heat, the two regiments succeeded in driving through the Japanese and secured the vital airfield west of the city. But the fight had been difficult, the naval troops putting up a more solid defense than even Ushijima had expected. But the

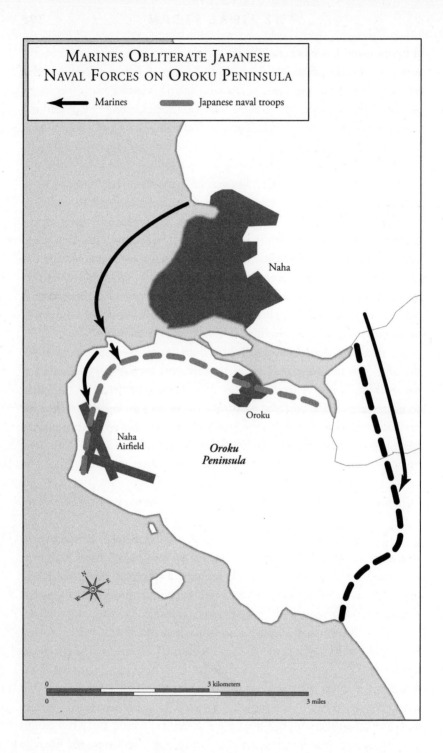

MARINES OBLITERATE JAPANESE
NAVAL FORCES ON OROKU PENINSULA

Marines   Japanese naval troops

Naha

Oroku

Naha
Airfield

*Oroku
Peninsula*

0   3 kilometers
0   3 miles

end had been inevitable, even if the Marines' casualties were, once again, brutally high. As a fitting conclusion to the battle, with the Oroku Peninsula securely in Marine hands, Admiral Ota did what he was expected to do. With Marine gunners zeroing in on his headquarters, Ota denied the Marines the privilege of capturing the senior naval officer on Okinawa. The admiral committed suicide.

To the south, what remained of Ushijima's army had mostly dug into the heights of the Kiyan Peninsula, and the delay from General Buckner in driving the American forces southward had been brief, much briefer than Ushijima had anticipated. The two army divisions now in the line, the Seventh and the Ninety-sixth, pressed from the east, allowing the battered Seventy-seventh to pull back for a rest and refit. In the center and right, the Marine First Division drove straight at the defensive positions, and with a more narrow front to contend with, the more compact Americans rolled into yet another slogging fight against high ground, a frontal assault that drove the casualty counts high on both sides. Once Oroku was secure, the Sixth Marines moved down the western coast, moving into position on the right flank of the First Division. But the losses on the Oroku Peninsula meant that all three of the Sixth's regiments were so badly chewed up, they could not assist their brethren with the force everyone hoped for. Thus for the Sixth, the front for the last great assault was narrowed even more, the Marines once more shoving southward along the coast.

"Well, whatya know? Things must be worse than they're telling us. They're sending crack-ups back out here."

Yablonski spoke from inside a foxhole, rose up, Adams staring at him with a weary fatigue, thought, some things never change.

"Yeah. They figure the guys up here ain't pulling the load, so they're scraping the barrel to find guys like me. You rather have a bunch of moron replacements?"

Mortensen had moved up behind him, said, "Speaking of . . . replacements. Over there, our new lieutenant, Gibson. Go report to him, let him know who you are, that you're with me. You wanna fight so damn bad, show off the shotgun. Once we move out, you'll be put right up front."

Yablonski perked up, climbed from the foxhole, his mouth stuffed with a chocolate bar.

"You got a shotgun?" He caught the weapon in Mortensen's hand as well, said, "Dammit! You didn't bring more? Come on, Sarge, that's the best damn weapon out here."

Mortensen ignored him, and Yablonski saw Welty now, eyed the third piece.

"Oh, for God's sake. That's all it takes, haul your asses back to some cushy hospital and they give you a reward? Hell, I'm going AWOL first chance I get. You girls know how to use that thing? The sucker kicks, might hurt your shoulder, you know. You need a man to handle it for you?"

Mortensen turned, moved closer to Yablonski, towered over the man, said, "This *girl* knows exactly what to do with it, and if you get in my way, I'll give you a lesson you won't like. You hear me? Now shut the hell up! All of you! Let's move out. We got a job to do."

Adams followed the others, had no idea what the orders had been, where they were going. Down at the far end of a bare field a pair of jeeps were parked end to end, a half-dozen men gathered, the familiar scene, a map spread on one jeep's hood. Captain Bennett was speaking to several other men, and Adams noticed one man with his hands on his hips, staring out at the Marines as they moved past. Beyond the jeeps were four big trucks, shirtless men unloading crates. Adams had seen those crates before, thought, grenades. I guess it's time to load up. He looked again at the cluster of men around the jeep, the one man still watching the procession, the attitude of the man *in charge*. Adams slid closer to Welty, said, "Who's that? You know?"

Welty whispered, "Hell, I guess you ain't heard. Sometime during the fight over Sugar Loaf, Colonel Schneider got relieved by General Shepherd. Word came back that Schneider had kinda fallen apart up there, wasn't doing the job. Scuttlebutt said that the big brass had to find somebody to blame for us taking so long to capture the place, and I guess Schneider didn't have too many friends. That guy over there's Colonel Roberts. He's the regimental CO now. I hear he's a pretty good joe." Welty paused, both men joining the flow toward the trucks. "You saw a bunch of it, Clay, but sure as hell, it didn't get much better after we pulled you out. A bunch of the brass never made it off the hill. The other units got busted up as bad as we did. Lots of new lieutenants now. And I heard that a bunch of ninety-day wonders got busted up on Oroku, hadn't been on the line for more than a couple days. The Twenty-ninth and the Fourth both took a lot of damage. We lost more guys than I want to know about. Be happy we got gathered up by the sarge. Mortensen's a good guy, even if he tries too hard to be a badass. Right now I wouldn't trust anybody in clean boots." He glanced at Adams. "Well, hell, you know what I mean."

Adams looked for a convenient mud puddle, thought, I can fix that part right away. But the land had dried out, more heat than wetness now, the sun already up over the far hills. Adams lowered his voice, said, "What do you know about ours? The new looey."

"Gibson? Damnedest southern drawl you ever heard. Someone said he's a VMI man, talks a lot about Stonewall Jackson. I guess we'll find out what kind of *stone wall* he is."

Gibson stood to one side, motioning his men toward the trucks, and Adams moved away from Welty, approached the lieutenant, knew better than to stand at attention, and though no one had heard a sniper in the area at all, Adams erased the word *sir* from his mind.

"Begging your pardon. I'm Private Adams. Sergeant Mortensen's squad. Just got back up from the field hospital. I'm happy to be back."

Gibson nodded, didn't seem to really see him, said, "Fall in, Private. You do your job, I'll do mine. Right now you need to load up on phosphorus grenades. We'll be mopping up for the boys up front, cleaning out some caves. I want to see some dead Japs."

Gibson was matter-of-fact, no smile, no real energy behind the words. Adams digested the word *Japs,* rolling out of Gibson's mouth with two syllables. *Jayaps.*

"I'll agree with that, uh . . ."

"Git on back to your squad. I want everybody loaded up with plenty of ordnance."

The conversation was clearly over, and Adams slipped away, no salute, Gibson not seeming to expect one. Adams mulled over the man's slow drawl, thought, God, if we're under fire, I hope like hell I can understand his orders. He tried to guess Gibson's age, thought, not as old as the sarge, that's for sure. Hope he's up to snuff. He searched for Welty, moved out next to him, said, "Phosphorus grenades. They're giving us something new."

"Not new. But nasty as hell. Best way to nail the Japs right in their hidey holes. Just don't get any of that stuff on you. Burns right through skin, bone, everything else. Hey, we got company."

Adams saw where Welty was pointing, a squad of men dropping down from an amphtrac, all with large tanks on their backs. Adams had seen plenty of those before, thought, flamethrowers, and a whole bunch of them. Damn, this is gonna be fun.

NORTH OF MEZADO RIDGE, SOUTHERN OKINAWA
JUNE 17, 1945

The prisoners filed past, a dozen men, wearing what looked like loincloths. The Marines who marched them back seemed disgusted by the job, and in front of Adams, Yablonski called out, "There's a damn cave back around the curve. Dump 'em there."

One man responded with a spit toward the prisoners, moved past Adams with dead eyes. Adams scanned one of the prisoners, the man rail thin, barefoot, a twisted mess of black hair. The man glanced at the passing Marines, seemed terrified, moving in halting steps, prodded by the next man in line behind him. Yablonski kept up the chatter, said loudly, "We'll be eating you boys for dinner tonight. Ha!"

"Knock that off."

The voice came from the rear, Mortensen keeping his squad together, spaced the usual five yards apart. Yablonski's shoulders hunched, the man clearly angry, but he seemed to appreciate that Mortensen had plenty of temper for all of them. The prisoners were past, and Adams saw a series of low hills, and beyond, a rocky, scrub-covered ridgeline. The rumble of artillery rolled down from the east, and Adams soaked that up, couldn't just let it pass. The thumps seemed to land somewhere very far away, and yet, inside his own brain, the smoke and smell of burnt explosives drifted through him in hot stinging waves. He focused on Welty, directly in front, boots kicking up coral dust, the heat drumming down on them. He stared at the nearest hill, thought of the shotgun, no use at all at this range. What the hell were we thinking? He saw another column moving out beyond the far side of the hill, saw men suddenly dropping down, scattering, and he caught the single crack of rifle fire. Now a Nambu gun rattled out that way, the awful sound too familiar. The lieutenant called out from in front.

"Double-time it. Move up to the hill, spread out!"

The men obeyed instantly, and Adams scrambled after Welty, saw cuts in the earth, shell holes, debris scattered in every direction. As before, most of the vegetation was obliterated, some burned into rough stubble, some uprooted, blasted trees, the blobs of earth at their base making for good cover. The Nambu began again, still on the far side of the hill, and Adams followed Welty's lead, dropped low, held the shotgun at the ready. But there was nothing to shoot at, no sign of activity, the churned-up ground showing swirls of dust from a light breeze.

Behind him there was a sudden rip of fire from a Nambu gun, a man's scream, and now movement through a brush line, flickers of fire. The men fell flat but the Japanese fire was coming from every angle, holes in the ground suddenly revealing their occupants. Adams hugged the shotgun, the crack and whistle from the Japanese weapons close overhead, heard cries from all across the hill. The sound of thirties erupted behind them, a machine gun platoon coming up to the base of the ridge. But the targets were elusive, the men close to Adams keeping low, no one returning fire. A man ran past him, the quick scamper of footsteps, and he heard a single thunderous blast close by, Welty, the shotgun. Adams turned, frantic, saw the Japanese soldier tumbling down, Welty pumping a new shell into the shotgun's breech, lying flat again.

"Got him! Dammit! These sons of bitches . . ."

The thirties kept up their sporadic fire, desperate machine gunners trying to find targets, the Japanese mingling in with the Marines. But more of the Marines were finding targets of their own, some suddenly caught in a hand-to-hand struggle. Welty fired the shotgun again, and Adams peered up, a burst of Nambu fire close over his head, driving him flat again.

"Jack! Nambu to the right!"

"I know! You want me to shake his hand? I can smell the damn powder!"

Adams felt his breathing in heavy gasps, red dust on his face, choking, rolled over, thin brush his only cover. He waited for the Nambu to go silent, thought, change belts, right? Reload . . . right now. He leaned up, sitting position, searched frantically, saw the barrel of the Nambu, movement behind a thick bush. He raised the shotgun, no time to aim, fired, the brush blown into pieces, leaves falling. He pumped the shotgun, fired again, the Nambu silent, the barrel suddenly rolling to the side. Welty was up, crawling quickly, moved to the gun, shotgun pointed in, fired, no sounds at all from the Japanese gunners. He waved back toward Adams, a shout, "Here!"

Adams crawled as well, a crack of rifle fire over his head, kept moving. He reached the brush, close to Welty, saw the gunners, four men, a heap of blood and shattered flesh, the Nambu on its side, one man lying across it, his face nearly gone.

"Good work!"

Welty slapped his arm, then crawled in among the gunners, settled low, said, "Here! Good cover. Bodies!"

Adams slid in beside him, shoved one man up on another, a small embankment of human flesh, felt the slick wetness, blood on his hands. A single thump impacted the body closest to him, sickening sound, the smell of the blood and the stinking Japanese bodies engulfing him. He was breathing heavily, his heart racing, said, "What now? What do we do?"

Welty peered up, cold fury in his eyes, placed the shotgun up on the bodies, a perfect perch, said, "Sit right here! Watch for Japs, anybody moves close, blow 'em to hell. Reload your shotgun, you fired twice."

"No, just once."

"You fired twice! Reload!"

Adams was ready for the argument, a ridiculous debate, thought, I know how many times I fired the damn piece . . . and he thumbed one shell into the magazine, tested another, which slid in easily. Yeah, okay, fine. How the hell did he know that? He stared at the shotgun for a long moment, lost in some other place, his brain trying to take him away, the roar of fire across the hill chasing him. But he fought it, kept his stare on the shotgun, felt the power in his hands, the burst of fire that took a man apart, that left no doubt if you had *hit* him. The voice rose in his brain, pushing aside the need to escape. *Do it again.*

Across the sloping ground, Marines kept up their push, some firing point blank into spider holes, Japanese soldiers still rising up, some throwing grenades, shot down almost immediately. The thirties were still seeking targets, one burst splitting the air close above Adams, and he ducked low, his face close to the Japanese uniform, filth and blood. He wanted to back away, the smells sour, gut turning, thought, good cover. Welty stays, you stay.

There were voices across the hill now, the lieutenants pulling their men up from whatever cover they had found. Adams peered up carefully, and Welty said, "Time to go. Damn, I liked this place."

Welty jumped up, and Adams followed, stepped up and over the stack of bodies, his boot pushing down into soft slop. He ran, following Welty, saw more Marines all out across the ridge, some firing toward Japanese soldiers on the ridgeline, some throwing grenades, fire in both directions. The brush thinned toward the top, the Japanese mostly in the open, some running, some ripped down by the fire from the Marines, some from the thirties down the hill. The grenades arced over from the crest of the hill, the same tactic the Japanese had used so many times before. Closer to the ridgeline, the Marines tossed over their own, the deadly, ridiculous game. Welty still ran, Adams desperate to keep up, the rocks difficult, clawing at his boots, a body underfoot, a Marine, and Adams flinched, tried not to step on the man, was past now, movements to his right, close beside Welty, a Japanese soldier rising up, a bayonet, Welty unaware. Adams shouted, but there was too much noise, no time, and he leveled the shotgun at his hip, fired into the man from a few feet away. The soldier collapsed, folded over, the blast ripping his gut. Welty glanced that way but didn't slow down. Adams ignored the man he had killed, too many Japanese troops rising up from their cover, some tossing grenades. He aimed the shotgun, sighted down the barrel, scanning, waiting, and one man rose up suddenly, half visible behind a bush, the grenade in his hand, thumping it on his own helmet. Adams fired straight into the man's face, the helmet blown away, the Japanese soldier collapsing in a heap, the grenade going off right where the body had fallen. The dust and smoke was rolling past, thicker toward the ridgeline, no visibility at all, choking stink of powder. The machine gun fire from behind had stopped, the Marine gunners seeing too many of their own on the hill. From beyond the crest the mortars came, more grenades, one arcing toward him, bounding on the rocks, right to Adams's feet. He kicked at it, panic, shouted out, but the grenade just smoked, no explosion, a *dud,* and Welty grabbed his arm, said, "Hit those rocks up there! Get ready . . . there's Japs right over the top!"

Welty threw himself forward, flattened, and Adams did the same, could see Marines lining up along the best cover, rugged coral rocks, whatever brush they could find. To one side Adams saw Mortensen, the tall man curling his legs in tight, one small boulder protecting him, saw Gridley, the BAR, the squad somehow keeping close through all the chaos. The firing was mostly one-sided now, Marines finding targets down the far side of the ridge, the Japanese scrambling away, some dropping down into holes, the mouths of caves, mostly hidden.

Mortensen called out, "Watch behind us! Those bastards might still be in those holes!"

Adams glanced back down the hill, many more Marines spreading out through the rocks, still some Japanese soldiers, one Nambu gun off to the left, silenced suddenly by a grenade. Marines continued to fall, fire coming at them from far to the side, the thirties now aiming that way, seeking new targets. The panic tried to return, Adams jerking back and forth, looking over the crest, back down, nowhere to go, another crest, another ridge with fire on all sides, too many men going down. Mortensen's words echoed through him, and he said aloud, "They're everywhere!"

"Shut up! You see one, you blow him to hell!"

Welty's words calmed him, the jerkiness easing, and Adams remembered the soldier he had killed, *reload,* slid a shell from the cartridge belt, slipped it into the shotgun's magazine. Welty suddenly fired, shouted, "Duck!"

Adams obeyed, the grenade blast coming a few feet away, a shattering of rock that blew over him, punching and slicing into his side. He rolled that way, ran a hand down his arm, his side, his jacket ripped, shreds of cloth.

"Ah . . . I'm hit!"

Welty was there, on top of him, rolling him over, feeling, said, "No you're not! Just tore up your fancy new duds."

"You sure?"

"No blood, you idiot. You feel dead?"

Adams felt the rips in the jacket, dry, pieces of gravel against his skin, not quite hard enough to blow into him, to . . . shatter his arm. He stared at his hand, saw only the dried crust of blood from the Japanese soldier, thought, damn, that was lucky as hell.

"Thanks!"

Welty rolled away, said, "Yeah, I get a medal 'cause you got lucky. Just keep your eyes open. We won't be staying here long. The brass will want us to keep going."

"No, not now."

The voice came from below Adams's feet and he saw Gibson, the new lieutenant crawling on his knees and elbows, the carbine cradled in his arms. "Stay right here! They're sending up another unit to go past us." He raised up, shouted out. "Everybody, you all stay where you're at. We're supposed to hold this crest—"

The man's helmet popped off and he slumped suddenly, facedown in the rocks. Adams stared, frozen, and Welty shouted, "Corpsman!"

"Here!"

The corpsman scrambled up the hill, and Adams caught sight of the medical bag, could see it was brand-new, the man staring at him with sweating terror. Adams pointed, said, "There, they hit the looey!"

"The what?"

"Right there! The man that's down!"

"Yeah! Okay! What do I do?"

Welty scrambled past Adams, below his feet, jerked the bag from the man's hand, shouted into his face, "How long you been out here?"

"Don't know. Just got here!"

Welty didn't respond, rolled the lieutenant over, turned away quickly, said, "Never mind." He handed the frightened corpsman his bag, said, "Keep your ass down, right here! We'll need that damn bag!"

Welty moved back up beside Adams, and Adams saw the furious glare, Welty mumbling, "What the hell's going on back there? They send us children to play doctor?"

Adams stared at Gibson's body, the feeling too familiar now, sickening helplessness. Welty said, "Right between the eyes. He never felt a thing. Let go of it. Do your job!"

"Yeah . . . sure."

Adams looked back down the hill, could see a new wave of Marines coming up, men carrying thirties, mortar crews. The ridge was still peppered by firing, but most of the Japanese troops had either pulled away or were among the scattered dead. Already stretcher bearers were coming up, gathering up the wounded, the sounds of the fight replaced more by the sound of men, the voices, sharp screams, curses. Beside him Welty said, "Hey, Clay. Your new boots look like hell."

23. ADAMS

The company had stayed on the ridge, the fortunate men sleeping in foxholes. The others made do with shelter halves, some with ponchos for pillows. They had stayed alert, the two-man buddy system again, but if there were Japanese there at all, they had mostly seemed content to stay in their holes. By dawn, another wave of Marines had passed through their position, a new attack on the next ridge, a place someone called Kawanga. The ridges ran like fingers out across the rolling rocky ground, each one a little taller, a little more rugged. The Sixth Marines were moving forward in a progressive wave, on a compact line that bordered the coastline. To their left, inland, the First Marine Division was pushing hard into more of the Japanese lines of resistance, while farther to their east, the two army divisions did the same. The sounds of the ongoing fighting were everywhere, some of it from the sea, shelling from warships that were taking up position around the base of the island. Word had come from Marine lookouts near the shore that the Japanese had attempted amphibious operations of their own, small boats and barges loaded with commandos who had attempted to slip along the coastline after dark, to come in behind the Marines and soldiers closest to the sea. But the naval lookouts had done their jobs, patrol boats aiming spotlights into every hidden bay, every rocky nook where those enemy boats could hide. Even the small spotter boats were armed with heavy machine guns. Supported by heavily armed gunboats offshore, the Americans made quick work of the Japanese commandos, none of whom reached their targets.

On Mezado Ridge the caves were everywhere, the nerves of the men tested by the certain presence of the Japanese beneath them, as well as the constant sounds of the fight far up in front of them. All through the day the Marines had pressed forward through the ridgelines, and in every case the Japanese had made a good stand, but the enemy could not hold back the power that the Marines brought to the fight. Bennett's company was one of several charged with the job of mopping up, of making sure that any Japanese soldiers hidden in the caves, in any kind of underground lair, were brought up, or dealt with according to how the Japanese themselves responded. From many of the holes Okinawans emerged first, manic chatter to the interpreters, some begging for mercy, for food, some telling the Marines that soldiers still lurked below, back in the caves. Some of those civilians were led away quickly, grateful for anything, if only the promise of food. But others had stayed below, and when the caves were blown, either by explosives or the blistering fire from the flamethrowers, the Marines were astonished and sickened to find women, children, even babies, horrifying groups of bloody corpses alongside the Japanese soldiers, the same men who had so brutally dominated the Okinawan people and their country.

Before the Marines could begin their own work, muffled shots and grenade blasts would ring out from inside the cave, ending often furious arguments between those Japanese soldiers who favored surrender and those who never would. More often the Marines would discover a cave occupied by corpses who had settled their differences in the bloodiest way possible. The same fate befell those few Japanese soldiers who sought the sanctuary the Americans were offering. Japanese troops emerged from caves, hands high, a show of gratefulness to their captors, but many of those men did not survive long enough to matter. From small spider holes Japanese snipers waited for the opportunity to execute the Japanese soldiers who attempted to surrender. To the disbelief of the Marines, the snipers seemed to regard that mission even above killing their enemy. Marines stood unharmed, startled, while a Japanese prisoner would suddenly drop from an unseen assailant. If surrender was the greatest act of dishonor a Japanese soldier could display, there were Japanese marksmen who would enhance their own honor by eliminating them.

"Easy now, take it slow. Where's that damn interpreter?"

Captain Bennett's order was repeated, a shout echoed back across the open ground, and Adams saw one man coming quickly, an uneven run, negotiating his way through the jagged rocks. Bennett waited impatiently, the interpreter struggling to make the climb, and Adams saw the man's lumpy gut, surprising. But he had seen that before, knew the look of rear echelon. Bennett pointed to the cave, a jagged hole in the rocks, lined with thickly webbed branches.

"Right here. One of the boys saw somebody drop down into this mess. Give it a shout."

The interpreter moved closer, obviously skittish, shouted, *"De-te-koi! De-te-koi! Shimpachina!"*

Adams stood close beside Bennett, Mortensen on the other side, both with their shotguns aimed at the hole, and Mortensen asked the question that rolled through Adams's mind.

"What's he saying?"

Bennett responded, " 'Come out, come out, wherever you are.' Or something close."

Mortensen said, "He should try, 'Come out or we'll blow you to hell.' "

The interpreter was still nervous, looked back at Bennett, said, "Again, Captain?"

Bennett gave the man a scathing stare, said in a low voice, "You call me *captain* again and I'm going to have every man in this company fall in, call you *general,* and give you a big salute. You know what a sniper is, you jackass?"

"Uh . . . yes . . . sorry."

Noises came from the cave now, a woman's voice, fast jabbering. Adams gripped the shotgun with cold, anxious fingers, felt the stab in his chest. No, please God, not a woman. She appeared now, a filthy billowing dress, bowed several times, terror in her eyes. She dropped to her knees, crying fitfully, the interpreter moving up close, low talk, something comforting.

Bennett said, "Get back away from her, you stupid—"

The blast erupted into both of them, the woman's dress flying into shreds, a bloody mass, knocking the interpreter backward. Bennett shouted, "Grenade! Son of a bitch! Corpsman! Get a corpsman up here!"

Adams stared, shocked, helpless, Mortensen watching beside him as a corpsman rushed forward, leaning low over the man. Another moved up close and Bennett said, "Stay back! Just need one. Too damn dangerous. Could be more grenades on that bitch."

The interpreter was screaming, and Adams saw bloody rips across his chest, one leg ripped open, a huge empty gash in his gut. Bennett turned to Mortensen, said, "Spread your men out around this hole. Those bastards are still in there. They just sent this one out for laughs. You got phosphorus?"

"Yep."

"Use it."

A voice came from the sloping hillside beyond the cave's opening, one man waving, pointing downward.

"Here! Air shaft!"

Bennett called up, "You have phosphorus?"

"No. All out!"

The captain pointed to Adams, surprising him, said, "Take a phosphorus grenade up there. Drop it in."

Adams scrambled to obey, climbed up along the rough ground, toward the Marine who had made the find, saw now it was Gorman, the older man. Gorman was excited, pointed his M-1 down toward a round hole, a piece of pipe, just barely above the level of the ground.

"I love this. Stupid bastards think we're blind or something. People wonder how these sons of bitches live in caves. Here's how, kid." Adams saw the pipe, no more than four inches across, hidden by a small clump of brush. Adams pulled the grenade from his jacket pocket, felt an odd shaking in his hands, had not used the brutal weapon yet. Gorman said, "Phosphorus? Good! Let the bastards have it!"

Others were gathering and Gorman seemed jumpy, giddy, unusual. Gorman pointed into the hole.

"Listen! You can hear 'em! They know we're up here! Hurry up. They might blow this whole damn hill! They could have a ton of explosives down there. Listen to 'em. Chatterin' like birds."

Another man moved close, said, "Dead birds."

Adams knew the man, another of Bennett's sergeants, and he looked at Adams, saw the grenade. "Do it, kid."

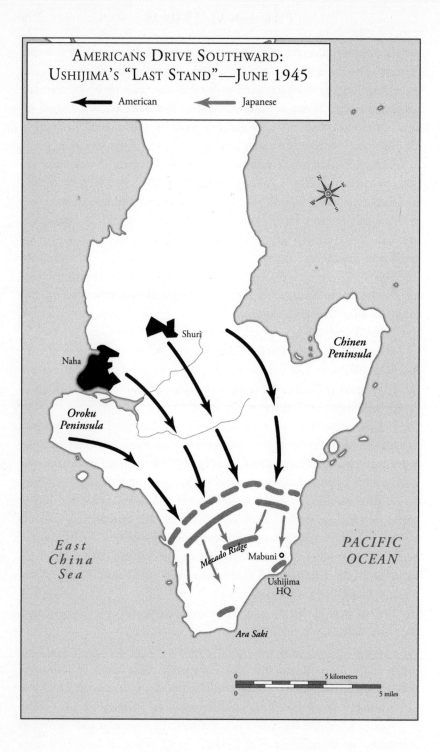

AMERICANS DRIVE SOUTHWARD:
USHIJIMA'S "LAST STAND"—JUNE 1945

American   Japanese

Shuri

Naha

Chinen
Peninsula

Oroku
Peninsula

East
China
Sea

PACIFIC
OCEAN

Mezado Ridge   Mabuni

Ushijima
HQ

Ara Saki

0   5 kilometers

0   5 miles

Adams leaned close to the pipe, could hear the voices plainly, men and women, some crying, angry shouts. He glanced down toward Bennett, saw more men moving around the mouth of the cave, rifles aimed, Mortensen backing them off. Welty was holding the shotgun at his waist, staring up at *him*. Adams knew what Welty was watching for, thought, this is a damn test. He's wondering if I'll do this. Adams held the grenade over the hole, pulled the pin, still gripped it, felt a shivering hesitation. He stared into the hole, the voices coming up in a chorus of sound, arguments, orders, more crying, and he waited another second, Gorman standing above him.

"Go on, son. Do it."

Adams dropped the grenade.

He jumped back, waited, and the explosion rumbled beneath them, the mouth of the cave boiling with white smoke. The voices were screams now, but not many, and Adams backed away, wouldn't hear them, the other Marines moving up, taking his place, cheering for the white smoke that spewed up through the pipe, a hot flume coming up through the narrow chimney. Men were cheering, M-1s in the air, saluting him, and Adams moved back down toward Welty, the others still aiming the rifles at the cave. To one side, Bennett glanced at him.

"Good job."

"Thanks."

He looked at Welty, saw cold eyes, a slight nod. Adams caught the smell of the phosphorus, moved farther away, upwind, but the smoke was already in his clothes, his hair, on his skin. Fire had erupted near the mouth of the cave, white phosphorus igniting brush, the men reacting by wisely backing away. The cave was spewing smoke, and nothing else, no one emerging. There was another rumble, a sudden burst of fire from deep inside the cave, something combustible igniting. Adams still walked, his hands shaking, and Welty was there beside him, said, "Now dammit, Clay, don't go all *Asian* on me again."

Adams held up his hand, still shaking, and Welty said, "Whoa, what the hell's with you? You okay?"

"I did it, Jack. Wiped 'em out. They never had a chance."

"I know. That was the idea. Bastards won't come out, we sure as hell ain't going in there to get 'em. You saw what they did, using those damn Okies like booby traps. They got no reason to live, none at all."

Adams was breathing heavily, sweating in the hot dusty air, the shaking rolling all through him. But it wasn't fear, nothing about the grenade, the smoke, the screams, and the death that bothered him at all. The shaking wasn't fear. It was excitement.

"Over here!"

Adams turned, saw a cluster of men waving from a crevice in a brushy hillside, and Bennett motioned for his men to advance, leaving a small party behind to keep tabs on the smoking hole. Welty began to move, said, "Look! They're coming out. Let's get there quick!"

Adams could see civilians emerging from the cave, another group of women in filthy dresses, some breaking into a run, escaping as quickly as they could. The captain was on the radio set, an angry demand for more aid workers, for interpreters and prison guards. Another interpreter was there, moving up quickly toward Bennett, no one bothering him with details of what had happened to the last man. Mortensen moved up within fifty yards of the new cave, held the shotgun high above his head, holding his men a distance from the cave's mouth.

"Give 'em room. They keep coming, let 'em come."

To one side Adams saw a pair of Marines moving up, a flamethrower team, the weight of the tank of napalm on their backs a hindrance as they staggered quickly through the rocks. Mortensen's squad was gathering near their sergeant, and Adams moved into place, focused on the man hauling the long spout of the flamethrower. This ought to be something, he thought. Ringside seat. Close by, Yablonski was watching him, said, "Hey Nut Case! Don't let these Okie ladies scare you!"

Welty moved past Adams, toward Yablonski, and Adams could see Yablonski's response, both men bowing up. Welty slung his shotgun on his shoulder, said, "I've heard about all I wanna hear outta your big damn mouth!"

"What you gonna do, Four Eyes, kick me in the shins?"

Mortensen shouted, "Knock it off, both of you! There's a boatload of these bastards in this hole! Stand ready!"

The flamethrower crew moved closer, the man with the nozzle looking at Mortensen, waiting for the word to fire. The sergeant shook his head, kept his eyes on the cave, said, "Not yet. Let 'em come."

The women continued to flow up out of the cave, more than two dozen, and now men appeared, ratty uniforms, hands on tops of heads. Mortensen yelled out, "Watch 'em! Any bundles at their waist, shoot 'em! Anybody drops his hands, shoot him!"

Adams wanted to move closer, better effect with the shotgun, heard

Yablonski saying something to Welty, some stupid vulgarity, Welty ignoring him. One woman emerged from the cave, men flanking her, close, as though making sure she didn't run, and Adams realized there was something different, the dress not as dirty, a shawl over her head. She looked up, eyes calm, scanning the men, focusing on the men with the flamethrower. Adams couldn't look away, something in her eyes, watched her, wanted to say something, what? There was something wrong, and now he understood. It wasn't a woman at all.

"Hey . . ."

She seemed to trip, falling forward, and Adams could see the Nambu gun strapped to her back. Behind another man dropped down, carefully planned, the machine gun beginning to fire, flashes of light, the distinct chatter. The Marines dropped low, some returning fire, but the Nambu had spread its deadly fire in a wide spray, finding its mark, the men with the napalm tanks down, others going down. The M-1s responded, peppering the machine gunner, the Nambu silent now. Adams rushed forward, Mortensen pushing ahead of him, one blast from the sergeant's shotgun, the body of the gunner jumping from the impact. The other Japanese soldiers had withdrawn, scrambling back into the cave, and Adams caught a last glimpse of them, faces, some near the cave's mouth, huddled low, firing still. He shouted out a warning and Mortensen dropped low, fired the shotgun into the cave, backed away, others firing as well, the heavy rumble of the BAR, shouts and chaos all around him. Adams saw Yablonski running to the fallen flamethrower, Yablonski shouting out something, curses. He ripped at the straps of the napalm tanks, freed them from the dead Marine, slung the tanks up on his back, yelled out, "Move aside! These stinking bastards . . ."

He raised the snout of the flamethrower, fumbled with the mechanism, and behind him, Mortensen yelled, "No . . ."

But the liquid flowed out, straight into the mouth of the cave, then up, higher, Yablonski losing control, the nozzle rising, pushing Yablonski back, the man tripping, falling backward. The napalm still spewed out, a fountain straight overhead. It ignited now, a thick burst of fire, seemed to hang airborne for a long second, then fell, coming down on Yablonski, around him, the man screaming, the fire enveloping him. Adams stood frozen, nothing to do, Mortensen shouting out, "No you stupid . . . no!"

The Japanese troops in the cave had disappeared, and more of the Marines moved up, no one talking, the men trying not to see the horror,

Yablonski's charred body still wrapped in fire, the grass and rocks around him smeared with burning jelly. Adams saw the second flamethrower crewman, wounded, his shoulder covered in blood, moving up on his knees to his buddy, dropping down. The man with the nozzle had been ripped apart by the Nambu, his buddy curling up with grief, a corpsman there now, working to treat the man's wounds. Adams felt drawn to the flames, moved up toward the dying fire, stared at all that remained of Yablonski, black twisted flesh, saw Mortensen still eyeing the cave, and the sergeant said, "Can't just shoot the thing like a rifle. It kicks like a mule. You gotta be prepared for the kick. Stupid bastard."

Men were coming to life again, focusing on the job at hand, gathering in a wide arc around the cave's opening, some moving up higher, searching for any ventilation hole. More men were moving up, another flamethrower crew, and Adams heard orders from Captain Bennett, the second flamethrower moving up close. The Marines stood back, all of them staying clear of the dying flames around Yablonski. The flamethrower operator aimed the nozzle, braced himself with one leg behind, the nozzle spewing a thick stream right into the mouth of the cave, then igniting, the men doing the job the way it should be done. The Marines kept back, some cheering, but the energy was gone, most of them just staring at the flames, knowing that if the men inside did not die by fire, seared lungs, they would die by suffocation, the flames sucking the air out completely. Adams watched alongside the others, rolling the words through his brain. Roast you bastards. *Roast.*

"Private!"

He held his stare toward the cave's mouth, raised the shotgun, searched for any movement, but nothing came from the cave but black smoke, brush burning around the opening.

"Private!"

He backed away, turned toward the voice, saw Mortensen down on one knee. Adams saw that the hillside near the dead flamethrower was littered with bodies, the effects of the Nambu gun. Some of them were wounded, corpsmen moving up quickly, Captain Bennett moving among them, guiding the medical men to the ones who could be helped. Mortensen called out again, "Private! Here!"

Adams realized the sergeant was calling *him,* and he moved that way, Mortensen staring at him with thick tired eyes.

"Your buddy."

He saw now, the red hair, the glasses askew, Welty's helmet off, lying in the grass. Adams dropped to both knees, shock stabbing him, and Mortensen said softly, "Sorry. He was a good man. Those dirty bastards."

Adams couldn't breathe, stared at Welty's face, the eyes partially closed, blood pouring up through Welty's chest in thick bubbles, one round red hole in Welty's throat, more blood. Adams yelled out, "Corpsman! Doc! Get the doc here!"

No one responded, and Adams grabbed Welty's arm, tried to pull him up.

"Come on Jack! It'll be okay! Come on!"

He couldn't hold the tears away, felt Welty's arm limp, no response from the man's eyes, the blood on Adams now, too much blood. Bennett was there now, stood above him.

"He's gone, son. The Nambu took out a half dozen of us. We need to tend to the ones we can help."

Adams didn't respond, stared through tears at his friend, pulled the helmet back, put it on Welty's head, straightened his arms, saw the shotgun lying to one side, the stock broken, shattered.

"What do I do, Jack? What do I do now?"

"Come on, Private. We've got to keep moving. They'll take care of him. You know his family?"

Adams looked up at the captain, shook his head. There was sadness in Bennett's face, acceptance, and Adams realized that the captain had seen this before, too many times, had already lost most of the men he brought to the island.

"Let's go, son. We've got more caves to root out."

Bennett moved away, and Adams looked across the open ground, the black stain that had been Yablonski, the stink from the cave, the Marines moving on, mopping up what was left of the Japanese resistance. He tried to stand, no strength in his knees, stared at Welty's face, could not stop the tears, wanted to say something, anything, some kind of goodbye. But there were no words, his thoughts a jumble of pain and grief. He put a hand on Welty's arm, a thought flickering in his brain, and he raised Welty's shoulder, saw the backpack, reached in, fished his hand around, felt the cardboard box, the K rations. He pulled it out, ripped it open, scattering the contents, picked up the small round can of stew, stuffed it in his pocket.

24. USHIJIMA

The letter had come from General Buckner on the seventeenth, but the date on the paper showed there had been a week's delay in reaching Ushijima's hand. That made perfect sense to the Japanese, since Yahara's plan of retreat had depended on Buckner making the mistake of believing that Ushijima was still at his headquarters beneath the wreckage of the castle at Shuri. The letter had been gracious, polite, as though the American general was trying to reach out with a hand of sympathetic understanding, offering a warm handshake, while the other hand held a grenade.

> The forces under your command have fought bravely and well. Your infantry tactics have merited the respect of your opponents in the battle for Okinawa. Like myself, you are an infantry general, long schooled and experienced in infantry warfare. You must surely realize the pitiful plight of your defensive forces. You know that no reinforcement can reach you. I believe, therefore, that you understand as clearly as I, that the destruction of all Japanese resistance on the island is merely a matter of days. It will entail the necessity of my destroying the vast majority of your remaining troops.

Ushijima had tossed the letter aside, the others on his staff reacting with loud derision and insults. But Ushijima's reaction had surprised even his staff. The note made him laugh, the first real laughter he had enjoyed in many weeks. Buckner's letter seemed to offer a compliment for Ushijima's skills while also showing what seemed to be pity. It was obvious that Buckner assumed that Ushijima had options, one of which was surrender. He had not replied to the letter, could think of nothing at all that would educate the American commander in the ways of his army, his culture, in the vows that bound the Japanese to only one outcome. Now, as he sat alone in his room, reading the transcript of the radio message from Tokyo, he had another laugh, different this time. For the first time, Ushijima felt pity for the man whose complete ignorance of the Japanese had now resulted in an extraordinary piece of history. Ushijima had not believed it at first, assumed that the dispatch from the High Command was pure fiction, still more propaganda flowing out of Tokyo that only insulted the truth. But on the ground out beyond his headquarters, his own communications officers confirmed what the message said, others, artillerymen, reporting to Ushijima what they had seen. The final confirmation of the news had come from the Americans, the Japanese listening posts picking up amazingly blunt transmissions that echoed across their positions.

It had happened as so many monumental events happened, by pure accident. On June 18, Ushijima's artillery spotters had caught the glimpse of a cluster of men gathered in an American observation post, a small clearing that was guarded by tall boulders. The Japanese had known of the place for days, Americans staring back at them through binoculars, a guessing game that might result in a duel between the vast power of the American guns and those few that remained tucked into Ushijima's defensive line. The Japanese had no reserves of ammunition, and so wasting shells on an observation post made little sense. But on this one day, the officer in command of Ushijima's only remaining heavy gun along that part of the front had sensed that what he saw through his glasses were more than observers. And so the Japanese gun had fired five shells in quick succession toward the fat rocks that offered protection to the Americans. The gun had been rolled back quickly into hiding, the officer knowing that five bursts of fire were all he could dare before the Americans would find him with guns of their own. What that artillery officer could not yet know had come to Ushijima days later from Tokyo. In the American observation post, one of those men had been General Buckner himself. As a result of the accuracy of Ushijima's gunner, or more likely, by pure dumb luck, Buckner had been struck by a blast of shrapnel from the rocks and the shells themselves, and had died in a matter of minutes.

Ushijima sipped from his teacup, thought, it is arrogance, the same arrogance that put the pen in General Buckner's hand, daring to tell me how hopeless my situation must be. It was arrogance that took him to his own front lines, puffed up by the need to strut among his troops, displaying his plumage, like some fat peacock. What inspiration has his army drawn from their commander's stupidity?

Ushijima set the cup down, tried to find some comfort on the hard mat beneath him, the wetness in the earth around him sucking any joy out of the moment. He had watched his staff react to the news of Buckner's death with outright joy, and Ushijima thought, that is appropriate, certainly. Is that not what war is about? My equal, my *foe* has been destroyed by my guns. Not so long ago that would mean victory for my army, the enemy crushed by the mere symbolism of it, the slicing off of their head. Throughout history, how many wars have been lost by the death of a single man, the leader who would inspire his army by bearing the mantle as his army's greatest warrior? But, no, the times have changed. The warrior has been replaced by the weaponry, so that even the coward may destroy his enemy from great distances. Even the unwilling can be ordered onto the battlefield, protected by steel. A single general cannot claim any victory, no matter what General Cho might believe. By pure chance we killed one arrogant fool, and there is not even a pause in the fighting. Already another fool has taken his place. Ushijima had received those reports as well, that Buckner's position at the head of the American Tenth Army had been filled by the Marine general, Roy Geiger. So, he thought, what has been lost? Buckner will be denied his victory celebration, his promotion, the glory of a parade in his honor. And still we sit in mud and our own sewage, infested with lice and dysentery, waiting for the final battle. Or has that battle already been fought?

The cave that Yahara had secured for the new headquarters faced away from the enemy advance, with its primary entrance on a spectacular promontory that offered Ushijima a serene view of the wide-open ocean to the south. The hill overhead was yet another lush tropical landscape, the slopes bathed in sago palms and low pines, coral and rock chiseled by millennia of tropical storms. From the main entrance Ushijima could view the flat sugarcane fields to the west, a panorama of the small villages that dotted the coast. Though the cave was a poor comparison to the relative luxury at Shuri, Ushijima knew that Colonel Yahara had done his job, had located the most suitable place available, and there would be no complaints, not even from General Cho. But the serenity was short-lived, and already the Americans had disturbed the beauty of the ocean with their warships, and very soon the ground across the peninsula where his troops found new shelter was tormented by the ongoing assault of the American navy's enormous guns. With the dryer weather, the planes came as well, daylong bombing attacks, strafing from the fighter planes, no safe place for his men to be, except the dark stinking holes in the ground. The fight to the north and east of his hill was going as badly as he had expected, the American army divisions there delayed only awhile by the valiant spirit of those few men he could place on the line. That spirit was no match for tanks, and from their caves the Japanese troops could not hold back the relentless push by American troops who knew that the end of this great fight was drawing closer every day. In a few short days after the retreat from Shuri had been completed, the lush hills around his own headquarters had become targets. The Japanese withdrawal had put his troops in a more compact defensive position, making them an easier target for the overwhelming American wave. There was no sanctuary at all, not even for Ushijima and his staff, the rumbles filling the caves, artillery and bombs already blowing away the vegetation, the hillsides above and around him churned up and denuded of anything green. The tropical paradise had been replaced now by the rotting corpses of his own men, too many for anyone to retrieve, too many for the meager memorial he knew they deserved. There was simply nowhere else to put them, and so they would be left where they fell. Each night now, instead of retrieving bodies, the patrols had one primary mission. The caves above Mabuni had no drinkable water at all, so patrols had to be sent down to the farmland for fresh water and anything edible, mostly sugarcane and sweet potatoes. Ushijima's staff had been reduced to eating filthy balls of rice, the barest minimum to maintain their stamina, and the vegetables had been welcomed as a rare luxury. Even Ushijima had been forced to limit his own meals to the same fare his men relished, along with a few remaining cans of pineapple. But there was no illusion that his soldiers were enjoying even that much luxury. Along the front, food was usually nonexistent, some men scavenging any way they could. That might include stripping the bodies of dead Americans for the precious K rations or ravaging what remained of the food that might be held by the desperately terrified Okinawans. Reports of brutality reached him, but Ushijima chose not to punish anyone. There was no longer any time for courtesy to the farmers, to anyone who was not a part of his dwindling army. Ushijima had erased any thoughts of the civilians from his mind, had rationalized their plight completely. On every battle-field across the island, the Okinawans had experienced the consequences of staying put.

He swallowed the last of the tea, thought, they are an amazingly inferior people. They observed all the work we did, did much of it themselves, giving up their tombs so we could anchor machine guns among their ancestors. They chopped and shoveled to build Yahara's caves, they saw our guns, they saw our soldiers, and when the Americans came they suffered the bombardments worse than we did. And yet, through all of that, so many of them have kept to their soil, their meager homes, their primitive protection, as though they believed all of this *noise* would just . . . pass them by. When we left Shuri, we warned them what would happen there, and yet so many of them chose to remain. We told them we were occupy-ing these heights, and yet, right here, in these villages close to this hill, they still keep to their huts. Are their lives so miserable, so limited that their only source of hope comes from staying in their homes? *Hope* is not a part of anything we do now, and the Okinawans should know that. If they do not, it is not my fault. If they insist on remaining in the line of fire, that is a choice I cannot help. If my men find them to be of use, either in fighting the Americans or in other ways, then my men shall have what they need. He knew that his soldiers carried a new desperation, that the urgent retreat from the Shuri Line had crushed their morale. He had stopped paying at-tention to any protests from Okinawan officials, who begged him to give protection to their people. There are only so many caves, he thought, and only so many places where my men can fight the enemy. That will take pri-ority over any civilian's safety. Yes, civilians have been massacred, some in their own homes, some huddling beside the urns that hold their ancestors. But there is no time for pity. I have nothing to give them, and Tokyo has nothing to give me. There is no more mercy, for any of them, for any of us. It is, after all . . . war.

For the past two days, as the Americans understood that Ushijima's di-minishing army was now anchored in a much more compact area, the in-tensity of the American bombardment had increased dramatically. Worse for the Japanese, the Americans were using a new weapon, napalm,

dropped from aircraft on those places where the Americans suspected anyone could be hiding. Often they were accurate, the gelatinous fire engulfing the occupants of a cave, usually with no survivors. The blessing, of
course, was a quick death, and Ushijima had convinced himself that it was
the best way, that his soldiers accepted that as he did. The Yasukuni Shrine
will welcome us all, he thought. There need not be suffering in this life for
men who have done their duty.

Outside, the American loudspeakers could be heard, broadcasting
messages in perfect Japanese, that his soldiers surrender themselves, that
no one would be tortured. The civilians were receiving those messages as
well, a rain of paper leaflets in every populated area, urging them to come
over to the American positions, where food and safety awaited. Ushijima
doubted that many of the Okinawans would believe the promises, the people too ignorant and too easily swayed by the Japanese propaganda that
had been fed to them even before his army had arrived. Reports had also
reached him of mass suicides, civilians and soldiers both, assembling in
groups within the caves, grenades most efficient when detonated amid a
tightly packed gathering. For his soldiers it was the proper way to die, to
pass on to the afterlife without the humiliation of capture. For the civilians
. . . Ushijima pondered that for a moment. I have no explanation for what
they do. They believe the enemy is evil, and so I suppose that death is a
preferable choice to capture. Whether they have honor at all . . . he stared
at the earthen walls close to one side of him. I have no idea. Some of them
serve us in honorable ways. For that we should be grateful. The women,
certainly, and not in the ways Cho uses them. The nurses, yes, I do respect
the nurses. He felt better now, as though some part of his conscience had
been addressed.

The few doctors still serving his army had long exhausted supplies of
useful drugs for treating the wounded, and even bandages were rare. Now
those same doctors had begun to respond to the misery of their patients by
administering one of the few drugs they had in their arsenal, cyanide.
Some was used to silence the worst of the suffering, but more was given to
those who asked for it, soldiers who might survive the caves, who would
not accept that their fight was over. Some of the doctors had dealt with the
overwhelming futility of what they saw by using the cyanide on themselves. Beyond the wounds there had been new suffering, outbreaks of
every tropical ailment imaginable, diseases birthed by the deepening pools
of blood and filth. In the larger caves, where hundreds of men might be

packed side by side, those few doctors who kept their spirit were aided by nurses who suffered from the same disease and who endured the filth and starvation diets alongside the soldiers and medical men. But there had been a singular tragedy as well, a note brought to Ushijima that even he could not dismiss.

From one of the high schools on the island had come more than one hundred fifty young Okinawan girls who had volunteered to serve the Japanese as nurses, though their medical skills were nonexistent. With the number of sick and wounded increasing dramatically, with stacks of corpses and every kind of misery infecting everyone in the caves, the girls endured the same suffering as the dying men and overburdened doctors. The Himeyuri girls were relegated to the worst tasks imaginable, and what had once been carefully guarded innocence had been ripped away by the filth and horrifying duties they were forced to perform, the most basic tasks for the sick and broken men who could do nothing for themselves. When the Americans approached the cave where the Himeyuri girls were hiding, most of the soldiers who occupied the miserable place were already dead, or too sick to respond to the American calls to vacate their hiding place. The loyalty from the girls meant silence, and silence from a large cave brought the usual response from the anxious and exhausted Americans, who had already endured booby traps and all forms of deadly trickery. With few inside willing to surrender, the cave was bombarded by phosphorus grenades and blasted by flamethrowers. Nearly all of the girls were annihilated. In time the Okinawans who became aware of the astounding tragedy were calling the blasted hole in the ground the Cave of the Virgins.

Ushijima set the teacup aside, thought, girls die. Boys die. Babies and the elderly. The Okinawans can mourn their own, their farmers and their fishermen, their virgins and their grandmothers. I did not bring this upon them, and I will not accept that any of this is my fault. That is another antiquated notion, that the general will be blamed for the deaths around him. My *army* is dying, is nearly dead now. Even for that I will accept no blame.

He felt suddenly defiant, thought of the High Command. They accept none of the responsibility and yet it is their orders that put me here. They make the decisions. So they must bear the burden. Instead, they wash their hands of failure and ask the emperor for forgiveness. And he will oblige them. That is what he does, after all. He will accept this defeat as his own, and as long as we have served him with loyalty, we shall carry none of the guilt. For that we should be grateful.

It wasn't working, nothing in those words soothing to him at all. That speech had been driven into him for too many years, but his faith in the perfect logic of his own culture had been battered. He had been surprised by his own reaction to the sight and the astounding smell of the dead from his army, spread out on the hillsides close to the cave. The unmerciful heat of the Okinawan summer was working quickly, driving their smell inside, into every small room, every dismal corridor. No, I do not care about virgins and farmers and goat herds. But my army . . . no, there will be no asking forgiveness from the emperor for what has happened to us here. I will not stand up and explain that we have done our *best,* not when Tokyo has forsaken us. These men have done what I asked them to do. How can any one man expect so much loyalty . . .

"Sir. Forgive me."

"One moment, Colonel."

Ushijima turned away, retrieved a silk handkerchief from his pocket, dabbed at his eyes.

"I can come back later, sir."

"No, come in, Colonel."

Ushijima saw gloom on Yahara's face, the same expression the man had worn for days now.

"You bear no responsibility for our defeat, Colonel."

Yahara seemed puzzled by the comment, said, "Thank you, sir. I do not agree, but I bow to your authority. I have been speaking with many of the officers. Your message to them was received with much appreciation. They have communicated that to their men, whenever possible."

Ushijima nodded.

"Thank you, Colonel."

The message had gone out two days earlier, a broad offering of congratulations for the fighting spirit of his army. But there was one line that sat heavily inside him even now, the message that he knew some would dismiss.

Now we face the end.

"They are fighting, still?"

"Of course, sir. It is the only course. We have mobilized a force to rush the enemy positions closest to the headquarters."

Ushijima felt a stab of alarm.

"How close is that?"

"That is why I am here, sir. In the east, the enemy has broken through our last defensive position. Reports have come that they are within a thousand meters, and we do not have the means to hold them back. Their tanks are . . . unstoppable."

Ushijima felt a hint of a spark in Yahara's voice, said, "And so, you have a plan?"

"I have assembled those troops who are positioned in proximity to this cave. It is a strong platoon force." Yahara paused, and Ushijima caught the meaning.

"A single platoon?"

"Lieutenant Matsui has volunteered to advance into the village of Mabuni. All reports indicate that the enemy has occupied the village. Sir . . ." Yahara lowered his head. "They will be here very soon. We must make some effort to distract them, and possibly to drive them back."

"With one platoon?"

The cave shook suddenly, a deafening blast. Yahara stumbled, dirt falling on him, and Cho was there, at the doorway, shouted, "They have struck the primary entrance. A direct hit!"

Cho moved back out into the narrow corridor, and Ushijima followed. There was only silence, little movement, most of Ushijima's guard already sent to the front lines. One man rushed toward him, emerging from the smoke, choking, a brief stumble. He held a rifle, dirt crusted on his face, made an attempt to stand at attention.

"The cave opening . . . there is great fire."

Ushijima put a hand on the man, calming him.

"Return there. Gather up the troops you can find. Fire means a shell, or a bomb. But the enemy troops might follow. Be alert!" He looked at Cho. "Probably from a ship, a lucky blow. But make sure the enemy troops are not coming at us on the cliffs below."

Cho bowed crisply, moved away, the soldier following him. Yahara said, "Sir, please. We must get you to safety. If the enemy succeeds in breaching this cave from the land side, you and General Cho will be most vulnerable. The shaft must be sealed off from that direction. The main entrance that faces the sea . . . if you are correct, sir, and certainly you are, there is less danger there. The enemy will not come at us by those cliffs. We can defend that section with a minimal force."

Yahara waited for a response, and Ushijima chewed on the word.

"A *minimal* force is all that remains, Colonel."

"Then perhaps, sir, we can make our escape by the routes that lead down the cliff. There are still boats, and in the dark we can make our way to sea."

Ushijima looked out toward the primary entrance, could smell the smoke from the blast, but there was no shooting, no other sound at all.

"Gather what troops you can, seal off the smaller openings that face the enemy."

"Is that all, sir?"

Ushijima looked into the eyes of the man he admired, knew that Yahara would find a way, would do whatever it took to secure the safety of his commander.

"I will not seek escape. I should not have to tell you that."

Yahara looked down, and Ushijima could see the emotion.

"What would you have me do, sir?"

There was a sound at the entrance to the room, and Ushijima saw Cho, sweat on his face, his uniform ragged, covered in dust.

"You were correct. The enemy fired a lucky shot, probably from off-shore. They are not on the cliffs."

Ushijima looked again at Yahara.

"Colonel Yahara has a gift of genius, wouldn't you agree? Has he not demonstrated a loyalty we should admire?"

Cho stepped into the small room, said, "Yes. Without any doubt. His loyalty to the emperor is beyond question."

"I am not speaking of the emperor. I am speaking more of this command. Colonel, it is essential that someone in authority survive this battle. Tokyo must know what happened here, in the kind of detail only you can provide. General Cho and I will face our duty soon enough. But you . . ."

"Sir, I would not disgrace myself by offering myself to the enemy, or by abandoning this command."

"There is no disgrace in following orders. You *will* make every attempt to escape this place, and make your report to the Imperial High Command."

Cho rubbed his chin, nodded.

"Yes. I agree. This army has fought a gallant fight, and their story must be told. A full report must be made." He looked at Ushijima now, a stern glare. "I would not be so hasty in judging this battle to be lost, sir. With all respect, of course."

"I make no such concession. I only wish Colonel Yahara to make preparations, that if events call for him to make his exit, he be prepared to do so. You will carry out my order, Colonel."

Yahara glanced at Cho, seemed to fight the emotions, kept his head low, then bowed.

"I will obey. But I will not make such a plan while there is still a fight to be made."

Ushijima looked up, reacting to the thumps above, the cave echoing with a new round of incoming artillery.

"Then make your fight, Colonel. For now, there is little else we can do."

JUNE 22, 1945

It was not yet midnight, but the lack of daylight meant very little inside the dismal cave. Above him the thunder of artillery had been replaced by new sounds, machine gun fire, sounds both familiar and foreign. He knew what was happening, that those officers still remaining who controlled enough men to make a stand were doing so right above him. It was a desperate attempt to drive the Americans off the hill. In the dark corridor, men had been assembled, a scattering of stragglers from various units close by, brought together by staff officers, the only officers these men could find. He knew that Yahara was there, could hear voices, the frantic words of men who were preparing for their last fight. Yahara was at his doorway now, the only light a candle to one side, and Yahara said, "We are prepared, sir. Major Matsubara has given the instructions, and Lieutenants Tsubakida and Yabumoto will coordinate the effort as best they can. We have the advantage of darkness, and the enemy cannot withstand our will!"

Ushijima waved him away, knew the plan was already in motion. There was nothing else to say. The commotion beyond his room increased, the men ordered out toward the main entrance. Ushijima sat silently, stared at the flicker from the candle, thought, at least he did not call this attack a banzai. I would rather them die with dignity, killing the enemy. There is no glory in hurling oneself into the abyss.

He had no illusions that this attack would be successful in removing the Americans from so close to his headquarters. But his troops were still willing, had accepted their role in this horrible drama with as much honor as anyone could hope for. He glanced at his pocket watch, the dial reading just after seven o'clock, completely wrong. Wonderful, he thought. Even my timepiece fails me. He tapped it gently, useless, slipped it back into his pocket. There were no voices in the corridor now, the only sounds coming from above, the muffled struggle rolling across the hillside a few meters above him.

JUNE 23, 1945

He found sleep, the steady roar of the fight offering him a strange comfort. But now there were voices, and he lurched awake, blinked in the darkness, the candle extinguished. A light flickered outside, and he pulled himself up, straightened his uniform, the light close, illuminating his room. The voice came softly, one of his aides.

"Sir, I beg your forgiveness. You asked to be notified when it was three o'clock."

"Yes. Please summon General Cho."

"As you wish, sir. Shall I leave the candle?"

"I prefer you not stumble about. I will be fine in the dark."

The man was gone, the light flowing away. At first Ushijima's room had received a single lightbulb, hanging tenuously from an unconcealed wire. But the power was out now, the cave no more than a warm, damp tomb. The fight still raged above but seemed to slow, the machine guns and thumps of mortar fire exhausted by the long night, a battle of attrition that had spent itself in blood and the death of too many men. He stood, moved in the dark space by memory, thought of Cho, the room next to him, the man's thunderous snoring apparent even through the thick dirt walls. He heard commotion from that way, knew that Cho had spent much of the evening consuming a generous amount of spirits, and Ushijima had no patience for that now. After a long minute, the candlelight returned, and Cho was there now, said, "Sir. It is time, yes?" Cho's words were slurring, and there was a strange cheerfulness to the man, something Ushijima had seen before. "I have been waiting for you to awaken, sir. You took a good rest."

Ushijima fastened the buttons on his coat, said, "You as well, General. Your snoring carries more thunder than the enemy's guns."

Other aides appeared now, and Ushijima knew it was the work of Yahara, that word had been passed. Ushijima saw a familiar face in the candlelight, said, "Captain, summon Colonel Yahara."

Cho stumbled into the room, sat heavily on a small bench to one side, and Ushijima could smell the man's drunkenness, saw the bottle still in his hand, something stronger than sake. Cho said, "So. Who will go first? You or me? Shall I die first and lead you to another world?"

"I will take the lead."

Cho laughed, took a slug from the bottle.

"Sir, you will go to paradise, I to hell. I cannot accompany you to that *other* world."

Ushijima ignored the comment, could see more men gathering outside the room, emerging from the offices that spread out down the musty corridor. One man stepped forward, dropped to his knees, soft cries.

"Please, sir, accept my respects. It is my honor to serve you."

Another man came in, one of the staff officers, and the man seemed drunk as well, said aloud, "Sir, I wish to inform the general that our final message has been transmitted to Imperial General Headquarters. I need not read it. The words are imprinted upon my brain, as it has no doubt been received so many times by those in Tokyo. 'Your army has successfully completed preparations for the defense of our homeland.' " The man laughed, slicing through the somber mood of the others. "Is that not what we are supposed to say, sir? Is all well here? Victory within our grasp, then?"

Ushijima retrieved his newest uniform coat from his trunk, said quietly, "Thank you for your service, Major. You will retire to your room."

The man stumbled into the others, took some of them with him, the crowd thinning, nothing else for them to say. Yahara was there now, and Ushijima saw his face in the candlelight, the colonel not hiding the tears. Ushijima pinned a large medal upon his own chest, something he had not displayed in over a year, the uniform coming together in a grand show that few in this command had ever seen. He looked toward Yahara, the man seeming to wait for him to speak first.

"Colonel, is there any change?"

"No, sir. I have not been outside myself, but the last report I received indicated that the enemy was massing near several entrances to the cave. We have blockaded them as effectively as we could, but with their high explosives, and the guns of their tanks, I do not see how we can hold them away. The flamethrowers will certainly follow, sir."

"They shall not capture us, Colonel, and they shall not have the satisfaction of destroying us." He paused, looked at the few remaining faces, flickers of candlelight, saw many tears, and now the face of Captain Sakaguchi. "Captain, I am pleased you have come. Are you prepared?"

"I am at your service, General."

"Then it is time. General Cho, are you able to walk?"

Cho ignored the insult, removed his coat, tossed it on the floor, was now opposite in appearance from his commander, who stood now for a long silent moment, straight backed, one hand touching the display of medals on his chest, each one a small memory of some ceremony, utterly meaningless now. Cho stood unevenly, and Ushijima moved past him, past the others, out into the corridor. The candlelight followed him, lighting the way, and after a short march the cave's wide opening was visible. Without any order the candle was extinguished, no opportunity offered the enemy to target the entrance from some lookout at sea. Ushijima stood at the opening, felt the warm breeze, could see moonlight on the water, felt a mist rising up from the cliffs below, a spray of salt air. He stepped outside, a ledge to one side, saw that the preparations had been made, exactly as he had requested. A soft mat had been spread on the rocky flat ground, a white ceremonial cloth draped on the rocks just behind. He moved without a word, sat, curled his legs in, faced the sea. Cho followed, settled down clumsily beside him. Cho leaned low, as though peering off the edge of the cliff, one last glimpse of something Ushijima knew nothing about, and he avoided the thought that somewhere below, a woman huddled low in some shacklike corner of this grotesque hell. With Cho's back revealed to the moonlight, he realized there was writing on Cho's white shirt, large brushstrokes, the details made clear not just by the moonlight, but the hint of dawn just rising in the east.

With bravery I serve my nation; With loyalty I dedicate my life.

Ushijima said nothing, thought, he is right, of course. There is nothing more valuable we can claim, no greater message to bring our ancestors. He stared out at the water, knew that very soon the daylight would reveal this piece of ground to the American ships, the white cloth a highly visible target. There was little time to waste. Ushijima turned, a half-dozen men standing close to one side of the ledge, and he saw Yahara, the man's head low, more tears.

"Colonel, please compose yourself. You may order the staffs to depart. And you will carry out my order for yourself."

Yahara snapped to attention, made a short, crisp bow. He turned, the word passing quickly, quietly, the men emerging from the cave as though awaiting this very moment. They moved in a single line, no hesitation, dropping onto the steep pathways that wound down the cliff. Ushijima turned again toward the sea, could hear new sounds now, from above, the thump of grenades. He felt a pang of urgency, his fingers fumbling, then finding the control, loosening the buttons on his coat, and then his shirt. His abdomen was bare, and beside him, the small grunts told him that Cho had done the same. He turned to see Sakaguchi, who held the sword at his chest, the sword that would bring the final blow to both men. Ushijima saw the strength in the man, trained for this ceremony, the man who understood exactly what his duty would be. But first there was a task that only the two men could perform themselves. The aide was there, dutiful, nervous, holding the white cloth that held the ceremonial knives. Ushijima slid one toward him, stared at it for a long second, heard a sharp blast meters behind him, the hillside awakening with more of the fight. Men were shouting on the hill above him, and a Nambu gun erupted a few meters to one side, just beyond the curve of the hill. Ushijima forced that from his mind, did not look at Cho, held the knife out straight in front of him, stared at the point of the blade, aimed just below his heart. He closed his eyes, a brief second, but a soft breeze brought the smell of the salt air up the cliff, erasing the stink of powder, and he opened his eyes, one last glance at the sea. But there was no serenity now, the dawn revealing the spatter of so many ships, the vast display of power from the enemy he could not hope to defeat. He gripped the small sword, let out a breath, and jammed the blade hard into his stomach, twisted, fought the gasp from his lungs, ripped the knife to the side, slicing across. His hands gave way now, dropping down, warm wetness flowing, his mind weakening, the ocean gone, his head falling forward. Close behind him the swordsman raised his blade, swung it down with a mighty shout, finishing the job.

25. ADAMS

The mopping-up phase was continuing all across the peninsula, men who did their brutal work in proximity to the narrowing front, some on the hills that bordered the ocean. Flamethrowers and grenades continued to be the weapons of choice, and there was little mercy shown to any Japanese soldier who still showed a willingness to fight. The casualties continued on both sides, Japanese snipers finding targets, carelessness punished, just as before. The officers and medical personnel were still prime targets but performed their work with no hesitation. Often the dead in the caves included civilians, Okinawans who were still afraid of the Americans, and kept up a loyalty to the Japanese that no American could explain. Even in surrender the Okinawans could be complicit in the most treacherous acts, and so the American soldiers and Marines who continued to press forward were kept on a razor's edge. From every cave death might emerge in the guise of pitiful innocence, pockets of Okinawans or Japanese offering their surrender, only to ignite hidden grenades as their captors moved in close. The civilians were often not civilians at all, thus the Okinawans were considered to be the enemy still, some eliminated before questions could be asked. Some of the dead inspired a furious guilt in the Americans who had killed them before discovering how innocent they truly were. The dead included mothers with their babies, the sick and horribly wounded, the feeble and the old. Some of the Americans vowed compassion, to be more careful, more selective before unleashing a horrible death on those hidden in the caves. That care would lead to hesitation, or an act of kindness that might explode in their faces, so the conscience would be shoved aside by the anger, the hate, the viciousness.

It was the face of war.

Many of the Americans had seen too much, had slept in the blood of their friends, had wiped brains and guts from their faces, had suffered through the worst of human behavior, enduring an astounding struggle against an enemy who kills because it is his only reason for existence. Many of the Americans responded in kind, any sense of mercy erased by hatred for an enemy that had become less than human. There had been prisoners, Japanese soldiers offering their surrender with hands high and no treachery. But those were not nearly as plentiful as the number of desperate civilians. It had been a painful lesson for the Americans all across the Pacific that the Japanese troops who surrendered were doing so with the understanding that they were disgracing themselves and their ancestors, and that if they were ever returned home, their shame would make them outcasts. Even those who accepted the kindness shown them by American doctors rarely showed joy. If there were no smiles, there was certainly relief and stoic gratefulness from men who had been hungry or wounded for days, marching out into sunlight, to find, not cannibals and torture, but medicine and water and food. As the caves were exposed and the enemy obliterated, the Americans began to explore, shocked that the shattered remains of the dead were not always the worst that awaited them. In many of the caves, stolen American equipment and food was found, trinkets and souvenirs that showed very clearly that the Japanese showed no mercy either. Letters from American wives and mothers lay among the ruins in the caves, along with photographs of children, Bibles and notebooks, diaries, the forbidden journals written by American GIs who had kept them out of sight of their officers, personal thoughts recorded on burned pages that no one would ever read. Some of the caves held American weapons and K ration boxes, canteens and dog tags, what some must have thought the appropriate spoils of war. But the Americans responded in kind, gathering their own souvenirs, some with a horrifying disregard for the humanity of their enemy. On both sides gold teeth were pulled from the jawbones of the dead and dying, jewelry ripped from fingers and necks. Some of the wounded were killed by torture and physical abuse that caused comrades to turn away in disgust. The fight for Okinawa had brought out the worst in everyone involved, but in that it was not unique. The veterans had gone through this before, some of them itching to begin again. To some the end of the fight was anticlimactic, the stirring in their gut needing to be fed by a new fight, another invasion, more blood, more death to the enemy they knew only as the *Japs*. There was very little doubt among any of those men that the Japanese who awaited them on the next island, the next landing zone, felt exactly the same way about them.

ARA SAKI HILL, SOUTHERN TIP OF OKINAWA
JUNE 21, 1945

The American command had received no response to General Buckner's letter, no hint at all that any Japanese officer was ready to offer a surrender of his troops. So the fights went on, mostly in isolated holes, ravines, and hillsides where Japanese troops had lost all contact with their senior command. The Americans had pushed all the way through the Kiyan Peninsula, entire units of Marines and soldiers reaching the southern coastline, finding they had no more enemy to pursue. In response the American command had declared that effective June 21, Okinawa was *secure.* But that designation meant very little to the Japanese, or to the Americans who engaged them, the sounds of various fights echoing still across the hills, pockets of resistance, clusters of Japanese who clung to their duty, who still offered a deadly strike against the unwary.

The men climbed the hill in a slow procession, some noticing with comfort the others out along the perimeter, formations of men in every direction, guarding the procession with rifles at the ready. The tanks stayed below, no sounds, the engines shut down, jeeps and trucks nearby, some men huddled there, groups who kept their talk low. To one side there was a chattering of machine gun fire, far distant, beyond another ridgeline no one could see. There was smoke as well, small arms fire, the faint thumps of grenades and mortars, a battle that seemed to contradict the strange peacefulness of this procession. But the order had come from above, General Geiger reinforcing his edict that the victory had been won, and so the ceremony would take place exactly as the commanders decreed it.

Adams moved behind Mortensen, walked in slow steps, saw a hand go up, holding the men back. Mortensen stopped, Adams beside him, the taller man seeming taller still. The ground to one side fell away, a sharp cliff that dropped to the ocean, the ships offshore seeming to stand in silence, observing the moment as did the Marines from the Twenty-second Regiment who moved up high on the hill. At the peak of the rugged coral ridge was a mound, and Adams felt the thick silence close by, the distant shellfire seeming to fade away for a long moment. He looked out across the far hills, smoky ridges spreading inland, away from the sea, tried not to think of what was to come out there, how many more fights there might be, the desperate and dangerous enemy. But his thoughts returned to the moment close by, his eye caught by a procession of four men moving up, climbing to the center of the mound, the highest point. Three were Marines, men he didn't know, the fourth a navy corpsman. They carried what seemed to be a skinny tree, long and crooked, stripped of branches, chopped at one end by a rough blade. The men moved slowly, appreciating the silence and the solemnity of the audience who watched them, appreciating that out beyond this one piece of high ground, men might still be dying by the hand of the enemy.

He had seen the photograph, they all had, the symbolic raising of the American flag on Iwo Jima, a photograph that so many letters from home spoke of, a photo that had graced the front page of every American newspaper. No one on Okinawa thought ill of that, no one cursed the good show that the photo offered, the American people allowed to absorb and enjoy that single moment of triumph from a fight that was far more brutal than the newspapers would say. But it was not the only triumph, and Iwo Jima was not the most deadly fight.

Adams felt the wind picking up, watched as the rough tree was jabbed hard into soft ground, the men steadying it with careful hands, hovering close, and now another man moved up, raised a bugle. The notes cut through them all with mournful familiarity, and Adams stared through tears as the men unfolded the cloth, attaching it to the tree, releasing it now, the flag fastened securely to the top of the makeshift flagpole. The bugler completed his task, and Adams heard soft cries, sobs close by, Mortensen, and Adams fought it no longer, held his hand up in a brief salute, the tears flowing hard.

On the mound, another man stepped up, older, an officer, and the man spoke out through strained emotions.

This has been a hard fight. In raising this flag we pay tribute to the memory of those brave men who have fallen in action. We shall ever be mindful of their glorious deeds as we continue along the road to Tokyo, and victory.

Beside Adams, Mortensen grunted, seemed to compose himself, and Adams felt his gaze, turned that way, saw the sergeant looking at him, a hint of respect. The sergeant's eyes were past him quickly, out toward the others who stood along the windy cliff. After a long moment Mortensen said, "Tokyo. Well, we better get ready, boys. There's gonna be one more fight."

Adams saw the others beginning to move, Mortensen turning away, the ceremony concluded. He followed his sergeant, fought the memories, the faces he could never forget, stepped over rugged coral, stayed in the footsteps of the others, moving down off the hill, Mortensen's words still inside him.

One more fight.

PART THREE

26. TRUMAN

The swells were gentle, made more smooth by the escort ship that broke the waves before them. She was the USS *Philadelphia*, another cruiser, designated not only as escort to smooth rough waters, but one more powerful piece of security. He was, after all, the President of the United States.

He stood against the rail, weary of meetings, the various officials mostly belowdecks, some sleeping, certainly. He knew there was seasickness, but not much, and the men who traveled with him would be unlikely to admit it to their boss anyway. The sea didn't bother him as much as he had feared, but the memories did. He had made this crossing before, in the first Great War, as an artillery officer. In 1917 the training had been brief and virtually useless, no one in his small command having any way to know what awaited them in that place they called the Western Front. But the fear was there, would stay there throughout the entire campaign, something an artillery captain could not admit to anyone, certainly not to the men who looked to him for authority, for leadership. He stared out at the swells, the hint of moonlight, thought, it is no different now. Well, maybe it is. This time I have a hell of a lot more authority, and a hell of a lot more people looking at me for answers. Three months ago I didn't even know the questions.

He had served as vice president for a total of eighty-two days, and during that time it had been made plain to him that President Roosevelt was not exactly his best friend. Vice presidents were chosen to help win an election, and Truman was under no illusion that his greatest benefit to Roosevelt's fourth campaign came from geography. FDR was a New Yorker, an *easterner,* something that concerned the campaign strategists even though Roosevelt's election to a fourth term was never really in doubt. But *balance* had always been the key word, and they had sought a midwesterner to round out the ticket. The previous vice president had been another midwesterner, an Iowan, Henry Wallace, but Wallace had caused rumbles around FDR's closest advisors for what some said was a kind of bizarre religious zealotry. It was the excuse made behind closed doors why Wallace should go, but Truman knew that the more likely reason Wallace had been replaced on the ticket was that Winston Churchill despised him. Whether Truman, a plain-spoken senator from Missouri, would do any better job than his predecessor seemed not to matter. The key for the political strategists was whether Truman was a liability to Roosevelt's presidency. Truman had never considered himself a liability to anyone, but then, his own career in politics had been turbulent only on a level that was invisible to anyone outside Missouri. And since Roosevelt's death, Churchill had surprised Truman by accepting him with far more helpfulness than Truman had any right to expect. It was a sad irony to Truman that Churchill seemed willing to support the new president with even greater zeal than many of the men in Washington, who were now Truman's subordinates. The grumbling about him in the halls of various government departments had not been a surprise. While Roosevelt was alive, Truman was very much a fifth wheel, kept outside FDR's inner circle, the president rarely conferring with Truman at all. The vice president's job had included presiding over the Senate, and Truman was perfectly content in that role. He was comfortable there, the familiar faces, the familiar squabbles. But on April 12, the world had changed. The man who was so much the country's grandfather had suddenly gone away. Truman had seen clear signs of Roosevelt's physical decline, but the reality of that had not sunk in until the president's sudden death. Truman the anonymous was now Truman the president, and more important, to the men who confronted the astounding challenges of waging a world war, he was Truman the Commander in Chief.

The air was warm, the only breeze coming from the movement of the ship, and he treasured the solitude, so rare now. He knew his plush quarters belowdecks was the appropriate place for him to be, catching up on whatever sleep he could. If the sleep wasn't there, the worries were, so many details about policy and personality, who among his party were dependable, and who were just along for the ride. He pushed his shoulders back, felt the first rumblings of a headache, thought, if my posture was sound before, it is miserable now. People bitch and moan about carrying the weight of the world on their shoulders. I can honestly say, I am one of them. But I'll put my bitching up against anybody's. Try this job for a few weeks, pal. See how *your* shoulders droop. FDR suffered through that with more grit than anyone I've ever known, and no matter how much adulation or respect he earned, he refused to let it go. I suppose he believed that no one else in Washington could do it, no one had the *shoulders* for it. He may have been right about that. I don't know of a single senator or anyone else who was worthy, no one who could have pulled the country together. Well, most of it, anyway. Now, in every corner of the globe, the question being asked is whether I've got the shoulders, whether I'm worthy. Hell if I know. Damn if I can find the instruction book. My job is to . . . do my job. Lead, for God's sake. Keep my nose out of places where the machine is working, and stick it in deep where it isn't. Thank God this war is on the downhill side. At least, they tell me it is. We won in Europe, we're winning in the Pacific. Maybe the biggest challenge I'll have to face is figuring out how to manage the peace. I can't leave that to military men.

Already a dark cloud was forming over Europe, the very reason for this voyage. His destination was Potsdam, near Berlin, a formal summit with Churchill and Joseph Stalin. Truman winced, thought, Old Joe has made it pretty clear that his best interests are in *his* best interests. Our best interests are an inconvenience. Tough nut, this one. Screw this up, Harry old boy, and we could find ourselves in another war. Europe needs a little quiet for a change, a few cities allowed to rebuild themselves, the people allowed to find some kind of life again. No one needs the kind of crap Stalin is inflicting on those people. How in hell do I stop that? Do I? With Stalin you either need extraordinary diplomacy . . . or a baseball bat. I think he's bigger than me, so the bat would have to be a surprise. But so far, every communication I've had with the man tells me he's got the big bat, and the big glove, he owns the ball park, and the umpire's in his pocket. Thank God for Churchill. At least he knows the man, knows how to talk to him, knows what to expect. But we're not getting any respect from the Russians for what we did to the Germans, for the help we gave Stalin's people. Respect? Hell, they don't even acknowledge us. That's not blind pride either. It's calculated. He's going to push us as far as he can, and that might mean he's going to push us right out of Europe. That won't happen. Can't. Churchill knows that, but he's not in a position to stand up to the Russian tanks like we are. From what they tell me, Old Joe has one hell of a lot of tanks. We have Ike, Marshall, Bradley, good people. And a few tanks of our own. *Tanks.* He pondered the sight of that, what it must have been like for the Germans to watch a sea of Russian armor pouring into Germany, crushing their army, their cities. We did most of that kind of work from the air, I suppose. Germans learned the hard way, that no matter what your boss is telling you, you aren't going to win a war when your factories are getting blown to hell every night. And the cities. And the people. Tough decision, there, Franklin. How do you bomb cities and not accept that you're bombing the civilians right along with the munitions plants? Churchill pushed FDR hard on that one, had every right to. Hitler was happy blowing London to hell, and we had to return the favor. It was sure as hell the right decision. And it worked.

And now we're going to do it again. Been doing it, of course, those puff-chested boys out there in their B-29s, torching every square mile of Tokyo and anywhere else they can find a target. Keep it up, that's all I can say. That's working too. Now . . . it might work even better. I've given them the *okay*, and if what they tell me is accurate, this war oughta be over pretty damn soon. If they're wrong, we've gotta send a whole bunch of American boys into Japan, to fight the most fanatical people who've ever tossed a grenade. No, not *we*. I.

Batter up, Harry.

He turned, looked up at the lights from the bridge, could see more lights beyond the bow of the cruiser, beyond the pair of three-gun turrets that aimed past the *Philadelphia*. The warships had no need to run in darkness, a wonderful change from the days of the U-boats. But there were no other escorts close by, no aircraft overhead, no great fleets of patrol boats keeping an eye on the new Boss. I wanted this trip kept secret as long as possible, and, by damn, they obliged me. I rather like that, asking for something and nobody arguing about it.

Truman caught a shadow, a brief flicker of movement back near a row of steel drums. He knew it was a Secret Service agent, knew there were more, and probably some naval guards, lurking in every dark hole. Truman turned again to the water, thought, yep, I suppose there's somebody out there who'd do whatever it took to knock a hole in my head. Jap agents all over the damn place, so they tell me. Well, not out here. If there were any Jap subs puffing around anywhere in this whole damn hemisphere, they wouldn't let me hang my face over the side of this ship like some gawking tourist. But in Washington . . . watch your step. They hated it when I walked to work, couldn't wait for me to move my ass from Blair House to the White House. Hell, I liked walking to work. Hardly anybody recognized me, and the mornings can be damn nice in the spring. Once the Secret Service started clearing off sidewalks, shoving people aside, well, that took all the fun out of it. I liked Blair House too. There are too damn many offices in the White House, too many people who insist on talking to me. Everybody's in a hurry, their pressing matter more *pressing* than the next guy's. At least the Secret Service is happy. I'm behind thick walls, makes it a lot tougher for some Jap agent to pop a rifle in my direction. Well, maybe we can put a stop to that business altogether, give those people a reason to go home. I oughta hear something once I get to Potsdam. Unless there are delays, some problem that rattles the physicists, some reason why Oppenheimer or any of the rest of them think we need to wait, to do more research. They're pretty rattled already, and I can't blame them for that. I'm rattled, and I don't have the faintest damn idea how this new bomb is supposed to work. They don't like to talk about it, but they're not sure the damn thing will work at all. Or, maybe it will work too well, and destroy the world. Now, there's a hell of a notation for the encyclopedia. *Harry Truman, Final President of the United States. Most Notable Accomplishment: Destroyed the World.*

For eighty-two days he had become accustomed to being on the outside, rarely included in FDR's most high-level discussions, especially with the military people. Truman wasn't bothered by that, knew that the relationship between the president and his vice president could never be chummy. Both men were, after all, politicians, and there was always life *after* holding office, and then you were likely not to be chums at all. Indeed, he thought, Washington is still Washington. He shook his head. Well, it's not always like that. But we're not used to having our president die in office. Now there's one damn good thing about the Constitution. Rules for this sort of thing. Otherwise somebody would just take charge, big mouth and big guns. We'd end up with somebody like . . . oh God . . .

MacArthur. Yes, thank you, Founding Fathers. Whether FDR kept me involved really didn't matter. But that piece of paper told everyone what they had better do next. There's a new guy in charge. Tell him all the secrets.

The meeting had come in late April, and after Roosevelt's death, it was the second shock Truman received. The messenger had been Henry Stimson, the secretary of war, and across Truman's desk had come the astonishing details of something called the Manhattan Project. Until that meeting, just days after FDR's death, Truman had no idea at all what the project was, no idea that the United States had been spending enormous numbers of man-hours, employing some of the finest minds in the world of physics, to develop a weapon unlike any ever known. Truman had faced the nervous Stimson, who seemed unhappy to be the one to inform the new president that the project had been so secret it was thought unwise to include in its inner circle the vice president of the United States. But Truman knew about it now, even if he didn't completely understand the physics of nuclear fission. Stimson had told him that the physicists were confident then that the first atomic bomb would be ready for testing within four months of that meeting.

He glanced up at the sliver of moon, thought, that's pretty damn soon. And damn it all, I have to go to this conference and stare down Joe Stalin, and keep my mouth shut about the biggest damn bomb ever built, a weapon that could very well stop this war. We're not even sure the thing will explode, and that's gotta be driving the physicists and their teams insane. Never been done before, ever. Might be a nice enhancement to my baseball bat if I could tell Joe Stalin that this damn bomb not only exists, it actually works. Hey, Joe, you get your damn tanks out of Poland or we might have to use Moscow as a testing ground.

He closed his eyes, a sharp shake of his head. Don't do that, Harry. This isn't a backyard spat, and this is a hell of a lot more important than punching a bully in the eye. This is a *secret,* and if there's one man on this earth who doesn't need to hear about it, it's Stalin. Churchill knows, thank God for that. He knew from the beginning, and I guess it makes sense that FDR would have brought him into the ring. The Brits were aching pretty bad, too much blood, too much gloom. Even if Churchill had to keep his mouth shut, at least we could let him know that we were working like hell to stick something new up our sleeve. The thing that stirs my coffee is that, from what we know now, Hitler was doing the same thing. Whether this big damn son of a bitch actually fires off or not, I'm a lot happier that we're testing this thing over some desert in New Mexico than some Nazi bastard doing it over London. God, I can't even think about that.

There had been additional meetings, some with the military men who stood guard over the Manhattan Project, some with the physicists themselves. With every piece of new information, Truman had become increasingly amazed that the secret had been as well kept as it had. This is *Washington,* for God's sake. Between Drew Pearson and William Randolph Hearst, you know damn well that FDR's enemies would have paid big to expose something as big as this. Jap agents had to be throwing money around every military base, every Washington hotel, trying to find out any little ditty they could. This one could have made somebody rich as hell. But so far, the secret is still . . . a secret. Damn impressive.

The latest word had come just prior to his boarding the *Augusta,* that the first test would come very soon in the desert near Alamogordo, New Mexico. The plan was for three bombs to be built, one for the test, and the others for use against targets in Japan. The arguments over targets had begun in earnest, and Truman knew that the military men would be the best qualified to make that decision. The city most favored was Kyoto, a city of such importance to the Japanese that its destruction would surely bring the Japanese to the peace table. But Kyoto's importance was the primary reason Truman vetoed it as a target. The city was more historical than military, a religious and cultural center like no other city in Japan. Truman had insisted that the target be someplace with more military significance, a direct strike into the heart of Japan's war machine. The list had been assembled, and the advisors had come up with four that made the most sense. Truman had studied the short list with no real sense of the priorities of each, though the military men had offered suggestions why each, or any, was important. Truman had the list still, studied it in his mind now. Kokura, Hiroshima, Niigata, and Nagasaki. I can't really tell them which one is the best target. I just don't have that answer. It might depend on weather, of course, and it might be the pilot's decision, the ultimate discretion, which target can be hit. Damn, what a place to put a bomber pilot.

Throughout the meetings, the physicists, especially Robert Oppenheimer and Enrico Fermi, had been adamant that this bomb would end the war. Even though nothing like this had ever been used before, and even though no one really knew just what might happen when it detonated, there had been no hesitation among those men that the bomb be used directly against a Japanese target. Truman agreed with the military men who had been enthusiastic about the possibilities of what this weapon could do. The Japanese had defined the moral argument from the very beginning, and as word reached the Western newspapers of what was happening in China, what had been done to prisoners of war at Bataan, or the civilians in every place the Japanese had conquered, the fury of the American people had grown substantially. The military had their own fury, of course, and yet throughout the war, the Americans had played as close to the *rules* as anyone could expect. But the kamikaze attacks against American sailors had seemed to be the final straw, confirmation that the enemy in the Pacific was nothing like the Germans. Not even the spreading news of the Holocaust had seemed to affect the American troops with the kind of visceral disgust for what the Japanese had done. Germany's sins could be placed too easily at the feet of Hitler and a few of his henchmen, but the astounding viciousness of the Japanese seemed to pervade their entire military culture, a culture that Truman knew was nothing the Americans had ever faced before. He had been astounded to hear a broadcast, forwarded to him from the monitoring stations that recorded Japanese radio. The speech had come from Japan's Prime Minister Suzuki.

> Should my services be rewarded by death, I expect the hundred million people of this glorious empire to swell forward over my prostrate body and form themselves into a shield to protect the emperor and this imperial land from the invader.

With such resolve being fed to the Japanese people, who would no doubt respond as their emperor hoped, the decision to use this extraordinary weapon caused Truman no heartburn at all. Quite the opposite. Without such a decisive piece of weaponry, the American invasion of Japan was the only viable strategy that remained. If the speculation about the power of the atomic bomb was accurate, Truman believed along with his generals that this one weapon could prevent the potential loss of an enormous number of American troops. But Suzuki's speech had offered up another reason for the Americans to avoid an invasion, something that many of the military advisors had given little attention. If the Japanese defended their homeland with the same ferocity they had inflicted on other lands, Truman had to believe that the loyalty of the Japanese people to their emperor might result in a fight that would cause the slaughter of millions of Japanese civilians, a moral nightmare for the United States, and especially for the young American soldiers who would stand at the point of the spear. To the commanders who had seen the barbarity of the Japanese up close, the morality of that was no issue at all. Increasingly there was a mood among the troops that Japan needed to be punished, *all* of Japan. It was an argument Truman could not dismiss. Throughout Asia, the people who had suffered such extreme depravity at the hands of the Japanese troops and their leaders had to receive at least some compensation, even if the best that could be accomplished was a weapon that some might see as overkill, an act of vengeance.

Though the military chiefs were mostly unequivocal in their support for the Manhattan Project, as June rolled into July, Truman felt that something had changed among the physicists, a slight whiff of what Truman felt was hesitation, or even pacifism. Truman suspected that the shift in mood was the result of the victory at Okinawa, the sense that the Japanese were beaten already, that this new weapon might be unnecessary. But the military chiefs had blasted that opinion to pieces, few believing that Okinawa would change anything in Tokyo.

A serious argument had been made for exploding a bomb off the Japanese coast, with no surprises, everyone notified well in advance, the whole world allowed to watch. If the Japanese High Command had any doubts about American superiority in arms, some said that this would clinch it, would inspire even the most fanatical Japanese generals to call it quits. But many of the military people thought that idea a waste of time, and there were two very good reasons why. Since 1942, Japan's newly acquired empire had been crushed around the edges, then crushed in the vicious campaigns that drove closer and closer to Japan. But every American commander who faced them saw for himself that the Japanese tactics and strategy had never seemed to change at all, no matter how much might and how much superiority in arms they had faced. No, he thought, if they won't even give up some pissant little island in the middle of nowhere, how can we expect them to lay down arms to give up their whole damn country, emperor and all? That one's pretty simple. Their losses have been staggering, and yet they've shown no hint of any willingness to accept defeat. Truman had been as baffled by that as the men around him. Okinawa had been a perfect disaster for the Japanese, and surely the Imperial High Command would know that mainland Japan was the next target. And yet the rhetoric from Tokyo had not changed at all. Truman had heard some of the Ultra intercepts, the Japanese communications codes broken early in the war. The code breakers had done the same with the German codes, which had given the Allies in Europe an outstanding advantage. Most of the Japanese communications had now become so primitive that the code breakers were hardly in use at all, since most of the bases far from Japan had been crushed or cut off. But Truman had heard some of the pronouncements, had been astounded that the Japanese people were being told of ongoing victories against the enemy, including their *magnificent triumph* at Okinawa. The Americans knew of food shortages, and that, for Japanese civilians, gasoline and many basic staples were nonexistent. And their *men,* he thought. Their sons and husbands and fathers are simply gone, and no one there sees a problem? So, no, we cannot expect that a demonstration of some new powerful weapon, no matter how dramatic, is going to change that.

The second argument was more straightforward. What if the bomb didn't work? Yep, that would be a good one. We tell Tokyo, hey, bring your emperor and half your army and come on out to Yokohama Beach, and watch *this.* And so they gather out there, with half the world's newspaper reporters, just to watch us drop a big damn steel ball into the ocean. *Sploosh.* I can just hear MacArthur, or even Nimitz. Uh, never mind, boys. And excuse us, but we've gotta go back home and help the president beat the crap out of every damn physicist we can find. As for the war, yeah, well, we'll get back to you on that one.

No, it's not funny. Not even close. The military says we need this, and it's hard to argue against that. Already we're mobilizing hundreds of damn transports, and gathering up every healthy GI for a beach party that will make Normandy look like a rainy day in Miami.

The noise that came from the Japanese High Command was as militant as ever, defiantly anticipating that the Americans would make their next move against the mainland itself, which was exactly what was planned. The invasion was scheduled for November 1, a massive surge into the harbors and across the beaches at several points near key Japanese targets. The operation had been given a name, *Olympic,* and Truman had been briefed by the joint chiefs that the first phase of the invasion would involve more than a half-million American ground troops, with that many more to follow close behind. George Marshall and the other planners assumed the operation would carry on through the spring of 1946. Despite the most optimistic estimates, it was apparent that the war would last for another year, possibly longer. As for casualties . . . Truman pondered that, all those estimates of American dead, some far more optimistic than others. Some of those boys think that if they feed me baby food, I'll give my okay to their plans without a second thought. Sorry, but no general has to tell me what a ground war looks like, because I've seen one. I know exactly what will happen to our boys. If I thought the Japanese could be convinced they ought to quit, fine, show me how to convince them. Nothing, not a damn thing has worked so far. We've been busting up their bases and driving their people into hell for better than three years, and no one's given me any sign that they're any less willing to die for their damn emperor today than they were in 1942.

It was disturbing to him that some of the very scientists who developed this extraordinary weapon were now hedging their bets by insisting it not actually be used on a target, but only as a demonstration, a show of force that could not be ignored. That's pure bull, he thought. Every report says their people are more enthusiastic about fighting now than ever. We won't be fighting just their army, we'll be fighting every damn Jap citizen. Call it what you will, their *Home Guard,* or militia. It means that sooner or later every GI will stand face-to-face with some *mama-san* holding a musket, or a pitchfork, and they won't just step aside. What will that do to our boys, faced with civilians who are as dangerous as the soldiers? How many more cities will General LeMay have to incinerate before he eliminates that threat? Hell, we'd do the same thing if the Japs landed a fleet of invasion ships on the California coast. American civilians would put up a hell of a fight if they were defending our homes in San Francisco or Los Angeles. Put anybody's back to their own wall and they'll turn up the volume. So, sure, if there's a chance to end this sooner . . . there's no argument that trumps that. We sure as hell don't need pussyfooting about this, not after so much has gone into it, and by damn, every one of those scientists and every damn general knows this decision is mine, and mine alone, and *that* order left my office a month ago. Right now it doesn't much matter which city it'll be . . . if this son of a bitch works, we'll hit those people hard enough to make even the emperor take a little pause.

Truman began to pace now, caught a glimpse of the guard in the shadows, moving with him. He stopped, hands clasped behind his back, turned to the shadows.

"Come out here. You're giving me the jitters."

The man emerged, two more to one side.

"Sir. Sorry, but you know our orders."

"No problem there, boys. But you can knock off the cloak-and-dagger stuff." He paused. "You know what I've done?"

The man seemed puzzled by the question, searched past Truman toward the railing.

"Not here, you . . . sorry. You know the kinds of decisions I've gotta deal with? Every damn day?"

"Yes, sir. Difficult decisions, sir."

"You have no idea, son. But there's one I've made that wasn't difficult at all. It has to be done."

"Yes . . . sir."

Truman felt a dangerous need to talk about it, a simple conversation, letting off some of the pressure. But his brain held him back, and he looked back out toward the moon, the low swells, heard the hum of the engines beneath his feet. Those damn scientists will keep chewing on this, he thought. But the decision has been made, and it might be the only time in this job when I'm completely sure I'm right. Just tell me that the son of a bitch works.

BABELSBERG, NEAR POTSDAM,
SOUTHWEST OF BERLIN, GERMANY
JULY 16, 1945

No matter what other goals could be met by a face-to-face meeting with both Churchill and Stalin, for the Americans the primary goal was to secure Soviet cooperation in the redevelopment of Europe. It was hoped, of course, that Stalin would allow those countries he now occupied to accept Western influence along with Western aid. But there was one other critical matter that Truman intended to put before Stalin. The Soviets had yet to declare war on Japan, for complicated reasons of their own that made almost no practical sense to anyone in the West. Truman intended to change Stalin's mind, and hoped, in the spirit of *Allies,* that the Soviets would understand that if the war was to drag on for another year or more, it was essential that the Soviets do their part. The carrot Truman offered was one he knew would matter significantly to the Soviets, one way to smooth over a major sore point for the Russians since their embarrassing defeat by the Japanese in the Russo-Japanese War, which ended in 1905. Russia had lost territory, islands north of the Japanese mainland, which no doubt Stalin wanted back. But if Americans were going to carry the load in any invasion of Japan, Truman was adamant that the Russians would have to make some significant contribution before they received any kind of reparations of their own. He went to Potsdam knowing that Stalin could not really be forced into backing away from anyplace he now controlled in Europe. But at least the Americans and the British might have something to offer that would soften the Soviet demeanor.

S talin had not yet arrived at the conference, and Truman had received a carefully worded intelligence report that the Soviet leader might have suffered a mild heart attack. The news had inspired a cascade of feelings, some of them distinctly unsympathetic, but very quickly after Truman's arrival, Soviet officials had come to call, assuring him that Stalin would arrive the following day. No one mentioned a heart attack.

The house Truman occupied was called the Little White House, a diplomatic nicety from the Soviets that mattered little to anyone, not the least because the house was yellow. But Truman's entourage was busy in every available space, spread out in other houses down the street. The officials who had accompanied Truman included Secretary of State James Byrnes and Truman's press secretary, Charles Ross. Military men were there as well, most prominently his chief of staff, Admiral William Leahy, who for a while had held the same position under Roosevelt. Leahy was the one loud voice close to Truman who objected completely to the construction and use of the atomic bomb, an unexpected voice against using a weapon of such magnitude. Truman respected Leahy, as had Roosevelt, but Leahy's viewpoint was distinctly in the minority, and the admiral seemed to accept that with a grudging acknowledgment, though he never failed to be a bug in Truman's ear about the fatefulness of the decision. I sure as hell don't need that right now, he thought.

Truman held the note in his hand, glanced at it one more time. For the moment all the important matters that the conference was to address seemed utterly trivial. He knew Churchill was housed about two blocks away, wondered about making another visit, this one unofficial, just to . . . talk. He studied the note again, thought, Churchill will know of this soon enough. This isn't about *gossip,* after all. Hey, Winny, look what we did!

He sat, but couldn't stay still, rose again, went to the window. Babelsberg had been a German resort town, thick woods, something of an artists' colony. But all that had been erased, the three-story house where he stood just one more piece of the Soviet occupation. The house faced a lake, and he stared at that now, imagined Germans swimming, a holiday, full of joy and whatever passed for carefree to Germans. But his heart was racing, and his eyes rose past the water, staring into blank sky, any thoughts of carefree far removed. He tossed the paper on the table, realized, right now, I have to just . . . shut up. But by damn, this is a day we will remember. Maybe the whole world. The paper seemed to float slightly, pushed by a gentle breeze from some open window beyond the door. He moved quickly, picked it up, folded it, stuck it in his pocket. He couldn't help the shivers, the strange excitement, knew that Leahy's doubts were about to be realized with as much gravity as the enthusiasm of the men who had pushed so very hard for the creation of the massive weapon.

The note had come to him in a specially coded message from the secretary of war, Henry Stimson. The wording had been cryptic and vague, lest any Soviet agent might examine it, but the code had been prearranged, and Truman knew exactly what Stimson was saying. It had happened at 5:30 A.M., in the bleak desert near Alamogordo. Under the gaze of the men who had created it, watched by military men and carefully chosen newspaper reporters, the first atomic bomb had been exploded. It had worked.

The man who could rightfully be called the Father of the Bomb, Dr. Robert Oppenheimer, had observed the extraordinary flash with one thought rolling through his mind, the words from the ancient text of the Hindu people, the Bhagavad Gita.

I am become death, the destroyer of worlds.

27. TIBBETS

The B-29 was warming up, the shimmy from the four massive engines shaking him down to his toenails. He checked the gauges, knew that Lewis, beside him, was doing the same. On the panel in front of him the instruments sprang to life, needles pointing where they should, temperatures and pressures rising. Behind him, he knew that Blanchard was watching every move both men made, making mental notes, or even paper ones, jotting down anything Tibbets and his co-pilot were doing wrong. Tibbets tried to ignore the man's presence, thought, *asshole.*

He pushed the throttle forward, the plane rolling toward the taxiway, the last stretch of pavement before the runway. The plane rumbled, shaking still, the roar of the engines growing louder, and Tibbets pressed the transmission button on the radio mike, said, "Dimples Eight Two to North Tinian Tower. Ready for takeoff on Runway Able."

The response was immediate, the voice crackling in his ear.

"Roger, Dimples Eight Two. Cleared for takeoff, Runway Able."

He didn't hesitate, jammed the throttles forward, the plane responding after a slight hint of delay, lagging just behind the immediacy of the command from Tibbets's hand. But the speed increased quickly, the plane bouncing, a slight swerve that Tibbets corrected. The B-29 continued to gain speed, the bounces more undulating now, no glance at Lewis. For now there was nothing for the co-pilot to do but watch, as he was, staring straight ahead toward the far end of the field, 8,500 feet away. He waited for it, felt it now, the nose rising slightly, the plane seeming to pause, gathering air beneath the massive wings, then smoothness, the wheels clear of the runway, the plane rising, pulling his stomach down, the sensation so familiar. He shifted his hands on the throttles, pulled one backward, heard the roar of the engines drop by a quarter, one engine shutting down, the prop feathering. He spoke into the intercom now.

"Engineer, confirm engine number one is shut down. Then feather engine number two."

The engineer, Duzenbury, replied, "Yes, sir. Confirmed. Number one feathered. Shutting down number two."

Tibbets smiled, would not look back at Blanchard, knew the man would be puzzled, possibly a full-blown panic. Just handle it, you jackass. I've got no time for chitchat, not right now. He struggled slightly with the plane's controls, compensated for the sudden loss of half the plane's power. To one side the props on the two idle engines had slowed considerably, propelled only by the wind speed of the plane, the B-29 held aloft now by only two of its engines. It had been Tibbets's plan, and his flight engineer had been prepared for the order, the entire crew knowing that their *special guest* was being given a demonstration of what the B-29 was capable of, and more important, what her pilots could do about it.

He looked to the altimeter, the plane rising past a thousand feet, then eleven hundred, gaining altitude far more slowly with half power. Suddenly Tibbets banked the plane hard, the silent engines now downhill, one wing pointing toward the blue ocean, and he said into the intercom, "Nice view, Colonel? Tinian's the hottest airfield in the Pacific. More B-29s fly out of here than anywhere in General LeMay's command. It's not the prettiest place, but we're making do."

He looked over to his co-pilot, saw Lewis glancing back toward Blanchard, a smile, no response from the guest behind him. Tibbets returned Lewis's smile, his eyes moving to the gauges again, keeping the plane in a steep bank. There was little drop in altitude, but he knew that wouldn't last, the bank too steep, the flight characteristics of the B-29 only allowing for so much lift before the plane simply fell out of the sky. The voice came now, high and tight, a slight stutter, Blanchard.

"Okay, Colonel. I'm satisfied. The engines are performing well. Can we complete the mission?"

Tibbets turned to Lewis, winked, said, "Certainly, Colonel. I thought I might shut them all down, show you our glide characteristics, but that can be a risky maneuver, especially at low altitude."

"No . . . not necessary. Please proceed with the mission." Tibbets focused on the restart of the two silent engines, heard a final word from Blanchard. "Please?"

The two engines restarted, belching smoke for a brief second, their props fully engaged. Tibbets pushed the throttles forward, the plane surging, climbing again, straight and level. After a long silence, Tibbets spoke into the intercom.

"Navigator, give me a time to target."

"Twenty-one minutes, sir."

"Roger, twenty-one minutes. Colonel Blanchard, please note your watch."

Blanchard didn't respond, but Tibbets knew the colonel would do exactly that. He leaned back, pressed himself into the seat, flexed his shoulders. Immediately behind him the gap was too small for a regular seat, and he knew that Blanchard's jump seat was far more uncomfortable. On Tibbets's order the crew had made a minimal effort to soften the man's ride by adding cushions to the meager padding. He felt Blanchard shifting around, a bump against Tibbets's shoulder. The thought came again. *Asshole.*

The meeting with Blanchard's boss, Curtis LeMay, had been on Guam, hours after Tibbets had learned that the test explosion at Alamogordo had been successful. Tibbets had expected to be there for the test, to see for himself just what this new weapon was supposed to do, but there had been an urgency about his return to Tinian, a sudden change of plans that infuriated Tibbets, and made Tibbets's own commander more nervous than either of them needed right now. Tibbets's superior was Major General Leslie Groves, the man who had headed up the Manhattan Project since its inception in 1942, and the one man who had more authority over the mission to drop the atomic bomb than anyone but the president. It was Groves who had transmitted the coded message to Tibbets, already back on Tinian, that the bomb's test had been an extraordinary success. Tibbets had enormous respect for Groves, especially for the man's hard-nosed resemblance to a bulldozer. The military chiefs respected Groves as well, appreciating that Groves was a problem solver, and a man who would pursue any project, no matter how complicated, to its conclusion. Though it had not been Groves's decision to name the pilot who would carry the atomic bomb over Japan, Groves had welcomed Tibbets immediately, quick to understand what many in the air forces already knew. Paul Tibbets was most likely the best man for the job. To the relief of both men, they had quickly forged a working relationship that rested on a firm foundation of mutual respect. Tibbets had not always agreed with the way Groves wanted things done, but even those arguments were never severe. Tibbets especially respected that if Groves saw he was wrong, he would listen to that and make corrections. Groves certainly had an ego, but he had been trained primarily as an engineer, with an engineer's mind. If the problem required a new solution, and that solution could be explained in ways an engineer's mind would appreciate, changes would be made. It had never hurt their relationship that Groves's office was in Washington, while Tibbets managed the intense training of the 509th in far-distant bases. The 509th had been established in the late fall of 1944, with its first base at Wendover, Utah. Security had been astoundingly tight, with a small army of highly screened guards, both in uniform and plain clothes, who kept a tight watch over the base and the men of the 509th, a tighter watch than most of them even knew about. But Tibbets knew that a host of unexpected security problems could plague any base located on American soil. With the enormous airstrips now fully operational on the island of Tinian, in the Mariana Islands chain, a few miles from Saipan, Tibbets had pushed hard for the 509th to relocate that much closer to their eventual target. Groves had not objected. The security of a base so far removed from prying eyes was only one reason Tibbets appreciated the move. He knew what many other commanders knew, that there was one enormous advantage being in the Pacific. You were no more than a teletype message or a radio relay from your superiors, but you didn't necessarily have to endure them looking over your shoulder.

The exception to that was Curtis LeMay, whose headquarters on Guam kept him too close for Tibbets to avoid. LeMay had known nothing of the Manhattan Project until a few weeks before Tibbets and the 509th had arrived on Tinian in early July, and even now LeMay knew very little of the specifics of just how this bomb was supposed to work. LeMay was far more concerned that a *very special* mission was to take place beneath the umbrella of his command, and he most definitely wanted to be included. That inclusion carried a heavy price for Tibbets. LeMay had begun to make loud noises that any special mission from Tinian should be flown by a flight crew selected by LeMay himself. With a nagging crisis possible from LeMay's increasing growls, Tibbets had been forced to fly to Guam himself, and had suffered through an explosion of a different kind, facing the caustic general by keeping a demeanor of calm that impressed even Tibbets himself. No matter what kind of demands or tirades LeMay might pour over him, Tibbets knew that he always had the upper hand. A single call to Groves, or better yet, to Groves's superior, the air corps chief Hap Arnold, would immediately produce the desired order for LeMay to leave his hands completely off of Tibbets and his mission. But orders or not, that kind of antagonism would never sit well with a bulldog like LeMay, and Tibbets knew that with so much at stake, it would be unwise to make an enemy out of Curtis LeMay. Tibbets had his hands full just keeping his own men segregated from anyone else on Tinian while he monitored their training and the ongoing secrecy of their mission, no simple task. None of the other wing commanders who flew missions out of the huge airfields had any idea what the 509th was doing there, and why they were not participating in the usual bombing runs over Japanese targets. Since the 509th's mission could not be revealed in any detail to anyone on Tinian, there was considerable hostility from the other bomber groups that these new guys were receiving some kind of cushy special treatment. And, of course, the rumors flew along with the B-29s. To many it seemed as though Colonel Paul Tibbets was being given plush special treatment for no better reason than that he had powerful friends in Washington.

It seemed to matter little to LeMay that Tibbets had once been the most sought-after pilot in Europe, had been the primary pilot for Generals Eisenhower and Mark Clark, and had scored more than forty successful bombing missions in the workhorse B-17. LeMay had his doubts that a pilot with no experience in the Pacific had any business commanding this kind of critically important mission over a target area he had never seen. LeMay knew that Tibbets had received a very definite order that he was never to engage in any kind of practice run over any part of Japan. Should something go wrong, from anti-aircraft fire or mechanical failure, Tibbets's capture by the Japanese could become a security disaster that might jeopardize the entire project. Tibbets took no insult from that. He had no interest in finding out just how much torture he could take from a sadistic Japanese officer, or whether his moral backbone could withstand the worst kind of interrogation the Japanese might inflict on him.

Even LeMay knew that Tibbets's orders came directly from Washington, and LeMay was sharp enough not to make enemies in places where his own career path might be decided. After the rage had passed, LeMay had reluctantly agreed that Paul Tibbets might be the right man after all, though LeMay had one *request*. For at least one training mission, LeMay wanted Colonel Butch Blanchard, his operations officer, to go along for the ride, just to see if these boys who had done most of their work over Utah knew anything about what it took to handle a B-29 in the Pacific.

T he voice came through the intercom from his navigator.
"Target dead ahead, sir."
"I see it, Captain."

Tibbets leaned back, made a slight glance at Blanchard, said into his intercom, "Note the time, if you will, Colonel. Unfortunately, my navigator has miscalculated. We're ahead of schedule by four seconds."

Blanchard said nothing, the message very clear. Tibbets looked to the altimeter, the plane straight and level at thirty thousand feet. He spoke into the intercom again.

"Major Ferebee, it's your bird."

The bombardier responded, "Got her, sir."

Tibbets pulled his hands back from the controls, scanned the skies to the front for any sign of Japanese anti-aircraft fire. The island of Rota was still in enemy hands, though no one, including the Japanese, seemed to give that much thought. The island was less than a hundred miles to the south of Tinian and for now made the perfect target for test bombing runs. Today, they carried a single five-hundred-pound bomb, and other than giving the B-29's crew one more opportunity to test their skills, Tibbets had designed this flight to serve only one purpose: a demonstration of the prowess of the men Tibbets already knew to be the best he had ever flown with. Impressing Colonel Blanchard would be fun.

"Ten seconds to target, sir."
"Roger."
"Bomb away."

Ferebee's voice was calm, none of the raucous cheerleading, no excitement from any of the others. Ferebee had been with Tibbets from his earliest days in the B-17s, as had his navigator, Captain Dutch Van Kirk. Both men knew exactly what this particular flight was about, and so far there hadn't been a single hitch.

With the bomb's release, Tibbets's hands moved quickly back to the controls, and in one jerking motion he pulled the plane into a steep banking move. It was a maneuver he had practiced a dozen or more times, knew already that the turn would reach an angle of 155 degrees, the best angle the plane could withstand to carry its crew as quickly as possible away from the bomb's eventual target. It was not a challenge any of them had faced before, but when the moment came, and the enormous power of the atomic bomb was unleashed over a Japanese target, no one, not the physicists, the military officers, not Tibbets himself, had any idea what would happen to the plane that dropped it. This one part of their training had appealed to Tibbets with perfect logic. Turn the plane as sharply as possible and get the hell out of there.

Tibbets had braced himself for the violence of the turn, knew the rest of the crew had done the same. Behind him, the one man who did not expect the maneuver squawked into the intercom, "What the hell? What's happening? We're stalling!"

Tibbets held hard to the controls, felt the tail of the plane sag, the natural reaction to such a tight turn. He suddenly had no patience for his passenger, said in a clipped shout, "We have to stall the tail. Only way to do the turn at this angle. You tell me if there's another way I should be doing it."

"Okay! Enough!"

"Not yet, Colonel."

Tibbets pulled back on the controls, the plane suddenly veering upward, nearly vertical, the engines straining, the nose skyward, the plane slowing, seeming to bounce softly on its tail. The plane stopped flying now, the perfect stall, nearly motionless, but now the violence returned, the nose suddenly swinging over to one side, the plane in a momentary free fall. The ocean below was in full view now, the plane in a steep dive, and Tibbets focused on the altimeter, heard a gurgling sound through the intercom, a chattering voice, "You're going to kill us!"

"Not today, Colonel."

He pulled back slowly on the wheel, the plane's nose rising, his stomach settling hard, the smoothness returning, the wings straight and level.

"Navigator, what's the heading to base?"

"Zero two zero, sir."

"Zero two zero, roger."

He could already see Tinian, could see the shape of the island, so much like New York City, *Manhattan,* and he wondered, did Groves know that? No, too much irony there.

"Tinian tower, Dimples Eight Two. Request permission to land."

"Dimples Eight Two, clear to land Runway Able. Winds eleven knots at zero eight zero."

"Roger, Tinian Tower. Dimples Eight Two out."

He nosed the plane toward the runway's western end, the B-29 responding with perfect precision now. He glanced over to Lewis, thought of letting him handle the landing, thought, no, let's keep this by the damn book. *This jackass behind me's probably puked on his shoes, and he'll still be looking for something to bitch about.*

The plane settled low, hovered slightly, then dropped the last few feet, touching down with a squeaking jerk. Tibbets pulled the throttles back farther, touched the plane's brakes, said, "Time, Colonel Blanchard?"

There was a silent moment, and Blanchard responded now.

"Yes, we're exactly fifteen seconds late. I've seen what I needed to see, Colonel."

Tibbets smiled, said nothing. The instructions came from the tower, but he knew the configurations of the taxiway, moved the plane that way, to the special security area, away from the other squadrons. He applied the brakes, the plane rolling to a stop, the engines shutting down completely. He sat for a moment, the roar of the engines still in his ears, fading to a soft hiss. Blanchard was up already, moving out from behind him, and Tibbets saw a smile on his co-pilot's face, heard Blanchard's voice.

"Thank you for the demonstration, Colonel Tibbets. It will be my recommendation to General LeMay that you and your crew proceed with your mission as ordered." He paused. "You proved your damn point."

HEADQUARTERS, 509TH COMPOSITE GROUP, TINIAN
JULY 26, 1945

He sat on the small porch of his quarters, the smoke from the pipe rolling up around him, carried off now by a warm breeze. The sun was sinking rapidly, and beside him the chaplain sipped from a china cup, the coffee

Tibbets knew was strong enough to melt tin. After a silent moment, the chaplain said, "How can you drink this stuff?"

"Iron stomach. Comes from training in a B-29. Never had any sweat in a B-17, like flying in your mama's lap. I've gotten all kinds of heartburn from these bigger birds. Some engineer took a few shortcuts, I guess. War Department probably got in a hurry, said, just build the thing, let the pilots worry about keeping them in the air."

Tibbets took another deep pull at the pipe, the smoke delicious, the most relaxed he had been all day. He glanced at the chaplain, said, "My old man still doesn't understand how any plane stays in the air. I've tried explaining it to him, he just . . . stares at me. But I'll never forget that first day . . . he bit his damn tongue and let me go up. Probably scared the wits out of him. Imagine watching your boy, a twelve-year-old for God's sake, going up in a biplane with some stranger you don't know from Adam."

"Where was that?"

"Miami. There was a promotion by the people who made Baby Ruth candy bars, and my father was the local dealer for the company. They were giving the stuff away, trying to get people hooked on 'em, I guess. The idea was to fly over the Hialeah Race Track, then the beach. It was summer, the places packed with people. Some old barnstormer got the job from the candy company to do bombing runs, swooping low over the crowd, dropping small bags of Baby Ruth bars, attached to little parachutes. Doug Davis. Yep, that was his name. He looked the part, the leather hat, the goggles, just what a twelve-year-old wanted to see. I jumped all over the guy, made myself as obnoxious as I could, let me go, let me go." Tibbets laughed. "He gave in, no matter that my father was probably begging him not to. But I had to work for it. Tied every damn one of those parachutes myself. Davis did the flying, I did the bombing. All I remember is that it was over way too quick. Greatest damn adventure any kid could have. No Arabian prince on his magic carpet ever had a thrill like that. Changed my whole damn life." He looked over toward the chaplain, drew another cloud of smoke from his pipe. "Guess that's pretty obvious."

"Maybe. Sounds to me like you were meant to fly, maybe before you were twelve. We all have our place. There's a path, and you were led to yours. You're fortunate to know that, to appreciate it. Most people never find theirs. Some poor souls stare at the right path, and then walk right by."

"So, Chaplain, I'm flying because God wants me to?"

"Didn't say that. If you're happy, truly happy, then God is happy right along with you. He doesn't create the path, just gives you the free will to find it for yourself. Make choices, live with a clear conscience, a good heart."

"Damn, Bill, you make me sound like I oughta be on some painting in the Vatican."

"I'm Lutheran, Paul. Don't spend a lot of time chatting with the pope. How's Lucy?"

Tibbets was surprised by the change of topic, knew too well why Downey had asked.

"She's okay, getting by taking care of the boys." He paused. "Well, hell, I'm not going to lie to a damn chaplain. Things aren't that good. She's not happy I'm so damn far away. I thought she enjoyed being at Wendover, having the family together and all, but even then I could tell there was a problem. Hell, I was gone all the damn time. The job . . . well, you know. They had me flying all over the damn place. Naturally, we can't have families out here, so now she's stuck back home, and sure as hell, she lets me know about that. What can I do, Bill? It's the job, and right now it has to be the job. She's gotta understand that. This'll be over one day, then maybe things will be all right."

"Of course they will. We'll all be better off once the war's over. She's not any different from every wife and every mother who's sitting home getting all they can from a letter every few days. They all want this to end, get all of you back home."

Tibbets looked at Downey, saw youth, the fresh face of a man who knew very little of family life.

"What are you, twenty-five?"

"Twenty-seven."

"Yeah, thought so. Tell you what, Minister Downey, you go home and have a half-dozen kids, then haul your ass to some seminary somewhere for six months. Tell me how happy they'll be about that."

"Sorry. Didn't mean to touch a nerve."

Tibbets took a hard pull on the pipe, the smoke turning bitter in his mouth, no comfort at all.

"You didn't. It just . . . never goes away. This isn't any kind of life for a married man. And the kids. Jesus, Bill, I miss my boys." He looked at

Downey, saw no change of expression. "Sorry. *'Don't cuss at the chaplain.'* Learned that in basic."

Downey started to protest, and Tibbets knew there was no offense taken at all. They all knew that the chaplain had enormous tolerance for the various adventures enjoyed by the 509th since their earliest days together, adventures that often included things best kept away from church. Tibbets had always liked Downey, though Tibbets had rarely gone to Sunday services. The excuses were always there, mostly unspoken. Neither man would believe that his absence at church was only because he just didn't have the time. But Tibbets was still self-conscious about his Sunday absences, had heard the occasional comment from some of the men in his command.

"I'd be at your services more often, if I could. It's just that . . . well, I've always felt that any time I needed to chat with God, I prefer doing it without a middleman."

Downey laughed, said, "Yeah, so you've told me. Tell me more about your sons."

"Toughest thing about being here. I miss 'em, sure as hell. They'd go crazy out here watching these big birds coming and going. I'd end up having to haul them both up one day. Well, Paul, anyway. He's nearly five. Gene's just a baby still. But I could stow Paul someplace where nobody'd see, maybe in the tail gun. Sergeant Caron wouldn't mind if I stuck him back there once in a while. Caron would get a kick out of teaching Paul how to squeeze off a few rounds with the fifty cal. I guarantee it would be just like Miami was for me. He'd never forget that. Hell, both my boys might end up flying. Gotta make sure they stick to the big birds though. Every damn kid who goes to flight school wants to be a fighter pilot. All that adventure, the silk scarf, the girls dripping off you. Bunk. You want adventure, try emptying a bomb bay over a Kraut city while flak cuts you to pieces and a Messerschmitt's on your ass."

"Maybe not as much fun as a Japanese city."

"Can't talk about that."

"I know. Not asking anything. Just wondering if this might be a good time for you to show up in church. You can still have your private *chat* with God. But it'll do the rest of the boys some good to see you there. There's a lot of nervousness here, a lot of uncertainty. I'm not talking about secrets, Paul. They've gotten used to all the cloak-and-dagger stuff. But they're getting hit pretty hard by the other crews all over Tinian. I heard about the rock throwing. Some of the other crews make it a point to toss rocks up your tin roofs when they come in from a bombing mission. The boys know they can't respond, not to that, or to anything else. That's tough, I know."

"They know they're in on something unique, something special. Not much else I can give them."

"Maybe. Let 'em know you're aware how tough this is. You're carrying some heavy-duty secrets around with you, and they know that. They also know they're being watched, they know someone's checking up on 'em, reading their mail."

"Can't be helped."

"Oh, I know that. Your Doctor Young came by yesterday, talked to me awhile. Asked a few questions that seemed, well, unusual, coming from a flight surgeon."

Tibbets knew exactly what Downey was referring to. For weeks now, Don Young had served not only as the 509th's chief medical officer, but as the eyes and ears for one more type of security. There had been growing concern that the stress of the mission, and the secrecy and shadowy rumors the men were forbidden to discuss, might be causing the entire unit to fray at the edges. Tibbets had given the order himself, that the doctor was to observe the men in every aspect of their routines, including their playfulness, temperament, their speech pattern, how they interacted with one another. If anyone's behavior was changing in a pronounced way, it might be cause to eliminate him from the final mission. So far the problems had been few, the symptoms of the stress not important enough to take someone off the team. But the doctor's observations were having an impact of their own, adding to the sense of jumpiness that was already affecting the unit well before they left Wendover.

Downey sipped from the coffee cup, then tossed away the last dregs, said, "It has to happen soon, Paul. They're winding tighter every day. You know the talk. This mission . . . well, I've heard the same rumors everyone else has, at least right here. Not sure what's flying around the rest of this island. But if you've got a chance to end this war . . ."

"*Can it,* Bill."

Downey was silenced, and Tibbets looked at him, tapped the pipe on the metal chair, cleaned out the spent tobacco. Downey nodded, said, "Not another word, Colonel. Just doing my job."

"I know that. Look, the mission will happen when it happens. No one needs to know more than that. Not even me, actually. This is being handled the way it has to, and when it's all over with, everyone will understand that. I can't coddle anyone right now. Sure as hell, no one's coddling me." He suddenly had a flash of an idea. "Tell you what. Write a prayer. When . . . or if the time comes, I want a eulogy, or an invocation, or whatever the hell you call it. Some sort of send-off, something to make the boys feel like God's watching over them. Something . . . kind. Oh, hell, maybe that's corny as hell."

"No, it sounds perfect. Absolutely. I'm flattered you'd ask."

"Don't be. You're the damn chaplain. That's your job."

Downey smiled.

"Yes, Colonel, it is. I'll get started right away. I assume I have a day or two, anyway?"

"Can't answer that."

Tibbets saw the figure approaching, was surprised to see one of his MPs. The man stopped short, stiffened, saluted.

"Sir, forgive the interruption. Oh, hello, Chaplain. Very sorry. I can come back."

Tibbets returned the salute, said, "Spit it out, Sergeant. What's up?"

"Sir, I've been told that you wanted to know when the ship arrived. It's docking now, sir."

Downey said, "What ship? Something I can ask about?"

Tibbets stood, stuffed the pipe in his shirt pocket.

"You can now. It's hard to hide a cruiser." He looked at the MP again. "You sure, Sergeant? The ship I asked about?"

"Yes, sir. It's the *Indianapolis*."

After absorbing the brutal effects of a Japanese dive-bomber in the waters off Okinawa, the aging cruiser had been sent to Mare Island, northeast of San Francisco, for refitting and repairs. But her service was not yet complete. On July 16, the ship was ordered back to sea, this time with two special passengers and a shipment of cargo that was not even detailed to the ship's captain. Tibbets knew the two men, and also knew the cargo. The first atomic weapon designated to be used over Japan was still an assemblage of parts, and putting all of those components in one place was considered far too hazardous, and far too great a security risk. The largest component was a cannonlike device that would be the bomb's core, a mechanism that would fire a piece of enriched uranium into a similar piece at the far end of the bomb, creating a sufficient amount of the material to trigger the chain reaction that would result in the atomic explosion. That cannon and one part of the nuclear material had been placed aboard the *Indianapolis,* guarded twenty-four hours a day by the two men, whose sole mission was to deliver the pieces of the bomb to Tinian. The men, Robert Furman and James Nolan, had accompanied the cargo without ever revealing their identities or their mission. Disguised as army officers, neither was in fact army at all. Furman was an engineer from Princeton, and Nolan a physician who specialized in radiation treatment. Their journey had begun in Los Alamos, New Mexico, under the authority of Dr. Robert Oppenheimer, the chief physicist for the Manhattan Project. Flanked by a convoy of heavy security, they made the first leg of their journey to Albuquerque, where the two men and their cargo were placed aboard a C-47 cargo plane. Escorted by two additional C-47s, they were flown to San Francisco. With an armed escort now in tow, the two men had accompanied their cargo to the wharf where the crew of the *Indianapolis* waited, none having any idea what their next assignment might be. Once on board the cruiser, Furman and Nolan had no other duty but to take turns standing watch over the lead bucket that held the enriched uranium. If the ship had gone down, there was no danger that the uranium would go anywhere else. The lead was welded to the steel deck of their cabin. Outside, the cannon device was housed in a crate that was lashed securely to the deck of the ship, guarded by continuous shifts of heavily armed Marines.

As the *Indianapolis* sailed for Tinian, the remaining components of the bomb were shipped by air on a four-engine C-54 transport plane, the big brother to the smaller C-47. With the uneventful arrival of the *Indianapolis* to the wharves at Tinian, all the pieces of the bomb had been gathered into a single location, put into secure facilities alongside the men whose job it would be to fly it to a target in Japan, a target they still did not know.

28. HAMISHITA

The men huddled together, one man attending the wounds of another, a torn shirt for a bandage.

"There, Doctor. I suppose you should take a look at that one. The others do not appear to have serious injury, though they are too stubborn to admit to anything. If they insist on keeping their pain to themselves, I will not object. They should suffer for their crimes." The captain turned away with a curt wave of his hand. "Do what you must, Doctor."

Hamishita moved through the open gate of the cell, the American prisoners watching him with emotionless eyes. The injured man was lying flat on the earthen floor, and one of the others spoke out to the doctor, words Hamishita could not understand. He responded by holding high the medical bag, the other hand held outward, a gesture of calm. Behind him the guards pointed their machine guns into the cell, a show of power Hamishita ignored. The prisoners will not attack me, he thought. I'm too old, and no threat to them. They know their man requires care, and surely they can see I am not one of the soldiers.

The Americans made room, five men easing away from their fellow flyer, cautious, watching Hamishita's every move. He looked at the faces, dirty, exhausted, scanned their limbs, saw no obvious damage beyond the rips and shreds to their clothes.

"I am a doctor. I am here to help."

None of the Americans showed any acknowledgment, no sign of understanding him. He moved forward, close to the injured man, opened the bag, then looked closer, saw blood thick on his shirt, a rag tied across one shoulder. He slid his hand beneath it, felt the gash in the man's flesh, his hand now in the wound, foamy and wet, the man not crying out. The Americans around him kept mostly quiet, one shouting something, a guard at the cell door shouting back. It was a ridiculous show, no communication at all, just the growls of injured animals, hatred and viciousness. But the Japanese guards had every advantage, and the Americans seemed to know they were powerless, had to trust this older man who claimed to be a doctor. At least, he thought, they will allow me to do my work.

He eased the bandage off the shoulder, and Hamishita frowned, the wound already festering. The smell rose up, spreading through the cavelike cell, mingling with the damp earth and filthy men. He took an instrument from his bag, scraped at the wound, the man still oblivious, no real consciousness. But the others reacted, some turning away from the gruesome sight, others watching his every move. No, I am not here to torture. If he can be cured, I will do my best. He probed the wound, saw fragments of bone, the slow pulse of an artery, opened now, the blood draining away through the man's rag of a shirt. One of the others said something, the man's tone more of desperation, a plea.

"It is not good. He has lost much blood. Too much."

Hamishita knelt upright, wiped the blood from his hand, put one finger on the man's eyelid, opened, saw the pupils wide and black, a small window through the man's blue eyes into a brain that was almost gone. The injured man was completely calm, no reaction at all, the odor from his wound overpowering in the cramped space. For more than thirty years he had treated every type of injury, and now most of those were wounds, many of them more severe than this one. He had never been bothered by the blood, by the opening of a man's flesh. But the smells had always affected him, the unavoidable stench of a man's inevitable death by the decay of blood and flesh, by the swift work of bacteria and vermin moving too quickly to be stopped. He removed a small vial of alcohol from his bag, sprinkled it on his hands, wiped again, cleaned as much of the man's debris from his skin as he could. He looked at the others, each one with the fear and the anger for what had happened to them. Hamishita would not think of that, had no hatred for these men, no matter their missions, no matter what destruction they might be responsible for. He had seen the pain of loss too many times, knew the look in the eyes, stricken with the blow of sadness, of the reality that a friend was dying. He tried to see who might be in charge, could tell nothing from their flight jackets, the uniforms looked the same, no insignia he recognized. One of the men seemed to feel the moment more deeply than the others, and the doctor caught his eye, slowly shook his head. Another man said something to him, a demand, hard words, and Hamishita ignored him, kept his eye on the man who was crying now, red eyes, fear, the man already missing his friend.

"I'm sorry. The infection is too pronounced. He has lost consciousness. I do not have the medicine that would save him. Even if he was in hospital . . . there is little I can do."

He closed the medical bag, stood, backed away, saw the fierce stares watching him, all but one, the friend, the man moving close, a hand on the dying man's arm. The American said something, soft words, and Hamishita heard a soft gurgle, one final breath, a faint rattle from the man's throat, the injured American injured no more. The others seemed to understand, another one speaking out, not as much anger, something to Hamishita, a short nod, some kind of gratitude. The doctor made a short bow, said, "I'm sorry. Your comrade is gone. I was too late."

He was out of the cell now, the guards closing the steel door with a hard clang, a stupid show the Americans certainly did not need. Hamishita moved out into fresher air, thought, they know their war is over. For those men, anyway, we are the victors. How many of us did they kill first? No, that is not your concern. Their friend died honorably, in the performance of his duty. If that is not important to them . . . well, it should be.

He had watched the raid from the bombers, a formation of B-24s doing what they always did, dropping strings of bombs that rained down like tiny insects. This raid had targeted some military barracks no more than a few hundred yards from his clinic. But two of the planes had not escaped, the first time he had actually witnessed accurate fire from the anti-aircraft batteries that kept hidden against the far hills. The planes had twisted and spun, wounded birds, and from each the parachutes had emerged like white puffs of cotton. He had watched them fall, their planes first, thunderous crashes into the woods to the north. The flyers came next, a dozen, slow and deliberate, and there had been gunfire from the ground, a rifle, but then the flyers were down, out of his view. He knew they had no chance to escape capture, the soldiers waiting for them before they even reached the ground. The six he had seen were among them, certainly, and it was not his place to ask what had happened to the rest. But the call to examine this group had been a surprise, a messenger from Captain Narita, and Hamishita had responded at once, a brisk hike from his clinic straight to the castle.

He was outside now, more guards, no one seeming to pay any attention to this one elderly civilian among a sea of uniforms. He saw Captain Narita, the man speaking to an aide, reading from a piece of paper. Hamishita moved that way, and Narita saw him, said, "So. Will they survive?"

"One did not. The others show no apparent injury. I am not certain why you needed me to verify that."

"You will do precisely that, Doctor. Verify that. I wish to have a written report from you, stating that the American prisoners are in acceptable condition, that we have not tortured or abused them. If you have time, of course."

Hamishita knew that the kindness in Narita's request was completely counterfeit, that the paperwork would be produced whether it was written by Hamishita or by someone else who simply added the doctor's signature.

"I will do so immediately, Captain. With your permission, I will return to my clinic. You shall have your paper by this afternoon."

"Is there a hurry, Doctor? Perhaps you will come to the commander's villa for tea."

It was another order, and Hamishita thought of the work that awaited him at the clinic, only a few patients, wounded civilians from the last bombing raid, one woman who had just given birth.

"Nothing urgent awaits me, Captain. I am honored to be your guest."

"Excellent. But you will not be my guest. Someone wishes to see you. You should be honored by such an invitation."

Hamishita was baffled by the hint of mystery, made a short bow, followed as Narita moved up the inclined path that led out away from the lower levels of the castle. He was still curious about the rest of the American flyers, if they had survived at all, if they were being held separately from the others, some kind of security, a place of interrogation perhaps. It was an odd request from Narita that the doctor provide documentation that the six men he had seen had not been tortured, that they had been given proper medical treatment. He knew very little of military matters, thought, perhaps they are to be traded, an exchange for some of our own. They would need to be in good condition, I suppose. That makes sense. The captain stopped, pointed the way, and Hamishita saw the grand home, guards flanking a narrow driveway, gates adorned with metal carvings. He knew of the place, a headquarters of sorts, had seen parades of officers coming and going. But today there was little activity beyond the presence of the guards. Narita said, "Your host is waiting. You may enter, on my authority."

The words were loud, intended for the guards, who made no movement at all. Hamishita turned to thank the captain, but the man was already moving away, back toward the castle, the activity there much more intense, a column of soldiers emerging from an upper doorway, more gathering in the wide grounds to one side. Busy man, he thought. I suppose . . . if someone was trying to drop bombs on my clinic, I would be busy too.

He moved up the walkway, past the guards, no one looking at him. The driveway was lined on either side by flowers, more greenery beyond. The house itself was very old, two stories, ornate carvings perched in various crevices in the stone architecture. There were more guards at the entryway, a heavy bronze door that was suddenly opened for him.

"Thank you. Very kind."

The guards did not respond, and Hamishita moved inside, caught the wondrous fragrance of food being prepared. For many months his own meals had consisted mostly of rice and dried fish, a necessity impressed on the civilians by the needs of the army. He had made his fights with the local military headquarters, protesting to anyone who would listen that the needs of his patients were a priority that even the local military commanders should understand, since he had been called upon to treat soldiers as well as civilians wounded in the bombing attacks. But so far there had been no promises of anything more than meager rations, and no other supplies at all, including the desperately needed medicines. He understood the needs of the army, but still he hoped that his status as a doctor would open someone's eyes to the necessity of a helping hand. Whatever medicines and supplies he had used on his patients had been scrounged from places the army would not have appreciated. It had been risky, but the doctor knew that each barracks was stocked with a first aid kit. Even the small doses of morphine or disinfectants would be useful, and if those kits were discovered to be missing, he had convinced himself, a doctor would be low on the list of suspected thieves.

The smells in the grand house were overwhelming him, erasing the sickening odor of the castle, and he searched for someone, anyone, heard a voice.

"Doctor! I have a small pain in my toe. I insisted that you be the one to treat it. There is no one in the empire more qualified to clip my toenails."

The voice was strangely familiar, and he saw the man at the top of the grand staircase, stared up into a wide, beaming smile.

"Shunroku!" He froze, saw the grandeur of the man's uniform, realized this was no time for such informality. "Forgive me, please. Field Marshal Hata! It is my honor to be in your presence."

"Yes, of course it is, Okiro. It is my honor too. I look in the mirror and announce myself every morning when I awaken. 'Hata Shunroku, you have the honor once more of adorning yourself with the uniform of a field marshal. Be worthy, or they will strip it from you.' How I manage to fill such enormous shoes is yet a mystery to me."

"I heard you had come to Hiroshima, that you were in command now. I have wondered how you were doing, but your fame has answered those questions. I never thought you would have time to see me . . . or even re-member me. It has been years."

"Fifteen years. You treated a member of my staff when we were on ma-neuvers, just before the Manchukuo affair began. I recall being impressed that my old friend should have accomplished so much."

"I am merely a physician, Field Marshal. You are so far above me . . . so accomplished. I could hardly matter to a man in your position."

"Why is that? Old friendships are far more valuable than new ones, and these days new friends are best avoided. Even the emperor knows this. He is avoiding anyone who does not smell like a friend."

A servant appeared now, a short, thin woman in a white silk kimono. She bowed deeply, her hands clasped tightly beneath her chin. Hata moved down the stairway, said, "Is the lunch prepared?"

She did not speak, her positive response coming in another bow. She turned quickly, moved away.

Hata watched her, said, "Perhaps we should even fear the girls. I should have you examine the food, test it for poison." He winked at the doctor now. "I am teasing of course. My staff is loyal to a fault. The *fault* is that they have chosen to be loyal to *me*."

Hamishita stiffened as Hata descended closer to him, and the field marshal stopped, seemed disappointed by the doctor's formality.

"Not you as well. I am treated like a deity by my soldiers. I do not expect such from one who has spent his youth swimming with me in the cold spring of that farmer, Gorito. We barely escaped that man without becoming a meal for his dogs. And me without my clothing! What would my colonels say of that?"

Hamishita tried to loosen his formality, but Hata's uniform was too imposing.

"Yes. I recall that. We were no more than ten, I suppose. The farmer complained to your parents. Your father did not spare the whip, as I recall."

Hata's smile darkened now, the words coming out slowly, quietly, "None of us will be spared the whip. Those of us in the High Command who have been so impatient for this war to end will soon enjoy the gratification of their wish fulfilled." Hata pointed toward a room to one side. "Come, my friend. Lunch awaits."

Hamishita followed, could not help admiring the field marshal's boots, a high sheen on black leather. The source of the smells was apparent now, a table lined with small bowls of steaming food, framed on each end by enormous vases of flowers.

"Sit there, Okiro. I shall assume my position at the head of the table. No one will be joining us but our ancestors. But even the spirits expect me to take my accustomed place. It will keep them from remembering a naked frightened child fleeing a barking dog. I should certainly have to answer for that once more when I reach the great shrine. What about you? What do you have to answer for? A respected physician, managing his own clinic. Did you ever imagine you would find yourself in such a position?"

Hamishita moved to the cushion where Hata pointed, sat, curled his legs beneath him.

"I have been fortunate. The emperor has blessed me. I have had a long and healthy life."

"Yes, the emperor. He wants only the best for his people. We are his children, yes? We should all grow old like you and me, in the splendor of this wonderful house."

Hamishita heard the sarcasm in Hata's voice, wasn't sure how to respond. The field marshal pointed a single chopstick at the bowls spread in front of them, said, "Eat. This is more nourishing than cold rice. I know what kind of rations you have, what you give your patients. It is a tragedy for you not to be more ably equipped. A man who cares for so many should be well fed."

Hamishita obeyed, sliding soft noodles into an empty bowl, the steam from a warm broth bathing his face. He absorbed Hata's words, thought, so, you know how little I have, down to the last detail? He wanted to ask about that, thought of so many young officers who had scoffed at his every request. But Hata was far too intimidating.

"Thank you for this invitation, Field Marshal. I am grateful that you allow yourself a moment's attention to my position in our empire. I am flattered."

Hata slurped at his own bowl, ignored Hamishita's gratitude, seemed lost in thought. Hamishita looked closely at his friend now, saw the age. They were both in their mid-sixties, the hard life of a soldier showing in Hata's face, the roughness of his hands. Hata looked at him now, said, "Have you been taking the training?"

Hamishita felt suddenly self-conscious.

"I was told my position as a doctor . . ."

"Stop. I am teasing you. Must you be so serious? You were the same as a boy, always the wounded one, the one who took offense, the one bitten by the insults. These days I should be the one who never smiles. My army carries the wounds that are far more serious than what an old farmer's dog could do. You and I carry wounds of happier times. I recall you falling from that old bent cherry tree. You broke an arm, your . . . left. I think we were both crying, and your father insisted that if there were tears, there had to be blood. I have always remembered that. There was wisdom in his cruelty."

Hamishita had tried to erase those kinds of memories, was amazed that Hata would recall them.

"If I may ask, Field Marshal, why have you summoned me?"

"Now you insult me. I have known you since we were in playpens, and I can feel your doubt, as though my intentions are dishonorable. My power and my rank causes me to be despised by everyone in my command, and today I merely seek out the company of an old friend. And would you please stop referring to me as *field marshal*? I need not be reminded that I command the entire Second General Army. But out there, this vast army that obeys my orders, there are not more than a handful of men who even know my familiar name. The emperor knows nothing of ten-year-olds making mischief in a farmer's barn, or stealing cherries from an old lady's orchard. I treasure those times, innocence and joy. Broken bones and dog bites. Very soon I shall enjoy that again, in another place. Those memories shall become reality again, as shall the best part of family. There shall no longer be sacrifice and pain and blood. Is that not what you wish as well? Would you not relish climbing that cherry tree? This time I would try to catch you."

Hamishita stopped eating, was uncomfortable now, began to see a hint of madness in the field marshal's rant.

"I . . . would very much like to enjoy my childhood again. Very much. But those days are gone. I have more . . . adult duties to perform. We all do."

"For now. Do not think for one moment that I do not take my duties here very seriously. I am honored the emperor chooses me for such a task. I spent so much time in his palace, enduring the twittering of all those neutered birds who flutter around him, so very careful not to say anything that might cause his heart rate to rise one extra beat. For so long the emperor treated me the same way, flowery kindness, rewarding my grand career with promises of great, lofty positions. Prime minister! How about that? If I had accepted that, then I too could become one of the fragile little birds. But I am a soldier. Forty-five years in this army, Okiro. That's why I am here. There cannot be much more time and I must fulfill my duty the best way I know how. That is why they despise me, of course. I make them work. But the emperor does not control my every waking moment, and he cannot tell me that, for one pleasant pause in my day, I cannot spend my time with a very old friend, sharing a simple lunch."

Hamishita made a short bow of his head.

"Please accept my apologies. But you are too famous and too powerful in this world for me to treat you as the boy I knew in Fukushima. You are a great hero to Japan. I know of your accomplishments, your career. I was so very proud of you, I cannot just toss that aside. When I learned you were coming here, I did not dare think you would even recall who I am."

"We all have our heroes, Doctor. I have followed your career as well. A long life in the army has its rewards, including sources of information. Look at you. You heal what I destroy. There is honor in that, far beyond what a soldier is trained to do." He paused, more serious now. "I was sent to Hiroshima to fortify the city, to add one more bastion to what will become the emperor's impregnable fortress. Such a duty does not result in *friends*, Okiro. At the castle, even now, they lurk in corners and curse my name, because I force them to be better soldiers. I order men to perform their duty, because if I do not, they will lie about and abuse slave girls. Yes,

I am despised. But if there is greatness to my life, it will come in what I do now. Our time is very close, Okiro. We have been granted Divine Opportunity."

Hamishita saw a glimmer of fire in his friend's eye, the soldier staring off for a second, absorbing his own meaning. But the doctor did not respond, wasn't sure what his friend was referring to. After a silent moment, Hata said, "I have always believed in a war of attrition. The military has made many mistakes. But now that will change. The enemy is coming, and very soon he will walk right into our parlor, where the knives await. It is so completely appropriate that it should come to this. The emperor has blessed you, my friend. He has blessed all Japanese, all of us who stand on our own soil, who will share the blessing of opportunity to greet the enemy with a violent death. The Americans will bring their ships and they will land their soldiers on our beaches and strike us in our harbors, and they will rely on the successes they have had against inferior commanders on far-flung outposts, absurd battles fought by men who never had the resources to prevail. But look around you. Look at this city! You know of the training, you have seen it, certainly. Every Japanese citizen, every one! The Americans cannot endure such a foe. They have become accustomed to smothering us like rats in caves, they have butchered our banzai attacks, they crush our feeble defenses in jungles where no man should ever fight a war. There are those in the High Command who continue to believe that all those many islands, all those nations we have subdued are ours still, that any talk of an enemy invasion of Japan is pure folly. But here is truth, my friend. Our empire does not rely on territory, on so many square kilometers of land we have taken from savages. The Japanese empire is right here, on this land, and in these people. In you and in me. The enemy believes that he is gaining victories because he chases outgunned and overmatched troops away from places where we never should have wasted our resources. I find no fault with the Americans. They have responded to our foolish errors by striking back at us. Those in Tokyo who believed we could match their armament were fools. Where we will prevail is in the heart, the soul, the spirit of what this empire means. They advance toward our homes having no idea what awaits them. They have no understanding what will happen to them here. None! And that is where I draw my energy. My father was a samurai, as was yours. They would understand what I do here. They are watching us, fists raised, knowing what will happen next!"

Hamishita felt the words engulfing him, the field marshal's energy flooding the room. Hata shoved a bowl of the noodles aside, seemed disgusted by the wordly presence of something so mundane.

"Perhaps you do not know all that is happening, my friend. I do not fault you for that. You are doing good work, you are healing the sick. You even treat prisoners of war. There are those who would toss those American aircraft crews to the dogs, to have them ripped apart by enraged civilians. I would rather have them fit and healthy. Witnesses, Okiro. They shall be witnesses to what we shall do to their brethren. No one will say of us that we are savages. I am sickened by the brutality of some of our generals. It is one thing to eliminate vermin like the Chinese, or to make good use of the strong backs of the Koreans. But when a man stands to fight you, and you conquer him, he should not be abused for that. A soldier should die like a soldier, whether he is captured or whether he leads his men in a great victorious charge. Either way he is still a soldier. And I want them to know, all of them, I want them to see what kind of soldiers we are. Not just me, not just this army . . . but all of Japan. We are a nation who has risen on the shoulders of the samurai, the code of the Bushido is a part of all of us." He paused, looked hard at Hamishita, smiled. "Physician. A man who heals the broken bodies. Your ancestors will be proud of you for your capable hands and your good heart. But there are many good hearts beating in this city and beyond. We are mobilizing the citizenry in every town, every city. Every man, woman, and child is being taught how to properly defend their country, and their emperor. A soldier is a better soldier when he is given the proper weapon. The same is true for *everyone*. A child, an old woman . . . they already have the spirit, the devotion to their country. But give them a *weapon*, teach them *how* to defend their country, and you have created an unstoppable force. I am one man, I can only do so much, but they sent me to Hiroshima because I do it well. I am truly excited by the future, Okiro. The entire island of Kyushu will become a bloody battlefield. In the countryside, farmers are being shown that precious gasoline does not merely drive a tractor. It makes bombs. They are being taught to create deadly traps for the enemy in every rice paddy, in every field. Every house can become a tomb. Imagine this. A home, armed with explosives, people armed with weapons. They are invaded by an enemy force, and by their own hand, the home explodes, the people inside ignite weapons of horrifying power. The enemy . . . he dies, swallowing his own blood. The civilian, the Japanese farmer, his wife, his child . . . they leave this life and move on with perfect honor. It is poetry, my friend. It is justice, and it is the legacy of this empire. I have never felt such enthusiasm for an attack. And the people! Their enthusiasm is most gratifying of all! Yes, the Americans are coming, and with them comes Divine Opportunity!"

Hamishita stared at his friend with open-mouthed awe, saw the man's hands shaking, the redness in his face.

"What can I do, Shunroku? I will train, as you say."

"No. You will do what you have always done, my friend. There will be wounded, a great many wounded. Repair them, return them to the fight."

The request sounded mundane, Hamishita feeling left out of something far more important.

"But . . . I want to do more. I want to help us win this war."

Hata sat back against a large cushion, smiled.

"Of course you do. Your loyalty to the emperor is well known, far more than you might be aware. But we will not win the war. That was never a possibility, not after the attack on the American fleet, not after we inspired so much patriotism from that race of mongrels. Despite all the bluster of those generals in Tokyo, all the claims of our superiority in numbers and in arms, all those radio broadcasts convincing the people how we devastated the enemy in every fight, there was never any other way this war could end. *Winning* was never an option."

"I don't understand. I thought . . ."

"There is much that I cannot tell you. But four years ago, when the Americans were attacked, there were many among us who knew we had made a fatal error. The emperor . . . he might have known that as well. But in war the loud voices prevail, and the emperor was swallowed by those voices. They are there still, calling for *empire* and *expansion*, denying even now that the enemy is anything more than a fly, easily swatted away. Those people . . . those *generals* are fools."

"But if you do not believe we can win . . . why do we fight?"

"Because we *fight*! Everything is the fight, my friend. Don't you see? It is not important that we defeat the Americans. What matters more is that they shall never defeat us! This war shall end and the foolish generals on both sides shall be swept away by their incompetence, their grand designs. Entire armies will cease to be. It is history, it is nature, it is the *way*. From the ashes new samurai will come, and Japan will rise again and be as she has always been. Oh, the war will end, make no mistake. The guns will fall silent, and all sides shall bury their dead, and there will be mourning and outcries. But no matter any of that, Japan will not lose. Our emperor is *eternal,* our empire is *eternal.* Armies come and go, men die, some with gracefulness, some with shame and cowardice. But Japan will always remain. That is what the Americans do not understand. I know something of their culture. They care a great deal about *winning.* But they will soon learn that wars do not decide winners and losers. Wars are where the honorable go to die, where the samurai meets his just fate. It does not matter that Tokyo has been burned, that our cities suffer their bombs. There is only one victory that is important, and no matter how many men must die, that victory will be achieved. The people know this, they are responding as I had expected. In every place I have been, every place where the training is taking place, even now, as we sit here, the people are rising up for the honor of Japan, for the blessing of the emperor, for the permanence of the empire. That, Doctor, is why we fight."

The lunch had not settled well in his stomach, and the long walk to his home had passed with more than one quick jaunt into the brush. All along the road, there had been many people, all on foot, going about their business with a kind of sad urgency, not quite the raucous enthusiasm for the fight that Field Marshal Hata had seemed to believe bathed every corner of the island. But in the fields Hamishita had been surprised to see assemblies, civilians gathered into formations, just as Hata had described. Not far from his clinic he had passed by a schoolyard, stopped, curious, watching a group of women, a hundred or more, young and old, standing in rows, attentive to the instructions from a soldier. Most carried bamboo poles, sharpened into spears; others held farm implements. But they obeyed the drills with increasing precision, while to one side another soldier called out the chants, the cheers, infusing them with the same astounding spirit Hamishita had heard from the old commander. He had seen children as well, a long column marching down the road past him, grim-faced boys mostly, holding broomsticks and tree limbs up on their shoulders, mimicking the march of riflemen. As he drew closer to his clinic, he had seen familiar faces, a group of old men, listening to a raucous lecture from another soldier, an officer Hamishita had treated in his clinic. The sounds of the mobilization seemed to grow in every crossroads, through every field, the great mission assigned to Field Marshal Hata taking place in every corner of the island, all across the city. Hamishita watched it all, slowed his journey home to absorb what Hata had driven into him, the pure and simple inevitability of what would happen when the Americans came.

He was close to the clinic, his attention suddenly drawn by low thunder. He turned, knew it was another bombing raid, the sounds rising up from south of the city. There are many factories there, he thought. The Americans have no lack of targets. The question rose in his mind now, as it had for many weeks. The Americans bring their bombers with perfect regularity, and yet I have never seen a response from the Imperial Air Force. The anti-aircraft fire is there, always, and sometimes, as today, the gunners are fortunate. He thought of a book he had read, translated from German, a gift from a friend who had traveled to Europe at the start of the war there. He had been fascinated by the exploits of the man they called the Red Baron, had read many stories of the other great aces who flew in the first Great War. We have men like that, surely. The government tells us of great victories in the air, of so many enemy planes shot out of the sky. Finally I saw it for myself, those bombers. And that was truly glorious, watching those huge machines break into pieces, fire and smoke. And parachutes. But we fire so much ammunition from the ground, and so much is wasted, so little success. Where are the Zeroes? It has been so long since they flew past here, great flocks roaring overhead, flying out to meet the enemy in some other place. Am I not supposed to think about this? Am I not supposed to wonder if the war has come to Japan because we have no way to prevent that? There was so much cheering about our conquests, all the islands, the great lands, the Philippines, China, Australia, even America. It was all to be part of the emperor's great destiny. Why has that changed? The Americans have driven our empire back to us, and my friend tells me it is all part of his plan. Hata says we are inviting them into our parlor. But would it not be better if we could destroy them in some far-distant place? Must our cities suffer, the old and the sick, too many for me to care for? He tells me my job now is to return the wounded to the fight. How many wounded will that be? How long will the fight last?

He had thought often of Tokyo, the horrific ravages of the firebombing that had destroyed so much of the grand city. His wife had gone there often, was there now, seeking out relatives, caring for the injured, a task that by all accounts had grown obscenely difficult. Years ago they taught us to fight the fires with buckets, he thought, long lines of citizens hauling water by hand. It seemed like the right thing to do, preparing us, organizing us to deal with a burning building, or a block of homes. But a *city*? Tokyo was a firestorm, and the men with buckets were swept away like so many pieces of straw in a bonfire. The government did not tell us that. I only know because my wife was there to see it. Officially, that disaster never happened. How many people were lost . . . unofficially? How much of what we are told is simply wrong? Hata is my friend, and he chose to share his thoughts with me. I should be honored by that. He is an important man, respected, even by the emperor. He surely knows what he is talking about. He surely knows what is best for us. He would not lie to me. Certainly *he* believes what he says. Can I?

He moved to the door of the clinic now, saw no one waiting for him, a relief. He hesitated, still felt the discomfort in his belly, his stomach in one great knot.

He opened the clinic door, caught the smell of disinfectants, comforting somehow. The front office was empty, and he glanced at the small clock on the desk, after seven, knew that his assistant had gone home. He thought of the young woman's family, her husband in the army, missing for months now, her child barely walking. What will *she* do when the Americans come? Will she stand and face them with a bamboo stick in her hand, while her child stands behind her gripping her skirt? Is that how *their* war will end? There is one certainty, he thought. If the Americans land here, we shall see for ourselves what this war will do to our *people*. Is that not as important as all this talk of empire? Surely the Americans will bring guns and tanks and great pieces of artillery, and their planes will lead the way. And if Field Marshal Hata is to be believed, we should stand proudly and face death with pride that we have fought for the emperor, that merely by the act, we have preserved the empire. I wish I found comfort from that.

He stood in the darkening room, heard talk from beyond the inner door, patients and his staff, the suffering and those who did what they could to ease it. Outside, a new chorus of rumbling began, more bombers, far away, another target, more deaths, one more day in a war he was simply supposed to accept.

29. TIBBETS

HEADQUARTERS, 509TH COMPOSITE GROUP, TINIAN
AUGUST 3, 1945

The thundering impact rattled the Quonset hut, and Tibbets flinched, felt the jarring blast rolling through the offices, his coffee cup spilling, a photograph on the far wall tumbling to the concrete floor. He pulled himself up quickly from the chair, rushed outside, saw the others there already, the darkness giving way to a bright orange glow to the north, the last flames of a great fireball.

"What happened?"

Ferebee responded, the bombardier staring fixed at the sight.

"Never made it past the end of the runway. You could hear the engine fail, sputtering like hell. They never had a chance."

He saw flashing red lights in the distance, fire trucks and ambulances, the emergency vehicles that waited close to the runways for every mission.

"Damn. The thing just lit up?"

Ferebee nodded, the others standing silently, still staring out to where the B-29 had erupted into fire. More of the crews gathered, and one of the others, the tail gunner, Caron, said, "Fuel ignited. Something had to bust up a fuel line, maybe in the wing. If the prop came off . . ."

Ferebee interrupted him.

"Nope. That kind of fire came from the bomb load. Incendiaries. I heard about the mission. It was just like last night. That's mostly all they're using now. General LeMay likes his bonfires."

Tibbets didn't like the talk, felt the gloom, the edginess spreading through all of them.

"Leave it be. That's not us, and it's not our problem. Those birds are old and beat to hell. We don't have that problem. Remember that."

In the darkness, another voice, familiar, the newest member of the crew to arrive on Tinian.

"That's right. Don't give it a second thought. As many hours as those planes have logged, it's a wonder more of 'em don't come apart. But we won't have anything to worry about."

Tibbets moved closer to the man, said, "Not now, Deak. Save it for the briefing."

To the others, Tibbets knew it was one more hint of mystery, this new man arriving along with the C-54s that brought part of the *special cargo* that sat now under intensely heavy security nearby. Tibbets put his hand on the man's shoulder, said, "My quarters. Let's have a chat."

They moved through darkness, away from the others, and Tibbets glanced out toward the guards, ever present, silhouetted against the lights from the distant runways. The sirens had grown quiet, little for any rescue worker to do, the wrecked B-29 likely no more than a pile of ash, along with its crew. The crashes were too common, and he knew that Ferebee was right, that the incendiary bombs meant that a plane's failure, whether from a fuel leak or impact with the ground, could produce a spectacular disaster. The crashes were common during the day as well, but those were the return flights, the planes wounded by anti-aircraft fire, or more likely, mechanical failure. Some of those never made it at all, adding to the casualty counts of those flight crews lost at sea, or the fortunate, rescued by the navy's flying boats or submarines. Some were more fortunate still, finding the landing strips on Iwo Jima and Okinawa.

He led the new man into the Quonset hut, to his own office, then past, to his quarters, where the pipe tobacco waited, along with a bottle of bourbon, a gift from General LeMay. The door was locked, and Tibbets pulled the key from his pocket, pulled it open, allowed the man to move inside, then closed the door behind both of them. Tibbets locked the door again, motioned to a small metal chair.

"Take a seat."

Captain Deak Parsons had been involved with the Manhattan Project from its earliest days, and some had said he was more qualified than General Groves to run the entire affair. He had spent most of the past month at Los Alamos, had witnessed the test explosion of the first bomb, but his role on the primary mission was something brand-new. The bomb's largest mechanism, the cannon that would drive the two pieces of the uranium together, the very act that would produce the atomic explosion, had to rely on the simplest of devices. The cannon was, after all, a cannon, and cannons were no more sophisticated than the explosive charges that made them fire a projectile, any projectile. Every artillery piece required a loader, even if that piece was centered inside the casing of the atomic bomb. Here the man who would load the cannon had been given the official title of *Weaponeer and Ordnance Officer.* Unlike the rest of Tibbets's crew, the man chosen for this job was navy, a captain, William Parsons. Everyone who knew him well knew him as Deak. And those who knew the hierarchy of the crew assembled at Tinian knew that Parsons was also *Commander of the Bomb.* If there was any doubt what that meant, no one had asked.

Parsons was forty-four, older than Tibbets by nearly fifteen years, and was one of the first men involved with the Manhattan Project that Tibbets actually met face-to-face. Whatever technical questions Tibbets or anyone else had about the bomb, Parsons knew the answers. With most of the physicists remaining stateside, Parsons was the one man Tibbets would need close to him throughout the entire mission. That meant that Deak Parsons would be aboard the B-29 when the actual mission began.

"Anything wrong, Paul?"

Tibbets poured from the bottle, handed one shot glass to Parsons, sat back in his own chair.

"I hate the crashes." He paused. "Well, hell, everybody hates crashes. But, dammit, every time my crews see a bird go up in flames, it has to dig their doubts a little deeper. I don't need any little speeches from you explaining all the technical reasons a B-29 can come apart. When the time comes, I'll have enough to keep me busy without my crew sweating out the takeoff."

"I've got news for you, Paul. I'm sweating out the takeoff right now. Anyone with a brain ought to be sweating it out. You know what will happen if we don't clear the ground?"

"Yeah. The mission is scrubbed."

"The whole damn island will be scrubbed. Every tree, every building, every B-29, every crewman. General Groves and I have been debating something for weeks now, and he's sticking to his guns. But I'm sticking to mine. Groves says that most of the physicists want the bomb assembled completely before it goes into the belly of your plane. They're concerned that every little bow should be tied, every screw tightened, before the bomb is handed off to air jockeys. General Groves has to listen to that, but I don't." Parsons lowered his head, said slowly, "I'll mention this in detail at the briefing if you want me to. The flight crew has to know exactly what I'll be doing to the bomb. Once the secret's out, there's no reason to keep anything quiet."

"Agreed. That will only happen when we're airborne."

"I understand that, Paul. But first, we have to *get* airborne. You know damn well that if we go down on takeoff, there are a number of things that can happen, none of them good. But the only way the bomb will ignite is if the two halves of the uranium collide. A crash won't guarantee that. But even without a crash, there are other possible problems. The bomb is going to be wired with two dozen circuits, every kind of sensor, monitoring every electrical signal, every battery . . . well, hell, you know all that. Point is, there's one system I'm not too happy with."

Tibbets leaned forward, the bourbon forgotten.

"What system?"

"The charges that fire the cannon. We've built in a duplication, two separate cordite charges. Obviously, if the cannon fails, so does the bomb. The redundancy is designed to cut the odds of the cannon's failure in half, obviously."

"Obviously."

"But if there is a short circuit, or the bomb jostles in some unexpected way, if turbulence on takeoff tosses the thing back and forth, any of that . . . there's always the chance that one of those cordite charges could be fired accidentally. If we crash-land, a fire in any one of the electrical circuits could ignite the cordite and fire the cannon. If that happens, *we* will be the least of anyone's worries. But I can't see the sense in risking this whole damn island, and several thousand men."

"What do you suggest?"

"Arm the cannon on the plane, once it's airborne, and clear of the island. If there's an accident, the only . . . um . . . *issue* will be how much dust is left of us. But . . . just us."

Tibbets sat back again, could see the perfect logic in Parsons's reasoning.

"Groves doesn't like this idea?"

"Groves is listening to the physicists who insist it will be too difficult to insert the cordite into the bomb once the plane is in the air. Mind you, not one of those boys has ever flown in a B-29, most likely. All it involves is a little . . . maneuvering. Can't say I've ever thought of being a contortionist, but that's what I'll have to do. Once we're clear of the island, I'll climb down into the bomb bay and insert both drums of explosives . . . on the fly, so to speak."

"Have you tried doing that before now?"

"Paul, no one's tried any of this *before now*. I'll work on it on the ground, practice the technique. It has to be this way."

"What about Groves?"

"He'll need to be briefed, I understand that. But you make sure he's briefed so close to takeoff, he won't have time to respond."

Tibbets tried to imagine the scene, Parsons sliding down into the bomb bay, perched on the bomb.

"You'll have to sit on the damn thing."

"Yep. Straddle it."

"Like it's a horse."

"Or a torpedo. Done that a couple times in training. One thing about becoming an engineer, you get to do things most people think are completely nuts."

Tibbets downed the bourbon, looked at Parsons, saw no smile, the man completely serious.

"This qualifies, Deak. But it's your call."

Parsons sipped at the bourbon, then downed it in one quick gulp. He shook his head, seemed to fight off the burn, said, "Ride 'em cowboy."

The choice of target came from LeMay's office. There had been considerable discussion between everyone who had the authority, communications between LeMay and Groves, Hap Arnold and George Marshall. The meetings had continued on both Tinian and Guam, the discussions involving LeMay and Tibbets, along with Parsons, Ferebee, and LeMay's own high-ranking staff, including the much-humbled Butch Blanchard. The list of potential targets had been narrowed to three cities, but the final choice could only be made en route, once the weather conditions over each city were determined. Once Kyoto had been eliminated by the president, the most favored site had become Hiroshima. There were several reasons, but Tibbets understood that militarily that city held a number of important targets, installations and barracks for Japanese troops, as well as a network of smaller factories and plants that continued to provide assistance to the Japanese war effort. But there was one more reason why Hiroshima seemed ideal. The city was situated in something of a valley, mountains framing one edge, so that the blast would be contained, and not allowed to dissipate over a wider, flatter area. Though no one was certain just what the bomb would do, the geography of the city suggested that the blast would be more compact, and thus more effective.

Once the bomb left the bomb bay, the electronic connections would be severed, the bomb then controlled by automatic systems Parsons would be monitoring. The switches that would fire the cannon had to engage while the bomb was still in the air. A ground-impact explosion was out of the question, primarily because the delicate mechanisms that controlled the inner workings of the bomb would be shattered to rubble, making the entire system unpredictable. In the many tests and studies, the various calculations made by mathematicians and physicists, it had been decided that the bomb would be programmed to explode at an altitude of 1,890 feet. At that altitude, the explosion, if it occurred at all, would spread out in a pattern that would cause a wider devastation zone over the heart of the city. Certainly, detonating the bomb at such a precise altitude was an engineering feat all its own, but there was one nagging problem that had plagued the test runs of various dummy bombs from the first training exercises over Utah. No matter the expertise of the men like Parsons, the proximity fuse that would determine exactly when the bomb exploded had been notorious for its failures. During test runs, two of the electronic fuses had ignited immediately after the bomb left the bomb bay, an unnerving experience for a flight crew even with a bomb weighted with concrete and charged with nothing more than TNT. Occasionally the fuse had failed altogether, the dummy bombs never exploding at all. That was certainly better for the crew, but far worse for the entire mission, the "pumpkins" of TNT impacting the Utah desert without any ignition at all. Once the test runs began out of Tinian, the bugs with the proximity fuses seemed to work themselves out. That gave great comfort to the engineers, especially Parsons. But the crews knew that a failure on a training run was a frustrating annoyance. If the fuse failed during the actual mission, the threat to the crew would be a minor problem, compared with the collapse of the entire program. Keeping the Manhattan Project secret would become much more difficult if the Japanese suddenly had pieces of some strange new device littered about the streets of Hiroshima.

In studying the aerial photos of Hiroshima, Tibbets and his bombardier, Tom Ferebee, had noticed a peculiar landmark at the city center, a T-shaped bridge that would be clearly visible at even the highest altitudes. For a bombardier, it was a perfect AP: *Aiming Point.* As long as the skies were relatively clear, everyone involved in the decision agreed that Hiroshima was the primary target, and now Tom Ferebee, the man who would guide the plane into position for their sole opportunity for a successful strike, knew exactly what to look for.

The strike plane for the mission had come from the Martin assembly plant in Omaha, Nebraska. It was a natural decision, based on the problems of airworthiness of so many of the heavily used B-29s, that the primary aircraft chosen for this unique mission would be brand-new, well tested, and would be handpicked by the man who would fly her. Tibbets had gone to Omaha himself, touring the assembly plant, learning more about the nuts-and-bolts construction of the planes than he had ever thought possible. Once his choice had been made, Tibbets had left the job of ferrying the new plane to his co-pilot, Captain Bob Lewis. While Tibbets continued with his various jaunts between Los Alamos, Utah, and Washington, Lewis had piloted the new plane to its training bases, first to Wendover, then on to Tinian. With a myriad of details to occupy every moment of his day, Tibbets had not paid any attention to rumblings from Lewis that Lewis actually expected to fly the primary mission himself. Tibbets was, after all, the man in charge, in command of several crews, all of whom had a specific part of the mission. From plotting the routes of weather observers to putting rescue planes in position, Tibbets had embraced every part of the operation. This planted the notion in Lewis's mind that Tibbets would remain on Tinian as the chief administrator, while Lewis, who had flown the specially equipped B-29 on many practice runs, would actually drop the atomic bomb. It was only when the plane had been given a name, with no input from Lewis, that the controversy had come to a head. For Tibbets it was one more piece of the aggravation trying to keep the cap on the psyches of men who had endured an astonishing amount of stress, training for a mission whose details they did not fully understand. Tibbets set Lewis straight. Bob Lewis would co-pilot the plane, with Tibbets in the pilot's seat.

Throughout the training, the strike plane had undergone modifications that most pilots who flew the big bombers would have found strange, if not completely unnerving. Tibbets himself had observed that a plane without machine guns maneuvered with far more dexterity and could actually reach an altitude nearly four thousand feet higher than a typically armed bomber. The strike plane thus would carry only a pair of fifty calibers in its tail. In addition, there was a panel of electronic switches and gauges installed in proximity to the bomb bay itself, separate from the usual radio and navigational panels. The strange configuration included heavy electrical cables that fed from the panel directly down into the bomb bay. Two dozen wires would feed from these heavy cables and be attached directly to the casing of the bomb itself. There was only one man who understood the importance of the wires and the panel that would monitor them: Deak Parsons.

On the outside of the plane, Tibbets had put into motion the handiwork of the bomber group's chief artist, the man charged with adding the distinctive decorations to each one of the planes. Until now, the strike plane was simply known as Number Eighty-two. But Tibbets knew that every plane in the group carried its primary pilot's distinctive mark, some piece of the man himself, his personality, his background. Tibbets had given that decision of naming the plane a great deal of thought. He recalled Miami, his first flight, the decision to become a pilot, to fly when few around him thought he would survive his first week. The greatest doubt had come from his father, but through all of that, it was his mother who had supported every decision the boy had made, even if it meant putting his life at risk by taking to the air. It was the perfect choice, to thank her, to memorialize her, to dedicate this special plane and its unique mission to the woman who had been his most ardent supporter. Her name was Enola Gay.

30. TIBBETS

The word came with little fanfare, the usual matter-of-fact reporting that every senior officer expected. That word was passed from the offices of General LeMay on Guam, directly to Tinian, first to General Tom Farrell, the ranking officer associated with the Manhattan Project, a man who, like Tibbets, answered only to Leslie Groves. The word had been passed quickly through the offices to Tibbets, who read the teletype dispatch with a hard knot tightening inside him. The report was as simple as every report of its kind. The weather over Japan had cleared, and there was minimal cloud cover over all of the three target cities. The time was now. The mission was a *go.*

NORTH TINIAN FIELD
AUGUST 5, 1945, NOON

They moved at an agonizing crawl, the trailer rolling down into the specially dug pit. It had been a requirement from the first time Tibbets had seen the size of the bomb, that a hole had to be dug, the bomb placed below the surface of the ground, so that the B-29 could then be rolled over the top of it. There was simply no other way to load the massive bomb into the plane's bomb bay. Inside the bomb bay, the shackles that held a typical bomb load were long gone, replaced by a massive steel hook. He watched, moving closer as the bomb was rolled down into the pit. Only then, with the bomb hidden from any distant eyes, was the tarpaulin on the trailer removed. Tibbets stood close beside the pit, stared at the amazing sight, four tailfins encased in a thin steel box, attached at the rear of a massive gunmetal gray trunk, ten feet long, more than two feet wide. The bomb weighed nearly nine thousand pounds, far larger than any single weapon ever dropped by an airplane.

With the bomb now in place in the pit, the *Enola Gay* was towed over the hole, precisely in place, and immediately the technicians were at work, chaining the bomb to the hook in the bomb bay, the crew working in rhythm to raise the bomb slowly upward, until it disappeared into the great plane. Tibbets watched it all, felt frozen to the spot, numbers still running through his head, all of those specifics given him by Oppenheimer, the others. There had been a great deal of talk about just what this weapon would do, and Tibbets had heard often that the bomb carried the punch of twenty thousand tons of TNT. He marveled at that still, though the impact of just what that meant was no more than a fog. There was one piece of the math he could relate to, that this bomb was the equivalent of two hundred thousand of the bombs he had dropped over Europe and North Africa. But the numbers were just exercises now, dancing around the brains of the physicists. Tibbets brought himself back to the moment, watched as the bomb disappeared upward, the bomb bay doors closing, the *Enola Gay* just one more aircraft in a vast field of hundreds more. The plane's mechanics were there, the specially picked men, seeing to the last details of the loading, the men who already knew the plane's every screw. As soon as the bomb bay doors were closed, one more man came forward. He had given barely a nod to Tibbets, had boarded the plane holding a hard stare that told anyone around him to leave him be. Tibbets complied, knew that Deak Parsons was headed straight for the inside of the bomb bay, and in short minutes would begin practicing the arming of the cannon inside the bomb, a job that no one had ever attempted. Tibbets still watched the plane, the tractor's empty trailer now up and out of the pit, most of the men moving off to tackle another task, seeing to the other planes in the group. But Tibbets stayed put, bathed in the warmth and the urgent silence, knew that inside the bomb bay the heat would be stifling, getting worse by the minute, and that a sweating Parsons would suffer for it, cutting and nicking fingers, drawing blood and cursing as he probed and twisted and clamped wires together, inserting the dummy canisters into the cylinder until they were perfectly situated. Then Parsons would pull the canisters out, disconnect the wiring, and do it all again. He would keep up the practice until there was no time left. Tibbets glanced at his watch, a little after noon. You've got a couple hours, Deak. Then I need you.

He turned toward the Quonset huts, saw the guards, knew there would be more, MPs mostly, and others, some of them civilians. Not all the security for the project had been military, guards watching guards. There were more civilians there as well. Scientists had been arriving for the past couple of days, sent by Dr. Oppenheimer to see the bomb's final journey for themselves. More than one of those men came with a cloak of arrogance that he would actually take the ride, see the bomb's delivery for himself. But Tibbets knew better. Even on Tinian there were any number of men who had the authority to order themselves aboard any bomber at any time. But not this time. The crew was his, and the *passengers* were limited to just two, Parsons and his one assistant, the men who had one very specific job to do.

He walked away, but not far, was drawn back to the plane, examined her once more. He'd noticed the fine work of the artist, the name painted near the snout with simple black letters. On the tail of the plane was painted a large *R* inside a black circle. That was Tibbets's decision as well, to blend the *Enola Gay* in with the hundreds of other B-29s that spread out on the fields across Tinian. There would be nothing to single her out, no special insignia to attract a Japanese saboteur, or, should the plane go down in Japan, nothing to tell the enemy that the plane was anything but one more unfortunate bomber who would not return home. He felt satisfied with that, but looked again toward the bomb bay, pictured the feverish work Parsons was trying to accomplish. Tibbets had always admired passion, and knew this navy captain had more than his share. Tibbets shook his head, thought, nothing else for me to do out here. It'll be time for the briefing soon, and I'd rather not go in there smelling like I just ran a couple hundred laps around this field. He started away from the plane, and the question came to him, nagging him yet again, one of those decisions over which Tibbets had no say. The answer would be found at Los Alamos most likely, and Tibbets knew it was a question he would have to ask Dr. Oppenheimer, or even General Groves. Surely someone would have the answer. He walked toward the shade, toward his quarters, thought, largest bomb ever dropped on an enemy. Why in hell would they call this thing *Little Boy?*

From Los Alamos to Washington, from Guam to Tinian, the briefings were many and often, intense information sessions, conveying news or engaging debate. For months the meetings had occupied the time and the thoughts of every man who had any association with the Manhattan Project. At each briefing some of the men already knew the details of what they were to discuss, others arriving at a briefing only to learn something they had not even imagined before. It had been the same with the men of the 509th, the pilots and their crews finally learning the date and time of their mission, and what each crew would be expected to do. With the final go-ahead for the mission, Tibbets had scheduled one last briefing, this one for the flight crews of the various B-29s who would take part. Three of those would take off an hour ahead of the *Enola Gay*, serving as weather observers, to confirm the conditions over each of the target cities, Hiroshima, Kokura, and Nagasaki. A fourth would fly only as far as Iwo Jima, then land and taxi to a position close beside a pit in the ground that had been dug exactly as the one on Tinian. That plane, the *Top Secret*, would serve as a spare, in the event some mechanical trouble developed on the *Enola Gay* on the outbound portion of the flight. An additional plane would trail the *Enola Gay* by several miles for the primary purpose of dropping sensor equipment by parachute after the bomb's blast, gathering data for the scientists, several of whom were allowed aboard the trailing plane to witness the immediate aftermath several miles shy of the final target. Tibbets also knew that on that plane, *The Great Artiste*, cameras would be in high gear, every man who had one certain to use up as much film as he could capturing the moment and its aftermath.

The final briefing began an hour before midnight on August 5, the first time Tibbets revealed to the flight crews details of the mission, which, rumors aside, the men knew very little about. For the first time, the men were told of the destructive power of the single bomb that hung in the bomb bay of the *Enola Gay*. The response was much as Tibbets expected, silence, the men digesting the numbers tossed out at them by Deak Parsons, numbers that were of such overwhelming magnitude that Tibbets knew they would respond as he had, no one really able to grasp just what kind of power the bomb held. No matter how many charts and graphs the physicists displayed, none of the men who had dropped bombs on enemy targets could fathom just how much more potent this single weapon would be. As if to emphasize the point, Parsons began to distribute goggles to the crew of the *Enola Gay*, and the others, the men who would be closest to the actual detonation of the bomb. The men had their own, of course, the usual flight goggles to protect anyone from any frigid blast of air. But these were not flight goggles at all. The lenses were thick and dark, welder's goggles. The instructions were simple. When the bomb leaves the bomb bay, put them on and keep them on. There would be no exceptions.

When the briefing concluded, there was one more detail, a signal from Tibbets, the men surprised to see their chaplain, Bill Downey, moving up to the platform. Downey had done as Tibbets asked, and he pulled a paper from his jacket pocket, the men quick to understand why Downey was there. In the stark silence, Downey looked at Tibbets, saw the nod, Tibbets knowing that even those men who gave the chaplain little heed would be attentive now. Downey cleared his throat, seemed nervous, read from the paper:

> Almighty Father, Who will hear the prayer of them that love Thee, we pray Thee to be with those who brave the heights of Thy Heaven, and who carry the battle to our enemies. Guard and protect them, we pray Thee, as they fly their appointed rounds. May they, as well as we, know Thy strength and power, and armed with Thy might, may they bring this war to a rapid end. We pray Thee that the end of the war may come soon, and that once more we may know peace on earth. May the men who fly this night be kept safe in Thy care, and may they be returned safely to us. We shall go forward trusting in Thee, knowing that we are in Thy care now and forever. In the name of Jesus Christ. Amen.

After the ninety-minute briefing, there had been a preflight breakfast, a menu chosen mostly by Tibbets himself. For the first time in many weeks, the men were given real eggs, genuine pork sausage, rolled oats, and apple butter, with all the coffee and cold milk the men could hold. But Tibbets knew that, despite the wonderful aroma of the food offered them, his own lack of appetite would be no different from the appetites of the flight crews. They had become accustomed to eating preflight meals at ridiculous hours, and usually the food had been just one more detail, most of the men scarfing down whatever was offered them. But whether it was the briefing, or the gravity of the chaplain's prayer, the crews spent a tedious half hour in the mess hall they called the Dogpatch Inn, mostly poking and prodding the food on their plates, some of them not eating at all. The silence in the mess hall was one more sign that these men were still absorbing the shock that, after so many months of dead secrecy, after so much security and training with fake bombs and milk runs over nonexistent targets, the real mission was about to begin.

The coffee was hot, and Tibbets gulped it down, his fourth cup, pushed the full plate away, knew he might regret not eating much else. But on board the plane there would be the usual boxed rations, nothing different about that. What little talk there had been in the mess hall was wrung out of the men around him, no one able to hide their nervousness. He scanned the tables, saw no one eating, some men checking their watches, a contagious gesture. At one end of the hall Tibbets saw the cook, Sergeant Easterly, his hands on his hips, a look of obvious disappointment on his frowning face. Tibbets rose, said, "Don't worry about it, Elliott. When we get back, these boys will be ready for a full-blown feast. See to it."

The sergeant nodded, grumbling quietly, forced to accept that all his work preparing the *special meal* had been mostly for naught.

"Yes, sir. Will do."

The mess sergeant moved out of the room, a prearranged order, the man no part of any briefing. Tibbets moved away from the table, others taking his cue, rising with a clatter of metal chairs. The crews of the three observation planes moved more quickly, their takeoff time set for 1:30 A.M., a full hour ahead of the scheduled start for the strike plane. They passed by him, some nodding to him, almost no one speaking. Tibbets was surprised by their tension, their part of the mission seemingly harmless, a casual flight over targets that likely wouldn't even respond to their presence at all. The Japanese had long understood that above thirty thousand feet, their anti-aircraft fire was virtually meaningless, and though larger formations of the great planes would still draw fire, single bombers would attract almost no attention at all. But the tension in the men's faces told him how involved they felt in the mission, a brief moment of gratification. No one feels left out, he thought. They know how important they are, every damn one of them.

"Paul? This a good time?"

Tibbets turned, saw the group's flight surgeon, Don Young, holding a small box. But Tibbets knew exactly what it held, a conversation with the doctor days before. Tibbets said nothing, followed the doctor to one corner of the room. The box was opened now, and Tibbets saw the capsules, knew that Young had made a precise count. There were twelve, one for each member of the *Enola Gay*'s crew.

Young made a faint smile, said, "Hope you don't have to use these."

Tibbets took the box, closed the lid, slipped it into his pocket.

"Not your concern right now. But the odds are in our favor."

He realized Parsons was watching the scene, standing beyond the closest table. Parsons nodded grimly, had been a part of that first conversation, and so was the only man among the crew who knew what the doctor had given Tibbets. In the event the *Enola Gay* was to go down over Japan, the contents of the box would be distributed to each man, with an order that Tibbets desperately hoped he never had to give. The capsules were cyanide.

Parsons moved close now, said in a low voice, "Can I have mine?"

Tibbets opened the box again, fished one of the capsules out, saw Parsons hold out a small matchbox, and Tibbets dropped the pill inside, the box disappearing into Parsons's pocket.

Beside him, the doctor said, "It's better than putting a bullet in your head. Just keep that in mind. No pain at all."

Tibbets held up a hand, didn't need any more of those kinds of observations.

"Thank you, Doctor. I don't plan on having to take advantage of either option."

TARMAC, NORTH FIELD, TINIAN
AUGUST 6, 1945, 1:45 A.M.

His crew had moved back through their quarters, quickly retrieving their flight gear, Tibbets not forgetting to grab a healthy dose of pipe tobacco. The jeep was waiting for him, the driver matter-of-fact, just another journey hauling four of the men from one aircrew toward their aircraft. But the black of the night was split wide by a vast sea of light, and Tibbets was stunned to see that the *Enola Gay* was bathed in spotlights, a far too obvious center of attention. He glanced into the darkness, knew that the island still had its Japanese holdouts, abandoned, desperate men who would scamper through dark fields to inflict whatever damage they could, or steal anything not secured. My God, he thought. They're getting a hell of a show tonight. I guess . . . sit back and enjoy it, boys. This is like some damn Hollywood movie premiere. The shock passed, and Tibbets felt annoyance rising, the jeep pulling up close to what was now a massive crowd. He saw cameras, perched on tripods, the popping of flashbulbs, eyes turning his way, calls for him to speak. There were many reporters, the event prearranged by General Farrell. In a few short hours, there would likely be no need for secrecy, and Farrell knew, as did Tibbets, that these men could take all the pictures they wanted, since for now there was no way they could share them with anyone beyond Tinian. What Tibbets had not expected was the carnival atmosphere that surrounded his plane.

He saw Farrell now, the general pushing through the crowd, men reluctantly making way. Farrell held out his hand, and Tibbets accepted it.

"Best of luck, Colonel. This is a hell of a moment. Hell of a moment. We could end the war, you know."

Behind Farrell, men were scribbling furiously, pencils on paper, jotting down his words. Tibbets didn't know what to say, suddenly didn't feel like giving these men anything to jabber about.

"Thank you, sir. Excuse me, I have to make the preflight checks."

"You bet. Don't let anyone get in your way."

Tibbets moved toward the plane, MPs struggling to hold back the eager reporters, some of them in uniform, the official army photographers. Others called out to him still, hoping for a photo of his face, some comment he would offer. Questions came as well, and he ignored that, tried to focus, went through the preflight routine in his mind, the automatic ritual, checking every cowling, every hatchway, the tire pressures, examining the outside of the four engines and the pavement beneath them, searching for oil or hydraulic leaks, any sign that all was not in perfect readiness for take-off. He moved around the enormous plane, tried to avoid being blinded by the brightest lights, moved to the hatch, saw Parsons pressed back against one of the fat balloon tires by a photographer.

"Just smile! Show me some teeth!"

Parsons seemed terrified, slid away from the man with a curse, and Tibbets saw that his belt was missing the forty-five. Tibbets waited for him, said in a low voice, "You need a sidearm."

Parsons looked down, cursed again.

"Forgot it. What do I do?"

Tibbets searched the crowd, saw one of the MPs watching him, waved the man over. The face was familiar, and Tibbets said, "Nick, I need your forty-five."

Parsons pointed sheepishly to his empty belt, and the MP complied immediately.

"Here you go, sir. If you don't mind . . . love to get it back. It'll be a hell of a souvenir."

Parsons hooked the holster onto his belt, said, "Yeah, fine."

Tibbets gave the MP a slap on the arm, said nothing, followed Parsons to the hatch, then both men were up and into the plane.

Parsons stood for a long second, seemed to get his breath, and Tibbets was close behind him, said, "You okay?"

"Yeah. Jesus. What a circus. Didn't expect that."

"Leave it to generals to make a damn show. Farrell's a good guy, but he likes to get his name in the paper. Hasn't been much chance of that before now. Let's go to work."

Parsons settled in at the special instrument console, his assistant there already. Tibbets had seen the gashes on Parsons's hands, fresh cuts from the practice at arming the bomb. He moved into the cockpit, thought, Deak will be fine. We'll all be fine. Just . . . do the job. Lewis was already in the co-pilot's seat, acknowledged Tibbets with a quick nod, no smile.

"Okay, Bob, let's go through the checklist. I'm ready to find some sky."

NORTH FIELD, TINIAN, RUNWAY ABLE
AUGUST 6, 1945, 2:45 A.M.

He ignored Lewis now, no banter between them, nothing at all. Tibbets kept his thoughts inside him, a stream of words, thoughts of the amazing weapon in the belly of his plane, the length of the runway, any detail on the checklist they might have missed. Eleven months, he thought. All that training . . . for this. Well, don't screw it up.

"Dimples Eight Two to North Tinian Tower. Ready for takeoff on Runway Able."

The response was immediate.

"Dimples Eight Two. Dimples Eight Two. Cleared for takeoff."

Tibbets released the brakes, the plane easing forward, slowly, far more slowly than he was used to. Just another takeoff, he thought. Just one more time. Outside the row of runway lights was something new, more lights blinking red. It was a fleet of emergency vehicles, fire trucks mostly, spread out the entire length of the mile-and-a-half strip. Wishful thinking, he thought. This thing noses in, those boys won't have much to do. They're just as likely to go up with us.

The lights on each side of the runway were moving past more quickly now, the plane's speed increasing, and he stared straight ahead, knew exactly where the end of the runway would be, and how fast he had to go to bring the plane airborne. He felt the sluggishness beneath him, more thoughts rolling through his brain, knew they were carrying four hundred pounds less fuel than usual, any effort to make the plane lighter. That was a damn good idea, he thought. Come on, just a little more speed. They were less than a thousand feet from the end now, and he felt the yoke in his hands move, knew it was Lewis, the man sensing a problem, pulling back, trying to lift the plane off the ground. No! Tibbets jammed the yoke forward, the clear signal to his co-pilot, just a little more! The end of the runway was a thick row of light in front of him, closer now, the plane hugging the ground, Lewis staring fixed, Tibbets as well, feeling the plane's gentle bounce, the nose starting to rise. He kept the wheels on the ground, the roar of the engines a part of him, filling his brain, the shouting in his ear, his own, *a little more* . . . The lights were right in front of him now, and he eased the yoke back, the wheels rising, clearing the lights by a few feet. The plane was flying now, climbing, and he felt the knot inside of him release, realized he was breathing heavily, glanced at Lewis, saw wide-eyed terror on the man's face. Lewis sat back in his seat, didn't look at him, and Tibbets nodded to himself, satisfied, thought, just had to make sure, that's all. He studied the altimeter, knew there was no rush, no need to reach altitude yet. The skies were total darkness, the moon not yet rising, and he studied the instrument panel, the pressures, the levels, the plane's attitude. He focused again on the altimeter, passing through two thousand feet, a steady climb, the roar of 'the engines constant, no shudder, no skipping, nothing to cause any of the crew concern. No machine guns, he thought. Great damn idea. Makes this a hell of a lot smoother. The plane continued its climb, and he glanced at his watch, saw that a quick ten minutes had passed, looked to the compass, the heading, three-three-eight degrees, knew that already Saipan would be beneath them. Jap soldiers still there, he thought, probably hear us going over. Some guy in a hilltop hole looking up, trying to see, maybe taking a potshot with his worn-out rifle. Not tonight, pal. By tomorrow, you might not have a war to fight.

He knew that Parsons was already down in the bomb bay, helped by the man chosen to assist him, Lieutenant Maurice Jeppson. I hope somebody put fresh batteries in his damn flashlight. He thought of using the intercom, a progress report. Nope, let him be. It took him about a half hour to do it in practice. Don't pressure him any more than he's pressuring himself. If there's a problem, he'll tell me. Or . . . we might never even know. One big damn puff of smoke.

The voice came in his ear now, Parsons.

"Working on it, Colonel. Tight squeeze . . . ow . . . dammit."

"I'll omit that last part."

Tibbets keyed the radio mike now, the prearranged transmission to General Farrell, a radio linkup that had been made to the communications center on Tinian, where the group of scientists waited for any kind of information Parsons could give them. Tibbets knew that Parsons was working from a checklist that included eleven separate steps, and as Parsons completed each one, he kept Tibbets informed. In turn Tibbets radioed Farrell, using their agreed-upon code word for the completion of each step. Tibbets tried to imagine the scene in the communications center, a dozen scientists scribbling frantically to capture every word, some of them already thinking of the academic papers they would write, or maybe some interview to get their name in the paper. Not much chance of that for a while. Not sure I'd want that kind of publicity while there were Jap agents hanging around. Some idiot physicist goes back to his university and starts prancing around like a big wheel and some Jap sympathizer might take exception, maybe a pistol shot at close range. Not my problem, I guess. Not anymore.

"Ow . . . dammit. Bloody hell."

"Easy, Deak. Take a breath. You got plenty of light?"

"Aye. Roger. Jesus, just hold her steady. This damn thing rides like a hobby horse."

"Ride 'em cowboy."

The messages continued with each success on the checklist, a slow countdown. Then, in his ear, Tibbets heard a strange crackle from the radio receiver.

"Radio, what's going on?"

The response came from Private First Class Richard Nelson, the lowest-ranking man in the plane.

"Sir, we've lost Tinian. We're flying too low to hold the signal."

Tibbets knew it was one very minor annoyance, keeping the plane beneath five thousand feet, so that Parsons would not require an oxygen mask in the bomb bay.

"Roger that."

Several minutes passed, Tibbets nervously tapping his fingers on the yoke. Then Parsons spoke again.

"Almost done. I want disability pay. Cut two fingers and ripped my shirt."

"I'll buy you the shirt. Just get the job done."

Tibbets could hear the tension in Parsons's voice, didn't comment. Just let him do the job his own way. He'll tell me if he needs anything. At least it's a smooth flight, but damn, I wouldn't want to take this trip riding bareback on that son of a bitch.

After a long minute, there was commotion behind him, and Tibbets turned, was surprised to see Parsons, sweat on his face, a broad smile.

"We're armed."

Parsons didn't wait for a compliment, moved back toward his own instrument panel. Tibbets glanced at his watch. Three twenty-five. The radio had been silent completely, and Tibbets knew that the other planes had taken off behind him, were all heading for the rendezvous point over Iwo Jima. The weather observers were far out in front, and nothing had come from them as well. Silence was a good sign, no problems, nothing mechanical. He scanned the gauges again, every one reading what he expected to see. He let out a breath, realized he was sweating, glanced over at Lewis. His co-pilot had said nothing at all, and Tibbets thought of the takeoff, the man's glimmer of panic. It's okay, Bob. You did it by the book. I used up every last foot because . . . well, I thought it was the best thing to do. I'm not gonna ream you out for it. He was already tired of the various comments he had overheard, grumbles from Lewis's own crew, the men who had flown with him when Lewis commanded various training missions, those men now left back on Tinian. I'm not in the mood for that, he thought. He wants to talk about it, we can do it later. Right now . . . we've got a lot of time to kill. A nap ought to be good. But I oughta check on those boys in the back, let 'em know I haven't forgotten about 'em.

"Take the yoke, Bob. I'm heading back."

Lewis nodded, still no words, and Tibbets pulled himself up from the seat, moved out past the others, Parsons and Jeppson. He looked toward the low light in the nose of the plane, the navigator's desk, Van Kirk writing in his log, keeping details of time and location all throughout the flight. Beside him, Ferebee, the bombardier, was reclining in his seat, smoking a cigarette. Farther aft, the radioman, Nelson, seemed to jump when he saw Tibbets, and Tibbets saw a small book in the man's hand, some kind of novel. Nelson glanced at the novel, as though Tibbets had caught him in some kind of illegal activity, and Tibbets said, "Easy, Private. We've got a lot of time right now. Relax as best you can."

"Yes, sir. Thank you, sir."

Tibbets was at the tunnel now, and he ducked low, took a long breath. The passageway to the rear of the plane was thirty feet long and less than two feet in diameter. No fat tail gunners, he thought. That's for sure. He was on his knees now, pulled himself with his elbows, making his way through the tight space. He reached the far end, saw a faint glow of light, four men gathered, one of them the tail gunner, George Caron. There was no surprise there, no reason yet for the tail gunner to be in his position at the tip of the plane's tail. Tibbets pulled his legs out of the tunnel, sat, realized that the radio countermeasures officer, Jake Beser, was sound asleep, his body curled up right on the flight deck. Close beside him, Joe Stiborik, the radar man, said, "Want me to wake him up?"

Tibbets shook his head, knew already that Beser could sleep anywhere and everywhere, and usually did. But Beser's job would come later, and Tibbets knew there would be no sleeping in the forward station where Beser would monitor any Japanese radar stations that tried to fix a lock on the plane's position. Tibbets pulled the pipe from his pocket, felt the plane veer slightly, a quiver magnified this far aft. He knew it was Lewis, engaging the automatic pilot. I suppose, Tibbets thought, he needs a nap too. Tibbets looked at the others, said, "All right, so you boys have been told we're hauling a hell of a weapon. You figure out the rest?"

Caron laughed, said, "You testing us, Colonel? We learned pretty quick that we get in trouble with security for thinking anything. I'm not gonna even guess."

"We're on our way, Sergeant. You can guess anything you want."

"Is it a chemist's nightmare? I read about some Brits working on a superweapon, some kind of chemical thing."

Tibbets was surprised by the question, thought, chemical weapons. Well, that makes sense, if you don't know anything else.

"No, but you're warm."

Caron seemed satisfied to leave it at that and Tibbets tamped the tobacco down in the pipe, pulled out his lighter. He paused, thought, no, wait until you get back up front. Tight space back here, and not everybody likes pipes. He stretched, looked back toward the tunnel, and he felt a hand tugging his pant leg. It was Caron.

"Are we splitting atoms today, Colonel?"

In all the briefings, in all the details revealed to the crews, neither Tibbets nor anyone else had used the word *atom*. I'll be damned, Tibbets thought.

"That's about it, Sergeant. I knew you were a sharp bird, but I wouldn't have thought anybody would have made that guess."

Caron shrugged, a hint of a smile on his face.

"As long as I'm guessing, sir. Oh . . ." He reached into the pocket of his flight suit, brought out a small camera. "That reporter, the one from New York . . ."

"Bill Laurence?"

"Yes, sir. He was pretty ticked off he couldn't make the flight, so he gave me his camera. Told me to take as many pictures as I could."

Laurence was one of the very select few allowed on Tinian, had a serious reputation as a writer of scientific articles. He had caught the attention of the Manhattan Project planners for a story he had done for the *Saturday Evening Post* before the war, a study of the experiments being done in Europe dealing with atomic fission. Tibbets knew that Laurence had cajoled everyone possible for a seat on the plane, but Tibbets would have no idle passengers. Instead he had agreed that his co-pilot, Lewis, would keep a log for Laurence, jotting down observations on a pad that the reporter could later use to write his own story of the mission. That assumed, of course, that the mission was going to be a success.

"Doesn't look too fancy. I figured a guy like Laurence would have some complicated super-camera. You know how to work that thing?"

"He just told me to push this button, and keep pushing it. Guess he figures that with me in the tail, I'll have a good view."

"Not sure how good a view you'll have with those goggles on. You got that, Sergeant? Don't forget the damn goggles. All of you. I've heard talk this thing might blind us all, goggles or not. No chances, right?"

They all nodded, Caron slipping the camera in his pocket.

"Yes, sir."

Tibbets moved away, made his way forward through the tunnel. The rest of the crew had very little to do, the skies still full dark, broken only by a hint of moonlight, low on the horizon. He passed by Parsons, sitting at his strange instrument panel, saw a row of lights, all green. He didn't ask, thought, unless he tells me otherwise, I've got to figure green is good.

He moved back into the cockpit, Lewis not looking at him, squeezed himself into his seat again. He saw a flicker of movement, Lewis writing on the pad Laurence had given him, and Tibbets thought, just tell the story. Tibbets turned slightly in the seat, thought of the naps that he often took back by the tunnel. Not tonight. Get some sleep, but figure out how to do it up front. You need to stay in the damn cockpit. This is a little . . . special.

OVER THE PACIFIC OCEAN
AUGUST 6, 1945, 8:00 A.M.

There had been very little sleep, the glimmer of sunlight to the east sweeping away any notion of a nap. He looked at Lewis, saw the co-pilot writing on the reporter's pad, felt a hint of curiosity, but the skies were full blue now, and Tibbets knew there was far more to do.

The flight thus far had been made at low altitude, but Tibbets knew that no matter the target, the bomb run would be made at 30,700 feet. He ignored Lewis, gunned the throttles slightly, eased back on the yoke just enough to feel the plane begin its climb. Lewis stopped writing, glanced at his watch, said nothing. The climb took several minutes, and Tibbets felt the impatience, wanted to goose the throttles more, held himself back, no need to waste fuel. He stared at the altimeter, desperate impatience, saw the needle rotating like a second hand of a broken clock, moving around the dial far too slowly.

"Three zero thousand."

It was the first word from Lewis in hours, and Tibbets responded, "I see it. Leveling out at three zero and seven hundred."

"Pilot, Radio. Coded message received from *Straight Flush.*"

"Hold on. I'm on my way."

Tibbets crawled up from his seat, saw anxiousness on Lewis's face, yep, I know. Now we learn something. He moved down toward the radio desk, Nelson reading a pad of his own writing. Tibbets leaned over his shoulder, saw Y-3, Q-3, B-2, C-1.

"Sir?"

"Easy as pie, Private. Cloud cover is less than three-tenths coverage at all altitudes. He's giving us advice too. Bomb the primary target. Guess I already knew that."

Tibbets straightened, felt a nervous rush, moved back to the cockpit, settled into his seat. He cleared his throat, keyed the intercom, said, "Boys, it's Hiroshima."

He saw Lewis point silently, straight ahead, and Tibbets saw it now, the first land they had seen. He knew the maps by heart, thought of Dutch Van Kirk, his navigator. Damn good work. That's Shikoku. And right past . . . the Iyo Sea. Son of a bitch, we're right on target.

He felt his hands gripping the yoke, couldn't help the sweat that gathered inside his flight suit. He keyed the intercom again, said, "Deak, those lights still green?"

"Armed and ready."

The clouds were scattered beneath them, no response from any Japanese gunners on the island below. Nope, we're just small fish up here. Pay us no mind. He glanced at his watch, 8:05, stared out through the windshield, the strip of water passing below, and now, through the wisps of clouds he saw a glimmer of sunlight coming from the ground, a scattering of reflections from the morning sun. They were buildings. It was a city. It was Hiroshima.

"Co-pilot, bombardier, navigator. I want confirmation. Do you all agree that the city in front of us is Hiroshima?"

The confirmation was immediate and unanimous, and Tibbets felt his hands gripping harder to the yoke. In his ear came the voice of Van Kirk, the navigator.

"IP dead ahead. Time to AP, ten minutes."

"Roger."

Tibbets knew the *Initial Point* from the many maps and photos they had studied, a point of geography obvious even from their altitude. The *Aiming Point* was drilled into him as well—the T-shaped bridge. He waited for Van Kirk's voice, ticking off loud seconds in his brain, and it came now.

"IP."

Tibbets turned the yoke, engaged the ailerons and rudder, turning the *Enola Gay* in a sharp left-hand turn, watched the compass, leveled out, heard Van Kirk, verifying what his own compass said.

"Course two seven two degrees. Speed two zero zero."

"Roger. Two seven two. Speed two zero zero."

"AP in ten minutes."

"Roger. Ten minutes."

"Winds south at ten."

Tibbets felt a stab of alarm. The prevailing winds over this part of Japan came from the west, and he cursed silently, realized Parsons was standing just behind him, nothing left for the man to do. Tibbets said, "Dammit, Navigator, give me a course correction."

"Working on it, sir."

The voice was Ferebee's, the bombardier fully aware how to correct for any variation in wind speed. Tibbets waited, agonizing seconds, heard Van Kirk's voice now.

"Correct to two six four."

Tibbets eased the plane slightly to the left, stared at the slow turn of the compass, said, "Roger, two six four."

Ferebee's voice came now, the man agitated, high-pitched, Tibbets not concerned, knew that even the most professional bombardier would feel *this* strain.

"Okay, I've got the bridge."

Van Kirk said, "No question about it."

Tibbets strained to see, knew both men had a far clearer view from the Plexiglas nose cone of the plane. He saw it now, the distinct T-shaped bridge, heard Van Kirk again, "Ninety seconds."

Tibbets said, "Bombardier, it's all yours."

He lifted his hands slowly from the controls, felt the plane quiver slightly, Ferebee taking control. Behind him, Parsons leaned low, said, "Forty-seven seconds. Remember that. From the time the bomb leaves, you've got forty-seven seconds to get the hell out of here."

"You get out of here! Get back to your damn lights. I know what to do!"

There was no time for an apology, Parsons backing away, and Tibbets wouldn't think of that now, knew no one would be pissed off by a short temper, not now. Tibbets sat back, gazed out across the vast sweep of the city, scanned skyward, no sign at all of enemy planes, no anti-aircraft fire. He had a burst of thought, keyed the intercom again, said, "Goggles. All of you. Put 'em on!"

Tibbets had his own resting up on his forehead, would wait until the final second. He knew Ferebee was working intensely with the bomb sight, the man wonderfully good at his job. Come on, Tom. One more job. That's all.

The tone came now, a high-pitched sound generated by one of the electrical connections to the bomb itself. Tibbets was startled, scolded himself nervously, knew to expect it. It was one small part of Parsons's instrument panel, triggered by a connection that had been strung to the bomb sight, controlled by Ferebee. When the bomb dropped, the wires would pull free, and the tone would quit. But Tibbets knew that when the tone began, there was one meaning. One minute to go.

Tibbets stared ahead, nothing else to do, felt a hand on his shoulder, Parsons, the hand letting go. All this time. All this work. Everything . . . and then he heard the violent rush of air, the bomb bay doors opening, and in an instant, the radio tone was silent. The plane suddenly lurched upward, the voice of Ferebee in his ear.

"Bomb away."

Tibbets took the controls again, paused for a glance at his watch, nine-fifteen and seventeen seconds. He pulled hard on the yoke now, the plane in a sudden steep bank to the right, the compass spinning, Tibbets struggling to hold tight to the yoke. The plane bounced, the tail settling downward, just as it always had, the *Enola Gay* fighting the unnatural angle, Tibbets fighting with her to prevent a full roll, keeping the tail up just enough to avoid the stall. He slipped one hand from the yoke, a quick jab at his face, the welder's glasses down over his eyes, total blackness, the instruments gone completely. Son of a bitch! He raised the goggles again, just enough, had to see, watched the compass, thought, hell I'll be going the other way. Forty-seven damn seconds . . . the image of the tail gunner flashed in his mind . . . Caron, you jackass, you better not forget those goggles. How many seconds has it been?

"Tail gunner! See anything?"

"Not yet . . . oh . . ."

The cockpit suddenly filled with a soft glow, and Tibbets felt his heart racing, felt a tingling sensation, had a sudden metallic taste in his mouth, thought, what the hell? He fought the distraction, kept his eyes on the panel, straightened the flight of the plane, glanced to the side, the blue sky changing to pink and purple, engulfing the plane, bathing the cockpit in eerie light. In the tail Sergeant Caron stared through the welder's glasses, tried to make out any detail, blinded by the light of ten suns, and he pushed the buttons on the camera, again and again.

31. HAMISHITA

Through the long night he had slept close to his wife, the tragedy of her trip to Tokyo hard on both of them. For more than a week she had sought out missing relatives, learning that two were confirmed dead, others not heard from at all. The refugees from the great city had been fleeing the destruction there for weeks, seeking refuge in the countryside, some with family, some homeless, traveling anywhere they could find food and shelter. Her return the evening before had brought a flood of tears, triggered mainly by the sight of her husband in his surgical gown, his hands thick with blood. The tears had been unusual, the product of so many days sifting through wreckage, the impromptu need for a nurse for some injured stranger. It had been nothing different from what she had seen before, and yet the magnitude of it had seemed to overwhelm her, the outpouring of her emotions triggered by little more than her husband with blood on his hands. He had tried to soothe her with words that belied his appearance, that he was the fortunate one, they both were, *healers,* in a place where so much was needed. On this one night he had to concede that the healing was not as helpful as it might have been. More often he spent his time in the clinic ministering to the injured, whether soldier or civilian, usually some wound from the collapse of a building, a direct hit from an American bomb. But there had been no bombing raids on the city for the past two days, and she had arrived just as Hamishita had completed an emergency cesarean on a pregnant woman. What should have been a small glimmer of light in a dark world had instead been a tragedy all its own. The baby was stillborn, the mother barely surviving. As a trained nurse, his wife had seen as much blood and as much tragedy as he had, but the death of the baby was one more knife in her emotions, one more weight for a woman who had struggled through too much of her own.

As quickly as possible, he had closed the clinic for the night, changing from the surgical garb, removing any sign of the sadness of his own day. They had eaten an evening meal in silence and candlelight. It had been common for some time, all of Hiroshima blacked out, logical precautions against an American raid. With the darkness swallowing the city and everything around them, she had pulled him to the bed, a woman who needed the secure arms of her husband. He had obliged her, had kept himself awake while he tried vainly to soothe her tears. His last thoughts were of the morning, that he would make some effort to find some flowers, something cheerful, to wake her to color and light and a smile. But his own exhaustion was overwhelming, and when he woke, it was to daylight. The shock of that had pulled him from his bed in a quick scramble, and he had moved outside to the comforting warmth still in his nightclothes. The day was bright blue, and he thought still of the flowers, knew she would not sleep late, would rise to find him gone. He moved quickly out the short walkway to the road, saw a spread of wildflowers beyond, sad, shriveled, thought, well, it will be something. There was no one on the road, the usual silence since the lack of gasoline had taken away the cars. He glanced down at his embarrassing dress, thought, well, who will care anyway? He heard the sound now, familiar, the distant drone of a great plane, looked up, thought, they come already? Can they give us no relief, not even for a few days? He searched for it, caught a glimpse of reflection, the plane very high, and he shook his head, thought, just . . . do it somewhere else, somewhere south of the city. Let me do my job today without the blood of wounded men. His eye was held to the plane, a dark speck falling from it, and he stared in curiosity, had not usually seen the bombs. He waited, watched, the speck falling, toward the center of the city, closer now to the castle. Strange, he thought. The sound of the plane abruptly changed, and even at that distance he could hear an odd pitch to the usual whine. He

saw the reflection changing, the sun catching both wings, a great silver bird
in a wide sweeping turn. He had never flown before, thought of the men
on the plane, no different from the men he had treated that week. Perhaps
you know of them, your own, left behind while you continue to do your
awful work. But . . . one plane? Are you here just to remind us what kind
of power you have? He thought of Hata, the old field marshal. He is not
intimidated by you. Perhaps you should be afraid of our power, of what we
will do to you when you finally have the courage to put your troops on our
soil. He felt a strange anger, looked toward his house, knew it was not
about planes and pilots, and the prisoners he had treated in the dungeon
of the great castle. Just . . . leave us alone. Hata, the generals, and admirals,
and all their speeches, their radio broadcasts. All of you. Allow us our love
for our emperor, to love all it is to be Japanese. Why must you all make
war? What have you done that makes our lives any better? End this foolishness. I will not be a part of Hata's bloody wall, and neither shall I surrender. I will repair the flesh, but I will not share your lust for a fight.

He began to move back toward his house, felt foolish, cursing at airplanes, cursing at his old friend. He ignored the plane now, stepped out in
the road, saw a group of men coming up from the town, soldiers, one more
march, one more drill into the countryside. He hurried his steps, moved
out of their way, and the sky seemed to burst above him, a blinding flash
of orange and purple, a low roar, growing louder. The roar drove him
down to the ground, deafening, a hard hand pressing him flat, the ground
beneath him moving, rumbling, a gaping crack, a ditch, his body sliding,
driven hard into a low place. The darkness covered the sky, he saw nothing
at all now, the immense brightness changing to black, smoke and dirt, then
no sky at all. He stayed flat, immovable, the darkness covering him, crushing in on him, obliterating the road, the flowers, and he felt a hard punch
of wind, ripping the ground around him, debris whistling past, a piece of
something hard striking his stomach. He tried to call out, turned to the
house, terror in his mind, thoughts of his wife, raised his head in the violent storm, saw the house suddenly collapse to one side, flattened. More
debris blew past him, and he tried to stand, impossible, was driven deeper
into the ditch, the wind still shrieking over him, dirt and dust and pieces
of everything covering him. He called out for his wife, but there was no
sound but the roar of the storm. He closed his eyes, felt heat now, tried to
curl himself up, too much wind, felt himself pulled up from the low place,
scraping the ground, dragged by an invisible hand, his clothes ripped away,

searing heat on his back. He rolled to one side, more debris falling, and he covered his face, but his hands were stripped away, his body beaten by the force of the wind. He slid farther along the ground, shoved into another hole, felt his legs crushed against a fallen tree, stopping his slide. He held to the tree, blinded, still crying out, nothing else to do, nowhere to go, his home and the sky and the city simply gone, filled by a swirling storm of fire and debris and the scattered bits of men.

He pulled himself free of the tree, dug himself out of a half meter of dirt and ash. He wiped the jagged roughness from his eyes, thought of his wife, the clinic, tried to see anything through eyes he knew were burnt. His hands slipped over the crushed limbs of the tree, and he saw shapes, one eye barely functioning. He put a hand up, touched his face, one side ripped raw, the skin around the eye torn and bloodied. He cried out, no pain, just . . . shock, knew he had to find someone, his wife, blinked hard, wiped at the blood, could make out more shapes. There was no sound but the wind, a steady roar from a massive cloud of black fog, he saw flickers of distant fires, one burst, the thunder driving toward him, an explosion far down near the castle. He stood, leaned against the shattered tree, his vision partially clearing, put a hand over the bloody side of his face, stinging pain. He stared toward the city, the landmarks, and through the smoke there was nothing else, the buildings flattened to rubble, or gone completely. He thought of the soldiers in the road, no sign of them, of anyone else, and the smoke swallowed him again, the hard stink of something he had never smelled before, his brain tossing out an image, burning fish. He was in full panic now, tried to walk, felt a sharp pain in his leg, tested it, stepped high, the leg unbroken. He struggled through the rubble, pieces of wood and stone, a crushed bicycle, pieces of fence, scratching at him, holding him. He cried out, choked on the dirt, searched again for his home, his crippled vision catching nothing but a flattened heap of splinters, bricks of his chimney, scattered away, strewn about like toys. His legs pushed out of the rubble, and he tried to reach the wreckage of his home, saw now that what remained of the clinic was a single stone wall, the beds and offices swept completely away. And the patients. He called out again, no response, and he climbed his way slowly to the house, shattered furniture, put a hand down on a lump of metal, saw it was his stove, on its side, and close to it, the icebox, crushed and twisted. He felt cold now, shivering in his chest, cold down his legs, knew it was shock, and his panic grew, his hands ripping at the rubble, his skin torn by his own desperation. He cried out, "Kiko!" He fought for more voice, pulled through the remains of his house, ignored the blood from his face, searching for his wife, called out again, "Kiko!"

He saw the twisted metal frame, the headboard of their bed, buried by a crumbled wall, moved that way, his foot ripped by something sharp. He ignored that, moved to the rubble, pulled it away, called out again, "Kiko! Answer me!"

He saw the cloth, soft silk, flowers, and he froze, his hand extended, knew it was her gown. He bent, knelt, more sharp edges, pulled at a piece of timber, but it would not move, and he dug with bloodied hands, saw her foot, part of her leg. He yelped, shoved himself into the rubble, felt her skin, the wetness, his blood flowing onto her, saw wetness around her, dirt and bone, the sweet sickening smell. He stopped, his strength gone, the sight of her bones freezing him, his guts rolling over in a hard spasm, and he vomited, then again, the grief consuming him, paralyzing. He sat, stared at the wreckage, his own home, the clinic, and everything beyond. There was pain in his legs, the cold increasing, and he looked down, fresh blood on his leg, a deep cut, his feet bare and bloodied, his nakedness. He sobbed aloud for a long moment, but new thoughts came, a great fist wrapping around his brain, his own will pulling him to the moment. There will be others . . . many others. You must help them. He looked toward the crushed walls of the clinic, saw a body there as well, a patient, her gown ripped away, the mother, her body torn in a grotesque shape. He turned away, searched frantically for any sign of what had been his office, something identifiable, thought of his medical bag. But there was only debris, his instruments buried, a broken microscope lying in a pool of something brown, bottles strewn into a pile of crushed glass. He fought to stay upright, looked again toward the heart of the city, saw more smoke, more fires close by and far away, no sign of anyone moving, no sign that Hiroshima had ever been a city at all.

The heat of the fires swirled around him, the cold in his legs passing, the shivering gone. His brain kept him there, and he wrapped his arms around his naked chest, squeezed, thought, stay awake . . . stay alert. The only sound was the firestorm, below, toward the center of the city, the flames coming together, one larger storm, smoke and darkness beyond. He thought of Hata, his old friend, in command of the garrison that would protect them, the man who knew so much of empire and power and the strength of will that would allow the Japanese to prevail. Hamishita glanced skyward, recalled the plane, the single reflection. It did not take an army to do this, he thought. It had to be . . . a weapon. And no matter what Hata or his generals believe, we cannot stand with our ancestors and pretend that our spirit is undamaged. The Americans will not be stopped by samurai. If they will do this to me . . . to Japan . . . we have lost everything.

H ata pulled himself to his feet, heard screaming down the dark corridor, stumbled, coughed in the dust, the air thick and smoky.
"What has happened?"
He fought to find the doorway, felt the heat rolling down through the dark caverns, more smoke, saw one man staggering close to him, an officer, no name, the man just one more wounded soldier. Hata moved past him, hugged one side of the earthen wall, felt the incline, pushed his feet up the hill, no sound but a strange roar, the smoke even worse, the taste of lead in his mouth, his body tingling, a swarm of invisible bees. He stopped, heard more screaming, somewhere in front of him, the stink and the heat driving him backward. Wait, he thought. There is safety here, down below. They must have made a direct hit on the castle. He thought of his men, the daily routine, drilling in the courtyard, men in formation for the morning rituals in the parade ground, his officers, the men who had come in from the outposts, gathering the night before for the strategy meeting. They are above, he thought, the guest quarters. I should go to them. Damn this smoke! You are in command, after all!
He pulled his coat off, wrapped it around his face, climbed again, furious at the ongoing screams, thought, some coward. I will deal with him. He could barely see, kept his eyes shaded with one bent hand, his bones aching, his legs stiff. Too old, he thought. They will tell me I am too old. But I am still the finest soldier in this city. I will show them that!
The smell of the fire engulfed him, a hard breeze, swirling directly down into the cave. He continued to climb, cursed aloud, thought, I will need to relocate my headquarters. The enemy has been fortunate this day. But they will pay for this rude interruption!
He saw light, the outside, surprising, the cave suddenly ending, far too soon. He expected to pass by the cages that held the Americans, but the

earthen walls simply fell away, nothing at all above him. He pushed up the incline, exhausted, burning in his lungs. He was in the open now, smoke blowing past, saw flames, looked to the hospital, a short distance away, nothing there, smoky air. He turned, searching, the castle so familiar, gone completely, obliterated into a mass of smoking rubble. For a long moment he stared at the destruction, close by, and far beyond, so much of the city either bathed in a dense fog of black . . . or gone altogether. He put the coat back on, tried to straighten his stiff back. He was furious now, searched for his officers, for anyone, to show them that he was still there, still in command, that if this was how the enemy would wage their war, the fight had only just begun.

32. TRUMAN

The Potsdam Conference was four days behind them, and Truman was desperate to return home to a place where intrigue and the annoying rituals of duplicity didn't infest every minute of the day.

He had sought out news every day of any Japanese response to the Potsdam Declaration, the joint communication issued on July 26 to the Japanese government, which spelled out precisely what the Allied powers expected from them in order that the war be brought to a close. Those who had signed the declaration included Truman, Churchill, and China's Chiang Kai-shek. Despite months of entreaties from both Truman and Churchill, the Soviets had been unwilling to actually declare war on Japan. Thus Stalin would have no say in just what the declaration called for. Truman's ongoing irritation with Stalin had been the greatest pill he had to swallow at Potsdam, and Churchill's continuing friendship and counsel had been extremely welcome. Churchill had learned that drinking Stalin under the table seemed to be the most effective way to win his friendship, and no one had been more suited to that effort than Churchill. Unfortunately for Truman, he could never keep up in anyone's hard-core drinking contest. Truman had quickly learned that Stalin had no interest in conced-

ing any meaningful diplomatic ground, and Truman had no reason to believe that putting the president of the United States into a drunken stupor
would have made much difference. As the meetings had begun to wind
down, Churchill's role had suddenly come to an abrupt halt. In a shock
that was still reverberating around the world, the British people had apparently had their fill of their wartime government. It was coincidence that
the British elections should fall while the Allies' most powerful leaders
were at Potsdam. For reasons no one in Truman's coterie could fathom, the
British electorate had tossed Churchill's party out the door. Thus, the
prime minister who had led the British people through some of the darkest days of their existence had suddenly been turned out to pasture, replaced by the likable but undramatic Clement Attlee. No one was more
surprised than Attlee himself.

Truman sat with the ship's senior officers, the lunch the usual fare for
senior naval personnel, something Truman had come to enjoy.

"I do not understand the British. How on earth they could pull the
rug out from under the man who . . . well, in my opinion anyway, has to
be the greatest statesman alive on this planet . . . well, I do not understand.
But that's why we have elections, and there are many in Washington who
are certainly anticipating that once my inherited term has expired, the rug
in my case shall be thin indeed."

The others smiled, polite as always, not even the ship's captain intrud-
ing onto Truman's conversation except by invitation. He had become a little annoyed by that, did not want to be treated as royalty, not by men he
had hoped would accept him as more down-to-earth than his predecessor.
The eating continued, no one responding, and Truman tasted the soup
again, thought, I suppose they have no choice. I'm the damn boss, and
military men respect that more than anyone.

The door to the captain's mess was pulled open by a young security officer, and Truman saw his map room officer, Captain Frank Graham, slip
quickly into the room.

"Sir, all apologies for interrupting your lunch. I thought you should
see this as quickly as possible."

"Let's have it, Frank."

Graham handed the paper to Truman, who read it silently, then sat back, felt a burst of energy, looked at the faces, the officers trying not to appear too curious.

"Gentlemen, you will hear greater details of this soon enough. Allow me to be the first to inform you. Probably appropriate that way. *'Following info regarding Manhattan received. Hiroshima bombed visually'* . . . well, a lot of technical details after that. *'No fighter opposition and no flak. Results clear cut successful in all respects. Visible effects greater than in any test. Condition normal in airplane following delivery.'*" He paused, saw puzzled looks, polite nods. "Gentlemen, you are being let in on the greatest secret this nation has ever hoped to keep. The shorthand version of this is that we have bombed the Japanese city of Hiroshima with a weapon unlike any the world has ever seen. No need for secrets now. I expect this will bring the Japanese to the peace table as quickly as they can button their trousers. Simply put, gentlemen, this is the greatest thing in history. Captain, with all respect, it's time for you to get us home."

The Potsdam Declaration had been specific and direct, had called for the Japanese to surrender or else face the most dire of consequences. The clauses included assurances that the Allies had every intention of destroying Japan's ability to make war. In addition there were specifics regarding boundaries of what would remain of Japanese territory, and those foreign lands Japan would no longer occupy. The Japanese would be expected to submit their military leaders for trial as war criminals, to answer for the astonishing variety and volume of barbarism that even now were coming to light. The declaration had been very specific that the Allies had no intention of enslaving or even punishing the Japanese people. There were also clauses allowing for Japanese industry to be supported in efforts to restore a healthy peacetime economy, and that a more democratic Japan, with freedoms of religion and speech, would be welcomed into the greater world community. Once the new Japanese government had taken hold, the declaration had promised that the military occupation of Japan by the Allies would end. But it was the final clause that Truman knew would have been pushed hard by Roosevelt, and thus Truman felt strongly he should press it as well:

We call upon the government of Japan to proclaim now the unconditional surrender of all armed forces, and to provide proper and adequate assurances of their good faith in such action. The alternative for Japan is prompt and utter destruction.

The word of the destruction of Hiroshima was spreading with light-ning speed through every world capital, carried on airwaves that sent Tru-man's announcement to every world leader. The success of the *Enola Gay*'s mission was now a dramatic and forceful punctuation mark to the resolu-tion agreed upon at Potsdam, a resolution that Truman and Churchill hoped would convince the Japanese that there was no reason whatsoever for continuing the war. If the Japanese leaders were truly aware of their military situation, they had to know that sending their people into combat was fruitless at best. Now, with the explosion of the atomic bomb, Truman expected that the ultimatum issued at Potsdam would crush Japanese re-solve, and that finally, even their most militant generals could be made to see that the war was truly over. Prior to Hiroshima, none of the Allied powers had received any direct communications from the Japanese, noth-ing to show that the Imperial High Command actually believed the threat the Allies were making. On the contrary, the Japanese response had con-sisted of the indirect broadcast of an address by the Japanese prime minis-ter, Kantaro Suzuki, which used the word *mokusatsu*. Those in the West who studied Japanese culture knew the term to mean silent contempt, as though the Japanese hierarchy considered the Potsdam Declaration and the final ultimatum to be beneath the dignity of any response at all. Tru-man was aware that the declaration had not made specific mention of what should become of the emperor, a technicality that might cause some prob-lems for a culture that the Americans truly couldn't relate to. But the con-cept of *utter destruction* had no hidden meaning in any culture. Now, with that promise fulfilled at Hiroshima, Truman felt confident that the Japa-nese understood quite clearly that the Americans possessed a new and hor-rifying weapon, and would use it with ruthless intent. But Truman was amazed that, even with the obliteration of most of Hiroshima, the Japa-nese government still did not respond at all.

On August 7 and 8, as though to emphasize that the Americans had more on their minds than a single weapon, a force of nearly five hundred B-29s made bombing raids both day and night on a considerable number of Japanese targets. With maddening silence still from the Japanese, Tru-man exercised his authority, and gave final agreement to the requests from Leslie Groves and Robert Oppenheimer, as well as the American military commanders who still faced the horrifying prospect of invading mainland Japan. The physicists and technicians of the Manhattan Project had thus far created a total of three atomic bombs. Little Boy, the bomb Colonel Tibbets had dropped on Hiroshima, had been a uranium device, fired with the least complicated form of ignition, the cannon projectile system. But both of the other bombs, including the test bomb exploded at Alamogordo, were altogether different. Those used plutonium, rather than uranium, and were ignited by an implosion method, where masses of plutonium would be fired simultaneously from multiple directions into a core of the material at the center of the bomb, causing the collision of a sufficient amount of nuclear material to create a nuclear explosion. Though more complicated than the Hiroshima weapon, the success at Alamogordo had convinced Groves and his teams that this plutonium bomb was just as reliable. The last remaining bomb was named Fat Man, its shape far more spherical than the bomb Tibbets had dropped. It was slightly larger and slightly more powerful than Little Boy, but its effects would be the same. On August 9, three days after the destruction of Hiroshima, and with no indication coming from the Japanese that they had any intention of accepting the Potsdam Declaration, Fat Man was loaded aboard the B-29 *Bockscar.* The plane was piloted by Major Charles Sweeney, who had piloted one of the support planes for Tibbets's Hiroshima mission. After struggling through deteriorating weather conditions over Japan, the primary target of Kokura was abandoned, and Sweeney flew his plane to the secondary target, the city of Nagasaki. With weather conditions threatening to scrub the mission altogether, Sweeney used radar as well as a chance visual through thickening clouds, and at 11:01 A.M., the second atomic bomb was exploded over a Japanese city.

Throughout the early days of August, the Japanese had been making entreaties directly to the Soviets, requests of influence that Stalin might exercise to bring an end to the war that would help the Japanese save face, by ensuring that the Americans did not tamper with the existing structure of the Japanese government, and that the tone of the Potsdam Declaration be modified to allow for the emperor to remain the spiritual and political leader of his people. Though Truman had pushed hard for the Soviets to enter the war against Japan, Stalin had resisted any such pressure. With the dropping of the second bomb, Stalin had a sudden change of heart. To the shock of the Japanese diplomats in Moscow, on August 9, the same day the city of Nagasaki was destroyed, the Soviets declared war on Japan. In what seemed to be mere minutes, Soviet troops that were poised on the border with China swarmed into Manchuria and immediately began to engage the highly overmatched Japanese forces there, sweeping them away with the same dedicated viciousness the Allies had witnessed in Germany.

Truman received news of the second bomb with the same optimism he had felt after the success at Hiroshima. The next day, August 10, that optimism was justified, though not as directly or as succinctly as Truman had expected. A message emerged from the Japanese government, delivered through intermediaries, the Swiss and the Swedes:

> In obedience to the gracious commands of His Majesty the Emperor, who, ever anxious to enhance the cause of world peace, desires earnestly to bring about an early termination of hostilities with a view to saving mankind from the calamities to be imposed on them by further continuation of the war, the Japanese government several weeks ago asked the Soviet government, with which neutral relations then prevailed, to render good offices in restoring peace vis-à-vis the enemy powers. Unfortunately, these efforts in the interest of peace having failed, the Japanese government, in conformity with the august wish of His Majesty to restore the general peace and desiring to put an end to the untold sufferings engendered by the war, have decided on the following:
>
> The Japanese government is ready to accept the terms enumerated in the joint declaration that was issued at Potsdam, July 26, 1945, by the heads of government of the United States, Great Britain and China, and later subscribed to by the Soviet government, with the understanding that said declaration does not comprise any demand which prejudices the prerogatives of His Majesty as a sovereign ruler. The Japanese government hopes sincerely that this understanding is warranted and desires keenly that an explicit indication to that effect will be speedily forthcoming.

Truman realized that the Japanese were balancing their conditions solely on the survival of their emperor and his full authority over the Japanese people. After consultations with his own cabinet and military leaders, Truman accepted the Japanese terms, so long as the Japanese government abided specifically by the Potsdam Declaration. The one fly in the ointment came from the Soviets, who, since they were now officially one of the combatants, added a last-second clause in the agreement that the Japanese would have to formally surrender to a representative of both the American and Soviet governments, as though to symbolize that victory had been achieved by the blood and toil of both nations equally. The maneuver was blatantly transparent, since Soviet troops were already galloping through Manchuria with virtually no opposition, seizing territory that Truman knew would be as impossible to pry loose from Stalin's hands as the territories he now controlled in Eastern Europe. Truman's response was definite and negative, though of course the language that was transmitted to the Soviets was couched in diplomatic niceties. Privately Truman had his own description of Stalin's ploy. After only one day's participation in the war against an enemy that for fifteen years had brutalized and massacred their way through Asia and the Pacific, Stalin expected to become a full partner in the spoils. Truman's response, stripped of its diplomacy, was a firm rebuke, otherwise best stated as "nice try."

OVAL OFFICE, THE WHITE HOUSE, WASHINGTON, D.C.
AUGUST 14, 1945, 7 P.M.

Most of his cabinet was in place, the members of the press corps squeezing in as best they could. Truman waited patiently behind his desk, would allow the microphones to be placed correctly, checked and double-checked, wanted no one left out. To one side he saw Bess, nervous, looked at her with a smile, a small nod, tried to reassure her with a gentle gesture, thought, she's as nervous as I am, and I'm about to drill myself through this floor. Don't show it though. This is one of those, well . . . perfect moments.

The room seemed to settle down, the guards at the door motioning to him that no one remained outside. He stood now, saw his wife jump, flinching, and he smiled again, tried to calm her from the short distance between them, but there was no time now for levity.

"I should like to read to you a message received this afternoon from the Japanese government in reply to the message forwarded to that government by the secretary of state on August eleventh. I deem this reply a full acceptance of the Potsdam Declaration which specifies the unconditional surrender of Japan."

There was much more, but through the room he could already feel the surge of energy, the thought flickering through him once more. Yes, a perfect moment. The war is over.

33. ADAMS

The train rolled slowly to a stop, the hard squeal of steel beneath him, the cars now jerking to a halt. Around him people began to rise, a burst of movement, suitcases pulled down from shelves above, a hum of activity surrounding him, keeping him pressed to the seat. He felt self-conscious about the uniform, had seen the looks, the attention of the other passengers, the long journey from San Diego seeming to take an eternity. There had been some attempts at conversation, the men mostly, curious, probing him in that carefree way, as though being male gave them some sense of sharing, that his experience was a part of their own, no matter that they had spent the war as civilians.

There had been other troops on the train as well, one sailor, who stayed to himself, two army officers, who ignored this young Marine completely, who spoke with a little too much brashness, attracting attention by the jauntiness of their caps. No matter where they had served, Adams knew it had been nowhere close to a fight.

The women had stayed quiet, one in particular, older, deep sad eyes, and he had avoided her, felt the attention coming from her as though she needed something from him, something too uncomfortable for him to offer. After so many hours it had come to him, a flash of understanding, that she had suffered a deep and tragic loss. He would not ask, would avoid speaking to her at all, and she had not tried to break that shield. But more than once he had seen her face cupped by a handkerchief, her grief ripped bare to the passengers around her. He finally understood she was reacting to his uniform. He felt some kind of responsibility, a flicker of guilt, had thought of talking to her. But his shield was solid and immovable, and no matter what inspired her tears, he could do nothing to take away her pain without bringing on his own horrific memories. Even in the crowded car he fought to keep their voices far away. He had no interest in eavesdropping on the trivial, someone's details of a trip to the doctor, a sister's wedding, all the while the older men seeking out some kind of story from him, something they could pass on to someone else, party conversation, chatter in a bar. Hey, I met this Marine . . . a hero . . . medals.

Even as he deflected their conversation, the question had come to him. What must they hear? Why do they care what I went through, how many dead men I saw, how many Japs I killed? This war wasn't for anyone's entertainment, for God's sake.

He had heard about the military hospital, a visit by the movie star John Wayne. It was pure Hollywood, some press agent's *good idea* that the star saunter into a ward of badly injured men in full Western regalia, as though by Wayne's heroic presence, a pair of six-shooters and jingling spurs, he would brighten the mood of broken and bloodied men. The response had shocked even the doctors, the wounded troops greeting this big-time star with a chorus of boos and catcalls. If I had been there, I would have done the same thing, he thought. Blood is not ketchup, a friend's death is not about dragging tears from the girl in the front row. Those wounded men are changed for all time, and some fake hero isn't going to erase anything they did, or bring back anyone they lost.

Adams stood, the crowd in the aisles thinning out, gathering outside on the concrete platform. He felt strangely nervous, reached for his seabag, would never look at the heavy green canvas without thinking of Guam.

The Marines had been sent there from Okinawa, mostly to rest and refit, and Adams had witnessed a scene that had stunned him. Massive piles of the green duffel bags, what the sailors and Marines called seabags, had been tossed into a pile, doused with gasoline, and set on fire.

There had been only one explanation. Those bags, and all they contained, had belonged to the men killed in action. According to some rule Adams would never understand, the seabags were simply burned. He had watched the pyre with a sickening sense of loss, had been forced to think of Welty and Ferucci and everyone else, wondering if their possessions were in that fire, wondering if someone had had the decency to sort through, to send home anything that the family might treasure. He did not stay there long enough to find out, knew only that his own bag contained no treasures at all. The only souvenirs he carried would not catch anyone's attention. He still had the single can of Welty's stew, and with that, the shattered eyeglasses that his friend had worn. He had no explanation for it, but Adams had seen the blackest pieces of his own heart, knew with perfect certainty that if anyone tried to take those from him, he would have killed them with his hands.

Soon after reaching Guam, the veterans had been given the astounding luxury of a thirty-day leave. Adams had absorbed that news with decidedly mixed feelings, but it had been Sergeant Mortensen who had kicked him hard in the ass, a dressing down about feeling sorry for himself. There was family, after all, all of them had somebody, and Mortensen wouldn't hear excuses from anyone lucky enough to get a leave. The Marines were offered a ship to San Diego and a train ticket to anywhere beyond, with enough time to make the visit worthwhile. Mortensen was not about to let any one of his veterans pass that by, especially since, in a platoon of fifty men, Adams was one of only six who had been with the unit since the invasion of Okinawa. The faces of the veterans were familiar, but no one was close, pure chance that any cluster of friends had long been shattered by the brutality of the fights. New friendships seemed nonexistent, the other veterans seeming to stay away from anyone else, just as he did. The replacements were learning quickly to keep their mouths shut, too many broken teeth pounded into the mouths of idiot recruits who did what they always did, asking for advice, or even more stupid, digging the veterans for some tale about the great adventure of combat. Adams had been lucky, so far. None of the new men on Guam had approached him, not even the *tough guys,* who heard talk of his reputation with the boxing gloves. There was something dangerous in the veterans now, deep beneath the calm and the distant stare. Even the captain had let him be, no suggestion that Adams should participate in the never-ending rituals of the boxing matches. For Adams those days were past, no desire in him at all to break another jawbone. That need had been fulfilled for the last time by a Japanese soldier on Sugar Loaf Hill.

If Mortensen's loud insistence on accepting the leave wasn't enough, the veterans had been inspired as well by word of their next mission. The entire Sixth Division was scheduled for a new assignment, occupying the seaports on the Chinese coast, and Mortensen had been as definite about that as Captain Bennett, that the assignment was open-ended, that the Marines might be stationed in some godforsaken hole in some bizarrely strange place for more months than anyone wanted to think about. The talk had rolled through Guam about that as well, the crude disappointment from the new men that they wouldn't join the *party* when it came time for the invasion of Japan. The invasion force would mostly be army, not Marines, and the transport ships were already in motion, some bringing men who had already done service in Europe. When the China deployment was announced, there had been plenty of outrage, the newer Marines making a good show of their envy for the soldiers who were going to *clean up* Jap-land.

And then, word came of Hiroshima.

Adams still knew nothing of their new president, but it had been Mortensen who had announced with vigorous passion that if the opportunity ever came his way, the sergeant would drop to his knees and kiss Harry Truman on the ass. The others had laughed, all but the veterans. Adams knew what those men knew, that this president wanted the war to end so badly that he was willing to use this astounding new weapon against the enemy. Adams wasn't as outspoken about it as Mortensen, but he imagined the same scene, Truman and Adams, in downtown anywhere, a million people watching, while Adams puckered up.

He stepped down onto the platform, the place noisy, crowded, too much chaos. The shouts came from paperboys and vendors, news about the bombing of Nagasaki, what Adams had already seen in a newspaper in San Diego. He hoisted the bag on his shoulder, searched the crowd, wasn't sure what he expected to see, smelled something wonderful, saw a hot dog stand, a man stabbing one of the thick dogs with a fork, stuffing a bun, squirting mustard all over the bun and his own hand, the mess handed to a boy who jammed it into his mouth. Adams was suddenly ravenous, hadn't eaten anything on the train, felt in his pockets, no change at all, nothing but military scrip. It had been his own mistake, forgetting to change the bills for real money, and he ached now, angry at himself. The crowd was more annoying to him now, too many happy people, people with hugs and kisses and hats askew. There were friendly greetings and slaps on the back, the two officers talking boisterously to another pair, big talk of big adventures, lies upon lies. Adams backed away from them, wondered what Captain Bennett would do to them . . . and now he heard his name.

"Clay!"

He wasn't sure, too much noise, too many voices, but it came again.

"Clay! Private Adams, you dumb son of a bitch!"

Adams turned, saw the crowd parting, some forcefully, saw the stocky thickness, the massive chest, a limp, unexpected, and the beaming face of his brother.

"Jesse! Oh my God!"

Jesse didn't slow, shoved himself right into Adams, picked him up, bag and all, crushing his ribs.

"You skinny-assed little peter! There's nothing left of you!"

His brother set him back down now, and Adams saw only smiles, strangers around them watching the scene.

"Mom's here! Come on, this way!"

Jesse pulled him by the arm, forcing their way through the crowd, people pushed aside, but the faces of the two young men told the crowd everything, their enthusiasm spreading all across the platform. He saw her now, a faint wave, the frail, exhausted woman, more frail, older, more gray hair. She was crying, still waving, and Adams slowed, Jesse still pulling at him.

"Yeah, okay, go give her a hug. If you'd have written more, she wouldn't be so damn worried, you know."

Adams ignored his brother's scolding, moved up to her, realized suddenly how short she was, and he felt his brother pull the bag from his shoulder, kept his eyes in hers, red and wet. He slid his hands onto her shoulders, then around, pulled himself to her, felt her thin bones, her soft voice, "My boy. God bless you. You're safe."

"Yeah, Mama. I'm okay."

They hugged for a long silent moment, and he couldn't stop the tears, didn't try. Finally, Jesse's voice was in his ear, "You can do that when we get home. Got someone you need to meet. Whole damn greeting party here."

Adams was mystified, still looked at his mother's tears, said, "Who?"

He turned now, saw Jesse move back behind his mother, pulling a young woman by the hand.

"Okay, I got a surprise for you, kid. Well, two surprises. But first things first. Nancy, this sorry-looking bag of bones is my little brother, Clay. He's a Marine, but we try to overlook that. Private Clayton Adams, this gorgeous example of womanhood is Miss Nancy Forbes. We're engaged." Jesse leaned closer now, faked the whisper. "She's a damn nurse. Makes my life a hell of a lot easier."

Clay saw the beauty in the woman's face, tears there as well. She held out a hand, said, "Clayton, it's a pleasure. Your brother's told me a great deal about you. Mostly things you wouldn't want repeated, I'm sure. He thinks paratroopers ought to rule the world, and Marines make . . . good busboys. Sorry. He insisted I say that."

Adams was overwhelmed, took the softness of her hand, caught the amazing scent of perfume.

"Wow. Engaged? Uh . . . well, it's nice to meet you." He looked at his big brother now, saw the pride, the smile, the couple looking at each other now with that gooey storybook grin. "Damn, Jesse, you serious?"

"Watch your damn language. Only first sergeants and paratroopers get to cuss around women, and I got both of those covered. Marines always need to learn manners. Yeah, I'm serious. We're getting married next month. Oh . . . one more surprise. We had room in the Nash, so this gal thumbed a ride with us. Said something about wanting to see you. Says she wondered if you'd remember her, and I told her you being all stupid and all, you'd probably forget what town you lived in." Jesse moved aside, still the smile, slapped Adams on the back, a quick grip on his shoulder. Clay saw her now, her hands clasped in front of her, a hint of embarrassment on her face, a polite hopeful nod. Adams felt something open up inside him, was stunned, his jaw falling open, her name in his mind for months. *Loraine Lancaster.* The fantasy had been with him from well before high school, the only girl he had thought about, the only girl who had ever stirred that hard ache that made him wonder if there could ever be anyone else. He had stared at her in school, on the street, and in his mind, even thought of her on the beach at Okinawa, that one odd day of blue sky and birds. She was also the girl he was very certain had no idea he was alive. He stared at her, saw more of the shy nervousness, and now she smiled. *At him.*

Jesse leaned close to his ear.

"Say hi, you idiot."

"Uh . . . hi. You needed a ride . . . ?"

Jesse slapped him in the back of his head, dislodging his hat.

"Miss Lancaster, will you please help get the glue out of his brain?"

She laughed again, still nervous.

"I was hoping you'd remember me, Clay. I heard you were coming home, and . . . I know it's only a short time, but maybe, when you've had a good visit with your family . . . well maybe, we could have a sundae or something."

Clay stared at her, felt something new, something he had not felt in a very long time. *Joy.*

"I'd love to. You came along . . . to see me?"

"Yes, Clay. Welcome home."

There was a hand sliding around his arm now, and he felt his mother's touch, her soft words.

"Looks like you'll be busy while you're here. I guess we should get to the Nash."

Clay looked at her, the tears still there, and he glanced at Jesse, his brother's arm around his fiancée, realized she was holding a cane.

"Jesse, you hurt?"

Jesse shook his head, shrugged.

"Tore up my knees. You paying attention? I jumped out of airplanes, you numbskull."

Adams felt paralyzed, the faces all looking at him, tears and smiles and happiness. Across the platform, a man began to shout.

"It's over! The Japs surrendered! It's over!"

The crowd responded with cheering, shouts, disbelief, a scramble for a fresh stack of newspapers. Adams stared at the mob scene, papers in the air, more cheers, a fat black headline passing by, someone slapping him, "Good work, soldier!"

Others were hoisting women in the air, the army officers down the platform waving their hats, others, civilians, tossing theirs high. Clay felt a burst of confusion, a fog settling in on him, too much emotion, too many shouts. The war can't be over . . . there's too many Japs . . . Guam, and then we gotta go to China. He felt a hint of panic, glanced to one side, the railroad tracks, thought of the rocks, the dirt, a shovel, the precious sanctuary of a foxhole. He looked at his brother, saw concern, the hard crust of the paratroop sergeant giving way, Jesse's eyes reading him, no smile now.

"Hey, Clay, I'll grab a paper, and we can read about it on the way. It's been coming for a couple days. You might not have known, traveling and all. You'll be okay. We can talk about . . . anything you want, maybe later. The old man's mostly gone, working some shifts at a mine down south. He doesn't mess with me at all. Knows better. It's real peaceful at the house. Let's head for home."

"Yeah . . . but I have to go back soon. I've only got a thirty-day leave. That's all."

Beside him, the voice of his mother.

"For now. But the war's over. And you're safe now. Soon, you'll have all the time in the world."

AFTERWORD

The sooner the enemy comes, the better. One hundred million of us will die proudly.

— Japanese propaganda poster, found in Tokyo

There was never a moment's discussion as to whether the atomic bomb should be used or not. To avert a vast, indefinite butchery, to bring the war to an end, to give peace to the world, to lay healing hands upon its tortured peoples by a manifestation of overwhelming power . . . seemed a miracle of deliverance.

— Winston Churchill

The use of this barbaric weapon at Hiroshima and Nagasaki was of no material assistance in our war against Japan. The Japanese were already defeated and ready to surrender because of the effective sea blockade and the successful bombing with conventional weapons.

— Admiral William Leahy, USN

You think of the lives which would have been lost in an invasion of Japan's home islands—a staggering number of American lives but millions more of Japanese—and you thank God for the atomic bomb.

— William Manchester (USMC)

On August 10, 1945, after absorbing the impact of the second atomic bomb, Japan's senior officials meet to debate what course to follow. They are almost evenly divided as to whether or not Japan should continue to fight the war. Led by Prime Minister Suzuki, the moderate faction pushes for surrender, but there are just as many, particularly from the army, who insist vehemently that the war be continued. To those highest-ranking commanders, including Field Marshal Hisaichi Terauchi and General Yasuji Okamura, surrender only betrays the army, those soldiers in the field who should still be allowed to end their lives with honor by fighting to the death. It is Emperor Hirohito himself who breaks the stalemate and orders his ministers to accept the terms of the Potsdam Declaration. Throughout the war, a fairly complacent Hirohito has allowed the Imperial High Command to operate mostly on its own terms. By stepping forcefully into the debate, he gives his ministers no alternative, and the Japanese government obeys their emperor. But radical elements of the army do not accept the emperor's order gracefully, and a coup is launched, an attempt to assassinate the emperor. The coup fails, the conspirators brought down in part by those generals who are still vehemently opposed to surrender. Even the radicals come to understand that, no matter the humiliation of surrender, the nation's outright suicide is not the most preferable course.

On Sunday, September 2, 1945, the Japanese formally surrender to the Allied forces on board the American battleship USS *Missouri,* at anchor in Tokyo Bay. The ceremony is stiff and somber, with signatures affixed to the documents by representatives of the United Nations, the United States, Great Britain, China, the Soviet Union, Australia, New Zealand, France, Canada, and the Netherlands. Signing for the Japanese are Foreign Minister Mamoru Shigemitsu, General Yoshijiro Umezu, and nine other officials. In one important gesture of concession, the American government does not require the document to be signed by Emperor Hirohito.

General Douglas MacArthur commands the ceremony, and signs the document on behalf of the United Nations. Immediately after the signatures are affixed, nearly two thousand American fighter planes and bombers roar overhead in mixed formations, a show of force that cannot be lost on the Japanese.

On the *Missouri,* a great many of the American generals and admirals
are present, including Admiral Nimitz, who signs for the Americans. But
no one's presence is more poignant than that of General Jonathan Wainwright, who surrendered the American forces at Corregidor, and British
general Sir Arthur Percival, who surrendered the British bastion at Singapore. Both men arrive at the ceremony just released from prisoner-of-war
camps in Manchuria. Their skeletal appearance is an appropriate symbol
of the suffering imposed on so many by their captors.

To honor his efforts as the Allied commander in chief, MacArthur is
invited to meet with President Truman in Washington, a gesture of gratitude from Truman, as well as an event certain to please the newspapers.
MacArthur refuses the invitation, and many subsequent ones, claiming his
duties are too numerous to be bothered with such ceremonial formalities.
It is a glaring insult to Truman and will lead to a great deal of controversy
between the two men that will only culminate in 1951, during the Korean
War. Truman will prevail.

THE JAPANESE

COLONEL HIROMICHI YAHARA

General Ushijima's confidant and the primary tactical planner for the Japanese defense of Okinawa escapes the collapse of the Japanese command.
Shedding his uniform, he makes every effort to blend in with a group of
soldiers attempting to pass themselves off as Okinawan refugees, intending
to find a boat that will carry them away from Okinawa. After several days
in hiding with groups of terrified Okinawans, the inevitable occurs, and
American soldiers discover them hiding in a cave. Yahara, who speaks English, beseeches the Americans to do no harm, and the entire group is captured. Passing through the refugee camps, along with thousands of others,
both Japanese and Okinawans, he is recognized by several Japanese soldiers, though his secret is not revealed to his captors for several weeks.
Finally he is interrogated by Japanese prisoners working in service to
American intelligence, where his identity is finally revealed. He continues
to be questioned by various American intelligence officials, all the while
seeking the means to escape his captors. But the atomic bomb changes his
mind. On August 15, he is shown a transcript of Emperor Hirohito's official surrender order, and Yahara realizes his war is over. He is repatriated to

Japan at the end of 1945, and reaches Tokyo Bay on January 7, 1946, on board the American transport USS *Gable*. He sees for the first time the utter devastation of the Japanese capital, few details of which had ever been communicated to his command on Okinawa. Still considered a high-ranking officer in the Thirty-second Army, Yahara is assigned to deal with the organizational paperwork that remains in repatriating those few soldiers who have survived. He reports to what remains of Imperial General Headquarters, which of course is completely dominated by the occupation forces of the Americans. Nonetheless, he makes his full report on the outcome of the battle for Okinawa to the highest-ranking general he can find, thus fulfilling his last assignment. By the end of 1946, he completes his wrapping up of the final paperwork for the Thirty-second Army.

Yahara is acutely aware of the disgrace that comes from being a prisoner of war, and never admits to any such status, convincing others, and himself, that the war ended with him still in the service of the emperor, and still trying to find a way to aid his country's cause. He agonizes frequently about his own survival, suffers frequent bouts of depression and guilt that his beloved commanding general took the more honorable way out.

As Japan organizes a national police force, Yahara is called upon to serve as instructor for new recruits, but his taste for uniforms has soured, and he refuses. Instead he writes his memoir, careful to define his role in such a way that there will be no shame in his capture, an awareness he carries even decades after the war's conclusion. The memoir is published in 1972, and surprises him by becoming a commercial success. He writes:

> A nation should never be sacrificed for the sake of its leaders. Japan's leaders got us involved in the China incident out of a sense of self-preservation. They started that war to preserve their own power, status and honor. Who would not despair knowing that soldiers were dying in the interests of such leaders?

He dies in 1981, at age seventy-eight.

DR. OKIRO HAMISHITA

Though grief-stricken over the death of his wife, he recovers sufficiently from the injuries received during the blast of the atomic bomb to fulfill his primary duty of caring for patients, and spends several days tending to the horrific injuries of those who survive the blast. But he cannot escape the unknown illness that afflicts so many of the bomb's immediate survivors, and succumbs to what we now know to be radiation poisoning on August 18, 1945, twelve days after the bomb is dropped. He is sixty-five.

FIELD MARSHAL SHUNROKU HATA

By a freak of fate, Hiroshima's senior military commander survives the bomb's blast, while most of his command, including nearly all of his senior officers, are killed by the obliteration of Hiroshima Castle. Despite his fiery rhetoric, he accepts his army's defeat, an unusual move for a senior military official, and surrenders to American occupation forces in late August 1945. He is tried as a war criminal by the International Military Tribunal for the Far East, the Asian version of the Nuremberg court. Found guilty, he is sentenced to life imprisonment. Hata makes very little defense of his actions, and later his captors feel he has shown sufficient remorse to atone for his crimes, and is thus granted parole in 1955. He dies seven years later, at age eighty-two.

HIDEKI TOJO

He consolidates his power throughout the war, amassing control of most of the Japanese government, even under the ultimate authority of the emperor, for whom Tojo has little private respect. Officially he is prime minister as well as chief of the Imperial General Staff, positions that give him virtually dictatorial power. But reaping the rewards for success also means accepting responsibility for failure, and when the Americans make their successful drive into the Mariana Islands chain, Tojo admits that his efforts have failed. On July 18, 1944, he resigns his position, and is never again an active force in Japanese politics or the war. Three weeks after the Japanese surrender, he attempts suicide, but fails at that as well. He is arrested by American agents and is tried as a war criminal before the International Military Tribunal for the Far East, which declares him guilty and sentences him to death. In his defense, he claims that he was merely following the orders given to him by the emperor, a claim no one takes seriously. He is hanged on December 23, 1948, at age sixty-four. Tojo is interred at Japan's revered Yasukuni Shrine, which creates considerable controversy that continues to this day.

THE AMERICANS

USS *INDIANAPOLIS*

After delivering the two technicians and the key components of the first atomic bomb, the heavy cruiser leaves Tinian for Leyte, in the Philippines, to rendezvous with the gathering fleet that will participate in the planned invasion of Japan. The mission of the cruiser has been so secret that she is unescorted both to and from Tinian, and thus sails alone through shipping lanes that the Japanese know well. Shortly after midnight on July 30, 1945, the ship is struck by two torpedoes, fired by the Japanese submarine *I-58*. She rolls over to starboard, and sinks in twelve minutes. Of the 1,196 crewmen, nearly three hundred are killed within those twelve minutes. The remainder go into the water. With few life vests or rafts to cling to, the nine hundred men begin an ordeal that subjects them to hypothermia, death from injuries, and madness. But there is one more ordeal they must suffer, which begins with their first sunrise: the relentless assault from swarms of sharks.

On August 2, midway through their third day in the water, the survivors are spotted by an American Ventura bomber, on a routine anti-submarine patrol. The pilot notifies his base at Peleliu, where a navy PBY Catalina flying boat is dispatched. Against orders, the flying boat lands near the men, trying vainly to rescue as many as can be retrieved from the water, men who are continuously being attacked by sharks. The nearest ship, the destroyer USS *Cecil Doyle,* diverts to the scene and rescues those who remain alive. Only 317 survive the ordeal. It is the greatest disaster at sea in the navy's history.

Because of the secrecy of their mission, there is no search made for the ship, since no one at Leyte knows just when to expect the ship to arrive. The captain of the *Indianapolis,* Charles McVay, is one of the survivors, and in December 1945, in what seems to many to be the navy's search for a scapegoat, McVay is court-martialed for "hazarding his ship for failure to zig-zag in good visibility." The conviction erases McVay's rank. The sentence is commuted by Admiral Chester Nimitz, and McVay is restored to active duty, though the court's verdict remains in McVay's record. It is a personal curse McVay will never escape. Strenuous efforts are made to clear his name, including ongoing accounts offered by his surviving crewmen as well as the Japanese captain who sank McVay's ship. But the navy does not reconsider the court-martial's findings, and McVay serves out a backwater career and retires in 1949. His personal torment continues, and he commits suicide in 1968.

Controversy swirls around the disaster for years. It is revealed that there was woeful negligence on the part of naval communications officers, who ignored a distress call made by the *Indianapolis* moments before she sank, and naval intelligence, which intercepted a communication from the *I-58* claiming an American warship sunk, a communication it ignored as well.

In 2000, the U.S. Congress passes a resolution absolving Captain McVay for the loss of his ship.

ADMIRAL CHESTER NIMITZ

To counter what Secretary of the Navy James Forrestal believes to be undue praise lavished on General Douglas MacArthur for success in the Pacific, Forrestal succeeds in having October 5, 1945, named Nimitz Day in Washington, D.C. With much fanfare, Nimitz addresses Congress, meets with President Truman (which MacArthur will not do), and enjoys a parade in his honor. Four days later he enjoys a massive ticker-tape parade in New York City. But Nimitz is never the publicity hound that MacArthur is, and he resists what could become a massive media campaign on his behalf.

Always an energetic advocate for naval power, he rejects the notion offered by some that the atomic bomb will make the navy obsolete.

He fights calls in Congress that the army and navy become joined into a single department, contradicting the belief of some that the United States will never again be called upon to engage in the kind of massive military action they experienced in World War II. His advocacy of a strong navy lands him the position of chief of naval operations, succeeding Admiral Ernest King. The appointment comes on November 20, 1945, the same day that Dwight Eisenhower is named to replace General George Marshall as army chief of staff.

In 1946 Nimitz begins to support the concept of nuclear-powered submarines, and throws his support behind Captain Hyman Rickover, the chief advocate for the development of the new technology.

Continuing his strong advocacy of a powerful navy, Nimitz writes nu-

merous articles and makes dozens of public speeches about the value of
that arm of the service. Such advocacy makes him enormously popular
among naval personnel, popularity that continues to this day. Despite his
penchant for writing, what he calls his "hobby," Nimitz never pens his own
memoir, believing it would put him in the awkward position of crediting
some commanders at the expense of others. He cites as an example the self-
serving memoir written by Admiral "Bull" Halsey, which does much to
alienate other senior commanders who shared in Halsey's actions in the Pacific. But Nimitz's love of writing does inspire him to contribute viewpoints to a general history of the U.S. Navy. The book, *Sea Power—A
Naval History,* becomes a much-sought-after text, in use especially at the
United States Naval Academy, though Nimitz will not accept any royalties
for his part in the book's creation.

In December 1947, his term as chief of naval operations ends, and he
retires. He and his wife, Catherine, relocate to San Francisco. His wife insists they keep a diary, which begins the day after his retirement. His first
entry reads, "I feel as if a great burden has just been lifted from my shoulders . . . how can we fail to have a full and happy life?" But there is little re-
laxation in his retirement. He is asked to serve as an intermediary in the
hotbed dispute between India and Pakistan over the territory of Kashmir.
He involves himself with other consulting duties with the United Nations,
but becomes frustrated with the squabbling of diplomats, and in mid-
1952 resigns the post. Though he is retired yet again, he accepts a position
as regent for the University of California.

In 1963 the admiral falls and shatters his kneecap, a debilitating injury
that keeps him from his beloved walks. The injury aggravates, revealing
that Nimitz also suffers from an arthritic condition in his spine. The condition worsens, causing him increasing pain, and in November 1965 he
undergoes a risky form of surgery to relieve his suffering. The operation is
a success, but in recovery he contracts pneumonia. On Sunday, February
20, 1966, he dies from the deteriorating complications, just shy of his
eighty-first birthday. At the moment of his death, he is alone with his
beloved wife.

His funeral is attended by thousands of onlookers and admirers, who
line the streets all along the route of the procession to the Golden Gate National Cemetery, at San Bruno, California. The admiral's body is transported through the cemetery by a horse-drawn caisson, escorted by a

dozen navy enlisted men. Once the caisson reaches the grave site, there is a nineteen-gun salute and a flyover by seventy naval jet aircraft.

Soon after his death, Catherine, his wife of fifty-two years, writes to a friend, "I'm not feeling sad. To me, he has just gone to sea, and as I have done so many times in the past, some day I will follow him . . ."

She does so in 1979.

In Nimitz's birthplace of Fredericksburg, Texas, the National Museum of the Pacific War is an unequaled site for memorializing and understanding naval history.

His good friend Harry Truman writes, "I came to regard Admiral Nimitz from the outset as a man apart and above all his contemporaries— as a strategist, a leader and as a person. I ranked him with General George Marshall as military geniuses as well as statesmen."

Private Clayton Adams

With the expiration of his thirty-day leave, Private Adams leaves New Mexico for San Diego, and is transported once again to Guam. On October 11, 1945, his unit is transferred to Tsingtao, China, where they begin the tedious duty of repatriating Japanese soldiers from the Chinese campaigns back to their home country. In February 1946 the downsizing of the Sixth Marine Division begins, and by April 1946 the Sixth is redesignated the Third Marine Brigade. On April 3, Clay leaves China, and eventually boards a transport ship that will return him to the United States for good.

From San Diego he once again embarks on the journey by train to Albuquerque, and is met this time by a one-woman welcoming committee. He and Loraine Lancaster marry four months later.

Like his brother before him, Clay has no interest in following his father's dismal career in the copper mines of western New Mexico, and where Jesse goes to California, Clay obeys his young wife's ambitions to travel eastward. The couple settles in Lexington, Kentucky, where they raise three daughters.

Clay graduates from the University of Kentucky and surprises Loraine by choosing the study of military science and history. After graduation in 1950, his combat experience lands him a position with the university as an instructor of ROTC cadets. Though he rarely speaks of his service experience on Okinawa, Clay is an outspoken advocate for education in the ranks of the military. By the mid-1960s the Vietnam War has made that philosophy increasingly unpopular. He speaks out frequently in support of the nation's efforts in Vietnam, and never fully grasps the nation's change of mood toward the military and its leadership. In 1970, a fire, presumed to be arson, destroys the facility that houses the school's air force ROTC. Disgusted, Clay leaves Kentucky for a position as an instructor of history at the Virginia Military Institute. His love of history deepens, and Clay begins extensive work on a biography of several of VMI's most illustrious alumni, and has a particular affection for Thomas "Stonewall" Jackson, but the effects of heart disease begin to drain him of strength, and the work is never completed.

In 1984 he retires and settles into the farm country of the Shenandoah Valley. He dies of heart disease in 2007, at age eighty-two. Loraine lives today in their family home near the New Market Battlefield, outside Harrisonburg, Virginia.

SERGEANT HAROLD MORTENSEN

The Sixth Division's downsizing does not affect the squad leader, who pushes hard to continue his career in the Corps. Mortensen is promoted to first sergeant in August 1946 and remains in service through the Korean War. When the brigade is revitalized as the reactivated Third Marine Division, Mortensen applies for and receives a commission as second lieutenant, and is awarded the bronze star for action in Korea. By the war's end he has been promoted to the rank of major. He retires in June 1955 and settles in Vienna, Virginia. That year Mortensen marries Constance Fowler, a secretary at the Veterans Administration in Washington, D.C., and she encourages him to seek a position there. Always an advocate for the care of ailing veterans, he agrees, and continues his work on behalf of veterans until his retirement in 1977. He moves to Venice, Florida, and dies in 2008, at age ninety-one.

GENERAL CURTIS LEMAY

The destruction of Hiroshima and Nagasaki is generally credited as accounting for the most cataclysmic loss of Japanese life, but LeMay's aggressive bombing campaigns produce losses to the Japanese citizenry that far exceed those two blasts. LeMay's *bomb 'em and burn 'em* philosophy reduces more of Japan to ash than both atomic bombs combined, and LeMay is somewhat justified in claiming that it is his airplanes that win the war, responsible for the destruction of sixty-five Japanese cities, causing more than a million Japanese casualties, and devastating more than ten million Japanese residences.

After the war LeMay is selected to head the United States Air Force command in Europe, and in 1948 is instrumental in the Berlin Airlift, which parachutes much-needed food and supplies into the German capital, breaking a blockade imposed on the city by the Soviets. Later that year LeMay becomes the first commander of the new Strategic Air Command, and works tirelessly to expand the role of the Air Force as a key component of America's military arsenal. He is promoted to full (four-star) general in 1951, the youngest to achieve that rank since Ulysses S. Grant. He heads SAC until 1957 and is widely regarded as the engineer of America's line-in-the-sand approach to the threat of Soviet missile attacks, thus ensuring that the Cold War remains cold.

He serves as air force chief of staff until 1961 and retires from active duty in 1965. Always a vocal critic of the "softening" of America's defensive shields, including what he sees as America's tentative strategies in the Vietnam War, a frustrated LeMay sees an opportunity to put his viewpoint on a loud pedestal. He accepts the opportunity to run as the vice presidential candidate as part of Alabama governor George Wallace's third-party campaign in the 1968 presidential election. Though Wallace has little expectation of winning, his high visibility brings out the most militant viewpoints of many in this country, who are mostly silenced by the vast outpouring of protest against the war. It is LeMay who uses that opportunity to express his support for the use of nuclear weapons in Vietnam, an incendiary philosophy that only helps polarize an already divided nation.

After the election, LeMay fades from public view, settles in California, and dies in 1990, at age eighty-three. He is buried at the United States Air Force Academy Cemetery, in Colorado Springs, Colorado.

President Harry Truman

The thirty-third president of the United States is a man both loved and despised during his terms of office, usually striving for what he believes to be in the nation's best interests as opposed to the will of the politicians who surround him. He seeks reelection in 1948 and scores a stunning upset over the heavily favored New York governor, Thomas Dewey. During his tenure, he supports his new secretary of state, George C. Marshall, a key force behind what is titled the Marshall Plan. From 1947 through 1952, the plan puts into action an outflow of American aid and other financial policies that rebuild Western Europe and thus do much to revitalize the economy of a significant portion of the industrialized world.

Though accused by his political enemies of being tentative in what many see as a crucial struggle to prevent the spread of communism, he adopts the Truman Doctrine, offering unwavering support to any nation that faces a blatant threat of Soviet expansion beyond those borders the Soviets seal off in 1945, what Winston Churchill refers to as the "Iron Curtain." In that same vein, Truman participates in the founding of the North Atlantic Treaty Organization (NATO) and vigorously supports American involvement in the United Nations.

In 1949, when the Soviet Union develops its own nuclear weapons, Truman recognizes the value of deterrence and supports the development and construction of larger and more effective weaponry, including the hydrogen bomb, which is significantly more powerful than the two bombs exploded over Japan in 1945. That policy remains controversial and is an integral part of international relations to this day.

In 1950 Truman vigorously supports intervention by the United Nations into an explosion of conflict in Korea. The nation, occupied during World War II by Japan, has been divided virtually in half by agreements and treaties that rarely involve the Koreans themselves, with an artificial border placed across the country at the Thirty-eighth Parallel. The north, influenced heavily by Soviet and Chinese politics and weaponry, invades the American-supported south, resulting in a response Truman labels a "police action." But the war in Korea stretches past Truman's own presidency, and fighting does not wind down until 1954. During the conflict there is considerable disagreement between Truman and Supreme Military Commander General Douglas MacArthur as to how the war should be fought. In August 1951 that conflict reaches its climax when Truman relieves MacArthur of his command, replacing him with General Matthew Ridgway. MacArthur returns home something of a political martyr and takes full advantage of a considerable volume of hero worship, at Truman's expense. The result, for a president whose popularity with the American people vacillates to either extreme, is that Truman leaves office with the lowest approval rating in history.

Truman's strength of will is consistently underestimated, and his homespun charm is often thought a sign of weakness. But what his political enemies view as weakness, the American public mostly takes to heart, and despite the various controversies, time heals America's perception of their thirty-third president. Truman becomes generally beloved, especially as the memories of his presidency fade, and he is today considered one of the twentieth century's more capable and popular presidents.

After leaving office, Truman and his wife, Bess, return to their home in Independence, Missouri. Truman will accept no compensation from any private corporation, and thus he and Bess subsist on his soldier's pension from World War I, little more than one hundred dollars per month. That an American president should be virtually destitute is an embarrassment the Congress rectifies, and in 1958 Truman is awarded a permanent pension of twenty-five thousand dollars per year.

He pens his memoirs, published in 1955, but signs a publishing contract that limits his royalties severely, thus he never receives the level of compensation appropriate to the memoirs' sales, which are significant. The two-volume set is regarded as one of the better presidential memoirs ever published.

Throughout the 1960s he continues to make public appearances, particularly to participate in official Washington ceremonies, but his health deteriorates. He dies in a hospital in Kansas City, Missouri, in December 1972, at age eighty-eight. He is buried at the Truman Library, in Independence, Missouri, where his wife Bess now lies beside him.

GENERAL LESLIE GROVES

If physicist Dr. Robert Oppenheimer can accurately be called the "Father of the Atomic Bomb," Groves is its godfather. By sheer strength of will and a personality that few find appealing, Groves succeeds in maintaining a wall of secrecy around the Manhattan Project that seems inconceivable in today's world.

At the war's end, he continues to lead what is still labeled the Manhattan District, which in 1947 evolves into the Atomic Energy Commission. Groves is awarded the Legion of Merit and promoted to lieutenant general (three stars) in 1948. Knowing he has consistently made enemies in Washington by the unyielding fierceness of his personality, which some describe as disgustingly rude, he realizes he can climb no farther up Washington's military ladder, and later in 1948, he retires. He moves to Darien, Connecticut, and goes to work as an executive for the Sperry Rand Corporation, until he retires again in 1961. He pens a memoir of the Manhattan Project in 1962 and returns to Washington. He lives out a peaceful retirement there and dies suddenly from a heart attack in 1970, at age seventy-three. He is buried in Arlington National Cemetery.

Captain William "Deak" Parsons

Immediately after the dropping of the bomb on Hiroshima, Parsons is promoted to commodore. For his actions he is awarded the Distinguished Service Medal, the Legion of Merit, and a Silver Star. In 1948 Parsons is promoted to rear admiral, and later serves as a member of the fledgling Atomic Energy Commission, but remains in the navy, and, appropriately, serves as assistant chief of the Bureau of Ordnance. He dies suddenly of a heart attack in 1953, at age fifty-two, and is buried at Arlington National Cemetery.

Colonel Paul Tibbets

Returning from the bombing run over Hiroshima, Tibbets finds himself the center of massive public attention, a position with which he is never comfortable. Immediately after the official surrender of Japan, Tibbets is granted permission to visit Tokyo, and learns that, while the airfields near Hiroshima are unusable, it is possible to fly into Nagasaki. Accompanied by two longtime friends, his navigator, Dutch Van Kirk, and his bombardier, Tom Ferebee, Tibbets logically enough keeps his anonymity among the Japanese, and learns to his surprise that the citizenry in Nagasaki is doing what citizens are doing throughout the rest of Japan (and Germany). They are making every effort to return to something of a normal life, even with the virtual destruction of their city. Tibbets comes away from the visit with respect for the civilians, writes, "I felt no animosity, neither did I have a personal feeling of guilt about the terror we had visited upon their land. It was unfortunate of course that these people had been obliged to pay such a price for a war into which their country had been led by a handful of ambitious and ruthless politicians and militarists."

With the war's end, Tibbets is still in service to Curtis LeMay, and LeMay orders him to leave Tinian and report to Washington, D.C. Along the way, Tibbets visits Roswell, New Mexico, where he offers a final farewell to many of those who had served the 509th as air and ground crews, most of whom are scheduled to be discharged from the postwar air force.

Expecting to return to something of a normal family life, Tibbets is dismayed to find that he is greatly in demand by newspaper and radio reporters. For the first year after the war's end, there is little controversy surrounding the dropping of the bomb, most of the attention focused instead on the practical peaceful applications of atomic energy, a topic Tibbets is woefully unqualified to address.

In 1948 Tibbets recognizes the coming of the jet age, and attends Air Command and Staff School to familiarize himself with the new technology. He soon becomes a staunch advocate of the new B-47 bomber, a six-engine jet that enters service in 1951, and he serves as a test pilot for the aircraft, which quickly becomes a primary tool for the increasing needs of the Cold War. As LeMay assumes command of the fledgling Strategic Air Command, Tibbets is brought along.

In 1952 Tibbets is amazed when Hollywood comes calling. Though aware that he has some celebrity status, he does not expect that his life story is to be put on film. *Above and Beyond* stars actor Robert Taylor as Tibbets, and reenacts the story of the bombing of Hiroshima. Tibbets learns firsthand that Hollywood's version of history can vary considerably from the truth. Tibbets responds to the film's mixed reviews and unexpected variations of fact with a standard cliché: "Well, that's show biz."

The fame that follows Tibbets adds considerable pressure to a marriage that has struggled for most of its seventeen years. In 1955, the struggle ends, as Paul and Lucy Tibbets are divorced.

Tibbets is named to serve on the staff of the American contingent to NATO, and with his marriage over, moves to France, settling in the town of Fontainebleau, near Paris. As part of a more international social scene, Tibbets is introduced to Andrea Quattrehomme, a French divorcée. Though there is a language barrier between them, that soon fades, and in 1956 they marry.

Bored with his NATO duties, Tibbets returns to the States in 1956 and is assigned to the 308th Bomber Wing at Hunter Air Force Base in Savannah, Georgia. He soon understands that the position is one of repairing an outfit with a dismal reputation, and his own reputation is enhanced by his success. Thus he is called upon to address the same challenge with other units, and is assigned to MacDill Air Force Base in Tampa, Florida. But there are rewards to this kind of service, and in 1959 Tibbets is promoted to brigadier general. Always on General LeMay's radar, Tibbets is called again to Washington, and in 1961 assumes leadership of the Office of Strategic Analysis for the Strategic Air Command, and a year later develops the National Military Command Center in the Pentagon, which serves as SAC's watchdog for any potential enemy activities that might threaten the United States. As such, he is now managing what is in essence the nerve center for secret military communications worldwide.

In 1964 Tibbets's career takes a completely different turn when he is assigned to the Military Assistance Group to India. But Tibbets's celebrity becomes an albatross, as India's government follows an increasingly leftist philosophy that brands the United States the world's most dangerous power. One newspaper in particular offers the opinion that Paul Tibbets "should not be allowed to breathe the air of India." Despite the political controversy, the government does accept the American military's assistance in modernizing India's air force, and Tibbets assists in the construction of a series of radar stations in the Himalayan Mountains, along India's border with China. Tibbets and his wife spend nearly two unpleasant years in India, and Tibbets is relieved when, in 1966, he is recalled to Washington. But he is offered command of the Department of Defense Transportation, which in effect makes him the port master of every American debarkation center, whether air, land, or sea. It is not a position that appeals, and Tibbets realizes that his thirty-year career with the air force should be concluded.

Tibbets and his wife take the opportunity for an unfettered vacation in Europe, but it is interrupted when he receives word that his mother, Enola Gay Tibbets, has died.

In the Vietnam War years, the tone of the nation shifts significantly against the military, and Tibbets finds himself targeted increasingly by antinuclear sentiment. He is stunned to read reports in European magazines that claim, among other things, that Paul Tibbets is confined to an insane asylum, resulting from his grief over the Hiroshima bombing. Though he tries to avoid the public spotlight, he becomes painfully aware that he has become a symbol of what some are insisting is America's darkest hour.

In 1976 Tibbets becomes president of the civilian Executive Jet Aviation Company, and relocates to Columbus, Ohio. The company has a troubled past financially, but Tibbets does for them what he has done for the various air force commands throughout his life, and within a short time the company prospers.

In 1986 Tibbets retires, and in 1989 writes his memoirs. But he cannot escape the occasional outbursts of controversy and vitriol aimed at him for his role in the war, and he responds aggressively to some of the criticism against him in an updated edition of the memoir, published in 1998. He writes:

> One must sympathize with any movement designed to reduce or eliminate human slaughter. Nuclear warfare is indeed inhuman and ought to be banned. By the same token, other forms of warfare, such as the dropping of fire bombs and the shooting of soldiers with cannon and rifles, are likewise uncivilized and should be outlawed. Those who try to distinguish between civilized and uncivilized forms of combat soon find themselves defending the indefensible. To suggest that one specific act of war is barbaric and thereby illegal is to imply that other forms of slaughter are acceptable and consequently legal.
>
> Interestingly, those who protest most vigorously our use of the atomic bomb against Japan deplore the killing of so many people in just two raids. One is given the impression that a thousand planes rather than two, should have been used to accomplish the same result.

Though many reports over the years suggest that General Tibbets endured his later years in an agony of guilt, his own quote on the cover of his memoir best sums up his feelings: "To me, [the bomb] meant putting an end to the fighting and consequent loss of lives. In fact, I viewed my mission as one to save lives rather than take them. The intervening years have brought me many letters and personal contacts with individuals who maintain that they would not be alive if it had not been for what I did. Likewise, I have been asked in letters and to my face if I was not conscience stricken for the loss of life I caused by dropping the first atomic bomb. To those who ask, I quickly reply, 'Not in the least.' "

He dies in Columbus, Ohio, in 2007, at age ninety-two.

> Actually, the bomb is no more revolutionary than the first throwing stick or javelin or the first cannon or the first submarine. It is simply a new instrument added to the orchestra of death which is war.
>
> —GEORGE PATTON

It is a sobering thought that our two bombs, feeble by today's standards, were the curtain-raiser on what many view as the supreme human tragedy. Mankind's best hope is that the prologue was so frightening that the main show will be canceled.

—General Paul Tibbets

ABOUT THE AUTHOR

JEFF SHAARA is the *New York Times* bestselling author of *No Less Than Victory, The Steel Wave, The Rising Tide, To the Last Man, The Glorious Cause, Rise to Rebellion,* and *Gone for Soldiers,* as well as *Gods and Generals* and *The Last Full Measure*—two novels that complete the Civil War trilogy that began with his father's Pulitzer Prize–winning classic *The Killer Angels.* Jeff Shaara was born into a family of Italian immigrants in New Brunswick, New Jersey. He grew up in Tallahassee, Florida, and graduated from Florida State University. He lives again in Tallahassee. Visit the author online at www.jeffshaara.com.

Jeff Shaara is available for select readings and lectures. To inquire about a possible appearance, please contact the Random House Speakers Bureau at rhspeakers@randomhouse.com.

ABOUT THE TYPE

This book was set in Garamond, a typeface originally designed by the Parisian typecutter Claude Garamond (1480–1561). This version of Garamond was modeled on a 1592 specimen sheet from the Egenolff-Berner foundry, which was produced from types assumed to have been brought to Frankfurt by the punchcutter Jacques Sabon.

Claude Garamond's distinguished romans and italics first appeared in *Opera Ciceronis* in 1543–44. The Garamond types are clear, open, and elegant.